NAGA BRIDES BOXSET

BOOKS 1-3

NAOMI LUCAS

 Created with Vellum

NAGA NAMES

Vruksha— Viper
Azsote— Boomslang
Zhallaix— Death Adder
Syasku— Cottonmouth
Jyarka— Diamondback
Zaku— King Cobra
Vagan— Blue Coral
Krellix— Copperhead
Lukys— Black Mamba
Xenos— Sidewinder

NEW EARTH
THE NAGA FOREST
The Observatory
Military March Camp
The Facility
March Rd
Krellix's Hideout
Eagle's Rest Base
Plateau
Azsote's Woods
Cottonmouth's Hollow
Zaku's Castle
Vagan's Grotto
Vruksha's Bunker
Zhallaix's Den
The Hills
N
W
E
S

VIPER

NAGA BRIDES I

NAOMI LUCAS

VIPER

Long have we been alone.

Without brides, without females to warm us during the long nights. Without sweet mates.

But we see them, from afar, brides that could be ours. Kept away from us by walls and weapons. Females we long for greatly.

Obsessively.

Human females.

And the one with red hair? I want her. I saw her first. I will fight for the death for her.

She is MINE.

So, we'll come together and make an exchange with their men that will benefit us all.

After that?

To the winner goes the spoils...

Let the hunt begin.

But the red-headed female is mine.

—-

One day I'm a confidant for our leader, and the next I'm escorted out of the settlement by armed guards. Before me now lies the vast and dangerous wilderness of Earth, ravaged by aliens that long ago vanished.

They left their devastation—and their technology—behind.

My leader wants that technology. He'll do anything to get it, even trading me to those who have it.

Serpent men. Nagas. Half-men, half-snake beast aliens rule these lands—misbegotten monsters warped by something we don't yet understand.

They want me.

Especially the ruby red demon that stares at me with such an intensity my soul quakes.

But I refuse to be any man's broodmare, especially an alien's.

If he wants me so badly, he'll have to catch me first.

Unfortunately, that was the whole point after all...

ONE

THE PACT

Vruksha

"Our truce ends after they release the females," I growl, peering at the males around me. The King Cobra's mane flutters, the Boomslang nods. Others react; some don't respond at all. I take their silence as agreement.

We're the strongest of our kind. The oldest. The deadliest. We saw the humans' ship breach our sky and land within our forest.

We're also competitors. The fact that we've all come together for this—*for them*—is a miracle. It shows how much we want *them,* how desperate we are to have *them,* and that we would risk our lives to make a deal with *their* keepers.

Their puny males.

Males who do not deserve the warmth of a female. They don't realize how lucky they are to have females, so we will take their females and covet them, mate them, make them queens to the lands we rule. As is how it should be.

There are many wrongs that need to be righted, and many mistakes in our past that need to be fixed.

My fingers tighten around my spear as I scrutinize the nagas gathered today, sizing them up. Some of us won't survive.

Humans are different from us, at least from what I've seen, and it's more than the way they look.

We thought them long gone. A species that had been eradicated when we were born on this Earth. Neither I nor the other naga males around me have ever seen a living one, not once, until recently.

They flew down from the sky in a large metal machine. Machines like the ones here, but not overgrown with weeds, roots, and vines. Not ruined the way Earth was ruined.

No, this machine—this ship of theirs—came to us clean of the forest and landed outside the old ruins of a civilization long gone, deep in the mountains. Other smaller machines came out with weapons and cleared the ruins. They erected a barrier and cut down the trees.

The humans restored the ruins into what it once was: a military facility.

Meanwhile, I watched the robots from afar, from the shadows of the trees, and soon found other nagas watching them too. We didn't know why they were here, or what they wanted, but we are determined to keep our secrets...secret.

At first, there were only machines. We didn't realize there were humans on the ship. The robots poured from their vessel in droves, destroying the terrain we once knew. A growl tears from my throat at the thought. The robots left us alone, though, having one singular purpose, a purpose we nagas did not know until several weeks after their landing.

They were making the facility ready for human inhabitants.

Thinking back on that day quickens my heart.

Her red hair. My fingers twitch. I can imagine the softness of it running between my fingers. I've never seen such a shade of red as my tail...

Zaku, the King Cobra, went to the humans when we realized they had females among them. He made our presence known. He wanted to meet them, court them, mate with one... We were stronger, larger than their males, and thought that because of it, they should be ours.

I did too.

Perhaps we could offer our help in return? Who knows?

Zaku came back enraged. The humans turned their weapons on him, refusing his request. They told him this land was theirs, as it has always been, and as long as he abided by that, they would not kill us.

Hah. I would like to see them try.

I'd wipe the humans from these lands but they have females...and for that reason, they remain alive.

I want my red-headed beauty.

I'll have to fight for her, kill for her. And I'm willing to do more than that, but I do not want her hurt. And fighting? I've seen enough death to know accidents happen. They have machines, and not all machines can be trusted.

It wasn't that long ago. Days, maybe? Seems like an eternity. The other nagas came together after word spread of what happened to Zaku. It wasn't hard to win me over. I would do anything for *her*.

When I first saw her, everything changed.

Gone was the bloodlust, the anger. Real lust took its place. Red hot desire, with a wild mane of red hair to match. Transfixed, I stared that first day as she descended from the ramp, realizing something more miraculous than machines had fallen from the heavens. She looked around with wonder and curiosity.

She had gazed at the sky and the clouds above. She had touched the grass at her feet. Her tongue poked out to swipe at her lips.

Her eyes had found mine, even as I hid beyond her barrier, in the shadows of the forest. From that moment, she was mine.

A human female, wondrous in her rarity, who with one look ruined me.

My female.

The way her eyes widened. The way her lips parted...

The fear on her face hadn't bothered me at all.

She was mine. I expected her to face her fear and come to me then, but instead, she turned away and rushed into the shadows of the facility, leaving me bereft, lusty, and angry.

She had looked at me, though, had met my gaze. She saw me, and that was all that mattered. Now I know I am in her head. She will always remember the first time she saw me. For I am a strong male, a vicious one, and refused to be forgotten.

It would be dangerous to forget me.

My anger returned after I lost sight of her, and my agitation at these human interlopers built. My need for this female stole my mind. Reclaiming the facility and this land meant nothing if I couldn't have her. I wanted both but only cared about the latter.

I saw her first.

She saw me first.

She was in *my* head. No other naga's head mattered unless they were hanging from a rope off my belt or lobbed off and impaled on my spear, decorating the entrance to my den.

Except whispers of human females spread through the forest—the mountains—the other nagas had similar thoughts. My female wasn't the only one, and nagas from far afield, males I have not seen in years, returned to see them, to steal them, to mate with them, and hoard them away in our respective nests.

The heat overcame us all like a storm. To conquer. These females came from the skies to be ours. We became very aware of our diminishing numbers, and with the threat of invaders from the skies on our minds...our biology altered against us, clouding our minds.

I started giving off a strange scent.

I wasn't the only one who changed, nor the only one desperate to nest. A piece within us unlocked, and it can't be undone. Some nagas feared the change and fled, hoping the change would reverse.

Less to die by my hands. I hiss out a breath of air.

Azsote, a Boomslang, snaps his tail. "And if they don't release them?"

"We invade with our weapons and strike them down. They need to know this land is not theirs, not without a price," Zaku snarls. Some of the other males snarl with him. The King Cobra is out for blood, one way or another. A king, even though Zaku wasn't one, doesn't like being told what to do.

Zaku's only king in name, and he holds no more sway or dominion than the rest of us.

"They will pay for it with females," I say.

Azsote snaps his tail again. "Yesss."

"They want our technology, our land... We will give them a little for a lot more," Zaku agrees.

I eye the facility far, far in the distance, through the trees and across the shattered landscape, hoping to see her. A splash of red among the green. But she's nowhere to be found from our vantage point way up on the cliffs.

I haven't seen her in many days. Venom leaks from my fangs. I need to see her soon or I may do something crazed, like storm the humans' barrier and take on their robots for just a glimpse.

She is the same color as me. I never thought such a female existed besides my sisters. One with Viper in her blood.

My hands tremble with the need to comb my fingers through her hair. My nose itches to burrow into her neck and languish in its warmth.

"We give them nothing, and they won't be the wiser," I hiss, "while they give usss everything in return."

The other males beat their chests and hoot in agreement. The coming hunt excites us. I feel it in my veins, the way my blood pumps heavy. I slam my fist against my chest and hoot with them.

"How many females are there?" Vagan asks when we settle. "Not enough, last I checked." His blue scales and long, slender body are like mine, except he is blue where I am red. Vagan is of the Blue Coral clan, a ruler of the dangerous waterways. He may be brightly colored like me, but to face him near water was certain death.

Of all the nagas gathered, Vagan is the one I watch the most. Him and the Death Adder.

Except Zhallaix, the Death Adder, is not here. He would rather kill us than work with us. An enemy to us all. He has no honor, nor allegiance. Ruthless and wild, he is probably fucking a mossy rock and spitting venom somewhere off in the hills. I have not seen Zhallaix since the ship first appeared.

"I have only seen three," Zaku answers. The King Cobra is fearsome, but I do not watch him like Vagan and some of the others. One bite and the Cobra could take out any one of us. I do not watch him because he has some honor in his cold veins.

Honor I do not know if I have. Zaku isn't just honorable, he's pompous and hard-headed. He's rash. Everything is beneath him, and it shows in his inability to help anyone but himself, even in this. If Zaku could steal a female human for himself, he wouldn't have gathered us. Sometimes I think he's not honorable at all, just overzealous.

I keep an eye on him anyway. If Zaku doesn't win one of the females today, he's going to destroy the world. Or die trying.

As for everyone else? They watch me.

I tighten my grip on my spear, meeting their eyes.

"Three? Three is not enough!" Vagan shouts. "There are at least seven of us here, and more yet in these woods. How will three brides appease us all?"

"They won't," I say. "We will fight for them when they are handed over."

Some growl, some hiss in agreement. We size each other up, considering who we could off now before the humans arrive.

The Boomslang with the shimmery green scales slips to the ledge, his voice lowering. "Why not fight now? Until there are only three of us left?" Azsote suggests, waving his hand.

"Why not let the females choose who they want to mate with?" another offers. I look at the naga and bare my fangs. It's the Copperhead. He is a quiet one. I'm surprised to hear him speak at all.

"No," I snap.

"That won't work," Zaku says at the same time.

"We will not honor their choices," I add. If my female chooses another over me, I would kill him and take her.

I am not honorable, after all.

The Copperhead nods. He knows what I say is true. The females can't have the luxury to choose, not now that their very presence has created a strange fervor.

Our members have filled up with unspent spill, causing pressure, bringing us pain. When I first saw my human, my shaft flooded with seed, seed that has been dormant for years, and I have had to milk my shaft nightly to relieve the pressure.

If I'm suffering, the other nagas are too.

"Three females is a problem," says Zaku. "But I have an idea. If we fight for mating rights to them, there is a chance they will run while we battle. It is paramount that the females do not come to any harm. Especially by us or our ways. They may be all there is, and we can't lose them. We must keep them safe."

We mumble in agreement. I love the red of my female's hair, although it is the only red I wish to see upon her. I do not want to witness her blood outside her moon cycle. If she is bloody, she is hurt, and that means I have failed...

Zaku continues, "If they run, the animals could kill them, the pigsss. They could get hurt—"

"So what's your suggestion?" Vagan interrupts.

"I suggest we spread out when the human males hand them over. So we do not fight. I suggest they run, we follow, and we hunt them down. Whoever catches the females first wins nesting rights to them."

Silence hangs over us as we ponder Zaku's words. It is a good suggestion, not the greatest. My redhead is already mine. But the other male nagas will want proof, and a hunt—because I know I will catch her —is a good way to prove it.

"I like this idea," the Boomslang speaks up first.

"Of course you do," Vagan snaps. "You are a hunter of the forest."

Azsote shrugs. "I am. That does not change that this is a good suggestion."

"And what about me? What about Syasku? We fare best in the water. A hunt over land cripples us."

Nobody cares about Vagan or Syasku. I don't say this aloud. My thoughts are strong enough. "There is water nearby, a lot of water. If the females head for it, then you have an advantage."

"And if they don't?"

I turn back to the facility, not caring enough to answer.

"I will accept a hunt," says Syasku of the Cottonmouth clan. *Good.* If the other water naga accepts a hunt, then Vagan has no grounds to argue it.

Vagan scowls.

"It is settled then," Zaku declares. "We will hunt for nesting rights to the females."

Another wave of shouts soars the air. I lift my spear and release a bolt of electricity to the sky. I like this. I will win. I have destiny on my side. Vicious, red destiny.

The other males pound their chests, and some release their well-hung and hard members from their scales. Tails coil and thump the ground. For a frenzied moment, excitement and real camaraderie return to us. It is a rare thing. We are deadly as a group.

We are deadly alone, but together... The world would tremble with fear.

The excitement does not last. I turn back once again to see if my bride is outside, if she's being gathered with the other females to be handed over.

And for a second, I see her. My heart stops.

She's being led to one of the flying transport machines. Another female is fighting, kicking, and screaming behind her. She's lifted off the ground and hauled to the machine.

My female goes calmly.

She knows her fate. Knows who awaits her

Me.

Venom fills my mouth. My heart revs back up.

The others have gone silent, and I know they are watching as well.

"She is the one I want," Azsote rumbles. My eyes flick to the Boomslang watching my female, and I slam my spear into his side.

I attack him, striking out with my tail, knocking him over. He evades my speartip, rolling away before I can plunge it into his gut.

"She is mine!" I roar, fury surging through me. "Mine!"

How dare he want her. How dare he even look at her! Azsote strikes back, hitting me with his fist, slicing me with his claws across my bicep. The sting of pain erupts. I barely notice, needing to see his blood splattered across the ground.

Hands grab us, pulling us apart.

"Enough!" Zaku shouts.

Fighting his hold, I spit venom in Azsote's direction. He pushes his capturer away and shrieks a battle cry. Furious, only his blood on the ground and his spine in my hand will appease me now.

"I sssaid enough! They're coming! Do not let them see us fighting." Zaku shoves me away, getting between us. Growling, I rise to fight the King Cobra as well, but he's facing the horizon.

Behind him, the humans' transport vehicle is heading our way. It glides soundlessly through the air.

All thoughts of Azsote and the others fall from my mind. My female is heading for me.

In mere moments, I will see her up close for the first time. My body tenses to not only fight, it wants to rut as well. It wants both, simultaneously, right now.

"Present the technology," Zaku orders.

Vagan hands Zaku a small metal box. A data collection. An ancient thing left here by aliens. Both this technology and humans once shaped this world, but for countless years, both have been ours. Times have changed and now the technology is wanted by these humans that have returned from the sky.

I don't care about the technology. I have my den, my weapon, and enough resources to last me into old age. These trinkets that we are giving the humans are nothing compared to what we keep hidden.

The transport flies past us to land on the clearing behind. Some of the males scatter, readying themselves for the coming hunt.

When the transport opens, the only ones left are me, Zaku, and Vagan.

I will not lose this chance to finally see my female up close.

My fangs drip. A male dressed in a powersuit steps out.
My spine stiffens when another man follows after.
Where are you, little female?
I clench my hands.
Then I see her, and my mind blanks.

TWO

THROWN TO THE SNAKES

Gemma

"Daisy, calm down," Peter says.

Daisy sniffles louder. "Fuck you."

"Crying isn't going to change anything. You're acting like a damn fool."

I glower at Peter, sitting across from us in the skiff, and tighten my arm around Daisy. "Can you blame her? You're throwing us to the wolves."

"Earth doesn't have wolves anymore."

"Fuck you." I agree wholeheartedly with Daisy here. "You said it would never come to this."

"No, *you'll* be the one fucking an alien snake. Not me. High and mighty Gemma Hurst, fallen from grace. You knew this course of action was in the cards the moment the locals offered a trade. What's at stake is too important..."

"It's only been weeks! We've barely begun our search—"

"Central Command does not want to wait."

I hold Daisy against me as I glare at Peter. I can't believe what a prick he's become. I've worked with the guy for nearly two years, and

I've never seen him be so cruel, especially to someone under his command.

Peter pointedly looks at the screen in his hand.

He can't even meet my eyes. He knows what he's doing isn't right. Maybe he thinks if I hate him, it'll be easier for both of us. It's not.

I get it.

I get it—and I hate that I do. Central Command is breathing fire down our necks, demanding a solution to *their war problem* and to bring them that solution fast, now that Earth is safe to travel to. Peter's feeling the heat. It's his neck on the line if he doesn't give Central Command what they want.

It's my neck too, and Daisy's. Except we're not as high-ranking as Peter. We don't get what he gets. We're expendable. At least more so than Peter.

What he's doing still isn't right, but I get it, in a deranged, depressing, horrendous way. Depressing because I can almost forgive him for this. He's desperate, and desperate people do shitty things.

Daisy trembles and any chance of forgiving Peter flies out the window.

"What about you, Collins?" I cut my eyes to Peter's second-in-command. Collins is gazing out the window, unable to look at me or Daisy, just like Peter. He doesn't even try. His face blank, unreadable. He's shut down.

None of the ranking crewmen can meet my eyes.

Because it's us that's making this sacrifice. It's the women who are being made to give up their lives to save the team, and we haven't even been on Earth a month...

"What about me?" Collins mumbles, avoiding my gaze.

"Don't you feel bad for doing this to me and Daisy? When it could be Shelby sitting here with us?"

Shelby is Collins' girlfriend, and she was spared because of it.

Apparently, Shelby's pregnant. That fact came out last night when Peter gathered the three of us women and locked us in a room together. Collins fought for her, sparing her. We can't risk a child—especially when that child could become a soldier one day.

Lucky lady. Shelby gets to stay. Hopefully, she'll reach Central Command and tell them what's happening down here on Earth.

Collins shrugs, doesn't answer.

Of course he doesn't. He saved the only one of us he cares about. He's not going to go to bat for anyone else, not with what's at stake.

Because we've been sent to Earth for one thing and one thing only: alien technology.

It's the only thing that can save us in the war against the Ketts, a species of blob-like aliens that are highly intelligent, extremely adaptable, and fully capable of consuming all organic matter in their path. They're always hungry, and humans make a great meal. Our bullets pierce their flesh except they leave no mark. Our lasers sear their gelatinous bodies but then are absorbed. We can't fight them with hand or fist, or weapons of old like swords and daggers. We can't even crush them...

They just reform.

We're losing the war.

The Ketts are growing, breeding, expanding at an exponential rate, hunting humans down like cattle because we pose the only threat to their existence.

It's only a matter of time before we find a way to hurt them.

Humans have a way of prevailing.

Which leads to me and Daisy being sacrificed. Whether the locals want to eat us, experiment with us, or something far worse... I don't know. And I refuse to find out—the same goes for Daisy.

She's a petty officer, whereas I'm Chief Communications Officer of our ship's bridge crew. *The Dreadnaut* is now outside the moon's orbit, hiding on the dark side so we don't alert the Ketts to our plans on Earth.

Until now, Earth has been a dead zone. A place to avoid at all costs. Occasionally humans ignored space law and visited the human mecca, though most never returned. The lucky few who did morphed into something... not human.

Alien technology did that, and a whole lot more. Long ago, back before I was born or humans even knew the Ketts existed, a species called Lurkawathians descended to Earth and made a pact with mankind.

For a while, their arrival had been good for humanity. Mankind established its first space port and got to study the Lurkawathians— dubbed Lurkers. We learned about the universe and reaped the benefits of their advanced technology.

They helped us develop as a cosmic society and introduced us to intergalactic travel. They cured our diseases and traded us resources that were in short supply.

In return, the Lurkers set up their own port on Earth and were allowed to study us.

Through all of this advancement, they kept their technology secret. The Lurkers gave us just as much as they needed for us to comply with them and no more. They took us into space but never helped us expand or allowed us a foothold elsewhere. They discouraged it. They resented us for trying.

According to my history discs, we were their special pets and they wanted to keep us that way.

As for my ancestors and the rest of humanity... Well, we don't like being told no.

I stare at Peter head-on. "Once Central Command finds out about what's happening, you're going to lose your title, your ranks, be stripped of your credentials. You won't even have the certificates to work as maintenance staff."

His brow furrows before smoothing. "You don't understand the pressure we're under, Gemma. The pressure I'm under."

"Try to make me understand. For all our sakes, try." I know he's taking heat...

But how much heat?

He shakes his head and looks out the window. Daisy wipes the snot from her nose and does the same.

I take a deep, unsettling breath.

Humans expanded anyway, despite the Lurkers' limitations. Relations with them soured. Sanctions, taxes, killings. In the end, the Lurkers, realizing that we couldn't be controlled, offered us a Trojan Horse of a deal. They offered to return Earth to its ancient glory. To purify our oceans, to give us back our forests, and to clean our skies.

The government accepted this 'gift,' not realizing that to do so meant our destruction.

The Lurkers unleashed devastation into the environment that manipulated and changed everything it came into contact with. Everything died. Everything.

Those humans out in space were the only survivors, watching as our blue and green world turned brown.

Afterward, the Lurkers left, never to be seen again. That was nearly fifteen hundred years ago.

Lurker technology remains on Earth though, and now that Earth is safe to travel to again, it's ours for the taking.

There's just one problem: finding it.

"Peter, please," I urge, trying hard to remain strong, when inside I'm panicking. My pulse drums in my ear. Peter ignores my plea. He ignores me completely.

The Dreadnaut and Peter's team—us—aren't the first to land on Earth in the last century, and we won't be the last. Though we're the first team to land near the old Lurker and human military base.

According to records, that's what the facility was, the same one now growing small in the distance behind me. We'd just begun to explore what was left of the ruins when a whole other problem presented itself.

A shiver of fear skitters up my back.

The locals.

THREE
SERPENT MEN

Gemma

My gut hollows out, and I swallow down the bile creeping out my throat.

A shiver courses through me, and try as I might to hide it, Daisy looks up at me. Our eyes meet for a moment, and she hugs me back. I take the comfort she offers.

All we have is each other.

Before yesterday, we had never spoken. Today, we're sisters.

I'm trying to be strong, but it's hard. I'm scared. I know what's awaiting us when Peter and Collins drop us off. I know what—who— will be there.

Him.

The red-scaled creature hiding in the forests beyond the facility. I saw him the first day I arrived. The facility had been deemed safe and clear, Peter and his guards inspected the place thoroughly enough, and the rest of the crew was given allowance to leave our transport ship.

I hadn't even stepped off the ship's ramp when I spotted him. He hid in the shadows of the trees just beyond our jurisdiction.

His dark eyes took hold of mine, and I knew it was a *him*, his large physique unmistakable. I've seen many alien worlds and have even encountered a Kett blob. Despite this, I've never met a being like the one in the woods. Like him.

Earth wasn't supposed to have sentient life on it. Or human life for that matter, but I can't deny what I saw.

A half-human, half-serpent male staring at me.

My skin prickles with the memory.

He had been large and ruby red, a red that I've never seen on another creature. He was a jewel, a bizarre, glistening beacon among the green of the forest, and I was shocked to discover later that I was the only one who saw him.

Because he was huge! With discerning human features and a male's chest, a man's musculature. Though I couldn't see all of him, I now know he has a tail because soon after I saw him, another one of the local aliens approached our compound to talk, causing a riot.

And the serpentine male who dared enter the compound had the largest, longest tail I'd ever laid my eyes on. Unlike the scary red demon from the trees, the one that visited the facility had been yellow with dark brown and black stripes. He had an enormous cowl.

I bite my tongue.

We'd trespassed on their land, and now they want reparations. Reparations or death.

The striped alien had the technology we came here for.

He knew where it was.

And he knew how to use it. Or so he threatened. It was enough to catch Peter's ear.

Right now, lost Lurker technology is the single most sought-after thing on this side of the universe.

Who cares if Daisy and I are the price for it? She's quiet under my arm now, and I hope she hasn't gone into shock.

Have I?

I glance out the window of the skiff as we descend. We've flown to a plateau with a clearing. The skiff lands soundlessly, and I immediately search for the locals.

Swallowing against the lump of fear in my throat, I see the red one, and my heart plunges to my stomach. Staring at me and only me, his eyes blacken out the color of him, stealing my awareness momentarily.

How can he see me? The glass is shielded.

His eyes are darker than I remember, black as the abyss and framed by deep shades of red. Above was a smattering of short black hair.

Holding a spear, he rises on his tail as my eyes trail down his body, strutting like he knows I'm looking at him...

He can't see me through the glass, can he?

I barely notice the two males beside him. I don't want to see them. I have enough nightmare fodder clogging up my mind already. One is the male who threatened us, his giant build and strange cowl unmistakable, and the other is a deep, sapphire blue—with a startling orange face that practically glows amongst the hue of his indigo scales.

The door to the skiff opens, and Peter grabs my arm, dragging me out. Daisy's hauled out next with a cry. I tear my eyes away from the group.

I don't quite know what will happen next, but I know I don't want the red one to catch me... Not him. When I run, taking the chance I can reach the transport ship, I don't want any of them to catch me, and that's especially true for the red one.

He eyes me like I'm already his.

He eyes only me. His gaze has not gone to Daisy or Peter or Collins, not once.

My throat tightens.

He's been haunting me. He's done terrible things to me in my sleep. He's made me scream, beg, and run as if my life depends on it. The only reason I'm not running now is that I don't want Peter to shoot me in the back. Because he will.

Daisy wipes her nose on the back of her hand and straightens. I'm proud of her. I wish I could be proud of myself.

I'm scared, a lot more scared than I'd care to admit.

"You still have the knife Shelby gave you?" I whisper.

Daisy nods. "Yeah."

"Good." If my voice trembles, she doesn't acknowledge it.

Collins glances over, and I go quiet until he turns back to the aliens. He's speaking to them. I don't listen, scanning our surroundings instead.

The plateau we're on is high up on a mountain, but there are possible trails along the ledges for a quick descent down from it. If Daisy and I ran for one of the ledges, they would return us to the facility the quickest, though we would be exposed for the entire climb down. Not only that, below is a river that we'd also need to cross. If we managed to make it there, we'd have the cover of the forest on the other side. There would only be one path from that direction—and every alien would know it because the forest lies in a gorge and on every side? Mountains.

Mountains and forest as far as the eye could see.

The cliffs stop Daisy and I from making a quick getaway back to the facility, but ahead and on either side of us, beyond the clearing, are ledges and the forest. We'll have to detour, find a different route, if we want to escape this fate.

We'll need the cover of the trees for any hope of that.

"We'll stick together," I tell Daisy. "We can get out of this."

"How?"

"The first chance we get, we run, we fight," I lower my voice. "Once we're in the trees, the ones to our left, we can hide. We'll make our way back to the facility from there."

"Pointless," she breathes. "Peter and Collins and the others will just give us back."

"Not if we get to Shelby first. Not if we sneak onto the transport ship and send a comm to *The Dreadnaut*. They don't know what's happening down here."

Daisy stops. "They don't know?"

"No." I can see the spark of hope that ignites in her at my words. It buoys my own hope. "We just have to make it there. That's all we have to do."

"Okay."

Peter and Collins turn our way, and I shut my mouth. They grab Daisy and me, forcing us over to where the aliens await.

We've been stripped of everything except for the clothes on our backs—Peter didn't allow us to pack, or bring our com-ware. Our knives were smuggled to us by Shelby this morning, slipped into the shower units we were allowed to use one last time before being forced into the skiff.

The big one with the cowl holds a metal box in his hands. He scowls when his gaze roves over me. He hesitates when he sees Daisy. His eyes harden, and his hold on the box strains. "You," he hisses.

Daisy cowers.

"Where isss the third female?" the male suddenly barks, jerking his head up. His cowl flutters.

Collins stiffens. "She is not for you."

"We were promised three females," another male says, the deep blue and black scaled one with a burst of bright orange coloring over his face. "Give us the third or we take our secrets to the grave."

"She is not for you," Collins snaps. "She is pregnant with my child, and we're soon to be married."

The blue one coils his tail. "Do you think I care? We still want her. She is oursss."

The red male comes forward. "The third female can remain with you. We will take these two."

I don't want to look at him. I don't. I try hard not to, but my eyes slide to him anyway. Our gazes meet, and my limbs lock up tight.

Sharp, exotic features fill my vision, thick arching brows and lean muscles covered in ridges and scales. Not several yards from where I'm standing, waiting for him to come forward and chain me, I'm transfixed. I couldn't run if I wanted to. And I want to.

I want to run far, far away.

He's beautiful, a deadly beauty meant for one thing: to lure idiotic prey like me.

Standing beside the other two, he's the tallest. His tail lifting him high off the ground. He may not be packed with muscles like the male with a cowl, but he's built. I don't think my little knife is going to help me.

"Just two?" the blue one balks. "Two to fight over? Do you know how many of us are waiting in the trees? Three was not enough! It will be a bloodbath!"

"Enough, Vagan!" the yellow and black one says. "We will not take a gestating female from her mate. The females are not to come to any harm, and that goes for the one out of our reach." He glares at the men. "For now."

Collins shakes despite his best attempts to hide it.

Vagan snarls but doesn't argue further.

"So we still have a deal?" Peter asks.

I hate him.

"We have a deal."

"Hand over the box, and we'll leave you to it."

I hate Peter even more—if that's possible. I want to wring my hands around his neck and squeeze.

The black and brown alien thrusts the box at Peter. "Take it then and leave."

In a blur, the next few minutes rush by. Daisy loses it when Peter and Collins enter the skiff, refusing to listen to her pleas. I stand stunned, fearful to move, wanting more than anything to grab my knife and fight. It's not until the skiff takes off and a tense silence returns that I acknowledge the three very big, very scary males staring at Daisy and me.

Their eyes feast on our flesh. Their stances are rigid and ready.

My chest constricts, and I turn my head away.

I shuffle to Daisy's side and help her stand, grabbing onto her tightly, locking my fingers.

"We need to be brave," I whisper, clutching her. "It's up to us now."

It's up to me. I outrank Daisy by a lot. She'll look to me for guidance.

I swallow my fear and stare back at the males.

"W-What now?" I ask, squeezing Daisy's hand.

"Now," the red one smiles wickedly, addressing me, and only me, "we hunt."

FOUR
SOFT FLESH

Gemma

I DRAG DAISY BEHIND ME, rushing through the forest. The trees are thick, the bushes so full my clothes tear, caught and ripping on branches at every turn. My skin opens up as sharp twigs abrade my flesh.

I don't know if we've been running for hours or minutes.

I don't see the forest or anything in it. I see him. His intense, serpentine eyes and sharp lips. I see the blue male's hard, bright orange cock, too long to fit in any human female without terrible discomfort. It was in that moment that I knew Daisy and I were to be nothing except slaves, or worse to this strange species. They don't want to eat us, or experiment on us... They want to use us.

A twig slices my cheek and I flinch, stumbling over my feet. Daisy catches me, and we surge forward.

Fuck reasoning with them.

Another large branch slaps me in the face, and I fall back stunned. Daisy tugs on my arm and forces me to keep going. "Don't stop! We can't stop!"

I love her more than anything at that moment. Shaking the pain away, I rush after her. I'd kill for her.

I hear hissing behind me.

"Daisy," I gasp. "They're catching up!"

"Don't stop!" she cries.

The hissing grows louder, and with it, the clash of males fighting. Their animalistic roars fill me with fear.

Spotting a ledge up ahead, we head straight for it. Daisy hits it hard, letting me go and pulling herself atop first. I catch her foot and push her the rest of the way up. When it's my turn, I jump and haul my body up, thinking Daisy will grab my hand and help me. When she doesn't, I claw the rest of the way over the rocks.

Rising to my feet, I search for her.

"Daisy?" I gasp between breaths.

No answer.

"Daisy!" I shout.

A shrill scream answers ahead of me.

"Daisy," I whisper, yanking my knife out from under the lip of my pants, where it's strapped to my leg. "Daisy!" I scream, hoping she'll respond. "I'm coming!"

She doesn't scream again. I call her name a dozen more times, receiving no answer. I don't stop shouting, even when I know she must be gone. I eye my surroundings wildly, hoping for signs of passage or tracks. A few minutes pass, my mania gaining momentum.

She's been caught.

And calling for her will bring the aliens down on me.

"Fuck," I breathe, coming to a stop. I try to stabilize, resting my hand on the trunk of a nearby tree wrenching my eyes shut. "Fuck, fuck, fuck." I've lost her.

Hitting the tree several times with my fists, I calm a fraction.

I can't stay here.

Looking around, there's forest on every side. I don't know what to do without Daisy. We never even had the chance to discuss what to do if we got separated. I can't even see the sky. I have no idea where I am or what direction I should run.

Tears bud in my eyes.

I won't be a broodmare.

I won't.

Shaking, I lift my knife and point it at my chest. I tremble, gripping the knife's shaft with sweaty palms.

I press the tip into me and grit my teeth. My hand shakes. "Do it," I whisper. "You can do it."

Something hits my hand, and the knife goes flying.

My eyes snap up to find the red male before me. "You will not leave me so soon, female," he growls. "Not now that you're finally mine."

I stagger backward.

His words are thick, accented, primal, but clearly in the common tongue. I fall back, hitting the tree behind me. I curl my hands protectively over my chest as the male slides my way. He's holding a spear in one hand. I vaguely remember seeing it on the cliff.

One long red tail dances behind him. A tentacle covered in ruby scales. I think I see blood splattered across them...

"I'm not yours. I'll never be yours," I rasp between breaths.

His brow cocks. "Oh, but you are. You just didn't know it until you met me."

He reaches for me. Covetous eyes lean closer.

I push as far back into the tree trunk as I can go. "I haven't met you."

"Consider this that time. We've now met."

His hand is about to be on me, and I turn my head to the side. Will it be cold or warm? Will it hurt? Will he rip my clothes off and take me? Or will he touch me softly?

I don't get the chance to find out. My vision blurs, and I'm yanked off the ground.

Air rushes over my skin. A roar explodes in my ears, below me. Gasping, I find it's not one hand on me, but two. They grip me tightly under my armpits, and I'm flying through the air.

Not the air... I'm bouncing through the canopy of the trees.

The red male is a spec on the forest floor as I'm jerked from one large branch to the next. Sparks of light shoot at us, coming from the end of his weapon. My belly curls and I taste bile.

"Azsote!" His terrible shout shakes the leaves. "You will die!" he screams. "I will see your blood seep into the dirt and your body rot! I will see the maggots feast on your entrails!"

My breath *wooshes* from my mouth. Leaves rush past me in a blur. It takes a stunned second before I'm struggling in this new male's grip.

"Stop," the one holding me orders, slinging from one tree to the next. "Or you will fall!"

I struggle harder, and when the male shuffles me under the crook of his arm, I kick and scream, clawing his scales wherever I can reach. I don't care if I hurt him. I want him to let go of me.

He grunts and curses things I don't understand, trying to get me to stop. I'd rather fall than have my choices taken away from me. The blur and the jerking, the pinching of my flesh weaken my attack. I flinch, hair blowing in my eyes.

"Female, you will fall!" He pulls me forward, twists me around until I'm face to face with a bright green male with black eyes. He squeezes me against his chest, and I draw back to pummel him with my fists.

"Let me go!" I shout.

"You are sssafe with me! I won't hurt you."

I don't want to hear it. "Then let me go!"

"Never."

"Azsote!" I hear the boom of the red male's furor. A voice filled with so much rage; it goes straight to the marrow of my bones. I finally still.

The green male stiffens as well, lips twisting into a snarl. There are small, shiny scales on the sides of his face, and they move with the wrinkling of his skin. I focus on them to stop my sudden dizziness.

I open my mouth to scream, and he spins me around and covers my lips. "Quiet," he demands. "Or *he* will hear you."

My nostrils flare.

Good.

Let the red one come and start a fight. It'll give me another chance to run for it.

I cock my head and bite the green male's hand as hard as I can. Blood gushes into my mouth as my teeth pierce his flesh. He shouts and jerks away.

I scream at the top of my lungs.

The male jerks me hard as I thrash. "I don't want to hurt you," he yells.

"You already have!"

A day ago, I was a respected member of the military. I was at the top of my field: Communications Director on the bridge of *The Dreadnaut*. A coveted position I worked hard to earn. I'd spent years working as a lackey, slowly rising in the ranks, taking classes, taking every training offered to expand my resume.

It was hard, grueling work. I sacrificed relationships, leaving my family to improve my chances of being bridge crew.

I earned my spot at the top and I intend to keep it.

It's mine.

I hadn't sacrificed my youth just to be used as a human sacrifice for Peter. I'm not just some piece of meat to be handed off.

I buck wildly. I see a flash of red coming straight for us through the trees, and it's enough for him to loosen his grip.

"No!" he shouts. But it's too late, I'm slipping down his sleek, scaled body. His hands grab the cloth of my shirt, ripping it as I continue to fall. "Vruksha! Catch her," he bellows. "Now!"

The air breezes over my skin as I'm freed from his grip. Yes! I wrench my eyes closed for the painful impact I know is coming. Whether it's branches or the hard ground, it'll hurt like hell—if it doesn't kill me.

Two large arms clamp under me, startling my whole body. They wrap around me protectively, holding me close into a steely chest of rippling muscle. I feel it under my cheek as I'm pressed into it.

It frightens me.

I still wait for an impact that's been denied me.

"You have tried to take her and have lost. Leave now or die," the male holding me says. "She fell, almost died in your grasp, within minutes of you having her. You do not deserve a female."

A hiss fills my ears.

"Ssshe is a fighter."

"All females are until they're nested."

Another hiss. "And you think you deserve that honor for catching her?"

"I have caught her twice and will catch her a third time if you try to take her again. Let us battle and be done with it!"

I pry open my eyes. The red male holds me close as the green one, Azsote, the red one calls him, is several yards away. His eyes meet mine. I can't help shying away from the fury—the anguish—in them.

I don't think I can escape him again. I see it. He won't make the mistake of letting me fall a second time.

"Do not be afraid of me," Azsote says, softening his demeanor. Maybe he sees my terror.

The red male clutches me closer. "Do not speak to her! Leave now or die."

Azsote juts his chin. "Why not let her decide?"

My eyes widen. *Choice?* Will they give me a choice? There's hope in that. That means they can be reasoned with.

"No."

"Let me choose!" I gasp, finally unlocking my joints to jerk in his arms. "Please?"

He tenses and looks down at me. There's doubt—and something else —is in his gaze.

They're smart, these aliens. Smarter than they have any right to be. They look like us, kind of. They speak the common tongue, even though they have a thick accent. What else can they do? What do they know?

A plan forms in my mind. I'll go with one, learn what I can, find the alien technology, and steal it. I'll bring it back to the facility and save Daisy in the process. And when I'm back with my people, I'll contact *The Dreadnaut* and tell them about Peter's and Collins' treachery.

Some of my fear vanishes as the plan becomes clear. I just need to keep my legs closed in the process. I just need to survive until I have the chance to see it through.

"Let me choose," I whisper again as the black eyes of the red male bore into me. He has scales on his face like the other, but he also has ridges on the sides of his jaw. Those ridges run down his shoulders too.

"You are mine," he warns. "You've been mine since you walked off your ship."

He remembers.

"Let her choose, Vruksha, and no blood will need to be spread. If she chooses you, I will leave you be, and if she chooses me...you slither away and take your chance with winning the other human female."

His *name is Vruksha.*

"Her name is Daisy," I say, still thinking of my plan.

"Daisy," Azsote corrects. "What a strange name."

He doesn't ask me for mine.

A branch snaps in the distance, followed by several others. A rustle of leaves, a scattering of stones. The males straighten. Tension fills the space.

Others are coming.

Azsote's voice lowers, hurried. "More are coming, Vruksha. We can fight, allow them to gain on us, and battle the others. Or we can let her choose and be gone before they arrive."

The red male—Vruksha, I now know for sure—continues to watch me. Hard. I wiggle in his hold because it's all I can do. I no longer have a knife to plunge into his heart. His dark eyes slide from my face and over my body, lingering on my ripped shirt. I reach over and pull it taut to hide my skin.

I don't like his eyes on me. I don't want to know what's happening behind them.

"Fine," he says. "Choose me, like you know you should."

"Let me down first," I urge.

"No."

"Let her down," Azsote rumbles.

"Never," Vruksha growls.

The rustling of leaves grows nearer.

"We don't have much time!"

More males don't sound ideal to me. The two I'm already facing are enough to contend with. I squirm even more, hoping for an escape.

"She's going to choose me, so why would I release her?" he snarls.

Fuck him. "I choose Azsote," I announce, finding my voice surprisingly level for my circumstance.

Vruksha's fingers wrench on my skin. His lips pull back to reveal two curved fangs.

"Give her to me," Azsote says, smiling, inching closer to us.

Vruksha doesn't look away from me. Is that betrayal etched in his features? My gut churns. I strain away from him.

Azsote is the better choice. He's more willing to compromise. He'll be easier to manipulate, I think this despite the sinking feeling in my belly. I'm good at judging people... *people,* not half-human, half-snake aliens.

"Azsote, is it?" Vruksha says, his voice so low it gives me pause. "He is who you want?"

I flinch.

"I want to go home," I manage. "I don't want any of you."

"She's made her choice! Hand her over and leave," Azsote snaps.

Vruksha tears his eyes from mine. His muscles bulge.

Azsote, noticing, bares his fangs in response. Their stances shift, tails sweeping forward with sharp tips. Vruksha hauls his spear in front of me, shielding me in, loosening his grip on me as he does so.

"Then we fight," Azsote mutters, slinking back.

Vruksha raises his weapon and swings it in an arc. The tip glows yellow and sizzles. It slices through the branches above, sending them crashing to the ground.

Azsote shouts, clearly offended by Vruksha's change to the battlefield.

Vruksha takes off, carrying me into the forest. He holds his spear out with his free hand to slice through branches and trees, clearing our route. I struggle to get free of his hold, and glimpsing the forest behind us, he leaves a wake of falling branches and trees.

I stare at the carnage.

Azsote's rage can be heard throughout it all, over the snaps and cracks and crashes.

Having a choice in the matter? Too good to be true... I press my hands into my eyes, stopping my tears from flowing, grasping for the modicum of calm I had reclaimed.

A short time later, Vruksha pulls his spear in, and the light from it diminishes. It's just a primitive wooden stick again. We're still slipping through the forest at breakneck speeds, and I can't get a great look at the weapon.

All I know is that I want it.

Destruction follows us for a time, and so do Azsote's yells.

When we outrun his shouts, Vruksha only speeds up more. The blur of trees makes me light-headed, and a little looney. The sunlight above dims, hailing night. I'm still not calm, but I manage to keep my tears in.

There's a strange, intoxicating scent that keeps stealing my attention. Turning my face into Vruksha's chest, it floods my nose.

Exhaustion hits me while breathing his scent in. There's no escape, not right now. Not at night. Not in the dark. Especially weaponless and in a strange land. All my years of training can't help me here.

I feel useless, and suddenly, exhausted because of it. I settle in Vruksha's arms and close my eyes. Tears bead them.

I don't want to escape, not anymore. Not while it's dark.

I will tomorrow.

I can't give up.

FIVE

MISCOMMUNICATION

Vruksha

My female slumps against my chest as we flee to my den. It's not close by, a day's travel from where the human base is located. I can get there if I journey overnight.

Though I contemplate turning back to collect Azsote's head, I keep moving forward. My honor and pride mean nothing to me right now, not while I have my female in my arms.

She has been sliced up by the whips of sticks and leaves. I smell the tiny dabs of blood on her scrapes.

She is not supposed to bleed, ever, unless it's her moon cycle. I am not equipped to see my female bleed in any other way. Returning to face Azsote is out of the question. I cannot risk more blood.

There are predators and darkness to deal with. Bloodlust is on my mind despite her wounds, and I hope we encounter bears, or better yet, the forest's monsters. My female chose another—Azsote, of all nagas. He is a contender like any one of us, though he is not as vicious or as fearsome as me. Instead, he is cunning and quiet.

But Azsote? A growl tears from my throat. *She chose him?* My bloodlust stems from needing to wipe his existence from this world.

I am lucky to have my spear. A weapon like mine is rare, and it gave me the upper hand against the Boomslang. Azsote could have camouflaged himself within the trees and struck a deadly blow without it.

My eyes flick up.

Azsote could be hiding in the branches above, quietly trailing me. I can't lose my head in memories and fantasies. He is a dangerous foe from the shadows, a sneaky snake. His coloring is meant for such an advantage. One bite from him will put me to sleep and upend the contents of my stomach. I'll be knocked out for hours.

My female will be taken from me. I can't let that happen.

The mere thought of it fills me with tension.

She sighs, settling further into my arms.

Heavy, triumphant warmth invades my chest.

I have never felt this sensation before, this madness that rises when I think of this female. It makes me want to turn back all over again and bash Azsote's head in for touching her, cut off his tail, and slice off his scaly hide. I would carry the Boomslang's skull with me always, as a lesson for any male who thinks about stealing my female.

And then I would burn his hide on a pyre until his scales shrivel and become ash, making my female watch.

He touched her and nearly stole her away.

I clutch her closer.

He may have even succeeded if she hadn't called out for me.

It had to be for *me*.

Oh, yes.

Her call was for me.

Still, this sensation in my chest pulsates. I want to kill, to claim, to mark my territory with the heads of the offenders and show off my beautiful prize for all to see.

Jealousy...

The word whispers through my head. *So this is what it's like to be jealous...*

It's not a feeling I enjoy. It's madness and frustration balled up in one. I'm already frustrated. I don't need to lose my mind in the process.

Not when my world is nearly perfect, and the future is bright. Why can't I shake it?

I take a short rest and glance down at my female to make sure she is okay.

Her eyes are closed and her breaths are light. *She slumbers.* Her face is cast in shadows, her nose pressed to my chest, her arms limp.

Tightness strangles my heart, squeezing to the point I'm nearly suffocated. She is everything I have wanted, everything I have fought for this long life of mine. And she is so small, with no scales, fangs, claws, or tail to defend herself with. I am already crazed with paranoia that I may lose her.

And it's getting worse, having almost lost her to another. On the first day.

She chose him.

My fingers curl.

It doesn't matter. She doesn't get a choice. She never had a choice.

Once she's within my den, she'll know she belongs to me and only me. I will care for her like a pet, and treat her like a female, a precious rarity. I will show her we are meant for each other. That I am a male, a warrior, and a master, and she is a woman. I will fill her with my spill and mark her with my fangs. She'll never look at another male again. Human, naga, or otherwise.

And if she does? It will be with revulsion.

The image alleviates some of my jealousy. I tug her sleeping frame closer to my chest, careful not to bruise her skin.

I have a female. A female!

My arms tighten even further. If she bruises, I will kiss them better.

If I have it my way, she'll never see another male again. She will see me and only me from this night forth. Her mind will be consumed with me; I will make it so. She will want nothing more than to sing my name, licking the excess spill off my scales.

I harden thinking about what's to come.

She'll apologize for her choice with her tongue, I decide. My jealousy vanishes entirely knowing how much she'll need to use it to be forgiven.

My eyes trail over her scaleless face, cementing it in my head. I had taken her in when she stepped off the small ship back on the plateau. Seeing her this close is different... I want to study her, but the forest isn't safe. It's quiet now, although it might not stay that way, and even the quiet brings monsters. With her in my arms, we are an easy target for any hungry beast.

I search for a safe place with enough moonlight to see her.

Spying a clearing to my left, I head in that direction. I come upon a rusty metal structure from the old world and test it with my tail. The structure is overgrown with plants. It holds when I thump it. When I move closer, I recognize it as one of those vehicles humans used to travel by. A car, a large one.

Outside the mountains, there are thousands of them scattered across the wastes.

I carefully set my female on the forest floor and search for the door, finding it quickly. I use my spear to cut through the stems, removing the vines keeping the vehicle closed. Once gone, I tug the handle.

The door comes off with a crunch.

My female moans.

I stop, waiting to see if she wakes up. Thankfully, she doesn't. I turn back to the vehicle, setting the broken, now crumbling door aside, and gently lift my female into my arms, slithering into the space, leaving the majority of my tail outside.

It's dirty and broken inside, and the seats are not comfortable. But the frame remains sound and the overgrowth on the sides makes it relatively private. There's a hole in the roof, and I push the vines aside to allow in moonlight. My sweet burden twists in my arms. I pause. She eventually settles back into sleep.

She's fascinating.

I've seen many human females, though I thought they no longer existed. I've grown up with their unused technology hidden all around me. It's everywhere if one looks hard enough. Even now, I see an orb on the seat next to me and pick it up, dusting it off. All orbs are connected like all the technology is.

There's a relay near the plateau that feeds power to the tech that remains, and though I have never seen it, I know it's there, hidden.

It belongs to Zaku.

The orbs I have collected are within my den, and I've watched videos through them, whatever I ask them to play me. And human females are often on them. These fake humans have kept me company since my father slipped into the forest, never to return.

To my dismay, the screens only show me things of the past and what can be immediately viewed in the present. They only work if they've been in the sunlight to charge, then they last for hours.

My father once told me that he, my sisters, and I were the only Vipers in the world, and though as a youngling, I didn't believe him nor understand him, I do now. I have never seen another like me. Not on an orb, not on a screen either.

Females of my kind... were not common. My mother was the only female Viper until she laid her litter, bringing me and my sisters into the world. And like all naga women back then who conceived a litter, she died giving birth to it.

Inhaling, I curl my arms around my female, trying to make her comfortable. I lean us back against the vehicle's interior frame.

If she is comfortable, she will sleep longer, and I will get more time to enjoy her.

I reach for her hair and twirl it with my fingers. It had been pulled back earlier though it's now tangled around her shoulders. I wish I could see the redness of it, but the moonlight and shadows bleed out the color. It's wispy and soft like gently flowing water.

The moonlight shines down on her face, stealing my attention from the feel of her strands, and my gaze shifts down. She wears blue-colored clothes that match. Using my free hand, I tug at the cloth, confused as to why anyone would wear so much at once. It is the hot season, and I can't stand any barrier on my skin in this heat.

Humans on the screens often wore clothes unless they were bathing —or mating. Since my female is sleeping, I let her keep them on. It can get chilly at night.

I notice a tag on her chest, and my fingers pinch it. Plastic? Something is written on it, and I spin it around to read what it says.

Gemma Hurst.

Bridge Officer and Communications Director.

She communicates with others? She is specialized in this?

I'm intrigued. How can someone specialize in communication? If her world is anything like the one I've seen on screens, then I can venture a guess...

I've seen a lot of miscommunication.

I release her tag, and it rights itself on her shirt. Sliding my upper tail under her legs, I bring her closer, reveling in the sensation of her against me.

Her body weighs little, though I felt the strain of her muscles pushing at me as I carried her earlier. She is strong despite her size, too strong. She fought me and Azsote and nearly got herself killed in the process. A rumbling leaves my throat. If she had died, I would have sought retribution. I would've attacked the facility where the other humans are and destroyed them.

I still might.

I would kill Zaku too, for spurring such a plan that resulted in her death. I despise the King Cobra as much as I am thankful he got the human females out of the facility for us.

Because otherwise, I would be gathering my weapons and infiltrating the base.

Hearing a soft moan, my eyes snap to Gemma's mouth. She sucks in and groans, shuddering once all over. It happens again with the next breath. Fear strikes me from the rasping sounds, and I shake her.

"Human? What's wrong? Wake up!"

The rasping turns into another moan as she startles and opens her eyes. She catches sight of me and—

I slam my palm over her mouth, muffling her scream.

She's tearing at me the next moment, and our limbs hit and knock the rusted walls around us. Some of it gives way. Dirt and dust cloud the air and falls upon us.

"Stop!" I snap. "You will alert othersss to our location."

"Let me go," she cries when I lower my hand from her mouth. "I won't be your plaything!"

I catch her fist before she slams it into my face and hold it tight, trapping her other arm next. She struggles until her burst of energy leaves her. I watch it happen, and the clarity of her situation returning to her eyes.

She's panting and stiff—fear and confusion etched across her face—when I loosen my hold. When she doesn't start hitting me, yelling, or trying to get away, I slowly relax. She doesn't, I notice. I miss her pliant body lying against me.

How fleeting it was.

She's watching me with fear and defiance, her confusion diminishing. She tries to curl her limbs into herself and make herself small. The space we're in doesn't allow it. No matter where she moves, my tail is pressed up against her, holding her open for my secret perusal.

If only she were naked...

I would like bare flesh on my scales.

I can't believe she's here.

She glares at me when she's done searching for a way to escape from my limbs.

"I won't let you go," I say.

"I know that now." Still, she scoots her feet closer, her knees to her chest. "I've forgotten..."

"Forgotten what?"

"That I don't want to escape."

I go still. Has she...? Has she accepted me? Chosen me? I can hardly believe it after she tore into me, but perhaps I scared her. Maybe she believes I deserve it. She did wake up in a new place and in the dark. "You will not fight me?"

"I didn't say that."

My eyes narrow. "Then you have not accepted what's between usss."

"There's nothing between us. I don't even know you. I don't know what you plan on doing to me..." she trails off.

So she doesn't know. Her males have kept her in the dark.

I puff out my chest. "I will give you shelter, food, clothing, and a place to nest," I announce. "A home where the monsters of this world cannot reach you or our future brood. I will provide everything you need and protect you."

"Monsters?" Her eyes shift to the darkness outside our small shelter, straining her neck. "Brood?"

I slip my claws along the column of her throat. "Do not be afraid. They cannot get to you now that you are with me."

She tears off my hand and shakes her head, grabbing it, burying her face in her hands. A dry sob escapes, and it hollows out my gut. I reach for her, but she shies away from my touch.

"I won't let them hurt you," I tell her, softening my voice.

She cries harder, shaking and rubbing her eyes. It re-emphasizes how tiny she is compared to me. She was the tallest human on the plateau, taller than even the human men. Yet, next to me, she is small. She is not safe in this world of mine, and she doesn't belong. She belongs in the sky, among the stars, where all hope and dreams thrive.

Unfortunately, she's here now, and I won't let her go. She will get used to it. I will help her.

I will be her protector. I will teach her the ways of this land. It will be difficult because she is unhappy. I will have to make her happy first.

She cries for a time, and I sway part of my tail to pet her in comfort. Her sniffles are the only noise breaking the quiet night. I wait, knowing she needs this. She cannot accept the future if she does not grieve the past.

An hour passes before her tears dry.

When she wipes her nose on her sleeve and looks at me, I know she's done.

"I vow it," I tell her. "Nothing will hurt you as long as you are with me."

For I am strong and vicious, and a master against anything that might lurk in these woods. She will come to see this soon.

"It's not that." Her voice hitches. "I had a life, a job, ambition—and then some fuckers took that all away from me like I don't matter, like I'm just a bargaining chip. And for what? Technology that may or may not help us with the Ketts? For something we may have discovered ourselves in due time?" Her voice gains steam. "Fuck them. Fuck Peter, fuck all of them. And to think I was friends with Peter? I thought he was a good boss, a good man—"

I grunt. If I see this Peter again, I will stab him with my spear.

"—and he does the worst, most cowardly thing a man in his position could do, forcing others to make all the sacrifices. I hate him. I hate all of them."

"You're better off with me, sssafer with me." *Yesss,* I coo, petting her hair.

"Am I, though?" Her voice lowers, her fury vanishing. "Are you going to rape me?" she whispers, hugging her arms tighter.

Rape? She thinks I would rape her? "I will have you," I growl. "I will have you in *every* way. But I will not rape you. I will never do that."

She looks away. "Then you will never have me."

My anger ignites. "You deny us? Still? I have caught you. You belong to me now! You ran and I caught you, my bride. Baring yourself to me and giving yourself over to my protection is all that is left!" I want to grab her, pull her to me, and shake her with sense. "It is what I have won! What I am owed!"

Her face shudders in shadows. "I owe you nothing. I didn't choose you."

I slam my hand against the side of the shelter. It goes through the metal with a pop, sending the metal around it crumbling down. How dare she? How dare she deny me? She thinks she can have my protection for nothing in return? She thinks her actions will not have consequences?

"Mates rut," I snarl, jerking my hand back. Her eyes widen. "They fuck," I say again, feeling my member pulse under my scales, using the ancient slang from the videos. "You understand this."

"Vruksha is it?" Her voice is hesitant, low. I nod. "Just because you say we're mates doesn't mean it's true. Let me go, and you will never have to see me again."

"Never."

"I will never *fuck* you. We are not even the same species."

"You will."

"Humans don't have mates!" her voice gains steam.

"They do now."

My agitation cannot be controlled. Finding the handle of an old door behind me, I jerk it open, snapping the vines on the other side. I slide through the shelter and out, uncaring of my female within, and grab my spear. If I stay, I will hurt her. I will bring the shelter down upon us both and bury us within it.

I am a Pit Viper. A dangerous foe. A red devil. She should be begging for my protection and all I have to give her. If I were taken to the stars and placed in her world, I would seek a master—a mate—for guidance so I may rule my enemies, but she doesn't even look at me as her savior—she doesn't want me at all!

I am trying to understand her... I can't.

"Vruksha," she says softly.

My scales straighten and stretch.

I can't look at her without mounting frustration. Instead, I swing my tail and lash the plants around me to shreds, expelling my fury like she just expelled her tears.

Tears. I spit.

I pivot to her. "You will come to realize your situation and the generosity I provide. I will let you fight it now because I do not think I can take you gently in my current state. But you will join with me. You will come to understand that Earth, this Earth, is nothing what it used to be, and that ssstarts with me."

I slip into the shadows of the forest nearby before she can respond. Her wary eyes find mine in the darkness.

If she does not want me, then she will have to watch me in my madness. She will witness what she does to me by her mere presence alone. She will see what she is missing, and I will show her that coming to me is the only way. Because the only protectors of this world are brutal and territorial, and I am kind in comparison to them.

My kindness has limits. Limits—that I have a feeling—she will test repeatedly.

For some reason... I am looking forward to it.

"What is your name?" I command from my place in the trees. I know it, but I want to hear her say it. I want to hear it aloud. I want to see if she'll listen and give me what I want. It would go a long way in soothing my agitation.

A prize, I convince myself, calming. *Her name is a boon.*

A gift.

She doesn't answer me at first, and despite what she said earlier, I assume she is considering running now that I have allowed space between us.

"Gemma," she says after a minute, loud enough for me to hear.

"Gemma," I repeat, my voice raspy. "This is what you do to me."

I slide out from the shadows and into a beam of moonlight. The scales at my groin pull back. With my spear gripped in my free hand, the other cups my hefty member, revealing it to her. It's heavy, engorged with seed, and painful; it's what she's done to me.

It's what I suffer for her. Weeks of torment, weeks of flooding torture as seed continously fills me, swelling my hide to the brink. Females do not suffer in the ways that males do, so we make them suffer by stoking their arousal, only to deny them. I have seen it.

Her gaze slides down to my middle, where my pelvis becomes my tail—where my shaft usually hides beneath. Except it's not hiding now, and her lips part as she takes it in.

"I am in pain," I hiss. "So much pain. For you."

SIX

A GAMBLE OF WANT

Gemma

I can't help staring.

An alien male is pumping his cock mere yards from where I'm sitting. Heat surges to my face. Uncivilized, quick to anger, but intelligent, Vruksha's nothing like the serpentine beast I believed he was.

And yet, he very much still is.

I catch a glimpse of his tongue when he hisses low and deep.

There's a small fork in it, and it vibrates on every S sound.

His intelligence and uncanny knowledge of my culture confounds me. It doesn't make sense. I don't care, not really, the nonsensicalness of it. Aliens are never what they seem upon first contact. I knew these locals spoke the common tongue, how could they not, having bartered for me? He can be reasoned with, and that is all that matters.

His hips snap forward.

I grip the vines inside my shelter as he releases his cock to my full view.

Dark red scales glisten in the moonlight, gleaming across his frame. Large arms, abs, and sharp muscles make up this strange, angry male before me. I barely take in his strangeness or otherworldly beauty because of the dick being presented to me.

It's a different color than the rest of him, darker, tumescent, and bulky. The shadows cast upon it hint of ridges and a large thickness in the middle of his length. He's long, longer than any human male should ever be, but only truly engorged at the center. Despite its shape, Vruksha's cock is ramrod straight and pointing up, bouncing a little when his tail shifts. The eye of its tip glistens with cum.

A drop slips out and falls to the forest floor.

I press my thighs together, nervous that his cum would somehow find its way between us, and if I don't stop it now, Vruksha's threats will come true. I don't want them to be true. I need to hold onto hope for as long as I can, and fight. Stay vigilant.

I can't help shivering, my flesh prickling. A man has never presented his dick to me before. I lean back into my shelter as my muscles tighten, because I'm watching closely all the same.

Because despite everything, he's physically alluring, and his smell is intoxicating. Sniffing, I can almost scent him.

I sniff again to make sure. His smell...is...really nice. Really, really nice.

He grabs his member, squeezing the thickness in the middle. His palm presses into it, and his fingers wrap tightly, massaging it. His gaze hoods, staring at me.

Staring at me and touching himself. Heat rises to my cheeks.

"Ssso much pain," he groans, rolling his S. The hiss rumbles through the air and tickles my ears.

Shock hits. I know what this is because I'm not averting my eyes and throwing things at him. My breaths shallow and as much as I don't want to, I stare. Hard.

I want to be that person who's righteous and virtuous, but I'm not. I never have been. Seeking spirituality and God is for those who don't have the kind of job I do. There's nothing virtuous or spiritual working on the bridge of *The Dreadnaut*.

He's an intelligent, sentient alien... My original, brief assumption of him is now mired in confusion.

Vruksha loosens his grip on his knot and pumps his length instead. His tapering tip, where his cum drips, is pointed and slightly curved, and could be a weapon in itself.

"Gemma," he rasps my name, and my skin rises even more. "Gemma," he mutters again when he slides his hand back down.

My heart riots. I turn away, but the motion is harder than I expected.

"Gemma, Gemma, Gemma," he continues. What he's doing goes against human decency, except he doesn't know or even care. "Gemma." He says my name with each thrust of his hand, his hips. "*Gemma.*"

I listen, his pace increasing. I steal another glance, practically mesmerized from the mantra of my name.

Primitive darkness glints his black eyes, bursting with fervor. His angular face tilts downward, arching, ribbed brows lower to show menace or... or want? I don't know, and I tremble. He looks at me like he really is in pain, and that the only thing in all the world that could relieve him is *me.*

I face him and the virility he's displaying. As I swallow, I find that my throat is tight. My mouth is dry, like I had been gaping.

His arm jerks, tempo building. The sounds of my name become nothing more than a guttural, animalistic gasp on his lips. The rasps he releases roughens.

He's showing me what he intends to do with me, and what's in store if I can't find my way home. Will it be bad? I hug my legs to my chest, making sure my ripped shirt covers me entirely.

Will it be...okay?

"Gemma!" he shouts my name one final time, bowing over as his hips thrust outward. His tail slams against the ground. The leaves above shake, some fall.

I jump, startling as he crumples onto the forest floor, thrusting still. I'm still watching this male jacking off, and I lean out to see if he's okay.

Something wraps around my ankle. "What are you doing?!" I shout as he drags me out of the shelter and toward his pumping hips.

I kick once, trying to dislodge his tail, but he lifts and grabs me, pulling me under his large body.

He pushes his hips between my legs, spreading them. I press my hands to his chest. His cock slaps against my stomach. I suck in.

It's hot and wet.

He pins me with his eyes as my clothes dampen with his cum.

"Do you sssee now what you do to me? What I need from you, Gemma?"

I swallow, holding still.

All I can think about is that my legs are open and his body is between them. I try not to press them closed, clenching, straining, uncertain.

"Why me?" I gasp, pushing at his chest.

"Because, my sweet little human, you are mine." His eyes twinkle. His tongue comes out and slides up my cheek.

My whole body shivers.

"And soon, you'll be licking me like how I'm licking you."

I gasp and the delicious scent of his smell invades me fully. I gasp again, sucking it in, needing more. Greedy little human that I am.

His mouth moves over my ear and I turn away, and then it's upon my throat. It's warm and wet and demanding. I hate that I clench again, that I grit my teeth because it tickles.

This isn't happening, I tell myself. Darkness or not, protection or not. Heat running through my veins or not. *I need...fresh air.*

His lips caress my throat. They're warm, soft...

I have a plan. He's just a means to an end.

Daisy.

The second Daisy comes rushing back to my head, I push at Vruksha, fighting to get out from under him. "Stop!" I yell, breaking through my shock, and the cage of his scent. He rises, and I scoot back until I'm pressed up against the shelter.

Darkness clouds his eyes. The twinkle, gone.

How could I forget about Daisy? I have no idea what happened to her or where she is. What she must be going through... If it's anything like this?

I pray she's okay.

Vruksha pushes his cock into the confines of his tail, the bulge in the middle of it now gone, and it disappears behind a slit of scales. I finally manage to turn away, shame rising to my cheeks. I rub the feel of him off my neck.

"Now that you know what you are in for, I suggest you get some sleep," he says. "Tomorrow, we will reach my den, and you will become mine. Sleep is of the essence."

I hear him slip away and I close my eyes.

I'll never be yours, I vow. Never. My time on this planet will be short.

I'll never become an animal like you.

Yet that heat... It remains. And his smell?

I shudder.

SEVEN

THE AIRFIELD

Gemma

I BARELY SLEPT, and I feel it. The little I got the night before hasn't helped at all. And I'm hungry. As dawn breaks through the trees, my stomach grumbles. I push onward.

My feet drag through the damp overgrowth.

I can't stop thinking about what happened between Vruksha and me last night. He came back to me when the Earth's sunlight broke through the trees, telling me it was time to move on. I thought he would regale me on his *need* again, instead, he handed me a cupped leaf full of water and helped me out of the shelter, asking if I was...okay.

Am I?

I told him I was. Should I have said otherwise?

The amazing scent coming off of him had disappeared during the night.

"How much farther?" I ask, hating that it's me breaking the silence. Again.

We haven't spoken more than a few words since we left the largely-broken shelter hours ago. When he tried to lift me in his arms and carry me after I finished the water he offered. I held him off. It made him furious.

I might be tired, but I've been carried enough by these aliens to last me a lifetime.

Besides, I don't trust him to not bring me up into the trees. Glancing up, I study the branches. They do not look like they could hold my weight, let alone the weight of a male like Vruksha.

A sigh escapes my lips. I rub my eyes with the back of my hand, wishing I hadn't lost my hair tie in the fight yesterday.

Massaging my neck, I still feel Vruksha's tongue. It's elsewhere too, or at least I'm imagining it elsewhere. Warm, wet, and mobile. Ticklish at the fork. It's a sensation hard to describe. I shake my head. His tongue tickles.

A blush rises to my cheeks.

If I were to be asked if these Earth aliens were voyeurs yesterday, I would've gifted a response of utter confusion. Today, I just want to laugh. Laughing is easy. The incredulous giggle tickling the back of my throat is all that keeps me walking forward, the only thing stopping my thoughts from drifting to darker subjects.

If I'm laughing then I'm not screaming or crying.

Vruksha threatened me with all of himself, showed me what he had to offer. No human man would've considered doing the same. They're all words, easy flirtations, and gifts. There's protocol in wooing a lover within the field—on a spaceship—and jacking off in front of them isn't part of it.

Perhaps it should be.

I've been asked out on dates and have gone out for a drink with men in the past. Sometimes I even enjoyed the flirty messages sent back and forth. Never has a man showed me his skill and stamina, or what he has hanging between his legs before a physical agreement, a contract.

Contracts are important legal documents, ensuring both parties are entering a physical relationship willingly. Oftentimes a relationship officer oversees them. Having a contract in place protects both parties. It protects the babies born between such unions too.

I can't get the scene of Vruksha thrusting out of my head.

My face scrunches.

"Through the trees," he answers, not even glancing at me. He's focused on the forest around us, checking the sky and trees constantly. I'm glad he is. At least one of us is. I hear animals but do not want to meet them. I'm not an idiot. If I do choose to run again, I know I'll have to contend with these *'monsters'* Vruksha mentioned. If

I run, it would be away from the one being who keeps me safe from them.

I eye his spear.

I want it.

I'm going to need it when the time comes. Bringing back a weapon like his—obviously Lurker-made—would be leverage.

"How can you tell where we are?" I ask, wanting to learn about the world I'm facing. Something hoots in the branches above, and I flinch.

"The land is flattening."

"Oh." Has it been? I hadn't noticed. All there's been is trees, trees, and more trees. And the occasional oddly-shaped structure overgrown with vines and leaves. It's not like the trees are strange to me. Most habitable planets I've seen or visited have trees like the ones on Earth.

"We are close, very close," he adds. Vruksha cants his head in my direction except he doesn't say anything more. He's been quiet since his show last night, and though it didn't bother me at first, it is beginning to now. Questions, so many questions are at the tip of my tongue, waiting to be asked, needing answers.

I want to ask so many things and each time I'm about to, I look at the alien who's captured me, his tail, muscles, and blatant, in-your-face strength and then intimidation thwarts me.

Nighttime didn't do Vruksha justice. The moonlight on his scales was beautiful, though it's nothing like seeing him in full light, in full view. I've gotten to watch him for hours, he's the only thing I've watched for hours. And my observations prove that this male is nothing like the men I grew up with. Vruksha intimidates me. Not even the captain of *The Dreadnaut* intimidates me. This half-man, half-serpent does what the most powerful man on my ship can't.

All my questions die on my tongue.

Vruksha is built, lean and long, and his tail seems to go on forever, flicking, wrapping, and testing the forest. He uses it like a third arm, a third leg, whichever he needs at the moment, and it's mesmerizing. I recall the sensation of his tail on my skin, his scales, sleek and soft although hard when pressed against. They're armor, and considering all the scratches on my arms, I envy him for that. My fingers twitch, hungry to explore his scales more thoroughly. To discover how strong they really are.

Can they be pierced with a blade? A bullet?

His scales shift as well, rising from his skin ever so slightly when a strange noise comes from the forest. Among them are ridges. Ridges that appear as inflexible as his scales.

And *oh*, is this male flexible.

Like an acrobat, Vruksha uses the world around him as a playing field. Using his tail and hands, he swings up into trees, slipping up to the very tops to peer out over the landscape at a moment's notice.

Yesterday, he carried me like I weighed nothing, and he carried me for *hours*.

It was probably easy too, I grump. With the length and size of his tail, that alone probably weighs three times what I do, if not more. He'd have to be mighty to climb with that weight hanging off him.

I'm not heavy, although I am tall, and I do have some curves. My weight should have hindered him somewhat. Recalling back, I don't think it did.

"We're here," Vruksha says, pulling me from my thoughts.

I see nothing but more trees around us.

I hug my middle. "Here? Please don't tell me you live in a treehouse."

"Treehouse? No, human, I don't reside in such an easily accessible place. I am not Azsote." Vruksha swings his spear out and moves the heavy branches in front of him. There's a clearing on the other side, a field almost. He moves aside and nods for me to pass through.

I hug myself tighter and walk past him, trying to avoid touching him. His tailtip brushes my leg.

A shiver goes through me, and I quiet it as fast as it rises.

Sunlight hits me, and the clearing widens as I move forward. Vruksha follows behind. He doesn't stop me, so I keep going until there's a field of intermittent trees extending beyond my sight. There are no bushes here, nor overgrowth.

It's like an orchard, but not entirely, instead there's just dirt and long fields of grass between the trees, and old, dead leaves covering the ground. And the ground? It's mostly level.

"What is this place?" I ask.

He slides past me and deeper into the field, toward a worn path on the ground where he's clearly moved many times.

"I think this used to be an airfield."

"An airfield? Like a landing port?"

"A landing area for planesss."

"You mean ships," I correct.

He shakes his head. "Planes. This was built for planes."

No one uses the term plane anymore. To know that at one point, humans were all stuck on Earth, without any access to space, unsettles me. The lack of freedom would have driven me mad. Where would someone go to get away from another? At least in space, the possibilities are endless. I could lose Vruksha easily if I had access to my tech.

I follow him deeper into the field. "How can you be so sure?"

"The robots have told me."

I still. My eyes snap to him. "Robots? What robots?"

"The ones still living and maintaining Earth."

"They're still here? They work?" How can that be? It's been... ages. "That's impossible."

Vruksha turns his head. "They are still here. They never left like humans did."

"Humans didn't leave. They were killed off. The only ones who survived are the ones who weren't on Earth when the Lurkers committed genocide."

"I survived," he grunts. "Yesss... the Lurkers."

"Were you alive when the Lurkers destroyed us?" I snap, knowing it was impossible. There are long-living beings in the universe, and none of them can survive for fifteen hundred years. At least none that humans have encountered thus far.

"No. I came after, when the plants and the trees returned to the world, according to my father. No naga remembers a time before that, before this world grew again," his voice lowers.

"Half this planet is still growing," I say. "Entire continents of this world remain without life. Only this mountain range has truly become acceptable. It's why I'm here, why any of us can be here."

"Ah yes, the dust wastes."

My eyes shoot to him. "You've seen them?" From my readings, the nearest wastes were a little more than a hundred miles from the facility, in every direction. It's as if the facility was the epicenter of this dead world's regrowth. It's why our team chose it as our base.

"I have seen them." He gives me an unreadable expression. "You may know more about this world than me, but you do not know this forest. This was once a place called an airport, and it is where I have made my den. A home I am eager to show you."

"But there are robots?" I'm still hung up on this. There'd been no working technology in the facility. In fact, the base had been practically stripped clean.

Which now I find odd...

"Come. I'll show you."

Vruksha glides to a half-bent tree that has a single large boulder beside it covered in moss. When I get closer, I realize it isn't a rock at all. It's a pile of... *something*. He swipes some of the moss off, and straight, angular edges reveal themselves. Man-made edges.

I move closer. "What is it?"

"What's left of a plane."

"Planes aren't robots," I mumble. I reach out and touch it, brushing off more of the moss. So much of it is bent and broken, and there's even some rust. I step back to get a better look. "This can't be a plane," I say. "It's not big enough."

"It's all that's left."

I stare at it, my belly churning, not liking his explanation. All that's left? I look around, trying to see what this place was like at one point. I can't imagine it. The past eludes me. I can only see a strange orchard with a strange growth pattern.

"There is more," he tells me when I finish circling the structure.

"There is?"

"Oh yes."

"Show me."

His eyes glint and something wicked darkens them for a second. He pivots away, and I chase after him to catch up.

EIGHT

A DEEP, DARK HOLE

Gemma

We don't go far.

Vruksha stabs his spear into the ground and reaches down when he comes to a random clearing. Turning, I can see the plane in the distance. He grabs something with both his hands and yanks. A thick metal hatch pops up from the ground, displacing a pile of leaves. Leaning forward, there are stairs on the other side of the hatch that leads down into a hole.

I jerk back. "I'm not going in there."

He reclaims his spear. "Yes, you are."

"Hell no, I'm not."

"My den is within. It is safe. The safest place in the world for you."

"I don't care. There's no way in hell—"

Vruksha grabs me, rounding his free arm around my back and tugging me to his chest. I squirm and fight, but he's too strong. He hauls me against him and carries me into the dark.

The walls close in.

"Let me go!" I shriek, kicking and batting at his chest. "Let me go!" He ignores me and shuts the hatch with his tail, closing off the remaining light. I'm blinded by darkness, and my fear returns tenfold. I got too cozy with curiosity. "Vruksha," I gasp, hoping that saying his name will help me. "Please!"

Then my world lights up, and the cold pathway reveals the walls on either side of us. There are small hanging glass orbs attached to them, and some glow, though most flicker weakly. He's taking me downstairs, down, down deep. The light grows brighter and brighter the deeper we get.

I'm still battling to get out of his hold when he comes to a stop at the bottom of the stairs where a long room reveals itself with dim lights and weak colors.

I spin away from Vruksha when he sets me down. I brandish my hand to keep him at bay. "Take me back out," I gasp, barely paying any mind to the colorful things around me. "I want out."

People go into holes to be forgotten about, or worse, to die.

"Soon, human. When you calm again. When it is safe."

"I am calm!"

"When you submit to me then," he says, his voice lowering. He sets his spear against the wall next to the stairs.

I swallow and back up another step. "So that's your plan? Keep me captive until I do what you say?"

"I will keep you captive regardless of whether you listen to me or not. I cannot let you roam the forest when there are predators, and there are always predators. Ruthless, bloodthirsty creatures who would like nothing more than to feast on your flesh."

My stomach sinks. "I refuse."

He slips toward me, and I back up even more. He continues until I fall upon a barrier and something crashes to the ground. It's not big. Regardless, I grab it and hold it in front of me as a shield. "Stay away!"

"Human," he hisses, rearing up and forcing me to strain my neck, to cower. "I will never stay away from you. If I did, you could be hurt, or stolen away."

"I can't stay here," I whisper.

"You are afraid?" He puts his hands on the wall on either side of me. "Why are you afraid this time, little female?"

"I'm..."

"You're?"

"I don't like being trapped," I breathe, pressing hard against the wall at my back.

Vruksha lowers his face to mine. "Then don't think of this as being trapped. Think of this place as a shield." He glances at the thing in my hands. "A better one than that," he mutters, taking it from me, whatever it is, and sets it aside.

My arms curl around my chest again. "I can't be in a hole, I can't. I know we don't know each other, but you seem... reasonable. Is there someplace else you can take me?"

I stop before I say Azsote's treehouse.

Vruksha's face snaps back before mine, and I startle with a hitch.

"This isn't a hole. It's a bunker. And if you take a minute to look around, you'll find it is not all that disagreeable," he growls.

He sounds unhappy.

Have I insulted him? I chew on my lip. Does it matter if I have?

Yes. Yes, it does, Gemma. You're now stuck in a hole with him. Don't insult those you're stuck in a hole with.

Even spaceships have port windows to help with claustrophobia. They have giant gardens with wild animals, and lagoons to swim. The nicer colony ships do at least. Those meant for higher castes of people.

Somehow, I know this place has neither gardens nor lagoons.

I'm not happy. I still haven't accepted my fate. There are correspondences I need to address, meetings I've made with my subordinates, and I have a checkup with the ship's physician in five cycles. Time is money, and lives, or so the higher ups say.

And there's this male here who unnerves me, a male who pulls out his cock and touches it in front of me.

No, I haven't accepted my fate yet.

I sure hope I'm not here long enough to do so.

"Are you calm now?" he asks, his head swaying side to side, his hot breath heating both of my cheeks.

But a hole? I can't do a hole. "No," I say, turning my face as Vruksha's sways. "I'd rather take my chances above ground."

He leans back, and my lungs open for air.

"Orb, initiate," he barks, looking to the left. My eyes follow to see what it is as I dash under his arms and move away from the wall.

A buzzing fills my ears, followed by a dry, mechanical voice. "What can I help you with today?" the orb says. A small, round ball drifts into the air. Lights come off it in flickers, like it's dying. Like the lights on the walls.

I've seen something like it before. We have similar speakers on the ship, although there they are integrated into the structure and appear more as holograms.

I think I remember seeing one of the other nagas on the plateau with one.

The old humans of Earth were highly advanced, this I know. And with the Lurkawathians guiding them, they had access to things far beyond anything we can currently create. Still... it unsettles me, seeing these relics of the past. I'm beginning to wonder if I'll know Lurker technology when I see it or if it's only old human tech that's left.

"Tell me what predators are nearby," Vruksha demands of the orb.

The lights on it twinkle once. "Scanning now," it says.

Vruksha turns to me. "This is why I can't let you leave." He reaches out and twirls a strand of my hair. I swat his hand away.

He plays with my hair a lot.

Vruksha recaptures my hair with his other hand. His eyes soften as he stares at the strands between his fingers, and this time, I don't swat him away. It's no use. He's going to touch me if he wants to. My scalp tingles as his fingers move and goosebumps rise on my arms. He's being gentle.

I hold still, waiting to see what he does.

His eyes lift from my hair and find mine.

Staring intensely, he brings my hair to his nose and breathes in. His eyes roll back and close as he groans.

My heart quickens, mystified. He hums next, like breathing in the scent of my hair is not enough for him, he tangles his hand into more of my strands and burrows his face into it, rubbing his cheek, his nose, against them. His groaning turns into a rumble, matching the thrum of my heart.

And then his tailtip curls around my ankle and wanders up my pants.

Startling, I dodge away and out of his hold.

He growls when I do, "Why? You are mine." He turns to face me.

I search for an escape but the space we're in is long and narrow. "No."

He stalks towards me and I'm back against another wall.

No. Not even if you look at me with softness, not even if you vow to keep me safe on this strange planet. I can't let his gentleness seduce me, nor his clarity, or his knowledge of my language. I won't be manipulated.

I've spent my entire life mastering a skill set to become an asset to my people. I clawed up the ranks and worked my way into a higher caste. Giving that all up for him and what he offers? I'll never do that. I can't let my blood, sweat, and tears go to waste.

His arms come back up to trap me again.

"Scanning complete," the orb announces. It couldn't be at a better moment. I turn my face away when Vruksha tries to lock me with his intensely hungry eyes. His muscles bunch, showing veins and tendons outlined where the scales are a little thinner. His strength is always on display.

I wish I could do the same.

I'm trying to be strong, except inside, I'm nothing but a little, lost girl, still wishing my parents were living on the same ship as me and wondering why it was so easy for them to give me away.

Depressing feelings rise, and I force them away before they take over.

"To the north lies several packs of wild pigs and a bear," the orb says as I ignore Vruksha's staring. "East is another, larger pack of pigs, heading south."

"Pigs aren't predators—" I whisper. I don't know what bears are.

The orb brightens, and a screen materializes in the air. I blink as it catches my attention, breaking the spell of Vruksha's gaze. We both face the screen. Whatever it's showing us is hazy, fuzzy, and dirty. Through the messy streaming, shapes emerge.

"There are three more bears west, following a herd of deer, and south lies two snakes," the orb finishes.

I take in the sudden imagery, hoping to get a clear view of what it's trying to show. I want to see these predators, what I might be up against when I make my way back home.

I need it to distract me from the way Vruksha is making me feel. I shiver.

Giant shapes appear. They are large, furry creatures standing on all fours. They must be these bears, since I know what pigs and snakes are. They don't look frightening to me, although their size gives me pause.

"Show the snakes," Vruksha demands.

The airy screen blurs, shuts off momentarily, then returns with a crackle. At first, all I see are trees. Nothing but thick branches, bushy leaves on some, while others have pine needles and cone-shaped baubles hanging from them. The same trees I've been seeing for weeks now.

"I don't see a snake," I say.

"Wait for it," Vruksha tells me.

Something emerges. It's slight at first, perhaps an appendage? Whatever it is, it coils around a branch slowly. Covered in scales of black and grey, it gets bigger and bigger. It reminds me of Vruksha's tail. Another one of his kind?

The tail slips out of sight, and I search for where it went.

One of the branches shakes and flings, and something large drops to the forest floor.

"A snake?" I gasp.

The rest of a serpentine tail comes into full view, and so does the male the tail is attached to. My gut twists.

"Death Adder," Vruksha murmurs. "Zhallaix."

The image wavers, but the male before me scares me to my bones.

He isn't beautiful like Vruksha, or even the green one, Azsote. He's large, scarred, and crooked, with stripes of thick black scales from chest to tailtip. His muscles are meaty and ripped, his hair is tied to the top of his head, and he wears garish white trinkets which are attached to his hair, arms, and waist.

Bones?

He's wearing them as trophies...

There's a scar trailing from one of his eyes and into his mouth, making it appear like he's scowling. There are more scars. Some of them are deep, as though there are chunks of his flesh missing.

His dark eyes whip in my direction.

My back straightens. I know it's not possible—I think—but the male is glaring directly at me.

His tail strikes out, and the image disappears. I stare at the air, waiting for the picture to return.

It doesn't.

"That's not a snake," I whisper.

"No, that's a Death Adder," Vruksha mentions that name again. I'm not a fan that *Death* is in this male's name. "One who will break you and use you, if he were to get his hands on you. Zhallaix, he's called. He's made his den in another bunker on the other side of the airfield."

I swallow. "Will he come here?"

"No."

I blow out a breath. "Are you sure?"

"He will lay traps and wait for us to come to him. Zhallaix does not hunt."

That's not better. That sounds worse. Much worse.

"Why is he called Death Adder? What's a Death Adder?"

"Zhallaix is gifted with exceedingly powerful venom. He is a rabid male who once tried to rule us with his power. We have all fought him at one point to keep our territory. He has survived us all. I don't believe anything can kill him. Especially not a small human female."

I tighten my arms over my chest. "How do you know he'll hurt me?"

My plan to run wavers.

Vruksha snarls. "You underestimate me if you think us understanding each other means we are not savage creatures. I have fought him and nearly died on several occasions, and I am sure we will fight again, he and I. He will hurt you because he does not use nor trust the mechanical beings of this world. He destroys all technology he finds. Death Adders are rapists, of his kind and technology, and the reason why there are no more females. He is a menace. A blight."

I don't understand half the things Vruksha says, but his mention of the females of his species stops me. My eyes shift to him. "Where are your females?"

"Gone."

My lips flatten. "Dead?" I ask warily.

He shakes his head in answer. "No. Show the other snake," Vruksha barks at the orb.

The orb glitters with lights again. "The other snake is no longer in range."

Suddenly exhausted, I turn away from both Vruksha and the orb to take a look at my surroundings. *Vruksha's den.* The hole I'm trapped in. He's right, I concede. Just because Vruksha isn't forcing me to mate with him doesn't mean one of these other males wouldn't.

For now, I won't fight him to leave. I want to live, because I know I can survive this.

I can survive him. *Maybe not the other...*

I try to forget Zhallaix. He's another problem I don't need, same with the bears. Getting Vruksha's spear is a requirement now—if I want to survive the trek back to the facility too. I won't take my chances on luck. Luck is for the wishful, for the unplanned. I'd rather plan.

Silence descends between us while I glance about, feeling the burn of Vruksha's eyes on my skin.

His bunker is long. It spans far out in front of me. It comes to an abrupt stop at the end, where there's a door. The ceiling is curved like a half-dome with ribbing, and between the cement ribs are lights—or what could've been lights long ago. None of them are on. And though there's light throughout, the longer I stare, the more it seems to dim to a comforting multi-colored warmth.

The main chamber is crammed with so much stuff it eclipses a lot of my view. There's no straight path from the stairway to the very back, and most of the stuff between me and the end, I know nothing about.

Wait, could it be?

I step deeper into the space as the thing I used as a shield catches my attention. It's a metal box with openings on one side, partially covered in dingy scuffs.

"What is that?"

It's not Vruksha who answers me though. It's the orb. "A toaster."

"Toaster?"

"A machine to heat and crisp bread."

"Oh..." That makes sense... The mention of bread makes my stomach grumble. "And that?" I ask, pointing to a contraption of bent and rounded metal pieces connected together.

"Parts of a bike." This time, it's Vruksha who responds. "Orb, off," he adds with a snap.

The orb's lights fade and it settles on a silver disk on a ledge beside the stairs.

Vruksha catches my eyes again as he slides forward, making me back up so I won't accidentally touch him. He scowls when I do. "Follow me."

His mood has only soured. For a moment, I stare after him and his winding ruby tail that remarkably avoids brushing against anything.

Master of his domain, Vruksha has skills I envy. In my job, knowledge is power. If I'm not constantly learning and honing the skills I've already acquired, I could lose my position to someone who has.

And then I feel it, the exit at my back, unblocked and beckoning. His spear is right there, waiting for me to grab it and flee. The realization strikes me like a heady force that steals my breath. Vruksha left the path open, and if I wanted to, I could make a run for it. I could turn and sprint up the steps and hope to the stars I get the hatch open in time before he catches me. I could use his spear on *him*.

I may never get another chance. A better time to make a run for it.

I follow Vruksha deeper into his den.

NINE

TO TRUST A HUMAN

Vruksha

I REPLACE the battery to my generator as I wait for the food to warm. My den is powered by a giant generator that I found long ago, locked away. I've come to understand it was once used for the airport. It doesn't fit in the main space where Gemma awaits. It's in a separate room off to the side.

It took me months to pry the door open. The claw marks on the metal is evidence of this.

The generator takes up the entire smaller room, giving off heat, giving off rich *power*. I used to stare at it, wondering how such a large, metal machine was made. It used to excite me, knowing it was mine, and no other naga knew I possessed anything like it.

Like Gemma.

Now such power doesn't help my mood.

After I led Gemma into my den yesterday, intending to take her to my nest, she could barely pick up her feet halfway through. She yelped when I carried her to a pile of cleaned pelts and encouraged her to rest. Except she would not do so with me so close... I was forced to move away so she would be comfortable enough to slumber.

She continues to deny us.

I see it in her eyes, etched on her face, and in the way she looks around as if searching for something to help her escape. Her cunning is easy to see because it's what I would do...if I were trapped with a being I didn't want to be trapped with.

I hiss.

Haven't I told her that she is safe with me? It is the world outside that is dangerous.

Gemma is not like the human females the screens have shown me time and time again. The broadcasts are from those final days before humans and all life was wiped from the face of Earth. Those females held their mates, their children; they fought for them, and their survival. They reported with fear as sickness took hold of them, they followed orders given to them, and they accepted their fates.

Gemma is not accepting hers.

I stuff the dead battery into a side pocket on the wall for it to charge. If I have learned anything living among the unliving relics of the past, it's that they would die if you let them, but if you don't, they continue to do their job. And this generator... it needed a lot of handling for it to continue.

Unlike many of my other treasures.

Treasures I have gathered, maintained and learned. Each piece I have found or fought for, collected from ruins across the land. Some are from my father and others were stolen.

My hoard comforts me and shows my wealth amongst the nagas. It also bestows security. *She does not care.* She would rather take her chances in the wilds. She'd rather sleep in crumbling structures, with little coverage from the elements and lurking predators.

She'd rather face all of that rather than being protected! She is not keen on being one of my treasures. I am trying to understand her...

It is not easy.

Gemma is nothing like the females desperately searching for security and safety on the videos. They screamed for it, they begged. I have heard those screams and begs so many times, I made certain if I ever met one, I would be able to provide them what they so desperately sought.

Safety and security I have spent years achieving. Years guarding, years perfecting. All in a terrible, primal need to strengthen my domain and keep others away. For what reason before? For me, for ghosts on screens, believing a female would never actually grace this space, but from the moment I first saw Gemma, my den has become something else entirely.

A nest. For her. For us.

Since then, if I wasn't watching for her, desperate for a glimpse of her while I scouted the facility, I was preparing for her.

Leaving the generator room behind, I find Gemma staring at the food on the burner, holding her ripped shirt and jacket closed.

I long for a peek at her flesh, if only because she's adamantly hiding it from me. I want it more with every breath. I sniff the air for blood just in case she might be hiding a wound. I have done so many times already, except I can't help the doubt that niggles me when she hides each time I near.

The food cooking on the burner though? It reeks of bear droppings.

My female seems to like the smell. Her nostrils twitch as I study her. Military rations, packaged and sourced many years ago, I brought them to my den in case of an emergency. And today? I have no interest in going out on a hunt for fresh meat. It's been nearly a week since I've returned to my den, not since Zaku approached the humans.

There is no fresh meat because of him.

Gemma's eyes find mine, and her back straightens.

I try not to scowl.

Why does she remain tense around me?

"I will not hurt you," I snap, and she flinches, her eyes going back to the food. I slide to the burner and roll the food over with my tailtip.

"Don't! You'll burn yourself," she gasps.

It's the first thing she's said to me today.

I pick up the food and set it down. "I feel nothing except warmth through my scales." Does she know nothing about this place and my kind? Wouldn't she have the same technology as I? Do I have to teach her the ways of this world, and the ways of *her* people too?

She shivers and leans closer to the burner. I leave to find a plate, bringing it back.

"I don't understand how it's working," she mumbles, still staring at the burner.

"Batteries. Power?" I pick up the ration and put it on the plate for her.

I may not burn easily, but she does. Humans—as far as I know—don't have scales.

"Batteries die, erode, and power needs electricity. Both are things that Earth should no longer have." She shakes her head.

I turn off the burner. She blinks, rubs her eyes.

Lost in thought, my female is. *Lost in thoughts that are not of me.*

"Earth has both. Though you need to know where to look for them," I explain. I like hearing her speak, the sound of her voice. It's not often I hear anything more than the buzzing of my machines or the hum of my heart, the orb, or screens in my den. A real human voice, with real inflection, is strange and exciting. "Everything living died, not the things made by the living," I add.

"But preserved without upkeep? For so long?" She pokes her ration. Steam wafts from the perfectly formed rectangular shape. "Human tech and Lurker tech?" She blows on her food.

A growl sounds from her belly when she does.

I settle across from her and watch. It will be interesting seeing her eat.

She visibly shrinks from my gaze when she realizes I'm staring.

I keep my scowl off my face. The tension between us bothers me. She is afraid of me.

"Both, perhaps," I answer.

"You don't know?"

"I never cared to find out what was made by who, only how the things worked and how they could be useful to me." My gaze shifts to the many objects around my den. "The rest has never mattered."

"And you? Where did you come from?"

"Me?"

Her face turns to my tail, to its long length, until she's facing me head-on again. "You are not human," she clears her throat, "Not entirely. Nor are you a Lurker or—or a Kett, or any other sentient species in the universe I know of, and I know all of them. Where did you come from, why are you here, and how do you know the common tongue?"

"You know little," I say.

Her brow furrows. "I assure you I know plenty."

"Yet you don't know what's around you, or the home you originated from, and your men are struggling to navigate both. That is clear. Even from the forest, that was clear."

"How would you know that? We've only just arrived."

"They would have never given you to us if they did."

A pink glow rises to her cheeks that compliments her hair. I ache to sink my fingers into those strands again and bury my face in her tangles. They would be beautiful spread across my nest. They would also be beautiful wrapped around my member, soaked in my spill.

"We can't *find* the technology. Using it isn't the problem."

"It will be. Eat," I demand. The steam rising from her ration has diminished greatly in the last few minutes.

She opens her mouth then closes it when a soft rumble from her belly sounds the space again. She gently picks up the ration and nibbles the side of it. Her eyes go distant as she chews.

I lean forward. She only has blunt teeth, no fangs. I'm amazed that her teeth are sharp enough to tear into the ration. My fingers twitch to pry open her lips and see.

Her throat bobs, and she lifts the ration to peer at it. "Interesting," she says. She takes another bite, this one bigger, more assured. I don't know how she does it. I've eaten these rations twice before when I could not rise after a terrible wound, and I had to force them down my starving throat.

I still don't know what was worse, the gash to my lower tail tendon or the taste of the ration.

On her third bite, I ask, "Interesting?"

"It tastes like chocolate. Really weak chocolate."

"I cannot stand the smell or taste."

"Chocolate is a delicacy for humans. It only grows on Colony 6." She finishes the ration, and her eyes meet mine. She flinches like she always does when she notices me watching her and wipes the back of her hand across her mouth. "We'll figure out how to use the technology once we find it. We have experts," she says, returning to the previous subject now that the food was gone. "People who have spent their entire lives studying Lurkawathians and their technology."

She licks her lips and my blood races. Her lips seem soft and sweet. The need to ravish them claws at me. To do more than that feasts on my instincts. Even if she tastes like rancid chocolate...

This is a dance I do not know.

I thought I knew how mating would work, and this is not what I imagined. It's confusing. After fantasizing about having her in my nest and taking my member inside her, the fact that I'm desperate for just a touch of her eyes eats up my insides.

She is repulsed—frightened—when I mention joining with her though.

She chose Azsote.

I do not understand why. I want to convince her that she should have chosen me all along, that I am worthy of her, but she wants to talk about other things.

Unimportant things. Things that simultaneously alarm me and bring back the curiosity of my youth. Questions I wish to not dwell on any longer...

I'm afraid that if I force her to confront her fate, she will only choose another male. Again. I will answer the questions she asks because I want her voice in my ears, but there are things on Earth that she does not need to worry about.

The Lurker tech being one of them.

That is why I can't let her leave my den, not anytime soon, and it has little to do with the bears, pigs, and the Death Adder nearby. Although the pigs worry me.

I don't know what pigs she has up in the stars, but the pigs here on Earth... They are intelligent, ferocious, and cruel. They will eat anything and chase prey for miles. They travel in large packs and are incredibly resilient. The best a hunter like I can do is kill one to distract the rest, because they will stop to eat their fellow rather than come after me.

Unfortunately, pig meat is the tastiest meat, which means I will be facing them again soon to procure some so I may hear Gemma moan.

I will feed my female the best food there is, and chocolate rations that must be a thousand years old are not the best.

She wipes her hands on her pants and stands. She peers at the stuff around us now that she's awake and fed, rising on her tiptoes to eye the items further down the bunker. My nest is in the back, hidden, and I wonder if she's looking for it.

I tense, my member pressing against my scales. I hope she is searching for it.

My nest. Where my scent covers every inch, where she will soon bask naked for me to gaze upon, getting my scent all over her. Where I will hold her down and claim her body. Where I can tie her up in my tail...

The mating act between humans is... feverish. I have studied what the screens have shown me thoroughly.

"Do you have any Lurker tech here?" she asks.

My hands' clench. She is not searching for my nest at all.

"Yesss."

"Can I..." She meets my eyes. "Can I see it?"

I sit back, mulling her question.

"No."

"No?" A wrinkle forms between her eyes.

"You and your people are here for their technology. You've made that abundantly clear." It's powerful and hard to find because the other nagas and I keep it hidden, although I know where there are caches of it, caches others are not aware of. "I want something in exchange," I decide on the spot.

She regards me warily. "Exchange?"

I nod, rising. Her eyes flip to my tail, which slides to coil around her. She pulls her limbs in. "I want to see you in exchange." I indicate her body. Perhaps she is hiding a wound that I cannot smell?

This is a fair exchange, but the way the blood rushes from her face tells me otherwise. She grabs hold of her torn clothes and bunches them in her small hands.

I will not relent.

"You want to see me?" she whispers.

She knows what I mean.

"As badly as you want to see this alien technology. And much more so."

"That's unfair!"

"Why?" I cock my head. "You have seen all of me. It is only fair I get to see you."

"You showed me your cock of your own volition, not because I asked," her voice quickens. "That's completely different."

"You are a communicator, aren't you?"

Confusion flushes her face. "Yes..."

"Then you know what making a deal is, and how deals benefit both parties? I will show you what you want if you do the same for me."

The blush returns to her cheeks. "My body is not part of any deal, especially one made between males who think they're unbeholden to anyone else."

Her words anger me. I keep it locked away. "There are no other males here, only me, Gemma. Only me. Only ever me. If your human males hadn't discarded you, I planned to steal you anyway. I was readying to do just that before Zaku approached the facility. Your body and who it belongs to will never be questioned again. It is mine by right."

"No, Vruksha, it's mine."

I slip my tailtip closer to her feet, and she doesn't seem to notice. "And the Lurker tech you so desperately want is *mine*."

She crosses her arms, pulling them to her chest. Another shield, one she uses often against me, though a weak one at that. It makes her chest rise, emphasizing her curves, and I like her curves.

We stare at each other for a time, and I can see thoughts running behind her eyes.

An hour passes in silence, neither of us backing down. She is considering the arrangement.

My pelvic region tightens, the scales around the sheath of my member itching to release it.

When I think she's about to give in and accept this perfect exchange, she rises, turns her back on me, and steps over my tail. I watch as she finds a corner between some of my treasures and curls up on the ground, facing the wall. Her stiff shoulders rise and fall for a while, and when they ease, the tension brought on by our exchange leaves her.

The little human has shut me out.

Again.

Impatience and curiosity settle within me.

Hours go by as I watch her sleep—or try to sleep—adjusting and tossing, again and again. At one point, I bring a large bear pelt from my nest and wrap it around her, and watch as she snuggles into it with a sigh, loving the way her red hair gathers amongst the fur. I debate picking her up and carrying her to my nest where I know it's most comfortable.

I wanted to the night before, but whenever I approached, she shrank from my touch.

My exhaustion builds as the day comes to an end. Still, I wait, keeping her trapped, unable to leave my post.

I want her answer. I have all the time in the world.

I know she's thinking about my proposal between her dreams.

That is why she tosses and turns. I grin.

How badly does she want what I have? What only I can give her? The warmth and protection I can offer? I only ask for one thing: her submission—for her to choose *me*.

When I finally manage to tear my eyes from her body, I leave my bunker to check the position of the sun, finding the world has returned to dusk. Our third day together is coming to an end—and I still have not claimed my mate.

I snarl at the rising moon and head back down.

She's sitting up, waiting for me as I descend the stairs.

She's decided.

My blood races through my veins.

TEN
PAST THE POINT OF NO RETURN

Gemma

I HATE HIM.

I repeat it again and again in my head as I try to sleep. Why can't I believe it?

I'm beginning to trust him. Giggles linger in the back of my throat at the absurdity. He hasn't hurt me or forced himself on me, he's fed me and given me a warm place to sleep, and now I have this pelt wrapped around my body... the largest, softest blanket I have ever experienced.

There's no reason not to trust him, right?

Soft fur tickles my cheek, and denying my comfort—the most comfort I've felt in days—is utterly useless. Vruksha scares me. There's no *denying* that. There's a glint of something dark in his black eyes... that I can't get past. But he hasn't used his strength against me, and that's saying something.

Human men love having power and rank for the very reason I'm beginning to trust Vruksha. If the wrong man had what Vruksha had *and* a woman at their mercy, they would take advantage, exploit the situation. I know because it's happened to me.

I've worked for many captains, and some of them were only captains for the power they can wield having that position. Fortunately, I'm not particularly beautiful, and so their attention never remained on me for long.

I can't shake the nervousness, that it's all a trap, and that once I begin to give in, Vruksha will do the same. Because there's literally nothing in this world stopping him from doing whatever he wants to me.

He wants to see me naked. Is it because he wants to know our differences? His eyes say otherwise...

I shiver.

Has anyone seen me naked? I tug the pelt against my mouth. I don't think anyone has. I've been with men before, though not so vulnerably. I could never risk being vulnerable when there was no telling if the men I let into my bed might someday be my subordinate, or worse, a future boss on the ship I made my home. Sex was about relief, and nudity didn't play into that. Not for me, at least.

I never knew if someone would record me or take a picture to use against me later. Staying as clothed as possible was prudent. Especially in my position of authority.

But Vruksha wants me naked. He wants to see what he thinks he owns. I scrunch my face. My back tingles, knowing he hasn't moved and is still watching me.

I wish he'd go away. I can't rest knowing he's right there, waiting for my answer. I also know I can't stay like this forever. I can't sleep forever.

Do it. Let him see you.

Get it over with.

He's going to see you eventually. You can't stay in dirty clothes forever either. And though Vruksha has allowed me to use the bathroom in private so far on our trek, I don't know if that will change going forward.

It might take weeks for me to escape this hole.

I hear him move, and then I hear him leave. I sit up, twisting to see where he's going. His tail slips out of view as he ascends the dark stairway. I relax, pulling the pelt over my shoulders. I didn't know how much tension was in my muscles with him so near.

I still feel his tongue on my cheek from days ago.

Warmth tickles my belly.

But naked?

Maybe letting him see me won't be so bad. Perhaps he'll find me disgusting, we are different after all. I don't have a tail, scales, or fangs like he does. Once he sees me naked, he might come to his senses, realizing fully that I'm not of his species and he doesn't really want me.

My heart twists at the thought, making me frown. I force it away. I don't want him to want me.

I nod, knowing it won't convince me even when I do.

Though, if he wants me, that gives me power...

And if he doesn't want me? I pull my pelt closer. If he doesn't want me and I can't make it back to the facility, what happens then?

For some reason, that question scares me just as much as everything else right now.

I'll have to figure out a way to survive on my own, and without catching the attention of other, more terrifying naga males who may not be like Vruksha at all. Like the black striped one from the orb's screen... or the one with a hood—Zaku, I believe—from the plateau.

My eyes glaze over as I stare at the stairway, realizing I'm waiting for Vruksha's return. He took his spear, which means I could be waiting a while.

My fingers go to the buttons of my jacket, tugging at them.

He's not going to show me the technology without me in return. I need the technology for leverage when I get back to *The Dreadnaut*. I need him to want me too... if my original plan fails.

I'm going to give him what he wants.

I suck in my stomach when the thought solidifies.

Seeing me naked isn't that much to give... He could have asked for much more, and he still might, if I keep denying him, and asking questions he clearly doesn't like answering. If I don't give him something, he might make me pay for every inch of his hospitality going forward.

I hear a noise and my heart ramps.

He's back sooner than I thought he'd be.

I sit up straighter when he appears, when he finds me and his eyes smolder.

He's beautiful. I can't get past it. All ruby and ribbed, so sleek with the way he moves. His prowess intrigues me. It's evident in everything he does. He knows how to survive. Men like that are incredibly rare above. They know how to manipulate, weasel, belittle, but truly survive? Unless they were trained as combat soldiers, they're just weak bodies, and weak minds under their suits.

I feel... lucky to have been chosen by Vruksha. Appreciative now that I've had food, warmth, and sleep. From what I thought my circumstances would be days ago, this isn't nearly as bad.

Truthfully, I thought I'd be dead by now, or broken and wishing for death.

Though there are still pieces of Vruksha that force me to temper the pull he has over me, refusing to accept that I even feel a pull at all. Like his fangs. Sometimes I think I see them drip with something, and I know that something isn't saliva...

Or the blatant lust in his eyes.

His delectable smell. My nose wiggles.

Has he ever been with a woman before? Before they all vanished? *Why* did they vanish?

He's staring at me again like he's waiting for an answer.

My hands shake when I manage to say, "You only want to see, right? Nothing more?"

His nostrils flare, his eyes dipping to my body hidden behind fur. "I want to spend my spill inside you." His voice is dark, gruff. "I will accept seeing you tonight. I would like to make sure you are not hurt."

Hurt? I shake my head. His words make me shudder. They also warm my cheeks. I've imagined what it would feel like with him inside me... How could I not?

Gooseflesh rises on my arms.

"Okay," I say.

I release my grip on the pelt and let it fall. My hands move to the buttons of my jacket again. Better get this over with before I think about it anymore.

"Wait," he jerks forward.

My fingers pause.

Vruksha stalks closer, and I stiffen. He stops several feet away, coiling his large tail under him. "I want you to stand."

Stand? "You'll show me the Lurker tech if I do?" I need to make sure.

"Yesss," he hisses long and low. "Little human, I'll show you whatever you want. I will give you this world if I could."

His voice is eager.

I rise to my feet, praying for calm. My fingers find my ripped jacket again. This time, when I unclasp the buttons, he doesn't stop me. His eyes are glued to me instead.

If I didn't know I was in a hole, on Earth, all alone with a strange male, I would think I was on a stage about to strip for all the rowdy men on *The Dreadnaut*. There were sex workers who did that very thing.

But it's just me and him—and the flimsy trust we've built. Too soon, I've reached the last button. I grab the lapels of my uniform jacket and tug it off, letting it fall to the floor.

Next, I reach for the clasp of my pants, loosening them. Vruksha hasn't moved, hasn't breathed. Heat flushes my cheeks knowing how intensely he's watching me.

I push down my pants to gather around my boots.

My belly swarms with nectarflies as his eyes roam over my bare legs. I kick off my boots, toeing the pants out from under me.

"No scales, not a single one," he murmurs. "How can you survive without basic protection?"

I don't answer. I can't answer.

I bring my now trembling fingers to the bottom of my top, clasping it. Before I can change my mind, I lift the fabric over my head and drop it onto the ground where my pants and jacket lie.

The scales on Vruksha's tail shift, straightening outward. His eyes sear my naked flesh, flashing over my body like lightning. I place my palms flush to my stomach, waiting for his response.

"I'm not young," I whisper, unsure why. "Not the type of woman most men want anymore." I hurriedly add, "I'm not old either." I've seen thirty-three standardized years, and where most women my age have already had children and are raising a family, I chose a career in a higher caste instead.

He may not know that. My body isn't perfect and sweet like it once was. I stay fit because my job demands it, though if I had it my way, I'd never leave my rooms on *The Dreadnaut*, reading and drawing all day, every day instead.

Those simple desires are denied me. Sometimes I wonder if I've made the right choices... I mentally shake the thoughts away. Having water rations and food is more important than books and free time.

"The rest," he demands when I pause. "I want to see everything. I want to check you for wounds." His forked tongue lashes out and steals all my thoughts momentarily.

You can do this, Gemma. He won't slip his tongue between your thighs when you're not looking.

Or will he?

He won't, I tell myself. I have not been able to wash since the day I was bartered away. I've never gone more than a day without being sanitized and scrubbed. Three days of being unclean? My nose wrinkles. Yesterday's morning dew is all I've had to scrub my skin since being here. Once he sees my scrapes and bruises, he won't want to look upon me further...

His eyes catch mine. "I want all of you," he says, gentler this time, as if he read my thoughts. "I am glad you are not hurt. I want to see what is mine."

Bringing my hands to my bra, to the clasp in the front, I unhook it. I let the bra fall down my arms, using one of them up to hide my breasts. My heart is racing. His hands fist at his sides.

"Drop your arm," he orders.

Anger rises, but I do what he says, letting my arms fall.

Air brushes my nipples, my exposed skin, making my shivers worse.

I pray he's not a liar.

Because if he is, there's nothing except the thin fabric of underwear, now several days worn, stopping him from taking me. I feel so unclean that no man or woman on *The Dreadnaut* would even get close to me right now.

Vruksha is not a man—or a woman—he's a primitive alien. What I might think is dirty, might be clean to him.

His member emerges from his scales, thick and throbbing. I take a step back.

"Don't," he rasps, shifting forward.

"You promise you wouldn't touch me." I shrink further as he nears to a hairsbreadth from me.

"And I won't—I will look my fill, see our differences, and show you how it makes me feel, unless you do not want the same allowance when it comes to your tech?"

My cheeks burn. I can't muster any words.

It's not fair.

"Now, the rest."

His body heat blankets over my skin. He's that close. This fierce, alien male. If I trip, I'd land on him, in his arms. If I stumble, it would be into him. If I breathe too hard, we'd touch. And if we did... I don't know what would happen. I focus on the bulge of his biceps, on the scars there I missed before.

The way his tail has curled back around me when I wasn't paying attention. He still isn't touching me but...

The hardness of his member, clearly deciding it *does* want me.

The wildness in his gaze.

I stick my fingers under the band of my underwear and slide them down my legs, almost taunting. When they're with the pile of the rest of my clothes, I straighten to my full height and lift my chin.

"There," I snap. "There's nothing between us anymore. We've seen each other."

I don't know if it's because I'm hyper-aware of the difference in power between us or because I hate him that I'm angry all of a sudden. It's definitely not the tickling, knotting, increasing heat dancing within me. The excitement of the risk I'm taking. His wickedness.

Vruksha's throat bobs. "You are..." he trails off.

"I'm?" I snap again.

"Fantastical."

My mouth drops at his odd choice of word. *Fantastical? A fantasy?* I've never been anything close to that to anyone in my life. No man, human or otherwise, has ever approached me like Vruksha, like he may die if he doesn't have me. But fantastical? No. I'm diligent, disciplined, and loyal. A perfect fit for the position I've earned. Not fantastical...

Fantastical people become stars and models. They are beings everyone in the universe envies. They are a caste all their own. They get to paint and draw pictures all day. They get to read and write their own novels during war.

No one envies me, no one wants my job with the stress of humanity's doom on their shoulders.

My eyes hood and I reach up to wipe them, finding my lashes wet.

I quickly rub them dry before Vruksha sees. I blink several times, clearing them, keeping my face downcast. I don't want to be here, where he can see me vulnerable. I want to hide in the big, fluffy pelt at my feet and vanish. And it's not my nudity that I don't want him to see. I don't want him to see my tears, not again.

He might not think I'm fantastical anymore if he does.

"Gemma," he begins. "You are a dream."

I stop him before he can say anymore. I step into him and hide.

He stills, and his member presses between our bodies, hot against my belly. He's warm, and here I can hide against him and pretend things were different.

His arms don't go around me, and that's okay. I don't need him to hold me; I just need him to hide me, at least for a little while. I lift my arms and curl them around his back, resting easier into him. His scales are velvety under my skin, under my fingertips, and I pet the ones on his back that I can reach.

"Thank you," I tell him, knowing he won't understand. How could he?

His arms go around me, pressing me into him. It's awkward and I don't mind.

I don't even mind the pulsing of his cock sandwiched between us. Somehow, I trust him.

"For what?" he rasps, clearly confused with what I'm doing. Clearly wary... of *me*.

I smile. Good.

"The compliment," I whisper.

We stand like this for a time, and I take in his scent. It's musky and raw, and something I can't place, but it warms me. It's not strong right now. It's not muddying my mind. It's perfect. It makes my skin prickle sometimes. It reminds me of this planet and all its mysteries. It suits him, I decide. I breathe him in, nearly shuddering when I do.

It's not a bad scent.

His cock remains hard, and as the minutes tick by, I grow increasingly aware of it. I can't hide against him forever. My tears dry up, and I swallow.

He's growing less wary of my reaction. If I want to attack him, I should do it now...

His hands slide down my back, pressing me harder into him, into *it*. A rumbling, breathy noise comes from his throat, and I can't help going rigid in his embrace. More of his scent floods my nose, making me warmer... everywhere.

I jerk away.

His nails scrape across my skin as I do, and he hisses, "Why?"

"I can't," I gasp, covering my body.

That hint of darkness glints in his eyes, and my throat closes up. He stalks forward, gliding, and I back up until I'm pressed into some sort of metal crate.

"You have been playing games with me," he growls. "I will be your fool no more." He pulls my arms from my body.

ELEVEN
NO PLACE LEFT TO HIDE

Vruksha

Her fingers tickle my back.

Chosen.

She wants me.

She comes to me bare and presses her warm body to mine, and even pets my scales. Her breath fans my chest. Her cheek rests upon me. The soft touch of her fingers on my scales steals my mind.

Gemma has come to me.

Why? She has fought me thus far, so why now?

Regardless, I hold back a roar of triumph. I want to rush to the surface, shouting to all the other males who did not claim a mate, that she is mine.

Chosen.

I wrap my arms around her small, trembling frame.

I will treasure you. I will shield you.

A groan of pleasure rumbles through me with her body tight against mine. A groan of worry joins it, knowing how delicate she truly is and how the only way I can keep her is if I protect her with everything I have. I vow it too. I will die for her. After spending so many countless moments alone, this is worth dying for. I'll never be alone again.

I squeeze her in my arms
She tears out of my hold.
She slips from my hands and gifts me a look of stunned surprise.
"I can't!" she cries.
I blink back my shock, and my frustration rises as she flees from me. My fingers twitch with loss. Does she think I'm a fool? Does she think she can tease me with what I want most and then take it away? My gaze sharpens.

Or is this a mating dance?

I move forward to reclaim her, to end this contradiction once and for all. "I am done with your gamesss," I hiss.

Her eyes widen, and they glisten like they've been wet. I trail her face. Her cheeks are ruddy, and her hair is a mess tumbling down her shoulders and over her pale, scaleless body.

She covers her breasts and mound with her arms and hands. "I'm not playing games."

I realize... *She came to me when I told her what she was, what I see her as...* I swallow my frustration, trying to understand.

"Why did you embrace me?"

She shakes her head.

"Why?" I demand.

Her eyes shift elsewhere, her body pushes back onto the metal crate she's nearly perched on. She doesn't want to answer me. *Gemma Hurst, the Communications Director...*

Humans do not communicate at all!

"Why?" I ask, louder this time.

"I—wanted to hide," she answers. Her gaze has landed on my tail and she's staring hard at it.

"Hide? What do you need to hide from?"

"Everything."

Cocking my head, I study her. She looms with uncertainty, her skin rising with prickles as my eyes caress her naked curves. Her thick, shoulder-length red waves have gone limp, but her hair retains its gleam. I have an urge to pull it back and have her face clear before me. I don't want her to hide. She should never have to hide, not while she's with me. My voice lowers, softens. "Hide from everything? Why would you need to do that?"

Is she in some sort of danger?

Her arms tighten across her chest. Tearing them off her body and tying them behind her back so she may never cover herself from me again would be a service to us both.

"You wouldn't understand."

"You can hide here. With me. No one can find you here, and if they do, I will kill them. You have nothing to fear."

Her eyes meet mine. Her lips tremble.

Oh, how I want her lips to tremble upon mine.

I shift closer, and she doesn't startle away. "You may hide as long as you want, but never from me. I will give you what you need." My desire for her makes me her begging slave.

A glittering tear beads on the corner of her eye. This time when she nods, I accept it. I want to know why it's there, why she's suddenly changed, except I don't ask. I curl my finger and bring it slowly to her face instead. She stiffens but doesn't move as I catch her tear, softly wiping the skin under her eye and taking the tear away.

I lick it from my finger.

I watch her while I do it. Dewy lips parted and eyes wide as black stones—filled with confusion—fill my vision. I savor the salty taste of her. She tastes like fresh prey, the sun on my scales. She tastes how I would imagine the blood rushing through my veins during an exciting hunt would.

"You're not like any man I have ever known," she breathes.

"Do not speak of other males," I growl as a fresh wave of jealousy invades. "I cannot bear it. I will not have it." No new tears form on her lashes. No more salt. I settle back to enjoy her nudity once more. "Drop your arms, Gemma. No more hiding. There is no reason to anymore. Your clothes offered little protection. Your hands and arms, less."

She hesitates, and I wait for her to decide. Slowly, she lowers her arms again. My scales flutter down my back. My mate, naked, for me and only for me. Only ever for me. How I've imagined this countless times, in many ways, but none of it was as delicious as the real thing.

Gemma will always be naked in my mind, with nothing except her red hair to cover her.

Her breasts are shapely, and the rosy tips are pointed, readied to be teased. The way they appear on her chest makes me hungry to take them in my hands and explore. Seeing her breasts reminds me of my young self, viewing a naked female on a screen for the first time.

A strand of her hair slips to fall upon her chest, and my muscles tense.

"Vruksha?" she says my name in question. I check her lashes and see no new tears.

"Yes?"

"Have you ever been with a woman before?"

My head cants. "Woman? Females are gone." I thought I told her this.

"Why? Where are they?"

It is not a subject I want to speak of. "They die during birth. Long ago, those who were left fled together from these lands, never to return. That is all I know."

"Oh."

I slip my gaze back to her body, lower this time, dropping down until I'm eye level with her sex—the enticing mound between her thighs. A mound with no hair. I see the peak of her little, swollen nub. She clamps her legs together.

"Open them," I demand.

"You can—"

"Open them. Do not make me ask again."

"I need to wash!"

I shoot her a look of uncaring frustration, and her mouth closes tight. She scents of heaven and rain to me.

For a short time, all I hear are her breaths. "You won't touch?"

This time, it's me who shakes my head. "I won't, unless you're hurt."

She inhales and shifts her feet apart. It's not enough to sate my curiosity. "Where's your hair?"

"I... don't have hair there. Not anymore." Her voice is no louder than a whisper.

I hum, staring at the milky gift. My prize.

"Can I close them now?"

"I want more."

"More?" she squeaks. It's a funny sound coming from her throat. My eyes snap up, and she's staring at me dumbfounded.

"More. I demand to see it."

Her cheeks redden feverishly. "I can't."

"Yes. You can."

"No one's ever—"

"I will, now," I snap. "I will see it, and all of you, now."

Her chest rises and falls, and she's hidden her breasts behind her arms again. She'll lower them when I demand it, I am sure of this now.

But I grow impatient at her continued hesitation.

"Gemma," I rasp, "Let me see what I have won. You are a prize, one I will die for, die to keep, and I will see what I have won." If she backs out now, I don't know what I'll do.

A terrible tension is filling my loins. It's the same tension that filled me the first day I saw her. Then, it nearly destroyed me, weeks later, I have conquered it. Though the continuous creation of spill is burdensome.

Her feminine heat is so close, it's upon my face, where I am as a servant before her. Her scent, purely female, is in my nostrils. My member is engorged, swollen with spill and dripping.

She shudders at my words, like they tickle her, and her legs twitch. To my surprise, she drops her arms to grip the edge of the crate, hauling herself to sit up upon it. I rise as she does, and she deliberately spreads her legs. Choosing to show me what I want to see so badly. She leans back.

At once, I'm at the crux of her thighs, staring at her center with a strangled growl.

Luscious nether lips meet my gaze. Pink and succulent and precious. They cling together with glistening arousal, obscuring my view of her center. Her female button is on display, framed by two indents of flesh. It's tiny and perfect, and my mouth waters to press it, to get a reaction from her.

What would she do if I touched her and did just that?

I close my eyes and groan.

Her legs slam closed, but her knees catch on my arms. In a flash, I'm pressing them open with my hands, flush and spread against the edge of the crate.

Gemma jumps, struggles and I hold her still. Her hands grip my hands, tugging. "You said—"

I squeeze her thighs. "You touched me first, twice. It goes two ways, little mate."

Her nostrils flare, and her hands go white where they're gripping mine. She shakes under my grip. I dive back down between her legs, uncaring.

Her folds are open now, and they are slick.

The little hole that'll take my member is sweetly on display. It's tight and closed. Primitive, hungering need slams into me.

She's so tense I can see her quiver as I stare at it.

"Mine," I breathe.

To be this close to my mate and not have her?

It's heaven and torture all at once.

I do not envy the naga males who did not capture a female. I do not envy them at all. Because if they knew what they were missing...

Paranoia hits me as hard as my mating fever. If the other males had an inkling of what they were missing, they would never stop coming after us. My tongue slides over my fangs.

I need to claim her, mark her. My eyes dilate.

She gasps. "Your smell... it's doing something to me."

Tearing my gaze from her sex, I meet her hooded eyes. I don't know what she's talking about. As I keep them, I slide my hands up her thighs.

Her brow furrows. She is so tense, holding herself prone, she refuses to accept the blatant arousal gathering between her thighs.

She also doesn't stop me.

I continue sliding my hands until they're right at the dent of her thighs. Gemma still grips my hands under hers and with an inhale, she releases them.

Triumph.

My member rises, and my tail coils onto the crate, enclosing her in my circle.

Triumph. *Yes.*

"Yes, female," I whisper. "Let me in."

She closes her eyes and leans back on her hands.

With a growl of elation, my fingers inch between her thighs, diving in as I snap forward and suck her tiny button between my lips.

TWELVE
STRETCHED AND

Gemma

I GASP, bending back. He said he wouldn't touch!

I don't stop him as he penetrates me, as he pushes his face between my legs and sucks my clit between his lips. Sensation zips up my spine, pleasurable warmth joins it. It feels good. There's no pawing, no rough handling, it's just... nice.

Vruksha's touch banishes all my worries.

Somehow... a part of me doesn't want to stop him. I inhale deeply, taking in the musk wafting off of him. Dizzying, I feel my body... warm.

A niggling thought scratches the back of my mind far too quickly and I grasp onto the pleasure he's giving me. How does he know we can even have sex together? I don't want to think about it. His rough mouth sups at my bud, and the question vanishes. Gasping again, he rolls and hooks his finger inside me, touching my special spot. That elusive spot...

"Rough and wet, like I knew it would be," he says, mouthing my clit.

My nerves vibrate.

He pushes a second finger into me, and I grab his head at the invasion. My fingers press into the scales around his hair.

His tail slides across my behind.

I should stop this. I should. I should insist on washing first, but I can't, because if I do, I know my morals will return and stop this from ever happening again.

Vruksha doesn't seem to mind, and I don't understand why. Does he want me this bad? I nearly forget to breathe at the thought. My nails bite into his scalp, digging under his short black hair. He's voracious and overwhelming, a vampire with his fangs, the red of his scales and skin, could easily be mistaken for blood.

Any woman on *The Dreadnaut* would kill for such a male to want them how Vruksha wants me.

I'm lucky... in a way...

No, I'm not.

I think this even as I bend forward, wrapping my legs around his head, leveraging my body to move against him.

I'm fantastical. A prize. This alien male wants me. It's heady and strange and wrong. He wants to protect me with his life. His words are like rare candy to my ears, and I want more of it. His curious, rough fingers roll, curl, and scissor me deeply, doing a number on me that's not wholly pleasurable. I like it. My head clouds. Rolls. Spins. I gasp his aroma into me and my sex constricts.

It's been so long since someone touched me like this.

So long since someone sought to give me pleasure without insisting on something in return. There's no sex contract with Vruksha, and that should terrify me, but he won't hurt me. I think.

My toes curl as I lean back again, lifting my hips.

"Yessss, female." Dark and gritty, his voice makes me squirm.

If I don't think...

His fingers push deeper, expanding, shooting me up in the air. Zaps of pain mix with excitement at his roughness. He does it again, and I gasp as he pulls me forward with his tail. His head lifts, catching my eyes when he does it again.

"Tight," is all he says. "Too tight."

Swallowing thickly, heat rises to my cheeks.

My fingers twitch on his scalp where they clutch him, afraid his features might cut me. Vruksha holds me pinned. My legs are on his shoulders, his mouth wet with my arousal, and his tail braced behind me, finishing the trap. His fingers expand inside me again, and I strain for what's to come.

Madness. I try to thrash, to shimmy for more or less. I don't know anymore.

He holds me still.

Wicked black eyes pierce my soul. "You're too tight for me, female," he rumbles.

His fingers expand, and I flinch, hips shaking, wanting to beg him to stop. But then his fingers close, and I sag, forgetting the pain, pausing in pleasure.

"Not for much longer..." He pushes a third finger inside me. "I will make us fit."

"Vruksha!"

He responds by snapping his mouth back over my clit, suckling it. A scream tears from my throat. Tension radiates through me, and as it pulses up from my core and throughout my body, building, his tailtip wraps around my side, under my arm, to curl around my left breast.

Gooseflesh blankets me from the sensation. I glimpse his tailtip flicking my nipple, and my eyes go wide.

He's not even human! Three fingers expand inside me, and I shriek again. I shouldn't be doing this with him.

He's.

Not.

Human.

"Almost," he mutters before sucking on my clit again. "Almost there..."

I brace for his fingers to spread, and this time when they do, throbbing pressure blasts through my body, sending me spiraling. I don't cry out or scream. I'm silent as he forces an orgasm from my body.

Abrupt and hard, I wasn't ready for it. Rocking wantonly against his face, frantic for more of what he's giving me, my mouth opens to release one long, shocked gasp. Spikes of raw pleasure brutalize my swollen sex.

His fingers expand outward hard and I cry out.

"We will fit, Gemma," he growls almost threateningly.

I'm a shaking, stunned mess when his mouth leaves my clit, when he pulls his fingers from my sex, when I feel him move away.

My hold on him loosens. I sag.

For a time, I give in. Even when his body shifts under my legs. I got what I needed, and all I want now is to come down from the sudden high at my own time.

I'm raw. My thoughts are scattered.

Vruksha rises over me, his tail slipping from where it's propped me up, I lay back on the crate, staring at him through hazy eyes. His hands wrap around my thighs, spreading me wide, and I muster a sated smile.

Pulsations from my orgasm continue, and it hits me... *It's been years.*

I haven't had a night alone since I was given this mission to go to Earth. They've all been sleepless with work.

Vruksha's dark eyes return to steal mine, nearly rabid, staring between my legs with such intensity my body goes rigid. My soul shivers. With his grip on me tightening, something hard presses between my legs.

I gasp as my eyes tear down to see his thick, alien cock pushing into my opening.

Spreading me wide. Much wider than his fingers.

"Wait!"

He pauses with a pained grunt. My lips part and I clench around him. He grunts again. The tip of his shaft is buried, and the rest of him remains poised to join it.

It's thick and red, but it's the thickened middle of his cock that tightens my stomach.

It's not going to fit. Not without discomfort. His cock is really big.

"Female..." Vruksha says, shaking.

Sweat beads his scaleless brow. Wrinkles cover his forehead as he bares his fangs. He licks one, and blood drips onto his lips.

I suck in, sitting back, pulling from his grip.

He doesn't let me go. He shifts with me, keeping his tip buried, like he may die if it slips out. Part of me wants to let him thrust into me, for me to push on to him, to feel the sensation of his bulge as it enters, but I can't...

Because I'm terrified.

Something snaps, and I grab his hands, pulling them off my legs. "I can't," I gasp, wiggling away.

This time, he lets me, pulling his cock's head out with an anguished grunt. His small claws graze my skin, leaving red marks behind.

I push my legs together and pull them to my chest, wrapping my arms around them, hiding my chest. His gaze shifts to my face.

"You deny us? I am heated, and you deny us?"

I shake my head. "I don't know you," I whisper.

That's not the real problem... That's not why I'm afraid.

"Why?" he hisses, leaning back over me, lust burnishing his face.

Lust and misery. His forked tongue licks at the blood on his lips, making me shiver.

"I'm...not ready."

His chest expands. "Have I not prepared you? Do you need my tail to stretch you? We will fit, little human, I will work your sheath until you take me comfortably."

I startle. My spine tingles from his words. The perversion of being penetrated by him, of him 'working me' in such a way isn't sending me running like it should.

Instead, I clench damnably. "I can't."

"Then I will prepare you some more," he declares, cupping my knees.

He spreads them.

"Stop! I mean I can't right now. Right now," my voice hitches as I push him off me again and move out from under him, standing. "I need to bathe first. I need to bathe," I say again, backing up. I don't want to make him angry by telling him the truth: that I'm scared. Of him, of what will happen.

Of what a creature like him could do to me.

And now, of all things, I think of his tail. I glimpse the tip and quickly turn away.

He follows me as I try to put distance between us. "A bath? You need a bath? If you think I am bothered by your arousal... I like you wet."

My eyes widen with embarrassment. I am wet, really wet. I feel my arousal trickling down my thighs.

I shake my head, searching for sanity.

As far as I know, there's no way to wash down in the bunker. There's no running water. He'll have to take me out of this hole for one. This is perfect. If it takes time to bathe, then—

"I will give you a bath, if that's what you need, if that's what will make this work."

My belly jumps. "How?" I reach for my clothes on the floor, trying not to think about the tail he's curling around my leg and the way it makes me tremble. "Where?"

"There is a creek."

"Okay," I say, before thinking more on it.

"Tonight."

"Tonight?"

"I will bathe you, and you will take my spill tonight."

The hunger returns to his face as he licks the rest of the blood off his lips. I watch as this large, serpentine male grabs his cock, squeezes the bulge in the middle, and pushes it back into the scales at his pelvic region. I blow out air in relief.

It doesn't last long.

My pulse, which was beginning to slow, thrums back to life. "Isn't it night right now?"

"Yes, female, it is."

Great. Just great.

I turn around and dress, feeling the burn of his black eyes fucking me, unable to get the image of his tail penetrating me out of my head. I've gained a couple of hours with my lame excuse... How am I going to survive another night? I can't sleep or pretend to sleep forever.

"And then I get to see the tech?" I say, far too absently for my liking. I press my palms to my eyes.

"Yesss."

At least I'm getting out of this hole. I can run again if I must.

He'll bring his spear...

"Okay," I breathe, scurrying to the bunker's exit when I finish putting on my boots.

His arm wraps around me and pulls me close, lifting me off the ground. I shriek, being pressed flush against his hard form.

He's never going to give me the chance to run.

THIRTEEN
A BATH

Vruksha

My mate confounds me and is destroying everything I thought I knew about females—human females. The screens left much out.

The taste of her arousal is in my mouth and her warm, wet sheath wrapped around the tip of my member allows me to forgive the lies of the technology I've lived my life by. Perhaps every female is different, and that is why the screens didn't tell me the difficulties of getting one to submit.

The tension within me is growing worse by the day, but I won't let it rule me. I can't. Gemma is easily hurt.

I can wait a little longer.

"Let me down, Vruksha," she grumbles.

"The sun is setting. It is easier to carry you than allow you to stumble through the overgrowth now that it's getting dark."

"I can see well enough."

"We are almost there."

She startles. "Already? The creek is that close?"

I peer at her. Why does she sound surprised? She must be eager. I know she wants me. She let me touch her, let me explore her sex, even let me taste it. Is she not ready for more?

Her sex had been tight, incredibly so. It worries me, and I can't let that show. She needs a master, a male to nest her, care for her. If I am too big for her, how will she forgive me? I do not want her to hurt, for her to feel pain with our union. It's not going to be easy to sink inside her, but I will make it work. Three fingers may not be enough. Four, or all of them perhaps?

My tailtip will do the trick. If she can take my tail, she can take my member. First, she needs a bath, or so she says. And the water will be a great way to make her extra slick for passage...

I scan my surroundings, listening to the quiet rustle of leaves in the evening's breeze. The creek is not in the airfield. Though it's nearby and a place I have gone to daily since I first established my den.

Unfortunately, it's the only creek near here, which means roaming predators use it as well.

Including Zhallaix.

He will steal Gemma if he sees her, or worse. I am certain the only naga who knows I have a female is Azsote, and I want to keep it that way. I can handle Zhallaix—because of his proximity to my den, I know him better than any other naga—but it will be deadly if the others find out.

I will risk it though, to make Gemma happy. She will get her bath.

My mouth waters at the thought of seeing her wet.

I have been dreaming of her for so long. For years and years, before I even saw Gemma, I've been dreaming of her and the life we will have. The loneliness she will make disappear.

I will feed her from my hands, gift her items I have foraged, and provide her every comfort. She enjoyed the bear pelt, and there are many more where that came from. I will introduce her to my nest when we return.

If she likes one bear pelt, she will like my nest. She will like all I have to give.

Tonight, she will be naked in my nest.

I don't know why I've become like this. A male obsessed. For years after my father died, I reveled in the fact that there were no females anymore. I celebrated that they were all gone and I would never have to come in contact with one, nor suffer one. I saw what my mother's death did to my father. It destroyed him. He explained to me when I was old enough that the male he was afterward was not the male he had been when she was alive.

He suffered guilt when he looked at me, but he still kept me close, teaching me of the dangers of this world. Of how unfortunate we are as a species, of how lonely it was because we are so few.

He gave me my spear, taught me how to use it, taught me how to find, repair, and take advantage of the technology across the land. He told me to stay away from the very facility the humans recently took over.

He said there were things in that building that weren't right. Things that could hurt us. He said that's where he found my spear. It was the last gift my father gave me.

It was the only tangible gift he ever gave me. And now, all I have are memories. Not even the orbs can show me his face...

The noise of rushing water pricks my ears. Gemma shifts in my arms.

"Sssshh," I tell her.

"Is there something?" she whispers. "Do you hear something?"

"No, but I must check for predators." I keep my voice low as I set her on the ground. "I will be too distracted once we are in the water."

"We?"

"Wait here, Gemma. Do not leave this spot while I scout the area. I will be right back." I cup her face and force her to look at me. "I will know if you run." The shadows are heavy, but the moonlight is out. Even in darkness, she is beautiful. She is Gemma.

I wait for her to nod before I release her, slinging up into the branches above. I still suspect she will run when she has the chance, despite this, I am beginning to trust her judgment. She won't run in the dark.

I slip from tree to tree, searching for signs of recent activity or lingering animals, staying within hearing distance of my female and the water.

It is strange, patrolling like this.

Before the arrival of the humans, I never wanted the burden of a female or the companionship of another, knowing the cost it would demand of me.

Seeing Gemma and her red hair, I discovered how profoundly lonely I was... How large my nest was—and for no reason whatsoever. My world shifted that day at the facility, spun, and shook me to the pointless life I've been leading. Where other naga males journeyed to find the female nagas, I stayed in my forest. Where other males succumbed to madness or melancholy, I smiled, viciously devouring another meal.

All those smiles were fake.

I've been lying to myself for years... I know that now.

I'm not liking how Gemma's presence is making these feelings emerge.

I won't let what happened to my father happen to me. Or what happened to my mother happen to Gemma. I will keep her safe—at all costs —and happy whenever possible. This bath is dangerous, but my need for her is strong, and how can I deny her when she offers herself so willingly?

Once I have claimed her, then I can relax. When she is nestled in the shield of my tail, plump with spill and sleeping soundly, I can finally sleep. Weeks with little rest is wearing on me.

Finding the creek and area around it empty of predators, I return to my mate.

She is where I left her, staring up at the stars.

Sliding to her side, she turns her head at my arrival, though her gaze doesn't leave the sky. My eyes search for what she's looking at.

"Earth's moon is so bright," she says, her voice soft.

"Are there other moons?"

She makes a noise. "Yes. Many. Every colony has at least one, some have dozens, but none of the ones I've seen are as bright as this one."

My eyes slip to the pale column of her neck and the way her hair tumbles over her shoulders. Her red hair is the reason I know she belongs to me. We share the same color. She wears my color.

Only my female would have my coloring.

"I wonder what life would be like if the Lurkers had never come to Earth, if they'd left us alone and sailed on by, if we'd still be fighting the Ketts with everything we have... Still failing."

I don't know what she speaks of, what or who these Ketts are, only that they are the reason Gemma is here on Earth. I rub my fingertips together. They're not her problem anymore. They're not here. I reach up and cup her neck, reminding her who is.

She tenses, her gaze dropping from the sky. I catch her in my arms and pull her close.

"Vruksha—" she starts.

"The area is safe," I interrupt, "for now. I do not wish to stay long. You are preciousss in these lands, and I can't risk losing you again."

She doesn't say anything more as I lift her in my arms and carry her to the creek's edge, to the deep, clear pool where I've often come to for hydration. I carry her into it.

She squirms. "I should undress first."

"I will undress you."

In the deepest area, I lower, enjoying the chill of the water gliding between my scales. Gemma's trying to get out of my hold again. I submerge us both, and she gasps.

"Cold, cold, cold," she squeaks. She pushes from my chest, slips out of my arms.

I catch her leg with my tail when she moves from me. I draw her back into my embrace. "I will warm you, little human."

She doesn't fight me, not like she has been. My member pulses, excited from the act of submission. Grabbing the edge of her jacket, I tug it off her shoulders.

"Vruksha, I don't think this is a good idea. Maybe we should go back and wait until morning if it's so dangerous."

"We are here now, and I can't wait any longer."

"But monsters?"

Didn't she hear me tell her it was safe? "Have you changed your mind? They're not here, and if they come, they will have to deal with me."

She shivers and raises her arms reluctantly, letting me take off her jacket. I toss it to the shore, reaching for her pants.

"I can do it," she says, pulling my fingers away from her.

I growl and put my fingers back. "I will be the one to undress you this time."

She drops all pretenses with a sigh. Excitement returns to me as she kicks off and wiggles out of her pants. I gather them and toss them next to her jacket.

How could I ever not have wanted this? Companionship? Quipping conversation? Pouty lips when they're not getting their way? My member has only ever known my hands sheathing it, and now it will know her. It's had a taste, and it's even hungrier than before.

Gemma curls her arms over her chest, where her remaining layers cling to her enticingly. She lowers into the water to hide.

I'm an idiot.

What's the point of living without a female to live for? To share my exploits with? To warm me during the coldest nights and fill my den with her soft voice?

To drive me mad with desire—and with jealousy.

She is so beautiful it hurts. Wet and shivering in the shadow of my body, where I can touch her at my leisure. Her hair is wet at the ends, and her chest rises and falls rapidly. Even in the darkness, I see her skin flush.

My shaft emerges from my tail.

I take her hands and pull her arms away from her chest.

She licks her sweet lips. I grasp the bottom of her shirt and tear it off her.

Now she's only in her underthings. Ridiculous clothes that shield her from me. Not for much longer...

I reach for her underwear. She slaps my hand away.

I reach for it again.

She slaps my hand again.

I hiss. "You can't bathe dressed."

"I can't bathe at all with you watching me like that."

My lips twist. "I will watch you as is my right as your mate."

"We're not mates."

Frustration fuels me as she turns away, lowering herself into the water, hiding from my eyes. Again. Pain bubbles up to join the frustration, but I push it away. Yet the thought niggles still. *She chose Azsote...*

Not me.

If she had, would she be naked in my nest this very moment? Because she chose *me?*

If I had let Azsote take her, would she be inviting his member into her right now? Would they have already rutted on the forest floor? In the very clearing in which he and I battled? The picture of them together enrages me, eats at my insides. I can't stand it.

I slide my tail around her, and she steps away from it.

I can't handle it and dive toward her, dragging her to me roughly, holding her wet body to my chest. Facing her away from me, her bottom slips across my member.

She makes a noise.

"You have accepted me," I remind her. "You spread your legs and cried out as I penetrated you with not one but three of my fingers." I slide one hand down her body to cup her sex hard. "You thrashed and cried and grabbed my head as my lips framed your nub, rubbing your sex into my face, or have you already forgotten? It was not Azsote working on your tight sheath to accommodate him," I growl.

I push her wet underwear to the side and find her hole, caressing it.

She writhes against me. "I need to bathe—"

"I know an excuse when I hear one."

My fingers push inside her. Gemma bows over my arm as she takes them. She's drenched, wet from the brook, and slick from her arousal. Beyond heated with her readiness to be claimed.

She is mine.

Mine.

I am undone.

My tail curls up her body, trapping her completely. My fingers find the rough spot in her sheath and rub it. *She liked this last time.*

"Vruksha!" she screeches my name and then gasps. And if she wasn't thrashing before, she's thrashing now. I rub harder, quickening my movements, sending her into a frenzy, enjoying the way her body shudders against mine.

She gasps again. Her little noises excite me.

Human legs are wonderful. She is soft and receptive, and her sex is never fully hidden. I can just spread her thighs to find it... I arch my member against her, sliding it through the curve of her butt as I roll my fingers inside her.

"Female," I groan, spreading them. "It is time." I decide I do not want to wait until she's in my nest.

She cries out and jerks in my arms. A wail releases from her lips, and her sex constricts around my fingers. She's cumming. She's releasing pent up tension because of me.

Only I will ever get the glory of seeing her succumb.

Not Azsote, not any other. *Me.*

Pleased, a grin pulls at my lips. "Yes, female. Like that. Like that. Yesss."

Her sheath clutches me, and I know it's time. Her legs buckle, and I slip my tail forward between her legs so she may squirm on it as well. I want her everywhere. If it's not her tongue, then it will be her sex dewing up my many scales. I bend her over further, holding her to me as her shaking subsides, until she's on her hands and knees in the shallow part of the creek, bowed over my lower tail. Her body is partially wrapped around it, facing away from me, just like how her sex will soon be wrapped around my member.

Rearing up behind her, I slip my fingers out of her channel, and after one last rub of her wrinkled spot, after one last pleasured, shocked cry tears from her mouth, I line my member to her opening.

"Vruksha," she moans my name, sounding almost defeated. And I pause, but then she lies her head forward, resting it on my tail as she pushes her butt outward. My tip sinks into her.

Tight, hot, soft. Pleasure blasts through me, and I take a moment to gaze down at her back.

Gemma, submitting to me. Waiting weeks of hell for this was worth it. Her hair is wet, plastered to her back, falling forward into the water. Her sex is open, ready for invasion, and clenching in the moonlight. It's tight, spread around my tip, and I push forward. I press my tail to support her chest and body. She wraps her arms around it.

She moans, straining. I watch as I sink deeper, pushing against flesh that fights me but quickly relents.

"Tight," I grit out, cupping her cheeks and spreading her as wide as I can. Will she be able to take my knot? It is softer than the stem of my shaft. I have worked it so it's not so big.

I press forward until her hole is up against it. It's twice the size of her opening, and doubt fills me. My bulge is not as hard...

Part of me wants to pause, to use my hand to expel some of my spill, and make things easier, but I don't. She's perfect where she is. If I stop, I'm afraid she might not let me mount her in such a way again.

"This will not be easy for you," I warn. "You will take it, and I will soothe you. I promise this. The world is yours."

"Vruksha," she moans my name.

I push inside her, not waiting for another response. It is better this way. I force her to take my knot, shunting forward. Immediately the tight pressure makes me spill. My throat closes around a guttural rasp from the pleasure it brings me.

"It's too much," she gasps, straining, buckling, and shuddering. She shimmies forward, and I force her back, arching my tail upward. "Oh, god!" she cries.

I pet her back, pulling out of her, untrapping my bulge. "Again." I thrust back in.

She moans with a hitch, grabbing me closer. She brings my bulge halfway in.

I pull out once more and thrust harder this time, pushing through the tight flesh that continues to fight me.

"Vruksha!" she screams as she takes the entirety of my member.

My mind blanks when I'm seated.

It is bliss. *And hell.* The way she squeezes me, the way I barely fit. The way her channel contracts and every movement her body makes, every sway... My shaft feels it all.

"Female," I grate, gazing where our bodies are joined. Drool slips from my mouth, so crazed am I with the need to move and thrust.

Tense and trembling, nails biting the scales of my tail, she whimpers, "Too much, too big!"

I run my hand over her spine, comforting her. "It will get better," I purr.

I grit my teeth and pull my bulge out from her, spilling even more as I do.

She slumps heavily. "Thank you. I don't think we—"

I line my shaft back up and thrust back in.

She stills with a shocked scream. "What are you doing!?"

"Easing you." This time there was no fight to my invasion. Her channel constricts.

I do it again before her body can try and reject me. The fourth time, a roar tears from my mouth and joins her whimpering. She's wet and tight and slicker than before, easing her was the right thing to do. Coupling with a human isn't straightforward, not from what I've seen of men taking human females on the screens in my den. I know how much larger and stranger I am compared to them.

But she's accepted me and I will worship her for it.

Lifting her until her back is to my chest, I wrap my arms around her body.

Gemma hitches but doesn't say a word as I start jerking my hips, pounding into her from behind. I twist, rising on my tail and then back down as madness takes over my mind, addicted to the sting of her tight sheath.

It grows with each pump, with each moan. My spill surges forward, flooding my bulge to the brink of pain. I speed up. Gemma shakes, grabbing me as I sway and move her body around, lost in the feel of her upon me. I free her breasts and cup them.

They are soft and sweet. Her tight nipples press into my palms.

Slapping my tail on the water, she slumps in my arms as I thrust harder. Her moans grow wilder. Her sex tightens for a third time this night, for *me*.

Such a sweet mate she is.

I spill. I spill all of the deep seed stored inside me.

Stars blast my vision as it jets into her. I snap like a rabid animal in heat, needing her to take it all. There is so much, and my body is only producing more. The way her channel milks me, and her soft moans are music in the night, I know she wants it, needs my spill just as much as I need to give it to her.

Even though she won't say it.

Holding her in the air onto me, I empty into her womb. Her body weakens from the effort. I lay her on my lap, settling into the water, and move us back into the deeper end, sure to remain inside her the whole time. I don't want to leave her, not now that I've claimed her. She may not let me back in.

For a time, she rests against me, with only our ragged breaths sounding between us.

Satisfaction rules me. Satiation. My jealousy vanishes, frightened away by Gemma's acceptance of my seed.

I curl around her, tangling my tail with her limbs, and hold her close. Spill pumps into her now and then as my loins produce more. They are sated, I am sated—and obsessed.

Yet my body only continues to make more, and her sheath quivers each time my bulge grows large inside her, stretching her back out.

No wonder my father mourned my mother. No wonder males search endlessly for the lost naga females.

It's perfection, mating. Contentment settles deep into my bones. I rest my chin on Gemma's head and close my eyes.

Sleep finds me swiftly.

FOURTEEN
DEATH IN THE SHADOWS

Gemma

Bone tired, I stare into the shadows of the forest at the edge of the creek. I dozed for a little while, surprisingly. I was even more surprised when I woke to find Vruksha sleeping as well, his chin resting on my head.

I don't move. The slow dance of the water across my skin feels nice. It washes away the sweat, the dirt, the sex...

The sex. I suck my lips into my mouth.

I knot up. *He's still buried deep inside me.* Vruksha groans, shifts, and I relax, not wanting to wake him. Especially in that way. He might want a round two, and I don't know if I can do that.

I ache. A lot. I throb.

He took me mercilessly. I will feel him for days, if not longer. He saw through my stupid excuses.

The cold water dulls my discomfort immensely though, but his bulge remains inside, and I'm almost afraid to move because it *will* move, and whether it's pushed further in or comes out, I'm twitchy about it. I gingerly reach down between us and massage the skin of my sex stretched around Vruksha's prick, soothing the ache. I tweak my clit afterward for a little pleasure.

It dawns on me that he won, he was right, that I submitted. Three days. It only took three days. *And I wanted it.*

This isn't like me.

But his scent is so delicious...

There's nothing in this universe that could've prepared me for this, for Vruksha. Or an alien at all—since no alien we have met can join with humans.

Lifting my head out from under his chin, I look at him. The moonlight shines brightly over his features.

Not an alien. *A naga.*

His eyes are closed, his sharp lips slightly parted. His breath is warm and fans my cheek. His chest moves with each shallow inhale. He doesn't look nearly as frightening when asleep. I reach my hand up from where it lingered between my legs and caress his cheek, touching the smooth scales there. His head slumps forward.

My heart warms...

I jerk my hand away.

I'm not staying. Not for a moment longer than is necessary. Once I have access to the tech he has, I'll need to make a run for it back to base. I have to. I need to find Daisy.

I can't grow attached to him. If I do, it'll be hard to leave.

He wanted me so badly...

He nearly killed for me.

The warmth in my chest expands.

I'm an idiot for letting him have my body. I groan, pulling back a little more. His hold on me tightens, and I press my hand to my chest, hating the warmth growing within.

I've never given into the protection of another, not since I left my parents to finish my training on *The Dreadnaut* at age thirteen, as dutiful humans to the war effort commonly do. That was almost twenty years...

I wanted to dislike him, but I don't. He makes me feel things I would rather keep buried. In the short time we've been together, he's seen me at my worst, and not once at my best.

Yet he looks at me like I hang the triple suns of Elyria.

No one's ever looked at me the way Vruksha does. It bothers me. I've never needed protection before, and I do now, and it scares me horribly. I want his protection. I think I like his adamance.

Shuddering, I inhale quietly. I force Vruksha from my thoughts, ignoring the warmth in my chest that's growing ever more when I think of him.

I don't need anyone's protection.

I've been gone for three days. Someone from command has to be asking about me, someone has to be wondering what happened to Daisy and me. Peters could tell *The Dreadnaut* we died, but then they'll demand an investigation—hopefully—and insist our bodies be brought aboard the main ship for burial rites.

My gut churns. I don't have family aboard the main ship. Daisy might though.

And if *The Dreadnaut* investigates our disappearance, what would they do to Vruksha and the other nagas if they come down? If the military lands? Will they hurt them? Want to study them?

I shake my head. That'll never happen.

They might send a few fighters but the military deploys for one thing and one thing only: Ketts.

I can't stop the thought from taking root. Earth isn't some random planet in the universe. It's our homeworld. Sentient creatures here wouldn't have the protection they do elsewhere. They'd be seen as invaders to be analyzed and, if need be, disposed of.

I stare hard at Vruksha's peaceful face.

He knows much—far more than makes sense—but he doesn't know humans. As someone entrenched in the constantly shifting ethics of a desperate government, and a bloodthirsty military made up of men and women seeking revenge. He doesn't deserve to be thrust into that world and all it demands.

Will he follow me into the stars if I leave?

I chew on my lip.

A twig snaps and my eyes shoot to the forest. Thick shadows and wild branches meet my gaze. They twist and dance in every direction, thickening the shadows. I peer into them, searching for the source of the noise.

Vruksha's soft breaths breeze across my neck. I listen for a while, letting them comfort me.

When I start to look away, certain there's nothing in the shadows, something behind the branches shifts. A massive coiled shadow rises into the heavier foliage above.

A face appears in the darkness and my throat constricts with terror.

It's a face that only has one eye because the other has been knifed out.

The Death Adder.

"Vruksha, get up!" I jerk out of his arms. His cock tears out of me, and I flinch from the pain.

Vruksha thrusts me behind him, and I fall into the chilly water. Recovering quickly, I scurry to the opposite shore. I force the water from my eyes and find him facing the Death Adder.

"Zhallaix," he hisses.

Vruksha's tail strikes out, snatching his spear from the creek's edge and bringing it to his hand.

"Vruksha," the other naga says, his voice a sharp whisper of warning. My skin rises from the sound. It's rough, guttural. Broken. "What do you have there?" The naga tries to get a look at me.

I reach for my clothes when his head snaps to the side. I jerk my hands back to cover me, bringing my clothes to my chest. It's not fast enough.

His eyes widen and dance across my body, purple in the moonlight.

The next thing I know, Vruksha tackles him to the water, thrashing his tail. I shriek and fall back, taking my clothes with me. A tail rises into the air to bash at the other pinning it below the water. Water sprays everywhere, making it difficult to see, but I spot Vruksha's spear come down again and again.

He doesn't see the tail that's about to strike him from behind.

I scream his name. The tail strikes.

"Run!" he shouts in pain. The word dies in his mouth as his body drops to the side with a splash.

The Death Adder shoots upright and turns to me.

I spin and run.

Pain shoots through me as my feet catch on everything, stabbing my soles. Sticks, twigs, and leaves whip my skin and tangle in my hair. Shouts follow me for a long time, echoing through the trees.

I don't stop. Not when my lungs are about to collapse, or when a particularly sharp branch slashes my side. The fervor returns, and I'm back in time, flashing back to three days before when I was terrified I'd be caught by a frightening alien male.

I don't stop when the night lifts and the moon lowers, when the first rays of the sun streak through the trees. And when I'm about to topple, stumbling from one tree to the next, I see a familiar sight.

The broken shelter Vruksha took me to the first night.

I drag my body to it, fall on my knees with a sob, and crawl inside.

I curl up into a ball and cry.

FIFTEEN
SURVIVE

Gemma

TIME BLURS, my sense of it vanishing with my control. I don't leave the shelter for a day, maybe more, drifting in and out of sleep, praying for a time that death will come while I'm unconscious. It doesn't, and each time I wake, I'm weaker, and still alone. My terror sticks. My body hurts.

I keep hoping I'll wake from this nightmare.

I moan and rub my eyes. I can't sleep anymore, and I curse everything. I even curse my stubbornness and self-discipline for refusing to die. Rising onto my arms, I peer through the shelter to make sure the forest is clear outside.

I wish it wasn't. *I wish...* I shake my head with a frown. Vruksha isn't here.

I need food, water.

I'm easy prey for any predator right now. I have been this whole time but just didn't have the strength to do anything about it.

I'm covered in cuts, some worse than others, and my feet...

When the forest remains clear, I shudder and push open the broken door and slide out, my body protesting. I try to stand but fall, sobbing in pain. I curl up on the ground, grabbing my bloody feet.

I want to survive—I need to survive—I can't be selfish. I'm not allowed to be selfish. I strain. My wounds are too much though. I find my bundle of clothes I've been gripping to me since my collapse and tug them on.

The cloth chafes my skin and I cry out again.

Vruksha fought for me. He fought, and I watched him fall. And I ran.

I let my tears fall as I wish for death to find me anyway.

It does, but only in my head. The Death Adder's broken face rises there, and I shiver. I don't know how I got away from him, though I'm certain it was because of Vruksha, and now I owe it to him to survive.

I prayed he'd come and find me, that when I fell into a fitful sleep, he'd be there when I woke. Except he wasn't, and I can't wait any longer, hoping he'll come. My heart is heavy. I still feel him inside me and it hurts.

His seed is still trickling out of me. It hasn't dried. I grab a leaf from the forest floor and wipe it from my skin, bringing it to my nose to sniff it. His scent makes me clench despite everything. I toss the leaf aside when I'm done, lifting my head. Even naga seed is alien to me.

I hope he's okay.

My boots are long gone, left somewhere by a creek far from here. I wouldn't be able to put them on anyway... My jacket's not here either. Nor do I have underwear or a bra. When I'm dressed with what I have left, I rest my brow on the ground.

You need to move.

I push up onto my arms, pick a direction, and begin crawling. Glancing behind me to memorize my surroundings, I leave the shelter behind. I hope I'll be able to find it again but am not expecting it. I was damn lucky to find the shelter in the first place, and that little bit of luck has given me hope.

I have a sense of where I am because of it. I don't know which direction the facility is or Vruksha's bunker, but I'm at least a half day from either.

I can survive a half day of travel. I just need food, water, and rest first.

I amble forward aimlessly, snapping upon twigs as I move, leaving an obvious trail of my passing. For a time, all I hear is the rustle of plants as I brush past them and the chirping of Earth's birds above me. Resting now and then, I listen to the noises of the forest, knowing they'll help me.

They're not the noises of a spaceship.

Burying my head in my hands, I groan.

I don't have a pocket knife, don't have shoes... I don't have anything except the clothes on my back. I've never trained for this in the academy. Survival on an alien planet wasn't a skill I ever thought I'd need.

I drop my hands.

I roll onto my knees and continue.

I hear a splash. Stilling, I stop breathing. I've found water! The splashes don't stop, and I brace for whatever is beyond my sight, begging the Gods that it's not a naga. I grab a nearby stick and curl my fingers around it.

As quietly as I can, I crawl toward the noise.

A giant lake appears through the bushes. My mouth drops as beautiful blue water spans outward before me, and across the lake are giant snow-capped mountains rising high.

Earth is beautiful.

I don't stare for long, searching for the source of the *splashing*.

There. Below me, a small feline-like creature pounces on fish swimming through the rocks on the shore. It's red, has a pointed nose and a bushy tail. It's cute. The creature snatches the fish between its claws and wrestles it to shore, biting into it.

I lick my lips.

Grabbing my stick, I call out, startling the feline. It flees when it sees me, leaving the fish behind.

I stumble to the bank, falling next to it. There's a bite taken out of the fish's side, and there's blood, but I'm starving.

Clutching it between my hands, I snap the fish's body to finish the kill and lift it to my mouth. Sinking my teeth in, I will my bile to remain in my belly. I leave nothing but bones and the head behind when I'm done. Stomach churning though full, I drag myself to the lake's edge.

I gulp down so much water that when I'm done, the taste of the fish is rinsed from my mouth, and I'm so bloated I can barely move. I lie in the shallow water, letting it wash away the grime. I stare up at the sky.

Wisps of white clouds slowly drift by, too thin to block out the sun's rays. For a while, it feels nice. As the minutes tick by, my skin heats.

I picture Vruksha's sleeping face and my heart twists.

He can't be dead...

I need to go back and find him. I don't know how I'm going to do that, but I have to try.

Rising on my elbows, I peer about. The shore is vacant of animals, though there's something large on the far side, across the lake. I can't make it out fully, only that it has antlers.

Water brings predators.

With that in mind, I wash my body, my wounds, and the dirt and dried blood off me. I scrub my hair and between my legs. I stay until my fingertips are wrinkled and the sun dips, watching for predators the entire time.

Finding the fish head and my clothes to dress, I retrace my path, climbing onto my ruined feet. Dusk shadows the forest by the time I find the shelter. I crawl inside and curl up into a ball on the back seat.

Vruksha's face reappears when I close my eyes. This time his gaze is wicked and hungry. My heart thumps. I debate climbing out and finding the leaf I cleaned his seed off with earlier so I can get another sniff of his scent.

"Vruksha?" I whisper.

He doesn't answer me, though something else does. A fuzzy crackle fills my ears.

I sit up.

Looking deeper into the shelter, a tiny light winks at me through the shadows. The crackling is coming from it. I push through the vines and overgrowth falling from above to see what it is when the light winks out. Rooting for it with my hand, my fingers curl over something round.

An orb.

I clutch it to my chest and clean the dirt off it, thrilled at my luck today.

"Orb, initiate," I say, my voice fracturing.

The lights wink back to life. A wheezy voice from the orb answers me, but I can barely make the words out. It quickly dies.

"Orb, initiate," I say again.

One crackle is all I get. It's dead. Frustrated, I throw the orb out of the shelter. I hear it thump, and then I don't hear it at all. Curling back onto my side, I close my eyes.

Sleep finds me for a time. I dream of my apartment back on *The Dreadnaut,* the paints that I bought last year, and how I never got a chance to use them.

I awake to another noise. This time, it's definitely not of the electronic variety. It's snorting. Something hits the side of my shelter, and the flimsy frame makes a terrible crunching sound at my feet. I tug my legs to my chest and clutch them, burying my face into my knees.

Pigs.

Fear takes hold.

More snorting breaks the night.

I relax a little. There's nothing to fear from pigs. One nudges my shelter behind me, and the whole thing rocks. The orb from Vruksha's bunker listed pigs as predators. I remember the large pack of them, and how gigantic they were.

My shelter shakes again as another one nudges it. Dirt falls on me. I hold my breath and stay as still as possible, hoping they don't discover me and will eventually move along.

Based on the cacophony of snorts, there has to be a dozen or so outside. Or more...

If they find me, and they are predators, I'm dead. I'm too weak to run.

I bring my hands to my lips, close my eyes, and go back to praying.

Morning brightens the forest before they finally leave.

Exhausted and numb, I wait before I risk moving. After checking that they're gone, I crawl back out of my shelter, fear twisting my gut, and I can't tell if I'm hungry or nauseous, or both. Turning back, the shelter is broken, punctured, and has shifted a couple of feet.

I can't stay here.

I was waiting for Vruksha... but he hasn't come. I have to believe he's still alive. I don't think I can live with the guilt if I caused his death. My heart aches, and I reach up to rub the feeling from my chest.

First Daisy, and now Vruksha.

Carefully, I rise on my wounded feet.

The pigs stamped out much of the overgrowth during the night, and I can't immediately figure out which direction they went. My trail to the lake is gone, and though I desperately want to go and fill up with water, I also know the pigs likely moved toward it for the same reason.

I wish Vruksha was here.

Shaking my head, I banish the thought. I can't rely on him anymore, it's up to me now. How things change so quickly.

Turning full circle, I wish for something—anything—to guide me, to lead me to Vruksha's bunker or the facility. I eye the trees, hoping one will be easy to climb, but they're tall and the branches are higher up. There is nothing.

Picking up a nearby stick to use for a crutch, I decide to follow the direction of the sun. It's as good a direction as any. I don't take more than a couple of steps when my foot rams into something hard.

Flinching, I sink my teeth into my lips.

My eyes land on the orb.

I pick it up.

"Orb, initiate," I whisper.

Under the streaming sunlight above, it comes to life, rising from my hand to hover in the air.

"What can I help you with today?" it says.

My eyes widen.

I remember how to smile.

SIXTEEN

CONSEQUENCES

Vruksha

Sunlight streams through the pines of the forest to greet me. I groan, staring at it.

"You're awake."

My gaze cuts to Zhallaix sharpening a knife across from me. I struggle to strike him with my tail, quickly finding I can't move. I'm bound. Ropes have been tied around my wrists, pulling them apart and anchoring me to the tree at my back.

"Gemma," I hiss. "Where's Gemma?"

Zhallaix puts his weapon away, hooking it with the bones he wears on his bicep. "Don't try and move."

"What have you done to my female?" I struggle against my bonds, searching the forest for Gemma.

"Ssshe ran."

I wheeze out a breath. Relief and horror hit me hard. "She's not in your clutches," I rasp. But she's also not here, which means she's alone, in the forest, completely at the mercy of the wilds and beasts that roam it.

Zhallaix hums, unconcerned.

"Let me go," I urge, nearly shaking.

Zhallaix cocks his head. His one eye hoods as he watches me.

"I need to go after her."

"She did not have a tail," Zhallaix responds.

"Of course she didn't!" I hiss. "Releassse me!"

"Where did she come from?"

I snarl. "I don't have time for this. She's not safe alone in the forest. She does not have claws, fangs, or venom to protect herself." She does not have me!

"Humans are extinct, and a naga female hasn't roamed these lands in over a hundred years. How is it possible you have one at all? What is she? A robot?"

I stop fighting my bonds when it occurs to me that Zhallaix does not know about the humans at the facility or the ship that descended from the sky. How humans came out of it took over the old ruins—that there were females amongst those who landed.

He has no idea about Zaku's deal to trade technology for their females. He doesn't know.

Zhallaix destroys all tech he comes across.

I stop struggling as an idea forms. "I'll tell you if you let me go."

"Or I can leave you tied up and find her myself."

"You could... or you could have one for your own, one who isn't already claimed and filled with spill," I growl.

Zhallaix crosses his arms, and I know I have him. The threaded muscles of his arms bulge, stretching white and red scars. Some of those are scars I've given him. There's a gouge on his side, half-strung up with plant fibers to keep it closed. Blood gushes from it. I did that.

I have a few open wounds too, but Zhallaix didn't string mine up.

Why would he? He'd prefer me dead.

So why am I not?

"Where did she come from?" he asks again.

"She may be the only one," I lie. "Or not."

Zhallaix glares at me and reaches behind him. He brings my spear forward.

I release venom at the sight of it. Zhallaix is not only putting Gemma's life in danger but also has my spear? Anger floods me seeing his hand wrapped around the shaft.

I hiss as he nears, bracing for whatever is to come. He stabs down on my tail.

I shout in pain as it pierces deep into my muscle. He digs it in before sliding the sharp tip out. I thrash to free my arms, making no progress. I slump with a grimace when my bonds hold. My blood pools around me as he lifts my spear to stab my tail again.

"Tell me," he rumbles.

"Release me."

Zhallaix stabs and twists.

I grit my teeth, holding in an agonized groan when the tip hits my tail's spine. Sweat pools down my face, agony radiates up my tail and runs straight through my whole body.

He yanks the spear back out. "Should we keep going?"

I scowl, spit.

"I don't want to hurt you anymore, Vruksha," he says, calm as ever, as if he isn't torturing me for information. "But what you did was unforgivable..."

"What I did? I don't know what you're talking about," I sneer.

Zhallaix lowers until he's level with me. Hatred burns for him and the situation he's put my female in. Hatred that he still roams these lands despite the numerous attempts to take his life.

But it's the same situation *I* put my female in for taking her out at night. For falling asleep...

Zhallaix continues, "Mating a female kills them. They do not survive gestation. Only a wretch would satisfy his cravings knowing the outcome. Tell me where you found her."

"Humans are not nagas."

"Have you mated a human female before?"

My nostrils flare. "Of course not. None of us have."

"Then how could you know?"

"And you do? I know what you've done, what you are. I know what your father did, raping female nagasss for his pleasure. I'm nothing like him. None of us are—only you."

His hand goes white where it's clutching my weapon.

"He taught you everything he knew," I continue, "didn't he? He brought you along as he single-handedly—"

"Enough!"

"—bred unwilling females across the region, even those not Death Adders, killing them—"

"Enough!" Zhallaix raises my spear and surges forward, aiming the tip at my groin. "I am not my father!" He slashes down.

I twist to the side, narrowly missing the spear's edge. Zhallaix jerks from the impact, and I'm finally given my opportunity. I spit venom into his eye.

He roars, rearing backward, dropping my weapon. He clutches his eye. He slithers away, shrieking as he hits a tree, sending branches flailing. I shimmy the wound on my tail toward my bound hands, drenching them with blood.

With the ties wet, I fight my way out of them.

One of the ties snaps, releasing my arm. I claw through the rest of the binds. When I free my limbs, I grab my spear and use it to help me rise.

Zhallaix thrusts his tail out to keep me back, unable to see me.

"I ssshould kill you," I growl, leaning over him.

One black and red eye peers wetly at me through strained fingers. "Do it!" he says.

I lift my spear over him.

"Do it!" he screams.

I stab him in the gut and twist. Blood gushes, as I yank it out.

Zhallaix drops his hand from his eye, hisses, and slumps. He doesn't move again but continues to watch me through his ruined eye. Slowly, the color fades from his scales, and his eye closes.

I stare at him for a short time, making sure he stays down. I take no pleasure killing one of my own, even though I have before and know I will again.

"You should have killed me when you had the chance," I say, lowering my spear.

I flick my spear clean of blood and take to the trees, not giving Zhallaix another thought.

The creek is nearby. I hear it rather than see it, and from my viewpoint, I notice nothing out of the ordinary, nothing that will help me find Gemma. I need to find her. I don't know how long I've been out, only that it's dusk now, which means many hours have passed since Zhallaix's attack. If not days.

I rush to the water, hoping there'll be a trail, wincing from the pain of my wounds.

I follow the creek north until I'm at the place I was last with Gemma. I see her boots. Grabbing them, bringing them to my face, I inhale her scent.

She's out in the forest alone, without me, the male who vowed to protect her. She doesn't know how to defend herself; she knows little about my world. There's so much more than animals and monsters...

I battle against the pain in my tail that threatens to slow me, slipping it in the water to wash the blood off as I frantically search for her trail.

Sticks are broken, leaves crushed on the ground. Someone hit the overgrowth hard, head-on.

It had to be Gemma. Imagining her fear as she fled infuriates me. She took to the dangerous forest in the darkness without a plan. My claws dig into the material of her boots, leaving the creek behind.

As I track her, I fear I'm going to stumble upon her broken form and a madness takes hold of my mind. But as the hours go by and the moon rises, I never do. She ran for hours...

Was she running from me as well? My tail coils, shooting spikes of pain up my spine at the thought. I refuse to believe it.

The moon ascends and deep shadows blanket the forest so thickly I lose the tracks.

My anger and helplessness coalesce into a roar. *"Gemma!"* I roar her name.

I'm answered with silence.

I stab my spear into the ground and gather wood to make a fire. If she's nearby, she'll see the light and will come. It gives me something to do while I wait for the sun to return, and the flames keep my mania at bay.

The night lasts an agonizing eternity. I do not sleep. Not with my female out of my reach and not knowing where she is.

Dawn has not yet risen when I take back to her trail. I lose it several more times throughout the morning because her tracks have begun fading. Backtracking and finding where it picks up, makes me lose precious time. The sun is past its zenith, the heat sweltering, when I'm plowing forward again.

I shout her name.

And again, rage takes hold at her loss. For losing her, and worse, for not being prepared to take on a human female like I thought I had been. I should have known better.

Why did I take her out at night when I could have taken her to my nest?

I could have her coiled up in my tail right now if I had.

Something blue appears in the distance, and I move toward it. Her jacket. I grip the material tightly to my chest. It's torn and dirty and yet, still in good shape.

A sign.

My hope returns.

The landscape changes, sloping downward, and her trail picks back up for a while. She slowed here. I have to lower to the forest floor to find her passage. Moving from tree to tree, I see dried blood upon the leaves. Though as I do, I see something else, something far worse...

Pig tracks.

Dozens of them. Hoofprints everywhere, pig shit amongst them. The smell of their passage makes the forest reek.

My heart plummets knowing they caught her scent and that I will lose Gemma's trail completely amongst the pigs'.

My fingers clench. She has to be close. Tearing my eyes off the forest floor, I look up to see where I am. I know this area, I realize. I've traveled through here countless times. Pig tracks or no, if she's here, I'll be able to find her.

Unless the pigs have gotten to her first... If they had, there'll be nothing but blood where they caught her. They eat everything.

I'll kill every last pig in the land if she's met such a fate.

The sun hits the horizon far too soon, and the diminishing strength of my tail begins to impede me. Blood still gushes from my wounds, making me sluggish. I keep going.

When I hear the pigs, I slip up into the trees and find a mid-size pack of swine in the distance.

One raises his head and sniffs loudly. He smells fresher blood now that I've arrived.

I streak my short claws over the wounds of my tail and give them more of it. Pain soars through my nerves, and I grit my teeth. If the pigs come after me, I can lead them away and kill them off one by one. Within minutes, there's a pack of swine beneath my branch, swarming over each other to reach me.

Lying flat on the branch, I position my spear and, gripping the handle tight, stab at the one nearest me. My speartip sinks deep into fatty flesh. The pig squeals, startling the others to do the same. I wrench my arm back and stab again. I hit another pig.

The pigs flail and scream, blocking out all other sounds. They frenzy, and some run off, the smart ones. Most remain because there's a meal to be had. I brace and stab again.

Soon, they're no longer after my blood, but their own. Snorting and snuffing, they turn on each other, too dumb to move away from the spear poking them from above. Blood fills the air.

Something catches my spear and yanks it from my grip. I recatch it moments later as one of the pigs jumps after me instead of his brethren. Glimpsing down, I find two large, intelligent eyes gazing up at me with hatred. I spit venom at the leader, and he shakes it off.

The others around him begin to notice that I'm still above; they see me now that their bellies are full of their friends.

It's time to go.

I coil and lift off the branch, slipping to the next tree over. The large pig follows me, while several others follow him. If I don't lose them, they'll chase after me until either I'm dead or they are. And from the look the big one is giving me, he wants my hide.

As long as it's me and not Gemma.

I lead the pack out of the area, killing as I go, stabbing through the night until morning breaks through the trees.

I need to find Gemma, and soon.

I push off the trunk of the tree I'm on and silently move back to the place I was when I found the pigs the night before. The place where I last had Gemma's trail.

In the dawn's light, I see nothing except half-eaten corpses and blood. The bushes, branches, and plants were decimated in the feeding frenzy. If there was a trail before, it's gone now.

I bite out a curse.

Something swishes past my head. I catch sight of it just before it vanishes into the forest. It's rusted, dirty, and broken, but I know what it is.

A drone.

Excitement rips through me.

My exhaustion disappears as I take off after it. Someone initiated drones...

Gemma.

SEVENTEEN

DANGER ON EVERY LEDGE

Gemma

I RUN my arm over my brow, wiping the sweat gathered there, and push forward. I've been running for hours, trying to get away from the sounds of the pigs behind me.

Soon after I found the orb, I heard them again.

They're getting closer. My pulse quickens as the sun crests.

They never left.

I catch hold of a branch, curling my bleeding toes into the dried leaves. I stumble to the next tree.

Ahead of me is a ledge, and I make a faltering sprint for it. Through the trees, I see the slope of the mountain I'm heading toward.

The landscape has become increasingly rockier and hillier. I didn't get lucky, I failed to pick the direction toward Vruksha's bunker. I curse continuously. I don't know how I ever thought I was going to find alien tech and run it back to my people.

I didn't know what I was truly in for. I was stupid to think it was a good plan, even with Vruksha's spear for protection.

God, I'm an idiot.

I reach the ledge as a snort sounds behind me and pull my body up, barely managing to get off the ground when something snaps at my foot. Jerking my limbs into my body, I twist back.

Behind me is the largest, angriest-looking hog I've ever seen. Three times my size, the hog could eat me whole. I hold in a scream as it claws and tries to climb the ledge, snapping and snorting in a frenzy.

I take my stick and jab its head.

My stick breaks.

"Fuck," I gasp, pulling my half toward me. I stare at the broken tip. Movement catches my eye. Two more pigs run out of the trees joining the first. They barrel into the ledge.

I recoil, turning around to find an escape. The slope is steep but rocky, and I can climb the boulders leading up the mountainside. That'll lose the pigs. *I hope.* I shiver and massage my aching hands, examining the jagged edges, deciding on the best route.

I try not to think about how tired I am, nor how I'll probably fall to my death. My gut cramps. I can't do much climbing, I won't be able to lift my body in the state I'm in.

I wish I was facing several horny naga males over this. *Anything* over this. The pigs I know are nothing like the mindless, brutal animals clawing at the ledge.

"Fuck," I whisper, breathing the word out between my teeth, tossing my broken stick to the side.

There are now five pigs at the ledge when I glance back. One's climbing on the back of another. I struggle to my feet and take to the slope.

Slipping, my clothes tear, while sharp rocks abrade my skin. My bleeding feet stain the rocks. My hands are raw, and my world spins. I cry and pray and beg. I'm hungry, thirsty, low on energy, and I don't have much fight left in me.

But pigs?

I'm not letting pigs be my end. I fight my way higher and higher until I fall face-first onto a ledge toward the top, collapsing. I still hear their snorting below me. There's more now. I roll over and stare at the sky, panting.

Even if I get to the top, what do I do next? My eyes catch the orb still hovering beside me. To my disappointment, it has spent more time 'updating' than answering my questions. At least it followed me.

"Orb," I rasp. It blurs as my vision wavers.

"What can I do for you?" it asks.

"Where is the..." I don't know what to ask to get the information I need.

"I don't understand. Please repeat."

"What predators are around me?" I finally say, repeating the question Vruksha asked in his bunker, all while trying to solidify a cohesive thought in my head.

The orb lights up and my eyes shift back to the sky. I don't expect it to give me any sort of answer.

So when it does answer, I'm stunned.

"Scanning complete. There are several packs of pigs scattered around this region, two families of bears, and three snakes."

I push up on my elbows. I smack my lips, swallowing even though my mouth is dry. "How do you know that?"

It doesn't answer.

"Orb, how do you know what's nearby?"

"I am connected to three major relays in this zone. Additionally, there are over eighteen hundred orbs signaling feedback in a fifty-mile radius around my location. Another fifty-six hundred are powered off. We are a linked data sharing maintenance system, used for the benefit of military security and the humans and the Lurkers working here."

I stare dumbly at the orb.

What?

"Orb," I cough, light-headed. "Do you know where Vruksha's bunker is?"

The snorts are growing louder.

"I do not understand what a Vruksha bunker is. Please repeat."

I reach up and cup the orb, bringing it to me. "Orb, is there a military base near my location? Anything?" I rub some of the dirt off its plastic frame.

"There's the Caret Center two miles east and Eagle's Rest base five miles north. We are currently within Eagle's Technological Zone."

A squeal pierces my ears, tearing my attention away from the orb. Rolling to my side, I look down the mountain.

I hear another cry as a second pig falls, tumbling hard against the rocks. There's more now, at least a dozen, and they're using each other to climb to my location. I drop the orb, letting it levitate, reaching for my stick before remembering that it's gone. I find rocks instead.

Picking one up with both hands, I drop it on the nearest swine. The pig rears up and runs, skidding down the side before it falls off. It rights itself at the bottom and flees out of sight. I find another rock.

A bigger one.

I aim for a second pig. "Take that!" I shout, throwing it.

The rock smacks it directly on the head, killing the animal. It falls over, twitching.

I suck in, excited by my kill, before the pig closest to it stops climbing and tears into the corpse. I slink back over the ledge, disgusted and scared. Glancing up, there's not much more I can climb without likely falling. There's also not a lot of rocks left to throw.

I turn back to the orb. "Orb," I hurriedly initiate, "is there anything near here that can help me get out of this situation?"

I reach over and pull another rock toward me as I wait for it to answer.

"I'm sorry. I do not understand your question."

I close my eyes, press my brow to my knees. I don't want to die here, not like this. I inhale and lean over the side, aiming my rock at the closest pig.

I miss.

I try not to cry. The remaining pigs, I count eleven now that the one that fled has returned, are between me and safety. I don't have enough rocks left for half of them...

"Orb. Help me. *Please*, help me."

I'm not expecting a response. I gather the remaining rocks to my side, preparing to die fighting. I can't even kick the pigs off the ledge if they get close... my feet...

"Sending help to your location."

Tears fill my eyes at the words.

"Help will be arriving shortly," it says.

My fingers curl into my palms. I can scarcely hope that what the orb says is true; I don't know what help is left to be had. But as I watch the pigs climb, trampling each other to reach me, a bang goes off, and blood hits my face.

I startle, shocked.

I don't move as I'm drenched in the sounds, hearing shots go off one after another. The pigs scream and squeal. I fall onto my back, listening to the sweet sound of gunfire. Because that's what it is: gunfire. I would know it anywhere.

"Female!" a voice roars, startling me further.

Vruksha?

I twist to my side. "Vruksha!" I scream. All I see is red. Everything is red.

A bath of blood and pig gore.

Something moves through it, sliding up the ledge at stunning speeds. I call out, near delirious when Vruksha's striking face fills my vision. It's the most beautiful sight I've ever seen. I immediately start sobbing.

I grab him as he reaches for me, planting my face into his chest. His smell envelops me, and I sob harder. His scent immediately starts numbing the pain.

"Sssshhhh, female, sshh." He gathers me into his arms. "You're safe now."

I gasp through tears, rubbing my face against him. "I thought you were dead."

"As long as you're alive, female, I'm alive. I'll always be looking for you."

He carries me away from the mountain, the blood, and the pigs.

A NAGA'S PLEA

Gemma

I WAKE to crackling and the smell of meat. My body curls deeper into the soft warmth that's gathered around me. I don't want to move. All I want to do is remain here, where I know it's safe. In my dream, I was standing in a quiet, undecorated apartment, staring at paints I longed to use.

My belly roils, howling from prolonged hollowness. I groan and cling to the fur gathered around my mouth.

"Wake, female, and eat."

I open my eyes to Vruksha holding a spit with meat hanging off it. Smoke rises from the meat.

I turn over and vomit, hacking up air. Vruksha gathers my hair and holds it away from my face. I cough until my empty stomach stops churning. I shake, barely able to hold my body upright.

Rising slowly from the furs, Vruksha helps me into a sitting position. He places the meat at my mouth, and I nearly gag again. I cup his hands to steady them and take a bite anyway, sinking my teeth into crisp perfection.

Meat this fresh, this good is rare, even for someone who works on the bridge of a warship. It's for the rich and the planet dwellers who refuse to give such luxuries up. I tear into it after the first bite, not stopping until I finish.

I hope it's one of the pigs who tried to eat me.

Vruksha pulls the spit away when I'm done, otherwise, I probably would've eaten it too.

"Thank you," I say.

He hums and slips away, returning soon after with a cloth. I wipe my face and hands, and flinch from the cuts there.

"You are feeling better," he says.

Am I? I glimpse the space around me, recognizing the inner shell of the bunker. But I'm in a different part of it, deeper in, I think. There are still crates perched about, cement walls, and the flickering lights above. I'm in a circular bed—or cot—and there are warm pelts gathered on every side of my body.

There are also pelts hanging from some of the walls and strange baubles and artifacts of Earth. There's a whole row of orbs on a built-in shelf opposite me. I see my dirty, bloody one at the end.

My gaze returns to Vruksha. He's watching me, poised close to my side. I stare at him for time, dazed and so happy to be alive, to see him alive. I continue to stare as the meat settles in my belly, needing the extra moments to decide I'm not dead, and he saved me.

"What happened?" I ask, my voice a broken whisper.

He moves at my words, taking my cloth and setting it aside. "You passed out after I found you. You've been asleep since."

"How... long?"

"Several days."

I reach up and feel my crimped hair, my face. "Days?"

Has it been days? I test my limbs and wince. It feels like minutes.

"You're hurt, Gemma. You nearly died."

My brow furrows. I push the pelts gathered atop me off.

I'm naked. I quickly bring a pelt back to cover me, but I glimpse the damage to my body.

I'm wrapped in bandages up and down my limbs, covered in so many bruises that my flesh is unrecognizable, and my feet... My feet are covered in balls of cloth. I wiggle my toes and gasp. *There's the pain.* I sink my teeth into my lower lip.

But I realize I'm clean, my hair is soft around my shoulders, if not tousled, and for the first day since I was abandoned by my people, I don't feel grimy. "You cleaned me."

"You wouldn't stop bleeding. I feared infection."

My eyes slide back to Vruksha. "Thank you." How can I ever repay him?

The look he gives me is grave, pained. Tired?

Has he slept, taken care of himself?

"Drink this," he rumbles, handing me a cup.

"What is it?"

"Tea, made of local plants and herbs that will dull your pain. A recipe was given to me by one of the orbs," he adds.

I swish the cup and take a sip. I recognize the taste. Hazy memories of Vruksha pouring the liquid down my throat return to me. I finish off the tea, already feeling better. The heat of it slips through my body, soothing me.

He takes my cup away and places several pelts back atop me. "Sleep, female, you need rest. You can not regenerate without it."

I lie back and drift off, not needing to be told twice.

The next time I wake, I cry out in pain. It radiates up my legs and through my feet. I grip the bedding but find only one pelt beneath me, the rest are gone.

"Sssshhh. This will be over soon."

Vision blurry, I find Vruksha leaning over my legs, pulling off my bandages and cleaning my skin. He gathers my feet and places them into a basin of water.

I gasp, tears brimming my eyes. "It hurts."

He slides a cup over to me with the tip of his tail and I take it, downing the contents before he has the time to tell me what it is. The pain tempers.

I slump and stare at the ceiling as Vruksha takes care of me. Shame fills me as he cleans my wounds and massages my aching muscles. He slowly makes his way up my legs, taking his time. I'm naked, and it bothers me. I'm weak and needy, and I hate it.

I can't be weak, I can't be needy. Weak, needy people can't help others and can't hold a high-ranking position...

But it's his washing of my body that I can't handle the most. He's an alien male, a species with no given name as far as I know by humanity, and he is not beholden to me. I don't want him to think I'm helpless. I reach down and grab his wrist before he dips his hands between my thighs.

"Please," I say, I beg, pulling at the cloth with my other hand.

His eyes pin me, but he lets me pull the cloth from his grip. I clean the rest up myself.

When I'm done, Vruksha hands me another ration of meat. I try to take it from him. He growls, not letting me.

"What? Why?" I ask.

"I will feed you."

"I can feed myself..." I touch my mouth. "It's not hurting like the rest of me."

"It's not whether it's hurting or not, I want to feed you."

"I'm not a child."

"No. You are my mate, and I nearly lost you." He lifts the meat to my mouth and gently presses it to my lips. "It will make me happy to feed you. It will calm me."

I think about fighting him out of pride, but I don't, because it's not my pride that hurts with being fed. It's the vulnerability. I glance down at my nude, broken body and know I've been at my most vulnerable for days.

And he's still here.

He saved my life. He's saving me still. I owe him everything.

I part my lips and take a nibble of meat, watching him. Vruksha moves closer and slides his tail behind me to support my back. I rest against it and take another bite.

I don't understand why he puts his life in so much danger for me, why he's going through all this effort to keep me alive—even comfortable. I get that there are no females here anymore, but to risk his life for one because of that? I don't understand it.

If I'd been in this condition back up on *The Dreadnaut*, only family would've stayed by my side and I don't even have family on *The Dreadnaut*. I haven't seen my parents since I was thirteen.

Vruksha is an enigma.

I watch him watching me, swallowing thickly. Seeing him as a man for the first time, rather than an alien. Or a monster. Or some mindless beast, viciously attacking anything that comes near me.

We continue staring at each other long after I finish the meat.

It's not just mere curiosity anymore, I want to know him—really know him—and how he came to be here on this ravaged world where there shouldn't be any sentient life to begin with.

I've seen no alien spaceships.

"Will you get me a blanket?" I whisper.

His eyes dip for a second, and I cover my chest. But then he's gone and soon returning with several pelts. He hands me one and tucks the others around my body, saving the last one to bind my feet. Afterward, he bandages my deeper wounds with fresh cloth and cleans the strips of the old ones in the same basin my feet were bathed in. We settle in the front of the bunker.

"You should rest," he tells me.

"I've slept enough."

"You're still recovering."

"And what about you?" I see the wounds on his tail and the cracks in the scales around them. They're fleshy and red and swollen. They look painful.

"Me?"

"Your tail." I reach out and touch it. "You're hurt too, Vruksha."

"I heal quickly. This is nothing compared to what I can truly endure."

"I don't…"

His eyes snap to mine. "Don't what?"

"I don't want you to endure anymore on my part," I whisper and look down, unable to hold his eyes. It's the truth. It pains me seeing he's hurt too. That he's suffering and not resting because of me. I'm such a burden.

You lose your job if you become a burden. You lose everything else after losing your job.

"Female," he growls. "I will endure far more than this for you. This —" he indicates one of his gashes "—is nothing compared to what I'm willing to sacrifice for you. What torment I'm willing to face."

"You shouldn't have to sacrifice anything at all!"

I don't know where the words come from, but it's true.

He slides up against my body, and while I try to lean away, his tail is still behind me, holding me upright. I'm trapped.

"I have nearly lost you twice. Once with Azsote. A second time with Zhallaix. And if I hadn't gotten to you in time, I would have lost you a third time. Do you know what I would do if I lose you?"

I shake my head.

"I would kill everything in my path until something or someone puts me out of my misery. I never wanted a female because of this, of how they make their mates crazy. I saw what happened to my father, but as I grew and he left, I realized why females are so important. It is why I would do anything, *anything* to keep you. Now that I have known you, I wonder how my father lived for so long after my mother died."

"I—" I swallow, asking the one question that has plagued me constantly, "Why me?"

"Life, sweet mate, there's no life without you. Not on this world or any other, I am certain. What's the point if there's no life? You are my life."

My brow furrows. "I don't understand..."

"How could you? Living up in the stars where there are more worlds than this to choose from? My people are dead, long before we thrived. We are lonely, without ever knowing companionship. I don't want to live without life anymore. I don't want to be alone.

"When I saw you walk off your ship, at first I did not know what I was seeing. Another human male? A robot? But it was your hair that captivated me. And the way you lifted your face to the sky and smiled? I was mesmerized. You glow in the sunlight, little female, and I have never rested my eyes upon anything so sweet. Why you, Gemma? Because you stole my breath. You stole my life when you turned and found me in the forest."

He says this with a haunted expression that weakens me. I tear my gaze away. I do not glow. It's hard to look at him when he stares at me like I'm the reason the stars exist. He's completely devoted himself to me.

My throat tightens. It hurts. He makes me hurt. I press my hand to my chest, gazing at the ruby scales of his tail.

How I wish I could paint him... Though I do not think I own a vibrant enough red to do Vruksha justice. I could keep him with me forever if I painted him. "I know what it's like to be alone," I say quietly.

I don't know how else to respond.

"You do?"

I rub my lips together and nod. "Not like you, here. Loneliness is different up in the ships most humans live on. You're surrounded by metal, plastic, glass, and cold space. And it makes you cold too because there's no warmth up there. We're crowded together, and there's no escape, so it's easier to put walls up, to keep everyone at a distance despite being surrounded all the time. Everyone is alone up there because everyone has these walls around them..."

"Then take them down?"

"You can't. If you do, you get burned, you lose respect, and you lose rank. But it's easier being alone amongst others, than being alone without anyone." I force my gaze to meet his eyes. "Vruksha, I'm sorry."

"Why?"

I bite down on my tongue, trying to find the words. "Because…"

"—Don't. Don't say it, Gemma."

I inhale.

"I don't want to hear it," he hisses.

He lifts me in his arms and carries me deeper into the bunker, back to the pile of furs and pelts. He places me gently atop them.

And suddenly, I'm bone tired. And sad.

He knows why I'm sorry.

That despite everything he is, the marvels of this place, and everything he has done for me, including giving up his life, I can't stay. I'll never be able to stay.

Not while Daisy is out there, lost. Not while Peter and Collins remain on Earth. And not when there's a chance that others from *The Dreadnaut* will come looking for us.

That they could hurt him.

I can't keep Vruksha, because of this.

And he can't keep me.

REFLECTIONS AND BLOODY KISSES

Vruksha

GEMMA PLANS ON LEAVING ME.

I see it in her eyes every time she wakes to eat, have her bandages changed, or tries to take a step. I'm always there to catch her when she falls.

My only comfort is seeing her on the mend. It has been over a week since I carried her limp, lifeless body back to my bunker, and in the days since, she has gotten better—stronger—every day.

Some of the fury, the guilt has lifted watching her get better. Though I know it will never fully go away. I hope it never does.

I failed.

She was wounded... Wounds that, if I had been more diligent, if I had been keener, she would have never received. Zhallaix should have never been able to sneak up on me. He should have never been close to Gemma. I'm not comforted by his death, but I am glad I won't have to worry about him any longer.

No wonder she chose another male over me.

She's all I think about. My mind is clouded with thoughts of her. It's a poor excuse though it is true. She is my weakness. I have never been weak before, not until she entered my world. Now, it is all I am.

I've had plenty of time to think while she healed. I've spent so much time watching her sleep, lost in thought as I've tried unclouding my mind.

Flicking my eyes over her, she's burrowed in the soft pelts of my many, many kills. She's chosen the thinnest pelt to use as a dress since her clothes are beyond repair. They had plastered to her skin from blood and sweat, and I had to tear them off with my fangs to undress her. Now they are nothing but shreds of cloth buried deep in the ground.

I curl my finger under a strand of her hair and twirl it.

The thought of her leaving worries me.

She only has one place to go...

Back to the facility where there's a ship to take her to the stars. Far, far from me. To a place I couldn't follow her. Not unless she takes me with her.

A soft moan escapes her parted lips, stealing my attention. She is so beautiful that it hurts. Staring at her in my nest, where she's firmly mine, I can't imagine not having her here. I do not want to gaze at the stars and wonder where she is among them.

It's true what I told her. Loneliness hurts, especially since I know what it's like to not be that way. Especially when, until recently, there was no hope for anything except a lonely existence.

I gently pull her hair from under her head and span it out on the fur above. I work the tangles out of her strands. Worshiping her this way eases me. I can't keep her knowing she is hurting, but I can have this. I can groom her to my heart's desire. She is in my nest, after all, and a naga male is king to his nest.

I nearly lost her. Again.

The recollection of her on the mountainside, curled, bloody, and trapped with nowhere to go sickens me. With the amount of blood and her pallor flesh, I thought she had died, but she's a fighter, my female, and she managed to survive long enough for me to find her.

I kiss her hair, breathing in her scent.

A shiver streaks through me, hardening me with lust.

How can I lose her again? She wants to go back to her humans. To her puny males. To a world where she is clearly not treated like the precious jewel she is. She has told me some about her life, and it sounds miserable. I am better than what awaits her there.

So why does she want to go back?

I pull away and find her looking at me when I do.

"Vruksha," she says my name with a softness that rends my heart into pieces.

"I did not mean to wake you."

Her face scrunches cutely, and she brings her hands up to rub the sleep from her eyes. In doing so, her pale breasts lift upward. They beg to be devoured and suckled until peaked. I hold off, knowing she is not ready for such attention.

"I'd like to try and walk again today."

I grab the cup with my tail and hand it to her. "After your bath. I've made you some tea."

She pushes it away. "Not today. That stuff makes me sleepy, and I want a clear head today."

I put the cup away. I like her sleepy, I like her like this, needing me. If she's awake and alert, she may want to take risks again, and knowing her, she needs to be watched at all times because of this.

I've learned.

"Later then," I say.

Gemma rises from my nest, sitting up. Her silky, wavy hair falls around her shoulders to tease me. Her strands caress and brush her upper breasts, her tips, and my mouth waters. I still don't push her into my furs and devour them.

It's taken days for her to be comfortable enough to be naked around me.

And as an obsessed male, her nudity tortures me constantly.

I like her needing me so, but *burning tech*, I want her healthy again so she will let me spill my seed inside her. I need to claim her, to reassure my soul she is well. I need to cover her, coil my tail around her, and clear my head of the dark thoughts of possessing her.

She nearly died.

If I had not gotten there in time...

Gemma grabs her dress-pelt and wraps it around her body, tying the lanks I'd cut days earlier to keep it in place. I hand her the other ties so she can position the pelt more securely. She moves to rise, and I catch her in my arms.

She gasps. "I wanted to try walking."

I cradle her close, carrying her away from my nest to the tub of water I have waiting. "Bath first."

"I just dressed."

"Perhaps you ssshouldn't have."

She grumps and kicks her legs halfheartedly in reply.

I set her by the tub and picking up a fresh cloth cut from one of my oldest pelts, I dip it into the water.

"You only want to bathe me so you can touch me." She says this as she moves onto her knees. "I've figured you out."

I ring out the cloth. "Mmm."

She tugs it from my hand. "I can do it."

My nostrils flare as she presses it to the bruised skin of her shin. The glistening water left behind entices me to lick it off. She works the cloth over her arms, neck, and finally under her dress.

My hands clench.

"Can I have a moment of privacy?" she asks sweetly.

My eyes snap to her face and discover she's studying me shyly. Her cheeks are pink. I grunt and turn my head.

"More privacy than that," she demands less sweetly. "It's not like I can go anywhere, Vruksha."

"Until you do," I growl, slipping away and to our nest. Her quiet movements reassure me as I straighten out and repair the pelts. I haven't felt comfortable using our nest while Gemma recovered, but perhaps tonight, I will join her in her sleep. I sniff the blankets she's been sleeping in, sucking her scent deep inside me.

I groan.

"I'm done," she calls out.

Dropping the furs, I return to her side. She's dressed and wrapping her feet in fresh cloth when I do. I tug her fingers away and finish the job for her.

"You don't have to keep caring for me so much…" she murmurs.

"I like it."

"But I can do it myself."

"And that matters how?"

She laughs, startling me.

"You're not nearly as terrifying as I thought you were. If I'd known that first day what I do now—" She laughs some more, pushing her hair back. "Maybe I would've just followed you home instead of running away."

"Perhaps you would have chosen me instead of Azsote." I don't know why I say it, but I do, the old jealousy returning viciously.

She's quiet until I finish up with her feet.

"I didn't choose him because I wanted him…"

I look at her. She's digging her finger into the material of her dress, eyes downcast.

My heart ramps at the submissive posturing.

"You didn't want him?" I ask gruffly.

She shakes her head, still not meeting my eyes. Oh, how I want to dominate her until she vows to let me rule her. If she allowed me to take over, I would impale her on my member and bind her body to me as I rutted her continuously for days on end. I'd make sure she'd never make it to the stars.

"I chose him because I thought he would be easier to manipulate."

She goes quiet again, but I want to hear more.

"Go on."

Gemma sighs. "I was terrified. For a minute there, I thought suicide would be a better fate than what awaited me. Males who barter for women like we're nothing more than items to own are not good males. When Azsote snatched me, I wanted to get away from him just as badly, but in the frenzy... and when you came for me... Azsote seemed less likely..."

"Less likely to what?"

"Eat me alive."

"If I ate you, then you'd be dead, and that is not my plan for you."

She laughs again. "Oh, I know that now."

She's in a good mood today, a talkative mood. It's odd. I like it. "You chose him," I snap anyway, bothered still.

Her eyes finally meet mine. "If I could go back in time, I would choose you."

"Why?" Give me more. I'm a greedy male.

"You're..." Her eyes flick over my face, even briefly to my chest. I straighten, showing off. "You're kind," she says.

I guffaw, slumping. "I am not kind."

"You are to me. I... I don't know anyone else who would have done for me what you have."

"I am your male."

"That's not a good reason. I still don't know many human males who would do what you did. Maybe my dad."

"Your males are pathetic," I growl.

She swallows. "Maybe you're right, but it's not their fault. It's how life is up there."

"Do not make excusesss for them," I hiss. "They do not know what they have lost when they gave you up, and as a male who knows what he has gained, they will always be lesssss than swine to me."

Her lips twitch. "You have a way with words."

I don't understand her meaning, but I don't care. I lean forward until my face is all she sees. I want to be all she sees. "Let me show you what you mean to me, female."

Her lips part, and it takes great willpower to not capture them and taste her.

"I think," she whispers. "You already have." She tries to pull back, and I let her, knowing exactly that she has only one place she can go.

Down.

I lean over her, corralling her as she leans on her arms, further still, chasing her with my mouth until she's flat on her back. When I have her where I want her, trapped beneath me, I close my eyes and breathe her in.

Honeyed and sweet. Her chest rises and falls as her heartbeat drums in my ear.

"Vruksha," she says my name. But it's not in warning or fear... It's something else.

I want to believe she likes this.

Me.

I want to show her that I'm not like any other male, that I am the best. That if she stays, I'll give her everything, and she'll never be hurt again. I'm a fast learner. An avid one. I've done nothing but study and watch her, protecting and caring for her. Trying not to touch her, letting her heal. She's healed now. Mostly.

I'm desperate for her to choose me. Perhaps it's because no one has before, not really. Why would they? I'm a lone Viper male with a vicious streak. It was only a matter of time before I left my father of my own volition, instead of the other way around.

I plant my palms on either side of her face, caging her in. My fingers reach out, curling into her red hair haloed about her face.

"I want to keep you, Gemma."

Her lips part to speak.

"Let me keep you."

I search her face, needing her to see the truth. I pour every desperate want and every feeling I don't have a name for into it, needing her to see it. Needing her to say *yes*.

She cups my face and brings my lips to hers.

TWENTY

BEAUTIFUL SCREAMS

Vruksha

HEAT ERUPTS, surging through my spine. My fingers strain, gripping her hair as she presses her mouth to mine. This is a kiss. I know what this is. I've seen them on the screens. It's affection, a human act of mating, a show of desire, and trust.

She trusts me enough to kiss me—a male with venom. I push my mouth against hers.

Her lips part and her tongue comes out to play. Lust soars through me, and my member springs out from my tail to stab at her body as I lower and press into her. Her legs fall open to the sides, forcing her makeshift dress up.

I ram my tail between her thighs, making sure she won't be able to close them. Now that she's open, the primal male in me, the one that wants to coil around her body and rut her into oblivion, needs her open. I have waited for this since the creek. I never finished spilling all I have inside her then, and my bulge still aches.

It's because of the seed she coaxed my body to create when I first laid eyes on her. The pressure is unending, the agony a constant torment.

We're surrounded by earth, cement, and metal here. There's no other male but me.

Only me.

Yet I can't fully relax. Groaning, I deepen the kiss.

My tail straightens out until it knocks at things behind me, scattering them as the need to thrash and bellow constricts my throat.

"What's—" Gemma gasps, pulling back, but I catch her with my mouth. I swallow her mumbled words.

I cup one hand under her neck, squeezing it as I open my mouth to ram my tongue into her. And just like I hoped, her tongue retreats and relents to my dominance. I lick it, rub mine to hers, petting it, tasting her inside. I want her to always submit to me.

The new scent my body creates when she is near floods the air.

Her hands grab my head and she deepens the kiss. She moans, and her tongue starts to fight back, pushing into mine. My little human fighter.

She gasps, her body going rigid, and blood coats my tongue. I jerk back as her hand covers her mouth. She looks up at me with wide eyes. I lick at her blood, swallowing it down. *Oh, yesss.*

"Oww," she whispers, pressing her fingers to her lips. "I forgot you had fangs."

"Keep your tongue out of my mouth in the future. I don't want to poison you."

"You can poison me?"

"I'm a Pit Viper. I'm highly venomous." So, she didn't know. "I can control it."

"Thank god."

I grab her hand off her mouth and trap it against the floor. I lean down and lick the blood off her lips.

Her breath hitches and her knees come up to press against the sides of my tail. I coax her mouth back open with my tongue. She tastes delicious and flinches when I find where my fang poked her. I lick the area until she settles. It's a promise that any hurt, big or small, I'll be here to take care of it.

Her mouth moves on mine, forcefully, and I deepen the kiss again, thrusting my tongue. Wet and hot, kissing a human female is exactly how I imagined it would be. I curl the tip of my tail and tug down the top of her dress, freeing her breasts.

I tear my mouth from hers and lift to see them. Gemma pants, eyes hooded as she gazes up at me.

I watch as she inhales deeply, taking my scent into her. Her skin flushes.

I drop my eyes to her breasts. I've seen them every day in the last week, but they're still enticing. Plump, symmetrical, and pale, all I want to do is lash them with my tongue. Her legs hook around my middle. I thrust against her.

Her breasts bounce, the peaks rise and fall, and the soft warmth of her body teases my member until I'm thrusting against her again. Her chest arcs, her nipples pop up like they want to be suckled, and I hiss, squeezing her hand under mine.

She is naked, without scales, without armor, and barely wears a pelt from one of my many kills. I couldn't get harder, but I still do.

"Female," I grate with painful desire.

Gemma arches her back higher, giving me my answer.

I place one hand on the center of her chest and push her flat to the floor. "Don't move."

She wraps her fingers around my wrist. "Why?"

"You're still hurt."

I dive forward and capture one of her waiting nipples. She cries out and tries to free her hand from mine, but I won't let her. I poke her flesh gently with the tips of my fangs but don't pierce her. After a moment, her tension eases.

Her other hand falls to the floor. I pull her nipple into my mouth, taking all that I can, loving on it. The soft, the tight, the honeyed flavor of her skin floods me, and I cup her other breast with my hand while my tailtip plucks her saliva-slick tit.

She shudders and I release one nipple to suckle the other, poking the wrinkled flesh around her tit with my fangs.

She trusts me.

I could destroy her and she still trusts me.

I dip my head between her breasts and graze my fangs down the center of her chest, down further still until I reach her belly button, which I dive my tongue into. I release her hand and cup her thighs, placing them on my shoulders. My heavy, seed-swollen member hits the floor.

Rolling my tongue, plunging in and out of the tiny indent on her belly, I rut it with my tongue the way I want to thrust between her legs.

Gemma trembles and I ram my tongue into her navel harder.

"Oh!" Her shocked cry drives me to a frenzy, shunting my pelvis hard against the floor as she grips my head and writhes. "Lower, please, lower." She squeezes her legs closed, trapping my head between them.

I tear them open and bend her up, holding her legs prone until her sex is spread and bare to my view. I press my face into it. Slick, warm arousal dampens my mouth, nose, and cheeks as I nuzzle it. "Female," I rasp.

"What are you doing!?" she whimpers.

I spill a little as she tries to pull her legs from my grip. I hold them tighter and keep them where I want them. Spread wide.

"Worshiping you," I rumble, breathing in her arousal. She squeaks cutely when I plunge my tongue inside her. Stars blanket my vision as her taste explodes in my mouth. A dark fervor grips me, and I rut her little, quivering hole as hard as I ravaged her navel. My member scrapes across the floor.

She dances wildly, her cries higher, louder, with each rough flick. I push my tongue as deep, licking everywhere. I've bathed her every day, though I never got to clean her here, inside her, the place that, when I think about it, makes me little more than an animal. I wanted to slip my fingers in and feel her here. My aching member dreamed about burying deep as she slept, only to wake her to mindless bliss.

If she woke to bliss, then she wouldn't wake to pain.

I stayed away, not wanting to hurt her further.

She's close. Her nails dig into the scales on my shoulders, and I curl my tongue to lick the rough spot of flesh that makes her scream. Truly scream. She tenses, her thighs gripping my head hard, and I thrust my member frantically.

"I'm going to—I'm going to come!" she shrieks.

I coil the tip of my tail around the middle of her body and squeeze her—simultaneously, I reach between us and pinch her nub.

Her whole body strains, her sex constricts.

And then she pierces my den with her beautiful scream.

Yesss!

I jerk back to watch her come undone. Gemma writhes, limbs tense, and cries out, grabs me, and tries to bring me back between her legs.

"Don't leave me," she begs, arching up and slumping, only to arch her back again. Seeing her like this excites me. Seeing her sex tremble makes me spill across my floor.

She begs me some more to return, riding out her bliss. When she begins to come down, I sink two fingers into her, stretching her brutally once they're seated in her quivering sex. She flails, and I quickly catch her wrapped feet with my tail. I hold them in the air, lifting her lower back off the floor. Her makeshift dress comes apart and falls off her body.

"What are you doing?" she squeaks again, her arms now above her head as she tries to free her legs from my tail. She fails.

"Preparing you," I grunt.

I plunge my fingers in and out of her as I grab my member and position it, lowering.

Her wide eyes meet mine, and sweat sheens her brow. Her shocked expression stokes me into a frenzy. I want to sink my entire soul into her and remember this image of her so caught and trapped and open before me. Her legs are straight in the air, her knees locked and trapped in my tail holding her prone. Her head lifts to stare at me as I thrust my fingers deep into her.

I thought I wanted her to use her tongue all over me, but I like this far more. I prepare her with my hand, guiding my member to her as I do. I slip my fingers out of her swollen hole and start pushing my shaft into her.

I loosen my hold on her legs so her knees bend to the sides, opening her up as far as I can so she can take me easier. I sink in to my bulge.

My nostrils flare as she clenches me, pulling me closer.

"Mine," I hiss, cupping her thighs and slamming my large bulge into her, pushing through muscle that fights to keep me out, stretching her more than my fingers ever could.

I roar as she takes it all, as her head drops back, and she cries out for me. My name echoes through the bunker. I sway my hips side to side working the rest of the way into her.

Heaven hails me as she takes everything I give her. It's my own shock that stops me as she constricts around my bulge, putting painful pressure there. I snarl.

"Female, you take risks," my voice is guttural, rough.

"Thank you," she gasps in response, confusing me, clenching again.

"What?"

"For saving my life."

I release her legs, dropping down atop her, forcing her back to the floor. "Don't thank me," I snap. I don't like it.

But she squeezes around me again, and I forget her words. My head drops beside hers, and I roll my hips hard. She moans, and I do it again.

I lose myself.

Jerking out, thrusting back in, snapping my hips. She takes my bulge with each hard shunt, and I make her do it again and again. Each time, a mewl leaves her parted lips, addicting me. I speed up as her body adjusts to accept me. She works our rhythm too, squeezing and releasing.

Before long, I'm rutting her in a craze, unable to keep control. Her noises excite me, her accepting body tormenting me, and all I want is to possess it.

If I'm inside her, then there's no place she can go that I won't be there with her.

My member surges and grows.

"Gemma," I moan, coiling further around her body, bending painfully. "Gemma," I repeat her name with each hard thrust.

She claws at my back, and I erupt.

Spill drains out. The intensity drowns out everything else. Her limbs grip me as I grip her back, and I shake, filling her with everything I have. More and more spill drains from my member, shooting pleasure up and down my spine. I sag into her, unable to hold myself up, as the last of it leaves me.

My loins produce more seed as my orgasm slowly fades, never fully allowing the pressure in my bulge to end.

I turn my face and nuzzle the hair plastered against her neck. I lick her throat.

She shudders, pushes her chin down, and slides her hand between her throat and my tongue. "Tickles," she breathes.

I lick her fingers instead.

"Stooop," she wails weakly. I rise over her.

Her brows are wrinkled, and she's hiding her neck with her hands. I snap forward to try and taste her neck again, but she squirms away. "Nooo!"

I slip out from between her legs as she tries to flee, and I grab her, dragging her back under me. "Stay."

"No more licking my neck!"

I tug out the pelt from under us, pulling it around her, curling her up in my tail and against my chest. The tension in her limbs eases as she settles into me. I reach up and streak my fingers through her hair.

She nuzzles my chest the same way I nuzzled her sex. A smile twitches my lips. She knows what I can give her. She knows that my world isn't just dangerous but pleasurable too. We can make a life here, she and I, and it will be good.

No, there's no other male for her, not here on Earth or above in the stars.

When she falls asleep, I carry her back to my nest, where I finally allow myself the honor of sleeping next to her.

TWENTY-ONE
QUESTIONING THE PAST

Vruksha

OVER THE NEXT SEVERAL DAYS, I leave, hunt for fresh meat, and bring back fresh water for Gemma's baths. I won't let her topside, and she knows not to fight me about it. At least, for now.

She spends her time making clothes out of pelts, first by ripping the old ones into strips. Then she uses those strips to tie other, thinner pelts into place. I help when I can, though my knowledge is limited, never needing clothes to cover me.

We fall into a pleasant routine.

Since our rutting, she looks at me differently, and I don't know why. Her expression seems distant sometimes yet always focused, and I can only imagine the thoughts running through her head. I try not to worry about it.

When the silence lingers a little too long between us for my liking, I pull her close with my tail and make her moan.

So when she stops trying to make clothes and starts wobbling her way around the bunker, examining my treasures and trying to figure them out, I stop cleaning my gutting knife and follow her, catching her every time her legs give out, curious as to what she's doing.

What she is learning.

"What's in this?" she asks, moving to yet another large crate pushed up against the wall of my den. They've been here forever, filled with supplies from when I first discovered this place. Half the crates had been opened and looted when I first arrived, and there were bones of humans who died down here, preserved after the destruction. I don't tell her this.

It was long ago that I cleaned this place out. A long, long time ago. Those ghosts are gone.

"Medical supplies," I tell her. "This one has syringes, radios, and flashlights."

She cocks her head, and a strange expression crosses her face at my response. I wait for her to say more, but she glances around the bunker like she's trying to figure something out. It's the same expression that eludes me.

"Vruksha, how do you know the common tongue? It's been bothering me, all of this." She waves her hand at the bunker. "We were told there were animals, ruins, and a broken world awaiting us... We were never told of you. How are you here? Where did you come from? Are you... a Lurker?"

Her questions surprise me. "I've always been here. I'm a naga, not a Lurker."

Doesn't she know what a Lurker looks like?

"But what's a naga? That doesn't make any sense to me. A thousand years ago, trees and vegetation were just returning to Earth, and you, well, you're half-human, half-serpent, and sentient. You say all your females are gone... How is that possible?"

"They left, together, those that remained."

"Where did they go?"

"I don't know."

"Why did they leave? Should I... should I be worried?" She looks at me.

"No, female, you shouldn't be worried," I say, going to her. "They left because they were dying when they mated. All of them. My sisters... All the nagas of my generation came of age around the same time." Now that I say it, the timing is a little strange. "Our mothers died giving birth to their litters, but we were not communicating much then, and so this travesty wasn't known until after they were all gone. To lose a mate... to outlive your female... It shamed my father, and so I assume it shamed the other older males as well, so they never spoke of it. It wasn't until my generation came of age that we realized what was going on. Our females were dying during birth, *all* of them."

"Oh," Gemma whispers.

"After it was known, we couldn't save those who were already gestating, and tensions rose. Females stopped taking mates, and we had to fight every day to keep those that remained alive. There were males who... did not care. And mates who tempted death just to lay with a female. And it was those males who valued rutting over the lives of females who destroyed us. The clans tore apart and those, like me and Azsote, who forsook females, embraced the strife it caused because we knew that death would inevitably follow. The remaining female nagas decided to leave. They left their mates, their families, and have not returned. They went west, and no one has seen them since."

"And the males who drove them away?"

"Hunted down and killed."

She exhales. "Have you or anyone else ever tried finding them?"

"Some have. Most who make the pilgrimage return alone, and the rest never return at all. I never wanted to find them."

"Why?"

"After growing up with a father who missed his mate every single day, I did not want the burden of a female."

Her face falls but then it's gone, still there's a wrinkle in her brow left behind.

"Where is he now?" she asks quietly.

"He left. My sisters were gone. My mother, gone. I like to think he found my remaining sisters and is with them now, wherever they are."

"You don't know?"

"No."

Gemma sits back. "Vruksha..."

I trap her in a circle of my limbs. "Female," I say gravely. "Do not get any ideas. I will not let anyone else leave me." I know what I'm saying to her, I know what she intends to do. I need to make it clear that I cannot accept it.

Her face shutters. She turns from me.

"So, you were born here," she says.

"Yes."

"And your parents?"

"What about them?"

"They were born here too?" Her curiosity has already returned.

"Where else would they be born, if not here?"

"Your grandparents?"

I stare at her, confused. Grandparents? "I don't have any."

"Your father never spoke of his parents? Ever?"

Now that I think of it, no. "Those questions angered him."

Gemma's brow wrinkles. "Hmm."

"Do not worry about my past. It is the past. It is unchangeable."

I see thoughts running through her head and the confusion in her eyes, and it bothers me. She asks questions I haven't thought of since I was a young naga trying to understand my world. With Gemma here, there's something not entirely right about it.

I've always known something was off though I never dwelled on it. I didn't want to. Where was I going to find answers anyway? The screens never helped. The orbs never understood. My father and other nagas only ever gave vague answers, if they answered at all. Did they even know? Did they wonder too?

Someone must know... right?

An idea forms.

"Let me show you something," I rasp, changing the subject, moving my mind from where it wanders. I want to hear her laugh again. I pull my tail to me and rise, scooping her into my arms.

Though what I want to show her might not make her laugh, it might do the opposite. Still, it is something I think she needs to see.

"Where are you taking me? I can try walking there if it isn't far."

"You'll see," I tell her, heading for another door. It's hidden behind several large crates that I push away.

She wiggles in my arms. "We're leaving the bunker?" There's excitement in her voice.

I open the door with my tail. "Yes, but we are not going above."

Darkness meets us on the other side, and I carry her into it.

TWENTY-TWO

ORIGINS

Gemma

VRUKSHA CARRIES me into a dark hallway, through a door I didn't even know was there because it was blocked by crates. There are so many crates, so many old things. I've learned Vruksha is a collector. Of random odds and ends.

Old human kitchenware, furniture, and even little knickknacks that have no meaning. Things that have survived the last fifteen hundred years and a planetary apocalypse. Some things he doesn't even have a name for, and when we asked the orb, it didn't know either.

I'm coming to understand how Vruksha knows the common tongue, finding my answers on my own. The orbs speak it. And some of the 'better maintained' orbs can even project a screen.

The longer I'm in it, the more his world makes more sense to me. There's so much more potential here than I think the rest of humanity realizes. I'm a little surprised it's taken humans so long to coordinate an official expedition, but then I remember the pictures and stories of the previous times humans returned to Earth. Extra limbs, growths...

Tails?

I chew on my lip and push the thought away.

Even if Vruksha might be a descendant of humans who may have broken space law and returned to Earth long ago, I don't think I'll ever know for sure. I don't see records lying around. And it's obvious a history like that wasn't handed down or talked about with Vruksha.

The way he speaks of me going to the stars, though...

The darkness closes in as he takes me deeper. This isn't just another side room like the one with the generator. It's a tunnel, and as a chill breezes my skin, I snuggle into Vruksha for warmth.

I can walk later, I decide. I'm getting better every day. The pain in my body has dulled to a throbbing ache.

And now that I ache between my legs as well, I spend less time thinking about my torn-up feet. The tea he gives me helps too. He's taught me how to make it—with something called Willow Bark—that he collects and brings back from above.

A blush rises to my cheeks as my mind wanders to the near-rabid way he gets when he knows I'll accept him. His eyes darken and glint with hunger. When he pushes his cock's bulge into me, forcing me each time to take it, he loses his mind.

I woke this morning to his tailtip pushing inside me, his fangs grazing my backside. He said he wanted me to wake up to pleasure rather than pain.

It's why I ache between my legs right now. I've accepted this thing between us. Curiously, maybe eagerly.

At first, I thought it was animal magnetism and my own lack of connection for so long. Only for me to be thrust into Vruksha's arms— literally—at my worst moment. I could explain away these feelings as a result of being vulnerable and afraid, but now... I don't feel so vulnerable anymore, and I still want him.

I like how he makes me feel. Safe, cared for, cherished... All things my job on *The Dreadnaut* used to make me feel. Although, I know now it was all an illusion.

I wiggle in his embrace, knowing he'll grip me harder when I do.

His fingers tense around my limbs, and I smile.

I like Vruksha. A lot. He is straightforward, honest to a fault, and headstrong.

Blinking back the darkness, I take in the shadows hiding my new surroundings.

"We should go back for a flashlight..." I say quietly.

"They don't turn on without batteries, and the batteries they need, I don't have."

"Oh..."

Hmm.

I'd rather he take me into a dark passage than continue telling me about the females of his species. Anything over that. The haunted look on his face as he spoke unnerved me. What he told me was heartbreaking. To lose your entire family the way he has? And not know what happened to them?

I can't imagine. I said goodbye to my parents at a young age because that is the way of life during wartime. I've barely thought of them since. But I know they're still alive and working on *The Grimstep*, a colony ship focused on the strength and longevity of the military—including militarized advancement. They've had several more children, none I've ever met, but I think they all left around the same age.

I'm not... sad about it, I don't think. I frown.

I don't know anymore.

I don't want Vruksha to have to relive the pain of his past because of me. I feel guilty asking about it at all. Even if I want to know him and understand this world he's living in.

Where he came from...

He frightens me sometimes still—especially when I glimpse the fervor in his gaze when he's staring at me when he doesn't think I notice. There's a wildness in his eyes when he does, and it makes me tense.

It's those moments that remind me he's an alien, with alien views, and alien laws different from my own. An alien species that thrives outside society. Vruksha's a starved male animal, ready to pounce. I smile softly.

The shadows fade, pulling me from my thoughts. Light returns, and it's far brighter than what we have in the bunker. Soon, flashing beacons of every color are around us, driving back the darkness, and large shapes materialize on either side.

"What is this place?" I ask.

"The tunnels," he says, sliding us past the blinking lights.

"And these things?"

"Old tech, robots, I think... they're called server towers?"

Servers? I push up in his arms and stare at the towers. I know what servers are.

"How are *they* still on? Are they actually running? Is there another generator?"

"They run because energy is being fed to them, as to why, I don't know. Perhaps there are more generators down here, better than mine. I have never found any. You seem surprised to find the tech running here. Why is that?"

"Because systems die, metal corrodes. Maintenance is needed to sustain tech."

"The Lurkers didn't destroy the tech. They destroyed the life surrounding the tech."

I shake my head, and he continues moving through, like none of this is out of place. "So, you know about the Lurkers." I strain my neck to stare at the towers behind us as they fade back into the darkness and we turn a corner. We've turned multiple corners...

"And these tunnels?" I pry.

"What about them?"

"Do you know why they're here?"

"The same reason why they're everywhere I assume. The tunnels have always been here."

"Everywhere?"

Vruksha hisses softly. "They ssspan for miles in many directions. So many questions."

I look around. How did I not know this? Do Peter and the others know? They couldn't. We all had the same briefing. The military facility we came down to investigate was chosen because it was once specialized in Lurker technology. If we were going to find this anywhere, it would be there. Underground tunnels were never mentioned.

Vruksha stops, and I hear the groan of a heavy door opening. The chill deepens when he takes me through it. It shuts behind us.

And then there's nothing. Nothing except darkness.

I fidget. "Vruksha?"

Light bursts forth, blinding me. By the time I can see again, buzzing has filled my ears. He carries me into the room as I rub the last of the fuzzies from my sight.

My lips part when I get a good look at where I am. I push away from Vruksha's chest.

"Let me down," I say, my excitement skyrocketing, and he gently sets me on my feet. I lean against him and his tail coils around my waist.

Screens. A bank of screens covers the far wall, and below them is an old system of computers. Some are blacked out, some are blinking, while others are blurry with static. The majority of them work it looks like, though not all. Images appear on those that do. Pictures of the forest, the landscape, and even the facility. Live feeds of the entire region.

This is a... "Security room."

A well-hidden one.

Vruksha slides to the control panel where there's an old leather swivel chair. He pushes it over to me, and I grab it.

"Sit," he orders.

I purse my lips and sit. "Are these the screens you always mention?" I ask, staring at the one overlooking the facility. I see the ship, the tents, the robots, and guards scouting the perimeter. There's more now. I even see the skiff that carried me and Daisy away from the place.

My stomach churns despite my excitement seeing it all. Knowing life has gone on without me... like I was never important at all.

My fingers tangle together, and I hide the wave of hurt that hits.

"The screens I mention?" he repeats. "This is only a few of them. There are screens everywhere if you know where to look."

"There are? Like these, not the orbs?"

"Yesss."

He moves to the control panel and types something in. I watch raptly, awed to see this wild, primitive male, who I once thought was no better than a beast or a monster, use a computer like it's second nature.

The screens change when he's done typing, and words appear in large letters across them, but so do people, and images, and... destruction.

Aliens.

Large, lumbering bipedal beings covered in leathery green skin. They're nearly human in appearance if it weren't for their tails or the reptilian faces. Some are holding spears eerily similar to the one Vruksha carries.

"I don't know why I'm here," he says, returning to the question I asked earlier, as I stare at what's playing out before me. Explosions, fires, devastation, men in gas masks shooting guns, miles of forests disintegrating into ash, people running. And Lurkers, thousands of them, ignoring the humans begging them for help, ignoring the crying babies. "I've never seen someone like me, ever, on any screen. I have never heard another naga speak of our origins either. I assume we have always been here, though perhaps that's not the case. If what you say is true."

I'm watching the final hours of news feeds of Earth and realizing this, my stomach drops further. This is something I thought I'd never see. Never wanted to see. Has anyone seen this besides Vruksha?

There had been calls for help, messages from Earth that survived and were archived in history logs, but so much was lost, never to be found again. And live feeds? None of that made it to the colonies. But here it is, playing out in front of me, stored like it has been waiting all this time to be found.

It's the images of the Lurkers that frighten me the most. The death.

"What I say is true?" I repeat absently. My heart grows heavy.

"That maybe we're not supposed to be here. That Earth isn't supposed to have sentient life, female." Vruksha straightens, and my eyes cut from him back to the screens and the death playing out there.

So much death.

"Vruksha, you have watched this?"

"Many times."

The man reporting is sweating bullets as *'Breaking News'* flashes on the screens. He wipes his brow as a new video feed rises behind him, showing thousands of ships taking off from Earth.

I know it's the Lurker ships leaving like the monsters they are, abandoning all to die. There are other ships, thousands of human ones, and at once, the Lurker ships assault them with their weapons, destroying all of them.

Every last one.

The sound cuts out as the Lurker ships vanish, leaving nothing but dust clouds behind. Silence fills the room as only a picture of Earth from orbit remains, slowly graying, dying before my eyes.

Billions of lives lost in hours. It took two more days before those that escaped were able to contact the colonies. By then, there was nothing left to be done. Nothing anyone could do. And the years after? Only more death.

Humanity was nearly wiped out to extinction.

It'll happen again if the Ketts can't be held back.

"Turn it off," I beg.

A rumble leaves him as he does what I ask. The gray Earth disappears as the feeds of the forest return. I sag in the chair. "Why did you show me that?"

"You asked me, earlier, if I was a Lurker. I'm not. You also asked what a naga was, and I can't tell you that... because I don't know. I don't know what I am, and this—these old images—is all I have, all any of us have here in explaining our origins. I can't tell you because I don't know, and I would like to... know."

I swallow as I take in Vruksha. He's looking at the screens like they hold all the answers.

"I want to know too," I whisper.

He turns to face me. We share a look, a despondent one. The truth is likely ugly. Do we actually want to know?

"I need to go back," I say.

Vruksha's face hardens. "No."

"You don't understand—"

"What is there to understand? I won't let you leave."

"The facility might have the answer." I glance at the screens. "Daisy is somewhere."

His tailtip coils around my wrist. "No."

"You just said you wanted to know about yourself, and my people need this information. They need to see this."

"They need history? And not the technology that wiped you out the first time, the same technology you're trying to uncover, right? It's what you want to steal from us."

My face scrunches. "It's not like that. It's also not your technology."

"It *is* our technology," he snaps, sending shivers down my spine. "We have protected it, learned a little from it, valued it for what it is— but we don't use it. It is evil. Explain to me why it's so important that your people would trade you for it, female."

"We're in the middle of a war," I blurt out. I rise to my feet but nearly fall and catch my body on the chair. Vruksha's tail releases my wrist and curls around my middle again. I push it away. "A war that could do what you just showed me all over again, but this time, on an intergalactic level. And you do use the tech," I accuse. "The Lurkers on the screens carried the same spears you wield!"

Vruksha's nostrils flare, and he moves to meet me head on. I straighten.

"You are mine. You belong with me. I won't trade you for an answer to a question I didn't care about yesterday. No amount of curiosity will change that. This is all the past, the past! Not the future."

"Then you shouldn't have shown me this," I say.

Because now that I know, I have to do something.

"I will not allow your life to be endangered again."

"That isn't your decision to make. You were so willing to trade your precious knowledge with us for *me*. Why can't you do it *for* me, instead?"

Vruksha hisses. "You are not being fair."

"What is it you gave them, that first day? In the box?"

"Scraps. Odds and ends that have no use."

"Scraps," I guffaw. "My people can't use scraps. They'll be back for more. You understand that, right? Once they figure out what you gave them was useless, they'll search for you."

"We'll kill them if they do. We'll kill them all."

"Kill us? There are millions of us." I can't hold back my shock, my fear. For him. "You live in ruins. Humans have battleships the size of the moon. How can you hold us back from taking the technology from you by force? We outnumber you."

Darkness etches across Vruksha's face, like he and the other nagas have already thought of this. It confuses me until I realize why.

They knew what they were in for all along.

They knew and they still risked themselves for me? For Daisy?

He slides to me, silently, like a shadow, and towers over me. "We have our ways."

All at once, the part of Vruksha that frightens me, returns. The exacting intensity he wields sharpens every scale and ridge of his muscled body.

"Ways?" I whisper, mouth going dry. "You not only know where the Lurker tech is," I breathe, remembering what he just said, what he said and I ignored. "And you know how to use it as well..."

The Earth turning to ash, the leathery reptilians ignoring the cries of children as their giant ships blast all of ours... the images unfold again before my eyes. It was like we—and all that humans had achieved—were nothing.

Whoever had that kind of power—terrible power—could cause massive destruction and should be feared.

Vruksha and the other nagas aren't just part of a primitive sentient species. They hold that power. The power humankind thinks could change the tide of war.

Something flashes across one of the screens, stealing my attention. Vruksha says something I don't quite make out. Familiar faces distract me. "Something's happening," I say, focusing on the flurry of activity. Vruksha goes quiet beside me.

It's the facility. My eyes narrow.

Men and robots rush across the cleared yard and toward the forest, past the barrier. I see Peter, Collins, and even Shelby. They're scrambling and pointing, screaming at something I can't make out.

"Can you enlarge it?" I stumble forward, using Vruksha's tail to keep me upright. "Where's the sound? Does this have sound? I need to hear what they're saying."

"Not the live feed," he rumbles, leaning over the panel again. He presses a couple of buttons, and the footage from the facility takes over the whole wall.

The skiff appears. It's trying to take off but is far too close to the forest to clear it. The others chase after it. Peter is barking what I assume are orders for the robots not to shoot it down. Whatever it is that's allowing me to see what's happening focuses on the skiff, following it as whoever is in the cockpit tries to fly it too high too fast. They're trying to take off.

"You're not going to make it," I breathe, my heart thundering. The bottom of the skiff hits the tops of the trees. "You're not going to make it!" I gasp.

The skiff jerks upward, hovers, skims more trees, and jerks again. It clears the next several trees and bounces higher. My fingers curl into my palms as it steadies. I forget my colleagues at the facility and focus on the ship, trying to see who's flying it.

A shock of long blond hair is all I can make out through the blur.

My throat constricts.

"Daisy."

TWENTY-THREE

MATE

Vruksha

GEMMA REFUSES to let me carry her back to our nest.

She struggles in my embrace as I do so anyway. She's not always going to get what she wants.

"I shouldn't have shown you," I growl. I regret giving her a view into the secrets of this place, this world I live in. The tunnels are known by all the nagas, like the Lurker technology and the old human ruins, but the secrets within them? Those of us who know of it, always kept those close.

Because what you know, what you have, makes you powerful in my forest.

The little bit of technology we handed over to the humans had been nothing more than cast-off bits and baubles of broken tech that no longer respond to us. To anything. Zaku and Vagan had made sure of it.

"I'm glad you did, except that's not the problem right now. Daisy is. That skiff can't save her! She'll never make it past the stratosphere, not without a miracle. We need to go back! Please, Vruksha." Her voice heightens. "You would have kept this from me?" she says, straining in my arms. "Something so pivotal?"

"It's not your passst."

"How can you say that? Of course it is. It belongs to humans," her voice trails off at the end, and I peer down at her. Shadows distort her face, although I can see enough of it clearly to know she's thinking.

"Or perhaps it belongs to no one and should be forgotten," I grit.

We slip through the tunnels in silence going forward. When we're back within my bunker, and I shut the door behind us, some of the tension leaves me. I set Gemma down on a crate, and she swings her legs over the side, stands, but quickly leans back against it.

I glimpse my spear perched against the wall by the exit.

I always knew it wasn't made by humans. When I wield it, it's like an additional limb, one that not only uses the muscles trained for it, but also your thoughts. Only Lurker tech does that, not human tech.

And Lurker tech never deteriorated, not like the cheap creations of the humans. Which, like Gemma's brought up, usually rusts and corrodes, or loses its power source.

I never minded showing Gemma the tech until now because I didn't think there would be any harm involved in doing so. It intrigued her so. Besides she's mine, and that alone once assured me she could never, or would never, use it against me. Now I'm not sure.

"Maybe you're right," she says abruptly. "Maybe some of what you and the others guard is too dangerous... But that won't help Daisy right now."

"Mmm." I coil my tailtip around her leg. "Who's Daisy?"

My female throws her hands up in the air. "The woman who was with me on the plateau! The other female who ran from you, terrified for her life."

"I forgot there was another female."

"How? Err, never mind." She rubs her brow.

"I've only ever seen you." I do recall this other female now that she mentions it, though I recall nothing else about her. No other female interests me.

"If I wasn't so upset with you, that might have made me happy, but as it is, there was another woman, and we need to save her."

I grit my teeth. I know females are rare, but this other one isn't my problem—or Gemma's. "Another naga will save her."

"You can't know that."

"Yes, I can. If she hasn't been caught, she soon will be, and I assure you there are many malesss right now—"

"That makes it so much worse. She doesn't want to be caught by a male, Vruksha. I didn't want to be caught. If she's running, she won't stop, and if she's been out there all alone for nearly two weeks... I can't imagine the state she's in."

"We're not going after her. Nagas will fight to the death for a mate. She will come to no harm."

"But you've said so yourself... there are evil naga males. What if she's been caught by one and is running from them?"

Tension streaks down my spine, and I slip my tailtip from Gemma's leg to coil around her back, closing her into a circle of my making. I understand she may care for those in her past life, but she should forget them and move on. She never will, not if she sees them and they remain near.

I tear my eyes from her pleading ones and snarl at my spear. "We destroyed the evil ones long ago." Thoughts of my father rise to my mind, and the way he'd stare off into the forest for hours as if he was waiting for my mother to come slipping out of it. I remember the sadness that always followed when she never did.

My mother was never a victim to a Death Adder or a Black Mamba or a Boa, but so many others were. I lost my sisters because they feared for their lives and chose to flee instead of becoming victims.

"Can you be sure of that?" Gemma whispers.

I snap my eyes back to her. "Yes. We were thorough."

"Thorough enough? What about Zhallaix?"

I bare my fangs, hearing the Death Adder's name. "He is dead."

"If you do this for me..." Gemma sinks her teeth into her lower lip, stealing my attention briefly, but it's the lost expression that remains etched on her face that has me questioning... "If you do this for me, if you help me save her, I'll stay."

"You never had a choice," I remind her.

Her face scrunches. "I could make your life a living hell by fighting you."

"I'll bind you."

"And I'll scream, kick, and battle you and us every single day until you have no choice but to relent. You'd become what you destroyed."

I hiss, frustration and anger pouring out of me. "You are not being fair."

"Neither are you."

Fury to match my rising rage meets me in Gemma's fierceness. I believe her threats, knowing she could deny me the life I want so badly with her. The affection, the company, the warmth, and the love of having a mate to coil up with in a shared nest. She could take that all away, and though I'd fight back, reminding her constantly why it would be easier to give in, I know she'd only come to hate me.

Because the humans are still out there. The other nagas are as well.

And there would be no peace inside my den or outside it until that changes.

"I am nothing like those rabid males," I grate.

"Help her," she begs. Gemma reaches up, and I go stiff, bracing for her to try and squirm out of my circle, but she cups my face instead, pulling me down. "Please do this for me, as your *mate*."

She seeks to call me mate now? Anger swells up inside me. "You ask much of me." I can't help but lock her in, gripping the crate on either side of her. I press into her, my anger growing.

She leans up and places a kiss on my lips. "I know."

It's gentle, soft, a whisper of a touch, and a tendril of her warmth. It's everything. I know she's manipulating me but her lips move, and I'm now the one who's lost, deepening it, uncaring. Because if I don't, I'm afraid she'll slip through my circle of limbs and vanish.

And I will become my father.

If I can't make her happy, then what kind of mate am I?

I cup my hand behind her head and capture her completely, sinking my tongue into her. Gemma's taste floods my mouth, reminding me of everything I have to lose. How fragile what I have really is.

Her hands fall from my face to grab my shoulders. She presses her nails gently into my scales there.

Something in me snaps.

I grab hold of her dress and tear it down her arms, freeing her breasts. She startles as I fill my hands with them and squeeze, pinching her nipples between the sides of my fingers as I do. "Female," I say, desperate and furious, "you will be the death of me." I don't give her the chance to respond, recapturing her mouth. I slide my hands down her body and grasp her butt, lifting her onto the crate.

I push my hips between her legs, and she opens up for me. Reaching under her dress, I tug off her undergarment. The weak ties holding it in place snap and fall away. I throw the annoying scrap across the bunker.

Holding her open, I line up my tip to her hole and thrust my member into her to my pulsing knot, groaning as I push against her tight flesh keeping me out.

"Vruksha," she cries, digging her nails into my arms.

"You ask too much of me, female. You seek to manipulate me," I snarl, pulling out and thrusting back into her. Her lips part, but I don't allow her to speak.

"You want to risk your life, again, and you haven't even recovered!" My hips snap. My tail curls around her hair and pulls it back until she's forced to lie on the crate. She gasps and her back arches. I rise over her, thrusting harder. Mastering her.

"And now you want to go after another female and bring her back to our den. I won't share you!" I roar. This time when I pull out, I shunt forward with brutal strength, pushing the entirety of my bulge into her in one go.

Gemma cries out, gaspy and harsh. Guttural, animalistic noises rip from my throat. Pleasure surges up my spine, and her hips tweak from the pressure I'm putting on her. Her legs tense around me, flailing from the force. She doesn't ask me to stop, and I don't. She lets me take my frustration, my lust out on her beautiful body.

Her sheath clenches around my bulge, and my tail drops, uncoiling from her hair. It straightens out behind me as far as it can go, climbing up the opposite wall, knocking things over.

Her hands fall to grab my hips as she buckles.

Sweat beads my brow from her little movements, teasing my aching prick into a furor. It grows.

Brutally, I rut her, enraged that she seeks to manipulate me. She gifts me hitches and moans, and I take them. My thrusts grow wilder, her cries louder. Seed swells my bulge painfully, and I can't hold back.

I bring my tailtip back to me, thrashing, spilling inside her. I drop atop her, catching my body with my hands, as I give Gemma everything. She takes it. She takes it all.

"We will sssave your friend," I breathe heavily into her ear. "But you will stay with me, you will obey me, you will never run again. You will not ask about the Lurker technology again, nor about the humans in the facility, you will never return there. You will never leave this planet, and every night, you will wait for me in my nest, open just as you are right now. You will forget all else."

Gemma whispers my name.

"I'm not done," I growl, rising on my elbows, pinning her with my gaze. "We will go after your friend, though she cannot stay here. This den is mine, and only what is mine is allowed inside it. If she cannot be found, and cannot be saved, thisss," I point between us, "isn't going to change." I span my fingers and tangle them into my female's hair.

Gemma purses her lips, lips that are red from my ravaging. My body pumps more seed, and I spill a little more inside her.

"Thank you," she gasps. It's all she says.

It hurts.

I rut her again, harder this time.

TWENTY-FOUR

THE HUNT FOR DAISY

Gemma

Vruksha checks the ties on my shoes for the third time.

I grasp his hand. "They're fine. I can manage."

"I don't want anything more to happen to them," he snaps. He's been angry since the tunnels, and so have I, but there's no solution until we find Daisy. I don't know what's happened, why she would steal the skiff, but I have to find out. I can't do anything knowing that if the roles were reversed, Daisy would help me. I know she would.

And what if she's not trying to escape from something? Maybe she's not running from a naga or our old coworkers. What if she's looking for *me*?

And risking herself doing so.

I barely know Daisy but after what we've been through—being betrayed by our peers—she's the closest friend I now have. I may be all that she has too.

War and tech be damned.

It's nice being ignorant of what's happening until it's not. Daisy could've been suffering, alone, exposed, or worse and I'd only given her a handful of thoughts while I rested in warm pelts and let Vruksha care for me.

While he made me cry out in bliss...

I clench and wince, throbbing from Vruskha's recent attentions. He's upset, and I've made him that way. He's a vicious alien—that I think might be in a rut—and I often forget that he's a different species now.

I can't help that I'm in heat just being around him... The way I'm acting. I like what he does to me...even if it makes me ache afterward. I shake my head.

And all I cared about stupid war tech that may or may not be useless. I scrub my hands over my face. I want it to be useless. I'm hoping it's useless, but I can't quite convince myself. Still, Vruksha's right. It doesn't matter. He and the other nagas have hidden it. They're guarding it, wherever it is, and for now, that works for me. Until I know more, or something happens, it's enough.

"They're mostly healed," I say, wrapping my hands around the walking stick Vruksha found for me. It's sturdier than any stick I've sourced so far.

He rumbles and drops his hands from my shoddy makeshift shoes. None of my new clothes are great, only held on by ties that never seem to get tight enough, but they're better than nothing, and each day I fiddle with them, they're more wearable.

Vruksha grabs his spear and ties our supply bag over his shoulder.

I swallow, rubbing my thighs together. They slip, still wet with his seed.

I care for him.

A lot. It's beginning to hurt how much I care. I press my palm to my chest, to the tightness there.

He hisses and slips up the steps, and I drop my hand. I follow behind him, watching the way his long tail moves back and forth. A *creak* sounds in my ears, and a ray of light bathes us, temporarily blinding me.

I inhale the fresh air, making my way up the last of the steps, using the wall to guide my spotted vision. It feels good.

Freedom.

The moment I step outside, Vruksha's tail coils around me and lifts me off the ground.

"What are you doing?" I ask.

He brings me to his arms and cradles me within them. "I'm not letting you walk. You are too slow even when your feet aren't hurt. I want this to be quick. I do not like the idea of you being out here where you can be further hurt."

"Then what's the point of the shoes?" I jest.

He scans our surroundings. "Protection," he answers me dismissively, ignorant of my teasing. An orb comes up to hover beside him. "Are there predators nearby?" he asks it.

The orb does its thing and we wait. Bears, a coyote this time, a snake, and pigs. Always pigs. My stomach sickens.

"What snake?" he asks.

The orb hums, and a hologram appears. It twinkles in the sunlight, making it hard to see the image. Something slowly appears, a familiar broken tail and scarred face.

"I thought he was dead," I whisper.

Vruksha hisses, holds me closer, and goes silent for a time, watching Zhallaix. "I always think that too, but he never is. As long as he keeps away, he can live with the pain of his wounds for as long as he likes." And at breakneck speed, Vruksha surges forward.

My hair flies as he slips us through the airport's ruined orchard and into the thicker forest. I grip his hand that's cradled around my arm. "Slow down. Your tail is still healing." My words are lost in the wind.

He doesn't stop.

The day was already halfway over when we left the bunker. Vruksha needs nothing but his spear, but I'm not so easy. He packed two day's worth of rations. He's not planning to search for Daisy long.

I turn from the glinting scales on his chest to the blurry landscape. I know it well enough now that it'll become less flat as we get closer. But when the trees close in and the overgrowth thickens, I'm not prepared for the fear that wells up in me.

Sooner than expected we reach the area where the pigs were, where I almost died. Where I ate raw fish...

Vruksha slows down, working his way through the foliage, careful not to let any branch, leaf, or twig touch me.

I can still hear the snorts and snuffs of the hogs like a ghost in my ears, reminding me how close I came to being eaten alive.

"Don't stop," I whisper. "Not here."

Vruksha pulls me into his chest, and I close my eyes, turning to press my brow to him.

"They're dead," he says as if he knows. "I killed every last one the drone missed. Do not be afraid."

He makes me feel safe.

For a time, I lose myself in the swaying of his arms, feeling the air on my skin. I wake from a fitful doze when he sets me on my feet sometime later.

He's taken me inside the ruin of an old building. One without a roof, with half-crumbled walls and metal piping sticking out everywhere. He sets me under a large slat of cement, leaning against one of the sides, forming a small alcove. I rub my eyes. Vruksha fills up the entire entrance, trapping me within.

"Why have we stopped?"

"Night will be upon us soon, and you need to eat and drink. I want to check your feet," he mutters, clearly still unhappy with me. It bothers me. A lot. I feel like I let him down.

But time is precious.

I knew it was a long shot, despite this, I can't help worrying. I know we're vaguely headed for the facility, but it feels like we're wandering aimlessly, a skiff could travel anywhere...

My heart thrums as we stare at each other. The ache between my legs hasn't gone away, and I crave him. He doesn't judge me, and I never realized how much I've been holding back all these years, fearing judgment.

My chest tightens.

Vruksha curls his tail under him, and he settles just under the opening of our alcove, placing his spear nearby. He reaches for my legs, and I give them to him. In the waning daylight, he unravels my bandages, checks my wounds. Most are nothing more than red blotches now, scabs, and yellowish-green bruises, but he's adamantly keeping track of how fast they're healing.

I lean against the side of the building as his hands prod my skin, aware of how they linger and inch up my legs.

"If I'd been hurt like this on *The Dreadnaut*, I would've opted for the pod," I laugh.

"Pod?" Vruksha lifts my foot and begins wrapping it back up.

"It's a medical thing," I say to fill the silence. "It eliminates the need for so many doctors and nurses since they're all needed on the frontlines. And so the rest of us get the cold love of a health pod. It's an oval-shaped device humans lie in when they're sick or injured, and the pod—which runs through AI software—heals you. They also put you under, stabilizing you for long distances of travel."

"Ah, yes. I know what you're talking about."

I peek at him as he sets my freshly bandaged feet aside. "You do?"

"I've seen something like it, once, where a—I think it's called hospital—used to be."

"I didn't think we had tech like that back then." We lost a lot in the centuries following the end of Earth.

"It was broken. There were human bones all around it."

Silence falls between us as the shadows give way to full darkness, and the only light comes from the moon rising through the trees. It would be peaceful if it wasn't for Vruksha's brooding, blocking much of my view. I reach for the bag slumped off his shoulder and dig out a ration.

His eyes never leave me.

I take a shy nibble, suddenly feeling like nothing has happened over the past two weeks and this is our first night together in his bunker all over again.

"Tomorrow..." I start then stop.

Vruksha continues to stare at me.

My fingers tangle. "Tomorrow, we should head for the facility and start there."

"No. Tomorrow, we'll get *close* and I'll check out the facility, search for her tracks. We are not entering the facility's grounds."

"She...won't have any tracks. She stole the skiff. And what if Peter and the others found her? They'll take her back to the facility."

"She hit the trees, breaking them. I can climb to the tops and know which direction she went in, and if they found her first, then we return to our den."

"I need to speak with her."

Vruksha growls. "That's not what we decided, *mate,*" he lingers on the word. "If she is safe, that is all you need to know. If she is within the facility and back with the other humans, there is nothing left that you or I can or will do for her."

Silence settles between us again. I finger the wrapper of my ration, hating it.

"Get some sleep," he says, startling me.

"You should be the one to rest." I sit up. "I can take the first watch."

Vruksha grabs his spear and ducks out of the alcove with a hiss. "I'm going to scout."

He slips away, and I stumble out, going after him. "Wait!"

Vruksha twists back and catches me just as I trip and fall.

"Female, you will hurt yourself further," he growls.

I push off his chest. "Why are you upset? What's wrong?" I hate seeing him this way.

"Everything," he quips, squeezing my shoulders, steadying me while being brutally honest. He grabs me against him and carries me back to the shelter.

"I understand you're mad because of Daisy, but I can't live knowing she's out here alone, possibly in desperate need of help, and I did nothing. I'm not doing this to hurt you." I need him to know this. I don't know why, I just do. "I won't leave. I promise."

"I would never let you leave," he says. "I have told you this again and again."

I search his face. "Why are you so angry then?"

Vruksha keeps me in his embrace, even when we're back inside. He clutches my chin between his fingers and brings my face to his. "Angry? You think I'm angry? I'm furious," he seethes.

I flinch.

"You," he begins but stops. "You..."

"Me what?"

"You didn't choose me!" he roars. He drops my chin and pushes me to the ground. His face is a mask of darkness as he leans over me. The outline of his fangs, his scowl. It steals my breath. He takes my hands and traps them above my head.

Like an animal about to devour his prey, he pants, holding me down. His powerful body trembles. Warmth rushes to my cheeks. An ache swells between my thighs.

My legs fall open unwittingly. "I did choose you."

"You chose Azsote, your humans, this Daisy, and even old tech over me, female. You haven't chosen me."

My brow furrows. "I—" How can I answer that?

He lifts off me, and I scramble onto my elbows as he leaves the alcove again. "Sleep," he orders, his voice gruff, agitated. "You'll need your strength."

Grabbing his spear with finality, he slinks into the forest and vanishes. I bring my legs together and hug them, feeling more alone than I've ever been before. Hurt that I offered my body to him and he rejected me.

My heart aches.

He's right.

I lean my face into my knees.

Now he knows I'm truly not fantastical after all.

The next morning, I rise bleary-eyed, rubbing my joints where they locked overnight. When I'm done, I find Vruksha perched on the ruins of the building, his tail hanging down the side, watching me.

I inhale sharply.

He could've been there all night while I waited for his return, and I would've never known. He jumps down and, without a word, checks my bandages. He slips our supply bag over his shoulder after handing me a ration.

"Eat."

"Last night—"

"We'll talk later," he says, rounding his arm under me to help me stand. He lifts me, but I push him away, keeping my feet on the ground.

"I can do this."

For once, he doesn't argue. Instead, he takes the lead, leaving me his tailtip to grasp if I need it. And for the rest of the trek, we're climbing, moving from one ledge to the next, working our way up. Each step is easier than the last. He doesn't speak, and so I don't either.

He intimidates me, I realize. It's not that I fear him; I'm intimidated by him. I don't know how to... make things right. Every time I want to, my tongue grows big and my throat constricts.

I try and focus on our surroundings while I swallow all of my words.

The trees have grown thick and tall, and there are fewer of them with leaves and more with green needles and cones. As we journey higher, I catch glimpses of the horizon and survey the terrain. There is a giant lake far in the distance, and I see streams and ponds. There are mountains around the facility—I knew this going in—and the forest is thick. But peering down into the gorge we were in earlier, I find dead spots here and there. Little patches where there are no trees but ruins.

We've come across many things, broken structures, overgrown buildings, and even items in the forest. I try to commit them to memory so I can use them as landmarks in the future.

Vruksha always seems to know where he's going, despite how many miles we travel, even without a compass or a mapping system. To me, it's amazing.

Seeing a spot of color by my foot, I lean down to pick up what appears to be a doll. Brushing the dirt off it, Vruksha pivots back to me and tugs me into his chest.

I tense, waiting for him to tell me what's wrong, but when a minute goes by and he doesn't, I start to get afraid. I whisper, "Do you hear something?"

"Another naga." Holding me hard to his chest, he moves us to a nearby tree, ducking under its low branches. He scans the canopy above us.

I search with him. "They're still out here?"

His eyes slide to me. "They live here."

"So close to the facility? Isn't that dangerous?" I shiver.

"This was our land first."

"What do we do?"

"Move quietly and not alert them that you are here."

My eyes go wide. "And if they find out I am?"

"I kill them and you run."

I drop the dirty doll and grip my walking stick. "Fine. Okay."

"Stay close to me."

I nod.

Vruksha helps me out from the branches and pulls me close. We continue our climb, a little warier of the noise we're making, and slow down, taking our time to not make any additional sounds.

Another hour goes by, and the tension eases from my shoulders. We pass by another series of ruins when something pricks my ears. A voice far off in the distance. Vruksha and I stop at the same time, waiting to see if the voice comes again.

I move under his arm and into the curl of his tail before he can tug me to him.

"What was that?" I whisper.

It sounds like someone, or something is—

"DAISY!" They're shouting her name.

I jump. Vruksha plasters me to his side.

"Daisy?" I gasp.

"DAISY!" Her name comes again, sounding from elsewhere, roaring through the trees.

Gooseflesh rises on my arms. "Daisy! Someone is looking for Daisy. She could be nearby."

Vruksha's eyes darken.

"We have to look for her!"

He nods, curling his fingers around my wrist, and we take off after the voice.

It seems like hours go by before it's loud enough to eclipse the sounds of the forest. Still, the quicker we move, the farther the voice seems to get. I want to call out but don't.

"DAISY!" The roar comes again after a short while. We reach the summit of the mountain and stop.

"Which direction did it come from?" I ask, huffing. I can see everything from here.

"It's Zaku."

I shake my head, wiping the sweat from my forehead as the naga with the large, spiked cowl rises in my mind. "Great."

The trees beside us shake. I stumble back just as something large and green drops down from them. Vruksha swings in front of me.

A naga male, shimmering vibrant green, rises, catches my eye, and puffs out his chest.

"Azsote," Vruksha snarls.

"Vruksssha," the other male hisses in answer.

"DAISY!" the roar comes again, startling the three of us.

"Take your eyes off my female," Vruksha's voice lowers, sending a shiver down my spine.

Azsote looks away from me and at him.

"I'm not here for her," he tells Vruksha. "I'm looking for Zaku." Azsote's eyes cut to me again though, making Vruksha hiss.

"Why?" he snaps.

"I've found the other female."

I step forward before Vruksha can stop me. "You have? Where is she? Is she okay? Take us to her."

Vruksha pulls me behind him, coiling his tail around me. "Is she safe?" he asks.

"She's hurt, burned up."

My lips part. Burned? The skiff didn't make it... "Take us to her, now," I demand, clutching Vruksha's arm.

Azsote flicks his eyes to me.

"DAISY!"

All three of us flinch. Zaku's roaring is further away now—we're losing him.

"She's not asking for you, female," Azsote says. "She asks for Zaku."

Azsote looks at Vruksha, and I see something pass between them.

Vruksha lowers his spear, and Azsote slips into the forest, vanishing so swiftly it was like he was never here at all.

I twist under Vruksha's arm. "We're following him, right?"

I think he's going to fight me, tell me our job is done, but to my complete surprise, Vruksha nods, picks me up, and chases after Azsote. It's not long before he catches up to the silent green male, joining him in his swift hunt for the king.

TWENTY-FIVE

DAISY

Vruksha

I SLIDE through the trees after the Boomslang, holding my female against me. I've missed having her in my arms. My mate's softness warms my scales, and her scent invigorates me.

She is mine, and I adore it.

"Thank you, mate."

I curse as the words snap into my head.

They haven't stopped repeating through my mind since Gemma said them. I didn't know how badly I needed to hear her call me mate in return, until she did.

Then they stung, and now, each time they repeat, the thrill of it muddies further. She called me mate so I would help her find her friend. And once that thought entered my head, I haven't been able to push it out. I've been mulling it over all night.

I don't feel like I'm her mate. Not entirely. Not yet.

Gemma's mine, but I'm not hers. Glancing down, I find her eyes are closed, her forehead wrinkled, face scrunched up again. She gets this way when I sprint through the trees and it's almost... precious.

She would not like being held if I swung through the trees as Azsote does. The branches above us shake as the Boomslang slips from one to the next, catching and bracing with his tail muscles.

Zaku's roars heighten as we catch up to him.

"King Cobra!" Azsote yells when we're close. "I know where she is," he calls out, dropping from the trees. I come to a stop a short distance away. Gemma wiggles in my arms.

Azsote won't try and steal her. I read it in his eyes. And if Zaku is after the other female, then Gemma is at least safe from these nagas, but if there are more nearby, brought out by Zaku's shouting, I want to keep a hold on her so they know she's been claimed.

I could coax her into a rutting for everyone to view—to establish who is her mate, the one who caught her—but I neither want Gemma naked in front of them nor want to share her sweet secrets with males who may try and risk taking her from me anyway.

If I were made to watch such a beautiful female open up her arms and accept her mate with a moan, I would want to steal her for myself— nothing would stop me. Not even another naga's prick sinking into her.

It would be the last thing he ever did.

"Zaku!" Azsote yells once more, coiling his tail around the trunk of a nearby tree.

Noises of passage strike my ears, snaps of sticks, and the rustle of leaves. Zaku's giant form bursts into the clearing, tackling Azsote to the forest floor. The Boomslang slides himself out from under Zaku, using his hold on the tree.

"Where is she?" Zaku claws at him. "Take me to her!" Zaku's nostrils flare, his cowl expands, and the spikes of it straighten out. He's covered in dirt, eyes fierce, and I bare my fangs. But the King Cobra doesn't see me.

Stupid male.

Azsote hisses and drops from the tree to put his tail between him and Zaku.

Gemma pushes out of my hold, answering before Azsote can. "She's hurt. Azsote's taking us to her. He's been looking for you. We've been looking for her."

Zaku's eyes swing to my female, and I brace for an attack.

His crazed gaze flicks over us, and he wipes the back of his hand across his mouth, taking us in. I notice a new wound on his chest that's swollen and red.

I hiss in warning when it appears Zaku isn't going to calm. "I will strike if you get close."

Zaku swings back to Azsote. "Take me to Daisy!"

"And them?" Azsote indicates us.

Gemma tenses. "We're going too, I demand to see her. If you try and stop us, you'll have to deal with me," she threatens.

Zaku grabs Azsote's neck and jerks the Boomslang close. "Take me to her. I won't ask again. I don't care what they do."

Azsote tugs Zaku's hand from around his throat and twists, dashing away. Zaku takes off after him, and I surge forward to follow. Gemma's hair flies against my chest, tickling my scales.

From one tree to the next, we rush through the forest. No one stops us. No one even comes out and tries. Three naga males against one is certain death. Invigorated, I feel part of a clan for the first time since my sisters left. A hunt with my brethren for the precious, rare females we all desire.

I suck in the warm air, grasping my female close.

It's at this moment, as the forest gives way to a long stretch of land and I watch Zaku rush after Azsote, that I forgive her for choosing her friend over me. I remember what it's like to care for more than my own hide. I had forgotten the strength there is in numbers.

If we came together, no human, beast, or otherwise would be able to stop us. And if what Gemma says is true, and the humans will never stop searching for the tech... then rejoining my brethren is imperative for all our safety going forward. Using the tech that we hide would be easier united.

Because this land is ours.

And no one can make us leave.

"Smoke," Gemma gasps. "There, see it?" She points to a ribbon of it rising from the trees in the distance. I smell it when she does. "Please be okay," she whispers, low enough she probably doesn't think I hear it.

"She will be okay," I rumble.

She rests her head against my chest. I feel her tremble.

By the time we make it to the smoke, Azsote and Zaku are already there. It's worse than I thought. The trees are charred, some are still burning, and a clear streak of land has been cleared out from the skiff.

The skiff is in ruins. The majority of the smoke comes from it. Part of its side is crumpled, and the windows are shattered. There's metal and debris everywhere. No one could've survived such mechanical violence.

"Daisy," Gemma breathes.

I hold onto her as she tries to break from my arms.

Zaku's silence is deafening. Another naga male is there, staring at the smoke. As a breeze wisps some of it away, familiar brown and beige scales appear. I grip my spear, bringing it forward.

Krellix, the last Copperhead. I haven't seen him since the plateau. Azsote snarls at him but doesn't stop, moving through the wreckage. Krellix glances at the rest of us, stopping to stare at Gemma. Zaku goes after Azsote.

"Vruksha," Gemma whispers. "We need to get to Daisy."

I don't take my gaze off Krellix. The male twists to face us head-on. The way he looks at my female forces a growl from my throat. Heat, desperation, and lust appear all at once, etched over his face.

He slides closer. His muscles bunch. Through the smoke, I smell his cloying scent. I tense, immediately acknowledging it as a scent I've recently been giving off too.

I set Gemma down. Her arm comes up around me as she moves under my shoulder. "Get behind me," I tell her, readying my weapon.

"You can't have me," Gemma snaps, glaring at Krellix. "I'm already taken." She shoots Krellix a withering look.

I go still, shocked by her words.

The Copperhead cocks his head. "You are a feisty one."

"And I'm Vruksha's, so don't even try it. If he doesn't kill you, I will. Now move. My friend is hurt and needs me."

Krellix's lips twitch.

"Move," I warn.

He finally looks at me. "You are lucky," he says, slipping out of our path and disappearing into the trees.

I'm skilled, vicious, and a little reckless, but lucky? I hiss. It wasn't luck that won me Gemma. It was fate. Gemma stretches up and hooks her arm around my neck. I haul her back into the cradle of my arms. We take off after the others.

We don't have to go far, finding Zaku and Azsote on the other side. Zaku is emerging from a fox hole with something in his arms. A broken, ashen thing I barely recognize as human, let alone a female at all.

"Daisy!" Gemma cries out. She pushes from my arms and stumbles toward Zaku.

The Cobra snarls before I can stop her, rushing up behind. Gemma doesn't notice. She's entirely focused on the crumpled form in Zaku's hold.

A weak moan leaves the creature's lips.

"We need to get her out of her clothes and cleaned, quickly! We need water!" Gemma yells, turning to Azsote. "Get water!"

The next hour is a flurry of activity. Zaku doesn't leave Daisy's side, and my female takes over, ignoring anyone who tries to stop her. We get Daisy away from the wreckage and bring her to a creek that Azsote leads us to.

Zaku and Gemma hover over her, cutting off the remainder of her burnt clothes. It's not until her screaming starts that Azsote and I shoot into action to secure our perimeter.

Azsote darts up into the trees, disappearing, while I take ground cover. I run into Krellix, who's returned to the wreckage, stamping out the last of the flames with his tail. I leave him to it.

The screams continue until they abruptly cut off. They will haunt my dreams for years to come.

When I know the area around us is clear, I head for Gemma, who's bandaging her friend with as much care as possible. Gemma's hands are bloody, and ash has gotten all over her hair and skin. She turns to me when I approach and wipes her hands on the grass at her sides.

The grass is covered in blood.

"You said you know of a medical pod? You've seen one?" Her face is strained, worried.

I coil my tail around her. "It's unusable." I glimpse the other female. She's naked save some strips of cloth, and half her face is mottled, bright red with purpling splotches. She's burned from the left side of her face, down her chest, to her navel. If she survives, it's a wound that will never fully heal.

I'm sickened. I see Gemma in her place, and bile rises.

Zaku's tail is ringed around where she lays motionless, leaving just enough room for Gemma to get close. His hands are white, his expression is a mask of worry, desperation. I see the pain, the fear.

I've never seen either from him and of all the naga males, he's the closest to me. Not in distance, but in history. He and Vagan.

"I have a pod in my den, but it's far from here," he rasps, his eyes on the female before him. "Her screams when we move her... They destroy me."

"You have a pod?" Gemma turns to him. "We need to get her there. Now! While she's unconscious."

I shake my head. "It'll be dark soon."

"Daisy can't stay out here in her condition. She needs shelter, a place to rest, food, and medicine."

Zaku growls. "Then we go." He pulls his tail under him and begins to slowly push his hands under Daisy.

The female's eyes fly open, her mouth parts, and she shrieks. Zaku roars and jerks his hands away. "I can't help you here!" he yells.

A sob leaves the female, and her entire body convulses.

"Try again," Gemma stammers. Her face has gone whiter than the snow-capped mountains.

Zaku's hands shake.

Gemma leans over her friend and coos, petting her brow where she is unharmed. The Daisy's cries lower to whimpers. "Shhh, sweetheart. We're taking you to safety. You have to be strong, okay? If the pain gets to be too much, let it take you away." Gemma looks at Zaku when Daisy blinks out tears. "Again."

"I can't," he chokes.

"You can. You can do this, Zaku. You can do this. She needs you." Zaku and Gemma share a look, and my first reaction is to pummel Zaku to the ground and kill him, but I force my mind to calm.

No one's ever talked to one of us the way Gemma is talking to Zaku. She's comforting him. She's doing it while she's still hurt and afraid, wearing clothes that are falling off her body, her feet bound. She's showing more strength than Zaku, than any of us.

"Zaku," she orders when he doesn't move, her voice hardening. "Lift her. We don't have time to waste."

Zaku's nostrils flare. He looks down at the female and closes his eyes. I place my hand on Gemma's shoulder, curling my tail around her as Daisy screams again.

My soul winces.

Azsote joins us, and together we make the arduous, devastating journey to Zaku's den.

TWENTY-SIX

BETRAYAL FROM ABOVE

Gemma

THE NEXT SEVERAL days are a blur. I barely sleep. I don't leave Daisy's side once we make it to the King Cobra's lair. Zaku's *den*. He doesn't leave her side either, which means, Vruksha, Zaku, and I are hovering over Daisy day in and day out.

I rub my eyes.

If it wasn't for Azsote, I don't think any of us would take the time to eat.

I drop my hands to stare through the plastic screen of the medical pod. The buzz of it soothes me, and I'm just so thankful it works. It works, and Zaku has one. He didn't like what it did to Daisy when he turned it on, how it stuck her with needles and shot her up of questionable stuff, but Vruksha and Azsote managed to hold him down and keep him away long enough for it to do its thing.

I wasn't thrilled about it either, but I managed to keep it to myself. A pod over a thousand years old going to work on my friend? I can't help but hope for the best and be terrified and suspicious at the same time. But suspicion is better than helplessness. And whatever the medical intelligence did... it worked.

Daisy hasn't screamed since we laid her down.

She's stable. Resting. And the pod, though not perfect, is keeping her clean. Zaku's robots are keeping her fed... The burns on her flesh appear less angry every day.

I sigh and turn my head from where it rests on my arms and stare out the window. Vruksha is gazing out of it too, facing away from me. His glistening ruby scales dazzle me with their beauty.

It takes my breath away. He's gorgeous in the light. My naga male.

I would paint him just how he is now, how I see him when he doesn't notice me looking, gazing over the land he's conquered. I would paint him with the sun at his back, and his spear held high, casting lightning upon his foes.

The picture would hang over my bed. I'd stare at it and touch myself.

He wants to go home. I feel it. He's not comfortable here, in Zaku's domain, and it shows. He's always touching me in some way, like right now, his tailtip is curled around my ankle. He doesn't let me talk to Zaku or Azsote without him. And when I'm about to faint from exhaustion, he winds me up in his tail and forces me to sleep on him.

I'd enjoy Vruksha's concern if it wasn't for the beds Zaku has. Beds with cloth blankets and sheets. He also has piles of clothes in every size and has let me have whatever fits, including shoes and undergarments. He has... luxury. His home is clean, bright, airy. He has dozens of working robots as well. They manage the place.

Except Zaku won't let any of us leave the front rooms, and I'm becoming curious about what he has hidden within his strange, ancient human home.

Outside his home, it's different. It's almost calm. The terrain near Zaku's place is rough, sprawling, but still serene. There's a view of the gorge, the mountains, including the one Daisy crashed into. We're at the peak of one, and the view goes far. It's nice as long as I keep my eyes off the lawn, where there are skulls everywhere and a pile of rotting pig corpses. But it's easy to ignore them being as exhausted and numb as I am right now.

When my thoughts grow bleak, I can just look out the window and feel better. I forgot what it's like to see trees, grass, and animals through a window. Even dead ones.

It's usually stars, nebulas, asteroid fields, and planets.

We're far from the facility, farther still from Vruksha's bunker. I've been trying to map it out in my head. Zaku lives in the opposite direction from the facility, in a mansion built into the side of a mountain, like a king.

King Cobra...

I didn't like Zaku at first, blaming him as the reason Daisy and I were sacrificed, but I've decided to hate him a little less.

He cares for Daisy. He never leaves her side, just like Vruksha never leaves mine. He worries constantly, and though he's obstinate, almost bullish, and I want to slap him even when I'm sleeping, I can forgive him. He gazes at Daisy as if she's his entire world.

I keep my doubts anyway. I still don't know why Daisy stole a skiff. I wonder how long she flew it before crashing, where was she trying to go?

I hear a moan and I sit upright, flicking my eyes to her. Zaku is asleep across from me, sprawled over a cushiony chair, his large tail draped over the glass shield of the pod.

Daisy twitches. Her chapped, peeling lips part slightly, and another moan escapes.

"Daisy?' I whisper.

One of her eyelids cracks open and finds me.

I sit forward. "Daisy?"

"Gemma?"

"Yes, it's me."

She shudders, and her eye closes. She tries to raise her hand, and I stop her.

"Don't move." Though as I say it, the pod goes into action and a screen of Daisy's current vitals appears in the glass. A robotic arm from the side injects her with something that makes Daisy sigh.

"Where am I?" she asks when the pod returns to normal.

"Zaku's... house? Den," I correct. "In his medical pod."

Her one eye looks around, stopping on the large naga tail above her on the glass. She follows it over to the male snoring on the seat beside her. He's still asleep, and I have a feeling his snores are drowning out our whispering. I debate waking him, but I want to speak to Daisy first.

I sense Vruksha at my back.

Daisy stares at Zaku.

My brow furrows, trying to read her. Her face is swollen almost beyond recognition. Is she afraid?

"Is there anything I can do to make you more comfortable?" I ask.

"Anything at all? I'm glad you're awake. We were terrified for a bit there... You were in so much pain."

Her tongue pokes out to taste her lips. "I don't feel anything right now."

"I think the pod is pumping you with painkillers."

Daisy's eye shifts back over to me. "I crashed."

My face falls. "Yeah."

"I shouldn't be alive." Her voice is barely more than an airy, strained whisper.

"But you are."

Despair washes over her, and my heart squeezes. "Daisy," I continue, "you're alive and you're going to stay that way."

But I need to know, I need to know if Zaku can be trusted. If she's safe with him. I won't leave her here if she isn't. I've been watching the King Cobra, and though I now like him okay, it doesn't mean he's not a monster. Peter turned out to be a monster.

"I shouldn't be," she chokes. "I fell so far. My escape pod wouldn't eject..."

"Don't think about it anymore. It's over. I have something I need to ask you, something important."

Her lips tremble. "What?"

I lower my voice, leaning right up to the glass. "Are you... Are you with Zaku?"

Confusion flutters across Daisy's face for a split-second, and then it's gone. "He caught me."

"Do you want to stay caught?"

Her eye turns glassy, and she looks up at the ceiling. "He calls me his queen."

"That's not what I'm asking..."

Her gaze goes to Vruksha. "Do you like him? His smell?"

I don't think I could explain how I feel about Vruksha to another. Being with him is like being sated, free. It doesn't make sense. My breath whizzes through my teeth. "I like him a lot," I tell her. "His...smell included."

A lot.

But does she feel that way about Zaku? I eye the naga male.

"I'm glad," she croaks. "Gemma..." Daisy says, dodging my question.

"The crash wasn't your fault."

"I was shot down."

Shot down? My brow furrows. Daisy shudders, clearly upset, and all I want to do is hold her, tell her it's all going to be okay.

"Who?" I ask.

Daisy shudders again.

And a streak of fear bolts through me, constricting my throat. The ship here on Earth, the transport ship we took from *The Dreadnaut*, isn't equipped with weapons besides a couple of turrets that can only be used while landlocked to protect it from thieves...

So that only makes one other option.

"*The Dreadnaut* shot me down," she whispers.

Zaku groans, his tail slides on the pod. He's waking.

"How? Why?" I ask. "They wouldn't do that. Captain Michal would never fire on our own."

Daisy's eye goes wide, flicking between Zaku's tail and me. "Gemma, I was trying to reach them. Tell them what's happening down here." Her hand shakes like she's trying to rise again. "They know."

She did what I was unable to do.

Daisy cries out just as Zaku snaps to attention, taking over. Daisy closes her eye as Zaku speaks to her in a soft voice. He hisses at me to back away. I reach behind me, and Vruksha clasps my hand. His tail coils the rest of the way up my leg.

Vruksha leads me away.

If what Daisy says about *The Dreadnaut* is true, my fears have been made real. Vruksha isn't safe, and it appears neither are Daisy and me. I squeeze my eyes shut, suddenly overwhelmingly exhausted.

If Central Command knows what Peter has done, then there's no help for us. We can only help ourselves. I turn in Vruksha's embrace and rest my head against his chest. His hands tangle in my hair, his short claws grazing my scalp, prickling me with comfort.

"It's time to go," he says.

"I know."

I have a promise to keep.

And more than anything, it's one I want to keep.

TWENTY-SEVEN

THE ONLY CHOICE

Gemma

WE DON'T LEAVE Zaku's den for another two days.

Daisy begs for me to stay longer, and so the males fight each other for dominion. Vruksha is forced to give way to Zaku, because we're in the Cobra's territory, and the longer we remain, he gets a little more crazed.

By the end, I'm with him more than I am with Daisy, soothing his sensitive serpent manhood. Though we're never truly alone, not with Azsote lurking around. The Boomslang is always watching when he's not out hunting. I see his envy building.

Zaku and Vruksha have noticed it too.

Last night, I found Azsote watching me change into softer clothes for sleep. It was the Boomslang's bitter scent that alerted me to him. Vruksha tackled him, injecting Azsote with his venom, forcing the Boomslang down. Azsote was then dragged out of Zaku's den and tossed over the side of the mountain.

He's been banished.

Though I know he's outside, waiting, and now that I know he's there, that he's willing to invade my privacy to see me naked, I don't leave the front rooms of Zaku's den.

I can't be with Vruksha the way we both need.

I crave him. I crave the way he moves my body. The way he takes control of my limbs, winding me up in his tail and making me forget everything but him. Nothing else matters when Vruksha and I are alone.

So when I stuff my bag full of all the clothes and items Zaku's given me, I'm hopeful.

Daisy wakes several times a day for short periods, and the pain in her gaze eases more each day. Whatever the pod is doing to heal her, it's working. Even her burns have mended a great deal.

She dodges my questions every time I bring up Zaku. She won't speak to me about him, but she also doesn't seem to fear him. It's possible I'm being overprotective, assuming a closeness she might not feel.

She's chosen to stay and heal. I don't know what that means when it comes to her and Zaku, though I take it she doesn't know either.

"Are you sure you have to go?" Daisy asks. She's lying on her good side today, facing me. The swelling around her eye has gone down significantly.

"I promised Vruksha," I've told her this before.

"I'm going to miss you."

"I'm going to miss you too, but we'll see each other again. I know it. We'll be back soon, I promise."

Though Vruksha is one word away from doing to Zaku what he did to Azsote, I know he and Zaku have an understanding. They trust each other; I can tell. They may never admit it, may not even realize it themselves since both males are reluctant to show weakness of any kind, but it's there.

"I hope you're right."

"I am. Are you sure you want to stay?"

Daisy nods. "I want to heal."

I purse my lips, search her face. "Okay. Enjoy this great view you have and think of me when you do, okay?" I hesitate to leave her. "I'll search for a way we can communicate," I tell her. It's been on my mind. Peter took our personal comm ware before he gave us over to the nagas, and I want it back. There's stuff here that can help us, I know it. I just have to find it first. "When I find it, you'll be the first to know."

Daisy smiles then her face winces in pain. "Good," she rasps.

I rise. "No more dangerous missions without me? If you run again, wait for me?"

"We'll see."

"She's not going anywhere," Zaku growls.

Glimpsing him on the other side. "Bye, Zaku," I say. "Vruksha and I will be back," I warn.

He hisses.

With one last lingering look at Daisy, I make my way to the exit where Vruksha waits for me. I pass through the barriers of the den's entryway and find Vruksha on the broken steps leading away outside. The doors close behind me with a resounding, finalized *thud*, and glancing back, I'm surprised Daisy managed to escape this place at all.

She's stronger than me.

Still, I can't help but think there's something Daisy isn't telling me. Something about Zaku she's not sharing. What's behind the doors of his den, the ones he won't let anyone pass through?

I chew on my lip. I'll find out, I decide.

Vruksha snatches my bag, and I look up to find his eyes glinting. His scales are rigid over his knuckles where he grips his spear.

He scents the Boomslang's tension. *Tension* is how he describes the mating heat he feels since he doesn't have another name for it. The way he gets—his bulge expanding—when he's near me, tastes me, or sees me naked. Tension. The pressure of the seed, almost unbearable, filling his cock until spilled.

There's no way of knowing what Azsote will do if it gets bad. Lately, he's been giving off a smell that wrinkles my nose.

I didn't know this until two days ago.

Apparently all the naga males have a knot on their cocks, one that expands and fills continuously until they spill the contents.

No wonder why I feel beyond stretched when Vruksha's inside me.

"Two days," he says. Vruksha's eyes go to my feet. Fortunately, I've found some proper boots. "Can you walk? For now?"

Curling my toes, I nod. I take the long knife Zaku gave me, palming the handle of it where it's sheathed at my belt. We make the slow descent down his mountain.

For the rest of the day, we're scaling down one mountain, only to climb another. We stop occasionally to rest and eat, though never for long. Vruksha won't let us. He's tense, and as the hours pass, the muscles of his back and arms only bunch further.

When the sun lowers, his countenance darkens even more. It's making me nervous.

He's been cold since we left his bunker, and now that it's just the two of us, his mood has only soured. My stomach twists. We have to talk; I know we do. We've kept our conversations to the here-and-now while with Daisy and the others, but they're gone now. Nothing is stopping us but the trek—the wilderness.

I keep my mouth shut.

Vruksha is focusing on our path and staying vigilant. I'm right there with him. Every snap of a twig, every gust of wind, even the chirps of bugs and birds keep me on edge.

People lived here. I trail the heavy growth of trees with my eyes, pushing through several branches. *My people.* We were landlocked here for thousands of years.

I can't comprehend it, not having the freedom of space, being stuck on a single small planet, where if I wanted to get away from someone or something, I could only put some land and maybe an ocean between us. I'd rather there'd be millions of galaxies.

I thought it was amazing that Vruksha's bunker, the tech, and even the animals were still here, but after seeing Zaku's home, there's nothing left to surprise me. He had running water, silver walls edged with stones, and so much more. I'd gone through a time machine, back to when my ancestors thrived.

It's while I'm thinking this, having finally stopped worrying about Daisy, that Vruksha leads me into the ruins of a building.

A large one. One I haven't seen before.

Vines and moss cover it, but floors remain, and the rest of it? It's scattered amongst the trees as far as I can see. There are rusty bars, shattered windows, and trees that shoot from the ground through the pieces that are left. We've passed numerous buildings and ruins, and each one is interesting in its own way.

Vruksha leads me deeper into the building, and I'm met with centuries of dust and decay. Looking around, it appears stripped of objects that might be collected, except for random bits and pieces left behind.

He stops, leans over a counter, and brushes some of the debris aside with his tail. He rises and points his spear to the spot. "We camp here tonight."

I peek over the counter to the hard, dirty floor on the other side. It's not great, though I like the walls on every side. Vruksha drops my bag of clothes. It's a good spot.

"I'm going to secure the perimeter." He slips away before I can stop him.

I rub the chill from my hands, open my bag, and pull out a ration to eat. I take it with me when I decide to familiarize myself with the building.

There are broken chairs, decaying pictures on the walls, and drooping plastic plants. I try to imagine what it would have looked like before the Lurkers, but I can't, not really. The place was made to be comfortable, and there's no comfort left.

I hear something behind me, and I turn, finding Vruksha. He stops when he sees me. There's a dead bird in his hand, and he shows it to me. "Food," he says.

"I ate a ration."

His tail curls. His brows arc. He takes me in, and I straighten, wondering what he's seeing. He lifts the bird to his mouth and starts eating it raw. My nose wrinkles.

I've seen him do it before.

He stares at me as he eats it, licks his fingers.

I shiver.

"I'm going to keep watch," he says when he's done, wiping his mouth with the back of his hand. "Stay here and get some rest." He turns to leave again.

"Wait," I call out quickly, not wanting him to go.

"What?"

I take a step forward. "You've been... distant since we left the bunker."

Vruksha cocks his head.

"You've been upset."

He hisses. "Your friend is sssafe, female."

"That's not what I mean. I know she is. This isn't about her."

"Then what is it about? Tomorrow, you will be back within my den, in our nest, and you will completely give yourself to me. Forever."

He continues, stalking toward me. "Unless you've changed your mind?"

"I haven't changed my mind," I say. I don't want to break my word, but also, I can't imagine what he'd do if I did. My naga is reasonable, intelligent, and strong, but he's also lawless, and quick to temper. He stops in front of me, eyes ablaze. I chew on my tongue, straining my neck to meet his gaze. "I want to know what's wrong. With you."

For someone who rose through the ranks as a comms officer, I'm sure as shit at failing at communicating now, when it matters most.

Maybe that's the trick about communicating. When it doesn't matter, it's easy, and when it does... It's the hardest thing in the world to find the right words—the right time.

"Wrong, female? There is nothing wrong. Once I have you safe, where no other male can either see you or get to you, we can talk. Tonight? I do not trust what could be waiting in the canopy above." He pulls away again.

I grab his wrist. He stops, tensing where I touch him. It's the most we've touched all day. He doesn't shake me off, so I move into his arms and press against his body, curling my arms around his back. I inhale his earthy scent, and his soft scales tickle my cheek. I close my eyes hard and shudder.

"I miss you," I whisper.

His arms close in around me. "I've never left."

"I need you," I say, holding in my tears. Words fail me.

His hands tangle into my hair. "I'm here, female."

"Don't leave me tonight. If you do, take me with."

Vruksha pulls me into his arms. "I'll stay."

He carries me to our spot behind the counter. And for a time, he just holds me, giving me everything I've missed, I've needed. *This. Us.* I burrow hard into him, relishing his body, his warmth. Whatever may be outside can stay there, but tonight, it's just the two of us in this building. I curl my fingers against him as he winds his tail through and under my legs.

I could never leave, even if I wanted to. I could never leave the heaven of his arms.

Not for rank, not for paints, not for anything.

Anything... Fantastical I am not. Perhaps, that will be my greatest secret. That I have chosen Vruksha over everyone.

His hands grip my hair, they run up and down my back, and his heart thunders under my ear.

"I miss you always," he says softly, holding me tighter against him. "Every time I take my eyes off you, I miss you."

A laugh bubbles up. "Is that why you're always watching me?"

"I always watch you because you are beautiful, and you glow in the light. But perhaps I also watch you because I'm afraid if I don't, you'll disappear."

My chest tightens. "I won't." I mean it.

Silence returns for a time. Vruksha sways his tail, caressing my body, keeping me warm.

"I want you to choose me," he says after a while.

I lift to look at him. "I have chosen you."

He meets my eyes in the darkness. "I need you to choose me." His voice roughens. "Every day."

"Every day, I will choose you."

His finger caresses my cheek. "I need you to really choose me."

My lips purse, confused. I pull away a little further so I can see him better, trying to figure him out. "Is that why you're unhappy?" I ask softly. "I've chosen you over everyone, I lo—"

He interrupts me. "I'm not unhappy."

"You've pulled away from me."

"I haven't."

"Then explain it to me. What's going on? I choose you, Vruksha," I declare. "I'm not going anywhere. You're the only one I trust." It hurts to say it, admitting the betrayal of my people, but it's also liberating. "Should I scream it?" I deadpan.

His finger drops from my cheek. "Your trust is a gift," he says.

"You're deflecting."

He hisses.

I hiss back at him.

His lips wrinkle, gifting me a brief glimmer of a smile.

Vruksha is handsome when he smiles. I grin, hissing once more. "I can do it too."

"Yesss, you do it well."

"Now explain it to me," I demand. "If we're to be mates, we can't have any more secrets."

His chest puffs out, and he exhales. "I've never been chosen," he begins.

I give him all my attention.

He continues, "I told you about my father, my mother. How he stayed to raise me and my sisters, though, I know now he died the day my mother did. He chose to live, to protect me and my siblings, and that was enough for a young male like me. I didn't know better, not like how I do now. How that choice he made, to stay with us, was everything. A sacrifice I can only start to comprehend. Except it didn't last, that choice he made, and when my sisters chose to go west, I knew it hurt my father gravely. That day, he lost them, like he lost my mother.

"I wasn't enough.

"For years, he stayed with me, teaching me to hunt and use the tech. He showed me how to live, but he was already dead, and those final years, I knew being with me killed him. He worried about my sisters. I wasn't surprised when he decided to go after them. Once he made his decision, he became happy, and I realized how much being with me was hurting him. He chose me, but not really. Those days before his departure, the happier he got, the more it hurt."

"Did you tell him this?"

"How could I? I'd never seen my father smile before. I couldn't take that away."

I can't imagine. "I'm sorry." I could say it a thousand times, but it would never help.

"I watched him leave me, never to return. He never asked me to join him."

I lean my head against his chest.

"After he left, it seemed he left not only me behind, but his darkness, his grief. And that grief went into me instead. I mourned the loss of my sisters, but it was not the way I mourned the loss of my father. For years, I was alone, never seeing another soul, not until Zhallaix established a den near my own, and in doing so, brought Zaku and the other nagas out of their territories and into mine. He and the others distracted me, and I moved on, forgetting what it was like to be lonely, that my family abandoned me.

"And then a ship came out of the sky, and with it, humans."

"Me," I whisper.

"You, sweet mate. I was lucky enough to see the ship land and go after it. Many of us did. Then, one day, you appeared, walking from the confines of that vessel and into my world. I noticed your hair first, the way it shimmered in the sunlight, its brilliance. I looked down at my scales and realized we were the same color. You wore my color, and I knew you were mine. Nothing else mattered. I had to have you. There was nothing else. And when I took a second glance, our eyes met."

"I remember." I shiver thinking of that day and how afraid I was when I saw Vruksha for the first time. I like hearing him tell it from his point of view though. It makes me happy. He hadn't seemed real, not with his shock of red amongst the trees. "You scared me. I thought you were covered in blood."

"You stood there staring back at me for a long time."

"I thought if I moved, you'd come out of the trees and eat me."

"I wanted to, but not in that way."

"Did I give you *tension?*"

Vruksha rumbles. "Yes."

I smile.

"After you left, running from me and into the facility ruins, I knew there was no way I was leaving without you. I planned to steal you."

"You did?"

"I scouted the perimeter of the facility a hundred times, searching for weakness, for a way in and out where I wouldn't be caught. I searched for you constantly, hoping for another glimpse. Each time I saw you, I became more obsessed, more certain you belonged with me, and during my plans, I found other naga males doing the same. They saw you and the other females within and wanted you too. I was desperate. We fought because we all wanted the same thing—you. When we realized attacking the base was a bad idea, Zaku decided to approach your males—"

"And make a deal with Peter," I snap.

"What else were we to do? If we attacked, you and the other females could be hurt. You could escape into your ship and leave? The very idea of those possibilities stopped me and the other nagas from sneaking in alone, from attacking at all. The risk was too great."

I shake my head. "It wasn't right."

"Yes, it was," he growls.

"And if I fought tooth and nail? And still fought you right now? What then?"

"I would make you see."

I sigh.

"This isn't why I was... unhappy, Gemma."

I sigh again and play with the scales on his chest. "Go on."

"After it was all said and done, and I finally had you, you chose Azsote."

Sitting back up, I glare at him. "I told you why I chose him."

"You did."

"I wish I could go back in time and make a better choice... I can't."

"When you had to make a choice again, you chose Daisy."

My brow wrinkles. "She was in trouble."

Vruksha shakes his head. "You called me your mate when you did. It was bliss, hearing you say it aloud, but then it infuriated me. I hated it. Helping your friend is one thing, but in doing so, it brought back everything."

My heart sinks. "I didn't mean—"

"Stop. I understand why you did it now. I also realize you didn't do it on purpose. I'd... forgotten what it was like not being alone, being a part of a clan. I... liked it. I remembered when we met up with Zaku, Azsote, and even your friend, how there's strength in numbers and there's comfort in sharing your worries with others who are like-minded. It's been years since I last saw my father, and I'd forgotten."

"What about today?" I whisper.

"You haven't called me mate since," he tells me.

I close my eyes hard, finally understanding. I manipulated him, used his insecurities to get what I wanted. I hadn't even realized what I had done until now. I knew how much he wanted me, how protective he was, how paranoid he gets, and I must've known calling him mate in return was a priceless gift. Even subconsciously, I knew. I did it anyway, not thinking if it was the right place or time.

And I used that power he'd given me to force him to take me to Daisy. I can't stop the thick ball of guilt squeezing my heart.

I sit up and lean back. His arms loosen around me.

"I choose you," I say, almost gasping the words.

His eyes hood. "What?"

"I choose you," I tell him louder. "Mate," I add.

"You don't—"

"I'm saying it not because you want to hear it, but because I need to say it and you need to hear it again. Because there's nothing else I want. Only you. There's nothing else I want than to be your mate. I will tell you every day if I must because it's the truth. I'm not going anywhere. I will prove it."

"Your humans are still here, and so is their ship."

"I know."

Vruksha searches my eyes. His tail closes in tightly around us. "You won't try and run? Like your friend? I couldn't bear it. Not after seeing what it did to her... Her screams."

"I won't run," I promise him. "I love you."

"Love," he says. "That's a strange word."

"You'll hear it from now on. It won't be strange for long." I've never felt how I do for Vruksha for anyone else.

He pulls me close, resting his chin on my head, and I settle against him. Moonlight shines through the cracks of the building, and I watch the flurries of dust in the dim silver light. It's such a simple beauty, but one I'll never take advantage of again. Earth may not be the place it once was, and there may be obstacles in our future, but for now, I'm exactly where I'm supposed to be.

I know what's at stake. What's been given up, and I vow to protect what's left with my life. There's something wrong with this new Earth, and I'm going to figure out what it is.

While I do, I'll be with Vruksha.

He gently brushes his fingers through my hair, lulling me to sleep.

"Love," he whispers.

It's the last thing I hear before sleep. Then his warmth takes me away, leading me to dreams of mountains and the alien men who rule them.

TWENTY-EIGHT
ONCE A SECRET

Gemma

WE LEAVE the building before the sun rises the next morning. He's eager to be back home, and so am I. I want the pelts and the warmth of Vruksha's nest, and he wants me to prove that I'll keep my word.

He doesn't have to say it; I know it.

I want to prove it too. Baby steps, rights? He's earned my trust, now I need to earn his.

For how alien Vruksha and his naga brothers are, they're still a conglomerate of softness and insecurity beneath their rough exteriors. Even Zaku, I bet.

I hope Daisy's made the right choice staying with him, but even if she regrets it already, now that I know where she is, I'll check in on her soon.

Even if it means facing the wilds again. Vruksha will take me, I'm certain. He's going to need to teach me how to hunt and defend myself anyway. It's not like there are working orbs everywhere I can beg for help. And still, if there were, I wouldn't. Gunfire is loud and imperfect. The drones here may no longer have the calibration software for perfect aim.

I got lucky, really lucky. I can't rely on luck going forward.

The next time... the drones may not come at all. I need to know how to survive and avoid another situation like the pigs.

I'm also anxious to explore this forest and clean out Vruksha's bunker. I'd just begun digging through his stuff and learning about my history before we left.

I want him to show me his screens again.

I want to know everything. Even if it's hard, even if no one survives. I've decided it's my job to make sure the information is protected, cataloged, and saved. So if humans do return to Earth, they'll know what's at stake, what we've lost, and that we still have so much left to lose. I've only just gained a little of it back myself.

I want to honor those who died.

As for the Lurker tech... I'm fine with it staying hidden until I understand more, keeping it far from anyone who might misuse it, even my own people. Because if *the Dreadnaut* did fire on Daisy...

Sighing, I push through the branches of a large bush, following Vruksha's trail.

I exhale loudly, seeing a steep hill ahead of me.

Why does it have to be steep?

As I've traveled by Vruksha's side, I've watched for the signs of the land flattening out, of the trees thinning, of the vague landmarks I've already come to know. But the land doesn't flatten out like I expect. I peek up at the sky and grasp Vruksha's tail. He hauls me up a ledge. It seems like we've been climbing for hours when I'm certain we should be on flat land by now. I wipe the sweat from my brow.

I had to be physically fit to work on the bridge of *The Dreadnaut*, but apparently I'm not as fit as I thought I am. Even after all the time I've spent on Earth, I'm pushing my limits every day. My injuries don't help.

It's getting easier though.

"I hope this is a shortcut," I groan. "I need a bath, even if it means risking running into Zhallaix. I have a knife now."

Come at me Zhallaix, I am not in the mood. I narrow my eyes.

"We won't make it to the bunker tonight."

"I knew it!" I throw up my hands. "I knew we weren't heading there when we kept climbing." I don't know if I want to cry or collapse. The past month has been hard, and it needs to stop. The hardness, that is. "Where are you taking me?" I ask, wheezing a little.

Vruksha turns to me, throws his muscled limbs around my body, and hauls me into the cradle of his arms. I slump like a damsel in distress.

"We're almossst there," he says.

He continues the climb with me holding onto him, only using the strength of his tail. Sometimes I forget how powerful it is, as he easily lifts us both up on it, coiling and shifting its weight for his needs. I've taken that power between my legs... Perhaps I'm powerful too.

It's been too long since our last time together, and I need him. But climbing all day? It really takes the *oomph* out of having sex. This is why I want a nice, cold bath, and some rest, because the next time it happens...

My eyes widen. I'm going to ride him. I'll show him that human females can be full of *tension* too.

I even miss the dangerous graze of his fangs sliding across my flesh. Especially now that I saw what his venom did to Azsote—I know the risk.

I wish I had venom of my own. Maybe then I could've bitten Peter and thrown him over a mountain too. I run my tongue across my blunt teeth.

Now that I know we're not going to make it to the bunker tonight, I continue studying our surroundings, looking across the land below, trying to figure out where we are and where we've been. My messy mental map suspects the bunker is far from here.

"This better be worth it," I mumble.

"It is."

For the next bit, I play with the scales on his chest. It's not until the steep ledges flatten out entirely and the trees are pushed back that I realize we're on a road, or what might have been a road. Now it's just weeds, grass, and cracked cement stones, with the occasional stubborn tree growing through it.

Vruksha follows it until it ends, stopping at a cave-in deep in the side of the mountain we've been climbing all day.

He sets me down.

"What is this place?" I ask, shielding my eyes from the sun.

"You'll see."

He slides to the rocks and shifts a few aside. Before long, I notice the rocks he's moving have been moved before. They're placed differently than those that fell naturally. A door slowly emerges.

Vruksha pushes the last of the stones away and turns back to me. "It's a hole."

I wipe my palms on my pants. "Like your bunker?"

"Deeper, darker. Bigger."

I suck in, staring at the door. "Is this..." I hesitate. *Could it be?*

"Yes."

"The tech?"

"Yesss, female."

I take a step forward. "You're showing it to me?"

"You said last night that mates don't keep secrets from each other. You have a right to know. And we made a deal once, not that long ago, a deal you have delivered on," he says as he swipes the tip of his tail between my legs. I startle but shudder with pleasure at the same time. "Now it's my turn."

"Vruksha," I gasp, glaring at him until his tailtip retreats, shuddering again. I've been inhaling his scent all day. "I didn't mean..." I shake my head, trying to focus on what he just said. "I didn't mean it like that. You don't have to show me this. Mates don't keep secrets from each other, but this—this is something else." He snaps his tailtip back between my legs and swirls it, and I stumble away. He catches me before I drop to my knees.

It's dangerous, the tech. I know that now, and part of me doesn't want anything to do with it. I don't think I want this responsibility.

He lifts me and turns my body to face him. "I know," he says with a throaty rasp.

"Then why?"

"Because what you said was true—mates shouldn't keep secrets from each other. Are you ready, Gemma?"

I swallow, look at the scuffed door, the forest behind us, and even the sky. I look to the wispy clouds and the faraway twinkle of stars beginning to emerge behind them.

To the bright moon ascending and the giant warship I know is hiding behind it.

I recall the way the Lurkers looked in the video, their leathery, scaled flesh. Their reptilian features. Their black, emotionless eyes.

"I'm ready," I say.

Vruksha pushes the door open, and darkness greets us.

EPILOGUE

Vruksha

Two weeks later.

"I choose you today, Vruksha," Gemma yawns, stretching in our nest. Her breasts rise as she takes in a deep breath, teasing me to play with them. I do, often. The marks around her nipples are proof enough for that. They're pink and swollen, perking up to meet the tips of my claws and my rough fingertips.

I show her my love with caresses and sweet kisses. I make her *take* my love with daily vicious rutting, and my unending need to spill my soul inside her.

"And you, female," I groan, tickling my tailtip between her legs where she's wet. She's always wet. I think my scent makes her that way but I'm not sure... If I want her, and she's not in the mood, I pull her close to breathe me in, and she melts—always. She opens up like a flower. But if my seed isn't trickling from between her legs from our last rutting, she's wet from my saliva, if not arousal. I am a lucky male.

A hungry one as well.

I rise over her as she opens her bleary eyes. She spreads her legs with another yawn, and I push my tailtip into her relaxed sheath. I reach down and pull out my shaft, curling my fingers around the bulge in the middle. It never gets large anymore. It never has a chance to, not with my Gemma.

But she is much smaller than me, and we are different species. No matter how much, or how rough we get, I have to coax her body to accept me. She's tight, cursedly so. I do not want to bring her discomfort when all I feel is sweet agony when her brow furrows and she accepts me.

I ready her now, pumping my tailtip in and out. She grips me, quivering around it.

"Vruksha," she moans, lifting her arms above her head, threading her fingers into her messy hair.

It's enough to make me spill. It's enough to make any male insane. My seed shoots out all over her breasts and stomach and I hiss, annoyed. I wipe the clear, watery spill off of her stomach.

Gemma smiles lazily at me and spreads her legs further. Her little hole constricts.

"Female," I rasp. "You tease."

I slip out my tail and sink my fingers deep inside her to rub the spot that makes her squirm and balk. When she does, when she writhes, I replace my fingers with my prick, thrusting hard.

She gasps, tensing, and I snarl. I spill again, and her legs hook around me, keeping us locked.

It's the last straw. I drop my weight, trapping her, thrusting violently. I take my mate the way I need to. I take her until there's nothing left in her entire world but me, and only me. I thrust until she's screaming, until any trace of sleep is banished from her body. And when she clenches around me, making me roar, I flood her full of seed.

She's kept her promise.

She's stayed.

And every day her laughter gets louder, her smiles more forthcoming, and I find that laughter and smiles have returned to me as well. I want them always.

I also want her screams.

She's a well-loved mess by the time I rise off of her.

"Now I'm not going to be able to walk again today," she moans, bringing a pelt up to her chin, throwing her leg over the side of it. "I have so much work to do, dammit!"

"Tell me what you want done, and I will do it." I turn on the burner to heat the bunker. It's closer to our nest now. Gemma has rearranged everything in the weeks we have been home.

Gone are the stacks of crates, the makeshift spaces between, and the items I collected over the years. Everything worth keeping, we moved into the tunnels, cleaning out the space. Now, the bunker is segmented with different 'spaces' down the long length, with a straight path to the back where our nest lies.

Gone are the baubles that don't work and the flashlights that no longer have batteries. Now there's only stuff we need—or stuff Gemma wants to fix. The walls are covered in pelts she didn't want to use as blankets, and even the flickering lights have been taken down.

There are only dim lights now, and we know we will have to find a better source of light at some point when those die too.

That's for another day.

"I wanted to start going through the crates we removed and empty them. It'll be good to have empty boxes at our disposal," she says this lying back and yawning again, loudly.

"Easy enough."

"I need another bath now too."

"Yes. You do." She is covered with my spill. It glistens her skin.

She needs a bath every day, apparently, and taking her to the creek has gotten easier. I rarely bathed before she entered my life. Now, I swim with her each day. Water is foreign to my scales, but I've come to enjoy the leisure time. I've never been a naga who prefers water over the forest, like Vagan. The Blue Coral rules the lake near here, and so I stick to the creeks, brooks, and streams when I need water.

Perhaps that will change.

"I want to talk about checking in on Daisy too, if that's okay?" she asks, sitting up. She goes to stand, and I give her my tail to help.

"Too soon."

"It's been two weeks... ish. Not soon at all. We don't have to stay long, just enough to make sure she's still recovering, and that Zaku isn't—"

"The Cobra won't hurt her."

"I can't help worrying."

I pull Gemma close. "We will discuss it tomorrow. Today, we bathe and empty the crates."

She sighs and nods while I wrap her up in my limbs. I don't want to share her with anyone, not Daisy, the other humans, and especially not Zaku or the other nagas. I need all of her attention, all of her affection. I am a greedy male.

My member strains to be released from my tail again. To show her that she should think of me and only me. And it.

Gemma is still gloriously naked, pressed up against me, and I can't resist. I lift her in my arms, wrap my tailtip around my member, and sink it back inside her. She tenses and squirms, her sex trying to keep me out, but then she sighs, moaning as I work her up and down my length, mating her again. She throws her arms around my neck and rests her cheek on my chest while I use her.

I am the luckiest male.

Ropes of fresh spill jettison inside her.

I use her three more times before we even make it to the creek for her bath. My body demands I swell her with my litter and until she is, I will remain crazed to do so.

And she? Gemma doesn't wear undergarments anymore. I keep destroying them.

Later that day, we're in the tunnels, separating empty crates from those that remain full. We've been at it for hours, deciding what should be kept, what needs to go, and where to drop what we don't want. Gemma doesn't like clutter and neither wants to keep the cast-offs in the tunnels nor outside our bunker.

I agree with her in keeping the entrance to the bunker clear. The way it is right now, it's hard for anyone who isn't looking for it to find it. It keeps trespassers away. And any naga male who may want to risk his life.

None have come so far, not even Zhallaix, and I hope it stays that way.

My female's gone quiet, and I look up from what I'm doing. She's staring into the darkened corridor that leads to the deeper tunnels.

We only have enough solar lanterns and torches to light up the part we're working in.

"Gemma," I rumble in warning.

She startles and turns to me. "I just want to watch them once more. Just a couple of hours?"

"No."

"Even if I promise?"

When we first returned to the bunker, she convinced me to take her back to the screen room—a room I once spent many months in during my youth—to watch the end of her world again and again. She became obsessed, wanting to go back every day until I pointed it out, and she stopped. But there's more than what I showed her that first day. The screens have... everything.

Videos of things I didn't understand at first. Plays and drawings and music. All things archived from the past. When she found out there was more, it was hard to get her to leave.

Music is a treat. The reenactments are enjoyable. They don't belong in this world, but they're here anyway, and I hope nothing ever happens to them.

Gemma particularly likes the idea of museums and the artwork within them. I told her some still exist and promised to take her to their ruined buildings.

That made her excited.

"Please?" she begs prettily.

I relent. "A couple of hours." We've gotten a lot done today anyway. What she wanted to get done.

It's been a change. Before her, I spent my days out in the forests hunting, scouting.

"Thank you!"

I take a lantern off one of the crates and pull her close.

She can't find the room without me—and I won't let her enter this space alone. The tunnels curve, break off and go on for miles in every direction. The lights haven't ever worked, and it's easy to get lost if you don't know the way. Some rooms splinter off on the sides as well. Most are empty or lead to the surface. Some are filled with crates like the ones I have, while others hold old human machines and items.

I don't know why they're here or what they were originally used for, but it's a dangerous place if you get lost. I searched them long ago, as have other nagas who have found their way here, and vaguely know my way through them.

If Gemma ever takes a wrong turn...

She can't see in the dark as well as I can. I shake the thought away.

We make it to the room with the screens, and I flip the switchboard on the desk overseeing them. Gemma tugs a pelt over her shoulders, left from the last time we were here, and I curl my tail under me, settling, pulling her close so she can rest upon it.

"What did you want tonight?" I mumble. "Not the final hours," I add.

"Can we watch something... fun? With music? I love the music." She leans back with a sigh of contentment. I wrap my arm across her middle.

I know just the thing. A human male appears, large on the screens, with an umbrella. We fall into a peaceful silence as he sings about the rain.

Such a simple thing to make a song about, such an easy thing.

Two weeks ago, I led Gemma into the dark mountain where a cache of Lurker secrets is hidden. We haven't talked about it since. She hasn't brought it up. It's something that's always been there for me, a secret revealed long ago, found by the nagas of my father's generation. Hidden by them, and for most, forgotten about.

Only a few of us remember the cache exists. And if anyone has found more, I'm not aware of it.

I never told Gemma. I fear the tech as much as I admire it. I wouldn't use my spear if it hadn't been given to me by my father. Overwhelming power radiates from these alien contraptions, and the way these things scramble my mind when I hold them... it is not always easy to endure.

It can be frightening.

But she... She seemed to know exactly what she was looking at.

Guns, bombs, and arsenal ware, she called them. Thousands, lined up on racks as far as the eye could see, vanishing in the distance. She picked them up, held them, even loaded a gun, but put it back when it wouldn't charge for her. I saw what the stuff did to her kind, and it has no place in the forests. No place in this world. I thought about leaving my spear behind.

I couldn't do it in the end, my spear is a fourth limb I do not know how to live without.

She said the guns weren't alien, though I'm not sure I believe her. I picked up the same gun she put down, and it immediately charged for me, scrambled my mind. And when she took it back? It died in her grasp.

That was when we realized she can't light the fire at the tip of my spear. Only I can.

Her kind wouldn't make weapons they couldn't use, right?

It wasn't the guns and weapons that scared her though, like I thought they would. Like how they make me and the rest of the nagas uneasy. It was the pods, much like the one Zaku had in his den. They were filled with liquid, with tubes and wires connected to a singular central orb in the middle.

Eggs, she called them, barely speaking above a whisper.

She wanted to leave after that.

We fled the cache, leaving the weapons and pods behind, putting the rocks back into place, and adding more when she demanded it. Since that day, I sometimes notice her looking at me differently, at least at first, luckily, the looks didn't last.

Once I got her back into my nest and made sure she had nothing else to think about but us, her quiet contemplation fell from her mind.

I would not have brought her to the tunnels again so soon if I hadn't seen the underlying fear in her eyes. I promised her protection forever, and I plan on keeping that promise. I'll keep all my promises.

And if I was born from one of those eggs? Or my father was, my mother?

I rest my chin on Gemma's head.

I'm not interested in finding out.

I have what I wanted, and I'm going to keep it. Whoever may come, whatever might happen, they'll have to go through me if they come here and try and take it away.

"Anybody out there? Is anybody out there?" a feminine voice says, crackling the music.

Gemma tenses and I lift my head.

"What was that?" she asks, turning to look at me. "It didn't sound like it was from the movie."

"I don't know."

We break eye contact and look around the room. In the background, the movie continues to play. A minute goes by, and the crackly voice doesn't return.

"Can you rewind the movie?" she asks.

"Please, answer! This is Shelby from *The Dreadnaut,* and we're in trouble," the voice, spiked with desperation this time, says again. It's coming from behind us.

Gemma shoots to her feet. "Shelby?" she gasps, searching for where the voice came from. I rise with her, pausing the screens.

We both turn to an orb, half-hovering, twinkling in the corner. It's one I thought as good as broken, and it hasn't been solar charged in months.

Gemma rushes to it just as I pluck it out of the air with my tail, grabbing it before it falls and breaks.

"How do we answer? Can we answer?" Gemma asks hurriedly.

The female calls out again. "Anybody out there?"

I turn the orb in my hand, asking it to—

"Connect us," Gemma orders.

"Connecting..." the orb responds. It works. It twinkles, glows.

Gemma grabs it from me. "Shelby, it's Gemma. What's wrong? I'm here. Are you okay?"

"Gemma! Oh, hell. You're alive! Thank god you're alive. It's good to hear your voice, any voice."

"I am." Gemma shakes her head. "What's the matter? What's happening? Are you okay? Where are you?"

"I'm trapped," the female answers on a hitch. "Under the facility. I'm trapped with *him*."

"Who?"

Shelby's voice lowers. "There's something you need to know. I've found something—" Shelby cuts off.

"What?" Gemma asks. "Shelby? Are you there? What do I need to know? Who's *him*?"

The orb twinkles one last time and dies.

"Shelby! Answer me!" Gemma yells, shaking it.

I snatch it from her before she hurts herself. "It's dead. She's gone."

"We need to find another!"

I nod, and we make our way back to my bunker at record speed, but when we reach the other orbs I've gathered, we cannot reach Shelby. The connection is gone.

"Scanning. Scanning. Scanning."

Gemma cries out in frustration, threading her fingers into her hair and pulling it away from her face. She turns to me.

"Vruksha..."

I already know what she's going to ask. I already know my answer.

I grab my spear.

Whatever comes. I'll protect what's mine.

"Scanning. Scanning. Scanning."

KING COBRA

NAGA BRIDES II

NAOMI LUCAS

KING COBRA

Daisy. Daisy. Daisy.

From the moment her name is spoken, it is all I can hear. Her tears of fear bring me anger. I vow to wipe them away and banish her fear. To make her my queen.

But I have to catch her first.

I have to convince her to trust me.

I have to show her she is safe.

But only with ME.

Because if any other naga male tries to take Daisy away from me, I will kill them.

And if she runs?

She'll find out there's no escape.

I've paid the price to mate her, and she needs to know a gilded nest is better than freedom in my world.

ONE

CAPTURED

Daisy

Gemma yanks my arm, and I stumble forward, my boots catching over a bush. Unable to regain my footing, I trip. Gemma turns back and helps me rise.

"Don't stop," she gasps, eyes darting left and right. "We can't let them gain on us!"

Panting, I chase after her through the trees but lose her.

"Gemma," I wheeze, bracing against a tree.

She comes back, grabs my arm again, and we keep running.

The forest is thick, filled with so much overgrowth it's hard to move through it. Leaves, branches, and thorns from alien plants abrade and rip at my clothes, exposing skin. Rasping, haggard breaths push my lungs to their limits, and still, I can't keep up with Gemma.

She's fierce, a fighter. She would have made a great soldier.

She's our ship's communications officer, and is being traded to alien men for tech. As am I. Gemma's presence is the only thing giving me the slightest hope of rescue. If she's here, someone on *The Dreadnaut* will notice she's gone.

Because I won't be missed...

Someone disgraced like me unexpectedly assigned to pilot the first team to our homeworld? It was legendary. I was going to be planetside for the first time in years, and of all planets, it was going to be on Earth. My father would have been proud.

My boots catch again as the land slopes down, and we both have to pause, eyeing the sharp descent.

"It's not safe," I croak, staring at the sharp ledge, the trees between us and the top. "We'll never get away." It's almost too painful to speak.

"We have to try!" She takes off to the nearest tree and flings her body against the trunk. She does it again, bracing her feet at an angle to stop from tumbling forward. From one tree to the next, she slowly makes her way down the mountainside.

Following her lead, I take it slow at first, shunting from one tree to the next. I see her reach the bottom, way ahead of me, and she glances back. "Daisy! You can do it!" she shouts.

I fall into another tree.

Something snaps behind me. I hear a breathy hiss.

No!

Pushing myself off the tree, I rush to the next one.

I fall forward, tumbling down the slope, crashing against the side of a bush. I stare at the branches above, stunned. Pain shoots up my side as Gemma's face appears above me and she tugs me to my feet. My hair snags on a branch and rips from my scalp.

"Come on, Daisy! You can do it!"

I don't know how long we've been running or how far we've gone. The shadows are lengthening. We started running when the Earth's sun was at its zenith, when Peter and Collins dragged us out of the skiff, exchanging us for a box from the large alien male who made all of this happen. Then Peter and Collins flew away, leaving Gemma and me at the mercy of the aliens.

The big, scary one had come right up to me. He leaned down, looked into my eyes, and scowled.

He scowled like he was furious at what Peter and Collins presented him with. Me. As if he knew I was an outcast. That I was weak. And all I could do was stare. Even when Gemma grasped my hand and jerked me behind her, all I could do was stare.

Because despite how giant and frightening the alien was, he smelled really, really good.

Something crashes behind us, and Gemma sprints forward, leaving me behind. I try to keep up. I claw at my chest, grasping my jacket. I can't lose her. She's the only thing keeping me from losing my ever-living mind.

The noises grow louder. They're getting closer. A tear rips from my eye.

I can feel hands grabbing at me, catching my hair and capturing me. I'm about to scream for her when I run into her back. She stumbles forward as we nearly tumble to the ground. I drop to my knees.

She grabs my shoulder and squeezes, and I almost lose it.

"We have to climb," she gasps. "Go!"

I look up to see what she means. Right before us is a ledge and a short rocky slope of boulders. It's the only way we can go.

The sounds of pursuit continue to grow. They're coming from multiple directions. I snap to my feet and take to the ledge. Gemma catches my foot and pushes me up. I pivot back to grab her hand, eager to finally help her, when something yanks me off the ground.

No!

I scream as Gemma gets smaller and smaller below me. My hair whips across my face as I'm jerked brutally around and into a hard, muscled chest. Pain lashes my side as a thick arm presses hard against it. The scent of musk invades my nose as trees blur past me.

The smell makes me vomit. It's bitter and sickening, like sulfur. I try to twist back to Gemma. Bands of steel stop me.

My arm snaps back as I'm flung through the air. The thing holding me hits a tree, jerks me higher in his arms, and jumps to the next one. I glimpse his face and shriek.

Yellow eyes, yellow skin, and even yellow lips. Two large fangs eclipse my vision before I'm tossed violently to the side.

Fighting with every last shred of strength I have, I kick and scream, tearing at him. He clutches me to his chest, ignoring my attempts to hurt him. My teeth snap together the next time he jumps. My neck wrenches.

He's going to kill me.

I'm going to die.

I scream for Gemma.

My nails drag across rough skin, catching on scales that rise as I touch them. Slamming my knees into the male's tail brings me more pain, and has little effect on the brute. Growing desperate when we hit the next tree, I manage to get my hands up his chest to wrap them around his neck. I don't want to die.

Tough flesh stops me from choking him with any real effect.

"Let me go!" I shout, returning to my thrashing.

He grabs a section of my hair and forces my head back. "Ssstop making noise," he hisses, snapping his fangs at me, his eyes devoid of intelligence.

I thrust back, terrified he's going to bite me when he drops us to the forest floor. Limbs locked from the sudden weightless and abrupt stop, the male releases me and forces me to the ground.

Claws rake down my body, shredding my uniform in a single sweep. Chilly evening air breezes my skin as the male tears my clothes from my body. I realize what he's doing when he gets to my boots and his nails aren't able to shred them.

I kick him hard in the face.

Rearing, the alien arcs back and grabs his face. "Rabid female!" he bellows thickly. His tail slams the ground beside my body, and the ground trembles. "You will submit! I am in pain!"

Twisting over, I hold what's left of my clothes to me as I crawl away. I don't get far. Fingers curl around my ankle and drag me back. "Gemma!" I scream for help, clawing at the ground, knowing there won't be any.

He thumps his giant, sickeningly yellow tail next to my head again, and I flinch. It's so huge it blocks out the forest, creating a wall of scales beside me. He rips my undershirt next. I try to hit the male again, but he catches my fist and forces it to the ground. The chill of the evening air hits my bare chest the same moment his hot breath does.

Shoving at his body, he's completely undisturbed by my struggles as a forked, meaty tongue lashes the air. "Female," he groans, tasting my terror.

I kick harder when he slides down my body, tearing off what remains of my pants, exposing my legs.

"Please!" I wheeze. "Please, don't," I beg.

He rips my pants off.

Something hard, hot, and thick falls upon my shin, and I cry out.

"Female," the alien groans, sliding the hot appendage up my leg. "You are mine."

I turn my head and brace for what's to come. The fight has left me. I can barely rise and can't catch my breath. All I can do now is hope I survive.

Hope it doesn't hurt, hope it doesn't last long.

The soft sensation of smoothed-out scales chafes my inner thighs as his tail forces my legs apart. His tail is so large, it forces my thighs and knees to the ground. I try to close them but can't, trapped under a wall of undulating muscle. His giant genitalia is lodged between us.

Closing my eyes with a whimper, I glimpse something shiny next to my head.

The knife.

This morning, while taking my last shower on the transport ship, Shelby, forced to guard Gemma and me so we didn't run or send a message to the Central Command, slipped a knife under my unit. I'd hidden it under my clothes...

A wet tongue slides over my breasts, fingers snaking around my neck as the alien pushes his cock to my open, dry sex. The male hisses when he's unable to easily thrust into me and bows his head down to peer between our legs, completely unaware of the knife.

Sliding my hand over to it, I grasp it, wiggling it free of its sheath and aim. Shaking terribly, I miss.

He doesn't even notice, gripping his member and trying to get it inside me. He's going to have to rip me in two to make it fit.

I bring my hand back, and a fleeting calm washes over me. I aim again.

And with everything I have, I sink it deep into the side of his neck.

I drop my hand as blood gushes from the wound.

The male jerks, his tail swipes out wildly, and he rises to meet my wide eyes as his hand releases my neck. Snatching my hand to my chest, he grabs the hilt of the knife and yanks it out of his neck.

Blood spurts from the wound and all over my face.

Run.

Twisting onto my front, I scurry out from under him as he brings the knife forward, pausing to look at it.

I don't wait to watch. Reaching down to grab at the shredded clothes next to me, I crawl away, putting as much distance between us as possible. I pray the wound is enough to stop him from chasing me.

I don't know how long I run, how many times I stop to listen, or when I find the strength to get back to my feet. I keep going until the sun sinks below the horizon and darkness blankets the forest. It's not until I'm about to faint that I collapse and curl up on my side. Bringing my ruined clothes to my chest, I sob until sleep takes me away, until my nostrils fill with the sweet scent of a different male...

TWO
ZAKU, KING OF THE FOREST

Zaku

I GIVE the human male his box of broken tech and dismiss him and his guard from my mind. He flees back to his ship and leaves. *Coward.*

Good.

Cowards are easy to control. *Yesss.*

If it weren't for their weapons, I would kill them and the rest. Only I do not know how powerful they are. I want to see them dead. I wish them all dead, or at least exiled. I am king of these lands and I do not suffer interlopers. The humans are trespassers and should not be here. They had their shot at Earth, and they will not get another. I'll make sure of that.

But the females... the females can stay.

Heading for the human ones now, I scowl as the crying one, the one with long light-colored hair held back from her face, flinches as I approach.

She cries? Why does she cry? A beauty such as her should never have a reason to cry.

Standing across from me is the most enchanting female I have ever seen. And she is not even nagakind. Except she is crying? Her glistening eyes glance at me before cutting away to the others. My scowl deepens. I want her eyes on me, and only me. Even if they are wet, even if they show fear.

They return to me like they hear my thoughts. *Good female. Keep your eyes on your king.* They widen as I move closer to get a better look at them, and it's the terror etched deep there that brings my anger to the surface.

I will not be feared by you! I growl.

Human, naga, or otherwise. Females are valuable. They bring males power, and power is all that matters. Dominion. Control. I am a king, and a king cannot rule without his queen. I have waited decades for my queen.

She holds my gaze as I stare. Pools of soft brown glitter and glint, framed by dark lashes that cling together. A teardrop forms, slipping down her soft, pinkened cheek. I curl my fingers into my palm, wanting to catch it.

I flick my tongue out for a taste.

The red-headed female comes forward and hides the blonde behind her back. My tail thumps.

"What do you want from us?" she demands, but there's a tremor in her voice. Is this one also scared? Is she trying to hide her fear?

What have their males done to them that they fear males so much? Better males at that.

Agitated that she hides the fearful one, I face her. "You will submit to one of usss."

"We'll never submit," she quips. "We're not items—we're not yours. We'll never be yours."

My brow arcs. "You will be hunted, and the best of us, the one who captures you, will covet you within his nest."

Vruksha hisses, stealing the red-headed female's attention. I stop from striking him down and starting a brawl here and now. How dare he interrupt me? This is my deal with the humans—mine! It's only out of fairness that I allow the other nagas to have a chance at one of them.

If I want both, my subjects should bow their heads and move out of my path.

"Run," Vruksha snaps. "So I may catch you," he tells the red-headed one, rising over her, urging her to flee.

"What?" she says, recoiling.

Vruksha presses into her until she's stumbling backward, trying to get away.

"Daisy," she gasps, keeping her hold on the crying one. "Run!" she shouts, and then both females are stumbling, catching their footing, fleeing into the forest.

Hoots and shouts rise up from the males, a cacophony of all the nagas hiding in the forest, waiting for this moment. This once-in-a-life-time chance to have a mate of their own. Trees shift, branches shake, and pine cones fall. One moment I see the females, and the next? They're gone.

Vruksha surges forward, and I miss him with my tail, but I catch Vagan before he hits the tree-line. The Blue Coral spins back to me. "Zaku," he snarls.

Twisting my tail up his before he can react, I sling him over the cliff. I hear a yell, a thud, and then nothing.

Then I'm in the clearing alone.

Taking off, I sprint after the others.

Something stabs at my right, and I fling to the side, glimpsing the Cottonmouth. He rams into me and bites down on my cowl. I rip him off me before he unleashes his venom. *He is not a king,* I hiss. *He's not worthy of a female before me!* I fall atop him as he rises, raking my claws down his chest. Bellowing, he hits my back with his tail, and I use mine to wrap around his head.

He thumps me with his tail again as my grip tightens. The Cottonmouth thrashes as his skull breaks under my coiled limb.

I encounter Jyarka of the Diamondback clan next. For a moment, I pause, thinking Jyarka died long ago. Below him lies a squirming Boa that he's beating. Blood is everywhere, and my cowl flares as its metallic scent invades my nose.

I sneak up behind him and sink my teeth into his shoulder. Venom gushes as he tries to tear me off him. Wrapping my body around his, I hold him prone until paralysis takes over his limbs. He drops atop the lifeless Boa.

Four down.

I hear a noise and head in its direction, finding Xenos of the Sidewinder clan hanging limp and lifeless over a large branch. Three vicious bitemarks rent his upper back, and entire chunks of flesh are torn from his body. I smell Vruksha's venom. Slipping past Xenos, I follow the noise.

It continues ahead, leaving messy tracks for me to follow. *The females,* I lick my lips. No naga would leave such blatant marks behind.

I will kill all the other males until I catch one, eliminating my competition. I have felled hundreds, vastly diminishing our numbers over the years, I will destroy more.

"Gemma!" a feminine voice cries out. It's in the distance. My head snaps up. It's the voice of the crying one. Soft, shrill with fear, it vibrates through my chest. Her terror stabs me, constricting my heart. She does not need to be afraid.

I will make certain she knows this.

No queen of mine should ever feel fear.

I surge in the direction of her call, forgetting the tracks entirely, coming across another male I'm forced to dismember.

Soon, the sounds of the chase vanish. One by one, males are taken out by each other, and while I come upon either their corpses and broken bodies, I don't reach the females. As the minutes pass by, my frustration rises.

The slopes grow steeper. The shadows lengthen. Minutes become hours.

Where are they? My heart quickens uncomfortably.

I am like Vagan; I am not a tracker. I didn't fear this because a king is never second to anyone. There is nothing for me to worry about. I want to wring Vruksha's neck for telling the females to run before my queen had a chance to deny all others and come to me.

She was about to. I know it.

No male would take the mate his king demands. Especially when it's their king who bartered for them in the first place. They are my right. Both females are.

But I am a generous ruler and only want one.

A *king* can only have one queen. Harems breed discontent and strife. Wet eyes fill my head, and pale, ruddy skin. My tail goes rigid, forcing me to stop as the female's face consumes my thoughts. If I wasn't sure who my queen was before, I am now.

It is not the red-headed one.

Wiping my hand down my slick chest, I look down at the shaft emerging from my tail, long and thick. Spill floods into it hard and fast. The sensation rips a groan from my throat. Cupping the appendage with my hand, it grows larger until I grit with pain.

I squeeze the knot forming in the middle, overcome with intense pleasure. I knead the pressure away. I squeeze harder, wrapping my fingers as far as they'll go, and sink to the forest floor. Slicing my hand furiously, I rub violently, maddened with the onslaught of sensation.

Tears, brown eyes and soft skin is all I see, and the tension escalates. Unbelievable beauty. How was I not aware the humans brought us such a gift from the sky? I never saw this Daisy—a flower—while I scouted the facility's perimeter these past weeks. If I had...

More spill jets into my shaft. More spill than my knot as ever endured.

What—what is happening to me?

I curl on my side, brought low by something I've never experienced, needing this human female—to the point of torture. Mouth gaping, rabid hissing escapes through my clenched teeth. I rut my hand, imagining tears slipping over soft cheeks to drip from a slender jaw. Mine?

Mine. Oh yes, mine.

I take my member with both my hands and shunt into them, writhing and coiling. Imagining glistening brown eyes beneath me as I thrust savagely. I spill all over dry, dead leaves. My knot immediately fills back up. I pump it again with an annoyed rumble, using both hands to take it on, vaguely aware I need to find my mate before nightfall.

Why is this happening to me?

I release a raspy breath, my tail coiling tight around me, I beg to whatever tech is out there to make my seed stop. My pleas go unheard. The shadows deepen, and the sound of crickets takes over. Grunting, I force my hands from my swollen member and push it into my tail. Collecting my thoughts, I rise. I am wasting precious time.

I stare at my seed that's now covering the leaves beneath me. Never have I done such a thing. My member has never reacted the way it just did. *Like it sensed its mate.* I glance around, expecting to see her.

All I see are shadows, trees, and bushes. They press into my sides.

Snapping back into action, I don't know how much time I've lost. I will not let my queen spend her first night alone—or with another. Clenching my fists, I take off.

I come across a trail, and I follow it. Heart thundering, the moon rises and the light fades. Each moment, the forest darkens more and more. I must find her before it gets any darker.

Fear niggles its way into my gut, and my muscles bunch. Darker and darker the night gets, so dark that I lose the trail and roar to the sky. This is not what I planned. By now, I should have had her coiled up in my limbs. I remember my wasted spill and hiss.

I slam my tail against a tree, snapping it in two.

The tree crashes to the ground, and I spy something pale in the corner of my eye. Venom floods my fangs as I turn toward it.

A Python male lies unmoving in the brush. I recognize his pale yellow coloring and scent his blood. Poking him with my tail, he wakens and groans. His head lolls to the side. I don't recognize him. He may be new to my forest or maybe we just have not yet encountered one another. Beside him, hovering at his head, is an orb. Its blinking lights brighten his face.

"Where are they?" I demand.

Eyes glazed in the moonlight, he lifts his bloody hand and reaches for something in the grass. Turning, I find a small object wet with blood. I take it before the Python can, discovering a knife.

A human knife. It's wet. I bring it to my nose and sniff, relieved to find that it's not human blood on it, but the Python's.

She's near. I puff out my chest.

I pluck the Python's orb out of the air and reset it so it recognizes me as its master instead.

The Python hisses low. "Are you going to kill me, Cobra?" he chokes out, blood leaking from his mouth.

"King Cobra," I correct him. "The female didn't want you," I say, turning away, happy in my knowledge that the human females should not be taken for granted. They bring weapons. They are strong and crafty.

I will not underestimate them.

I take off into the forest, leaving the wounded Python behind.

THREE
DAISY WAKES UP

Daisy

I don't sleep long. Moaning, I peel open my eyes, wishing I could go back to sweet oblivion, but the cold night air stops that from happening. I hug my ruined clothes, wishing for a lot more than sleep.

My bunk on the transport ship is one of those wishes, and having never left *The Dreadnaut* is another. A blanket, a cup of coffee, and the annoying chatter of the two kids who live in the rooms next to mine would be nice as well. I like those kids, more than anyone else in the universe, despite the noise they make. I promised to bring them back a souvenir...

Faces of other kids rise in my head. I shove the memory away.

In slow, jerky movements, I untangle my clothes, trying not to cry out. Placing my hand on my chest, my heart still pounds. Only now that my adrenaline's gone, the cold has crept in.

Feeling my jacket, I straighten it out and slip my arms through the sleeves. The front is torn to pieces, but after I tie the ends together, there's enough left to cover my chest. I grab my pants and breathe a thank you to whatever god is out there when I unravel them. The sides are ripped, but there's enough cloth to band it around my waist.

I slide one pant leg between my thighs and bring it up to tie it with the other one. It takes me at least a dozen tries before I manage to form some sort of loin cloth-like covering. I pause to feel between my legs and make sure I wasn't hurt... *there.*

Everything hurts. Who am I kidding? Thankfully, there's no pain when I probe my sex. I exhale. I curl up and burrow my face into my sleeve.

You were trained for situations like this, I remind myself. *Hold it together.*

Growing up in a military family, with a dad who's considered a hero —a brilliant commander before his death—it was apparent I'd be entering into the service as well, joining the fight against the Ketts. While I'd gotten into all the best academies and did okay in all my courses, I never felt any pride. I knew the entire time I was in training that I wasn't made for war. I wasn't made for death.

The first time I shot down a ship, I couldn't sleep for weeks, haunted by the beings inside it.

Still, it was *my* life, and it was expected that I give it to the demands of the greater good. There was no gilded cage for the daughter of a war hero. I was meant to sacrifice. I was not shielded. Ever.

Violence, torture, exploitation, mind control, cannibalism, and rape. I've seen it all in one way or another.

The Ketts, though unrepentant, bloodthirsty eaters, didn't torture, exploit, cannibalize, control minds, or rape. I was conditioned to it regardless, and far more, far worse.

I press my face harder into my sleeve. A cadet never knew what colony they were going to be sent to for field training, and humans were as despicable as any other alien species. Some alien cultures are worse still.

I never want to encounter a Gestri, a horse-like species from the planet Illa that can manipulate and control a human's mind with ease. I once saw a video where they forced a man to rape himself... and then eat his genitals. It was punishment for a crime he committed, a murder of one of their elders. Still... It was a lot. It was horrible.

I pull my hand out from between my legs and wipe my fingers on the grass.

I got lucky.

But I don't have Shelby's knife anymore. I curl my knees tighter into me and wince when my scraped knees rub against my jacket.

I don't have clothes.

My boots are still on. I wiggle my toes. *And I'm hungry, dehydrated, and cold.*

I'm alive, though.

Gemma's gone.

I'm...alone.

Thoughts tumble through my head. I'm not fully aware when the Earth's sun crests, but as the shadows weaken, tweeting and chirps sound in the air. None of the noises from yesterday return. There's no hissing or shouts of pain, no hoots or calls. Just the breezy rustle of leaves and the calls of animals. I look up to see the sky through the trees. It's grey and gold.

Yesterday was a nightmare, only a nightmare... I wish I believed it.

Watching the sky change to a light, airy blue, I sit there numbly. My throbbing muscles are bearable when I hold still. Maybe if I remain as quiet as possible, the forest and everything in it will forget about me.

I peer around, and every direction looks the same. Fat bushes with berries press against me on either side. There are tiny thorns on their stems that prick my skin. Twigs and leaves are caught in my hair, and there's something wet. I reach up to touch the side of my head, and my fingers come away sticky.

Red berry juice smears the pads of my fingers as I rub them together. Sniffing it, my nose wrinkles. I wipe my fingers on the ground again and pluck a berry from the bush, spinning it. Reddish-pink, the dimpled orb has an indent.

I set it aside, not yet willing to risk being poisoned. I'm not starving... yet.

Closing my eyes, I take a deep breath. *You can do it. Just stand. You can stand.*

I shift onto my hands and knees and my body screams in protest. I bite back a groan. When I'm certain I'm not going to topple over, I bring one foot forward and shift my weight onto it. It takes me several grueling minutes.

Walking is easier—I have no idea why. I pick the direction in front of me and start heading that way. I'm on a gentle slope.

The facility is outside the gorge. There's forest on every side of it and mountains nearby. Going down is better than up, I decide. I'll know soon if I'm in the gorge or outside it. Doubts emerge anyway.

I can't be more than a couple of miles from the facility. If I can evade the aliens, I'll find my way back to it. I frown, imagining it.

Seeing the barriers, walking in, hailing the team members... And coming face to face with Peter.

Peter might give me back to the aliens.

Should I go back?

Stopping to rest, I head for a tree with large, low branches and climb under them to get out of the sun.

I need a plan.

Captain Peter will give me to the aliens again if I go back—perhaps for even more tech. The facility isn't safe for me or any human woman, and Earth isn't safe either. The only women on the planet are Shelby, Gemma, and me, and Peter wanted to give all three of us to the aliens.

The Dreadnaut will care about Gemma, since she's ranked and knows those in command, but I'm just a petty officer. A pilot. No one of real importance, and exiled. No one is coming for me; no one's going to save little ol' Daisy from the aliens. I'm insubordinate, I *care* too much, and I have too many emotions. It was my compassion that sent me from the front lines of the war against the ravenous Ketts and to serve an old support warship colony like *The Dreadnaut.*

Not even my father's legacy shielded my compassion. I tried for years to numb it, and for a time I had...

Instead of joining my teammates to battle the encroaching blobs assaulting Colony 4, coming on like a tidal wave, I spied a pair of children crying on the roof of one of the buildings below. No older than four world spins, a little boy was cradling his younger sister, a babe, behind a water barrel.

I saw the Ketts coming, the fire, the blasts. I heard screams for reinforcements in my earbuds, instead, I turned back, landed, saved the babies, and took them to base, leaving my battalion behind to fight and die alone. And they died. Every last one of them.

Within hours, I was stripped of my rank and sent to serve *The Dreadnaut,* billions of miles away. I would have been killed but my father's name saved me.

Still, those in higher castes will never help me.

I rub my face. This shouldn't be my problem. I shouldn't be here. *I'm just the fucking pilot.* I know very little about Earth. I'm not part of the team here, not really.

A branch snaps to my right, and my head shoots up. Tensing, I pull my limbs to my body and listen, hearing more snapping and the heavy fling of a tree branch. Fear hits me hard, and everything from the night before comes crashing back.

The terror, the anxiety, the assault.

Something moves through the forest ahead of me. Something giant. I force my joints to unlock and slowly slip to the ground, trying to hide, and praying the simple movement won't alert it.

It's one of them. I stop breathing.

A very long, very large tail slides by, revealing pale beige skin with thick black stripes. I recognize the coloring immediately, recalling the monstrous serpentine alien with a cowl on the plateau. He handed the tech to Peter; he stared at me and scowled like I was a disappointment. I've seen that same look so many times... My chest tightens, and I close my eyes waiting for him to pass.

I get a whiff of his scent, and my throat tightens. I nearly moan.

I dreamed of this scent. His scent.

It angers me. I want to grab my nose, tear it off, and scream.

Something like him, even his smell, shouldn't be lingering in my head, not with how awful he is, bartering for flesh like it isn't against intergalactic law. Even those in the lowest castes, like me, are protected by that law.

His tail continues sliding by me, unending. It's big. This alien was the largest of the males on the plateau. Of all the things I recall about him and the way he looks, I recall his size. *One thump of that tail could crush me.*

I hold still, waiting until he passes and I don't hear him anymore. And then I wait a little longer before crawling out of my hiding place. Ignoring my throbbing muscles and bruises, I head in the opposite direction from where he went, hurrying my steps. Trying to be as quiet as possible, I fail horribly.

When I don't hear the sounds of pursuit, I start to breathe easier.

I lost him.

Another handful of minutes pass, scurrying as far as I can, when I see water between the trees. Excited, I dash forward until I'm at the edge of a lake.

I saw this lake when I landed the transport ship a month ago. I flew over it.

I'm still close to the facility.

Except I'm in the gorge, not outside it.

I've spent hours studying the maps of this region.

I clap my hands together at my luck and slide down the small bank to the lake's edge. I glimpse my haggard reflection as I cup a handful of water and bring it to my mouth. I'm covered in dirt and flecks of dried blood, and my long hair is a cloud of knots with sticks and leaves caught up in it. The water ripples from my hands and my reflection blurs.

I swallow greedily. When my belly is about to explode, I glance around to make sure I'm alone and scoop up water to clean my face and hands. Coyly, I clean between my legs as well.

If I follow the lake north until it ends and then go northeast from there, I'll be right back at the facility. I look behind me at the mountain slope I just came down. If I go back up toward the plateau, I can get to the facility even quicker.

I push to my feet.

"I've found you," a deep voice says.

My stomach plummets.

I slowly turn. Up on the ledge, the big one with the cowl is staring at me. The giant. The barterer. Our eyes meet and my soul shrivels. *Not him.*

I scream.

FOUR
MY QUEEN

Zaku

I'VE FINALLY FOUND HER.

I can barely hiss, barely breathe. My wicked loins leak with seed, spilling out from behind my scales. I am an idiot for taking the time to dismantle the others, for spreading my seed, when I should have been hunting for my mate.

The Python's orb mentioned only one female is near me, and I hoped it was the one who's mine. The one who hurt him... It excites me.

I feared it would be the redhead I would come upon. She seemed more likely to fight back. But it's not the redhead who has invaded my every thought; she's not the one making my body turn against me. I don't want her, even knowing the rare creature she is. She is not my queen.

My queen is scared, though not scared enough to not sink her blade into the neck of one who would have her.

All night, I searched. All night, I cursed, wanting to shout to the sky, fearing I'd lost her. Even when I used the Python's orb and it told me there was a single human near my location, I feared.

A king does not fear.

Stumbling through the forest and toward the big lake, she does not yet know that she's been found, that she's been caught, and soon to be claimed so thoroughly that her mind will become as clouded as mine.

I saw her under the tree. I saw her staring at my tail. I've been trailing her since, learning what I can about her. Because I've begun to give off a different smell since my body turned against me, and I don't know why. She has done something to me and I needed to make sure it wasn't another attack of some kind. A sneaky attack. Something else I could admire about her.

Studying her, she looks harmless. My tongue tastes the air.

Her long, light hair is a wild mess down her back, with sticks and leaves poking out of it. Her legs are bare now, and the way the muscles move under her skin as she dodges branches captivates me.

How strange it must be to have legs instead of a tail. How limiting... How does she climb trees? Or protect her backside? Does she not have a single scale to protect her joints?

I slip through the forest behind her, keeping her in my sight, searching her skin for them.

She does not have scales that I can see... not a single one... Worry fills me. These humans have no natural armor. They have no fangs, no claws, nothing to guard themselves against those that wish to prey on them. I've seen human women in images and on the tech, and I have always wondered how such a species survived for so long without natural protection.

I shudder, imagining how easily she could be hurt.

It doesn't matter. I will keep her safe now. I have enough armor for both of us. I dig my claws into my palms, noticing the dirt and grime on her next, the smattering of blood.

It's not hers.

She dashes to the lake's edge when it comes into view. I hear her moan of pleasure, her gasp of wonder when she stops and looks across it to the mountains on the other side.

She comes from the sky... Do they not have lakes in the sky?

She drinks from the lake and washes her flesh. She dives her hands between her legs, rinsing there as well. Did she have to touch her body last night, like I? The thought thrills me. Clasping my member, I squeeze it once more before tucking it back into my tail. She is a small thing. She will bring me greater pleasure than my hand ever could.

Except I failed her.

She endured a cold night in the forest without me, unprotected. A queen should never have to endure such a thing.

She rises to her feet, pulls her yellowish hair away from her face, and smiles softly. My heart slams against my ribs as a streak of sunlight brightens her small form.

I must claim her now before another sees! Before another arrives, wishing for death!

Puffing out my chest, I slip out from behind my tree. "I have found you," I declare, claiming her outright for all to hear, making it known.

She twists toward me, and I expect her to gift me her shy smile. Perhaps her hands will go between her legs again...

Her smile falls. She screams, stumbles back into the water, and trips.

Confused, I jerk forward and reach for her.

"No!" she shouts, blue eyes wide with terror. "No!" She slips through my hands. Water splashes in my eyes.

No?

I hiss, reaching for her again. She evades and splashes to the left, moving further out into the lake.

"The hunt is over," I say, my voice straining as I try to catch her. More water hits my face, and I'm forced to pause and blink it out.

She ignores me, moving further away. I slice my tail to catch her, but her bare skin slips easily over my slick scales. I push through the shallows, hating the feel of the water sliding through them.

"Don't!" I bellow when she dives under and I lose sight of her.

I draw my tail back, flinging the blasted water off my limb. The lake is too big for her to swim across. Only a Blue Coral or Cottonmouth could manage such a feat. And there's no spare tech around for her to use. Gasps fill my ears as she emerges farther out and begins swimming into the deeper waters.

She's going to drown. My jaw pops, searching for something on the shore to catch her and bring her back. There's nothing.

Why is she running from me? I am a king.

The king. The only king.

Growling, the divide between us grows. Desperation strains my limbs as I stare helplessly after her. To keep her from drowning, I'm going to have to go in. I push into the water and dive forward, biting back my disgust. My tail sinks to the filmy lake bottom, scattering stones and silt. The water pulls at my limbs.

Closing in, I grab her ankle, and she shrieks, kicking me in the face. I rear back and slice my tail forward, but the water stops me from striking out and coiling around her.

"We will both drown," I choke, pushing my tail to the lake bottom instead to keep my body above the water's surface.

She dives under again, and I lose her. I thrash, searching the water, scanning the broken waves we've made. With the water so deep and clouded with disturbed silt, I can't see her. I can't see anything.

Water is my weakness. I hate it. There's only one pool I swim in, and it's heated, private. It's nothing like the lake early in the morning. Waving my arms wildly, I search, feeling for her. I will not lose her so easily.

I won't fail again.

She emerges again several lengths ahead of me. My lips twist, and I dive after her.

This time, when I catch her, she doesn't slip through my grip. My fingers close around her arm, banding around the delicate limb.

"No!" she screams again, kicking at me.

We drop into the dark depths as I tug her to my chest, and I feel for the lake's bottom to push off of it. When we break the surface, she's clinging to me, gasping.

"No more, female, no more," I tell her, spitting out lake water. I swim us back to shore.

Holding her tightly to my side, I fall onto the bank and pull my tail out from the lake. My mate pushes off me and rolls away coughing. I do not let her get far, coiling my tailtip around her ankle. She shivers violently and continues to cough. Turning on my side, I press into her back, seeking to warm her.

"The water freezes overnight," I rasp into her ear. "It is not a sssafe place to swim."

She shakes, pressing her limbs to her body, straining away from me.

"I will warm you," I continue, wrapping my arms around her small frame and pulling her into me tightly, draping my tail to slide up her front and closing her in. "My black scales catch the heat. Touch them. Let them take away the cold."

She's tense and doesn't say a word as we lie there in partial shade. She also doesn't touch my scales. I wish she would. I would like to make amends. If she is the one who stabbed the Python, she might be in shock from the kill. Her silence and shivers stop me from prying.

There will be plenty of time for that later. I am content just holding her, knowing the hunt is finally over.

I listen for predators as the sun rises higher, drying us. My member tries to emerge, but I keep it locked away. I won't mount my queen out in the open, on the dirty forest floor, drenched in lake water. She will mate me in my nest, one I have prepared for her, one where she belongs. She will wear my jewels and my collar when she opens her slit for me.

"Are you going to hurt me?" she wheezes after a time, her voice weak and winded and filled with so much sadness it startles me.

"I will never hurt you."

"Then will you let me go?"

I lift my head and study her. She's facing away from me, avoiding touching me any more than I make her. Brows wrinkled deep, there's a hand over her mouth as her eyes stare at the scales of my tail. Even like this, she is beautiful. So beautiful I almost believe I don't deserve her.

Ridiculous. I shake the thought away. I reach down and brush the wet hair on her cheek away.

She flinches at my touch.

"There is nowhere for you to go but to my nest," I say, hoping to soothe her with my words. "There you will rest and eat, and we will mate."

She falls silent again. I spend the next few minutes gathering her wet hair from her face and brushing it out with my claws. Strands of it dry and curl into soft waves around my fingers. I gently squeeze the water out that's gathered in the rest of it, enjoying the simple act of caring for another.

She is in my arms. She is protected. This is good.

"I waited for you for countless yearsss," I hiss. "I will never let you go. Never. You are safe."

She closes her eyes and whimpers.

She must still be cold... Rising, I cradle her in my arms, nuzzling her shoulder.

And with the sun warming my back, I carry my precious treasure home.

FIVE

CAPTURED AND CARRIED AWAY

Daisy

I LET the alien male carry me to wherever it is he plans to take me.

Fighting him, as weak as I am right now, is futile.

Wincing from the built-up water in my ruined jacket and the sun's rays burning my exposed legs, I'm hoping the elements kill me before we get to wherever we're going. They won't. I'm on Earth, after all. Humans evolved here, surviving on this planet for thousands and thousands of years. Somehow, I fear I won't die so easily. If there's anything I've learned growing up traveling through space, it's that humans are remarkably adaptable.

Even after attempted genocide.

Earth has been deemed safe now that the radiation levels have returned to normal. People stopped morphing into gross amalgamations after illegally landing here.

A shiver passes through me. Those first humans—those brave or stupid enough to return—whether for religious, scientific, or greedy reasons, had all suffered for their choice, growing extra heads, even brains, arms, toes. One human turned green before his bones dissolved.

Those humans all survived, which was the most horrifying thing of all. They suffered until death finally came.

Which means I'm probably going to survive too, and it makes me wish I had grabbed my knife when I ran. I stare at the forest canopy until it blurs.

If I hadn't let my compassion win, if I hadn't saved those babies, I wouldn't be here. I'd be dead, and they would be dead too. I take comfort in the fact that they're still alive and so am I.

Hours pass by. Not once does the alien stop to take a break or eat. He carries me like I weigh nothing, slithering away from the lake, through a forest that thickens, over one small mountainous hill, and toward a larger one—the largest mountain on the horizon. It's impossible to miss.

His hands clutch me, reminding me of the male who tried to rape me. This male could be taking me to a private place so he can do what he wants and not have to worry about being attacked.... That would be the smart thing to do, right?

I think I doze for a time, once I realize he's not going to immediately throw me to the ground and assault me. I don't want to sleep, but I'm so tired I can't help it, and the soft swaying of being in his arms. It's annoyingly soothing. I try to sniff him and get a whiff of his scent. It's gone.

The lake water must have washed it away.

I hope... My chest tightens. *I hope he won't hurt me.*

I startle awake when he sets me on the ground. Sitting up straight, I brace. Instead of attacking me, he moves away, perches on his ginormous tail, and yanks several shiny red orbs off of a tree. Once his hands are full, he returns and offers the orbs to me.

I turn away.

"Food," he says, his voice a low rumble.

I stare at the forest. Eventually he hisses, sets the red orbs down, and goes back to pick more. Soon there's a pile of them beside me.

"Eat," he says again, lowering on his tail to wind it behind my back. "Humans love these. I've seen it. They are called apples."

My brow furrows. That doesn't make sense. Humans don't live on Earth anymore. And unless he's seen them iconified from some of Earth's relics, how would he know they liked these apples?

"There's no humans here. You're lying," I say, facing him. I take in his bare chest, his groin region, where there's only smooth scales. My throat tightens. He's naked, except for his scales, and it's very obvious.

A body like his—minus the tail—would be favored by the military. He'd ascend in rank from his size alone.

Lucky bastard.

"I am not a liar," he barks, clearly annoyed at being called such a thing.

The other male had a big cock sticking out of his tail where this one is smooth. Do they not all have cocks? My pulse races as I hope for the miraculous, that he's a eunuch.

He did say we would mate...

I stare at his tail, unable to help it, too dazed to realize how long I've been doing it until the male shifts, startling me. My eyes cut to his face, and my cheeks heat with embarrassment. He's watching me intensely, his cowl pulled taut and framing his pointed face. His tail starts to move, and it's like I'm in a whirlpool of limbs.

My stomach twists and I pull my arms and legs closer.

"Why are you staring at my tail?" he asks a little too thickly for my liking.

I part my lips, closing them again after a second. I shake my head. "I don't want to mate you," I say. "I'm not going to mate you. Let's get this out of the way now. You'll have to force me, like the other one, if that's all you seek from me."

His expression shifts, morphing first to confusion and then to fury. Dark, slitted irises streaked with gold, blaze with emotion.

Fear breaks through my numbness, and I go rigid. Struggling to hold my tears in, I want to fight, to run, but I know I'll never get away. Not again, not without food and rest. I don't even know where I am or how far we've gone, and if it's not him who breaks me, it'll be the wilderness.

"Force... you?" he says slowly. "Force you to do what?" His cowl flares and the scales on his shoulders shoot outward. His face continues to darken.

I lean away, too frightened to answer. His tail shifts again, and I scramble back, pressing against it. He continues to rise over me.

I gape.

"You...were forced?" he growls.

He's so huge. One sweep of his tail would knock me across a room. One hit and I'd be on the ground. He could pin me beneath it and crush me. My fear becomes something more, something harder to fight. Dread.

Rational thought drops from my head as I shoot to my feet, sprinting head-first into the trees. Something snags my ankle. I kick hard and manage to break it off.

He roars.

I run, dashing through the forest in no direction except the one before me. The trees aren't thick anymore, and the bushes are gone. I sprint faster, realizing there are no hiding places. The terrain has changed since I fell asleep.

The ground begins to slope down, and I pick up speed, stumbling over my feet. There are noises behind me—loud, low hissing—and I know he's right there.

I'm not going to get away.

Stopping suddenly, I sag to the ground and sob, curling into a fetal position. My chest hurts so much. I can't breathe. I wait for him to strike me down, to do his worst.

So when he lifts me and cradles me gently, I lose it.

"Ssssshhhh," the male tries to comfort me, making everything worse.

"Why are you doing this?" I gasp. "Why me?"

He begins moving again, and I cry. I inadvertently press my nose to his chest seeking his scent and then whip my face away, disgusted with my actions.

"There are no females left in these lands, no females like me," he says softly, his fingers petting me where his hands clutch me. "You are precious and should belong to a male who deserves you. There is no one more deserving than I. You are beautiful. You are my chosen queen. My —" he clears his throat "—loins recognize you as such. The mere thought of you has filled them with seed. I will avenge you."

I cry harder. He has a cock and plans on using it. I'm disgusted and angry at his words, angry at myself for being too stupid to hope my luck hadn't run out yet.

Numbness claims me again when my tears dry up.

I don't know when it happens, but my mind blanks as the Earth's sun descends below the trees. As the moon climbs in the sky, I realize the trees are all but gone now and he's carrying me up a sloping mountain ledge. We're so high that by peering out over the horizon, the forest, the mountains, and even the lake comes into view. Untamed wilderness with deep greens and blues meets my eyes, cast in the golden hue of twilight.

It's so striking it should hurt. And yet, I just stare at it because it's something to distract me as he winds up the mountain.

To his home. To where he's taking me.

You can survive this, Daisy.

SIX

AN ANCIENT CASTLE AND HIGH-TECH TRAPPINGS

Zaku

THE PYTHON FORCED HER.

It's all I can think about. I want to topple the trees, tear out throats, and crush bones. I want blood in my mouth and my gore under my claws. It was dark when I came across him, and I had not taken the time to interrogate him, nor check if his member was out. If it was wet with human juices.

I'd smelled blood, only his blood. I did not think...

I had thought my female hurt him because she refused to be *his*. Perhaps that is what she means by "forced." But the way she whimpers, the way she turns from me, and what is clearly between us, tangles my mind with doubt. It brings back memories of the naga females who were forced to mate males against their will. The fear they had of *all* males afterward, the paranoia, and the sadness.

A dark, agitated, and furious rumble vibrates in my chest.

If that is what my female has suffered on her first night in my world, I have failed far more than I'd thought. Doubt niggles in the back of my skull. Perhaps Krellix was right...

Maybe we should have let the females choose.

I instantly dismiss the thought. I would not stand it if my female chose another over me; I would kill him and take her anyway.

If the Python forced her, then he committed the only crime we have.

The worst thing a naga could do.

I thought I was rid of them. The ones who destroyed us. I thought there were no nagas left who would risk doing such a wretched thing as raping a female. The dishonorable ones should've been gone from these lands. *I've killed so, so many...* The ones who cared nothing for life and only thought about themselves and their needs. It was because of these savage nagas that the naga females left. One forced mating could result in gestation, and gestation has always led to death.

Not humans, though. I cradle Daisy closer. I will make sure the Python is dead, that his meat is given back to the land. It's my duty to keep the others in line.

Scanning my surroundings with fervor, if any naga happens to be trailing us, he will die. My trust is gone.

Glancing down at my mate, I am certain if I spill my seed inside her, she will survive the litter that will result from our union. I have a human medical pod in my den to ensure her survival.

I've prepared—for years, I prepared—with hope that eventually she would come to me. I had nothing else to do but wait and prepare.

The naga females journeyed to the west, long ago. My mother had been dead for decades by the time it happened, and I had just matured, the only one she birthed before she perished. There is not a day that has gone by that I don't carry the weight of her death.

I didn't realize then what I do now. How dearly the males left behind would miss them. If I had, I would have followed the other females west. Some tried to follow, only the females killed them or forced them to turn back. Brothers, fathers, friends...

However, if I had followed, I'm sure they would have let me join them. I am a king, after all. Nothing is higher than a king. A king is beloved by all.

My mate has been quiet for some time, and I don't know if I like it or not. She gazes off into the distance, her face emotionless.

What did the Python do to her? Did he force his member inside her? Did he spill?

Disgust fills me at the thought.

I should have made sure he died. I should have taken the time to kill him or at least cut off his tail so he would suffer, crippled, until death finally came, until the monsters of the forest found him and finished him off.

"I will gift you his head," I growl, swallowing the venom leaking from my fangs.

Her chest rises as she inhales deeply before her breathing returns to normal. It is the only response I get from my declaration. I tear my eyes away from her.

Seeing the broken path to my den ahead, I hasten only to stop, knowing that if another naga is still hunting for a mate and knows one is with me, he may have staked out my den. It is what I would do if I were not a king and had to use other, trickier means to get what I want.

Daisy looks up at me, then around, noticing I've stopped.

"Do not make a noise," I warn, lowering my voice.

I scrutinize the few trees and boulders one might hide behind as I start heading for my den again. Unlike most nagas, my home isn't tucked away, fully hidden from the world. It's out in the open, built into the side of the tallest mountain, and can be seen from certain vantage points from miles away. Though it is camouflaged to a degree, the glass walls sometimes glint while looking upon it far in the distance.

Someone important lived here once, someone who wanted to oversee all the land below.

Someone with wealth and power. Because that is what this old human home is, a place of vast power. Through a secret tunnel, one connected to the room my nest is in, is a relay. A piece of technology—a machine—that is still working from the old world. I don't know how it works but based on research I've done from the books in this place, it helps connect all the technology in this region together.

Many males have journeyed here at one point or another, seeking to take my den from me. All have failed. And they do not even know of the power source I reside over. They do not know that their precious information orbs would stop working if I wanted them to. They do not know that I keep the Earth from dying.

Me alone.

They do not know how generous I am. Only Vruksha knows, somewhat, and it is because we once hunted down dirty rapists together.

Though my home is out in the open, it is secure, and I am not an easy male to beat in a fight. Skulls litter the ground around the entrance, a warning to any who seek to take something from me I am not willing to give away.

As I near, I see nothing waiting for us in the shadows, nothing except rocky steps, tall grass, skulls, and piles of bones. I finally relax when I reach the security panel at my den's entrance. Typing in a code, the door opens.

I carry my mate into my home.

Triumph washes over me when the door shuts. Sliding to the seating area in the large living space, I lower her upon it. She pulls her arms and legs into her, curling up as if she's trying to make herself small.

She is already tiny enough. She does not need to be smaller!

My nostrils flare.

I reach out and thread my fingers into her hair. "I am not like the Python."

She turns her head so she doesn't have to look at me. "And the bones?" she asks numbly.

I hiss. "Filth I have purged."

When she shrinks further, I realize I'm going to have to prove it to her. She doesn't know me, nor my people. She doesn't know if she can trust us. She didn't even recognize the fruit I offered her. She jumped into a frigid lake at first light...

Tonight, I decide, I will go back out and collect the Python's head.

"Rest," I say, pulling back. "I'll feed you."

Staring at her for a moment longer, until I'm certain she won't meet my eyes, I head for the kitchen. Lights turn on when I move through the wide central space of my upper den. The front of the entry space is made of glass and can be seen into by anyone who braves to get close enough. The inside is minimally decorated. The humans who built this place did not like *things*. Which is why I don't mind leaving Daisy's side. There is little she can hurt herself with, and there's no escape.

White and silver, sleek with old tech appliances, the kitchen, like the rest of my home, has glass walls and a view of the mountains and forest below. Most of my den does. The walls to the outside are either glass or the rocky mountain interior.

I hear movement, and I see my mate sprinting to the exit, yanking the handle. She shrieks when the door doesn't budge, slamming her fists against it.

"It's locked," I rumble.

She runs to another door, throwing it open and ducking inside. Something crashes from within, and she shrieks again, angrier this time.

My hands clench as I hear a sob, and she comes out of the room a few minutes later. She looks at me only to avert her eyes, striding from one room to the next in the hallway off the living area. She's not going to find anything but spare rooms. This place is like a labyrinth of nothing. Quiet, perfectly preserved, nothing.

It has barely changed since I took ownership of this place. The house won't let it change. I have destroyed it before—during times of wrath. The robots that live here just rebuild it. They are as much a menace as they are generous to the house's inhabitants.

There is another frustrated scream.

Trying to calm, I force my hands to uncurl and go to open the kitchen's icebox. Inside are slabs of raw meat from my recent kills. I place the juiciest one on the counter as she heads for the last door in the back hallway.

The red one. It's thicker than the others and has a lock like the front.

She's no longer running now that it's clear I'm not going to stop her. This den is hers now as much as it's mine.

I silently slip up behind her as she tugs the handle to the immobile door.

"My nest, little human, is beyond that door. It's locked for that reason."

She startles and faces me, pressing her back to the door. Her eyes are wide with renewed fear.

With my hands slippery with meat juices, I reach beside her and type a code into the panel next to the door. The door opens, and she slinks back onto the threshold, watching me warily.

"Our nest," I declare, "lies within the spaces the robots have chosen to block off from outsiders."

Whoever once lived here... was an unusual being. The secrets of my home are why I decided to stay. That, and the robots have decided I am the home's new master.

Her eyes hood as she turns to look within. Tension radiates through me. I've waited for this moment for years. For her, and her alone, I've helped preserve the best nest in all the world. I want to see that spark of wonder finally hit her eyes when she realizes she is beloved. No one but me has gone through this door since I claimed this space.

My mate is the most beautiful. Beautiful creatures should be worshipped and surrounded by the best. It is the least a king can do for his queen.

She glances at me, and though she scents of sweat, her skin is grimy, and her hair a tousle of tangles, I still see her beauty beneath it all. She doesn't look queenly right now. She needs a bath.

I did not see, nor smell, spill on her from the Python. It may have washed off at the lake.

Was that...why her hands were between her legs?

I grit my teeth, sickened and horrified that I touched my member while she cleaned him off of her. I need to make sure she is entirely clean of him and his repulsive fluids. I want her adorned in my wealth, and as pure as the first moment I laid eyes on her. Right now, she is dirty, and it was not me who has made her that way. I don't like it.

If I want her dirty, I'd make it so. I don't, I want her beautiful, surrounded by beautiful things, and fresh to touch.

I will not only bring back his head, but I will also bring back his member, his spine, and his hands. I will rip him apart.

"Your nest," she whispers. "Not mine."

"Take a look," I encourage her, hiding my fury.

She trembles, peering down the dark, windowless hallway and the winding stairs at the end. Until she goes down those stairs, there's nothing to see except for some pictures hanging on the walls. She turns back and evades me, denying it, us.

Hissing low, I bristle.

She doesn't seem to notice as she sidesteps and heads for the kitchen. Agitated and curious, I trail her. She stops when she sees the meat.

"Food," I growl, passing her, rubbing my tail over her legs, marking her.

She jumps away. "What is this place?"

Does she not listen? "My den."

Watching me intensely, she crosses her arms, making her jacket leak with water. "How is this possible?" she says, near cowering, keeping the counter between us. "Everything is—" her eyes flick around "—brand new. This doesn't look like a... home."

Using my claws, I cut the meat into slabs. "The robots preserve it."

Her eyes dart left and right. "Robots?"

I call out, "House, initiate cleanup." Buzzing sounds fill the space and several wall panels open to the left of me. She turns as tall, thin machines with extendable arms and screens come out. They spread out as red lasers shoot from their limbs. They probe and pick at things, straightening them or dissolving them from existence. They come out on their own to keep the house the way they want it. They also come at my command.

She watches the robots, her mouth dropping open as one comes up to her and lasers the stone tiles at her boots. The water that dripped there sizzles and evaporates. I move around the counter while she's distracted.

Stepping back, she lands against my chest.

I embrace her, but she flings herself away.

Clenching my hands, I hold in my growl. "House," I call out. "Obey her." I indicate my mate. "Make her a master of this place." I turn to her, lowering my voice. "Tell them to stop if you do not like what they're doing."

"Stop!" she sputters out, and at once, all of the robots halt what they're doing. She moves further away as she takes notice. The more I watch her, the more her responses confuse me. "You'll let them respond to me?"

"Yes."

She reaches out and touches one of the robots only to pull her hand away soon after. "They will not hurt you, nor will they hurt anyone else. They will protect this place, though, keep it how it is, and that is all."

"Unlock the front doors," she says.

One of the robots heads for the door.

I grab her arm before she can bolt after it. "Stop!" I yell, making the robots pause. "Never respond to that command. Turn off," I order them next, and they retreat to their spots in the walls. Pulling Daisy into my chest, she struggles futilely. "Stop," I command again. When she continues to thrash, I spin her and grab her wrists.

"Do you understand what would happen if you run? You are far from the plateau and your human ship now. The forests are no longer clear for the hunt. The predators will have returned by now, brought in by the lure of fresh blood in the air. This mountain is home to bears, giant felines, and far worse. Even if you do not trip and fall by descending in your current state in the dark, you will inevitably face them. What will you do then?" I scan her small form. "You have no weapon, no armor, you have no scales, claws, or even fangs to defend yourself."

Her face has gone white, and I loosen my hold on her wrists. "How can you say that? Your walls are made of glass. Nothing about this place is safe," she breathes. "How do you know my name?"

I let go of her and grab the metal dining table, lifting it above my head. With all my might, I throw the table against the nearest glass wall. A loud clang pierces the quiet space of my den as the table strikes the glass and clatters to the floor.

The glass holds.

Snagging the table with my tail, I bring it back to me, right it, and settle it back into place before the robots get to it. "See? It holds. It will always hold. Many have tried to take this place from me," I rasp, "and all have failed. I leave their heads, their bones, outside as a warning to others. I am Zaku, King Cobra, king of this mountain, king of the forest, and king of all you see before you now fading in the darkness the moon brings. No one has fought me and lived. No one."

She freezes with my words.

"Now, female, you will eat, or I will force you. I will make you beautiful again."

I turn on her and take her stunned form into my arms.

SEVEN
THE SECOND NIGHT

Daisy

HE NEVER TOLD me how he knows my name...

Sitting stiffly, I stare down at my hands in the water. Warm, clear, luxurious water that fills the giant tub I'm in.

Warm water.

A tub that's within the most decadent bathroom I've ever seen. Creamy stones make up the floor, leading to a jet-black stone basin in the center. One wall is entirely curved and made of glass, but I can't see anything out of it right now. It's dark outside, and the bathroom is lit up in a golden glow.

Like the rest of Zaku's home I've seen so far—glassy, sleek, bright, and beautifully open—the bathroom is much the same. It's off one of the side rooms, and Zaku led me here after I refused to eat any more than a couple of bites from his hand. I had let him lead me, having exhausted my pride with the shame of being fed like a child.

He could hurt me here as easily as he could hurt me anywhere in this place. It doesn't matter which room he wants me in.

The alien forced me to eat and demanded I bathe. He calls me beautiful. He calls me a queen. I grab my head as it spins.

He tried to get me inside a medical pod, which was in one of the side rooms, saying it would help me heal. He did this with a scowl on his face and his eyes staring at my legs. While I'd go in any pod on *The Dreadnaut*, I'm not about to go inside ancient technology.

Zaku hissed and took me to this bathroom instead.

He forced me to eat from his hand. I try shaking the whole episode from my head.

Instead of forgetting it, I recall the way his eyes darkened as he pressed the meat to my lips, when I relented and took a bite. I drop my hands from my head and scrub my lips clean, pumping more soap as I do.

There are gleaming silver spouts beside me, and each one is labeled in Old Human. The common tongue's origins are Old Human. *Soap, shampoo, and something called conditioner.* Testing the conditioner between my fingers, I sniff it. Vanilla fills my nose. It's nothing like the chlorinated, chemical stuff I'm used to.

It's nothing like Zaku's scent...

Pulling my limbs close, staring at the closed door and the wooden chair I leaned up against it after he left, I lather the conditioner between my hands and scrub it into my hair.

I don't know if he'll change his mind and barge in. There are no weapons in the bathroom, at least nothing that could be used against a beast like Zaku. I searched thoroughly under his gaze—as he filled the tub. He did not seem to care.

Which is concerning. I suck my lips into my mouth. How have I gone from shivering and naked in an alien forest to this? I scrub my hair feverishly.

This shouldn't be possible. This bathroom shouldn't be possible. It's one thing to encounter sentient alien life, another that they could already speak the common tongue without a translator, but this? I glance around the bathroom. This is something else.

I don't know how to handle it.

Once upon a time, did humans live this extravagantly? I almost giggle. I have no idea. I'm in one of the lowest castes in society. I haven't been near such finery since I was a babe and under the control of my father's authority.

Zaku, King of the Mountain, has everything and more. This bathroom alone has more wealth than I'll ever make in my entire life. Captain Peter and Collins would give their souls to be where I am right now. Most people would.

If I bring Peter and Collins here, perhaps they'll let me return to The Dreadnaut.

My mood sours at the thought.

I'd sooner shoot them than help them ever again. I don't like what's happening with the Ketts anymore than anyone else, but I'm not going to give a prize to the men who practically sold me into slavery.

Or matehood.

Or sexual matehood slavery. I haven't figured it out.

"What is taking you so long?" he rumbles, his voice muffled behind the door.

Tensing, I stop washing.

I might not be as afraid of him as I was earlier, but I still don't trust him. Though, if he were going to hurt me, he would have done it by now. I saw what he did with the table...

He's strong. Really, really strong.

The fact that there's a door between us means nothing—he can come in whenever he pleases.

I'm going to have to answer him or he'll come in here. Just as I think this, the lock on the door clicks.

"Wait!" I shout, covering myself. "My hair takes a long time to wash." Bracing for his entry, I stare at the door.

I hear a low, raspy hiss, and the door closes without ever opening. "I will wait," he grates.

Bending my knees, I hug them to my chest.

Maybe not all these aliens are bad.

A tremble shoots through me, and I reach between my legs to feel my sex again. The other male hadn't penetrated me, except the pressure of his cock is still there, present as a ghost. Every time he comes to mind, I feel it. I hope it vanishes soon.

I yank my hand away.

I clean my wounds in record time, and afterward, when I'm drying and watching my dirty bath water drain away, I snag the tube of moisturizer on the bathroom counter. It smells of something clean, something sweet. I could never afford something like this on *The Dreadnaut.*

Stepping up to the floor-to-ceiling mirror across from the bath, I wince. My sides are mottled purple from where the Python gripped while swinging through the trees. There are smaller bruises on my legs. My knees are scraped up, and my legs are pinkening with sun damage.

You're alive.

I quickly go to my clothes, lifting my ruined pants and jacket off the floor. They're dirty and destroyed. Grabbing the towel I dried with, I wrap it around me instead.

Reassuring myself that I'm going to be okay until I almost believe it, I head for the door and stop before it. "Zaku—" I'm hoping I say his name right "—do you have something I can wear?" I hear shifting on the other side, and I curl my arms tighter around my body.

"Wear..." I hear him murmur. He doesn't say anything more.

Shifting anxiously, I peek out. The room on the other side is empty. Exhaling, I wait for him to return.

Soon, Zaku comes back with his arms full of various cloth products, ones vibrant with more colors and patterns than I've seen in my life. He sees me in the doorway and stops.

"Female," he purrs, his golden-glinted eyes searching my face.

"Daisy," I correct with a far steadier voice than I thought I had in me. "My name is Daisy, not female. If you know it, use it."

"Like the flower," he says.

My head tilts.

"Flower?" I ask hesitantly. "I'm not named after a flower." My father named me after my great-grandmother.

"Daisies are a common flower in my forest. They are beautiful and delicate, like you."

I'm named after an Earth flower? I furrow my brow.

Now, I long to see this flower. Flowers are rare. Swallowing, I eye the cloth Zaku is holding as the strangeness of our conversation makes me increasingly uneasy.

"Can you put those clothes on the bed?" I whisper.

He straightens and dumps the clothes without taking his eyes from me. My gaze goes to his tail. I haven't given it much attention, though I've noticed it... How could I not? Long, coiled, and scaled across a furnished room—it's so out of place. It threatens to fill the space entirely.

His tail is different from the rest of him, shifting from beige, brown, and black stripes upon his upper chest, becoming straight black as his scales reach his tailtip. There are still stripes at his tailtip, but they're thin. Even his tailtip is thick.

I'm suddenly grateful he doesn't eat humans like the Ketts. I could fit inside his tail several times over. He'd need to eat a lot of humans to sustain a body like his.

Zaku's chest swells when he notices me staring. He lifts slightly and straightens even more.

Is he trying to impress me?

"Why do you hide behind the door?" he asks.

I grip my towel tighter. "I'm not dressed."

Heat floods his gaze.

"I wish to see you," he says.

My fear returns. "N-Not yet. Can you please step—uh, slip out so I can dress?"

His eyes narrow and his mouth twists, like my request is ridiculous.

He thinks I'm beautiful and called me a... queen? An idea forms, and I add before he can tell me *no*, "I want to look my best. For you. I... wish to hide my bruises."

He pauses.

"Please? For me?"

For a moment, I don't think he's buying it. He looks like he wants to argue. His hands open and close, and my eyes narrow in on his small claws.

"I wish to lick your bruises, so dresssss, and do it quickly," he hisses, his eyes glinting, his cowl expanding. "I will not wait much longer," he threatens as he leaves the room.

I scurry from the bathroom and fumble through the clothes on the bed, not needing to be threatened twice. They're all women's clothes, and it makes me wonder if another woman lives here. Then I remember where I am and who I'm with. If there was another woman, why barter for me and Gemma?

I hope she's okay. I frown. I hope I'll be okay.

Finding a pair of soft white slacks, a white shirt, and a loose, drapey sweater, I drop my towel and dress. I'm tugging the sweater on when the bedroom door flies open.

I jerk and face the door.

Zaku fills the entire frame and then some.

Piercing eyes trail over my body. He licks his lips, his gaze more feverish than before.

"Little human," he rasps thickly, coming straight for me. "It's time to nest."

EIGHT

THE ROOM

Daisy

"Let me down!" I snap, pushing at his chest. Zaku doesn't budge. He carries me out of the room and down the hallway, toward the red door at the end.

"You will sleep in my nest and only in my nest," he hisses, his hold on me tightening.

I kick my legs and arch my back. It makes no difference. The doors flash by until we're passing the threshold of the red one and crossing the empty hall with walls covered in pictures. "I will not!"

"You have walked enough for today," he says, ignoring me. "I've allowed you your bath in privacy. I allowed you to dress. I have fed you and given you all you have asked, and now you will obey me. You will sleep in my nest, or you will not sleep at all," he warns, stopping and catching my wide eyes. I pause my thrashing. "What will it be?"

And then I feel it.

Pressing up, hard and probing to my backside, between where he cradles me to his chest. Staring into his shadow-gold eyes, stunned, it takes me a moment to comprehend what's rubbing and pushing up against my ass.

His prick. His straight, hard, cock.

Hell—I writhe upward—*how is that possible?*

Zaku clutches me to his chest as I thrash even harder. Where did his cock come from?

Where did he hide *that*? It's like a dagger to my back. *No, more like a club.* And it's hot, it nearly burns.

"Calm down!" he orders, his thick voice reverberating. "Or I will spill all over your backside!"

I cower, and he tucks me back into the cradle of his arms. When he begins moving again, the pressure of his cock is gone.

"I'll sleep in your nest," I utter, still coming to terms with what I just felt. "Just keep it—that thing," I stammer, "hidden."

Without responding, he takes me down a spiral staircase. My belly jumps trying to imagine how big his cock is. It's big enough to ram into my back as he moves. I thought the other male's cock was large...

A tremble shoots through me, the ghost of pressure between my legs returning. *I stabbed him. He's gone. He can't hurt me again.*

Zaku looks down at me, and I avert my eyes.

The spiral staircase comes to an end, and I realize that there are no glass walls or windows in this new room. It would be pitch black if it weren't for the small white lights above.

Another realization hits as I turn to watch the door shut behind us.

I'm never going to be able to escape this place.

He moves deeper, and I turn to see where he's taking me now. We're in a large seating room that's shaped exactly like the one above. Except this one has no view over a lush, alien landscape. There are no windows at all. Where the one above was bright, white, and airy—even at night— this one is the opposite in every way.

The furniture is black, the tiles and walls are a dark metal grey, and instead of a kitchen, there's a pool, lit up in a midnight purple glow. He takes me across the room and toward the only door.

"My nest," he announces, his deep voice teasing my ears as he opens it, and a dim, soft golden glow reveals the room beyond.

My chest constricts when he brings me to the center. Staring at the view before me, I can't look away. The entire back wall is a window, like above, but instead of darkness, I see Earth's moon in its glory and a sky filled with stars. I untangle from Zaku's arms, and he lets me down. I walk to the window, seeing my reflection in it as I press up against it.

A forest and a mountain range cast in silvery moonlight greet me. They span for countless miles in every direction.

But it's the abrupt drop outside the window that has my throat constricting. I try to peer downward, to see how steep it is, finding nothing except impenetrable shadows. I step back from the abyss as my stomach churns.

I turn, taking in the rest of the room, trying my best to ignore the giant male—a male who fills every room to capacity—watching me.

My eyes fall on the bed. It's huge, covered in a mess of spilled blankets and large pillows. It's near the ground, situated on a pedestal that only slightly rises from the floor. The blankets pour off it like inky black liquid, making it look overly full. Like its master.

Something glints in the corner of my eye, and I turn toward it. My brow furrows.

Gold prison bars fill my vision. They climb from the floor, stopping just before the ceiling where they begin tapering, curving to come together at a point in the center. They make a large, cylindrical shape, and inside is a swing. There's a barred door, left wide open to let someone inside it.

I notice the lock. "What is that?"

"A cage," he responds.

"Like for a pet?"

"For a human, I believe."

"Why do you have it?" I whisper, hugging my body.

"It was here when I found this place."

"What is *this place*?"

He moves to the cage and wraps his fingers around one of the gold bars as if testing it. "Do you not listen? A bedroom. My nest."

That's not what I mean but I don't say this. "And behind those other doors?"

His eyes return to me as his tail slips circles behind my back. "One is a bathroom, one is a closet, and the other, I believe the house told me, is called a playroom. I do not understand why."

I don't know what's going on anymore and it scares me. I don't want to know what constitutes *"play"* for someone who has a human cage. This isn't just a house and a bedroom...

There's something really unsettling about this place.

"I want to sleep upstairs."

"No."

"I'm not sleeping here."

"You are."

"If you think that, you—"

"My mate will sleep in my nest!" he snaps, making me fall back. He reaches for me, and I scurry away. "You will not fight me on this!" He shoots forward until he's directly in front of me, catching me. He clasps my chin and forces me to meet his eyes. "Here, female, I am king. Here, you will bow down to me and submit. I have hunted you, caught you, chosen *you* for my queen." He bares his fangs. "And now you will be one."

Gone is the male who lulled me into safety, who carried me, and gave me a false sense of exhausted comfort. His tail slides up the back of my body, trapping me in his limbs.

"I'm not your mate," I wheeze. "I'll never be your *queen*."

Fury flashes in his eyes, and I brace for him to strike me.

His mouth slams on mine.

Zaku's rough, velvety lips move against mine in a frenzy—sucking, plucking, and nipping at my parted ones. Shocked, I can't respond. I feel like I'm suffocating by what's happening. Vaguely aware I'm pushing at his chest, it's the only resistance I give.

He groans and it's thick and animalistic, making my flesh prickle. He's a predator, and I'm his prey. His growls fill my mouth and slip into my throat. They puncture my soul and vibrates it from within. It's not fair. He leans into me, pushing me against his tail. I strain my back. He's too large, too overwhelming. With his hard, muscled chest flushed to mine, he's devouring me.

I stir.

His lips move on me faster when I do, completely covering my mouth and then some, far larger than mine. Clawed fingers tangle into my air, tickling my scalp. They move downward.

His scales are hot, warming my skin where they're pressed to my skin.

He pushes my legs apart, sliding between them, and the club of his alien cock falls out. He undulates and his tail rubs over my sex. A spike of sensation rips through me, consuming my mind.

A forked tongue invades my mouth, and I gasp, finally responding.

"No!" I tear from his hold, from fingers whispering across my body, from the coiled tailtip tangled in my hair. "No," I whimper, feeling my eyes burdened with tears. I hate that they do. I reach for a pillow and grip it, using it as a shield.

I try not to cry, but my tears fall anyway.

Sobbing, everything hits me all at once, and it's like the floodgates opening. I was almost raped, I almost died. I murdered someone. Glimpsing Zaku's horrified expression as he backs away, makes it worse.

I was betrayed by my own people. Again.

I'm *lost*.

I'm alone. Again.

I'm alone when I finally fall asleep.

NINE

A BLOODY TRAIL OF VENGEANCE

Zaku

I CLAW my way out of my room and to the other side of my den, putting distance between me and my... Daisy before I do something I'll regret.

Why won't her tears leave my head? I head for the exit of my home.

She scrambled to the other side of the room, acting like if she didn't get away, I would hurt her, or worse. Tension radiates from me. It wafts in the air and my nostrils flare, scenting the new smell my body has begun creating.

She is mine! My body knows this—does hers not?

Then I remembered the Python. I remember the fear I incite in others as I near them. I'd forgotten in the excitement of seeing Daisy dressed in clothes I provided, of carrying her down to my nest for the first time that I am a male to be feared.

My member is swollen past the point of pain. All I wanted to do was grab her and shake her into her senses.

Jutting out of me now, my cock swells. I yank the wretched thing, squeezing the giant bulge expanding in the middle. All day, its pressure has tortured me. I wanted to jump my Daisy and mount her; I wanted to invade her bath and plant her onto my stem until it was she who bathed me, until she was even dirtier than before, a mess from my spill.

After, I would clean her at my leisure, satiated. I would lick her wounds and convince her to let the medical pod heal the blemishes on her skin.

Instead of heading for the exit, I turn for the bathroom Daisy had bathed in.

Waiting outside her bath, knowing she was full of the meat I hunted for her, knowing she was naked and her sex would be easy to see, easy to mount, was hellish. It had driven all rational thought from my mind. Staring at the room now, being cleaned by robots, I grip my shaft and force my seed out.

Spilling it all over the tiles, I yank my member until I'm able to tuck it back into my tail comfortably. The pressure will return, but for this moment, my mind is clearer. Shame hits, staring down at my seed.

My lack of finesse is unbecoming.

I scared her. Because another male hurt her. Because I am a male to be feared

She's crying.

Again.

My mouth fills with venom.

I tell the robots to take care of her—to *not* let her leave—as I head outside.

The sun is ascending above the mountains, and a soft pink glow is bleeding into the waning blue night when I leave. An early morning chill breezes across my scales. I hate dawn for this reason. I prefer direct sunlight.

I descend the mountain path with speed.

This is the first day Daisy is in my den. I should be with her, coiled around her. Instead, I am hunting. If I can't have her, I can at least have my bloodlust.

Only the Python's head, his spine splayed out, his fangs ripped from his skull, will sate me now.

His head will be the first of many gifts I give my female.

She will see it and worship me. She will know that I will destroy her admirers and her enemies.

Morning vanishes into noon. I know these lands like the pattern of my scales. And without a delicate, scaleless human to protect, I am unhindered. The chill of dawn fades in favor of a hot, summer day. Invigorated, I snatch a rabbit as it flees. It struggles for a moment before

I snap its neck and cut my fangs through its fur, stripping it off to devour the meat.

If the Python lives, I'll need my strength to finish him off. We are hard to kill. We regenerate if we're not adequately destroyed. It's annoying.

Fury fills me for leaving him—and the rest of the nagas—alive. I won't make that mistake again. Perhaps I should have obliterated all of them. If I had, they would not be the nuisances they are now.

Passing through the gorge, I angle in the direction of the lake. I climb up a ledge and scan the treetops, locating the general area I last saw the Python. If he hasn't slithered away or been eaten by bears, pigs, or worse, he'll still be in the area.

There are worse things in my forest than animals. Creatures like *me* that I used to spend a great deal of time hunting so they would not take over my land. When I was a young serpent, there were more monsters than nagas. Now, they are rare.

But if any monsters show up...

I will kill them like I always have.

The sun is lowering when I find the very spot I captured Daisy. Stopping at the shore, my member shoots from my tail, imagining her bare legs.

Hissing, I grab it and stuff it back in, following my old trail. When snake blood fills my nostrils, I pick up speed.

Bursting through the trees, I come upon ground soaked with it, but no male. The Python's gone. Slamming my tail against the nearest tree, I crack the trunk. In the light, my eyes take in the area.

Picking up a piece of cloth the same color as Daisy's ruined pants, I grip it in my fist and bring it to my nose, inhaling her scent. I glimpse more shreds of cloth nearby.

He tore her clothes.

He left her practically naked in the cold night. She is scaleless and small!

I roar. This male forced himself upon my female, tore her clothes. I gather up everything I can, making sure nothing of Daisy's is left behind. Everything of hers, is mine. I will cherish every piece of her. I tie the cloth together, using the shirt to band everything around my arm, as I glare at the bloody spot on the ground.

It is good he did not make her bleed. My breath wheezes through my teeth. I needed to see this.

Eyeing the blood, I notice a trail leading away, in the opposite direction of the lake, and back up toward the mountain slopes. Checking the sun's position, I realize I won't make it back to Daisy tonight.

He will pay for that as well.

Once again, I must make a choice... I hiss furiously.

I go after the Python.

TEN
A HEAD FOR A HEAD

Zaku

I follow the trail until I lose it in the darkness.

The Python continues to bleed. His wound is deep. Daisy nicked a vein, and thanks to that I'm able to track his path. By staying low to the ground, his blood is enough to lead me, even in the dark.

My female is fierce and direct. I will remember this. But I am certain I'll never give her a reason to stab me. That is a mess I wouldn't like to clean. Though my member is another story entirely. It wants to stab repeatedly.

I groan as it falls out of my tail again, too big to stay within comfortably, and absently tug it as I continue. At least the darkness is good for something. It hides my shame.

The scent of the blood builds, and I lift, narrowing my eyes. I spill my seed and shove my shaft away. There's too much blood to be distracted. I slow my pace and listen. Chirps of insects sound in my ears but nothing else. I continue on until I realize it's a different scent that's now leading me.

It's not just the Python's blood in the air anymore... I taste the air. *Pig*.

Coming across a pig's corpse soon after, I pause to check it out.

Mangled and broken, it's twisted into two halves. Chunks of flesh have been torn from the main part of the body—and it's still bleeding. A fresh kill. A recent one. From the way the body has been left behind, the Python caught it up in its tail and choked the life out of it. His clan wasn't blessed with venom, only strength.

If there's one pig, there's more.

Slipping into the shadows, I move on.

I come across several more in the next clearing. The branches are broken; the ground is flattened. There was a struggle here. One of the pigs wheezes, and I smash its head in with my tail. Tearing off its back leg, I don't let the fresh meat go to waste.

He's close.

I scan the shadows.

I scent him in the breeze, his sweat, his musk. There's also dirt and… rot? His scent is strange, like mine, and it churns my stomach.

Good. He's intact and alive.

I get to make him suffer. He needs to suffer. He's caused me much strife these last two days, and for that alone, deserves death. For hurting my mate, he will endure tremendous pain during his last moments in this world. Devastating, shameful pain.

Leaving my mate behind has to be worth something. She will forgive me if I bring her back the Python's head. She will look at it and smile, seeing the torment I caused in his dead eyes. And once her fear has been abated, she will embrace me and take all I have to offer. She will know.

I finish off the pig leg, flicking my tongue through my fingers to lap the blood.

Daisy won't have any choice but to accept me if I give her the head of the one who hurt her. Hissing, I slink forward. If she fears my kind, I will gift her all their heads.

Another clearing is ahead of me, and the sounds of slurping, cracking, and thumping reach my ears. Something moves, a dark shape amongst the leaves. It's bowed over another form, a twitching one.

The Python. I lick my fangs, readying for my vengeance.

Blood shoots into the air, and then it's gone.

I slither forward, careful not to make a sound as I slip my tailtip toward him through the overgrowth. He's had days to regenerate, his strength may have returned.

I hear an oink to the right of me, and a pig crashes through the trees.

I still as the Python jerks back and snarls. Rabid and angry, the pig attacks him head-on. *Dumb creature.* The Python snags its back leg and yanks the hog into the air. It squeals and writhes. Its leg snaps, tearing from taut tendons.

The Python holds it there for a moment, watching the pig's misery before he slams it onto the ground and coils his tail around its body. Another crack, a squeal and a crunch, and it's dead.

The Python returns to his meal.

Feral, savage male.

My fangs drip as I approach, snaking my tail slowly through the moss.

I grab his tail and yank it hard away from him. He startles and reacts, jerking his tail back, but not before I shoot forward and throw my body atop it. My weight is enough to hold it down. He is weak from his wounds.

Our eyes meet, and his bloody scowl greets me in the moonlight. He undulates to dislodge me, but there's no strength behind it.

"We meet again," I say, clawing my fingers into the stab wound on his neck. He screams and rakes at my chest as blood gushes over my claws. His tail thrashes and thumps futilely under me.

I curl my limbs around his, sinking my fingers deeper into him.

"Cobra," the Python croaks as I obliterate his larynx. He claws at my chest, his nails biting into my scales. Eyes wide, dark slits move from my face to stare up at the night sky as I drape the rest of the way over him, keeping him beneath me.

He does not get to see the sky again. He will see me when his heart stops.

I watch him die. It's slow and agonizing, twisting my claws under his flesh, mushing his insides, prolonging it as long as I am able. He grabs my hand weakly and tries to pull it out.

"You know your crime," I say as his gaze hoods.

I wait several more minutes, ensuring his pulse doesn't start beating again and his body doesn't try regenerating. When I'm sure he's dead, I climb off him, tug my hand from his neck, and get to work.

I tear off his head first, twisting it the way he twisted the dead pigs. As I set his head aside, atop a branch in a tree nearby, I listen for more pigs or other predators that may be nearby. This much blood will attract something. The subtle breeze across my scales assures me that the scent is potent in the air, and there are creatures with much better senses than I.

Even after I take care of the Python's head, my fury is only partially sated. I dig my hand into the stump of his neck again and yank out the Python's spine. His tail twitches and coils until it's gone from his body. I lay my prize on the ground next to me. Grabbing it, I roll it around a nearby tree so any naga who comes across it will know that this male broke our one law. Now that females are back within my lands, the old icon will be a good reminder.

None have challenged me and won.

I am undefeated.

When I am done, I turn back to the Python's mangled body. It is because of him that I am not with Daisy right now, that she cries when I try leading her into a mating coil.

Knowing something will come along and eat the male brings me some comfort. As I think this, my mouth waters.

I never understood, for so many years, why I hungered for the flesh of other nagas and forest snakes over all else. My father had too, and he even shared a tail or two with me when I was young. I knew it was wrong, except my body said otherwise. It wasn't until I came across an ancient book about Earth's reptiles that I began to understand why.

There was once a reptile on this planet that resembled me. How? I don't know, but as a king, I did not like seeing a base creature in my likeness. I vowed to not be anything like these other *King Cobras*, those that do not have any human in them. It was from that book I learned of our cannibalistic nature.

That book is gone now, cracked and withered into dust after my many read-throughs. There are not enough robots in this world to preserve everything from the past.

I grab the Python under his arms and lean him up against a tree, facing his spine. For a final trophy, I carve out some of his scales, tucking them in Daisy's ruined clothes on my arm. Afterward, I retrieve his head, just as I hear the snorts of pigs.

They can have their vengeance too.

I am benevolent.

ELEVEN
GILDED CAGE

Daisy

I slip my fingers across black silk, comforted by the feel of it. I've been awake for hours but haven't moved from my spot in the corner. I'm exhausted, my body hurts, I'm hungry, stressed, and sleep threatens to pull me under. I don't let it because I can't be so unguarded. Not with an alien male nearby who I don't know.

Zaku will be able to sneak up on me if I sleep.

He's not here, I remind myself.

My fingers snag on the silk—silk someone like me shouldn't be touching—and groan, knowing my exhaustion will catch up with me eventually, and then I'll truly be vulnerable. I scrub my face with my hands. I'd been trained for situations like these. All women in the military are. It's not fair, but war isn't fair. I should've been able to compartmentalize. I shiver, and I can't help it.

Zaku kissed me.

I raise my fingers to touch my lips. It was shocking... like everything else that's happened.

I reach down and clutch my new clothes—soft clothes—closing my eyes.

Zaku isn't like the other one.

Hours have gone by and despite my circumstance, I'm warm and sheltered and clean. Wrapping my mind around this has been hard. Maybe... maybe I actually am safe. He didn't have to help me. He could have hurt me instead, but he *has* helped me, and I need to remember this.

I open my eyes and I push upright, realizing it's no longer night. Endless blue skies and a bright, big sun are visible through the window, making the strange room bright and airy and open. I wince.

My gaze cuts to the door. It's still shut tight.

I glimpse the corners of the room. Stretching, I groan again. My bladder is full, and I'm going to have to get up and relieve it soon.

I eye the other closed doors. The ones I haven't been inside of yet.

He said one of them is a bathroom.

Standing, I keep my eyes on the main door. There are three doors in total. Two line the walls on either side of the window, and I assume they lead to more rooms with a view. The third door is beside Zaku's... *nest.* Though almost in the center of the room, the nest is still closest to the left wall. Between me and the nest, is the third door.

To the right side of the room is the human cage. Or an alien cage. I hope I never find out. There are people out there who like to fuck alien species, even if they're not compatible—as long as they're sentient—humans find a way. I don't know if that makes it better or worse.

Alien species have never been compatible with humans. I raise my fingers to my lips.

I haven't been kissed since I was in the officer's academy. Boys wanted to kiss me back then, hoping to steal the affection of someone who could help them rise in their careers. I stick out my tongue, remembering them. Once it was clear the military wasn't my calling—that I was too emotional, that I had no knack for violence—the boys vanished.

That was maybe... ten years ago? I took up piloting. It was a salvation I didn't know I needed at the time. I didn't have to interact one-on-one with anyone. And piloting didn't leave a lot of room for lovers. At the end of a shift in the sky, I was too tired for anything but bed, too worn down by death to want to do anything else except hide under my blanket and pretend the universe was a better place, a different place. One I could be proud of.

Petting my lips, they're dry now and nothing like Zaku's warm, full ones. It's strange being kissed again. It's been a long time.

I shake my head and walk to the door beside the bed. Testing the handle, it gives easily. Lights turn on when I stand on the threshold.

I gape.

Lucky me. It's the bathroom, but it's not like the one upstairs.

Leather brown, warm grey, and cream, one entire wall is a shower unit, with four large square spouts coming off the wall. There's no door on either side of the unit, making it easy for someone to slip in and out from either direction. Across from the shower is a long mirror with a table and sink beneath it. Upon the table are what could only be soaps, toiletries, and candles. Lots and lots of unused candles. In the back is a seating area with a sleek leather sofa, covered in silk black pillows, with a black glass table before it.

To relax and gaze upon people showering? I tilt my head. Why else would there be a sofa in a bathroom?

Like the bedroom, the bathroom's huge. I guess it has to be if a male like Zaku uses it. *His tail would fill up the whole of this space. It would run up the walls and curl over itself.*

I head for the toilet, which is in a mirrored alcove directly to my left. Seeing myself pee is something I never thought I'd do.

Whoever—whatever—once lived in this mountain palace was a strange fellow. It makes me curious about the original inhabitants and what their life was like. It's obviously nothing like mine.

I explore the bathroom for a weapon and find a nail file. Pocketing it, I wash my hands once again in wonder from the endless water. I shoot the shower a longing glance. There's no way I'm going to risk showering right now. There's also no bath. I decide I like the bathroom upstairs more. I re-enter the bedroom to find one of the robots.

It picks up the blanket from my makeshift nest in the corner, lasers it, and then positions it nicely on Zaku's bed.

Heading for the exit, I yank the handle. It doesn't give.

I yank it harder; the door holds. I search for a lock and find none. I slam my fist against the door, and it barely makes a thud. Trying the handle again, I call out for Zaku. Nothing. I pivot to the robot.

"Open the door," I say.

It doesn't respond.

I try again. "House, open the door for me."

The robot stops, scans me once over, and continues whatever it's doing.

"Hey, wait—" I follow it, waving my hand "—house, let me out!"

It ignores me.

When it enters the bathroom and begins lasering the toilet, I sigh and go back into the bedroom.

I wander to the window. There's not a cloud in the sky. I've never seen such open, clear skies in all my life. Flying toward Earth, looking down from orbit, most of the landscape was brown, beige, and dead. Though here, in this spot within the mountains, it's like the Lurkers had never touched it.

I can almost forget the dead wastes. The endless desert of dust and ruins I saw flying down from *The Dreadnaut*.

The lake is in the distance, a blue glint among the scattered mountains. It seems close, but it took an entire day of travel to get from there to here. That's a long time for me, considering I'm used to flying everywhere. I search for ships in the skies, exhaust tracks, and end with my gaze in the direction of where I'm certain the facility is in.

I wonder what's happening with the team. After a few minutes, I rub my face and turn away.

Ignoring the cage and the bed, I head for the other two doors. I aim for the one on my left first, the one on the same wall as the bathroom, saving the right door, the one beside the cage for last. I have a feeling that one is the *"play"* room.

And I'm right once again, entering a closet. I almost gape again.

The closet is twice the size of my room on *The Dreadnaut*, filled to the brink with clothes, shoes, and everything else a person could ever want. Silks and lace, velvet and leather, there are dresses and suits, underthings and casualwear. In the center is a large island covered in glass bottles, decorative candles, and jewels. Dazzled, I walk around the island, wanting more than anything to touch the beautiful things.

Why does Zaku need all of this stuff? None of these clothes would ever fit him, and there's not another woman here...

Taking a risk, I lift a sparkling sapphire necklace from where it's placed on a velvet frame. My lips part in awe. I've never seen something so exquisite...

Someone treasured this once, and then they died. I set the necklace down gently, ensuring it's perfect upon the velvet it lives upon.

There's a large locked jewelry box beside it. I test it. It doesn't open. Beside it, half covered in a swathe of silk, is a picture. I push the silk aside and take hold of it.

Several men are standing together framed by flags. Two of the men are shaking hands while facing the camera, like it's a staged moment. A photo-op. The main focus, the man in a crisp black suit, is beyond handsome with haughty features and keen eyes. I notice something is standing in the background, in the shadows.

My brow furrows as my eyes go to the creature half-hidden behind the flags. I squint, trying to make it out.

It's a Lurker.

I swallow, staring at frightening reptilian eyes that seem to stare right back at me. I've seen Lurkers in digital media before, except this one is different. There's something not quite right about it.

The word evil flits through my head. A quiet, ominous whisper.

The longer I study the Lurker, the more my uneasiness grows. Unsettled, I put the picture down and wipe my hands on my clothes, feeling icky, feeling...scared.

Glancing around the opulent closet again, I wonder why there's a picture like this in here.

This place of Zaku's has to be a human dwelling, not a Lurker one. The closet is full of human things. The knowledge doesn't comfort me. If I were in a Lurker dwelling, eventually Peter, Collins, and the rest of the team would find their way here, and I could use that to get back on *The Dreadnaut.*

For the next while, I dig through every corner, searching for a weapon. At the end, the nail file from the bathroom wins out.

The sun is setting when I finally leave the closet. The robot is gone as well, and my stomach is growling. I go to the bathroom and pour myself a cup of water from the sink. When I'm done, I'm still alone.

My stomach growls again, and I try the door to leave the room. It doesn't budge.

I call out for Zaku, and I get no response. I call for the house, and nothing. A niggling, uncomfortable sensation churns my stomach.

Where is he?

It's going to be dark soon. I chew on my lip.

Grabbing some pillows and several blankets, I set up my spot by the window this time and lie down, staring out across the landscape, hoping that someone might see me and rescue me.

No one comes.

No one.

I'm alone, and I don't know why... The Lurker in the picture steals my mind and try as I might, I can't push it out. I see it in the glass, staring back at me. Terrible, intelligent eyes that see right through me focus just enough on my soul to let me know that it's watching me.

There are scarier beings out there than the ones I'm facing. Scarier creatures that don't offer food, water, and shelter.

I fall into a fitful sleep, wishing I wasn't alone with *it*.

Wishing I wasn't alone at all.

TWELVE
ZAKU'S RETURN

Daisy

I HEAR SOMETHING BEHIND ME, and I shoot upright. Rubbing my eyes, I search for the source of the noise.

Is he back?

Moonlight bleeds through the room, and elongated shadows give the otherwise empty space an ominously quiet appearance. The bars from the cage cast dark lines on the far wall and the swing... It jostles from a breeze that doesn't exist. Seeing nothing out of the ordinary, tension leaves my shoulders.

I'm still alone.

Something moves by the door, and I pause as light pierces the gloom. A robot.

I slump, annoyed.

Facing the clear night sky and Earth's moon, I wonder why *The Dreadnaut* hasn't sent anyone else down. I shake my head and turn away. I haven't seen or heard any ships descend. And if I missed them while sleeping, they leave trails in the skies that last for days.

The robot moves toward me, and I snag my blankets and pillows close. "You can't have them. They're being used." If it tries to clean me out, it's got another thing coming.

My nose twitches, and I notice the robot holding something.

It sets a platter beside me and moves away. The wall opens up, and the robot vanishes within it before I can think of darting into the hole behind it. Dragging the platter next to the window, I scrutinize the plate.

Meat. My tummy roils with nausea even though the meat is cooked and served with one of those red orbs Zaku gave me the first day. I'm not hungry for meat or strange food, but I'm not about to let sustenance go to waste. I gorge, polishing off everything. When I'm done, I push the plate aside and go to the bathroom, wash my hands, and splash water in my face.

Sighing, I abandon the bathroom. The sun is cresting the mountains when I reenter the room.

I turn toward the last door.

The *"play"* room.

The one I haven't dared to peek inside of yet. Maybe it's because of the picture of the Lurker in the closet. Shaking out the fear that wants to drag me back down, I head for the playroom's door.

Clutching the doorknob, it gives under my hand, opening inward. I see my face staring back at me on the other side. Stepping inside the room, I'm surrounded by floor-to-ceiling mirrors on every side. There are only mirrors.

How odd.

Moving to the one before me, I study my reflection. My brow furrows and I glance around. Seeing something above me, I walk to the side to get a better look at whatever it is.

A hook. A small one. Like something is to be hung from it...

Deep, vibrating hissing floods my ears. I spin toward the door.

My heart ramps. Leaving the playroom, I return to the main room and close the door behind me. My gaze shifts to the locked door on the other side.

He's back.

I brace for it to open, taking a step back. I don't know which Zaku I will get, the one who looks at me like he's starving or the caring one who draws me a bath and cradles me in his arms.

Maybe it'll be neither. I shift further away as the hissing grows louder. It sounds like it's coming from all around me, piercing through the walls. My nerves vibrate with it, making my toes curl.

The knob turns and the door swings open, revealing a beast. One that is dark, dirty, and covered in... blood? Dark eyes catch mine in a trap, and I gasp, releasing a shriek. The Lurker is real! Scrambling to the window, I try to get away. It rushes me, grabs me, and lifts me in his arms.

The stench of blood invades my nostrils. Flailing, I strain away. "No!" I scream, wild with terror.

"It is me! Zaku! Your male. Your king. Calm down," he barks.

I hear him, but only see the dried blood caking Zaku's large body, covering his mouth, hands, and arms. He's a different color—his pupils golden and striking and wild. I kick out frantically as I mumble his name.

"Zaku?"

I stop kicking as I take in his face.

My...male?

His gaze searches mine. "I have returned to you."

Zaku slowly lowers me, placing me on my feet. The dirt and blood on his scales have diminished his yellow coloring to the point of unrecognition. And as he leans back, removing his hands from me, my gaze trails over his giant form, making sure it's really him.

Making sure he's not another monstrous naga seeking to hurt me, or something worse.

"Zaku," I say again, almost in reassurance. It is him. I reach out and touch him with the tips of my fingers to make sure.

He's disgusting. My nose twitches from the stench wafting off of him. He reaches up to grasp my hand and I tug it away, hugging it to my body, because the gore on him is all over me now too.

He lifts his hand, outstretches his clawed fingers, and brushes a tendril of my hair behind my ear. "Your fear will end today," he says. "I promise, little mate."

I flinch.

"What happened?" I whisper, bunching my sleeve around my hand to cover my nose. "Where have you been?" Why do I even care? I back away from him, wanting to put distance between me and the blood cloaking him, not liking the way he towers over me, intimidating me. It reminds me of my father.

Still... I'm relieved. I almost press forward to see if I can get a whiff of his scent despite the coppery tang of blood invading my nose.

Zaku's chest puffs and he straightens onto his tail, commanding all of my attention. I almost smile from his obvious peacocking. How did I ever see a Lurker? Zaku looks nothing like the alien in the picture.

And then I glimpse his enormous cock.

My mouth drops. *It's outside of his tail.* A shaft of sunlight hits it directly, saying: "look here!"

It's huge! I squeak, my eyes widening, and look away.

Was that—is that—possible?

I forget about the smell, the gore, even my predicament, because what Zaku's packing is big enough to eclipse everything else. Fuck. He starts to say something that goes in one ear and out the other; I'm too stunned by his... *monstrous nether region.*

Don't look at it, Daisy. I want to look at it. Damn the light haloing it.

"—I have battled and won—"

Educational curiosity?

I try to focus on what Zaku's saying all while backing away and trying my hardest not to glance at his package. If he thinks he's getting that inside me, he'll be sorely disappointed.

We don't fit. We never will. It's not possible.

"—your king has made these lands safe again—"

I'm vaguely aware of Zaku showing off his muscles and indicating his body to me like he's a god, but his cock has literally cock-blocked him; it won't even disappear into his tail. It jerks in the periphery of my view. It's begging me to look at it.

Zaku strains, rising up, peacocking some more, and I can't help it any longer. Fuck, fuck, fuck. My eyes drop back down to his *monster,* swaying and bobbing with every one of his movements. Staring hard now, I can't help it. It's not like he's *not* displaying it for me to gaze at anyway...

"—no female of mine should ever know fear from another, only me—"

Is it... getting bigger?

I tilt my head, narrowing my eyes. There's a bulge in the middle of it that's turgid and swollen, and I swear it's growing. He keeps moving, making it hard for me to decide. Regardless, it looks uncomfortable, and I don't envy him. I'd be an angry, bloodied-up naga too if I were in his boots—uh, tail.

Liquid beads on the tip and drips to the floor.

I hold in a squeak as his seed—alien snake seed—leaks from cock's head.

Zaku stills and so does his "monster" after a final bounce. My gaze shoots to his face, and he's staring at me with an intensity that makes my soul try to shrivel and hide. I tense up when I realize what he'd just caught me doing.

Gazing at his cock...

The golden spark in his eyes gleams and brightens, making the coloring of his facial scales darken further. I inhale sharply and snap my mouth shut, discovering his gaze tracking my lips.

Suddenly, I feel his mouth back on mine.

My heart jumps into my throat.

And then I see what he must see in his head—my mouth choking down on him.

I stiffen, straighten. I'm the only daughter of a great war commander; I'll never suck a man's cock. An alien's cock. Any cock. It doesn't matter how far I fall.

"Female," Zaku rasps. And though he couldn't pose himself kinglier, he somehow does, jutting out his chin, flaring his cowl wide, and straining his muscled-packed arms.

Something in me... shifts and stutters, pauses and ponders, and then starts to warm up. I would roll my eyes if I weren't appreciating his muscles so much. My lips part and I curl my fingers into my palm to stop my hand from reaching out and feeling Zaku's arms.

This alien man wants me. He wants *me*. I don't even need the evidence of his swollen dick to know this, nor do I need his words. I see it in his eyes. I shiver, losing my train of thought as I stare into them.

I recall his muscles pressed against me. I recall his warmth.

Inhaling, and that delicious scent of his, the one I smelled the first day invades my nostrils. My skin warms, lips part. I suck it into me like I'll starve if I don't. He's bloody, disgusting, and those smells are in the air as well. They no longer bother me. All I want is to move closer to him and breathe him in.

Wrenching my eyes close, I shake my head.

Why does he have to smell so good? My skin heats even more as I breathe it in. A sensation of emptiness knots my sex, and I think it's because of his scent...

Wait? What was he just saying? Something about not having to be afraid anymore? I cover my nose.

"I have brought you a gift," he announces, his voice low, his tail coiling forward.

"A what?"

I don't get a chance to brace for what comes next because I'm suddenly face-to-face with a sagging, horrifyingly bloody, dismembered head.

THIRTEEN
THE HEAD

Zaku

DAISY RECOILS, bringing up her hands. The color drains from her face.

I'd just watched her skin turn rosy. She was staring at my member, exciting me. Now her face is ashen?

Gripping the Python's scalp tighter, I lift his head higher. "He is the one who hurt you and mated you against your will, and for that, I bring you his head," I announce again in case she needs reassurance. "You do not need to be afraid anymore."

Now, she will accept me. Now, she will lead me to my nest.

Daisy bows over and heaves, clutching her stomach. I furrow my brows, dropping the head and rushing to her side. "Are you hurt?" She tries to shake out of my grip; I tighten it. There's spittle on her parted lips.

I slip my tongue out to taste the air before them, my tongue a finger's width from her mouth. I long to taste her again. She is delicious and sweet, and everything I would think a daisy flower should taste like.

I glimpse her horrified expression. "Are you hurt?" I ask again, worried and frustrated by her response and lack thereof.

"Let me go—please let me go. You brought me his head," she gasps, tearing at my hands. She's making a sickened face, and I notice the dirt and blood on her, how the mess is getting all over her. Hissing, I release her.

"I brought you his head," I agree. "So you will know that he is gone and will never trouble you again."

She scurries away from me as if she doesn't hear my words, and I clench my hands to stop them from snatching her up again.

"His head..." she utters with disbelief, refusing to look at the offering again.

"Yes. The Python's head," I grunt, tossing it to the corner of the room. I've forgotten what it's like to be with another. They do not always agree or do what I want.

I thought once her fear was gone, she would sing, she would submit.

"House, prepare the bathroom," I rumble thickly. I hear the shower turn on soon after. I will clean her, clean myself, and then present her with the Python's head again. Then, she can put to rest what happened, knowing he's in the bellies of pigs, probably scattered across the forest by now, and let me finally fill her with my member.

My mouth waters. I absently palm my knot as I think this. I hear Daisy's breath hitch. She's in the corner of the room where I left her the first night, watching me warily. Color has returned to her cheeks and she's holding her hand over her nose.

There wasn't wariness on her face when she was staring at my member moments ago. I could feel her eyes on me, petting me. I thought that she'd been pleased, earnest after my story about battling the Python. That I brought her a gift. That I planned to spoil her. Her cheeks had warmed, her eyes took me in.

I strain my muscles again, wanting her gaze back on them.

I go to her and she presses away.

My eyes narrow. "I will not touch you again while his filth is on my hands. For that, I apologize. I am—" I slip my tongue across the roof of my mouth "—eager to see you... settled."

But my frustration grows.

"Can you put that away?" she asks, catching my eyes and then glancing at my member. "Please?"

She wants me to hide *my want* for her? After I killed on her behalf?

"It no longer fitsss," I grate.

She regards me, closes her eyes hard, and opens them. Her hand tightens around her nose. I don't understand what she's doing, and at this point, I just want to get the Python's blood off of her.

I'm liking his smear on her less and less. I miss seeing her perfection, the glimpse I got of her when her tears dried after the ship left her on the plateau.

Why is the head not working? Her troubles are no more.

"I-It doesn't fit?" she asks. "Don't answer that!" She shudders, pivoting to the bathroom as if she could hide from me. "I can't believe you brought me a head!" The door begins to close, and I swipe out my tail to jar it. She hitches from within, a sound of annoyance. "I need to—"

I snap to the threshold, thumping my palm on the door, stopping her from tugging the door closed. She startles and meets my eyes. "Need to *what*, Daisy? Relieve yourself? Wash? I have been away for over a day. I am not ready for you to be gone from my gaze."

Sliding into the doorway, I block her in. She cannot get away from me, my limbs are too big.

She steps back, continuing to hold her nose and eye me warily. Steam fills the space between us. The golden mountainous rocks that make up the walls begin glistening with humidity. I suck in the heat, letting it bloom inside me as I sneak my tailtip into the room and circle it around her.

"Zaku," she says. "I... want to thank you... for not—" she stops and shakes her head. "I can't be this way with you."

Hmm. "What way is that?"

Her soft, flimsy clothes drape her curves enticingly, showing off hints of her body beneath. Even dirty, she is enticing in them. I catch her human nipples peeking through, and I hold in a groan. I've always been fascinated by human breasts. They are large compared to the females of my kind. They also appear softer, rounder, and easier to grab, grope, or play with. I read once that human females can produce milk for their offspring.

Human females are always covering their breasts in the images I've seen, and I never understood why. Naga women wore no clothes, remaining as free as their males.

Humans do not have scales to guard their flesh...

That must be why she covers herself. For protection.

"Well, I'm a human, and you're not? I mean, half of you looks human... You speak my language..." A blush deepens her cheeks as her eyes shoot to my member and dart away. "We're not compatible. Humans have tried being with aliens in the past. It doesn't work. And that," she says, indicating my swollen shaft, "is a lot..."

"Compatible?" I ask, not quite understanding her meaning. I enter the bathroom and she stumbles back. I catch her with my tail. Why is she trying to get away from me? She pushes out of my limbs and dodges deeper into the room. I close in, pulling the door shut behind me.

I am a large male, and my den was not built for one such as me, still, I fit. I make myself fit. My tail coils up the walls. It wants to coil around her.

"Well," she says, "humans are much, much smaller than you."

"And?"

She guffaws. "That should be reason enough!" Her eyes flick back to my member, and I shoot out a jet of spill just knowing her eyes are on it. She brings her hands up to her mouth after taking a deep breath. "Zaku, I'm not ready. You've been reasonable, you've... cared for me. It took me time to realize this. But this is never going to work. I'm not staying. The first chance I get..."

"Not staying...?" My eyes narrow upon her. "Where else would you go? If you try and leave me for another," my voice lowers, "I will kill every male, human, and naga in the land until I am all who remains." Daisy's eyes go wide as I say this. "You have seen the skulls out front. I have many kills. I am unbeatable—I am king. And you... you are the most beautiful female of all, and that means you're mine. My queen."

Her mouth opens and closes several times. My tongue licks my teeth, imagining her lips moving over my scales, her hair fanned out across my tail as I bend her body for me.

"You..." she whispers.

"Me?"

"You are—" she straightens "—really thick-headed."

I consider her words and decide she's right. My skull is rather thick. The cartilage of my cowl is heavy. "I am," I agree.

She sighs, but the hand covering her nose still remains.

Do I smell bad?

"How was I ever afraid of you?" She clutches her brow. "Because he's a headhunter, Daisy. You've been caught by a headhunter."

This word pleases me, and I pet her ankle with my tailtip. "I do collect the heads of my enemies," I say. "You have begun noticing things about me... I like this. I would decorate our den with them except the house robots..." I trail off. "You fear me because I should be feared, little female. I will be a good protector to you, the best protector. There is no other who is better."

As my tail touches her, she finally drops her hand and dances farther into the bathroom. I smirk, beginning to enjoy her now that it's not fear that keeps her from me. She just said so herself. She curses me and scampers around the bathroom as I follow her with my tail. When she climbs up on the sofa, shouting at me to stop it, I hook it around her and snag her around the middle, bringing her back to me.

"Zaku!" she pushes at my limb, legs kicking, feet straining to remain on the floor. "Let me go!"

When I have her in front of me, I arch my brow. "Never."

I carry her into the shower.

She fights, hitting me with her fists, her curses growing louder. She could never hurt me.

"I am not something that can be man-handled! I'm a military pilot, I know how to snipe, I should be feared too—" I put her under the water. She blubbers, stops fighting me and swipes her soaked hair out of her face.

I move her back toward the other shower faucet, slipping under the first, while shifting my tail behind her to keep her from escaping out the other side.

"How dare you!"

She starts struggling harder while I find the soap spout hidden in the crevices of the mountain rock, pumping the liquid in my palm. I lather it between my hands until it's bubbly. She's pushing at my tail some more but not nearly as hard as she could be; she's watching me instead. I think she likes the warm water. When I bring my hands toward her hair, she jerks back.

I pause. "I will wash you."

She shudders, then glances at my member again. "I can't give you what you want, Zaku," she whispers. "Even if you spoil me, take care of me, even if what you say is true... it can't be."

"It can. You are mine now. That's all that matters."

Her tongue peeks out to swipe at her wet lips. She's so stiff that I'm afraid she'll break if I move my tail too quickly.

"Submit?" she asks with hesitance. Water droplets gather in her lashes. She wipes her brow as water continuously showers her from above. I span out my cowl and rise higher, trying to shield her eyes, touching the ceiling.

"Yesss, female. I will take care of you, and your worries. You only need to let me. I can be your king too."

Her eyes flick to my soapy hands, then back to my face. "What happens if I submit? Will you... will you listen to me?"

"Listen to you?"

She glances behind me. "I don't want to be hurt again."

"I will never hurt you."

"I don't want to be locked up anymore either... I want freedom. I don't want to be left in the room alone with that..." she trails off.

"With what?"

She shakes her head.

"With what?" I demand.

"The head!"

I nod. If that is all she needs to give me what I want, then that is easy to grant. "You will have access to my den, and I will not bar you from any room, though the entrance will remain locked. I will not budge on that. You will not go outside without me."

"You said the land is safe, didn't you?"

I hiss. "Until it is not."

My logic is sound.

She searches my eyes, and my nostrils flare, waiting for her to finally accept me. My spine stiffens as the seconds lengthen, and my tailtip presses into the floor. Water continues to drench us, and the humidity thickens with the steam. The heat on my skin doesn't diminish the throbbing of my member as I hoped.

I know she is small. I know I am large.

That won't stop me from lodging inside her, from spilling my seed within her. From filling her womb with many litters.

"I want one more thing," she says slowly.

"Anything."

Anything. I will give her anything; I will give her everything except her release.

"I want to decide when we first mate."

"Fine," I snap, bringing my hands to her hair.

She startles. "Fine? Wait, what?" She tries to tug my hands off her. "You're not going to argue that? Wait—"

"No," I rasp. "No more waiting." I know she fears mating me. The Python made her fear it. I do not want to wait, even though I must for her sake. There are other ways to find relief until then. My mood sours despite my excitement. "She's mine, finally mine," I whisper to myself, awed.

Daisy winces. "I thought…"

Gathering the rest of her long yellow hair, I bring it closer to me, liberating it from the water, and soap it up. *The feel…* I groan as it catches on my claws. Daisy grows even tenser, holding her limbs close to her body, but she's no longer trying to get away. She looks deep in thought.

I will take it. It doesn't matter that she's holding herself prone and away from me. I don't care.

"I will let you decide when you wish to mate, but I will decide the rest. Right now, I will wash you, and you will wash me. Afterward, you will lead me to our nest and lie with me while I sleep. I have earned this. I will have you naked when I want, I will touch you when I want, you will touch me when I want. You will allow me to prove to you that I will protect you, that I will destroy your enemies. And you will stay and be my beautiful queen.

"You will help me rule these lands, and I will remain the envy of every male in our world."

"Zaku… You really are thick-headed."

"Yes. It is thick." I squeeze her gently with my tail. "If you try to leave me, I will know."

I *will* know.

Because from this moment on, she'll never be away from my side again. I tremble at the thought.

FOURTEEN
LIFE ISN'T FAIR

Daisy

He's so naïve it's almost painful.

Only there's a fire in his gaze that I can't ignore. His claws gently scrape my scalp, making my skin prickle. It's a lot. He's a lot. It feels good and I wish it didn't. Biting my tongue, I didn't expect him to so easily accept my terms, hoping his swollen cock would give me more time to figure something out.

Who can think straight when they're horny?

I'm not the craftiest person. I'm not creative. I'm reactive, living in the moment, with seemingly every instance ruled by my annoying emotions, so being trapped by a massive, turned-on male covered in gore has not been an easy moment for me to wade through. Not without appreciating the specimen who's trapped me.

If circumstances had been different, I'd be more open to Zaku's advances... *Maybe*. I like men who know what they want and aren't willing to manipulate others to achieve their goals. I like *kind* men. But I've given up thinking those types of men existed. I've been manipulated my whole life. I'm sick of it. Only, Zaku's not like any male I've ever known, stiff, cold, keeping his thoughts and feelings closed off. Seeing me as a means to an end, and then not seeing me at all after they got what they wanted. Which is usually something I never planned to give in the first place.

No, Zaku's an open book. Too open for my comfort.

It makes me nervous. I've never dealt with anyone like him. He's so blatant and forward about what he's thinking that I almost think it must be a trick. It has to be, right?

He doesn't seem like the type to be tricky, though.

He believes that by catching me during some cultural mate hunt, we're destined to be together. I get that now. Sleep has helped. Also, his insistence that he won't hurt me—over and over again—has helped a lot as well.

I believe him. I'm beginning to, at least.

He should keep his thoughts to himself... Zaku would never survive on a ship like *The Dreadnaut.*

But it means I can get free of him if I'm patient enough.

I inhale, remembering the rotting head in the bedroom, how he thrust it in my face, and the stench of decay coming off of it. I don't want to become what I hate. I don't want to manipulate Zaku, even if it means my freedom. I also don't know him very well. *He's the reason I'm in this situation to begin with.*

He's the one who came to the facility and brokered an agreement with Peter.

Thankfully, the water has taken Zaku's scent away. It was muddling my thoughts. Though I find I'm missing it, hoping for another whiff. I'll have to be patient. He's reactive too. He's willing to kill for me.

What else is he willing to do?

My belly flutters.

He's waiting for me to respond... His hands tug and grip my hair, lathering it, making my body warm. The water feels good.

"I won't run," I lie. I will, but not now. I can hold him off for a while, though I'm certain I won't be able to forever.

His tail coils tighter around me. *He's watching me.* Bubbly soap trickles from my over-lathered hair, soaking my shirt.

"I know you won't," he rumbles, his voice heating. His eyes go to my breasts again, as if he could stare so hard that he'll see under my arms and through my shirt.

"I will have you naked when I want, I will touch you when I want, you will touch me when I want... And you will stay and be my beautiful queen."

An idea forms. His claws softly graze my scalp again, and I stop the moan that wants to leave me.

I can ingratiate myself to him, give him what he craves—within reason—and maybe by doing so, he'll want me so badly that he'll give me whatever *I* want.

He says I will touch him when *he* wants, though he can't make me do that against my will. As far as I'm aware, neither the Lurkers nor ancient humans had developed tech that could control another's mind.

God, I hope.

If these nagas are anything like the Gestri...

Feeling empowered suddenly, I desperately want to hold onto the feeling.

Slowly, I uncoil my arms from my chest and place my hands on his tail.

His eyes glaze, and his kneading, tugging hands halt in my hair, tightening into fists. My chest constricts as a hungry fervor etches across his face. The water from above trickles down his cheeks, and I catch a glimpse of his forked tongue sliding over his fangs. His scales glisten, wet.

"I will touch you when I want," he says, as if reminding me of our agreement, his voice a mumble.

I shudder, and it's not because I'm scared.

It's because I want him to touch me. His hands in my hair feel good. I recoil at the thought and strain back. Only his hands untangle from me and cup my breasts instead. I go still, shocked. His hands are huge, his fingers having to curl inward to cup me better, covering the entirety of my torso. Every fiber in me is on edge. I don't know if I'll bolt or give in —my thoughts war. What I should want and what I really want are refusing to align.

He gently squeezes my breasts, and I'm still waiting to react. To run. To burst into tears.

I don't.

A low, guttural, and deep hissing fills my ears, blending with the patter of the shower. I press the pads of my fingers into Zaku's tail, testing, feeling the velvety grooves of his scales. His eyes flick to mine as I do so, and my fingers lift from his hide.

Without saying anything, eyes locked on mine, his tail around me loosens, and I bare down on my feet, able to stand on my own once again. The pressure between my legs diminishes from the loss, and my sex clenches, hoping to bring it back. I reach up and grab his wrists.

I can't even curl my fingers around them.

His hissing lowers even more. Suds trickle from my hair and down my body, gathering over his hands on my chest. They slip down his wrists, slickening them. I slowly, damnably slide my palms up over his hands and press them into me.

Giving in, just a little.

"Daisssy."

His fingers find the top of my thin sweater and the shirt beneath it, gripping the material of both. His claw grazes down, drifting down from my neck, ripping the fabric. I gasp. He grins and, with new vigor, tears both open, baring my breasts completely to his view.

He pushes me backward into his tail and puts his mouth on one of them, lapping wildly. I cry out, straining from the abrupt assault of his tongue. I grab hold of his cowl and arch my back, trying to find purchase—anything to help me when everything is slippery—but then the thick part of Zaku's tail pushes my legs apart, sliding between them.

This is more than a little!

Straddling him, half-lying backward upon his tail, Zaku's upper half rises over me, his mouth suckling my left breast, then my right, and then back to my left. He laps at me like a man starved, and I'm too stunned to do anything but let him do what he wants.

He hisses my name again, licking up and down, the fork of his tongue flicking my nipples. I hitch. His tail writhes under me like a wave, each undulation putting pressure on all the right spots.

I whimper.

It's not fair.

It's really not.

I turn my thoughts off and close my eyes with a moan. For a final moment, I glimpse the Python's head in my mind, then Peter's awful smirk, and finally Zaku's hungry eyes. His tail comes next, his enormous cock—that will never, ever fit. The images can bring me back to reality—

He pushes my breasts together and thrusts his tongue up and down my cleavage, forcing my eyes to snap back open. The spray of the shower dews my lashes, and I blink rapidly to clear them.

He looks at me as his tongue whispers over my breasts again.

"Oh, hell," I moan, digging my nails into his cowl. It's thick and hard, like the rest of him.

I can give him this. I can—

Zaku flicks my nipples faster. I squeeze his tail with my thighs, pushing up into his face. *This is wrong, Daisy.*

But his tongue...

He releases my breasts, sliding them down my body, moving so gently they don't even disturb the bruising on my sides. He tears apart my pants, pulling them off me.

Zaku moves my body between his, laying me fully on the length of his tail. His eyes are almost human, and for an instant he's just a man of my species, but then his forked tongue appears again.

"Beautiful female," he says, licking the air. "You have made me happy. I am honored. You rest naked and wet and open on my tail. I am *pleased.*"

I grow warm from his words.

I've pleased him.

Zaku's eyes drop back down to my chest, and further still, wandering to the rest of my body. I curl my toes realizing the position I'm in and how vulnerable I've become.

How did this happen so fast? How? His tail undulates again, and I feel him everywhere. His scales, his heat, his muscles...

Something hot splashes my belly, something much hotter than the water.

I strain my head to look between us and see his cock poised above my splayed sex, the head angled toward it. Seed is leaking from the tip and onto my body.

Fear returns hot and fast.

"No!" I jolt upright, pushing at Zaku's chest and climbing off his tail. I turn to face him, plastering my body against the glass wall that separates the shower from the sink, blocked in by both sides of the shower, by his tail. I curl my arms over my breasts again, a hand protecting my sex.

"No," I say again, almost whimpering. "We have a deal."

He reaches for me, and I turn away.

"I was not going to..."

His hands never meet my skin.

I hear him hiss—and perhaps inwardly curse me. "I can't," I whisper.

I need to know he'll be true to his word. I need to know he won't betray me like Peter, like my own kind.

I'm desperate... to be able to trust someone again.

I feel him move away, feel it in the way the shower sprays me as he slips out. The air cools without his presence.

Without opening my eyes, I sense that he's gone, that he's left me alone. I slide down the glass with a soft sigh... and suddenly I'm splaying my fingers through his seed on my stomach and rubbing it into my skin.

I've lost my mind.

But...

I can trust him.

FIFTEEN

CHAINS

Daisy

It takes me some time to wash the soap out of my hair and clean my body. I make doubly sure any grime that has gotten on me is scrubbed off. I don't have any open wounds, only scrapes. I clean them thoroughly anyway, not wanting to risk infection. An alien bacterial infection. I gulp. I don't want to get sick here on Earth.

I'm also hoping that if I scrub hard enough, long enough, I'll scrub the way Zaku's making me feel, scouring it right out of me.

It's his damned scent. I know it is.

Though I don't smell him right now, I still can't get him out of my head.

I can trust him. Hope constricts my chest.

Wrapping a towel around my body, I leave the shower and peek out the bathroom door. Zaku's on the other side, wet and dripping and splayed out in sunlight that's beaming into the room through the window. With his cowl wide around his face and arms crossed over his chest, he's leaning back on his tail. He looks like a god. A strange, alien snake god.

He straightens when he sees me.

And puffs out his chest.

"I need new clothes," I tell him, checking him out, sliding my eyes to his pelvic region. Relief fills me—and perhaps a little regret—when I don't see his *monster*. "I'm going to just... go to the closet over there." I point toward it. He won't deny me clothes, will he?

"I have something for you."

I suck on my lip. "It's not a head, is it?"

His eyes glint. "No, not a head. Another gift. One you might like better."

I see something in his hand as his fingers uncurl away from his palm. Whatever it is catches the sunlight and flashes with brilliance, shooting rainbows across the room. I flinch, shielding my face, thinking he's shooting me with something. When nothing hits me, I lower my hands.

Rainbows streak across Zaku's tail, his rippling muscles, all coming from the thing he's holding. My lips part. He jangles it, and the room glitters with another burst of brilliant color. Dazzled and curious, I blink rapidly, clearing my eyes.

Whatever he's holding doesn't look like clothes.

It looks like—I squint as my eyes adjust to the sparkling light—strings of jewels? *Maybe crystals...*

Or diamonds?

My whole body goes on alert. If what Zaku is holding are diamonds... adding that to the wealth of jewels I'd seen in the closet... he might be the richest being in this galaxy. Maybe all the galaxies.

Diamonds are exceedingly rare, especially those from Earth.

There's a whole other reason *The Dreadnaut* has been sent to Earth, and it's not entirely for lost technology. Every human in the universe knows of the wealth that's been trapped on our home planet, wealth that's unguarded, unprotected, and ripe for the taking. A lot of people want that wealth, and no one more than the government and the royals. I'd heard enough chatter in the academy to know that the government isn't just going to let people return to Earth and steal that from them.

Greedy bastards, all of them.

I hate working for them. I only kept piloting because there were innocents out there—children—who needed saving, and also because if I quit, I'd sink to the lowest caste. I'd be a dregger.

I'd do anything to not be a dregger. Dreggers have no rights.

Zaku curls his fingers, and the sparkles—the rainbows on the walls—vanish. My chest feels lighter once they're gone. He shifts from his cocky posturing and slithers to me and out of the sunlight. I sniff the air, and when I smell nothing, I open the bathroom door a little further, clutching my towel and stepping out.

His eyes drop to my body. I hold my towel tighter.

"You'll wear this," he hands me the glittering thing he's holding, "and I will enjoy the sight of you while I rest. I will enjoy your beauty."

Taking the sparkling thing from his hand, making sure I don't accidentally touch him, woven chains fall from my fingers, each attached to a black leather band. "This... isn't clothes." Stretching the thin chains out, my eyes go to the crystals. "This won't cover any part of me," I mumble, trying to see how something like this would even be worn, mesmerized all over again.

"I don't want you covered."

I gulp, bringing the jeweled chains to my chest. "I don't think this is safe. I can't accept this, Zaku." Not at all. Not. At. All. What he's giving me is little more than jewelry and nothing else. I'd be exposed, completely. The chains cover nothing.

I also don't think I deserve to wear such wealth, if my pounding heart has anything to do with it... I hope it's only crystals that I'm holding.

Zaku lifts his hand and twirls a strand of my damp hair with his finger. "If you're afraid they will chafe your scrapes, I will pet and soothe your skin. I will enjoy it. It will give me time to learn you."

"I can't."

"You can. You will. It is what your king wants."

"What about what I want?"

Zaku tilts his head. "Your freedom?" He indicates the door to the room with his chin and my gaze snaps to it. It's open. "The house is yours. The robots are yours. They will listen to anything you ask of them, except opening the front door. They will not release you."

I shiver. "And you promise it's my choice—" I lick my lips "—when, uh—" and I feel my cheeks heat "—when we—"

"Mate?"

My eyes flick back to his. I nod.

"It is your choice," he says.

"Can I go outside, ever?"

"With me by your side, you can."

I glance at the chains in my hand, the black leather band. "How long do I have to wear this?"

Zaku gently pulls the chains from my grip, letting them fall between us. "Until I have had my fill of your beauty. Until I have memorized you."

That's not a good answer. He may want to gawk at my human body for weeks—months. I startle, realizing I might be here for that long, or more. But my skin warms at his compliment, and I am intrigued.

If Zaku were a human, I would think he was playing a huge joke on me, except he isn't a man, and he's not. "Okay."

His gaze smolders at my acceptance. He lifts the chains above my head, unclasping the collar. "I will give you more gifts than this," he rumbles. "Gather your hair."

Digging my nails into my towel, I swallow thickly. "You don't need to win me with gifts. Kindness is enough."

"I have already won you."

My lips purse.

I eye the exit behind Zaku and swallow again. The room is warm, my cheeks warmer, and my belly is twisting up with starflies.

"I can be kind," he says. "I am out of practice, but I can be kind. I think."

My gaze goes back to him as he sends the starflies dancing.

I let my towel drop to the floor and gather up my hair, meeting Zaku's waiting eyes.

He keeps them despite my nudity and works the delicate chains over my head, over my arms. I shimmy, threading one arm through, and then the other, helping him out, knowing all the while, every inch of my body and all its flaws are exposed. Zaku positions the open band around my neck and latches it at the back. Once it's on, I let my hair fall.

Tense, neither of us move as silence fills the space between us.

I drop my gaze from his to look down at my new adornments.

There's one thick central chain that falls from the band, down to my navel where it forks, draping around my hips before returning up my back. Thinner chains drape from the collar, landing like necklaces, falling across my collarbone and breasts. They stop an inch above my nipples. From those thinner chains, two branch off, wrapping my upper arms, accentuating my neck and chest, my curves.

Throughout the piece, there are jewels. *Crystals*, I reassure my mind. More than I can count.

"Beautiful," he says.

I bring my arms up to hide my breasts. He's looking at me like I'm the sun, the stars, and the magical nebulas of space. His hands open and close. His tail coils around my ankle.

I wish my body was as beautiful as he says it is. I wish my bruises were healed. I'm glad he knows nothing about my past...

I lower my face.

His fingers clasp my chin and lift it, forcing me to meet his eyes. "It is time to rest now, Daisy. I am tired. I want to enjoy you. I want you to enjoy me."

"Okay."

What else can I say?

He smiles, revealing his fangs. "Good." His tail strokes the sensitive skin behind my ankle. "Lead me to my nest, female." His fingers drop from my chin. "It is time for my queen to give her king a gift in return."

I step out from his tail and start walking toward the bed. He grabs my arm.

"Take my hand," he says when I look back at him. His eyes trail across my backside.

It's only several steps. I grab the hand he offers me.

When I'm at the edge of the bed, I stop, waiting for another cue. Why am I so nervous? I realize I'm waiting for the ball to drop, for Zaku to do to me like Peter has, like others before him have. He slides into the bed and lies back upon the silken pillow. With his hands behind his head, he looks at me.

Once again, he looks like he could be a god. All gold, all big, all potently male.

His tailtip slices through the air and tugs my hair, making my whole body jerk. The sun catches the jewels on my chains, filling the bedroom with sparkling wonder. I gasp, and he lets it go.

Awed, I turn away from him and walk into the sunlight.

Zaku doesn't stop me, though his tailtip follows, stroking my ankles. Mesmerized, warmed, and feeling oddly freed, the rainbows streak over the floors and walls with every move I make.

After a while, I forget my nudity. I forget the aches in my body, the bruises on my skin, and even the circumstances I'm in, unable to look away from the splendor. I've never created anything before except tears.

The sun begins to set as my hair dries in silken waves down my back, as I hold onto this moment as long as I can.

When the sun lowers and my sparkles vanish, I press up against the window and watch Earth fall into a purple twilight. It looks empty and serene—peaceful—like no matter what happens, everything will be okay.

The room is in shadow when I face Zaku again.

He hasn't moved, though his gaze is hooded, dark, like molten fire.

He looks wicked.

I feel beautiful.

For an instant, I consider crawling up onto his tail and straddling him.

"Come here, Daisssy," he hisses my name when I just stand there.

I walk to the edge of the bed, and his tail coils up my leg. He reaches out for me to join him.

Staring at his outstretched hand, I slowly take it, climbing into the bed with him. *A bed he calls a nest...* Zaku shifts and herds me to his side, his giant tail moving to drape around all sides of me, closing me in. He presses me up against him, and I wait for him to do more as his hand cups my shoulder.

But his breaths even out and his hand loosens, slipping down my arm a short time later.

My heart calms, and I relax.

Sleep takes me away.

SIXTEEN

MORNING LIGHT

Zaku

I WAKE, warm and content. The past weeks have seeped from my limbs. Twirling a silken strand, I have the most beautiful female in all the universe at my side, her leg hooked over my tail and her hand on my chest.

She is asleep. Against *me*. I have never slept next to another. My mother did not birth a full litter, and so I never had to share my mother's nest with siblings.

I'm sharing my nest now, and it is everything I have dreamed about.

Rumbling a low hiss, I release Daisy's hair and play with the chains at her back. Her skin is flushed this morning, the red of her scrapes now a soft pink, and her bruises are yellowing. She will become more beautiful as she heals. I long to see her in all her glory.

I envy *me* for claiming her. No male deserves the most beautiful female in the land more than I.

I only want to be surrounded by beautiful things. I deserve the best.

My rumbles deepen. I have earned them.

Soon we will mate, soon my member will be lodged deep inside her, and she will remain on it, the flower to my stem, forever. She will give me young, gestate many litters—live well and long by my side—and raise our offspring.

It's been so long since I saw a young naga. Decades. The female young who were birthed were adopted by unmated adult naga females and taken west. Males, like me, were left behind with their fathers.

I do not have to worry that Daisy will die like the females of my kind. Humans have safely brought children into this world far longer than I've been around. They will continue doing so long after I'm gone. Her being here is proof of that. I have a human medical pod just in case...

Though... I have never seen a pod that could fit a naga. I wonder why.

Catching a new strand of Daisy's hair, I rub it between my fingers.

Seeing the humans' ship descend from the sky has changed my plans. I'd thought about journeying west again to search for the lost ones, to try and help them. I expel the old plans from my mind.

I am glad I waited.

Everything is perfect—everything except my swollen member. I glance down at where it's sticking out like a slightly curved pillar from my tail. I clutch the base with my free hand and slide my palm up my length, squeezing the bulge that has only grown. Seed bursts from my tip.

I grit my teeth.

Some of the seed drips over the side of my tail and onto the bedding between Daisy and me. Groaning, I do not want any more of it to go to waste. I gather what I can and rub it over her skin.

She mumbles and shifts. She doesn't wake up.

Excited, remembering our deal, I drop my hand, coiling my tailtip around my member.

I yank my shaft while I lift, shifting so I'm on top of her, gently positioning her below me. Arching my tail so my member won't bump her, I squeeze my length hard, imagining so much more.

I hiss low and deep. My nostrils flare as my knot grows from the attention. I gather as much seed as I can endure, staring at Daisy's slumbering, soft face. Slipping my tongue out from my mouth, I lash the empty air between our faces, wishing I was lashing her body. But if she wakes, she may stop me, and though I have every right to do as I will up to the point of mating, she might balk and try to flee.

I can't let that happen. This moment is perfect.

She's under me, soft and sweet, so small she could be nothing more than another pillow on my nest. Yet she's in it, and she remained in it the whole night, letting me enjoy her warmth. My gaze streaks to the chains bunched up around her breasts and the glittering diamonds that tease her nipples.

I grip the bedding on either side of Daisy's head, tearing it with my nails, rocking my hips, rutting my coiled tailtip.

She moans, brings one of her hands up, and swats her nose. Tensing, I go still, waiting to see if she wakes up. She moans again, and I lean on my right arm, deciding to shift to her side. I never get a chance to.

Her eyes flutter open.

Widening, they land on my face. The glare of sleep vanishes from her irises instantaneously, and her body loses all its sweet looseness.

We stare at each other. She's stopped breathing. Her lips part and I can tell she's trying not to scream—trying not to move. Because she knows if she does, even a little, she'd still be trapped under the cage of my arms, and right now, I'm barely touching her.

If she tries to flee, I'll grab her and pull her against me. Daisy fears our differences, I sense it.

Her eyes flick down between our bodies, stopping where my tailtip is curled around my shaft. She stares and takes a deep, shuddering breath.

I wait for her reaction yet all she does is stare. I puff out my cowl, delighted that she wishes to watch me. She takes in another deep breath. Pulling my shaft harder, I wonder how far I can go before she tells me to stop.

"What are you doing?" she whispers. Her hand slides up to cup her nose but not before her cheeks pinken.

"Relieving the pressure in my knot," I growl, releasing the tip of my shaft and spilling all over her thighs and legs.

She jerks, shimmying her legs, trying to get out from where my seed is leaking onto her. I reach down and clutch her hip. "You wear my diamonds—you will also wear my seed. See? It is nice when you wear it." I tilt my head at the glistening cum on her skin. "It is yours."

Daisy stops moving, her gaze snapping to mine. Her other hand comes up to grasp the chains tangled at her neck. I pet her cheek, pull her hand off her nose, and while she winces, she remains where she is, sucking in another deep breath. She even relaxes.

"Zaku... this is..." She inhales deeply again. "So wrong. We don't even know each other."

"Wrong?" I check to make sure I am not limiting her airflow, but finding I am still fully above her, I move my gaze back to her face. Her eyes hood and dart between us, down to where I hold my member.

"I..." She brings the hand I pulled off her nose to join the other one clutching her chains. "I'm scared," she whispers. Her chest rises and falls quickly.

My ardor cools, and I release her hip, bringing my hand up to cup her face. The other pets her tousled hair. "I know, but you don't have to be. Our deal still stands."

"Promise?"

"Yesss," I hiss.

Her eyes search mine. They're a light brown that complements her yellow hair and pale skin. I don't know why I haven't studied their depths until now, but they're as alluring as the rest of her.

I smile, caressing a line from her cheek to her lower lip with my thumb's claw. She relaxes a little more, and I lower my throbbing member to rest against her thighs, pressing my body to hers.

She tenses again, though it doesn't last. Her body is heated. She takes in another heavy breath, and her flesh warms even more. A delicious scent rises to my nose. It's one I have never encountered before. I like it. Immensely. I push my tail into her legs until she has no choice but to open them and let me lie between them. When she does, the scent blooms in the air.

I groan, my tail swaying gently.

It's her arousal.

She wants me. I have aroused her!

I am king.

Uncoiling my tailtip from my member, I thrust once excitedly against her thigh. The sensation of her flesh along my bulge forces a winded groan from my throat. I empty my spill all over her.

She gasps as I spill and spill and spill. There is little pleasure from the action itself except for the release of tension deep inside me.

I rise and, grabbing my shaft with my hands, staring down at Daisy beneath me, I spill even more. Daisy's gone tense again, but she lets me have this. Her fingers loosen on the chains and her hands drop to rest on her chest.

She's panting wildly. I notice dabbles of sweat forming upon her brow.

Thrusting into my hand, I cover her with my essence. Fluid falls over her legs, her belly, her arms, her chest. It pools and trickles over her curves and dampens the bedding. I spill until the aching bulge is gone from my shaft. And still, I clutch myself, wanting to soak her, working all the built-up tension from my loins. Releasing my member long enough to remove her arms from her chest, needing to see all of her, I groan, wanting more than anything to sink my fangs into her shoulder and mark her and engorge.

She squirms, rubs her nose, and gasps again, stopping this primal need of mine. I spread my seed over her breasts instead, her neck, and even smear it on her lips.

The shock on her face excites me.

When her tongue sneaks out for a taste of me, I lose it.

Grabbing her thighs, I press her knees to her chest, drawing back to plant my face between her legs, needing her taste on my tongue.

She cries out, and her hands grab a hold of my cowl. Heels dig into my back as she tries to close her legs, undulating her hips all the same. "What's happening?" she whimpers. "To me?"

I think I hear a twinge of fear in her voice and I glimpse her face to make sure. It's not fear I find. Her face is flushed with fervor and...excitement?

Have I excited her as well? Pride wells inside me.

"Pleasssure," I answer, helping her come to terms with this thing between us.

When she doesn't try and flee, I spread her open wide, and take in her delicate human sex. Yellow curls glisten with dew, framing a soft pink slit. There's a nub at the top that beacons my tongue, but it's her little hole that brings my saliva forth. It's wet and quivering. It's small and delicate. And it's open... For me.

For her king. Satisfaction joins my pride. I have chosen well.

"Zaku!" she whimpers my name, body straining against mine.

"Daisssy," I hiss back, petting her opening with my fingertip. I lean forward and slip my tongue into her, pushing through tight, tender flesh.

She cries out again and her hips shoot upward at my invasion. I grasp them and hold her there in the air. The angle gives me even better access to her sheath. Sliding my tongue everywhere, tasting her, drinking her, I learn her from the inside out. Pressing my fork as far back as I can into her tightness, I reach her body's end. I swirl my tongue.

A deep, satisfied groan bursts from my throat.

"Zaku!" Clawing and clutching my head, my cowl, her nails bite into my scales as she shrieks my name. Her little body writhes and she jerks her hips up and down like she's trying to dislodge me or seek more of my attention.

But my mouth is planted firmly on her opening, my lips kissing it, refusing to move. My tongue is lodged deep.

My little flower needs watering. She needs to bloom to fit my stem.

She is small. And so is her sex. She will need lots of watering.

Pressing her back down to the bed, I glimpse her overly flushed and stunned face, her wild hair. Her eyes are wide and heated. I lick harder, and she hitches.

She's not trying to remove me anymore—she's doing the opposite. I smile against her dewy folds. Daisy bears her sex down onto my face, gripping me tightly. Careful not to hurt her, I open her legs wider and push her back until she's sprawled out like a meal.

I could accidentally hurt her, so easily, a niggle of worry enters me. Perhaps her fear of mating is sound...

Her eyes close and her body hitches again, banishing my worry. She shunts into me, and when she does, I roll my tongue in deep circles. Her moans build, her gasps heighten. Her little noises excite me. Her body wants what I can give it. I know because her arousal thickens over my tongue. It gushes, and I quickly remove my tongue to swallow it, only to thrust my tongue back in for more.

Groaning, I feast.

Her hand comes down between her legs to pet her nub. Wondering what she is doing, I exhale a hot breath through my nose, staring as she works it. She moans, and I massage her thighs where I grip them.

The Python might have gotten here first, but I'll be here last.

I'd kill him all over again if I could.

I lick her harder, faster.

"Zaku," she breathes my name again, and my spine straightens, waiting for direction. There's a rigid spot inside her that makes her moan when I flick my tongue to it. I use it so she stays put. "D-Don't stop!" Her fingers quicken on her nub.

Good.

Her sex clamps down on my tongue, and Daisy arches her whole body, going abruptly silent. She flings her head back; and I look up, mesmerized. Her mouth purses as her chest arches. I'm tempted to pull away but I don't want to stop licking her. Her body convulses, and she takes my tongue with it.

She writhes on my face, and I give her the leverage to do so.

Sweet essence floods me.

My knot expands hard and fast from the assault, and I spill again, lapping it up.

Slowly, her convulsions subside, her breathy panting the only sound in the room. I hungrily swallow everything she gives me. If I could sustain my body with hers, I would. From this morning on, I will see if it's possible. I will drink her down and see if we're even more compatible than she wants to believe.

"Zaku…" she says, sagging into the bedding of my nest. She pushes my head out from between her legs. Sliding my hands up to grip hers, I swirl and lick her sex one last delicious time.

I will seed you soon, sweet flower. I kiss it goodbye and pull my tongue out, swiping at her outer folds as I do.

"No more." Clamping her thighs together, she turns on her side, bringing her hands to her face and rubbing it. "It's too much, too sensitive," she whines. "I need… I need to think."

I crawl over her until she's within the cage of my body, my large tail coiled around us. She's such a small thing compared to me. My worry returns. I have to be careful. So easily, I could ruin her. My hands, from claw to palm, span from her chin to curl over the top of her head. I carried her body for hours the first day, never tiring.

She's all soft curves and lush breasts, softness personified, and a perfect contrast to the hard scales and ridges of my body.

She also has no natural armor; I don't even know how she is alive right now without armor. I take in her scrapes and bruises. I take in the tangled chains gathered around her throat. I span my fingers out to grip them, pushing my fingers under the collar around her throat.

I will need to feed her well and often so she becomes more substantial. Daisy will need the extra sustenance if I plan to keep her nested for many years to come. If I plan to feed from her slit.

Her panting subsides as she slips her hands from where she has them pressed over her eyes to look up at me. The pink glow of her cheeks has yet to disappear.

"We're only just beginning," I say, leaning down and licking her jaw, gripping her collar.

But first, she needs food.

SEVENTEEN
A VISITOR

Daisy

THE NEXT COUPLE of days bleed into each other.

Pressing my palms to the glass in the foyer, I debate if I've been here for five or six days already. Maybe more? It's hard to keep track, even with the windows. Time is different on Earth than it is in space. Things are faster here yet somehow slower too.

Gazing at the bones in the yard, I make up stories about them in my head. Fierce battles, bloody deaths, and booming last words. Only for those words to vanish on the wind as Zaku ultimately wins. The more he wins in my head, the more I want him to win. The more I like thinking about it and imagining it.

Everyone has their heroes. Mine was supposed to be my father except putting him in that role in my head only infuriates me. I sigh.

Zaku's out hunting and foraging to refill his stores and I wonder if he'll battle today as well, perhaps bring home another trophy. I shudder, uncertain if I like the idea of it.

He says I'm too small and wants me to eat until I'm bursting. He needs more food for that.

I sigh, annoyed that I haven't even tried to escape now that I'm alone.

Being alone is easy, safe. I became a pilot for that very reason. I can spend entire shifts alone in my cockpit, never encountering another soul. Though right now? It's making me uncomfortable. Imagining a whole day alone churns my stomach.

I suck in a clear, unscented breath of air. With Zaku's absence, his scent has vanished. I curl my toes, not certain I like that it's gone. His scent makes me happy—happy, of all things. It does something to me. At first, it was frightening, but now, not so much. It's not always in the air. It's not always spinning my thoughts. I've come to realize the scent only comes around when Zaku's overly aroused. *I don't think he realizes...*

Most of the time, though, he's producing the smell. And, I, desperate to trust him—to trust in *something*—keep testing his limits, keep searching for a reason to distrust him like those I've worked for.

I'm waiting to be betrayed all over again.

Closing my eyes, I bring my hands to my face, rubbing it hard.

I should be trying to escape. I should be looking for Gemma.

Except all I want to do is pretend the world outside these walls doesn't exist. My hands fall from my face to clutch the collar around my throat. I haven't taken it off since Zaku placed it upon me. The diamonds and chains have been unhooked, but the collar remains.

I blush, remembering this morning how I gripped at his cowl and dug my nails into it, writhing on his face as he held me up on his shoulders. As his scent flooded my nose, warmed my body, made me ache feverishly, and almost had me screaming for sex. As his tongue slammed into me, dizzying my world.

Each day, I get to sleep for as long as I want, bathe in hot, scented water for hours, eat the freshest food, and *relax*. Throughout it all, Zaku's touching me, massaging the aches out of my muscles, and trying to part my legs for his pleasure and mine. I stopped caring because it's a distraction—*he's* a distraction.

I'm growing complacent.

My hands fall from my collar.

Sex is commonplace amongst agreeable, contractual humans. It's even encouraged to grow our numbers. Women, despite being soldiers, are still pressured to have at least two children in their lifetime. The father's identity doesn't matter. It's the numbers that count. There's always a need for more soldiers, for workers.

If I were to stay here on Earth, Zaku would be a great companion. He's strong. He'd keep me safe until I learned how to keep *myself* safe.

He's not cold. If he were human, he'd give me strong children—he'd provide for those children, I'm sure of it—except he's not, and inter-species relations have never resulted in gestation.

I can't be with him. I want to be a mother someday. I want to raise my children the way I was never raised. With love, affection, and perhaps... dreams. I want to prove there is more to life than war and death. My fingers twitch.

Who'd want someone like me? I can't offer anything anymore. The best I can hope for is a contractual relationship with a man who will impregnate me and leave, to impregnate another. I could do the same for a man who wants children, but then I wouldn't be able to keep my baby, which is out of the question.

I don't have the looks to entice a higher caste man. One who would willingly *life partner* with me. And then there's the problem of barely having enough rations to take care of one, let alone a child.

It's not in the cards, Daisy. It never was.

I inherited nothing from my father except his genes, his appearance. Everything he earned, he donated to the military. It was the first time I felt betrayed. When he died, I had no idea what was happening, begging for him, confused as to why I was being handed off from one official to the next. They didn't even let me keep one of his medals to remember him by. My father was there, and then he wasn't. He and the military taught me not to rely on anyone in the most brutal way possible, through innocent, childish confusion.

Zaku could teach me things. Different things. How to survive here. He could make *me* stronger.

Feeling my eyes grow heavy, I force my tears away. I've gone years without crying. Earth, Peter, and the Python unraveled all of my hard work and I hate them for it.

Zaku could show me how to use the tech. He could teach me about this land. I suck my lower lip into my mouth and chew on it, knowing I'm trying to convince myself of life here on Earth. That living here is a possibility. Glimpsing the scars on my hands that I've sustained over the years, guilt floods me. I brush them with my fingers. Zaku cares a lot about the way I look. I don't understand why. I'm not particularly beau-tiful for a human woman, but he doesn't seem to know that.

I can't help wondering if his affections can be easily shifted, and if they are—if there were more "options" —would he still think I'm beauti-ful? I scrunch my face.

You're not staying here, Daisy.

I groan, turning to the stake right outside where the rotting stump of the Python's head is decaying. It's been covered in maggots for days, surrounded by bloated flies. One of the flies crawls into its mouth. Looking away, my eyes go to Earth's sun.

Where is Zaku?

Does Central Command know I'm gone yet?

Is Gemma okay? Shelby?

I hear a sizzling sound behind me. Turning toward the kitchen, there's a robot preparing food.

Something thuds on the glass, and I twist back. A blue shimmer catches my attention as a rock tumbles away from the window.

Zaku?

Suddenly the blue blur comes charging toward me from out of the trees. My heart jumps into my throat and I fall into the room and duck behind the sofa. *A naga male.* The blue one from the plateau. I close my eyes and press my hands to my mouth.

Please go away.

There's more thudding on the window, louder than before, and I flinch. I press my hands harder to my mouth. I wait, even pray. After a few minutes, the thudding stops. I wait some more and it doesn't come back.

Slowly lifting my head, I peek over the sofa cushion...

I stiffen, and my chest constricts with fear.

The male sways on his tail when he sees me. He presses one of his hands flush to the glass. His palm is a brilliant orange, like his face, like his hair. Stunned, we stare at each other for a time, taking each other in. This one's not like Zaku at all. The only thing this naga and Zaku share are their forms.

Where Zaku is a giant with a cowl and dull colors, this naga has a short tuft of wild orange hair on his head that matches the brilliance of his face and his hands, his body bearing a longer, thinner tail. The orange upon him is striking with the sapphire and indigo blues of his body and scales.

His eyes are black.

I can't decide if the male is either stunning or uncannily terrifying. Or both. He reminds me of the lake. Of deep blue water and all the creatures hidden within it.

Swallowing, my fear ebbs. *The glass will hold.* It will...

The allure of his coloring, though, screams for me to keep my distance. If I've learned anything from visiting numerous planets, it's that the prettiest, brightest creatures are the most dangerous.

Wanting to get closer, I move into the open space of the room.

What will he do if I show courage? If I stand up to him?

Will he *fear* me?

I've met two of these nagas so far, and both were different. Maybe he will be too?

He stares at me intensely, and I curl my arms over my chest. When I'm standing mere yards from him, he says something to me that I can't hear through the glass. One of those little white orbs floats around his head.

He bares his fangs and says something more, the intensity going into his expression.

I shake my head.

He slides his hand down the glass, bringing the other forward. He's holding a knife.

Shelby's knife.

I forget the naga and search the yard for Shelby. A fist pounds on the glass, startling me. I look back at the male. His flaring nostrils, the frustration etched on his face, sends my pulse racing. I take a step back. He looks around, finds a large rock, and flings it at the glass.

Thump!

I recoil as the rock tumbles to the ground.

The male glances at something behind me, and I turn to see the robot holding out a plate of food. An idea forms.

Zaku programmed the robots to listen to me in all things except for letting me leave.

"Robot..." I say, pursing my lips, trying to find the right words to ask for what I want, trying to keep my anxiety from showing. "I want to speak to him." I indicate the male outside.

The robot scans me, scans him. Then it scans the white orb hovering beside him.

"Connecting," it says.

I glance at the trees around the yard, searching for Zaku. He could return at any moment. I don't know what he'll do if he sees this other naga speaking to me, but I assume he'll kill him and put his head on a spike with the other. Or maybe he'd just let it rot on the ground with the others scattered about. If his talk about domination is to be believed, he won't let this naga live. Facing him, I straighten my shoulders.

If he wants to risk his life, then so be it. He might have news of the outside world. He has *something* because he's holding Shelby's knife. I'll take something over nothing.

A crackling noise fills my ears, and then a voice.

"Female... where... Zaku?"

My flesh prickles with excitement. It worked! But I shake my head again at him. I sure as hell am not giving Zaku's location away.

I like Zaku.

More than most people or beings I've met.

"He's around," I say softly. "Stop making noise or he'll hear," I lie.

The male snarls at me. "Open the door," he demands. "Let me speak to him." His voice is clearer now coming through the house's robot. "I am owed."

Owed?

"I'm not an idiot. I'm not letting you in, and even if I wanted to, I can't," I say a little louder.

The male pounds his fist on the glass, clearly annoyed.

"Where did you get that knife?" I ask, pointing to the weapon in his hand.

He pauses, looking at it. "The forest."

"It's mine," I say, growing more confident.

His eyes come back to mine. "It's *mine* now. Open the door. I am owed!" he shouts, thumping his tail.

I flinch. Absolutely not. If he's near Zaku's home, where there are remains scattered everywhere, then he's not afraid of Zaku.

Maybe this male is that terrifying. Or maybe he's stupid.

But then if he's stupid... if I try the door with his help, perhaps I'd get *free*. I could trick him.

I could run.

I could make it back to the facility, take the transport ship, and return to *The Dreadnaut*. There I could find reinforcements, save Gemma, and get my vengeance on Peter and the others.

Zaku will never let me get that far.

I'm mad at myself for even considering such a terrible plan. These males aren't stupid...and if they were, they're strong enough to counteract it.

"No," I tell him.

The male's lips twist. His eyes go wild with desperation, making my heart race. The scales rise on his neck and shoulders. "He promisssed me a female!" The male strikes at the window again, and I take a step back. "He lied. I will have what I'm owed!"

A cold sweat breaks out on my skin. I shake my head again. The male hisses, flings his long tail like a whip upon the glass.

The window shudders, the sound louder than the thump of the rock. "I will have what I've been promised! I will have her!" his roar thunders through the robot, making my soul quiver. I back up until my butt is against the kitchen counter. "He promisssed me! A so-called king," the naga spits, "never breaks a promise!"

The further I back up, the angrier he gets. He slams his tail against the glass over and over. Harder, heavier, the pounding rumbles through my whole body, filling me with terror. He thrashed, beating at the window.

I hear the glass crack.

"I will have what I am owed!"

EIGHTEEN

BROKEN PROMISES

Daisy

GLASS SHATTERS, and I dart to the side, sprinting to the red door. I slam it closed behind me, frantically searching for a lock, a weapon, anything. There are only the paintings on the walls and the spiral staircase on the far end that leads to Zaku's nest. Nothing else.

Then I see the panel next to the door. Pressing buttons at random, I pray it locks.

I hear more glass shatter, growing louder by the second. *The glass isn't working*, my thoughts reel. *The door isn't going to keep me safe. I can't stay here.* I pivot to flee below when Zaku's voice stops me.

"Vagan!" he bellows, the sound eclipsing all else.

There's another crash, and I stop.

"I gave you what you needed, and you deny me my prize!" Vagan roars. "I bought her, not you!"

Bought...her? Anger streaks through me. *Who?*

Sliding my damp palms on my pants, I crouch as I hear more things break and shatter.

After a time a thunderous hiss pierces through the door and straight into me. *Zaku's hiss.* It slithers through me and over my flesh, entering me and invading every nerve ending. I lick my lips and open the door to peer outside.

Shaking, I find Zaku in the middle of the room, towering over the other male's form, and the naga, Vagan, coiled, glaring up at him.

Shelby's knife is sticking out of Zaku's chest. Fear rips through me.

They're poised, the both of them, waiting for the other to make the next move. Zaku's tailtip sways tensely from side to side above his shoulder.

I clutch the door as the blue naga hisses, "We had a deal."

Slowly, Zaku lifts his hand and grips the knife. "You dare enter my den? Attack my queen?" he grits. "Any deal we had is gone for your foolishness."

"Gone? It was my tech. Mine! I will have what I'm owed!"

Zaku's lips curl and he pulls the knife from his chest. "You are owed nothing. You did not capture a female. The hunt was fair."

"Fair? There was nothing fair about it. You threw me off the mountain. You denied me the chance," the blue one sneers. "I will take yours in compensation," he hisses.

Zaku lifts the knife and stares at it. Just like the Python had that first night. Blood spurts from Zaku's chest.

Transfixed, fear cramps my stomach.

Zaku's cowl flares, his eyes darkening when they return to the blue male. "You will never have my queen, Vagan. And for this intrusion, I will make you pay."

Vagan rises to face him. "Dishonorable sssnake," he says. "You're the one who will die today, and I will claim your female upon your corpse! I will take her as your punishment for your deceit!" He attacks, and I shove open the door, screaming when his tail snaps behind Zaku and comes down.

Zaku braces against the hit, tenses at my voice, and strikes out, thumping Vagan in the face. Vagan roars, and then there's nothing but a flurry of tails and limbs. I hear grunts, snarls, and groans. Vagan flings away and twists in my direction. He rushes for me.

He abruptly stops and is dragged back by his tail. I dodge behind the door and close it again, sliding down the frame with a whimper. I need to do something. I need a weapon.

There's no fucking weapon in this house!

"I will have what I'm owed!"

"She is not the one you want," Zaku bellows.

"You allowed the human males to leave without delivering her, without giving her to us! She is mine!"

"She is gestating. How was I supposed to know this? Do you want a human litter to fend for?"

"The human males lie. She is not gestating!"

They're talking about Shelby.

"I can't give you what I don't have. The hunt was fair, Vagan. Leave now and I will let you live," Zaku growls. "For the history we share, I can be merciful."

"Merciful? You don't know the meaning of the word. You owe me, King Cobra. You owe me. Help me! Help me steal her. Now that would be mercy."

"I'd rather see you maimed."

Abruptly fighting returns, louder, wilder this time, and closer to the door. I fall back when something crashes through it. It cracks, shattering, wood splintering everywhere. Fleeing, I race for the safety of Zaku's nest.

A tail wraps around my ankle, jerks me, and I drop hard to the ground, hitting my head. Crying out, I'm dragged across the floor and into a cage of arms.

"Release her," Zaku snaps, poised in the doorway, a hand clutching his chest where his blood spurts. Sharp claws press into my neck.

"I want my mate," Vagan wheezes against my ear, lifting me against him. Corded muscles press into me. His claws push into my skin and I wince.

Zaku strains but remains where he is, meeting my eyes. "Don't hurt her."

"I will do more than hurt her," Vagan threatens, "if I don't get what I want."

"Shelby," I rasp. "You want Shelby."

Vagan goes taut, his chest pushes into my back. "Ssshelby," he repeats her name. "The one with bright eyes."

Zaku's tail inches closer.

"Yes!" I burst out, focusing on it. "Shelby, you want her, don't you? Her eyes are special," I say, distracting Vagan.

"Ssspecial?"

I lick my lips. "Very special. They're... they're enhanced, her eyes." Vagan's claws lift from my skin slightly. "She's very special. Only one in a million have eyes like hers."

"She is," he agrees. "She excites me. She... she has turned my body against me. Why?" he roars, sending my hair flying from the ferocity. "Why is my body quaking!?"

Zaku's tail gets even closer. I feel Vagan's tail coil up my leg and something hard digs into my lower back, something more than his chest.

Knowing what it is, I try not to be sick. "How does she excite you?"

Vagan grunts and his cock grows harder, bigger, wetter. "She makes me want to mate. Tell me more about her eyes. Tell me anything. I want to know everything. I need—"

Vagan's hold on me drops, and I fall forward. Zaku catches me as Vagan is ripped back, pulled away by Zaku's tail. Zaku thrusts me behind him, and I tumble to my knees as he jumps atop Vagan's form, his fangs sinking brutally into the blue naga's arm.

Vagan screams, clawing at Zaku, refusing to give up. Zaku's entire body twitches, straining against the place where his fangs are deep in Vagan's skin. I scurry away and into the foyer, not wanting Vagan to grab me again. Zaku's fangs hold.

Vagan rolls onto his back, his eyes glazing over. They meet mine and he hisses weakly, "Shelby." Like he is satisfied dying on her behalf. For a woman he has never even met.

I frown.

Zaku slides his tail over Vagan's form, pulling his fangs out as Vagan falls unconscious. Zaku presses his hand back to his wound. Minutes go by—minutes that feel like an eternity—and Vagan doesn't rise.

Zaku slumps to the floor, keeping the heaviest part of his tail draped across Vagan's chest. His eyes hood, finding mine. They dull further as I rush to him. There's blood everywhere, pooling from his wound. It's all over his scales.

"Zaku," I whisper, spanning my fingers, uncertain if I should touch him.

"Vagan... will not be out long." He sags, his hand sliding down his chest. "You... must hide."

"We need to stop your bleeding," I say. I sprint into the front room, grabbing some towels from the kitchen, and when I do, I spot dozens of robots everywhere. They're picking up the rubble, the broken furniture, and the glass strewn about. Some are beginning to repair the walls. I don't wait to watch, returning to Zaku's side.

His eyes follow me as I press the towels to his wound, staunching the blood as best I can.

"We need to stop the bleeding. Do you have anything that can help?" I call for the robots when he shakes his head. Soon, several come to my aid. "Help me," I beg them.

One of the robots scans Zaku. "Emergency medical aid has been called. They are on the way."

Zaku reaches for me. "I will regenerate."

"Hush. The robots said aid is coming—we need to put pressure on your wound. We need to stop the bleeding. Try not to move."

"Aid isn't coming. I need... sleep. Rest. You need to hide. Vagan will not be down long. My venom—"

"Not without you. I'm not going anywhere without you."

He just saved my life. There's no way I'm leaving him, but if what he says is true and Vagan will soon wake, he'll kill Zaku and finish the job. He'll come after me. He'll go after Shelby.

I need a weapon. Straightening, I run back to the front rooms and find my knife. Covered in blood, I wipe it on my pants and return to Zaku.

He eyes me and the weapon. I go to Vagan's side.

I poise the knife over Vagan's chest and sink it in, putting my weight down on it to push it through the naga's muscles and organs. I hit bone. He groans but doesn't wake. I yank it out and stab him several more times in the gut.

"Shelby will never be yours," I whisper, "You'll never hurt her baby." Pushing my knife into Vagan once more, I leave it in. "You'll never hurt her or her baby."

I turn back to Zaku. He's slumped over, and I crawl to him. "What about the medical pod?"

"I... will not... fit."

Glancing at the robots gathered around us, Zaku grabs my wrist, forcing my eyes back to his.

Slowly, he lifts, pinning me with his eyes, towering over me, blood spurting between his fingers when the towels plop to the floor. Some of it gets on me. He tugs me to my feet, and my mouth slackens as he drags me toward the stairs.

"What are you doing?" I choke. "You're going to hurt yourself further. You'll die!" He leads me toward his nest, his grip tightening when I try to pull away. "Stop, Zaku! You're making yourself bleed more!"

"If you will not hide—" he wheezes. "I will make you hide."

Zaku falls against the wall, taking only a moment to steady his body with his arm. I gag, glancing back at the trail of blood he leaves in his wake, his tail slipping through it, half tumbling down the stairs.

"Please stop," I beg him. "Please. I'll hide, I promise, just stop!"

He uses the wall the rest of the way down.

A robot is waiting for us at the bottom. Zaku groans and stares at it. I try yanking my wrist from his grip again. "Why are you doing this?" I gasp.

"From this... point on," he hisses at the robot, "you will follow no one's... commands but my own."

My brows furrow. Zaku drags me into his room and toward the golden cage. He thrusts me inside. I catch my footing and turn as the cage's door closes.

"Sssafe," he says. He tumbles to the floor.

I rush to the bars. "No," I cry, reaching my arm through them. My fingers brush his scales. "Zaku!"

He doesn't respond.

"Wake up!" I scream.

Daisy

I LOSE MY MIND.

I scream, I rattle the cage bars, I curse. All the while, Zaku's blood slowly covers the floor, making the cage feel even smaller.

The stench of it fills my nostrils. I can't stop breathing it in, no matter how hard I try. I can't get away from it. My clothes are soaked with it. I shout for Zaku to wake up. I scream for the robots that no longer respond to me. I vomit up bile, nauseated with fear.

I climb onto the swing in the cage when the house robots enter the room, fearing it's Vagan back from the dead to finish the job.

The robots clean the blood. They wash the walls. They laser the ground. They even wipe the blood off Zaku. I beg them to let me out of the cage but they leave me be, cleaning what they can through the bars.

The smell of blood remains.

When the robots are done, I move to the lock and try it. Only I can't get a good look at the mechanism on the outside. I can't reach it with my fingers. Straining, pushing I still try, giving up before I hurt my hand. Holding it to my chest, I curse some more. My attention returns to the giant, unmoving male and my heart constricts.

He hasn't stirred, his coloring continues to diminish. The yellow, browns, beiges, and even his black scales have gone grey. I calm, staring at him, or go numb, I don't know anymore. His bleeding has stopped, but he's also still not moving. I gaze at his motionless form, begging for him to wake up and then cursing him for putting me in this situation. Eventually, the robots leave.

And I'm alone.

One returns and brings me food. It's the same plate from earlier. One look at it, and I hack up empty air.

Wiping my mouth with the back of my hand, I notice Zaku's chest quake. He expels a heavy breath, shudders, and goes still again. But soon after, he breathes once more, easier this time.

"Zaku," I whisper, expelling my fear. Deep-seated fear that's been drowning me from the inside, thinking he had died...

I clutch the bars, frighteningly relieved and excited. I grip the bars harder.

Safe? This isn't safe.

I can't do anything inside a cage. I can't even help myself!

And then it occurs to me that perhaps putting me in the cage is to keep Zaku safe. From *me*. It makes sense. Unconscious, I could easily stab him to death like I did Vagan, and he'd not be able to stop me.

I could also run. And right now, with the way I feel, I want to stab Zaku all over again for throwing me in here. My numbness gives way to fury, and for a long time, I glare at him. I glare and tell him if he dies to spite me, I am going to find him in the next plane and kill him myself.

The night comes and goes. I don't sleep. I can't. Sticky, cold, and miserable; there's not enough space for me to lie down without touching blood. Most of it is dry now, but that's not any better. It's crusted on my clothes, and I contemplate stripping, eventually deciding against it.

Resting my head on the bars, I begin telling Zaku stories I heard as a kid just to fill the deafening silence. Legends of space pirates, marauder kings, and princesses who fell asleep only to be woken up by a lover's kiss. He stirs, and I grasp onto the hope that he's listening, that he hears my voice.

"Live," I whisper. "I'm not worth dying over." I tell him if he comes closer to the bars, I'll kiss him. It's stupid, but maybe fairy tales have some truth to them. I'm willing to try.

He doesn't wake, he doesn't move closer. And before long, I run out of stories. I was never told very many of them when I was a kid. I try making a couple up, stumbling over words, saying silly, ridiculous things. I give up when it doesn't work.

My fear ramps up again in the silence. I've been around silence for far too long. I've been alone for longer, and I can't do it anymore. I don't want to be alone anymore. Tears fall, and I angrily wipe them off my cheeks.

When the picture of the Lurker pokes at my brain, when it finally makes its return, I sit in terror thinking that he's real... he's real and he's watching *me*.

So I fill the silence and tell Zaku about my horrid life, to keep my tears, the fear, and the silence at bay.

"My dad was a commander," I begin but then stop, sniffling. "I hate crying. I grew up in the military," I say, starting over. "I don't have any brothers or sisters, at least that I know of... My mom was... well, she had a contract with my father to give him a child. She wasn't in my life after I was born. I might have siblings," I ramble.

I lie down on the floor despite the blood, pressing up to the bars nearest Zaku where it's cleaner. "I was forbidden from seeking her out. Even after my dad's death, I was forbidden. I was my father's daughter and no one else's. There are rules. Strict rules where I'm from."

Why do I keep coming back to my dad?

I start over a third time. "I grew up on a ship called *The Prime*. A sister ship to the one hiding behind the moon right now, but newer, faster, closer to the front lines of wherever the war is taking place. It was an honor to be born on such a ship. I had access to the best training. I was born privileged, and I was told such every day. Not every child is lucky enough to be born into a high caste..." Pulling my limbs close to me, I curl them into my body, finding I'm able to keep from focusing on the Lurker in my head if I focus on talking. "But I hated it. I hated every single minute of my life on the Prime," I whisper.

"It was worse when my dad passed. I cried a lot. I missed him. I thought I hated him, but once he was gone, it was different. I was six. I had no idea about the world. No one cared. I had no friends, no family. And crying is a sign of weakness, and someone like me shouldn't have been weak. Not with who my dad was. Daisy Downer is what the other military kids called me. They tried to beat it out of me. I took up piloting to get away. I could be alone if I was flying a ship. No one would see me cry there, no one could hurt me. I didn't like being alone, but I learned to live with it."

I pause, swallowing, hoping Zaku will rouse so I don't have to go on. When he doesn't, I rub my eyes, hard.

"When I was thirteen, it was pretty evident that I wasn't going to live up to my dad's name. Everything got worse. I had to start paying my keep, so they put me in the field. I was sent on my first mission." I hate remembering those days and how terrified I was. I was just a kid. "I shot down my first ship on that very mission, killing over a dozen aliens."

I lift up and look at him, begging him to wake up. *Please, wake up.*

"And do you know what I did, Zaku? I cried. Fuck, it was the worst thing to ever have happen to me, my dad, and then *that*. I didn't want to live. I wasn't cut out to be a soldier. I had no idea who was on that ship, nor what they had done. I was confused and the ship's doctors told me that someday it would all be clear to me. It didn't matter. I had killed them. The guilt was horrible. I vowed to bury that Daisy forever. I didn't deserve to be sad, not after that. I didn't cry again for years.

"I buried my emotions, and life became... tolerable. I began to understand why everyone was so cold, so walled. They learned that lesson much sooner than I. I rose in the ranks and became a petty officer, and life was... okay. But the war caught up to me eventually, and I was shipped to the *real* front lines. My life is pretty boring, isn't it? Pretty sad. No wonder you won't wake up," I say, lying back down.

I stare at Zaku's tail. "Please wake up." He stirs briefly at my voice. I wait another minute hoping he'll stir again. He doesn't.

"I was sent to join a fleet of ships that were being deployed to help stop the wave of Ketts taking over Colony 4. I was supposed to die there, give my life to the war, just to hold them off another day. Only, I saw children on a rooftop as I was flying by." I press my hand to my mouth, guilt flooding me. "I'd be dead right now, if I wasn't so emotional... I should be dead. I'm not worth dying for. I saved them. I couldn't *not* save them. They were crying, like me, like when I was a kid. Everyone in the fleet died that day but me and those kids." Tears bud on my lashes, and I let them fall this time. "So many innocents died. So many lost souls."

Thinking of those babies, silence surrounds me again like a heavy blanket. "They had clung to me, wanted me to protect them, and I wanted to keep them," I murmur. So badly, it hurt. I wanted to be their mother from the moment I saw them. I wanted to give them the protection they sought but I never even made an argument for them because I knew it was futile.

No one was going to give me two healthy, land-born children.

I was a disappointment after all. A failed prodigy. I couldn't provide for them.

"Now I'm here. With you," I say. "Begging you to survive."

When the sun lowers and my eyes start to hood, when I'm bracing for another night in misery, for more silence, I hear a moan.

"Zaku?" I say his name almost hesitantly.

His tail twitches and moves, pulling into his body. I sit up.

He moans again, and his eyelids peel open. For a moment, he stares at the ceiling.

"Zaku?" I gasp, excited.

His tongue leaves his mouth to swipe his lips. His eyes slide from the ceiling to mine.

"Daisy?" he groans, tilting his head in my direction.

"You're awake," I breathe, unable to believe it myself. "You're seriously hurt, Zaku." I grasp the bars.

Zaku slowly lifts his hand from where it rests on the floor and presses it to his wound. He winces and then raises his hand to his eyes. It glistens with fresh blood. "Nothing I won't recover from," he rasps.

I guffaw. "You should've died. You bled—a lot."

He places his hand back on his chest. His gaze narrows as it slips from it to me, and over my form, checking me over. "Are you hurt?" He tries to coil his tail under him. More blood leaks from his chest.

"Don't move!"

He doesn't listen, pushing up, opening his wound even more, and coming to me.

"Zaku, you're going to make it worse."

"Are you hurt?" he asks again, his voice gaining strength.

"I'm..." I trail off, having no idea. "I'm hurt, all right! I'm furious!" Everything in the last day and a half expels from me. "How dare you," I growl, sitting up on my knees. "How dare you put me in this cage where I have no choice but to watch you bleed out! How fucking dare you."

He stares at me like I've lost my mind.

I've lost it, all right.

"You bled out all over the floor! You left me here to rot, all the while soaked in your blood, and for what? Safety? I'm not safe in here, nor are you out there! You stupid, stupid male!"

He doesn't say anything as I do, and only when tears burst from my eyes and I sink to the floor, does he reach through the bars. He catches a tear with his claw.

I hate him so much for it; I hate that the simple gesture comforts me.

"I could not lose you. I am sorry I've been asleep for so long... Do not cry."

"Fuck you! I'll cry if I want. A day and a half, almost two," I whimper. "Two days where I've been drenched in your blood, no idea if I was going to die alongside you." More damning tears fall.

"Vagan must have pierced my heart. I did not think it would be so long."

"Well, you should have thought about that before you passed out." I wipe my cheeks. "Please let me out. I promise I won't run."

He draws his hand out from the cage and presses it back to his wound. "I can't, not until I've gained my strength."

"What? I can't stay in here!"

Zaku rests his shoulder on the bars. "You are safe in there. My den has been compromised, and if something catches the blood in the air before the robots finish repairing it, that something will follow the blood trail here. Nothing can get to you behind these bars. They will have to go through me."

I'm still not sure I'm hearing him correctly. "You can't possibly leave me in here like this," I whisper.

His head rolls, his chin lowers to his chest. I sit up straighter.

"If I lose you..." his words slur, softening. "I will never let that happen—" He slumps.

"Zaku?" I say his name, getting no response. "Zaku?" I say louder.

I reach through the bars and shake his shoulder. His cowl shifts and his eyes are closed, and I notice the blood steadily trickling between his fingers.

"Zaku!" I shout. "Don't leave me in here!"

But I already know he's gone, and I'm once again alone, left to wait. Something snaps, and I scream and scream. I scream until sleep finally takes me away.

TWENTY
NO LONGER HUMAN

Daisy

Hearing a strange sound, I peel my eyes open. They're crusted, raw, and my face is dry. I rub my eyes hard and groan, pulling my aching body up from the ground to look around. I've gotten weak, being unable to eat and getting no rest. No good rest, at least.

My nose twitches. The air smells fresher.

Rubbing my face even harder, I wonder how long I've been asleep.

The first thing I see is a hot plate of food outside the bars, and a little further away, a large lump of fresh meat on the ground beside it. My brow furrows.

The kitchen is fixed? Why that comes to my mind first, I have no idea. But it no longer smells like blood. It smells like food. My stomach knots, and I'm suddenly starving. Hearing the robot leaving the room, I fixate on the food.

There's a large shape moving out of the corner of my eyes. I know what's happening—the sounds I'm hearing indicated as such—but haven't mustered the courage to look at Zaku head-on.

Wet groaning, rasping, growling, and hissing fill my ears. The sounds of a wild animal feasting on a kill.

Slowly, my gaze moves from the plate.

Zaku's hunched over, his hands clutching a red, dripping husk, and he's tearing into it. Chewing and ripping, ravenous hunger shudders his giant form, and I go still, awed by the sight of an apex predator. He sinks his teeth—his fangs—into the husk and yanks a huge piece from it. He doesn't even swallow it before he's ripping off another chunk.

And there's more blood. It's back upon his hands and all over his face. Forcing my eyes from his mouth, I notice hunks of meat surrounding him. As I stare, the wall opens up, and another robot enters carrying more. I press my hands to my mouth as the bloody leg of some animal is dragged across the floor.

I think about saying something but don't, lowering my hands. My stomach growls.

Zaku drops the husk he's holding and snatches the leg.

I flinch when the bones snap, as he devours the entire limb, including those bones. His throat bobs and expands, his belly growing bigger, pushing out his abs, and as it swells, the color returns to his scales.

His wound is closed.

His cock's out.

I swallow thickly, heat blooming my cheeks. My stomach growls again despite the gorefest. Staring at his turgid member, I appreciate it and the primitive nature of him. For a moment, I wish Zaku had been with me that day on Colony 4. If he had, those children would be mine because no one would deign to stand up to a male like him.

He'd protect them like I would have... Glancing at the bars around me, I see them differently. Maybe his methods are mad, but he still managed to protect me.

When the leg is gone, there are two more body parts already waiting for him. Where the robots are getting these limbs, I have no idea, and I'm not sure I want to know. I'm just happy they look like animal parts.

Zaku reaches for one, and I absently reach for my food. I eat my cooked meat as he works his way through the new offerings.

His eyes shift to me when the meat runs out. His eyes twinkle gold and then darken. I stiffen. His tongue swipes out to taste the air in my direction. He rises onto his tail, and his cowl flares outward, laying his large shadow over me. I straighten as he nears, as he does something with the lock, and opens the door.

He yanks me into his arms. I let him, even knowing he just ate my body weight in meat, possibly twice over. Even knowing he might still be hungry for more... I press my nose to his chest, and breathe him in.

And there it is. His musky, soothing smell. It's weak, but it's enough.

I moan, nuzzling him.

"Daisssy," he hisses.

"You're alive," I whisper, my voice dry. "Did you get enough to eat?"

He doesn't answer me, carrying me to the bathroom instead, and turning on the water. He slips us both under it and lowers me to stand. Keeping my hand on his chest so I don't fall, he tears my dirty clothes off with his claws.

Weak, I brace my other hand on the rocky wall, dropping my head to my chest, and simply enjoying the sensation of water and warmth, the heat building inside me, and his scent.

Zaku washes me thoroughly, reverently. His hands scrub my hair clean, tugging and pulling and gripping it. They move to my breasts, my arms, my belly, giving every inch of my flesh attention. I spread my feet when he moves to my sex, lathering it with slick soap. When that's done, he lowers and lifts one of my feet to wash it, massaging it as he does. Holding onto his shoulders, I moan when his thumb pushes into my arch. Then he moves to the other foot.

As warmth returns to my body, I lift my face to the shower and open my mouth, letting the spray fill it. I drink, lick my lips, and drink some more.

"My little queen is a killer," he says thickly, running his hands up and down my legs like it excites him. "I will have to watch you more carefully."

I hum, too tired to respond. I am a killer. In his world and others. I'm glad one of us likes it. I'm glad he's a killer too. If I'm going to be a killer like him, I hope it's only ever in self-defense.

His fingers sneak between my thighs. Turning my face away from the water, I peer down to see what he's doing. His giant tail is partially coiled around me, up against the walls, and the rest of it outside of the shower, filling the bathroom. Water sprays over Zaku's cowl and face, rinsing the blood off of him. His fingers swipe back and forth over my slit, teasing me, coercing me to open for him.

"Zaku," I breathe, leaning into the wall.

And then he finally answers me.

"I hunger," he groans.
"I know."
He pushes a finger into me, and I sigh happily.

TWENTY-ONE
COAXING DAISY

Zaku

Slipping my finger into Daisy's sheath, I shudder with need.

Every second I grow stronger, and it's because of her.

She chose me. She chose to save my life, and remain by my side. She will forgive me for the cage. I had not planned to kill Vagan, only maim him—he has many secrets I long to know, and we have history—but Daisy chose to protect us. How can her mistake anger me? When it was done to protect her mate?

Over and over I see her stabbing him on our behalf. I see his body slump.

No one has ever killed for me before. It is an exciting thing.

What a delicious gift she has given her king.

My member engorges with fresh, hot spill.

I heard her words, her story. I heard everything. Daisy is a killer, and I now know why she stole my attention on the plateau. She's a survivor. She's kept herself alive. She saved children.

She will make a great mother to our many litters.

And she made it across the vast skies to *me*.

My eyes fall to her collar, thick and banded, still around her neck. It's dirty. Even in the shower, she leaves it on. It's the only thing she wears. I did not have a tiara to give her—or a crown—but that collar and its diamonds are part of the treasures stored in my home, and I want them to be hers. I have kept them safe all these years. For her.

The robots can't replace everything...

Grunting, I swallow the saliva flooding my mouth. I am hungry. The meat my house robots brought to me was barely enough to sate me. Daisy will sate me instead. Her swollen sex will. Only... I have no more jewels that I haven't already given her, and she already has reign over the entirety of my den. Now that my strength is returning, I will give her access again, but only once I've made sure the robots are done repairing the walls and windows...

I have nothing left to give my queen—only my member and my devotion. Finding the rigid spot inside her that makes her thrash, I begin rubbing it.

She moans softly for me.

I growl, wrapping my tailtip tight around my aching shaft, yanking hard.

In the days she has let me explore her sweet sex—bringing me closer to my madness without realizing it—I have memorized it. I have pushed and pressed and licked and loved it with my fingers and tongue, wanting to know my female and what works for her best. If she is pleased, she will let me do more, and then we both get what we want.

I like getting what I want. I always get what I want. I want to spill inside her.

She insists it will never happen, insists that we'll never fit. Does she not see that I have been preparing her?

And now that I know she will kill for me, I need to claim her. I need it, or I might crumble into dust. If I can't claim her, no one can.

I almost lost her.

I can't wait any longer.

My mind is clouded, and I am making too many mistakes because of it, mistakes that will get us killed. I also made her a promise...

And she is a small, little thing. A breakable flower, unwatered, and in need of mastery.

I push another finger inside, forcing her to open for it, and join it with the first in petting the sweet spot within. Her sheath is tight, having lost all the work I've put into it, devouring her arousal for sustenance.

"Zaku!" she squeaks my name. But she pushes into my hand and I smile, knowing I will soon get what I need from her.

Her arousal on my tongue... I am also in need of watering...

I lick the air, tasting her despite the steam and water. She may have cursed me to death, but she will soon understand why I caged her. It's not even my cage, though I'm glad I have it. It is useful now that I have a mate to protect.

Rubbing her gently, I add a little pressure, letting her know I will take it slow. My wound still aches. It will take another meal to finish regenerating. That and another night of solid rest.

Rest can wait. Food can wait.

I haven't moved in days, and my muscles need exercise.

So do Daisy's...

"Zaku," she whimpers my name again when I stuff another finger inside her, forcing her to take it.

The worst of her bruises have yellowed and her scrapes are all but gone. I run my free hand up her leg, feeling the smoothness of her skin. She is bare of hair everywhere below her neck, and I... like it. She is like me in that aspect. Our differences are not as much as she fears.

I *will* master her.

Daisy rests her brow on the wall, languid with the pleasure I'm giving her. Her eyes are closed, her lips parted. When I press my fingers —hard—into her spot, she gasps, jerks, and tries pushing my fingers out.

My smile widens. "They are just fingers," I purr.

I release the pressure of my fingers and go back to rubbing her gently, stretching them slightly as I do.

Oh, how wet you are, little queen.

"Too much," she breathes. She brings her hands to the wall, placing her brow on them instead of the wall, and rubs her face against them. "I'm so mad at you," she mumbles weakly.

I hiss. I stretch my fingers a little more.

She will fit me eventually. Human females can expand, and expand a lot. I read it once in a book about human reproduction. She can take me. She will take me. Sliding my hand up and down her leg, I soothe her.

Daisy rubs her face some more against her hands, but her feet part to give me better access. Pleased, I speed up my fingers and contemplate adding a fourth.

"It was for your safety and mine," I groan.

"So you did... put me in there because you thought... I'd hurt you," she murmurs through soft moans.

"You would not have hurt me, but you could have run, and that would upset me. I will not have you run from me." I quicken my fingers.

"I—" she swallows, "I…"

"You?" I rub her harder, seeing her hands fist and her spine straighten. I yank my member hard before sneaking my tailtip up her front to slap her nub, sensing her imminent undoing. Spill dribbles from my shaft.

"I won't be your captive forever!" she cries out, pushing away from the wall.

Her sex clamps down on my fingers, squeezing them; her hips buck on my hand. She drops her hand to grab my tailtip, tearing it away from her nub as her body shudders deliciously. I grip her hip and steady her, keeping her upright as she bucks and quivers.

Her sheath dances beautifully around my fingers. "I need—I can't —" she gasps.

I pull her into me, stretching my fingers as wide as I can get them inside her. "Let me take care of you," I say, clutching her body, rubbing my swollen member over her backside. "You can take it."

I will not lose her. I will lie and beg for it. I don't think I can go another day without her.

If Vagan had stolen her from me… If I hadn't returned in time…

She moans loudly as I force a second orgasm from her body, but this next one is weaker. She is exhausted. If what she says is true, I've been unconscious for days.

The cage is not a comfortable place.

I resolve to remedy that after she's forgiven me.

"Freedom," I rumble in her ear. "Freedom for your surrender."

Daisy shudders at my voice, her legs splayed, and I'm half-holding her up by my hand, pressing into her back. I run my free hand up her chest, her breast, and cup her neck and the collar there, continuously working her sheath, waiting for my answer.

I will coax another orgasm if I must. I will coax a dozen.

"I will never cage you again," I add, licking her ear. It's a lie, though in truth, I hope it's not. I never want a reason to cage her again. I will if I must. "Forgiveness is next to godliness," I say, remembering reading that line somewhere long ago.

She grasps onto me, trying to support her weight. "You're using my exhaustion against me." Her head falls back onto my chest. Climbing over her to look upon her from above, I slip my hand from between her legs and cup her breasts, rolling her nipples between my fingers.

"You've gone through a lot, little mate. Give in and let me rule you. Let me take it all away."

A king should never have to beg…

"I will never give you another reason to cry," I purr.

She doesn't say anything for a time, resting against me while I roll her nipples and move my palms along the curves of her body. I wonder if she's asleep, letting me work the tension from her muscles, because her head rolls to the side. But when I lift her, moving my tail between her legs so she straddles me, she leans forward upon it. She rests her cheek on my scales.

Leaning back, I take her in.

She's facing away from me, and her ass, her sex is open and on display, dewy wet and being sprayed on by the water from above. Her feet barely touch the ground on either side, hanging off me where she sits. I slide my hands down her back to cup her behind, pulling her cheeks apart to open her up.

She wiggles, and I grip her hips, sliding her backward so her sex is flush against the length of my shaft. I undulate slowly, rubbing it back and forth over her slick folds.

She still hasn't answered, but she lets me play.

My hunger festers.

I won't let this gift go away. If this is what happens when I get hurt, I will seek pain to have her so amenable toward me. Just enough for her affection; not enough to bring her tears forth.

I rub my knot over her slick sex, piercing it with my fingers when she sighs, and it quivers for me. I thumb her sensitive nub and her backside, even after she swipes my hand away. I like her responses.

I am the luckiest male.

All the while, the warm water of the shower sprays upon her, while she cuddles my tail. Cuddles it!

It's almost too much for me to bear. She is teasing me, torturing me. She has no idea what she's doing to me, pushing me to the brink. I milk another orgasm from her body and yet, she still does not give me an answer.

I grit my teeth, sinking my fangs deep into my lip. I position my tip to her entrance. I nudge it.

She tenses immediately. "Zaku," she whispers my name, fisting her hands.

I grab my member and glide my tip up and down her slit, and when I'm done, I press it to her little hole again, sinking the tip in. "Answer me," I growl.

She looks back, blinking water from her lashes. I press into her a little more. Her sex clenches deliciously and I moan.

Her lips part.

We stare at each other. I don't move my eyes from hers as I reach out with one hand and pet her spine.

I dare to push a little further. Tight, swollen flesh fights against my invasion. I hiss, deep and hurried, as the pressure of her sheath tries pushing me out. I refuse to let it win, keeping my tip seated.

"Daisssy," I beg.

Hooded eyes staring at me is all she gives me. Wildly, my heart thunders, knowing how close I am to my own ruin.

"Freedom," I whisper, pushing a hand between us to tease her nub.

Her brow furrows.

Daisy

I HAVEN'T FELT this relaxed in longer than I can remember.

Zaku's finger rubs me, and I whimper. Overcome with exhaustion, I've been open to his gentle caressing, the orgasms he's worked from my aching body. I'll take the pleasure he offers greedily, having been denied any pleasure or comfort for days.

His tip is inside me. I tense around it, feeling it press back, keeping me stretched. It scares me, but I feel so warm... so relaxed.

And his smell... It's heady. The water washes it away, but it doesn't stay gone. I breathe it in, wanting it to fill me up. Except every time I try to inhale it deeply, there's never enough.

Zaku's hand pets my spine. We stare at each other. He's waiting for me to give in, he's taking advantage of me, and I should hate him for it, but I don't. I want the pleasure he's giving me to continue. He's alive. Yet...if I let him try to put his cock in me, my last defense against my captivity and my capturer will vanish. I'd be powerless.

Keeping my gaze, he dares to press further into me. I constrict, not ready to allow him access. I ache for so many things. I don't know what I want anymore.

He rubs my clit faster in response.

Gasping, I accidentally shunt back onto his cock. It sinks further in, and I strain backward. Zaku groans and I fist my hands harder. I jerk forward into his rubbing fingers, and his tip loses its purchase, slipping out of me.

He growls and stops flicking my clit, hooking an arm around under me and stopping me from moving. He pushes his tip back into me, lodging it in place, stroking my clit so I won't fight it.

"Zaku," I moan.

He answers by thrumming my nub hard and fast. Hitching with pleasure, I jerk upon him, feeling another orgasm build.

Terrible male. He's a terrible, terrible male. He's not being fair.

But neither am I. I have tested him, pushed him, using his want for me against him to see if he'll keep his word. It's worked against me just as much as him. Because I want him. I want him so badly it stings.

He's given pleasure, and more, he's saved my life. I've given him nothing in return.

He hoists me, taking my feet off the floor. I hold my body over him precariously, crying out as he works another orgasm forth, trying not to slip over his slick scales. I rock my hips, desperate to be... *full*. He stops his thrumming, and I cry out again, rocking on his tip. I press back, searching for the pleasure I've lost. He grabs my hips to help me, and his claws bite my skin.

"Yesss," he hisses as I shudder upon him. "Yesss. Use me."

Use him?

"Yes," I whisper.

My legs slip on his tail and he sinks into me. I hitch from the abrupt, brutal stretch as I fall onto him to his massive bulge. He goes rigid, his hands tightening on my hips, and I tense, alarmed by the sensation. His bulge presses against my opening—so big that I'm practically perched on it, seated on it.

I scrape my nails across his tail. "Zaku!"

He holds me upon him as I adjust to his size. I try to widen my legs but can't, my feet sliding, my heels slipping. His tailtip coils around my right foot and holds it away from my body.

"Don't move," he rumbles thickly, keeping me precariously over him. "You will make it worse. Trust me."

"Trust you?!"

I reach back and grasp his cowl. I try not to move, knowing if I do, I might slip further onto his cock. I might break.

"Trussst me," he hisses.

Hot, blistering heat shoots up inside me. Zaku growls, filling me with his seed. His scent returns thick and heady. I heave, taking as much of it as I can into me.

Squeezing around him, I brace. I want my orgasm.

"I need—" I gasp, "I need... more!"

TWENTY-TWO

A KING NO MORE

Zaku

"Zᴀᴋᴜ! I can't stand it any longer," she begs.

Daisy milks my member, twitching upon it, rolling her hips. I push her forward to lie down on my tail so she can relax.

"Relax," I order her. She's so tense. Her body is fighting me, making it harder for her to take me inside her. Even as she cries out for *more*, her sheath is refusing to accept *more*. I bare my fangs, staring down between us, where she's stretched upon me. Where the seed I've released is trapped.

Watered. I growl inwardly.

Her hole is tight around my girth, gripping it hard. There's no way I'm going to be able to push further in. My knot is thicker than the tip of my shaft. A lot thicker.

She can't take it. Already my bulge is pushed hard to her opening. It's so full it'll never breach her as is.

I groan as a niggling thread of doubt enters me.

"Please," she mumbles, and while I hold her still, she shakes.

I shake with her, salivating, tasting the humid air, the aroma of sex, her arousal, and my spill. A delicious miasma to drive me insane. Nudging further, her sheath gives me no access.

I dig my claws into Daisy's hips, trying to retain a modicum of control. She cries for more than I can give her, and my lips twist. I slip out and flip her over, trying again. It doesn't work. I bare her to the floor and try mounting her from above, finding I'm able to get even less of my member in her in this position. I swipe my tongue across my fangs.

No matter how much I spill, it's only ever gotten bigger. Glaring at it, I snarl where it's blocking my complete mastery of her.

She is right.

We do not fit.

Disappointment ravages me hot and fast. Hauling Daisy into my arms, I put her back on my tail to straddle me again. She shimmies her hips, undulating in tiny sways, reaching down and grasping my member, seeking what I can't accomplish. She pushes onto my bulge, and I grit out an annoyed moan.

She lowers but can only take half my shaft. She rides my tip, and it's almost too much for me to take... I need my knot inside her.

My tip is not enough.

Clenching my hands, I hold them away from her body so I do not accidentally hurt her.

Turning her head, she blinks the water from her eyes, finding mine. Her hair is plastered beautifully over her shoulders and onto my tail, and I love it. I just can't love it enough...

"Zaku?"

The way she says my name is enough to nearly turn me into a rabid beast.

I yank her off my shaft and place her on the ground.

"Zaku?" She calls out for me when I slip out of the bathroom. I need to put distance between us. I need to get away from her. I don't know what I'll do if I don't. She cannot fit me, and the pain of that knowledge is too much to bear. The pain in my loins will make me do something terrible. She's all I want, the only being I crave, and we are not meant to be.

We aren't compatible.

She doesn't follow me, and I'm glad. If she did, I might jump her, mount her, and destroy her. I do not want to hurt her. I never want to hurt her. Seeing my empty nest twists my stomach.

I am not a king.

I am not *her* king.

I am a naïve, monstrous male, one who seeks to force a union where there isn't one. I have wronged her. She kills for me, and I lock her in a cage because I cannot bear letting another have her, even if I perish. Fleeing, I head for the rooms above because if I turn back, I will force my knot inside her body, and she will suffer great pain. I hiss long and furiously, scraping my fangs across my lip.

Let her leave if she wills it. I snap. She has earned her freedom. It is the least I can do. It's not her fault that I am what I've been made to be. A brute, even to my own kind.

A murderer.

I strike out, slamming my tail against the nearest wall, reopening my wound. Gritting my teeth, I press my palm to my chest to staunch the new blood. The pain feeds my sense of failure. Not only must I suffer this loss, but I have to live with the scar of it until my last breath? I finish ascending the staircase and enter the hallway where Daisy stabbed Vagan.

It's as good as new. The pictures on the walls are perfect. There's not a crack, a scuff, a scrape from the fight. Even Vagan's body is gone.

It's what I expected.

The robots that maintain this place have always repaired it. They go into their walls and come back out with magic and lasers and materials from the storage hidden high in the mountain. Seeing them angers me. They can keep this place perfect, they can abide by my wishes, but I have never been able to fully master them either.

Like I can't master Daisy... *my* female.

The robots never stop. I have wrecked them, and they don't stop. New ones arrive and repair the ruined ones. I gave up long ago. I shove open the brand new red door.

The foyer, the kitchen, everything is back to normal. There are a half-dozen robots still working and I fall upon them, tearing them to pieces, scattering their parts across the room. Roaring, I turn my attention to the real source of my misery. My throbbing, swollen shaft.

My knot is enormous.

How had I not noticed? It's bigger than it's ever been, bigger now that I'm full of sustenance. Curling my fingers into my palm, I stop from tearing the whole appendage off and being done with it.

Wiping the sweat from my brow with the back of my hand, I calm, trembling, and cup my knot instead. I squeeze it until I grit my teeth from pain, and then I squeeze it harder, forcing the spill out. I take no pleasure; I feel no pleasure. My hand is not Daisy, and now that I've felt what it's like being inside her, I'll never find pleasure from my hand again.

I work my bulge, hissing like the base savage I am, spilling seed upon the clean floor of my home, wanting to ruin the robots' work.

I reclaim the space, taking back control, jetting out spill all over the broken robots, the furniture, and even the glass windows, trying to empty my bulge of all it has stored. It makes no difference. I curse my misery, thrashing my tail. And when my shaft is red and aching from violent fingers, when everything is marked and claimed by me, I take to the wilds outside. I leave Daisy and my den behind.

Tonight, I will be what I've always known I am.

Not a king.

Not an honorable naga.

But a primitive animal. A reptile. The one I've buried deep within. The one that needs to be far, far away from its mate. Because if it's not?

I shudder, not letting the thought of what would happen come to my mind.

TWENTY-THREE
ALONE

Daisy

Dropping to sit on the shower floor, I stare after Zaku, waiting for him to return. I press my hand between my legs and thrum my clit, clenching around nothing. The loss of his cock has me reeling. Zaku's scent vanishes. I was so close to the edge that now I'm consumed by the fall from it, but as the seconds turn into minutes, and Zaku doesn't reappear, I pull my hand away with frustration.

I stand and figure out how to turn off the showers, my nerves twitchy and pent-up. I'm tired, annoyed, and desperately pushing the last few days out of my mind. The blood and the cage—the Lurker—are invading my thoughts again.

I dry off and step into Zaku's room, wrapped in a towel. I expect to see him, but the room is empty. I avoid looking at the cage and the robot within, who's lasering the inside, and head for the closet.

And I pause, staring at the island of baubles, my gaze going to the picture. Feeling my blood pumping, I slowly go to it and pick it up. Hands shaking, I crush it between my fingers and rip it in half. *Stupid ghost. You're not even mine.* I tear it into tiny little pieces and cup them in my palms. Heading back to the bathroom, I flush them down the toilet.

A fitting end.

Returning to the closest, emboldened but still angry and confused, I put on some loose black slacks and a long-sleeved shirt. When I leave, I'm still alone.

My gaze falls on the open door across the way.

I still. Is it a trap? Is Zaku testing me? It has to be a trap, right?

Or is there really a ghost haunting me?

I walk to the door. Zaku isn't devious enough to try and trick me. He's practically an open book. Peering into the room beyond, my eyes go to the stairs. I hear the buzzing of a robot out of my sight.

"Zaku?" I call out. I get nothing except the robot's whirr in response.

Heading up the stairs, I frown, coming across the robot repairing the wall.

The blood trail is gone.

I slip past the robot and enter the hallway of the upper level of the house. Everything is gone from the fight. It's like Vagan was never here, that I never stabbed him, that none of that happened at all. There's no corpse to greet me, no rubble and plaster. There are only the sleek edges of a sparsely decorated home.

The red door opens when I turn the handle.

On the other side, everything is exactly the same as it was the first day Zaku brought me to this place. Almost.

Instead of seeing broken furniture, a shattered window, and the markings of a fight. There are broken robot pieces scattered across the floor. Some twitch and spark. Amongst them are several robots gathering the pieces and taking them into the walls of the house.

I recall Zaku mentioning the robots repairing it, but I never imagined they'd be able to do so to this degree...

When I step out, Zaku's smell floods my nose.

My skin heats furiously and my eyes contract. A whistle of air escapes through my lips as his smell falls upon me thickly. I bring my hands to my chest and drop to my knees, sucking in, needing more of it, all of it, right now. The world tilts, and my swollen sex quivers erratically.

My knees slide apart, slipping on the stone, and I press my hands to my sex. I moan loudly, practically salivating.

Zaku's scent has always warmed me, though it's never been like this, never been this overwhelming. I can't get my hands under the waistband of my slacks fast enough. My fingers slip through wetness, seeking my opening and my clit at the same time. Thrumming hard, shoving my fingers into my body, it's not enough. I paw at my sex, thrusting my hips helplessly. My arousal gushes.

"Zaku," I moan weakly, scared. My sex constricts around my fingers, and I lean forward until my cheek is pressed to the floor. It's wet and sticky, but down here, his scent is even more potent. "Zaku," I say again, calling out for him.

I push my palm to my clit, rubbing hard.

It's not enough. I lick the floor, knowing it's his seed beneath my lips.

He tastes as good as he smells.

Writhing like an animal, I inhale him. His smell is changing me. I don't know what's happening to me, and my fear builds. I need him badly. So badly it hurts.

Where is he? I whimper.

I clean the floor with my tongue. I tug my hand from between my legs with a cry and wipe my fingers through his seed, returning them to my sex and pushing it inside me. I don't know why I do it—it's just right.

And after I do, my body cramps. Pain tightens my stomach. I curl into a fetal position until it goes away.

My lust returns furiously, my sex crying out for more of his seed. For hours, I crawl from one puddle to the next, fighting the robots who come near me for it. A wild thing, inhuman, desperate for more. I beg for Zaku, but he never comes to me, never relieves my torment, and as the day falls to evening, the robots finally win out.

His scent slowly vanishes from the air.

I don't know how long I lie there, staring at the ceiling, touching myself. No matter how many times I come, it's not enough. It's not what I need. The robots clean me up like I'm part of the room, like they cleaned Zaku when he was unconscious. I'm too tired to stop them.

When it gets dark, I crawl up onto the sofa and pass out.

I wake with a start, forgetting where I am.

Snapping upright, my eyes darting around wildly. I yank my hand out from my pants where it must have wandered in my sleep and suck in fresh air, realizing where I am and how I got there. Heat and shame colors my cheeks.

Zaku would never let me sleep here. He always made me sleep in his nest.

He's gone.

The thought jolts me, and I push my legs over the side. It's day again, and the robots are gone. I look around the room absently. There's a plate of meat and fruit, and I grab the apple as I stand.

"Zaku?" I call for him again.

My eyes slice to the window—the completely fixed window—but he's not there. Instead, there's a pile of rotting corpses that weren't there before.

Squinting, I see pig corpses. Lots and lots of pig corpses.

What I don't see is Vagan's corpse.

"House," I call out. "Why are there pig corpses outside?"

A speaker answers from one of the walls. "The pigs entered the house, and as a source of meat that needed replenishment in the icebox, the house accepted the resource."

My fingers go to my mouth as nausea threatens. "What about Vagan?"

"I don't understand. What is a Vagan?" the house responds.

I walk down the length of the window, trying to see around the pile for a shimmer of blue. "The other creature that attacked the house," I say a little nervously. "I killed him."

"Except you, all beings who entered the house have either left or have been used to replenish the house's resources."

"And Zaku?"

"What is a Zaku?"

I sigh. "The house's master," I correct. "Where is he?"

"The current master left yesterday at 11:18 a.m. He has not returned."

11:18? I tilt my head. I don't know the ancient time system. But that was yesterday, and he still hasn't returned. It confirms that he did leave and isn't just hiding in one of the numerous rooms in the house.

Why would he leave? And in the middle of a shower? In the middle of... My confusion builds. Had I done something wrong? Had I said something?

Did he... did he not want me, once he had me? I couldn't take him, but...

I lift my hand to my nose. His smell did something to me, made me delirious, mindless, and lusty. As the memories resurface, I drop my hand. I would have done anything to take the heat between my legs away. I would've begged.

I licked the fucking floor. I scrub my face with my hands and run back to the kitchen. Grabbing a cup from the cabinet, I fill it with water, gulping it down and pouring another until my mouth feels clean again.

"Where did he go?" I ask the house, not expecting an answer.

"Relay Two's current master went west."

"West? Relay Two?"

A robot comes out of one of the walls and takes my empty cup away. It also lifts one of its long arms, and points in the direction of the gorge. "West is that way. Relay Two is one of three relays in this area," it answers.

Turning, I can just see over the cliffside outside the house's grounds. Searching the lawn, I realize the same rocky pathway Zaku climbed to bring me here the first day is in that direction. The same path I would need to take to go back to the facility.

"Thank you," I say.

"You are welcome." The robot drops his arm and leaves.

I check for Vagan's corpse again. I still don't see it.

Could he be alive?

My fingers twist, remembering the feel of stabbing him in the stomach, the way his muscle fought me. The pressure it took to sink the blade in. Zaku regenerated from a stab wound to the chest, a deep wound that bled for hours. He hadn't died. Instead, he went unconscious until the wound closed, only rousing when it had.

The Python's head... My eyes dart to the skulls on the lawn. There are some other bones among them, but they're mostly skulls.

Vagan could've regenerated like Zaku.

Impossible.

The blade nicked Zaku's heart...

My fingers twitch.

I swear I stabbed the Python in the neck and through his jugular. Both Vagan's and the Python's wounds should've killed them. Zaku's wounds too. Yet none of them had died.

Realization sinks in.

I only know for certain the Python is dead because his rotting head is on a stake. Swallowing thickly, I bring my hands to my mouth.

Shelby's in trouble.

A shudder zips through my body. Vagan's after her. He wants her badly enough to break into Zaku's home, nearly killing me, nearly killing him for *her*. Zaku owes him a debt for the tech. And Zaku's gone. They both are. My chest constricts.

Shelby's pregnant. She can't fight without risking her child. She shouldn't take the risks I've been able to. She can't risk the child.

Vagan doesn't care if she's with child... I saw it in his madness. The faces of the children I saved on Colony 4, their frightened eyes, their tears, their hopelessness hits me like a punch to the face. I see the Ketts approaching in the distance, the fleet unable to stop them.

I run to the door, praying it'll open, and when it does, I don't question it. I race to the ledge and look out.

I have to warn Shelby before it's too late.

I have no idea what happened or why Zaku left. *If he is with Vagan...* I shake my head.

I will protect Shelby's baby, even if it's from him.

TWENTY-FOUR
GONE

Zaku

I go to the human's facility in my torment. Intending to tear it down, to locate all the males across the land, human and naga, and rip their heads off. They deserve pain and my fury. For coming to my land and trying to steal it from me.

Hunger claws my gut.

But by the time I see the lights of the humans' ship and their strange robots guarding the once dusty ruins, my frustration wanes. All I want is to be back in my den with Daisy and coiled around her body. I worked the enormous knot out of my shaft during the journey, and my seed hasn't fully refilled it. The pressure, the tension in my groin has eased and with it some of my anger.

Except each time I glimpse my shaft, I snarl viciously, hating it. I am the biggest naga in all the land and for once, I hate it. Not even my father was as large as me. I used to revel in this knowledge, but I'm beginning to think I am cursed. *If I were a smaller male...*

Daisy is a small, human female. I don't want to bring her pain. If I bring her pain, she may not submit to me. She may refuse to let me touch her again.

She will see me as she saw the Python. I spit venom.

And I gave her freedom... I had done so as I left, unsure if I would ever come back, if it would even be possible with the tension wrecking my thoughts. At least behind the barrier of my home she would be safe, especially if I were to guard it and her from afar.

She could be the home's new master, keeping me and all else who might hurt her away from her. That way, I could ensure she is mine without fully giving her up.

I was an idiot.

If she locks me out, I will break the glass like Vagan had.

Until him, no other has ever been able to. But if Vagan can, so can I. Looking around at the shadowy forest on all sides, I clench my fists.

What if another male comes while I've been away? Or animals? Or creatures of the forest? What if she accidentally lets one in and I'm here at the facility where I know she is not? What if she leaves and gets attacked?

What if she comes looking for me?

I turn for home, leaving the humans and their creations alive, cursing my recent choices. Cursing many of the choices I have made.

It was idiotic of me to leave Daisy and my den. My body is weak and strained beyond its limit, from my mating heat and my wound. My head is a torrent of riotous thoughts. I dig my claws into my palms, seeking the blood under my skin. *I had her on my stem. I had her spread open upon my tail.*

And I left.

It's only proven to me that I am nothing more than a lowly, despicable reptile.

I wish I had never found that book.

She's the only thing that can cure me of these horrible thoughts and feelings. If I can't be a king for her, then how can I ever be a king again among my kind?

Slicing through the forest, across the gorge, I don't stop, needing to be back home, needing to see Daisy. I need to know that she is safe. The sun sets too soon, and it's dark before I reach the base of my mountain. Exhausted, I'm forced to stop. I can't risk ascending the cliff pass in the dark.

I can guard the path, though. Ensure no naga finds it, and protect Daisy from here. Pressing my hand to my chest, I lower to the ground, hiding within a pile of dead leaves. I've reopened my wound and fresh blood leaks through my fingers. Sleep finds me swiftly, despite not wanting it to.

I wake once, hearing movement but when the noises fade soon after, indicating it is not a large creature passing by, I fall back asleep.

The sun is high above me when I wake once more. I release a frustrated hiss. My knot is full to bursting again, but I find the pain in my chest gone. The wound has reclosed. I take to the mountain with renewed strength. What feels like an eternity passes before I see the glint of my den's windows.

I enter my home and dart my eyes around the space, finding everything the way it has always been, quiet and perfect, and...empty. Usually, I can feel Daisy's presence all around me. She's brought life into my world and into my home. Right now, my den feels lifeless.

A low hiss climbs my throat as my nostrils flare to take in the scent of the place.

There's no scent at all. I make my way to the lower rooms.

She is waiting for me there. She is always waiting for me.

I smile.

The door to my nest is open and I head straight for it, eagerness vibrating my nerves.

It's empty and perfectly made. The pillows, the bedding I once detested, all crisp and organized as it had been every day since the first day I'd come to this place. Slipping to the bathroom, it's also empty. I go to the closet next, and halt, seeing the collar I gave her, the diamond strings reattached to it lying where the sapphire necklace usually is.

Blood rushes through my veins.

It's the only thing in this wretched place that has changed—has ever changed. Floored, I stare at the diamond chains. Only noticing afterward that the picture of human males is also gone.

"Daisy!" I roar, leaving the closet. My gaze falls upon the cage.

I should have never let her out. I should have kept her locked in it forever, even if she hated me for it, even if she denied me, even if I never saw her smile again. I'd rather have my queen in a cage, where she's mine, where I can protect her and gaze upon her beauty, rather than free. Where she can be hurt, or worse. She isn't safe without me. She'll never be safe without me. I hiss deeply, reverberating my cowl.

Overcome with foreboding, I move to the playroom, hoping there's a slim chance she is within. But the mirrored wall is still in place...

There's nothing but cold silence and my reptilian reflection glaring back at me. My hands shake.

She's gone.

She left.

The noise I heard last night...

A growl bursts from my throat as I pivot and tear out of my house.

TWENTY-FIVE
THE PIT

Daisy

"DAISY!"

I startle, turning around as my name echoes through the gorge.

Zaku?

Goosebumps rise as I hear my name again. I can't tell which direction it's coming from...whether it's ahead of me or behind.

I can't let him catch me.

Even if he's not with Vagan, Zaku will never let me near the facility, he'll never let me warn Shelby.

I catch my body against a tree and clutch it, holding myself upright. Pushing off the tree, I aim for the river in the distance. It's attached to the lake. Keeping high on the mountain ledges, I've kept it to my left, knowing I'll need to cross it to get to the facility.

But not yet...

It's the only river, and I remember seeing it below the plateau the first day. I need to cross there to keep my positioning. If I cross too early, I could miss the facility entirely while in the forest. But if I can spy the plateau, keep it at my back, I can make it to the facility. I can.

"DAISY!"

I flinch.

But it's been hours and I still haven't located the plateau. I've circled boulders, ledges, even climbed one of the trees to get a view of where I am and where I'm positioned, but no plateau. The sheer edge and the steep climb to the plateau's bluff are unmistakable. There are no trees, no foliage after the dropoff.

Huffing out a ragged breath, I round another set of boulders, swiping the sweat off my brow.

And then I see it.

I nearly drop to my knees when I do. The plateau's sharp ledge.

I want to sob, half-terrified I was never going to find it, that I was lost, that I miscalculated.

I'm a pilot, not a ranger. I've been on and to many alien worlds, but rarely do I set foot on them.

It's time to cross the river and go straight north. Wiping my cheeks, I descend.

From one boulder to the next, from one rocky landing to a dead tree stump, I head for the river below. This side of the mountain has grown increasingly jagged with dirt and stone. There's barely any shade. Losing my footing on a shifting stone, I slip and land on my butt. Wiping the dirt off my palms, I try not to touch my face. My cheeks are burned from the Earth's sun. Sweat drips into my eyes, and I blink it out, wincing again.

When I hear the river, I sprint, wading into the reeds, and sinking into the water and mud. I push through the reeds until the water is up to my waist and the river opens up. Dipping under and cooling off, I wash the sweat off my face and drink all I can. I haven't encountered an apple tree or a berry bush in hours, and I need to keep my energy up for as long as possible. Hydration is key.

"DAISY!"

I lower into the water as my name echoes and then fades.

When Zaku's voice is gone, I glance at the barren slopes of the mountain behind me, expecting to see him charging down and toward me. When I don't, I say a silent prayer.

It's quiet as I dive into the water. It's a short distance to the other side. On the far shore, I position my back to the plateau. Taking a deep breath, I close my eyes and visualize the land, hoping to the stars that I'm right and the facility is in the spot I remember it to be.

I'm in the forest, on flat land. I have to be in the right area. I'll know for sure in a couple of miles.

I wring out my clothes and walk into the trees. Soon, the silence gives way to sounds.

Hissing fills my ears. First, it's on my right, and I drop and quiet my steps, and then it's on my left. My adrenaline surges and my stomach drops. *It's a good sign if I'm hearing other nagas,* I tell myself. I lick my lips and try to remain calm.

I should've considered there would still be nagas scouting the facility. If it's not Vagan who goes after Shelby, eventually one of the others might.

If they haven't already.

My fury at Peter—at this whole operation—slams through me. I grit my teeth and try not to scream.

I'll sneak in, find Shelby, and contact *The Dreadnaut. That's all you have to do.* Once Central Command knows what's going on, none of the rest matters. They'll save Gemma, they'll fire Peter, and they'll make a better deal with the nagas for their precious Lurker tech. A deal that doesn't include bartering flesh. This time tomorrow, the nightmare will be over.

I see the wall through the overgrowth and quietly move toward it. There's hissing behind me, though it's far off. But as I near, a low buzzing takes its place.

A scout. I crouch. Searching for it in the air, I spy the flying metal turret and let it see me. It stops, turns its guns on me, and flies in my direction.

I go still as it scans my face.

After a moment, it lowers its guns and I sag. The security systems still have me in their database. I move to the turret's side and open its panel, wiping the data off its system and powering the turret off, hiding it in the bushes. I turn to the wall afterward, heading for one of the entrances.

Something touches my leg.

Twisting around, I come face to face with a large, darkly-colored male coiled around a branch. Our eyes meet, and we stare at each other.

"Please let me go," I beg.

His expression doesn't change.

"My friend is in danger and so is her child. Please, if you have any mercy, you'll let me go."

"What is your name?" he rumbles.

"Daisy," I say, trembling.

"There's another calling that name." He tilts his head, glancing at the canopy. "It's on the wind."

"I know."

The male's eyes come back to me, darkening. "Are you in trouble as well?"

His question gives me pause. It's not something I'd thought one of these aliens would ever ask. *Am I? I am.* I am in trouble, though it's not the type of trouble a stranger could ever help me with.

Right now, all I want is to make sure Shelby and her baby are safe. And if possible, to reach Central Command and help Gemma. After that? Thoughts of Zaku flick through my mind.

"I...I'm okay," I say.

The male regards me for a time. Waiting for him to snatch me or let me walk away, my heart pounds wildly. I brace for the former, for a fight. Slowly, I slip my hand into my pocket and grasp the nail file.

It's always the former.

He draws his tail away from me and vanishes into the trees.

I sag. *Thank you.*

I turn and run through the entrance before he changes his mind, pivoting behind a barricade. I take a look around. There's only me, the robots, and the ships on the newly-cleared field. None of the team is outside. Seeing everything the same way it was a couple of weeks ago saddens me. It also brings me some relief.

I'm not too late.

Glimpsing the sky, the sun is heading for the horizon.

It'll be dark in a couple of hours.

The day shift is ending soon, if it hasn't already. Everyone will retire to their quarters soon. Shelby will be working within the old facility or on the transport ship categorizing recent data—she's obsessed with Earth and the Lurkawathians—a little too obsessed. We haven't had many conversations in our short time together though each time we have had one, she brings up her work. She lives for it.

She loves it.

Something I have never really felt about my work...

Sneaking onto the transport ship will be risky, and riskier still is heading to the ship's bridge to contact Central Command. It would be better to wait for the night shift for that, I decide.

I dash to the ruins before I can change my mind. I've never been inside them, but others have mentioned that the old building is big. If it's big, there'll be lots of places to hide and to wait.

Coming to a stop at one of the partially fallen walls, I duck inside. The inside is a mess of rubble, but it's been cleaned out of all organic matter by the robots upon our arrival here. Hallways and rooms of dirt, mottled items, and old rusty metal greet me on every side. There are also lamps and beeping machines throughout, attached to computers under tarps. They hum softly in my ears.

I climb through another broken wall, deeper into the space where there are more shadows, rather than take the cleared hallways, and search for one of the team members, or for a place to hide.

Hearing footsteps, I duck behind a tarp and press my hands to my mouth.

The footsteps move past me and I peer over the tarp to see who it is. Squinting, I make out Collins' uniform. He turns left, down a different hallway, and toward the outside. I decide to go in the opposite direction. I don't want to encounter Collins any more than I want to run into Peter. I might just kill him and rid the universe of his presence if I do.

Seeing lights ahead of me and an open space, I slow and slip to the wall to look inside. I find what may have been a large atrium at one point, maybe a gym. The ceiling is caved in, and there's digging equipment. In the center is a giant pit with rusted pipes and old infrastructure bent up and out of the ground. More tarps and spotlights are blazing down into it.

There's also a lot of sentinel robots protecting the pit.

They're guarding it.

My curiosity piques. I can't see into the hole from my angle. Glancing around the room, it's empty but for the robots. I check behind me and there's no one coming.

Having only two ways to go, I enter the space, dodging to the right. The sentinels don't acknowledge me, staying angled to the pit. My brow furrows, and I move a little closer to see what it is they're focused on.

Could it be?

Is it?

What we came here to find?

I don't see anything at first, just dirt, cement blocks, and more pipes and wires than I can count. A flicker of blue light emerges, casting upon rocks from under the biggest tarp in the middle, and I suck in.

"Shelby?" I whisper.

TWENTY-SIX

LIES

Daisy

"COLLINS, if you're trying to scare me, fuck off," she says from somewhere below and out of my sight. "I am not in the mood."

My heart goes wild, and I scramble down into the pit before I can think otherwise. "It's not Collins, Shelby." Heading toward the deepest part of the pit, where tarps are covering it from my view, the blue light of Shelby's eyes brightens. It shifts in my direction. Shelby ducks her head under the tarp and blinks, turning off the light of her mechanical eyes.

"Daisy?" she says, her lips parting when she sees me. She stares as I rush over to her, taking her into my arms and hugging her to me, hard.

She's tense in my arms at first but then throws her arms around me with a cry. We hold onto each other tightly. I don't want to let her go. I thought I'd never see another human ever again. If I hold her hard enough, long enough, maybe I'll never be torn away again. She's warm. She's alive. The journey was worth it just for this hug.

But she pulls back and I let her go.

Her face is dirty, smudged with dirt and dust, and she's shaking.

"Daisy? How—how are you here? What happened? We need to get

you to medical! Do the others know your back?" Shelby's questions fill my ears.

I grab her wrist. "I'm fine. I don't need medical attention. Though we need to go, and we need guns if they're around. I'll explain later, but we need to get you out of here. Now!"

The sentinels fly toward us from every side.

Shelby jerks her arm out of my grasp, stopping me. Fear lights her eyes as she looks at the sentinel drones. "I can't. Why do we need guns?"

The sentinels aim their lasers at me. "For protection. I'll explain later but right now we need to go," I tell her.

She shakes her head. It's then I notice the exhaustion on her face, the amount of dirt covering her. There are sweat stains on her clothes and her face looks long and winded. Her long hair is in a messy bun on the top of her head and some of her braids are slipping from it.

She's thinner than she was when I last saw her.

"What has happened to you?" I whisper. The last time I saw her, she was healthy, clean, and full of energy. Though angry too and filled with desperation for the situation we were in.

"I'm being watched," she whispers. "I can't go anywhere without guards, without Collins. Daisy, I'm so sorry—"

"I don't understand—"

"—I tried to contact Central Command, but Peter stopped me. I can't go anywhere without them." She points behind me. "They'll shoot me if I try."

I look back at the sentinels now hovering around us.

Shelby continues, "You need to get out of here. It's not safe. Peter is not..."

"Not what?" I ask.

She shakes her head. "If we don't deliver..." she whispers. "If *I* don't deliver... Peter's head is on the block. All of our heads are. The Ketts took out *The Mercy*."

I still. *The Mercy* was the ship my father once commanded before he retired on *The Prime*. It was where I was born. It's also one of the biggest colony battleships in the entire fleet. A whole army of battleships was docked there.

Nearly a hundred thousand people lived and worked on *The Mercy*. *Dead.* My heart stops. *They're dead now.*

"If Peter doesn't give Central Command what they want..."

I scrunch my face. "Stop. Just stop," I beg, reeling from the news. Losing *The Mercy* is a huge defeat, but there's nothing we can do about it here. "You're in trouble. There's a naga, a rabid one, coming for you. We have to get you out of here." I grab her hand. "I tried to kill him but these aliens don't die easily. They regenerate. We have to tell Central Command what's happening down here. Your baby is at risk."

Shelby tugs her hand from mine. "What are you talking about?"

"Vagan. I'm talking about Vagan. An alien who's after you, who's willing to kill me and—never mind. That's not all, the facility is surrounded by aliens. You're the only woman here. You're not safe and neither is your baby." I take her hand again and tug her after me.

"Daisy..." Shelby pulls from my grip. "I'm not pregnant."

I face her, not sure if I heard her correctly. "What?"

"I'm not pregnant," she repeats.

"Y-You miscarried?" I stutter.

Her face falls. "No."

It takes me a moment to realize what she's telling me. "You lied?"

"I was scared. Collins convinced me it was for the best. I've been doing everything I can to get you and Gemma help—"

"Wait. You were never pregnant?" I'm still not believing what she's saying.

"Daisy..."

I drop my hand. She's not pregnant. She never was?

"Are you okay?" Shelby reaches for me. Reeling, I turn from her.

She was never pregnant. My heart sinks further, and tears well. Shelby grabs my arm, I tug it out of her grasp.

She lied to save herself. She abandoned Gemma and me when our worlds fell apart. The fear I felt, the disbelief when Peter gathered Gemma, Shelby, and I to tell us what he plans on doing to us comes back to me. I had no lover, no friend, no one to turn to for help. Only two women, two strangers who served on the same ship.

"Daisy?" Shelby whispers my name. "I'm really sorry. I tried to buy an opportunity to help. I should've told you and Gemma. Collins said it was too risky."

I wipe my eyes with the back of my hands, hating the betrayal I'm feeling. I push through it. I try to, at least.

I never should have left Zaku. I should've waited for his return, should've looked for *him.* I should've searched for Gemma.

I clench my hands. What am I going to do now? Can I even leave the facility without getting caught, or find my way to Zaku's mountain? Will I ever see him again?

"Please forgive me," Shelby begs. "I tried to use it to help us." She waves at the sentinels with defeat. "I tried."

I finally look at her, exhaling the betrayal. It doesn't change anything. "I forgive you," I choke. My voice is numb after I clear my throat. "Vagan is after you. We need to get you out of the facility before he or another, or several band together and come for you."

"What do they want?" she asks, her voice lowering.

"Nestmates? I was almost raped," I wheeze as flashes of the Python return. I push him out and think of Zaku instead and even the male I met outside. "Some are not bad... I have no idea what Gemma is going through. You're not safe. You need to get onto the transport ship—to *The Dreadnaut* if possible. That, or join me. There's a place you can hide. A place you'll be safe. Zaku has a den..." I trail off. "It doesn't matter, as long as you're not *here*. I need to get to the ship and send a message to Central Command." I turn to leave.

"Wait! The sentinels."

I pause. "They're watching you, not me. They still recognize me as part of the team."

"They'll shoot me if I follow you."

"Okay. I can turn them off manually." I glance at the turrets poised on us, shuddering some more. "Give me a minute."

"Shelby, who are you talking to?" Collins says from somewhere above us.

Going rigid, my toes curl and I reach for my nail file again. Shelby's eyes widen, and she tugs me toward the tarps she crawled out from under. "Hide," she whispers furiously.

I duck with her under the tarps. I thought I could trust Shelby—I know I still can. The knife she gave me saved me. I owe her, but my debt is cleared. There's nothing left for me here. I rub my chest, feeling heaviness there. She can come with me, or find her own way. She's more capable than I.

But there's still Gemma, and Peter to contend with. There are naga males still lurking outside the facility.

I wish they would attack, tear the facility down, and humanity can prevail and defeat the Ketts—that they'd start evacuating the planets in the Ketts' path instead and fleeing into a different part of the universe to rebuild.

The government will never give up its resources and lands. The upper castes can't fathom losing their wealth.

I wish I had made a case for those babies.

I wish for a lot of things. They're all just wishes. Wishes never come true. Gripping my nail file tight, I ready to stab Collins in the throat.

Why did I come here at all?

"I'm just cataloging my finds," Shelby calls out. "Have Nick and his team made any headway on the data?"

Collins grunts. Rocks shift as he nears and his footsteps get closer. "They're still deciphering the text, so no. Captain says we're all working through the night again. He wants an update. We're having the night meal with him tonight. He wants another test."

"Another one?" Shelby's face falls as we hold each other's gaze. "I don't want to eat with that fucker," she snarls. She lowers her voice to me. "I'll distract him. Go," she says, pointing to an opening through more pipes behind me.

"What about you?" I whisper. "The sentinels?"

"I'll be fine."

Collins sighs deeply and it's right outside the tarp. "I prepared a test already, so don't worry. I have it covered. Eating with him on the other hand, I can't change. If he's willing to share extra rations with us, we need to take advantage of that. You need to keep your strength up."

"Tests?" I ask.

"Pregnancy tests," Shelby says, shooing me to the other side of her tarp tent.

"They'll find out you lied, Shelby," I tell her, ducking under the other side. I crouch. "You can't fake a pregnancy forever."

She scrubs her face with her hands, and I almost feel bad. Almost.

"I'll be fine. Go, Daisy, please. I can take care of myself. I have Collins. Get to the ship. Tell them what's happening. Save us."

I see Collins' hand as he lifts the tarp. There's no way she'll be able to follow me now, and waiting is too risky. My heart falls further.

"I stole some water from John for you," Collins says, lifting the flap.

"Go," Shelby begs. With one last look, we turn from each other.

Hearing the tarp drop, I crawl away, finding another way out of the hole. I check to make sure he's within the tent before I move to the outer walls of the atrium and head back the way I came. The shadows have lengthened and I hurry my steps, dashing down the hallway, deciding I don't want to be here when night falls.

"Hold," someone says behind me.

I stop. My hands shake.

"What are you doing in here, and without your uniform... Wait... Officer Daisy? Is... No..."

I turn and face Captain Peter, and our eyes meet in the gloom. There's a light behind his back that casts his face in shadows.

Hatred bursts through me, hard and fast. "Peter," I breathe his name through gritted teeth, taking a step toward him. Fury is giving me courage I wouldn't usually have.

Seeing his shocked face, all I want suddenly is for him to feel what I've felt, what Gemma's felt, what Shelby feels. I want him to know the terror, the hopelessness, and the helplessness he's made us experience.

"How are you here?" He's as still as stone, and I hope it's because he's afraid. I take another step toward him. I am done being a victim. "Where did you..." He reaches for his gun.

"I wouldn't do that if I were you," I warn.

His hand pauses. "Daisy, let's talk—"

"Talk? You want to fucking talk? Now?"

He shakes his head.

I continue, "We are way beyond talking, you piece of shit." I rush forward and tackle him. He falls back into the wall. I hit him over and over with my fists, and he tries to push me away, tries to defend himself. "You son of a bitch!" I scream, aiming for his face, drilling him in the nose. I grab my nail file and slam the tip into his hand, puncturing it. "I will kill you!"

"Stop!" he yells, pushing at me, jerking his hand away, taking my nail file with it. I hit him some more. Enraged, all I want is to hurt him as much as I can for as long as I can. Blood surges through my veins.

"I said stop, damn it!" he roars as I curl my fingers and try clawing his face.

"Stop?" I shout. "You want me to stop? You should've thought of that before you left me on a plateau at the mercy of aliens! You should have thought about that when I was nearly killed!"

He struggles to get his gun free from his hip, and I throw my weight over him, grabbing his hand. I don't see his leg before it's too late. He kicks me hard in the gut, and I tumble backward with a gasp.

"Stupid bitch," he growls, yanking his gun from his waistband.

I turn and run as gunfire rings. I hear shouting from Collins and Shelby, and the buzz of the sentinels and drones floods my ears. Peter fires a shot as I duck through a crack in the outer wall. A blast goes off next to my head, sending rubble flying. I stumble. Catching my footing, I sprint across the open field.

Seeing the facility barrier all around me, I'll never make it to the forest alive.

"Stop her!" Peter shouts.

He gives chase. Shots ring out, and the dirt around my feet explodes.

"Daisy!" Shelby screams. "Run!"

Ducking my head, I pivot for the skiff to my left. Throwing my body against it, I slap my hand on the security panel and pray that it still registers me. When the door slides open, I scramble inside, slamming the door closed behind me. A bullet hits the glass by my head, pinging the inside of the vessel. Peter aims his gun at me as the rest of the team runs out of the transport ship. Several sprint for the skiff.

Turning to the controls, I power them on.

"Come on, come on, come on. Faster," I beg. The controls light up. Something zips by the window, forcing my eyes up. Several drones are right outside with their turret guns. They shoot at the windows. I swallow back my vomit.

The thrusters come to life and I crank the switches. I push my palm to the central orb. "Take me to *The Dreadnaut*," I order, checking that the coordinates to the warship hadn't changed, waiting anxiously for the skiff to connect to the main vessel. Whether it takes me there or not, connecting to it is all I need.

Something hits me to my right, rocking the skiff. The ship falters for a moment, losing its momentum. "Come on!"

"This is *The Dreadnaut*," a woman's voice says through the controls. "You do realize you're asking for clearance for a planetary transport skiff, right?"

"It's an emergency," I snap, pressing my palm hard to the central orb, forcing the vessel up. Gunfire rings in my ears, but the ship hoists into the air. Seeing the forest and the mountains over the barrier, I push my palm forward.

"You do not have clearance, Officer Daisy. I recommend you land," the woman says. "The skiff will not be able to make such a journey."

"Do you know what's happening down here?" I shout. "Captain Peter is trading lives for tech!"

The ship jerks, the sentinels fly out of my path, and I push the thrusters to the max, yanking the controls back. I see the barrier loom before me.

I'm not going to make it. "Please," I whisper. "Please."

At the last moment, the vessel clears the barrier, though a wrenching, screeching noise bursts my ears as the bottom of it scrapes it. I hit the trees, slicing through branches, barely evading the thick trunks.

"Turn back, Officer Daisy. You do not have clearance to use this skiff anymore, nor do you have access to *The Dreadnaut*. You are being insubordinate."

Hitting tree after tree, I make it above them, and I sag a little, angling the skiff higher, toward the mountains to the left of the plateau. I see it and the lake for a split second before I turn.

"You don't understand," I say, stumbling over my words, sweat pouring down my face. "Captain Peter is bartering the women on his team, even Officer Gemma—"

"I know—"

"—we're in trouble, we need backup..." I trail off. "You know?"

"I recommend you turn around and land," the woman says.

I start to shake. "You know?"

"If you do not turn back now, I will take away your access to fly and the skiff will no longer respond to you. It will fall."

"You know!?" I scream.

I focus on the mountains ahead of me, the sprawling forest.

"Turn back, Officer Daisy. Do not make me take away your access. The skiff is expensive."

The skiff is expensive. I want to laugh and sob.

Tears brim my eyes. I think of Peter and Gemma, and Zaku. The last couple of weeks flit through my mind. Zaku. I'd been happy. *With him.* Despite everything.

He cared for me. Me, of all people.

"Officer Daisy, I won't ask again. This is my final warning."

"I'm sorry," I whisper. "I'm so sorry." Sorry about Zaku, sorry that I couldn't save Shelby, sorry that I didn't get a chance to end Peter.

I hear a sigh and then everything goes silent. A thunderous noise builds from there, hollowing out my ears. I close my eyes and take a ragged breath.

She did it. She really fucking did it, taking away my access.

Something hits the skiff, knocking the vessel sideways. Pushing my hand to the orb, the ship doesn't right itself. I wipe them off with the back of my hands, nose-diving for the mountain.

I'm sorry.

TWENTY-SEVEN

A NEW PAIN

Zaku

I HOLD DAISY CLOSE, as close as I can without hurting her any more than she is. Days, I searched for her. Days, I thought I lost her, terrified I would never see her again. Now I have her in my arms, and I've never been in more pain.

She screams.

And screams and screams. Her body is burned—black and red—her clothes are charred, and her hair is nothing more than singed, smoking wisps around a swollen and mottled face.

I want to hold her close and take away her pain, except each time I move, she whimpers. Her screams fill my ears, and I beg for her to lose consciousness again. It's only when she's unconscious that I can breathe, that I can think straight. She's not cognizant of the pain when her mind is blank.

I barely acknowledge the others traveling with me. I do not want them near her, I do not want to share her, but the other female, Gemma, insists on staying by Daisy's side. She is with Vruksha, as I suspected she would be—even I noticed how he fixated on her coloring. He has pined for his lost family for many years, and the other female's coloring is similar to that of the Pit Viper. He can be near Daisy, as he only has eyes for his claimed one.

But Azsote, the blasted Boomslang, is with us as well. He's the one who found Daisy, pulling her burning body from the wreckage of the ship she was in, and for that, he can live. For now.

He did not steal her while he had the chance. Instead, he sought me and brought me to Daisy's side. He told me Daisy said my name as he carried her out of the flames. Azsote wanted to honor her dying wish.

Her dying wish...

She will not die!

I will not let my queen leave me, not again! I will atone. I have to atone. I have made so many mistakes that I don't know where to begin. Making sure she lives and is comfortable is a start. Because if she dies... A shudder goes through me. If Daisy dies, there is nothing left for me to live for. I've been alone for so long before her, and I can't go back to that.

Azsote and the others are not the only ones who saw Daisy's ship fall from the sky. There are nagas in the shadows of the forest, lurking about. I need to keep her from them as much as I need to keep her alive.

Azsote and Vruksha bare their fangs at the others, saving me from the task of handling her broken form and guarding her as well. I am indebted to them.

Daisy shakes and screams, and I grit my teeth.

The trek back to my den is grueling, and it's not until Daisy goes unconscious and stays that way—when I fear she will give in and let go —that we finally reach my home.

Only the medical pod can save her. Gemma, the other female, insists it's our only option. It's either try the pod, or make Daisy as comfortable as possible until she succumbs to her wounds, or until infection takes hold and kills her.

Still, I can't let her go, and it takes the others forcing Daisy out of my arms and holding me down on the floor before Daisy is placed in the machine. With Vruksha gripping my arms and Azsote on top of me, Gemma—with Vruksha's tail for help—settles Daisy in the machine. Gemma scrambles around it, figuring it out.

I roar.

Watching the glass of the pod shield Daisy's body from me and fill with smoke, nearly destroys me. But then the smoke clears and I see her again. The arms within the pod go to work and I'm released. Moving to her side, I beg to the skies for her to live. The house robots have maintained this machine as they have everything else in this wretched place. It should work. I will bring this place to the ground if it doesn't.

You are strong. Stronger than me.

The tension in Daisy's body goes away after the machine pokes her with needles. I fist my hands, waiting for her to wake up and see me. Instead, she doesn't wake at all.

What if she never wakes?

"Zaku?" the other female says my name. I snarl in response. I do not want to be bothered. After a few minutes, she says it again.

"What?" I snap.

"She's going to be asleep for a while. You should get some rest."

I hiss, low and annoyed.

"Leave him," Vruksha says. "He will do as he pleases."

Hours go by. Time stands still. I don't move, gazing at Daisy, unable to look away. I'm afraid if I do, she'll vanish. The day comes and goes, and so does the night. The house robots try to feed me and I ignore them, unable to stomach food, unable to do anything except wait. It's not until much later that I catch Azsote enter my home without being stopped, that it occurs to me others are here with me.

Seeing him through the open door of the room I'm in, he drags in a deer carcass, hauling it to the kitchen. Once there, he and Vruksha strip its hide off.

Confused, I study them for a while.

I don't like that they're here. I like it less that Daisy hasn't woken up. I turn to the female sleeping in a chair across from me. She hasn't moved from Daisy's side either.

Daisy is alive because of her.

I recall her taking charge by the crash site when I couldn't. I owe the other female for forcing me to face what I did not want to.

My eyes fall upon her bandaged feet, her shoddy clothes, and I leave quietly so I do not wake her, coming back with an armful of garments and some footwear from the closet below. I place the offering by the female's side. A gift for her help.

I eat the meat the robots bring me in silence, studying my guests, lulled by the constant beeping of the machine. It has been many years since I tolerated a guest. Clenching my hands, I keep my body still so I do not strike out.

There have been many changes in my life this season.

"You should get some rest." The female across from me sits up from her chair and rubs her eyes.

I hiss in warning. No one tells me what to do.

She is unbothered by it, standing to check Daisy's vitals. "I'll be with her. I'll make sure nothing happens," she says. "I need her to live."

I slide my tail over the pod's glass. "Why?"

"Because this should have never happened. I should have been able to stop it, and Peter can't win." The female looks at me. "I care about her. If she dies, then I've failed."

The female's eyes hood, and she licks her lips. She curls her fingers on the glass beside my tail, keeping my gaze. "We both have failed if she diesss," I say. "Do you understand?"

"I do."

I nod. "If she dies, you will have failed me as well, Gemma."

Her brow furrows briefly, then smooths out. "I understand."

"Do not let the others near her," I add, tilting my head at Vruksha and Azsote. "I do not trust them."

"I won't."

With that, I settle down beside Daisy, pushing the rest of my tail over the pod. I close my eyes.

I wake to hushed voices sometime later. Female voices. I pull my addled mind out of the slumber it desperately needs when Daisy cries out.

The next second, I'm up and over her, gazing into her eyes. Or eye. The other is swollen shut. We stare at each other. There's so much I want to say, except my mouth doesn't open. Nothing comes out. She is not the Daisy I knew. She is different. There's pain in her that wasn't there before, and it's not physical pain. It's more than that, and I fear it's because of me.

"My queen," I say. "Forgive me."

TWENTY-EIGHT
A FRIGHTENING FACE

Daisy

The days blur. The pain ebbs and flows.

It's because of the pain that I know I'm alive. I wait for death to take me. I pray it does, I hurt so much.

Most of the time I feel nothing, stuck up with needles and tubes. I never thought I'd live, and each time I wake, the pain reminds me that I'm still alive. That I'm *going* to survive. It hurts, knowing I won't have an easy out. That whatever the medical pod is doing to me is working. When I woke the first time, it was to glass covering me, and Gemma's face. I finger the thin sheet draped over me, glad I can't see underneath it.

I've glimpsed my reflection in the pod's glass. It scares me.

I don't know who it is looking back at me anymore.

I manage to tell Gemma that *The Dreadnaut* knows what's happened to us and that they're in on it. At least someone in command is in on it. It means there will be no help coming, and I fear what it means in the future if they don't get the tech they're so desperately searching for. It's not like the war is over.

Earth is clear for travel. At least if sanctioned by Central Command. Others will come. It might take some time for them to get here, but they will come. The government is tyrannical, though they live by laws and codes. Others? Not so much.

But they won't be coming for Gemma or me. Or Shelby, or Peter, or anyone else.

Gemma says we have to help ourselves now. She's a flitting voice in my head. I think she's right. It's the last thing she tells me before she says she'll be returning soon, that she'll find a way for us to communicate.

I think I mentioned seeing Shelby to her as well, but I can't remember. I don't tell her about the lie. I tell her about *the Mercy*.

I beg her to stay. I fear for her safety. She says she is safe and not to worry about her. That I shouldn't focus on anything except getting better. She's a leader and I've always tested as a follower growing up. A sheep.

Gemma's been claimed by Vruksha, a red naga I sometimes see in a blur behind her. She has claimed him back. I see her leading him outside.

My head spins. The pod pumps me full of more drugs.

Zaku's claimed me... Have I claimed him too?

Should I claim him? He's sitting beside me, staring at me. I try to look at him but my eyes hurt. It makes me sad.

I wish... I stayed.

He's quiet, letting me rest, forcing me to rest. I don't want to rest anymore. I want to get out of the pod and get dressed. I want to bathe. I want to curl up in the coil of his tail. I want to pound my fists against his chest for leaving me when he did, of not telling me where he was going, of abandoning me after I spent days thinking he might be dead!

He won't let me do anything of the sort.

"Zaku," I rasp, trying to sit up. The glass shield of the pod moves back.

He shifts and gently puts his hand on my shoulder, keeping me down. "Do not move. You are not well yet."

I sigh. "I've been here forever." The fact that it's only been days should be astonishing to me. It should take me weeks to heal the way I am, months, years even. Then I remember it's advanced technology being used on me. This pod, while similar to those I've used before, is clearly superior. It's technology that humans like Peter are willing to sell their souls for.

Technology that can restore a human from critical condition to stable in no time at all, would be worth millions of credits. Zaku's home has more wealth than I can wrap my head around. I'd been flummoxed by the jewels, the warm water, the pleasure, when I should've been in awe of this pod.

I haven't been paying enough attention...

"Not forever, little human."

He settles back when I don't fight him. Managing to face him, fighting the taut wounds on my neck, I take him in.

He hasn't left my side, not once since I woke up. He gives me no privacy, hovering over me every second of every day. I don't think he's sleeping now that Gemma's left, and I worry for him. He's been wounded, and his chest is still healing. He needs sleep as well as food and rest.

"I wish I could regenerate too," I say.

"So do I."

Arguing with him to go take care of himself is futile. He won't do it, not while I'm awake at least. I've tried and failed. But I feel better today, stronger. Perhaps it's the recent flood of meds. The pod is helping me heal rapidly, repairing my skin, numbing my nerves. "At least let me sit in a chair. If I can just take a dose of painkiller with me, I'll be fine," I beg. "I'd like to sit upright. I'd like to look at the trees and the gorge below."

"No."

"Please? Just to the window?"

His tail winds over the top of the pod, giving me his answer. "Daisy, not only have you been burned—"

I close my eye. The other one doesn't open any longer. "I don't want to know."

"—you've lost sight in one eye. Your arm is broken. You've also lost a significant amount of blood and you have third-degree burns down your body from your face to your hip. You are not going anywhere."

"I didn't want to know," I whisper. I'm damaged. I know this. I don't think I have hair anymore either. I don't... feel it. I didn't see it in the glass. There's a wounded person in it, not me.

"You must rest," he says.

"What about you?" I ask.

"Rest."

Heartbroken, I let sleep take me away.

When I wake next, the pod is changing my IVs, and it's dark. A single candle is lit, flickering shadows across the space. Zaku's beside me, reading. I've never seen him read before.

When he notices me, he puts the book down.

"What is it?" I ask, though it comes out as a croak.

He lifts the book. "An encyclopedia."

"What's that?"

His cowl flutters. "I think... It's a book of many subjects. There is a lot in it about the old world."

"Is it interesting?"

"I have read it before, so no. But it has subjects on human health, and I have no other books on the matter."

He goes silent, studying me, and the longer he does, the more nervous I get. I can't read his expression; shadows cling to his features. My eye is out of focus. I can't even sit up. My heart quickens uncomfortably the longer he studies me.

"Please stop looking at me," I whisper when it becomes too much, facing away.

He shifts, and I try curling into a ball to make my body small. "Why?" he rumbles.

"My face—"

"Is the same as it has always been."

Tears spring. "No, it's not. I've seen it. I'm not *me* anymore. I'll never be beautiful again for you. I'm—"

"Look."

I open my eye to find a mirror posed over me. "I don't want to see," I cry, turning away.

"*Look*, Daisy."

"Please don't make me."

He hisses. "You have nothing to fear, little mate."

Mate. He still claims me. My heart cracks and swells and I shudder.

Slowly I look into the mirror. Tears escape when I do, slipping down my cheek. Bleary, I blink them back until I face my reflection. It hurts. It hurts more than what's happened to my body.

I've always been Daisy, the daughter of a great commander. I've always looked like my father. I've always been that, and nothing more, until I was an orphan, a disappointment, and then a pilot, and then nothing at all. But it was *my* identity and no one else's. Now, like everything, it's gone. I don't know who I am anymore.

I don't know what I am anymore.

Why does everything have to come to an end?

The face staring back isn't me. It's also not the fearful thing I'd seen in the glass. It's my face, only different.

My hair is gone on the left side of my head, and shorn short on the right. My left eye is scarred, swollen, and closed. There are blotchy red burns all along the left side as well that goes down to my neck, shoulders, and lower still under the sheet, but the char of my skin is gone. And the right side of my face is almost entirely untouched. I have no eyebrows, and the one eye I can open is still bloodshot and red, still... I see me—*me*—behind the burns.

"Every day, you are healing. Every day, the pod grafts your skin. You're mending, Daisy, and you will live. Tomorrow you will be stronger, and you will be better. You will be closer to sitting up and looking out the window. You won't be alone."

I fall asleep staring at my reflection.

When I wake next, it's bright, and the pod is vibrating beneath me. My gaze goes to the ceiling—which is moving—and then to the view of the mountains next. Trying to sit upright, the pod stops as the glass above me shifts, and Zaku's hand is back on my shoulder, stopping me.

I glimpse him behind me, seeing he's rolling the pod across the main room. "I can sit up," I say softly.

"Not yet."

Sighing, I slump, and Zaku removes his hand from me, rolling me to the window. Once there, the glass screen of the pod lowers once more, and Zaku moves to my side with pillows under his arm. Carefully, he helps me rise and places them behind me.

I'm not sitting, but I'm a little more upright. Looking out the window I'm reminded there's a world beyond this glass. When he tries to move away, I reach for his hand.

"Stay with me."

He coils his tail under him, and we stare at the landscape together.

"Thank you," I whisper, just to fill the silence. He doesn't respond, and I get twitchy. "Can you tell me about your home?"

"What do you want to know?"

"Everything. Anything? I know so little about this planet. I want to know more. I've got nothing else to do."

Zaku's eyes twinkle in the glass. His tongue swipes his lower lip.

He tells me about the animals that scurry past the window first. Squirrels, rabbits, birds, and once he's done with the animals we see outside, he tells me about the animals we don't see. The pigs, the bears, and the monsters.

"Fearsome beasts once wandered this land, but they have been gone for many years now. They attacked indiscriminately, viciously, and so I and the other nagas who were strong of body and mind hunted them down."

"But monsters? Not just other animals?"

"The orbs did not know what they were. They are not of this land."

"Do the orbs know about you?" I ask.

His eyes pierce me and he doesn't answer. I let it be, already knowing his species is not from Earth. They can't be. Fifteen hundred years is a long time for a planet like Earth to be uninhabited, something would've returned in that time. The plants had, even animals. Why not other aliens, aliens that also worked with the Ketts? Every couple of hundred years or so, humans encounter a new alien species.

Shivering, I ask him what these monsters looked like, and where they came from, trying to glean more from Zaku's origins, only he shakes his head. "I have never seen them in my books. I do not know."

He shows me his encyclopedia, flipping to different points of interest he finds fascinating. One is a map of Earth and the old oceans. He can't fathom an ocean but thinks they must be several times larger than the lake.

I smile. "Much, much larger."

He tells me about his favorite battles. The nagas he's killed, and the skulls on his lawn that he enjoys the most, one being the head of a Death Adder—a notorious rapist and killer—that he and several other nagas took down many years prior.

As the sun sets, Zaku feeds me berries from his hand and tells me about his father.

"I was searching for him. I had not seen him for some time, and we often kept in communication. One day, I scented his body in the wind. I followed the scent and came upon his corpse. It... was mangled and broken, but not torn and bitten. I could not figure out how he died. He did not have the wounds that would indicate another naga had killed him, or a beast from the forest. For days, I stayed by his side, trying to figure out how a king, a male that even I feared could be dead. I needed to know. I had to know. And until then, I remained and kept the scavengers away from his corpse. On the third day, I realized a truth I didn't want to accept. There were steep cliffs nearby."

Zaku goes silent.

"Why?" I ask quietly. "Why would he do that?"

"I have never known, until recently... He was not the king he thought he was." Zaku's cowl falls. "Our females were dying. They were beginning to band together and leave us, to travel west. Rogue males were appearing and much more was lost in the shift. My father chased after things that I did not care about nor understand. It was wet that summer. Water fell from the sky for the first time. The skiesss opened up and water poured for weeks on end." Zaku shudders.

"Rain?" I say.

"Yes. Water that comes from the sky."

"I know what rain is, but here? That's not possible. The oceans are gone. The water has to come from somewhere to rain." My brow furrows.

I never paid attention to my history lessons and had very few on the ancient home planet, though it occurs to me that there's a lake here, and that shouldn't be. I saw no other bodies of water from the sky. Maybe the water is coming from under the ground?

Is the lake big enough to make rain? It can't be. Glancing at the trees in the gorge, I wonder how they're alive at all.

Perhaps that's why Central Command wants the technology here so much. My stomach drops and I try to push the feeling of unease away. It's not my problem. Still, I look at my hands and the scarring on them, tracing them with my fingertip.

"I do not know. Are there not oceans and lakes in space?"

"Not... quite. On other planets, yes, but not in space. It's not in one of your books?"

"Not that I have found. I have never thought much about it."

I turn back to the landscape, recalling what I've been told about the Lurkers and their precious tech. Even so, no tech could control the weather.

"I'm sorry about your father," I say.

"I am sorry about yours too."

I go still, my gaze finding him. He's looking at me and not out the window. He reaches over and cups my cheek where I'm not burned.

"I would have chosen to save the young as well. In that, you and I are alike," he rasps.

"Zaku..."

He drops his hand when I nuzzle it.

"Rest now. It's getting late." He rises and moves away.

"Zaku, wait," I say. He stops and comes back to my side. I grab his wrist and curl my fingers around it. "Why did you leave me?"

He tilts his head.

"In the shower," I clarify. "Why did you leave? Where did you go?"

"You were right," he says.

"Right about what?"

Instead of answering me, he leans down, putting his face before mine. I fall back upon the pillows. I lick my chapped lips when his mouth moves close.

But it doesn't fall upon mine. It doesn't kiss mine. He presses his lips to my forehead and slides his wrist out of my fingers. "You will always be my queen. Regardless of what I am, you will always be that."

And with the silence clouding in around me, he rolls me back to the room, breaking my heart.

TWENTY-NINE
THE HARD TRUTH

Daisy

ZAKU MAKES me stay in the pod until it stops grafting my skin and administering painkillers. And even then, he keeps his tail over the glass until my vitals are normal and stable. We don't talk again. Not after that last time. I try to start a conversation, but he dodges. I have never been stationary for so long before. It's worse because Zaku's pulling away. He's different around me. The days come and go and with each new sunrise, I'm stronger, healthier, better. The pod's AI verifies it.

It begins administering steroids, boosters, and stimulants to help return my strength.

When it starts to return, it returns fast.

Afterward, the pod began signaling low on stores, making Zaku erupt at the house. Like it's the house's fault. Seeing emotion from him brings me hope. Managing to calm him, I tell him I'm going to be fine, that we'll replace what is lost, that unless every hospital on Earth has miraculously vanished, there will be ruins for us to scavenge through. Later.

And then it occurred to me...

I'm making plans. Plans *here*, with Zaku. I didn't have a choice when I was stuck, though now that I'm not, now that I'm free, I can't help but think about my future.

I'm not going back to *The Dreadnaut*. I want nothing to do with them and the people who are in command. I can't help but think of them all as child killers. Dream destroyers. Though it's not true. There are good people. It's just... you have to break down too many walls to find them. And I'm tired, so very tired of doing that. I see those babies on the rooftop often in my head. Hearing Zaku's response—that he even heard my story at all—healed me more than the pod ever could.

He'd save them too.

I don't have to wonder if I made the right choice any longer.

We should have evacuated Colony 4. Not try to keep it. So many lives would have been saved if we had. *So many children...*

I want to be with him. We're more alike than I ever imagined. Sucking in a breath, it's deep and satisfying...and scentless.

He's sweet, kind, and patient, and not at all the Zaku who pulled me from the lake weeks ago—who chased me down and caught me up in his arms. And it scares me. It scares me as much as my choice to stay has.

Staring at my reflection in the window, I gently trace the wrinkles on my skin. I'll never look the way I did before the crash. I'll never be what I once was. I stretch out my fingers, loosening the scar tissue that's stiff between them, peering between them. The pod has been unable to return my sight, and I'm slowly getting used to my altered vision.

Facing the room, it's empty. There are no robots, no visitors, and no Zaku. He's around. I think...I hope he's just giving me some space.

Now that I can move freely, he's gone distant. He stiffens when I touch him, only giving me his tail to use as a crutch. Besides that, he's avoiding touching me at all.

Is it because of the way I look? Is he afraid he'll hurt me?

Hugging my body, I walk to the kitchen.

He says it's because I'm weak. I don't believe him. I need him. I need him so badly it hurts.

I miss him.

I can *feel* around him and not have to be ashamed of it.

I want my Zaku back.

Does he still want me?

I rub my face, wanting to rub it all away. Stinging my skin, I drop my hands. I hear the scuff of his scales sliding across the floor, and when I look up, I see Zaku entering the room. He catches my gaze as he closes the red door behind him but looks away.

He approaches me with something in his hand. Reaching out, he offers it to me. "Fresh clothes," he says, his voice a rumble.

I take them and hold them to my chest. "Thank you."

He makes his way over to the door. "I am going to harvest berries."

"Why won't you look at me?"

He stops. I step away from the counter, and toward him.

"Why won't you touch me?" I try to keep my voice from cracking. "It's been nearly two weeks," my voice cracks anyway. "Why?"

He tilts his head in my direction. "I don't want to hurt you."

I take another step. "You've never hurt me before. Why would you now? Tell me the truth." My voice gains steam. "Is it because of the way I look? Is it because I... I look this way?"

He pivots in my direction and hisses furiously, forcing me to lean back. His cowl expands, shuttering my view of everything else. The gold flecks in his dark eyes spark with anger. "Never say such a thing! You are the most beautiful creature in the world."

"But I'm not. I never was," I whisper, unable to hold his eyes. "I'm this," I run my hand down my chest and clutch the loose shirt I'm wearing. "I'm scarred."

His tail coils around where I stand. Zaku's fingers clasp my chin, and I squeeze my eye shut. He lifts my face. "Look at me."

I crack my eye open unwillingly. "I hate when you say that."

"No one is more beautiful than you. No one can be."

"Your lies are pretty."

"They are not liesss. I do not lie."

I swat his hand off me and turn away. I never cared about the way I looked, but now, it's a ball of pain in my chest. It's building, and each day it gets worse. If he hadn't regaled my looks so much... "Why won't you touch me then? Do you not want me anymore? There's something wrong and it's been wrong since the shower.."

Zaku's hissing deepens. "Daisssy—"

"Go. Leave," I snap, suddenly needing space before I become the weak creature I'm feeling right now, the weak creature he says I am. I don't want Zaku to see me vulnerable anymore.

He grabs my hand and spins me back to face him. "You do not get to tell me what to do," he growls.

I growl back. "The same goes for you."

His brow cocks, and I try tugging my hand from his grasp. His hold on me tightens. "I will not have you think you are not beautiful. You are healing, little one, and I am..."

"You're what?" I ask when he trails off.

His eyes shift away, and he shakes his head.

"You're what, Zaku? What's wrong? What happened during the shower? Why did you really leave?"

He hisses, releases my hand. "Don't."

"Don't? After all you've done? After bartering for me? Stealing me? Keeping me trapped and then caging me? You ask me to... *don't?*" Anger fills me, replacing my doubt. "I will not '*don't.*'"

Zaku's lips twist.

"Tell me!" I shout. "You wanted a mate so bad—you should know that mates talk! Contracted couples communicate! How am I supposed to feel if I don't know what's going on with you?" I lower my voice. "How can I believe your words if I don't know if there's any truth behind them? Let me trust you again. I want to trust you!"

When he stares at me, saying nothing, the numbness I had thought long gone returns hard and fast. I refuse to be deluded any longer. I refuse to live in a world where I'm unwanted any longer. I might not be the prodigy my father hoped I would be, but I survived without him.

I can survive without Zaku too. My soul splinters. I can make it here on Earth. There are entire cities, towns, buildings scattered across the land, and technology that I'm growing more comfortable with every day. I'll scavenge, stay low, and make my own way.

Perhaps I'll head west and seek out the missing naga females.

Yes. That's what I'll do. I'll join them.

Sanctuary. The word fills my head.

"Fine," I say, heading for the door.

My throat closes as I approach it. I haven't tried to leave and I don't know if it'll open for me. A hand slams on the glass before I can try. Zaku's claws streak across the door before curling into a fist in front of my face.

I swallow thickly, and then I smell it.

It. His scent.

"You are going nowhere," he growls.

THIRTY

THE LAST KING COBRA

Zaku

How DARE she try to leave?

I push away from the door, seeking to calm my rage. *Calm!* It's not something I've felt since Daisy. There's no calm anymore, only her. Her and my failures and the hard truth of my existence.

"You want to know the truth? Is that it?" I snap.

She slowly turns to face me and I lower to face her.

"Yes," she says. "More than anything."

"I'm going to hurt you." I slip my tongue out to taste her cheek. I can't help it. Not with the emotion etched on her face. I've been needing to taste her, desperate for it. I was tormented before I ran, and before her pain. I am in anguish now. The need, the endless throbbing, it will not stop.

It was easy to ignore for a time. Not anymore, not with her mending.

"Hurt me?"

"I am trying not to." My words come out through a tightened throat. "Because I will. I will hurt you, and you will hate me. You will leave me, and I will have no choice but to let you go. That's the truth. I want you so much that I don't trust my strength, or my mind anymore. I am not..."

I trail off, staring at the streak of saliva on her cheek from my tongue, wanting to lick it again.

It glistens like a beacon.

She pulls her arms to her chest. It means she's nervous. She's done it often, shielding herself from me, and only recently have I begun to realize *why*. I hiss deeply and thrust away from her before I do more than lick her face.

Daisy jerks forward. "Wait—don't!" She throws her arms around me.

I go rigid. My soul stills. If I move... I will feel her and I will fall.

"Don't go. Don't stop talking. Please, Zaku, I want to know what's wrong. I do." She pushes her face to my chest.

Should I tell her that I know nothing about who I am? Shaking, I inhale and embrace her to me, risking everything. "I do not know how to live with another. I do not know how to take care of you. Since I've had you, I have only brought you further into danger."

She lifts her head and looks at me. Her hair is beginning to grow back, her scars are fading, her self-assurance returning, helped by the stimulants from the pod. I have read everything I have on the machine— everything. The meds it administers, the sprays it covers her body with. But I don't have all the information or the skill to help in her recovery. I am ill-equipped.

I always have been.

"You have. You've put me in danger. But you've also done more for me than you could know."

"Yet you said so yourself. I have done nothing but hurt you."

"The cage? Yeah, that wasn't good. Bartering for females against their will? That's even worse."

I close my eyes.

"You've also saved me," she continues.

"It wasn't me who pulled you from the wreckage. It was Azsote."

"That's not what I'm talking about, Zaku." She reaches up and cups my cheek, and I tremble from her touch. "You've helped me realize I can be strong too. That there's more to life than war and death and laws and codes. That... life is more important than all of that. You realize that, right?"

"You cannot have a life with me."

Her brow furrows, and I hate seeing the softness from her gaze diminish. The hurt that crosses her face. She snatches her hand back and brings it to her chest like she's been burned. "I don't understand," she says.

Groaning, I put distance between us, moving back into the room. "I will hurt you. There will come a time where I can't hold back, or I will make another mistake, and I will betray you. I have almost done it already. It... will happen again."

"I don't—"

"The shower!" I roar, spinning on her and baring my fangs.

She flinches but doesn't recoil.

She should be running!

"You told me we weren't compatible, and I refused to believe it. I tried to mate with you anyway, even after the deal we made. I used your wish for freedom against you. My mind is not what it once was. My body is not the same. It hasn't been, not since I saw you. Look," I growl, swiping my claws across my tail. "Look at me! I am an animal!"

My member bursts forth, barely contained by the scales that hide it. Red, thick, and swollen, my knot beyond recognition. I grab my shaft and squeeze, and even without touching my bulge, spill pours out of me. "Look at it, at us, and tell me I won't hurt you!" Tearing my eyes away from my misery, I force them to Daisy, needing to see the horror return to her. "I will destroy you," I say, my voice lowering as my torment builds.

Except it's not horror that crosses her features. It's not disgust, or fear, or even the sadness that has been plaguing her. It's... something else. Something unexpected. She's staring at my shaft, and her chest rises and falls. Her nose twitches. Her cheeks pinken and then redden, and when they do, her lips part.

She takes a step toward me.

My arm snaps out to stop her. "If you come any closer, I don't know what will happen," I warn.

"Zaku," she says my name absently and then her eye rips from me to look at the floor, her brow furrowing, and if I didn't think her skin could heat any further, it does. She shakes once all over and grasps her shirt with straining fingers.

Her reaction confuses me.

"This is why I avoid you," I rasp. "I have felt what it's like to have you, to have you kill for me! And I have been cursed ever since. It is the least I deserve." Sweat beads her brow, and I fist my hands to stop from diving forward and licking it off. "I am not a king. I am not anything. I am becoming something I never wanted to be, a primal, nasty naga, one who deserves to have his spine removed from his body and wrapped around a tree. That is why I left. We're not compatible, nor should we ever be. You are a rare creature, a human female, and I am nothing but a beast living in someone else's home, pretending to be something I am not."

She licks her lips and I nearly throw her to the ground and mount her. Pivoting to the door, I need to get away and now, or my worst fear will come true.

I grab the handle. "The place is yours. You will be safe here—I will make certain of it. I will keep these lands clear of any who might harm you and provide for you, but to ask me to stay? I can't. I would like to keep you, and I have tried, but I can't at the expense of your life. Do not ask such a thing of me. I am losing my mind."

I push the door open, shaking all over.

Daisy throws her arms around me. I crush the handle.

"Stupid, stupid, thick-headed male," she says against my back, her breath teasing my scales. I don't move, I don't dare, wrenching the metal between my fingers and closing my eyes. "You are so stupid."

"Is that...what thick-headed means?" I grit, remembering her calling me this. She climbs over my tail and pushes her body flush to my back.

It's too much. It's torture.

"Yes. That's what thick-headed means. I am not the weak creature you want to so badly believe I am. You are not leaving me. I am not asking."

I growl.

She continues like she has no idea that I am about to tear her clothes off and rut her across the floor. That I am about to add her bones to the ones outside. Agony floods me at the thought.

"I want to mate. I want to."

My claws crack, pushing into the metal. "I... It will not... work..."

"Then let me prove it to you. After everything, can you give me that?"

"A gift?" I wheeze, slicing my tongue with my fangs, swallowing blood and venom.

"Yes. A gift. One more gift."

How can I refuse?

"I will hurt you."

She laughs—laughs!—while pressing her soft lips to my spine. "No, Zaku, you won't."

My mind scrambles. I drop the metal shards and clasp her hand on my chest, feeling hope niggle its way into me. Horrible, damnable hope. She pulls away but takes my hand, coming to my side. I peer down at her.

Daisy gifts *me* a smile, and I am undone.

THIRTY-ONE
TAMING THE KING

Daisy

I LEAD Zaku back into his home. He's nervous, perhaps afraid? It's flattering and is giving me confidence. Confidence I have been in sore need of. I thought he didn't want me anymore. I'd been wrong.

"Wait," he rumbles, pulling his hand from mine. Before I can ask him why, he's slipping into the kitchen. When he returns, it's with a kitchen knife. He hands it to me and I eye it curiously.

"There are knives in the kitchen?" I've gone through every drawer several times over. I never found a knife. I assumed the robots had utensils attached to them, and Zaku used his claws for cutting the meat.

"They are kept locked and hidden."

"Why are you giving me this?" I ask, turning it over.

"So you have protection."

"I'm not going—"

Zaku stops me, lifting my chin with his fingers. "I vowed I would never give you a reason to stab me like you had Vagan and the Python, but..." His eyes glint dark and gold. "I need you to know you will use it."

"I can't possibly—"

"Daisssy," he says, hissing my name unusually long.

Stunned by the anguish in his voice, I can't help but nod. "Okay," I whisper.

He closes his eyes and when he opens them, there's only hunger. Feverish hunger. The anguish is gone. I curl my fingers around the knife's handle, anxiety swirling through me. *He really is afraid he's going to hurt me.* Glimpsing his cock, I know why.

It's gone from a smooth shaft with a knot in the middle to a swollen battering ram. Veins pulse up and down its length, pushed out by the seed flooding it. It leaks, milky and wet from his tip, blooming the air with its scent. I'm addicted to it. I don't know why I'm not flopping on the floor, but I'm glad I'm not.

I want to be. I feel my body changing because of his scent. The sensation is exciting and pleasant. Some alien species change during certain cycles... I should've gotten my period by now, but I haven't.

And ovulating? I take shots to stop that from happening. All women do unless they plan to get pregnant with a contracted partner.

I haven't had a shot in several months though... Shaking the thought from my mind, I've missed many monthlies due to stress in my old line of work, and the shots last a while.

Zaku shifts and I jerk, realizing I've been staring at his cock again. Forcing my gaze to his face, blood trickles from the corner of his mouth.

My palms dampen with sweat. I retake his hand with my free one and finish the descent. I'm going to claim him as Gemma has with her male.

With my confidence building, I approach the Zaku's nest. I haven't been in the lower parts of the house since the crash. First, because the stairs were too much for me, and then it was because of Zaku's indifference. I was afraid to crawl into it, only to lie amongst the soft bedding without him.

I stop at the edge, suddenly nervous again. I turn to face him.

"Remember the knife," he growls.

I look down at it in my hand and place it by the pillows. "I will. Lie back."

"Lie... back?"

"Yes," I respond quickly before I lose my nerve.

His eyes hood and my chest tightens. His tail thumps, but he listens to me, running the length of it against my leg as he moves past me. When he's positioned, leaning on the pillows with his arms folded behind his head, I gaze at him, unable to do anything else. *He's certain he's going to hurt me.*

He could. He's huge. I hear the door to the bedroom click close behind me, and I know it's his tailtip that has shut it.

It wraps around my ankle a moment later.

I pull off my loose clothes, avoiding looking at his cock. If I do... I'll just stare at it, and nothing will happen. The tension between my legs *wants* something to happen. It wants it badly.

His eyes shift over my naked body, and my spine straightens. He's seen me naked many times as the pod worked its magic on me. I'm not what I once was and he knows that. This is different though...

His tail tightens around my ankle. "Come here," he growls. "Or I will force it."

Heat rises to my cheeks. Crawling over his tail, I straddle him. His scent floods me, and my eye waters. Wetness leaks from me, and feeling his scales all along my sex, I push down into him. Male musk, sweet star-sugar, and every smell I have ever loved enters me. I stare at his bulge and saliva gushes.

"Daisss—"

I grasp his knot with both hands and moan. Spill shoots out.

Zaku thrashes, sending me bouncing, he hisses and grasps the bedding, shredding it. I hold onto his cock, my sex slipping over his scales. He roars.

My mouth falls open and I dive forward, so hungry it hurts.

Zaku grabs hold of me as I squeeze his cock, forcing his seed out. Pressing my lips to his tip, I drink it down. Starving, I wrap my mouth on him and suck, becoming an uncivilized creature like him. A primitive creature who needs to devour or die. His body shakes as I suck him hard, tensing my jaw, swaying my face side to side, lashing my tongue. Grasping his knot, I knead it, needing more. Cum flows into my mouth like a river, and I take it all greedily.

I jerk up with a gasp, flinging my head back, catching my breath. Diving back down, I go for more.

He bellows raw, animalistic noises, bowing his chest over me, clawing my back with his nails, and toward my butt, hoisting it up.

It's not enough.

His seed slides down my throat like oil and into my belly. Fire erupts there, and I grip his shaft, massaging it for more. His spurts have me swallowing constantly. Precious seed leaks from my mouth, and I roll my hips. Tickling sensations pet my nerves, knotting up my insides. He grabs my butt and digs his claws into my cheeks, pushing my brow to his abs.

Zaku spreads my cheeks wide, and I clench hard, emptier than ever.

Almost faint, I pop off his cock and rub it hard up and down. Like a fountain, his cum releases. It splashes my face. I lick my lips.

"You taste how you smell," I moan.

Zaku strains upward, slamming his shaft back into my open mouth. "Daisssy," he hisses between the rabid sounds he's making. I squeeze his knot as my eye waters.

His fingers paw my sex and thrust into me. I lift off him again and inhale, wiping the cum off around my eyes. "We need to empty you," I say.

He groans, thrusting his fingers in and out of me. "I have tried."

"I haven't." Locked between his tail and his torso, I swirl my tongue over his tip.

He trembles, and I smile. His fingers strain, scissor, and I lift my butt higher for more.

"You... are... killing me," he grates thickly. "I am dying."

I run my tongue over his knot. "Have you cummed, Zaku?" I ask between licks.

He doesn't answer at first, his tail going tense, then quivering. "C-Cummed?"

"Orgasmed."

"I am—" he rumbles "—always spilling, always since you. I am... tormented! Tortured!" He roars as I find the groove around his cock where it hides inside his tail. My fingers explore the warm skin inside, searching for where his spill is stored. All I feel is smooth, warm skin.

Zaku falls back, tearing his fingers out of me, and the bed bounces. He grabs my hand and rips it from his tail slit. "Don't," he grits, squeezing my fingers.

"Does it hurt?" I ask.

His eyes are crazed, diabolical. Blood is smeared across his lips. I lean up and press my sex to his tail excitedly, rubbing it over him.

"It's too much. Too muuuch. The knife. Use the knife."

I swipe the cum off my lips, taking my hand back. His body convulses when I do. "Trust me?"

His cowl extends out. He exhales slowly. "Yesss," he hisses. "No. I do not trust myself."

Keeping his eyes, I slip my fingers back to the groove around his cock. His pupils expand, and his chest swells. My poor king is lost.

Poor, poor king. I slowly lower my face, keeping his gaze trapped. I push my mouth to his root and slide my tongue to the groove. I lick him within. Zaku falls back, pushing his pelvis up. With my free hands, I wrap them around his cock and work his length.

I need to get his seed out of him before there can be more...

Beyond tense, he goes completely still as I lash my tongue, moving it around the base of his cock. The noises he made before are gone. He's silent, shaking, and I almost feel bad for putting him in this position. I'm sending him to the edge. I'm trying to at least.

Just in case, I slide my hand up to the pillows and grasp the knife, bringing it toward me. Déjà vu hits, and I lick him faster.

Slicing my hand over his length, his knot is growing, rather than getting smaller. His tremors are joined by a deep, vibrating hiss that thrums my nerves. Clenching and desperate, I lave him with everything I have. I need him inside me, I need this to work, taking so much more from him than I'm giving.

His hisses deepen.

My skin prickles, my spine arches, and I cry out. Grasping his base, I rise over him.

He doesn't stop me, watching me through slitted, serpentine eyes. Eyes I don't recognize.

"My gift," I gasp, reaching down and pushing my fingers to tickle his cock's base as I lower my body onto him. His tip sinks into me and I rub the sensitive flesh in his slit hard. He grabs my hips, shunting up.

And spills and spills and spills. It invades me deeply, overflowing, leaking out around his shaft despite how stretched I am. Zaku's eyes roll into the back of his head, and his tail slithers around my body, caging me in a trap of swarming limbs. I lose sight of him as it gently coils around my head. He holds me still, emptying inside me.

Tensing, I realize the knife is out of my reach. *Is he...* His muscled tail and velvety scales is all I see. A thick wall of scales and tendons. Pleasure blooms despite being caged in his limbs and I moan from the onslaught.

He won't hurt me.

When I can't take anymore, I cry out and shoot off him, letting it empty out of me as well. His tail shifts and allows just enough room for me to relax. He continues to come, and I palm his knot, helping him.

The moment my hand cups it, he thrusts me back down and forces me to take it inside me instead.

I cry out.

Minutes go by, maybe hours, and slowly the tension leaves his hands. We work the seed out of him together. Twitching, he lets me rise so his spill can trickle out of me again. My sex constricts. I feel what he's been feeling. Except it's me who's full now.

Gasping, his hisses remain deep and soothing and he tugs me off of him to lie me on his chest. I snuggle in, tracing the scales on his chest. I'm needy and hot, and I moan weakly. So tired and yet nowhere near as sated as he is.

Seed dries on my skin as he caresses my back.

"My queen. What a gift you have given me."

We drift.

THIRTY-TWO

GLASS

Daisy

THE GROUND SHAKES, and I open my eye. Zaku's over me, licking my neck, rubbing his cock against my leg. He's hissing again. It's that deep hiss I can't handle and I reach for the knife. But my eyes slice to the window where the glass is vibrating.

"What's that?" I ask.

Zaku's forked tongue dives into my ear, and I squeak. "My desperation."

Shunting my hips up, I tell him with my body that I need more than ear licks. The reverberating of the glass worsens, and my eye cuts to the window again, but then Zaku moves, blocking the view. Can his hissing do that? The tremors stop, though the nerve endings sparking throughout my body continue.

Vaguely aware that a robot is lasering the bedding, I try not to giggle from the absurdity.

Zaku sees my smile and gives me one back. I cup his face and drag it down to mine. Warm, thick lips cover mine—even his mouth is big—and he pushes his tongue into me. I moan, sucking on his tongue.

He's between my legs, held open wide by the girth of his upper tail. Something pushes between us and tickles me. Zaku rises slightly and that *something* flicks my nub. His tailtip. He pushes it inside me and flicks some more.

I moan, having been waiting for this for too long. Needing him to claim me. Even if it does hurt...

My mouth parts to tell him this, and Zaku slides his tongue down my throat, stopping me. Sputtering, I thrash, and he slips it out. I inhale quickly as my throat contracts. Tight and quivering, the muscles in my throat riot. His eyes glint wickedly. He knows what he's doing to me. My eyes water.

"You have broken me with your mouth, little female."

I swallow and he dives forward, thrusting his tongue back down my throat.

Gagging, I grip his cowl. Invaded from both ends and swollen with his seed. He groans and I feel it through my entire body as he pushes against me. I press up into him, lost in sensation, not sure if I want to get away or stay. My throat tightens around his tongue as I try swallowing my hitches, trying not to gag. He pulls out of me all at once, from both ends.

Bereft, I collapse into the bedding, coughing.

Zaku peers down at me, pleased with himself. "Beautiful," he says.

Because of him, I'm beginning to think I might be. I wipe the wetness gathering on my lashes off from his attack.

Gently, he caresses where my brow used to be above my blinded eye. "I will make sure you see again, so you can see what you are with clarity."

I hitch again for a different reason.

He rears and grabs my hips, rolling me onto my front, pushing against the back of my thighs. His prick nudges my sex. Curling my hands under my face, I brace for it. His tailtip returns and pets me, wrapping around my front. Needing something to hold onto, I grab it and bring it to my face and nuzzle it. The end flicks my lips and I lick it.

Zaku pushes his girth into me.

My sheath opens slowly for him, stretched tight, still half-fighting his invasion. I clamp my hands around his tailtip when he stops, when his bulge hits my opening, where it can go no further. I whimper.

"Let me mount you," he groans. "Let me in." His hands caress my buttocks, my backside, coaxing me. "Relax."

I take a deep breath.

Slowly, so slowly it's almost unbearable, he works his knot into me. I fight it unwillingly, moaning from the stretch, even though it's not nearly as big as it has been, it still stings. Liquid heat hits me deep within. He's already seeding me.

It helps—oh, how it helps. His spill is hot when fresh, and it ignites my insides. I bite down on the bedding.

His hips move to either side, stretching me further, working me open. Clenching hard around his shaft, part of me wants to fight him out of me, fearing it'll be too much. But then his hissing fills my ears and I relax again. I am not of his species. I don't know why his hissing, his scent is affecting me so much, but I'm grateful. His claws rub my opening.

"Relax," he rasps.

I take another breath, and when I do, he grips my hips and slams into me.

Rising, I scream. His knot pushes me from every side, his tip bottoms out, and I blanch. He stops once he's seated, petting me all over, whispering compliments all around me. Compliments and scales and heat and musk entrap me. A wall of masculine fervor and I'm nothing but a lost creature caged within, forced to worship it, having entered the trap of my own volition. It's too much. Panting, I hold my body prone, waiting for the pressure to end. It doesn't.

"Zaku," I cry.

He pushes me back down to the bed and lowers his body to mine. He nuzzles the back of my head. "We fit, my queen, we fit."

Tears brim my eyes again as time stands still.

Zaku doesn't rut. He doesn't do anything but lick my ear, my cheek, slipping his forked tongue all over my face and giving me the time I need to accept him. After a while, I can't take it anymore, shifting my hips to get him to release me, ready to give up. Then I feel it again...

Pleasure. Deep, strange pleasure.

My body eases.

He seems to sense it because he rises and takes me with him. Seated on his prick, he wraps his arms around me, pushes his tailtip between my lips, and moves me on him just a little. His bulge rubs my sensitive spot unlike anything ever has. It's not like his tongue, or his fingers, or his tip. It rubs it like a puzzle piece, one that's been missing my whole life.

Is this how Gemma is with Vruksha? Is this why she claimed him? Did she feel this too?

My thoughts swirl, and I constrict.

"Zaku," I whisper his name again, easier this time. "What's happening to me?" I'm not like him. This doesn't happen to human female bodies.

"You are ovulating. I am heated. I can scent it. I did not know it at first, though I am sure of it now."

Air *wooshes* out. He pushes his tail hard against me, undulating ever so slightly.

Ovulating...

Pleasure explodes through my body. Falling forward into his banded arms, my sex quakes as an orgasm rends me. Brutal and devastating, I scramble, squirming, so full I might burst. Before it ends, before there's an ease, another one hits. Screams tear out of me. Zaku lifts me off him and then seats me back on his length mid-quiver. His bulge expands and then loosens as my sheath milks it. He empties into me. He does it again, ripping me off him only to put my body back upon his length. It hurts. It stings. And then it's rapture.

I'm helpless as another orgasm pummels me each time he connects us. Hips dancing, sexes swollen and raw, I unravel.

"My little flower has finally found her stem," Zaku growls, his knot thickening again. "You have shown me how to water you, and water you, I will."

I trust him. The knife clatters to the floor.

He pushes me forward, wraps his tail under me, and mounts me. I grasp his wrists now on either side of my head and cry out for more. Lost in the shunts, the violent thrusts, I forget the war, my past, the dark things that haunt me.

We fit.

Please don't crush me.

THIRTY-THREE
THE PLAYROOM

Daisy

"What's the deal with the... playroom?" I ask, peering at the door between the cage and the window. "Why is it just a room of mirrors? Do you know?"

Zaku's fingers whisper across my back, his tail piled in around me from every side. He's leaned up against it like some cocky prince. The appendage slithers closer, indicating he doesn't want me to move away from him. I move to my knees anyway and rest my elbows on it, looking at the door across the way.

We've been in his nest for days, unbothered by the outside world, choosing each other instead. The frenzy of our first mating continued, only paused for nourishment and medical scans to make sure I am still on the mend and that Zaku's and my's eagerness isn't doing something it shouldn't. I'm getting better every day. I have strength. My mind is my own again. I can stop the stimulants and boosters today.

Though I ache unlike ever before. Zaku is merciless and needy. His body won't stop producing seed at an alarming rate, and mating regularly is the only thing keeping his knot from growing too big. It's easier to take him when he's purged.

We do fit... with work.

He's certain the heat will come to an end... if only he can rut me one more time...

Still waiting for Zaku to answer me, I face him and tilt my head.

He hisses, captures me in his arms, and dives his tail into my sheath. I gasp, jerking upward from the invasion.

"It'sss not just mirrors," he growls as he stretches me wide, stroking my inner spot, making me tremble. I plant my hands on his chest to hold my body upright from the attack. With focused hunger in his dark eyes, he pulls out his tail and guides me down on his girth.

I squeeze him, not wholly prepared. He pushes through my slit's weak refusal and forces my acceptance. "Zaku," I moan, annoyed and... pleased.

He rocks my body upon him, having more than enough strength to sate his need despite my laziness. I feel his knot expand, his tailtip teasing my behind, and with another annoyed groan, I rub my clit. I want my answers.

Zaku grabs my hand, taking over.

I don't know which one of us releases first, only that for the next hour I ride his undulating tail a lot more vigorously after the first release he gives me. We continue until we're depleted, until all I want to do is curl up against his side and go back to sleep. He leaves me on the bed— sprawled out, drenched, and thirsty—to get me water. I gulp down the pitcher he returns with and rush to the bathroom afterward to clean up.

He follows me, bathes me, dives his tongue between my legs, and soothes my aches away.

When we leave and I'm dressed, I head straight for the playroom and cross my arms, waiting for him to join me. My gaze goes to the nest, which is being cleaned by the house robots.

I've found Zaku is a reader when he relaxes. Books from the upper part of the house are stacked up around our nest, hoarded from the house robots who want to gather them and put them back in their place. I asked them to politely stop.

But all they say is that they have been given an order from the master—the original one—to keep the place perfect for when he returns.

The robots gather the books and carry them out. I sigh.

I had argued that the old master is *not* going to return because he's dead. Of course, they ignored me. Not all of the lost technology is perfect, I realized then, though the jury is still out on the Lurker tech. I haven't seen any of it.

I almost feel for Peter and the others. Hopefully, they'll decide it's a lost cause and leave.

A woman can wish.

Zaku scowls at the house robots as he comes my way.

I turn and open the door, walking into the mirrored room. He joins me, leaving the majority of his tail outside. The room is small.

"All I see are mirrors," I say, walking around the space. "How does someone play in a space like this? Were ancient humans narcissistic?"

"I do not know. What I know about your kind and Earth's history is all from books and the house robots. My father searched for information, which, I believe, led him here. We did not often see each other near the end of his life." He moves to the mirror directly across from the door.

I pause. "Your father died here?"

Zaku's cowl flares. "He jumped off the top of this mountain, and I found his body out on the lawn. That is how I discovered this place."

"Oh..." My brow wrinkles. "I'm sorry, Zaku," I say, joining him at his side in front of the mirror. "I did not know it was here your father died."

"It was long ago. Many seasons have passed since then, and I have lost count. I no longer think of him unless he's brought to my thoughts."

Still, I can't imagine living in a place where I'd be reminded of my father's body. *The lawn... with all of the bones...*

Is his father among them? I don't ask. I'm not sure I want to know. That will be a question for another day.

"You... don't know how long you've been here?" I say instead.

"It takes effort to count the seasons when there are so many of them." Zaku goes to the side of the mirror, where it ends in the corner, and hooks his fingers behind it. I hear a snap and the mirror opens inward. On the other side is an ascending staircase. It's not like the others in the house. It's a cement staircase more appropriate in a government building or... *Facility?*

I freeze.

A cold draft hits me as small lights upon the walls flicker on, brightening up the gloom. The air is fresher, like it's coming from a breeze off of the mountain.

"Has this always been unlocked?"

"It is hidden. It does not need a lock if it's hidden," Zaku says as he pushes the mirror against the wall within, opening the passage up for both of us.

"I suppose that's logical," I grumble. "So I was never trapped in your room to begin with?"

"As I said, it is hidden, and there's no escape this way, only old things, and a sharp descent and death."

"Is this...where the robots go?"

"Yesss."

I study the staircase curiously. "Where does it lead?"

"Come. Maybe you can answer questions I haven't been able to. I have not been up here since..." he trails off.

I look at him. "Since?"

"Your ship came out of the sky and your male leader demanded to know the secrets of this land." Zaku slides forward but stops before the stairs and turns to me. When I join him, he offers me his hand.

I stutter, "L-Lurker tech?" I recall the picture in the closet, the frightening alien in the shadows. A picture I wish I had never seen. A picture I destroyed. A ghost that isn't mine and I refuse to let haunt me.

"I don't know."

As if my curiosity couldn't get worse, it does. I don't care about alien technology. That's not why I'm here. I'm here because the good pilots— the obedient ones, the less emotional ones—are all on the front lines or in active duty.

But the Lurker tech brought Zaku and I together, and if he has it, knowing about it might save us in the future, when others arrive. I take Zaku's hand and we climb the stairs, and for a time there's nothing but our ascent to fill the silence. The stairs wrap around and continue. Zaku carries me when my legs shake. There are no doors, nothing to break the bleak passageway. I get lightheaded after a few minutes.

Eventually, we come to a room when the stairs end. Ahead of us are double doors, but one is cracked open, letting in wind. Sunlight streaks through the gloom, filling my vision with dust motes. There are two more doors, one on either side.

Zaku sets me down. Saving the open door for last, I go to the right one first. The handle is crushed, and I wonder why it hasn't been repaired. Peering inside, I find a cavernous room filled with dormant house robots. Several are milling about, repairing their broken comrades. There are crates upon crates stacked in rows at the back. *A warehouse.*

Well... Now I know where the house robots go. I hum. Except there are so many of them, it gives me pause. Hundreds, maybe thousands. Why are there so many of them?

I head for the left door where I find the handle also destroyed. Inside is machinery I have no idea what's for.

When I look for Zaku to ask what it is, he's at the open door waiting for me. I close the one behind me and go to him. He swings it the rest of the way open, and I step out.

The sky greets me. Wind whips my clothes, and I shiver from the cold. We've climbed above Zaku's house, and higher still. But my attention doesn't stay on the sky, it goes to the ground.

"It's flat," I say. It's also partially cracked. Taking a few steps away, it appears to me like a landing pad. Ahead of me and to the left is a circular railing in the center, covered in rust. There are strange grooves on the ground. "What's this?"

"The relay."

"Relay two," I mumble. "The house mentioned it. That you were its new master. What does it do?"

"It controls the power in this area. There are others, though I don't know where they are located. Vagan knows where one is."

At the mention of Vagan, my heart drops.

"The power?" I ask, moving the subject away from him. "What power?"

"Do not move," Zaku warns suddenly and moves back toward the doors. Beside it is another door, another space I completely missed. He goes in it and the ground trembles. I catch the railing.

"What's happening?" I shout.

Inside the railing the mountain opens up, dropping and shifting into the rocks. Buzzing floods my ears and a big machine rises from the ground, streaked in brilliant lights of red and blue. The air heats around me. And with the machine are turrets, dozens of turrets. They aim their guns at me.

Hitching, I stop breathing. I don't dare.

"Zaku?" I whisper for him.

The turrets turn away. My shoulders sag and I back up.

When the machine fully emerges, the buzzing stops and Zaku is back at my side. Still, it takes a moment for my muscles to ease.

"This keeps the tech running across the land," he says as if the active turrets aren't worrisome. "This machine feeds it information. It stores it, moves it, collects it, and keeps the power on—electricity, humans call it? I think it is magic."

My lips part. "Science, not magic. Perhaps a battery of some sort, a server?"

"I don't know," Zaku rasps, coiling his tail around my legs. "All the information I have on it is within the room I was just within."

"And the house robots?"

"Keep their secrets to themselves."

Stepping out of Zaku's tail, I walk around the railing, and as I do, something zips by my head. It comes to a stop beside the relay and hovers. An orb. Like the one Vagan had. More of them appear, flying from every direction to hover around the relay. And not just orbs, other things too. Other machines I don't recognize.

I continue walking around the railing, watching them gather.

One by one, they fly away.

When I approach Zaku, he pulls me against his side. "If I turn it off... the machines die. They fall from the sky, they halt in their tracks, they stop. Everything stops."

"What do you mean stops?"

"The power leaves them, and when that happens the Earth begins to die."

My spine straightens at his words. How simple they are. And yet... how many answers it gives. I think of Central Command and Shelby, Gemma, and the nagas. Peter and the others. "Let's make sure it stays on then," I whisper.

Zaku leads me back to the doors and enters the side area. The relay drops back into the ground, and any remaining machines floating around it zip away.

Zaku's home isn't a home after all. It's a front.

A military one.

Why...

Waiting for him to emerge, I look out over the landscape, saying another useless wish. *Leave us alone.* My stomach churns and vertigo hits. Walking to the edge, I peer down and see the entrance to Zaku's home below. Recoiling, I back away. Something strange catches my attention, and my brow furrows.

To my left, past the lake and beyond the smaller mountain next to us, in the same direction as the facility, there's smoke. Wispy and rising into the sky, it's undeniably smoke. My stomach sinks recalling the trembling glass the other day while in Zaku's nest.

"Zaku!" I shout, dread and nausea rushing through me. "Something's wrong!" I curl my arms over my stomach as it upends.

He's at my side the next second, trapping me in his limbs. "Daisy?"

Shaking, I lift my arm and point in the direction. "Look. The facility," I rasp, feeling another wave of nausea hit. "Something's... wrong. There's smoke."

The roiling in my belly gets worse. Swallowing thickly, I taste bile in my throat.

"Daisy?"

"The smoke, Zaku, something's happened," I burst out, ignoring the nausea. I glance at him but he's not looking at the smoke, he's looking at me.

"We have to do something," I say, my breath hitching, the pain in my belly worsening. I go to look back and he captures my chin, forcing my gaze to remain on him. I furrow my brow.

"You have gone white," he growls.

"I'm...fine. The...smoke—" I don't get a chance to finish. I drop to the ground and vomit.

Zaku catches me in his arms, hissing furiously. My world grows dizzy. I try to speak but cough and hack and cough some more instead, vomiting between breaths.

He roars my name, lifting me in his arms. My world spins.

I cry out in pain as he rushes me down below.

THIRTY-FOUR
EXPANSION

Zaku

I CAN'T GET to the pod fast enough. Barreling through my den, each door, each room is a barrier I crash through. Wood, stone, and other materials go flying as I curl around Daisy's shaking form as I make my way to the main floor.

"Zaku," she groans, straining in my arms. "There's—there's something wrong! My stomach!" She screams.

I curse the enormity of my den.

The red door flies off the wall as I plow through it, bouncing down the hallway. I crush it under my tail as I slide into the room with the pod. I lay Daisy within it and immediately the machine goes to work.

She rolls over onto her side and curls into a fetal position. Sweat beads her brow and I wipe it off with the back of my fingers as the pod's shield rises over her. Her watery eye finds mine as I draw my hand back and it finishes closing her in.

"Zaku," she moans, burying her face in her hands.

"I will fix this, little mate," I say.

Her whole body trembles.

My hands open and close, clenching and unfurling, uncertain what to do, what to say. The pod scans her and one of the arms comes out to grasp her arm, pinning it from her body so it can take a sample of her blood. She presses her knees into her chest harder.

The pod releases another arm to take another one of her limbs and she fights it.

"Let it help you," I say, keeping my voice as calm as possible. It's a feat. "Let it help."

Daisy cries out.

My tail coils tight under me. I lean atop the glass and cover her as best I can. "Let it help, Daisy," I plead. "Look at me."

She quivers and slowly lets the pod take her limbs. The pod straightens her out and shifts her clothes.

"Look at me."

Daisy squeezes her eye closed briefly but then opens it. She blinks rapidly, meeting my gaze. "God I hate when you say that," she moans

"Good," I encourage her.

"*Administering relaxant,*" the pod says.

I keep Daisy trapped with my gaze. She winces when the pod sticks her with an IV. Tears bead her lashes and I can see the worry cross her features, deep, concerning worry. The scales along my spine rise.

She begins to relax as the drugs enter her system. My claws streak the glass on either side of my head, trying to reach her through it to comfort her. I do it to stop from lashing out and breaking something. I don't see a wound on her body. There's no blood, no smell of infection, nothing.

Which means she's sick on the inside...

Have I mated her too roughly? Did we not wait long enough after her recovery?

"I cannot lose you, I will not lose you." Not again. Not so soon.

The pain etched over her vanishes and she inhales deeply. My thundering heart doesn't join her as she relaxes. I'm not sure if it ever will.

"*Scanning for infections.*"

"I'm feeling better—" she gasps, jerking, pressing her hand to her stomach. I jerk with her.

"Don't move," I order. It's as much for me as it is for her.

"Zaku! Something is happening, what's happening!" She tries to peer down at her belly. The pod's arms grab her and pin her flat. "It hurts!"

"*Please remain still.*"

I hiss wildly, wanting to tear my heart out of my chest with my claws. "What's wrong with her!?" I bellow at the machine.

Daisy's body strains.

The pod's glass lights up with color. It beeps and sticks Daisy with another needle. She fights harder against her bonds.

"Administering a higher dose of relaxants and calmers."

I tear away from the pod before I break it.

"Zaku!" she screams.

Grazing my claws down my face, I draw blood, trying to hold in the fear spreading through me. Venom leaks from my fangs and I swallow it, slicing them across my tongue. I have only had Daisy for a short time. Too short. I can't lose her.

I can't! I roar, striking my tail against the wall, unable to keep calm any longer.

When the pod beeps again, I turn to it, ready to destroy it.

"Scanning done."

I rush to Daisy's side and she's no longer fighting her restraints. She's breathing rapidly but the furrows on her face are gone. She's slumped, staring at the scans on the glass shield within the pod. Her lips part and she inhales once very hard. She stops shuddering. Her whole demeanor changes and some of my fear lifts.

The pod's restraints release her and her hands go to her belly.

"Daisy?" I ask, leaning back over her. "What's happening?" I don't look at her scans, unable to take my eyes off of her.

Her gaze meets mine.

"I'm pregnant." She brings her hands to her face and beams. "I'm pregnant!"

Stilling, unsure if I heard her correctly. "What?"

"Zaku!" She leans up on her elbows and the glass pulls back. She winces once but her smile quickly returns. "I'm going to be a mother!"

EPILOGUE

Zaku

A PING SOUNDS, and my body goes stiff. Tilting my head, I look at the entryway door.

"What was that?" Daisy asks.

I turn to her as she lifts her head from the book about advanced robotics she's reading.

She's fretting. She'd told me about this ship called *Mercy*. A ship where many humans have recently died. That is was the ship her father once commanded, and that she once lived on.

She told me of these...Ketts and how they are killing her people in droves. Females and children included. I flick my tail and hiss. They are the reason she's even on Earth right now. Humans are searching for an answer to a grave problem. They think the answers are here.

I'm not sure how I feel about this information. More humans means more females for the other nagas in search of a nestmate, but it also breeds uncertainty. Who will rule?

Daisy fears they will come. I am not so sure. No one has come before her. We have jewels, power, and knowledge, she says. This is all stuff her humans want and want badly. This, I understand. They will trade precious females for it.

She's nervous about the smoke. She fears for the human female called Shelby and her safety.

Above all, she's worried and excited about gestating. My queen wants to do something, anything, but I am against it. Over the last day, Daisy's spent a great deal of time in the robot room up in the mountain. She's decided it's her job to learn how they work and to reconfigure them before our litter comes.

She wants to use them as guards. Our personal army. She also wants to add a room called a nursery. She'd determined to get the robots to use their stored materials to build one for us.

First, the book on robotics, then I'll decide if she's capable for more than that in her current state. The pod says she's in her second trimester. Daisy is gestating quickly for a female human. Worry and excitement battle inside me as well.

Her stress is becoming my own. And so is her happiness.

I puff out my chest. Whatever happens, whatever comes, they'll have to go through me to get to Daisy and our litter. She has nothing to fear.

I always win.

"It's a visitor," I growl, severely unhappy at the prospect. If a naga is here to steal my female, I will string them up by their spine.

My den is camouflaged in the mountain and the pathways to this ancient place have long been overgrown with trees and bushes. I reassure her that she does not have to worry. Only the winding walkways along the mountainside are ever used.

Still... We have a litter to worry about now.

"A visitor?" Her face lights up. "Maybe it's Gemma. Maybe..." The color drains from her face. Her hands go to her stomach.

The ping chimes again, several times in rapid succession. Daisy stands, and I slice forward to stop her. "We don't know that. I will go first."

She nods.

Since her time in the pod yesterday, I have been edgy. I refuse to leave her side even for a second, fearful she will fall again. There are two in her litter, and as far as we both know, a human-naga child has never been born. We have decided to nest upstairs so she may be near the machine at all times. They are growing rapidly.

Already, she is showing.

The ping goes off again and again, rapidly, frantically. Daisy is right up on my tail, and I can sense her nervous energy. Each day, I am getting better at reading her, caring for her, loving her—as she calls it. I like it. It's a human thing, and I like it even more because of that.

I never told Daisy about the book of reptiles I once found, about the king cobra snakes within it, and how I resemble them. I'm not sure I ever will. I do not want her to see me as an animal...not with the family we are about to create.

A family.

I don't think I will believe it's happening until our litter is birthed, despite the proof. How fast things change.

"Do you think it has something to do with the explosion? The facility?" she asks. "I'm worried."

"It is not your problem anymore."

"I can't help it. You know I can't."

I turn to face her, cupping her shoulders, stopping her in the hallway. "You have to for the litter."

"Babies. Call them babies, I don't like you using the term litter. It makes me squeamish."

"Babies," I correct, holding her gaze. "It doesn't change my answer."

"I know." She sighs. "I have more important things to worry about. Still—"

"You will do nothing, nothing, until they are out of you safely."

"The pod says I'm healthy and fine. The babies are healthy and fine. I am gestating normally..." Her brow wrinkles. "Which is strange for the pod to say considering the circumstances."

"But I'm not," I tell her. "I am *not* fine." The corner of her lip twitches and the concern in her eyes diminishes. Grabbing her to me, I hold her close, shielding her with my body. "I am not fine and I won't be until I have you and our young coiled within my limbs."

The pinging continues.

"Zaku, you're emotionally manipulating me. I had a terrible case of morning sickness yesterday, that's all."

"Morning sickness is still sssicknessss."

Any sickness is bad in my mind. All sickness. Nagas don't get sick. It's a human thing. I've known Daisy was delicate since the moment I laid eyes on her, but illnesses never occurred to me. They didn't even occur to me after her crash. My mate can be hurt by things unseen, things I can't stop. This bothers me.

When the pinging of the door abruptly halts, Daisy pulls out of my arms. "The door."

"Stay here," I warn, pulling back. "Do not let whoever, whatever is out there see you. Not until we know it's safe."

Facing the entryway, I leave her in the shadows of the hallway. Outside, on the lawn, I see a flash of red.

Vruksha. I'd know his coloring anywhere. There is no naga left in the land that has his coloring. Slipping closer, his female comes into view. She's got her eyes shielded as she tries to peer through the window and into my den. She pulls back and steps away from the outer door when she sees me.

Of all the beings to disturb Daisy and me, at least it is the other human female and a naga I almost...*trust*. He helped me bring Daisy safely home. Regardless, I do not want them here despite this. Daisy is stressed, she worries greatly, and though seeing Gemma will bring her joy, it will ultimately cause her pain when they inevitably leave.

Because no one is allowed to live in my den that is not part of my nest. Especially another male who is not of my blood.

"Zaku!" Daisy yells, "What's outside?"

"Your friend."

She dashes out of the hallway and towards me. I knew she would.

Gemma throws her hands up into the air, clearly upset I have not let them in yet. Cowl flaring, keeping Daisy behind me, I unlock the door.

"Finally," the other female exclaims, barging in. "We have a problem." Vruksha's tail wraps around her middle, keeping her from going too far into my space. He slips forward and presses to her back, wrapping an arm around her as he meets my gaze.

"King Cobra," he says.

"Pit Viper."

We glare at each other. Muscles straining, we size each other up.

"We don't have time for this! The facility has been destroyed," Gemma says, pushing out of Vruksha's arms and going straight to Daisy, cupping her face. "I'm glad you're safe... you're mending fast." She pauses. "Really fast," she says, checking Daisy over.

Drawing back, I let Vruksha through. Daisy shakes her head. "I am, thanks to Zaku," Daisy says. "Destroyed? We saw the smoke. What about Shelby? Where's Shelby? Have you been there?" Her voice quickens.

Gemma faces Vruksha. The look they share isn't good.

It's then I notice how disheveled the other female is. There's dirt over her cheeks and hands. Her clothes are dirty and sweat stains on the front of her shirt. She carries a wooden spear with jagged metal plates at the end. *A weapon to defend herself with*, I presume. I glance at Daisy, realizing I have not given her such a thing. It is something I must remedy, and soon.

I cannot keep her contained in my home forever. She is a creature from the skies. She will not be content to hide behind walls.

I decide right then and there that I will not only make her bigger, but stronger as well.

Vruksha looks just as bad.

They have been traveling. Hard.

"Tell me!" Daisy demands when Gemma and Vruksha continue looking at each other. Gemma turns and walks to the seating area, sitting down and rubbing her hands all over her face. She peers at me.

"Can I have water, Zaku?" she asks.

I nod and move toward the kitchen. Vruksha stops me and pushes past me, retrieving the water for his mate instead.

Returning to Daisy, who's followed Gemma to the seats, I pull her into me, knowing what's to come isn't going to be good for my mate. Vruksha joins us after handing Gemma her water. She gulps it quickly and swipes the back of her hand over her mouth.

"The facility is gone. The transport ship is...gone."

"Gone?" Daisy asks, confused.

"Just...gone."

"There's no ship exhaust in the sky. We would've seen it."

Gemma shakes her head. "I don't think it went back to The Dreadnaut."

"What do you mean?"

"Whoever took it, if someone did, they're still here. That's my only guess. Ship's don't just vanish."

"And the facility? Shelby? The smoke?" Daisy asks quickly.

Gemma's eyes flick to Vruksha briefly. "We were wondering if you guys might have...if Zaku..."

I hiss. "We have been *here*. If you think I went back to destroy the humans who have caused my mate so much pain, I have not. Daisy is my priority." I don't say that I haven't thought about it, a lot. About slipping out one night and traveling to the facility and breaking all of the humans' robots and machines, burning their ship, and killing those who try to stop me. I have fantasized about it.

When I thought Daisy and I were not meant to be, it was all I wanted to do. I have not thought about it since my queen has proven me so very wrong...

Gemma nods.

"You're dodging the questions," Daisy snaps. "What did you see?"

Vruksha growls. "Ruins and dust. Smoke and fire. There was only blood by the time we got there—"

"But Shelby could still be alive? She could be in the ship, right?" Daisy looks between Vruksha and Gemma. "Right?" She asks again when neither answer her.

"There's a hole, a giant pit where the facility used to be," Gemma breathes.

"And?"

"We searched everywhere we could. We couldn't find her. I know she's alive, I'm certain of it."

I coil my limbs closer to my mate. "And what do you want us to do about it?"

The other female sighs. "I was hoping you could tell me."

Daisy steps forward. "We need to find the ship."

"I don't think Shelby's on the ship."

"Where else would she be?"

"We talked briefly, Shelby and I. That's how we knew something had happened. She somehow connected into one of the orbs." Gemma reaches into the bag on her shoulder and pulls an orb out.

"And?"

"She said she was trapped with someone. That she's under the facility. Except there's nothing there. We searched the pit. She sounded desperate, Daisy, scared. Shelby doesn't get *scared*."

My gaze cuts to my mate. She's gone stiff, her face white. I tug her back to me. "We can't help you," I fire to the other female.

"Vagan..." Daisy whispers. "I should've forced Shelby to come with me."

Gemma stands. "Vagan? Who's Vagan?"

"Another naga male. He was on the plateau with Zaku and I." Vruksha answers. Gemma nods in remembrance. "He took part in the hunt."

"He was here," Daisy whispers. "He was crazed. I thought I'd killed him. I had hoped…" She trembles. "We have to help her, Zaku," Daisy looks up at me, her eyes fearful and pleading. "It's my fault."

"No."

"But—"

"No." I lower and place my hand on her stomach. "Remember the risk."

I feel the others staring at us. Daisy clenches her hands, closes her eye and then stares deep into mine. "You're right." She faces Gemma. "We can't go with you. I'm sorry, but Zaku's right. We can give you supplies, though, and food, water, a place to rest before you head out. If Shelby sounded scared, I would start with this Vagan."

"I know where his den is," Vruksha says.

Gemma continues to stare at my hand on Daisy's stomach but rips her gaze away when her mate speaks. "We'll go?" she asks.

He hisses. "Yesss, because there will be no peace unless we do. Peace is what I want."

Peace? My brow furrows, bending my scales.

Peace. I like this word.

It is what I want too, I realize. Peace, with Daisy. Peace in my land. Just… *Peace.*

"Thank you," Gemma whispers to Vruksha, reaching out and placing her hand on his arm. She faces us. "Thank you. We'll take those supplies if you're offering." She glances at Daisy's belly again. Her fingers touch her own stomach before they fall to her side.

"Save her," Daisy says. "Please. Do what I couldn't."

Gemma straightens. "We will."

The next night, when I have my mate back in our new nest by the pod, after Vruksha and Gemma have left, and my den is our own once more, I pull Daisy to my side where she likes to burrow against me. Because it is her favorite place to be, it is my favorite place to put her.

"You are worried," I say. "Do not worry any longer."

She sighs. "I can't help it."

"Vagan will not hurt this Shelby."

Daisy tilts her head to look at me. I brush my fingers through her short hair when she does. "How do you know? He tried to kill you, tried to take me. How can you say that?"

"I just know." Speaking of other nagas, especially males, is not something I often do. "He is…not a bad male. He can be trusted. He was not himself when he came here." My fangs drip when I remember how he attacked Daisy and me. "Though I will kill him if he ever comes near you again. Do not think of it any longer." I do not want her thinking of other males. "I have a gift for you."

Her lips flick upward and some of the worry leaves her face. "Another?"

"Another."

She perches on her elbows as I reach under the blankets where I have hidden her stolen gift. A prize I came across during my hunt this evening when she demanded apples. A craving, she said. Perhaps the first of many.

A symptom of gestation she has told me...

"I hope it will ease your mind," I say, bringing my gift forward from its hiding place. Handing her the delicate trophy, I know I won't get the same reaction as the head, or the jewels, but I am looking forward to it, like I'm looking forward to what happens next.

Daisy gently cups the gift between her hands. "A flower?"

"A daisy."

Transfixed, enchanted, her face lightens. Her eye clears, the scars smooth out. Her luscious lips part slightly and a whispering breath slips through them. I don't move, terrified if I do, she'll remember I'm here. I have not always been my best with her, I have failed a lot, but I am evolving and will continue to do so. I may not be a king in this world, but I am a king to her, and that is enough.

"Peace," I form the word with my mouth, uttering it in the silence.

She gently touches the petals with one of her fingers, feeling them, then feeling the fuzzy center at the flower's middle.

"It's beautiful," she whispers, smiling.

I pull her close, because I can. Because she's mine and I am hers.

Beautiful. Like you.

BLUE CORAL

NAGA BRIDES III

NAOMI LUCAS

BLUE CORAL

When I see her, I have to have her.

The one they call Shelby.

But the humans have not given her to us. She remains behind the walls of the facility they have reclaimed. She remains with a male that does not DESERVE her.

This beautiful, enchanting creature with long black braids and bright eyes needs a real male, a master, a true protector. She needs me.

I will do whatever it takes to claim her.

I'll kill.

I'll cheat.

I'll steal.

No human, naga, or otherwise will keep us apart. Tonight, Shelby will be in my arms whether she wants to be or not.

To hell with the rest.

ONE

FALSE POSITIVE

Shelby

"Why aren't you showing?"

I purse my lips and switch off the feed from my eyes. Wiping away the sweat gathered on my brow, I turn to Peter. My captain. Except he's not my captain anymore. He's the prick who's working me to the bone.

"I'm still in my first trimester, *Captain*. Most women don't show until the second. Your question is inappropriate," I say, unable to keep the hatred dripping from my voice. Glancing at the sentinels behind him, on either side of him, and the ones now circling me, I try not to shake. Peter has them watching me night and day. Ever since a deal was struck with the locals—locals who shouldn't be here—and gave Gemma, *The Dreadnaut's* Communications Director and team's liaison, and Petty Officer Daisy to them. Our transport ship's pilot. The only one we had.

He's a fucking psycho. How are we going to get back to the main ship without her?

He wanted to hand me over to the locals too—for his precious tech, so he can please his bosses—but Collins, his second-in-command, wasn't about to have that.

Peter eyes me up and down. "I want another test done."

"I've already done three. I'm not doing another."

"This evening, come back to the ship and just do it."

Fisting my hands, I stop from hitting him. "Is that all, *Captain?*"

Peter glowers. He hates when I'm mad, and I'm always mad now. His face is blotchy with sunburn, his eyes are red, and there are dark smudges beneath them. He hasn't shaved in weeks, and a beard is forming upon his once smooth jaw. His short hair is tousled, sticking up from grease. He hasn't showered in days, weeks maybe, and it shows. Then again, neither have I. He's not wearing his captain's uniform correctly. His blazer is off, and the top of his shirt is open, revealing the hair on the top of his chest.

If Central Command saw him, they'd dock his pay for the crime, maybe even replace him. He looks tired and weak and not like a leader at all.

He's not, not anymore. At least not to me. He's a piece of shit criminal who has bad karma coming for him, and as far as I can tell, he knows it. Part of me wants to empathize, part of me wants to help, but then thoughts of Gemma and Daisy arise and all I want is to see Peter burn. I think of what I've done, and what my lies are going to cost me, and I hate him even more.

Because I'm not pregnant. I can't even get pregnant. It was part of the procedure done to me, a sacrifice I made for my work. No one seems to know that, though, and I'm glad. It's saved my life.

For now.

I think.

It hasn't done anything for the guilt that's plaguing me. Guilt that keeps me up at night. Guilt that whispers in my ear and hisses, telling me I should be out in the forest like the others. I should be suffering like they have, like Gemma still might be.

"What have you discovered?" Peter asks. "Any closer to the source of the electrical spikes?"

"Not yet. The diggers are excavating slower now, so I believe we're close to something. Besides that, I've discovered nothing new."

"You said we'd have something by now."

"I can't crack the data cube your friend gave us. Not without access to the ship's terminal. And you've taken away my access to the ship." I glower back. "I can't ramp up the diggers without compromising what we might find beneath the ground. If it's what we're searching for, Central Command will kill us all if we deliver broken tech." I turn on my eyes, and the blue light they cast falls upon Peter's face. They automatically begin recording him. "Tell me to ramp up the diggers again. Go ahead."

He scowls at my provocation. "Your insubordination is tiresome. You'll be doing double shifts until your baby pops if you keep this up."

"It doesn't change the facts."

Peter takes a step toward me. I brace. Is he going to hit me?

"I want an update this evening, and that test," he says, keeping his hands at his sides. "Central Command wants an update and they want it now. Keep the diggers level. I'll let them know I am trusting your expertise," he spits. "They put you on my team for a reason. But remember, Shelby, your circumstances will only get worse if you don't deliver. If you think I'm bad, you have no idea what can be done to you. I'm trying to be nice here. Supportive, even."

Right. Like trading me to one of the locals so they can eat me, or worse?

"Is that all?" I ask. Talking to him makes me tired. I'm already exhausted enough as it is.

"Tonight, Shelby," he warns, eyeing me once more. "I want something to give to Central Command *tonight*. You hear me? You better come up with something."

He turns and climbs out of the pit, taking some of the sentinel robots with him. He's been using them as his personal guard since Daisy's return and big escape. I'm proud of my girl for attacking him, for busting his nose. She did what I couldn't. What none of us could.

I just wish I could have stopped her before she stole the skiff. Seeing it crash into the mountain destroyed something in me, taking one more sliver of innocence from my soul.

You didn't have to die. Not for him, not for me, not for any of this. I told her to save us, I shouldn't have.

Not at the cost of your life.

Hearing Peter's footsteps fade, I slump and close my eyes hard. I'm the one who's supposed to save *them*. I'm the one who lied to do so. And look where it's gotten me? Nowhere.

Now Daisy's dead. Gemma might be too.

You just have to outlast him. Once Command knows what he's done, you'll be rid of him. You'll be rid of him, and they'll find Gemma and return her before anyone else dies.

I keep thinking this, but as the days come and go, it's getting harder to believe it. Peter has me guarded at all times so I don't rat him out. But someone else must have said something by now, right? The rest of the team is made up of men—Gemma, Daisy, and I were the only women on this mission, thank the nebulas—and not all of them like what he's done. I frown.

Collins hates Peter.

Collins still won't rat him out on my behalf.

I've known him for years, having encountered him again and again during academy training. He's the real reason I'm here at all. He recommended me for Earth's first excursion. And yet, he's loyal to the bone to his captain.

We had a short contracted relationship before the mission, and we terminated the contract once it was certain we would both be going landside. Jobs come first, after all. More so for him. And this job was important, extremely important. A dream job for me and a way to prove my abilities. A clear path to becoming a captain for him. We ended on good terms, laughing and flirting, over a drink.

I wasn't about to let our contract ruin our life's work, and neither was he.

Hours spent listening to Collins talk about his work killed any potential romance we could've had anyway, especially since he never gave me an ear in return when I wanted to talk about mine.

"Hey, what's going on? Are you okay? What did the captain want?"

Speaking of Collins...

Looking up, I spy him climbing down into the pit, past some of my tarps.

I stand as he nears. "Peter. Call him Peter, or scumbag. He's not a captain. He doesn't deserve the title. Do not call him a captain when it's just us."

"Scumbag then." His eyes soften on me. "You okay? I brought you food." He hands me a canister, and I snatch it from him, twisting the top off. The smell of oatmeal hits my nose, and I tip it back, letting the warm sludge slide down my throat. I swallow it all, feeling a little better after my stomach's full.

When I lower it, Collins is studying me. "You look tired," I say, handing him the empty canister. "Thank you."

"I wish I could have brought more. I hate seeing you like this."

"Peter still being flaky on the food?" I ask.

He sighs. "Now that Central Command wants to keep the team here for an extra month, yeah. Food is being rationed."

My heart drops. "Wait, another month? You're not serious."

"I am, unfortunately. I came to tell you. We can make it through. You can make it through." Collins reaches out and pushes one of my braids behind my ear. "You're strong. That's why I like you so much. What did Peter want?"

I push his hand away, uncomfortable with the affection he continues to show me. More so now that we're pretending we're having a child... a fake child that Collins seems almost giddy about. It's beginning to make me worry.

But another month of this? I try not to wilt.

Turning, I duck under the tarp before I give in to a moment of weakness. Showing any vulnerability is bad in our profession. Collins follows me like I knew he would. Inside are my excavation tools and gear, even a cot because I'm not allowed back on the ship unless requested. Radars and trackers, scanners and chemicals are organized neatly upon rocks with flat surfaces. I've set up a makeshift laboratory and workstation.

Everything I need to collect, examine, and study any alien or human technology I come across. Most are contraptions I created or have had a hand in creating. Alien technology can be volatile, and handling it takes someone with knowledge, care, and deep respect for it.

Lurkers nearly wiped us from existence. Who knows what the pieces they've left behind might do?

To my left is the hole at the bottom of the pit. Around the deepest parts are the diggers. They're carefully excavating through pipes, dirt, and stone. There are also my laser scanners collecting data, examining the hole continuously, sending it to the diggers and my tablet.

"Shelby?"

Checking over the current data, new readings are saying the ground is getting warmer and the electrical spikes higher. My eyes narrow. Moving to the hole, I peer down, seeing... My eyes narrow further. *Cement? Steel?*

Why would there be a foundation thirty feet under the facility?

A niggle of excitement rushes through me.

There is a sublevel!

"Shelby?" Collins cups my shoulder and turns me to face him. "*Dreadnaut* to Shelby, what did the scumbag want?"

I blink. "What?"

He snaps his fingers. "Peter, Shelby, pay attention."

"Sorry, got distracted—"

"I know."

My lips purse. "He wants me to take another pregnancy test—"

"Are you fucking serious?"

"Yes. He's suspicious."

Collins runs his fingers through his hair, dropping his head back in exasperation. "Well, fuck, glad I came to check up on you. Now I'm going to have to get into the damn lab without being noticed again. Fuck. A fourth test?" He paces. "What is wrong with that guy? Doesn't he know trading you to some alien savages isn't going to get him any closer to what he wants? Your expertise is priceless." His face contorts.

Even the complete mess Collins is right now, his sharp features are nice to look at. His light grey eyes are mesmerizing. He's always been nice to look at. Unlike Peter, Collins continues to put effort into his appearance. Thick biceps strain his jacket, his dark brown hair remains close to his head in the standard military cut, and there's not a single wrinkle in his suit. I've seen him chased by multitudes of women, only to ignore them. Why he ever wanted to contract with me of all people is a mystery.

"Yep," I agree. "You could tell Central Command this," I add with a mumble under my breath and look back into the pit. I knew there'd be a sublevel. I knew it.

"At least that means you'll be back aboard for the evening." Collins stops pacing and faces me. "I'll let you have my weekly shower slot."

"Do I smell that bad?" I huff absently, glancing back at him.

He smiles. "Like dirt."

"Thanks."

His hand cups my cheek, and I go rigid as he presses his brow to mine. "I like the smell of dirt," he says, his voice lowering. "We can try for real, you know."

Shuddering, I pull away from him. "You know it's not possible. I don't want children, not unless we defeat the Ketts. If that miracle happens, I'll get my eyes removed and my uterus replaced." Maybe.

"I'll defeat the Ketts for yo—"

The ground trembles. Collins and I shift apart. "What's that?" he asks.

I scan the pit. "I... don't know."

My machines start shaking, and rubble slips into the hole, displacing pebbles and debris. Tightening my hold on my tablet, the trembling abruptly stops. A few seconds pass, and the dust settles.

"What the hell was that?" Collins growls, walking away and lifting the tarp to check outside.

Heart thundering, I switch my eyes back on and lift my tablet to scan the readings. "A seismic wave maybe…"

"A what?"

The ground jumps under my feet, and I fall to my knees. I lose my tablet as the tarp drops atop me. "Collins!" I shout, struggling to raise it, to rise. "We need to get out of the pit! Now!" Catching my balance, I try to stand again, only to be forced back to my knees as the rumbling worsens. Flapping plastic hits my ears as the tarp flutters. In the distance, someone shouts. Someone screams.

"Shelby, where the fuck are you?" Collins yells to my left. "The ground's caving in!"

As he shouts, the dirt gives way beneath my feet, and I start sliding toward the hole. "Here!" I cry, rolling to my left, and grasping at the ground.

"Shelby, there's gunfire!"

Clawing away from the hole, the tarp envelops me, blanketing my vision. Sparks go off. A vacuous, hollow groaning hums through the air from every direction. I scramble toward Collins's voice, seeing him on his knees a few yards away. Wide, fearful eyes meet mine as the ground gives way under him.

"Collins!" I scream and dive forward as he plummets out of sight.

The tarp slides off me. Racing to where Collins had just been, the atrium walls of the facility crumble. I struggle to a boulder and shield my head as pits form on every side of me. "Help!" I scream. Seeing a sentinel above me, I reach for it, praying it'll hold my weight. "*Help me!*" I scream louder. "Somebody help me!"

Then I hear it, through the crashing, cracking, and violent shaking. My name, deep and hurried, hissed through rough vocal cords.

"Ssshelby."

A flash of brilliant blue streaks across my vision, coming toward me through the dust. The ground gives way under my knees just as thick arms clamp around my body.

Together we fall.

TWO

FALLING FOR YOU

Vagan

LEANING FORWARD, I shift my position upon the branch. Before me lies the facility, and I can see most of the ruins where I'm perched.

The leaves rustle, and a breeze slips through my scales. Pressing my hand to my stomach, I close my eyes. I've been here too long. I need to go back to the water and rest.

I've tested my limits and forced my body to go even further. I've never spent so much time out of the water, and it's weakening me. My mind spins as I think this. I should be dead. Zaku's mate stabbed me repeatedly in the stomach.

I woke anyway, dragged through shattered glass by a robot as a fire pit raged nearby.

Pulling my hand away from my wounds, I open my eyes and glare at the facility.

She is not going to emerge.

She has not emerged once in the weeks after the hunt.

Shelby. Her name slithers through my head like a beacon in the darkness. Peering at the last place I saw her weeks ago, I hiss, demanding she reappear. But as time passes and the breeze picks up, she doesn't. Just like yesterday and the day before that. It was like she never existed at all.

The tightness in my loins and the pain from my wounds assure me otherwise. Swallowing shallowly, thirst constricts my throat. I can't stay much longer, not in this state.

I'm going to have to leave again... A scowl twists my lips.

Thoughts of treacherous Zaku and his female, cozy in their castle nest, sting my thoughts. I wouldn't have to leave if he had any honor. My fangs ache viciously from his betrayal. Still, I should not have attacked his home and threatened his mate. I was not thinking straight, being crazed with lust and denial.

What is straight anymore? Eestys would be ashamed of me. I haven't had a clear thought in weeks, months. Has it been months? Or days?

Hours?

Glancing at the forest around me, it's still the summer season. I've thought of little else since *her*. Even time is eluding me.

The sight of a giant robotic structure descending from the skies drove me from my nest. I thought the monsters had returned to the forest. I knew other nagas would be gathering to destroy them and tear apart the strange, flying structure and I was eager to join in. But as I stalked toward my prey, braving the deepest parts of the forest, it wasn't a monster I came upon. It was a ship.

My orb verified it was a ship.

A swarm of robots appeared from it, entering the ruins of the facility it landed next to. They erected a barrier around it, closing the facility off from the forest and everything that dwelled within it. Like me.

Like the other nagas and their clans.

We had not fought each other or the ship, instead scouting the forest around the barrier and keeping watch. If there was knowledge to be had, power to be taken, I did not want to head back to my den without it. If these new robots had something I could use to give me an advantage on land, I was going to take it for myself.

Now I'm reduced to staring at the shadows of the facility, ordering Shelby to show herself. To face me. To come to me and ease my troubled mind. Like I have replayed it in my head a thousand times.

She doesn't appear.

She never does.

My hissing deepens furiously.

Those first weeks after the ship landed, there had only been robots that had left the ship. Robots that could fly, robots that could dig, robots that could lift, drag, and reach. They tore down acres of forest for their barrier, ravaging the land I once knew, and yet no one stopped them. I didn't.

I was curious. What did the robots want with the ruins of an old, empty building? A building that had been picked clean many, many years prior. I had almost lost interest—feeling the need to drench my scales in water—when the first human appeared.

A hush fell amongst the nagas that day. Not a hiss was breathed or heard. Those like me, who had stayed, gazed in awe as a human male walked from the ship and onto the new field the robots had created. Other humans had accompanied him shortly after, a female with red hair, more men, and then... she walked out...

Shelby.

I did not know her name then. Only that she was a spark. A mesmerizing beacon. She had been what I was waiting for, what I was born for. I had no idea why, only that she was beautiful and that I wanted her on a primal level.

I denied it at first, having accepted that I was never going to have a nestmate. My father abandoned me after his mate died upon giving birth to me and my siblings. My first memory is of him dragging her corpse away as I wailed. They went into the water, and I never saw either one again.

My siblings died next to me, perishing from hunger, from the elements, until I was the last one left. We were babes, our muscles unformed, our minds a blur of sensation. It took a while for my siblings to die... such is the curse of being able to heal rapidly...

If Eestys hadn't found me, I would have died with them on that bank. She saved my life, raised me by the water where I could thrive, and when the other naga females joined together to flee west, she stayed.

For a time.

Until I grew into the brutal male that I am today and pledged my life to hers. I owed her my life. But that very night, she vanished. I have not seen her since, and I know now she did it to save both our lives. That was many years ago, and I am glad she is gone because I would have taken her to my nest. Or tried to, at least. Now I barely remember what she looks like. She was not a naga like me, not a snake of the waters.

She had the patterning and mannerisms of a Boomslang.

Still, I owe her my life and vowed I would never take a nestmate on her behalf. That I would never become an evil naga like the rapists who forced her and the other females to leave.

My hands clench.

I'm going to break that vow. At least one of them. I have already tried breaking it and have nearly died twice because of it. *Eestys would be ashamed.*

Where are you, Shelby?

I hiss, frustrated when the two same males I see daily come and go from the ship to the facility. My hands clench harder.

Watching them, my vows to Eestys wilt in my mind.

Tension radiates through me as the male, the one who denied me Shelby on the plateau, walks into the ruins. I lick the air, wanting his blood pouring into my mouth.

He is the one who claims her, saying it is his litter she is gestating.

I will bathe in his blood and fill his body with my venom for his lies. I will watch his life drain from his eyes as I take her away from him. She does not know that I exist, but will soon, once I come up with a new plan.

Once I capture her.

Once I steal her away to my den.

Once I make her see that she has always belonged to me and only me. She is the spark in my eye. A growl tears from my throat. Whether she is gestating or not. I will take everything of hers and make it mine.

Even if it's a piece of him.

A deep hiss joins my growls. My body is not mine anymore because of this human female, and it curses her as much as it wants her. I tried denying it, tried to return to my nest. I couldn't, hoping for one more glimpse.

One glimpse. That's all I want... A glimpse.

Pleading to the forces of nature for such a gift, my eyes drift to the skies.

So, I stayed. I studied her, learned her habits, and found she goes into the ruins each day and heads back to the ship in the evenings. I found I wanted to know what she was doing within the old stone walls and *why*. At one point in my denial, I realized she was the only thing in my head.

It was windy the day when I caught a whiff of her scent.

My body hasn't been the same since.

Already enraptured, adrenaline raced through my veins when I first breathed her in. Blood surged to every part of me. My body tensed up, ready to pounce, and I fell into a jealous rage when she disappeared into the ruins for the day, leaving me in my miserable state of desperation. All day long, my member remained engorged. A bulge formed in the middle of it.

A knot that had never been there before.

I broke out into a terrible fever, barely able to see straight.

When she walked out of the ruins that evening, it expanded painfully, and I was forced to spill with thoughts of her long black hair—and braids like snake tails—and her dusky skin.

That was days before the hunt. It's why I'm almost certain she's not gestating the human male's litter.

Pressing my hand to the wounds on my stomach, I drop down from my perch.

She will not show this evening.

Rising on my tail, I grit my teeth, desperate for water. Turning for the river, I slip into the deepening shadows beneath the trees. If one of the other nagas finds me right now, I will be easy to kill. I have not cared about anything else but Shelby for far too long. Baring my fangs to the trees, she makes me weak.

Leaving the facility proves to be difficult. Questions puncture my thoughts. What if another male steals her while I'm gone? What if this is the evening she emerges and I miss my chance at seeing her? Doubts rip through me as I slip farther away. I will eat, cool off, and come right back.

I will be right back.

A scream tears through the forest. Halting, I twist to look at the trees behind me. It sounded like a male's scream.

I cock my head.

Thunderous noises boom, and the ground trembles. Grabbing hold of a branch, the tremors quickly worsen, and my gaze drops to the forest floor. It shudders, branches shake. I coil my tail toward my body.

It has been a long time since the ground shuddered.

Only monsters make the ground shake...

The monsters are dead. They have been for years.

Hearing another scream, I slice back toward the facility, discovering the barrier falling apart and crashing to the ground. Dust clouds and smoke rise into the air from the impacts. Beyond it, the facility's walls are collapsing. My throat constricts at the abrupt change.

Shelby could be inside.

I break through the debris and into the chaos.

"Get to the ship!" someone screams, sprinting across the field. They see me and startle.

Not Shelby.

"The facility is coming down!" another human yells. "Everyone get to safety!"

"Nagas are invading!" the first human cries.

Where is she? I look around frantically, searching for her, finding nothing but swarming robots and a few human males sprinting for the ship. Hearing a loud groan, my gaze tears to the ruins.

"Help me!"

A female's scream comes from deep within.

Dread seizes me.

Crashing through the collapsing building, I follow Shelby's cries.

"Somebody help me!"

Halting at the edge of a large hole, I see her. The ground is caving in all around her. There's no way out. She's going to fall.

"Ssshelby," I hiss, diving forward.

The ground opens up and swallows us both.

THREE
DARKNESS AND LONGING

Shelby

Crushing agony bursts through my head and I whimper, flailing my arms. Except my arms don't move and the sounds of shifting rocks fill my ears instead. I try to lift my hand to feel out the source, but it hits a hard surface before I can even raise it a couple of inches. Something is pinning my lower body to the ground.

My heart jumps into my throat.

Releasing a gasp, stifled air and dust particles coat my tongue. I cough, jerking my arms upward again, trying to roll onto my side, unable to do either. Covered in dirt and with sweat beading my brow, I blink open my eyelids with another fearful hitch. Darkness greets me. Complete and impenetrable, all I see is black.

"Help," I croak softly, trying to bring my hands to my face again. "Help," I rasp a little louder. My hands come upon a warm, straining... *body?* Whatever is directly above me is fleshy and alive.

I don't understand.

I hear a deep groan as I slide my hands up my chest, pressing my elbows into my sides.

I fell.

I'm alive?

"Collins," I murmur, "is that you?"

I blink rapidly, clearing the dust from my eyes, feeling a budding wave of terror form in my stomach. *If I'm alive... I'm... underground.*

I hear another groan. "Collins?" I say a little quicker, pressing my hand to my brow. I turn on my eyes. Blue light banishes the stifling darkness. Moaning from the pain in my head, jagged shapes and crevasses blur my vision. Sweat, dirt, and an unusual spicy scent accompanies it, giving me sensory overload.

The first thing that comes into focus isn't the rocks or the dirt, or any of my surroundings, but the large brightly colored male above me. Going still, I inhale, sucking in my stomach. An alien face, one strained with pain, is inches above my face.

Not... Collins...

My breaths quicken. A scaled brow, rigid with taut, deep wrinkles, and eyes wrenched shut steals my mind, making everything else come to a screeching halt. I wait for something to happen, for my mind to work again, but as the moments lengthen and fear streaks my subconscious, I dare to move, to shove the alien away. A groan emanates from him when I press my hands to his shoulders and push.

He doesn't move.

Turning my head, my breaths turn into full-on pants, and I dart my eyes right and left.

There's nothing but rocks and stones closed in tightly around me. I jerk my legs, finding them cushioned under the male above.

This isn't real. This is just a nightmare.

My panic escalates anyway.

Wailing in terror, I thrash out and cry. Adrenaline and instinct take hold of me. *I'm trapped!* Deep underground, surrounded by rocks, with no escape. I forget all about the male above me and scream. Every untrapped limb strikes out, hitting barriers on every side, desperately seeking freedom. There's no give, nothing but rock and stone.

I hear shifting dirt and tumbling rocks, and I arch my back with a loud wail. "Help!" I scream at the top of my lungs.

Buried alive. Buried alive.

I'm buried alive!

"Sssssshhh."

Buried alive.

"*Help!*" I scream again.

I'm buried alive!

Shaking uncontrollably, I press my arms to the male above me, pushing at him again. When he doesn't budge, tears sting my eyes and I gasp. I try curling into a fetal position again, completely unable to.

"Ssssshhh, female."

A soft hiss breaks through my terrified whimpers, and I let out another sob.

This is a nightmare. Just a nightmare. You'll wake up any moment now, Shelby. You're having the evening meal with that scumbag.

Peter can't see you crying. Don't let him win.

"Female..." a pained voice says, breaking through my panic, my cascading thoughts.

The soft shushing continues.

Slowly, my thoughts grow less erratic and I calm down. I put my mind elsewhere, waiting for the horror to end. Minutes, maybe hours go by, and my gasps ease. My racing heart slows. I test my limbs to see if I'm hurt anywhere besides the back of my head. Only feeling some aches and mild pain, relief fills me that nothing is broken. My lower legs are stuck and the pressure is extremely uncomfortable, but there's no pain.

Not yet, at least.

Taking another faltering breath, I dare to reopen my eyes. The male appears above me, same as before, face wrought with strain. I notice his arms on either side of my head, bent at the elbow, and the quivering of his muscles. There are scales on them, on his face, and they're covered in dirt.

He's keeping the rocks from crushing me. Closing my eyes once more, I let that terrible thought pulse through my mind.

I'm going to die. Blinking out tears, I face the male again.

"Why?" I whisper, tasting dust on my lips.

He doesn't respond. Searching his face, sadness clogs my throat. For me and for him, whoever he is. *He must be in so much pain.*

He twitches and the rocks all around us groan. I flinch and brace for death.

But the male catches himself and holds them up.

"Why?" I wheeze again.

We're going to die, yet, I still need to know.

His brow twitches, and his lips part. His teeth are gritted closed, his jaw locked. There are two sharp fangs. Liquid drips from the end of one of them and lands on my cheek. His face is... orange, though his arms and upper chest are a brilliant blue. He's covered in scales of many sizes, and they're not just on the sides of his face and arms. They're everywhere I can see. Mid-length hair, sodden with sweat, sticks to his brow. He takes a shuddering breath, and a forked tongue peeks out. His eyes remain closed.

I scan his face, unconsciously adding him and these facts to the cloud in my mechanical eyes.

"D-Don't answer if it's too much," I whisper to him as my lashes brim with tears.

"You..." he utters and stops. I try not to jump at his voice. It's rough and deep. His bicep jerks to my right, and I hitch. "You..." he wheezes. He grits his teeth again and groans.

"Don't, please," I cry. "Don't speak if it hurts."

I don't want to see him struggle. I don't want to distract him anymore than I have. Calming further, I try and ease my body, finding it incredibly difficult knowing that at any moment the male's strength will give way and we'll be crushed. I'll be crushed, *under* him.

He will kill me before the rocks do.

Studying him, guilt hits me hard. I thrashed and pushed at him. I was out of my mind—still am—barely comprehending his existence above me. His hot breath fans my face, his sweat drips onto my body, and I know why it feels like I'm in a furnace.

I should be preparing to die, to think my last thoughts, but all I can do is stare.

Focusing on him keeps me from losing my mind. And then I remember the pit, the shuddering ground, the rocks tumbling and trying to take me with them. I remember a flash of blue coming toward me right at the end.

And the strong arms that curled around me as I fell.

He grabbed me as the ground gave way. He wrapped me in his embrace and protected me from the rocks, the landing. We rolled, and I hit the back of my head before everything went dark.

He saved my life. Or tried to, at least.

Killing himself in the process.

Shaking violently, nausea churns my stomach.

"Thank you," I breathe out, knowing the words are shallow in our circumstances. Saying nothing seems worse, though.

His eyes crack open. They're dark, ebony orbs, glistening with the blue light cast from my glowing, fake ones. With how colorful he is, his eyes are anything but... They're haunted, devastating, and reflecting my stricken reality.

He's beautiful, this creature, and I know exactly who he is.

"Vagan," I utter his name.

His jet-black pupils narrow when I say it, and his body drops a millimeter. I gasp as his chest presses to mine. Rocks shift around us. He hisses furiously and releases a guttural moan, catching himself once again before he squashes me completely. His heart thunders against my chest where we're pressed tight. My heartbeat matches his, thumping wildly together.

Stay calm, Shelby. You need to stay as calm as possible.

I close my eyes and shudder, opening them to his dark ones once I regain some composure.

"You... know," he grates through clenched teeth, "my name."

Why do his words make me sad?

"Yes," I whisper. He's unmistakably the blue one Daisy warned me about. The rabid naga who was after me and me alone. He's the reason Daisy came back to the facility—to warn me, to save my... baby. He attacked her, scared her. He's the reason she died.

No... I'm the reason she's dead.

I told her to save us.

I sent her running to the skiff, not him.

My fingers twitch where they're curled under my chin. *It doesn't matter. We'll both be dead soon.* When I first arrived, I'd been very curious about the aliens inhabiting Earth and had planned to entreat with them to find out why they were here and where they had come from—what they know—but I never had the chance.

They weren't part of the mission. Despite how groundbreaking the discovery of them was, we were sent here for more important matters.

After Peter made a deal with them... *these nagas,* my research pretty much came to a halt anyway. And for more reasons than losing access to my lab on the ship. No matter how much I wanted to know about the Lurkers and what had happened in Earth's final days, doing it for that *scumbag* wasn't worth it. Peter deserved none of my work.

What I had discovered, I kept close to my chest.

Vagan's eyes don't move from mine. In any other situation, it would make me nervous. I stare at him back, searching their depths.

"How?" he grits.

"Daisy," I croak. I say her name again with resounding sadness. "Daisy..."

Confusion flashes across his features though it doesn't last. His expression says enough. He knows who I'm speaking of, and all that does is confirm what she told me was true. I can only guess he knows my name because of her too.

Except... He sacrificed his life for a complete stranger. Because we're both going to die, and we're going to die together.

The aliens I've studied have never done something like that before, especially for a human. And these alien males want human women to procreate with... It doesn't make sense. This one wanted *me*. A bead of his sweat trickles down the bridge of his sharp nose, and my eyes follow it. When at the tip, it drips onto mine.

It slides down the side of my nose.

For a moment, the smell of exotic spices invades me. I suck it in, finding comfort in the scent. My breasts push into his chest when I inhale. It hurts.

My face flushes.

We go back to staring at each other. He's strong, incredibly so, except the trembling of his taut muscles is growing. Minutes, maybe less, is all we have left. He's not going to be able to hold up the rocks for much longer.

I gingerly uncurl my fingers and cup his face. His eyes riot, searching mine. "What are you—" he begins.

I lean up and softly press my lips to his. *Thank you.*

Thank you for not letting me die alone. Tears well and fall.

Tasting the salt of his sweat, I brush my lips across his, pushing into them. His mouth, open from exertion, trembles. His breaths become shallow, and we breathe each other in. Our eyes remain locked as tears trickle down my cheeks.

"Thank you," I say against his lips.

"Ssshelby," he responds with my name. It reflects my remorse, spoken with the regret of a lifetime of missed memories.

My heart swells, and emotion slams into me. More tears fall knowing all we have left in our existences is a few minutes and each other. I thought my life would flash through my eyes but it doesn't; it's only him. Him and nothing else.

I'm so grateful and so terribly sad.

There's only him, and a journey we may have had together if things had been different.

"Shelby!" I hear my name suddenly yelled through the rocks.

I twist my head upward. "Collins," I gasp. "It's Collins!" Excitement races through me. "Collins! Here. I'm here!" I shout, blinking back my tears.

"Shelby?" he calls hesitantly. "Hold on! I'm getting you out of there!" he yells.

"Hurry!" I beg. "We don't have much time. Hurry!"

I hear stones moving and deep huffs. We're going to survive! I'm going to survive. And I was certain I had only minutes left to live. Collins's grunts fill my ears, and it's almost too much. Too much hope all at once. I hope. *Hard.* Nerves twitching from another adrenaline rush, I hear a deep hiss and turn back to Vagan.

The male who I've been staring at is gone, replaced by something... *else.* My hands drop from his cheeks as if burned. All I see is frustration, anger, and shock.

There's no relief. There's not even a glimmer of excitement that we're going to live. I furrow my brow.

Rabid male. Daisy's words flit through my mind again.

He's pressed up to my body everywhere. His chest is pushing into mine, his... *tail*... keeping my legs trapped to the ground. His body is warm and hard, and I feel every spasm of his muscles. And he has muscles, lots and lots of them. His biceps, which are taut beside either side of my face, are bunched and quivering.

He's keeping what I can only imagine are tons of rocks from crushing me... Strength such as his shouldn't exist.

I swallow thickly as my thoughts take a turn. His eyes flick to my lips, and I see his thoughts turning as well.

Where was the hero I was just about to die with?

I hear more rocks being moved, more grunts and curses coming from Collins somewhere above my head, but they fade into the background. The scent of spice blooms, and I suck it in, inhaling hot breaths. My nose wrinkles.

It's his scent.

It has to be. It reminds me of my mother's cooking.

"Shelby, are you still okay?" Collins shouts. "Say something!"

I part my lips to answer.

A rough mouth crashes onto mine. Hard lips, *desperate* lips.

Stunned, I push my palms to Vagan's bunched shoulders. Gasping, his tongue shoots into my mouth. Stunned, I falter, feeling the fork in it slip across my gums, teeth, and tongue.

He moans, and it invades every fiber of my trapped body.

Swept up in the sudden hope that we both might live, my tongue tangles with his despite the niggling fear. Delicious flavor coats my mouth as he slides his slightly thinner, more demanding tongue around mine, capturing it in a coil. My heart thunders wildly, pulsating from my skin to his and vice versa where our chests press together.

"Shelby! Answer me!" Collins's deeply worried voice startles me.

Realizing what I'm doing, I try to turn my face, to stop the kiss, to answer him. Vagan kisses me harder, keeping me captive to his mouth's whims.

The straining in his arm eases slightly, yet he doesn't give me more space. I'm still pinned.

"Shelby, hold on!" Collins grunts and more rocks move. "Hold on! Please, god, don't be dead. Don't be dead. Don't be dead," he chants. His desperate pleas bring more tears to my eyes.

A draft hits my cheek, and my eyes shoot to the sides. Vagan releases my mouth and slips his lips over my cheek. I turn my face as the last boulder by my head is hauled away.

Vagan still doesn't push off me, instead caressing my ear with his lips.

"You are mine," he whispers.

I see Collins's face, cast in the blue glow of my eyes, and his worry shifts to shock when he discovers Vagan.

FOUR

A RISK WORTH TAKING

Shelby

"Take my hands," Collins orders, grabbing and helping me untangle them from under Vagan. This time, Vagan rises, wrenching his eyes shut with the effort, lifting off of me enough to give me room to move.

Collins displaces more rocks and boulders at a speed I am desperately thankful for. Kicking the rocks lying above my head away, he yanks me out.

My legs being trapped under Vagan isn't lost on me, nor how I have to shimmy and twist to free them. Rubbing his limbs in all the wrong ways... It's also not lost on me how Vagan rises as much as he can to help me, his features still etched in pain, all the while staring at me like he either wants to yank me back under him or kiss me again.

Collins puts his arm around my shoulder as I bend over on my knees and drop my head, shaking violently from nearly being crushed to death. I claw my fingers across the broken ground and press them into the rocks. It stings, but it's a good sting. It helps settle me. It means I'm still very much alive.

I twist around to help Vagan.

I reach for him when I'm thrust away.

Gun in hand, Collins aims it at Vagan's head. Vagan cocks his head to look up at Collins. A broken hiss emanates from his throat.

My flesh prickles from the sound. It's deep and penetrative, lifting the hairs on the back of my neck.

"Stay still," Collins threatens. "I'll fucking blow your head off if you make any sudden movements."

I grab Collins's arm and force him to face me. "What are you doing? He just saved my life! We need to get him out of there."

Collins nudges me back with his shoulder, keeping his eyes on Vagan. "Did he? Or did he just save his own?"

"Put down your gun, Collins. If it wasn't for him, I'd be a heap of skin and shattered bones." I tug on his arm again, harder this time. "We have to help him. He'll die if we don't!"

Collins steps away, pushing me back with him as he does, his gaze only leaving Vagan when we're a few paces out of his reach. He faces me. "Help him? Are you crazy? Shelby, he's one of those creatures giving us hell since the moment we landed on this blasted planet. What do you think will happen if we free him? Think!"

I scrunch my face, but Collins makes me doubt. "He's..." I glance at Vagan, swallowing. "He's not going to hurt me." He won't. I saw his dark eyes shift with strained emotion, his will to keep me alive despite the pain, and the kiss...

I touch my lips with my fingertips without meaning to.

"What about me? His kind wants women, for god knows what purpose, but they don't need men, Shelby. They hate human men. We free him? He attacks me, kills me, and then he has full access to do whatever he pleases with you. I am not about to let that happen. We don't know him or his kind. It's too dangerous."

I frown. *He's right.* Vagan could do just that. He could attack and kill Collins. My stomach churns, and I rub my eyes.

"Think about Daisy and what she told you." Collins cups the back of my neck and forces me to face him. "What she went through."

Shuddering, I look back at Vagan anyway. He's watching Collins now with an expression I can't quite place. It's not just anger anymore... it's something else. Something raw and frightening. It proves what Collins fears.

Vagan will attack him, maybe even kill him.

Looking back at Collins, I know Vagan can't be trusted.

But I also can't just leave him to die. Not after... I stop my fingers from rubbing my lips and the pressure tingling there from our kiss.

Fuck.

I twist out of Collins's hold and rub my face hard. "I can't," I say, turning back. "I can't leave him. I'd be dead right now without him."

Collins drops his arm, sheathing his gun with a groan. "You'd be dead without me too, don't forget that. I guess I'm going to have to force the issue."

Confused, my frown returns as Collins pivots to me and grabs me against him, hauling me over his shoulder. I cry out, railing at his back as he turns and walks in the opposite direction.

Vagan growls, hissing simultaneously, bringing the prickles back to my skin. Trying to get a look at him, I see him struggle to free his body and keep the rocks up at the same time.

"He's going to die if we leave him! Collins, let me down!" I shout. Collins grabs me harder, and for once I hate how strong he is. Vagan's dark hissing fades the further Collins walks.

"You're not thinking straight," he grits almost calmly.

"I can't think straight because my head's upside-down! Let me down," I order, hitting his back some more. Exhausting quickly, I lift up to see Vagan one last time before I lose him behind a broken and crumbling cement wall. I inhale sharply. "Collins, please! We can't leave him to die, not like that! That's cruelty. We are not cruel!"

He doesn't respond. The nausea in my stomach builds, and I grab hold of his jacket, bracing my upper body with a whimper. Each step he takes, his shoulder presses into my stomach, making me flinch. I think about kicking, except I don't want to hurt Collins any more than I want Vagan to be left behind.

Collins continues walking and my head spins terribly from the jostling. Reaching up, I feel for the source of the pain near my crown. Finding it damp with blood, I groan.

"Collins, please, let me down. I'm hurt."

He lowers me to my feet the next instant. Catching my shoulders, Collins steadies me. "Where?" he asks.

I reach up. "The back of my head."

He tugs my hand away. "Let me."

I turn around, and his fingers shift through my braids. Flinching from the sting, I glimpse my surroundings for the first time. The scent of burning metal, copper, and musty terra fills my nose. Smoke sways in the air above me, pierced by the sparks from a partially hidden and cracked ceiling. Lights flicker from sources hidden behind the smoke, illuminating enough of my surroundings to not need the light cast from my eyes.

I keep them on anyway, recording everything.

We fell. We fell into the sublevel I was certain was beneath the pit. For weeks I'd been getting unusual readings from the area. It was why it was chosen for excavation. There had been so much rubble piled within the atrium that it appeared like someone had tried closing something off.

The deeper the pit got, the stronger the readings had become. I was getting electrical spikes. I knew there was still working technology here on Earth by then, but technology that was still active beneath the facility?

It didn't make sense.

Unless there was a sublevel or at least a basement. I'd take either. Since this place was the forefront of alien technology development—and an old military base at that—I was certain I'd find something here, at least something to point me in the right direction to what Central Command is after.

A way to defeat the Ketts. A weapon.

A key.

Lost technology. Salvation.

Hearing rocks fall out of sight, I swing my head in the direction of the noise, getting an annoyed grunt from Collins. Dust plumes the air, thickening the smoke deeper into this place, and I lick my lips.

We're in a large hallway of some sort. There are no doors or rooms, only a way forward and back. Behind, entire sections of the ceiling are caved in, and rocks still fall through.

It's eerie, reminding me of a spaceship after an attack. My eyes shift to the ground.

"Looks like you have a small gash. We'll need to clean it the first chance we get and keep it that way so it doesn't get infected," Collins says, letting my braids fall back into place. He wipes his fingers on his coat, smearing blood. "Try not to touch it until then."

"Thanks," I say.

He nods and sighs, rubbing his arm over his brow. "Look, I'm sorry. But it's too risky freeing him. I don't like it any more than you—"

I turn and start walking back the way we came.

"Shelby, stop!" Collins yells after me.

At his voice, I break out into a run, dodging burst pipes leaking fluids, sparks, and dust. I catch a glimpse of several more floors through the bigger holes above me.

What I don't see is the sky—or a way out.

"Shelby!"

Collins's fingers brush my arm, and I dash to the side, sprinting forward. Seeing Vagan ahead of me, he's no longer holding his body up but trying to crawl out of the rocks instead, his face back to being strained with pain. Surprise flashes in his eyes when he sees me.

"Shelby, don't!"

Ignoring Collins, I drop to my knees beside Vagan. I face Collins when he stops behind me. He reaches for my arm, and I pull it away.

"I am not leaving him. You'll have to fight me on this, and you know how hard that will be. I do not give up easily."

"Nor do I, Shelby," he warns.

We stare at each other, neither one of us willing to back down. This has been us, for so long, this has been *us*. Collins and I, reaching for the tops of our fields, encountered each other again and again throughout the years. The first time we met, it was in early development, when our caregivers taught us how to act, how to handle our emotions and to bury them. I had scraped my knee, and I was trying hard not to show my pain. When his booted feet stepped into my vision, I looked up just as a stray tear slipped down my cheek.

Collins cocked his brow and offered me his hand, never mentioning the tear.

He could have. He was older than me, training the younger kids. He could have ratted me out to our caregivers, or worse, the other children. He could've made my life a living hell. He didn't, instead taking me under his wing.

His hand is out now, except there's a gun in it.

A rock tumbles behind me, and Vagan grunts, breaking the tense moment.

"Fucking hell, fine," Collins snaps, moving away. "Free him, see what happens! I'm not helping you, though." He walks away and aims his gun at Vagan. "I'll be too busy watching his every fucking move."

I twist back to Vagan.

Collins curses under his breath.

Lowering until I'm eye to eye with Vagan, our gazes catch. My heart jumps into my throat, being so close in this way with him again so soon.

A shudder goes through my body, reliving the terror of being buried alive, of knowing death is imminent. I shake my head, pushing back my rising panic.

"I need you to promise me," I say to him as calmly as I possibly can. "Promise me if I help you, you won't hurt him." I point to Collins. "Or me."

His eyes darken. They never move from mine.

When he doesn't answer, my heart drops into the sick pit of my stomach. "Please let me help you like you've helped me. Please don't make me make a hard choice."

His eyes glint.

"I can't help you if you put my friend in danger," I beg. "Let me help you."

If it were just Vagan and I, I'd help him despite the consequences. My heart is swollen from emotion, emotion *we* shared. He's seen more of the real me than anyone in our shared experience of being buried. He saw the girl I'd hidden away under layers of pain and sacrifice.

And in those moments, I saw him, felt him.

His declaration slithers through my mind.

You are mine.

Now, more than anything, I need to see him safely out from a ton of rocks and boulders.

When Vagan doesn't answer me, I wonder if he doesn't understand what I'm asking... though I know that can't be true.

"I promissse," he hisses, catching me by surprise. My lips twitch into a pleased smile.

"Sure he fucking does," Collins huffs behind me.

"Stop it Collins," I say, searching Vagan's dark eyes for a lie. My shoulders rise and fall. "Okay," I say, wiping my hands together and leaning back.

It takes some time freeing him; the boulders cascade and tumble with each displacement. There's no easy place to put them as this part of the hallway is narrower due to the detritus of the punctured ceiling. Hauling rocks away takes its toll on me. The ache in my head builds with each heft, and soon Collins is begrudgingly helping me.

I knew he would. He's a good guy despite all that's happened recently.

When we get Vagan's upper half free, he hisses, shooing me back with his arm. "Stop," he rasps, forcing me to pause and back away.

Collins scowls.

"I've got my gun aimed at you," he threatens.

Vagan ignores him as he presses his palms into the ground and shunts upward. Collins and I scurry back a few more steps when rocks topple inward. Vagan drags his body out from under the pile. His muscles knotted and thick, I clench my hands, keeping my mouth shut, trying not to focus on the blood I see on his scales. Rocks continue to fall and shift as a partially limp tail emerges. It's long and thick. Thickest at his waist, and blue like his chest and arms, only to slowly taper.

"Collins, help me," I say, moving forward and grabbing one of Vagan's wrists with both hands. Vagan pauses when I do, looking at where I clasp him.

With an annoyed curse, Collins reaches for Vagan's other arm. Swiping Collins's hand away, Vagan growls, his expression turning murderous.

"Do you want to get free or not?" Collins growls back. "Make me happy and tell me to walk away. Please."

"Stop! Both of you," I huff. "For heaven's sake! No one's masculinity is at threat here. We have bigger problems right now."

Cowing them, Collins grabs Vagan's wrist. Vagan, suddenly tenser than when he was holding several tons of stones up, accepts it.

With a lot of cursing, we pull him the rest of the way out.

Dropping my hands to my knees, I pant, breathless. Head spinning, I close my eyes. When I open them a short time later, Collins is sitting against the wall with his head tilted back upon it, sweat pouring down his face, and Vagan is staring at me with his hands pressed to his stomach, his tail draped across the rocks behind him.

His tail is much longer than I expected.

Deep blues with spots of vibrant orange near the end. I've only seen one other of these nagas before, and he looked vastly different from Vagan. The other one was a literal giant, large and imposing, brown and beige with black stripes and sporting a cowl behind his head. *That* naga had bartered for Gemma, Daisy, and me, coming to the facility without fear. I'd gotten a good look at him as he conversed with Peter.

Vagan's large and imposing, though compared to the other one, he at least appears... less intimidating? Wilder perhaps, exotic even?

Curiosity plagues me, wondering why he and the other one look so different. There's a lot of variety among humans, ranging from every hue between black and white. Certain colonies have evolved my species to take on more exotic appearances. Could that be why Vagan and the other naga look different? They're from different places, both ending up on Earth?

Staring into his serpentine eyes, my brows furrow. My blood quickens.

Again.

I push off my knees. "Are you... okay?" I ask, breaking the hold his gaze has over me and eyeing his dirty tail.

He nods weakly, and I almost miss it.

Collins stands with a huff. "Now what?"

I look around, sensing the alien's eyes on me all the while, burning holes into my back. My flesh heats, and I try my best to ignore it.

He's big. He's strong. He smells nice.

He's affecting me.

We kissed. *Twice.* Expecting to die.

His words slither through my mind once more.

You are mine.

I hug my body. "Now... we find a way out of here," I announce.

FIVE

THE ARGUMENT

Vagan

I'M WEAK RIGHT NOW.

But *not* as weak as him.

He puts his hands on Shelby and she lets him, accepting his touch when he offers it, not flinching when his fingers brush her shoulders. He caresses her when he can, glaring at me, trying to lay his claim.

She's ignoring it. Does she even realize what he's doing?

The human male sticks his little weapon out, threatens me with it. My female stops him when he does. If he used it on me, I would have every reason to strike back. She knows this. I can see it when she glances at me and then quickly looks away. I see it when she licks her lips and eyes my tail. I could sink my teeth through this human male's grimy flesh and flood him with venom. I could kill him, snap his neck, and throw him aside, have him out of my life. And hers.

It could be easy. So very easy.

She knows this.

Yet she lets him close to her, threatening his life. No one touches what is mine. I will let them play their game, but when I decide the game is done...

It's done. Promise or not.

Shelby is right. We have more important things to worry about right now.

But I do not share. I do not like other males, human or naga. They are bothersome. Once I know she is safe, I'll take her to my nest where she'll see no other except me, forgetting all else exists.

There are no other males for her. She may not know this now, but she will soon.

Unfortunately, the human male doesn't use his weapon. He balks and puts it away when she begs.

Begs!

My female should never have to beg for anything, especially from another male. The only begging to ever grace her lips should be to me, to claim her.

Bristling, I keep from striking the human male and ending my frustration anyway. I made her a promise, and I plan on keeping it. I have no other choice.

She fears me.

I see it in her eyes amidst the curiosity. The doubt, the questions there. She looks at me and doesn't let her gaze linger. Not anymore. Not now that we're free. It's clear that she doesn't trust me, otherwise she wouldn't try to hide it. I may have just saved her life, and yet she doubts... *me.*

She knows my name, and I am still reeling from this news. Has she seen me before today? Has she spied me watching her from the trees? Or was it because of the other female? Zaku's female?

Pressing my hand harder to my stomach, I can't do anything about her fear, except prove to her that she doesn't need to feel that way.

And that wretched human male is here. My eyes shift to him and I settle against the nearest wall, murder on my mind.

Every move I make, my body threatens to give up. My spine radiates pain, the deep wounds in my stomach are agonizing, and there are parts of my tail... Some bones have splintered and broken. They stab and tear my insides, keeping my wounds from regenerating. The crash of healing sings its beautiful song, luring me to fall upon the stones and seek oblivion. I will fight it to the bitter end.

I need to be strong for her.

I swallow against a groan. I need water.

"What is this place? Part of the facility?" the male asks, squinting around. "I don't remember seeing it on the blueprints."

"It wouldn't be on the blueprints. The prep bots never found it," Shelby says. She glances at me again though doesn't hold my eyes. Tension floods my limbs.

She palms the back of her head as she steps over the rocks and tries to peer up into the floor above us. I want to stop her, pull her into me, and remind her who is in charge. I clench my hands instead. This is not the time or place to claim her. There's a hole in the ceiling from our fall, and a hole in the ceiling above that. After? It's just broken pipes and precarious debris holding the structure up from collapsing further.

All of it could come raining down on us at any moment.

"I thought the bots could sense disparities under the ground?" the male asks, kicking a rock out of his path.

"They can. But this place, whatever it is, is deep. They may have missed it. Look, Collins, we've fallen through several floors. My diggers were nearly thirty feet below the facility already when we fell." She strains her head, still peering up. "We're... much deeper now. I don't see any light. Maybe the Earth's sun has set."

"I know we're several floors deep. I fell only to have to dodge the walls that came down after. Going deeper was the only choice. Wait..." Collins says, eyes narrowing. "The readings you were getting, was it because of this place?"

Shelby glances at me before looking at him. My fingers curl when she does.

I do not like her looking away from me, especially at another male. She has the most beautiful eyes, glowing like the deep water near my den, and their light shouldn't be wasted on those beneath her.

"I think so," she mutters. "I suspected there was a sublevel..."

"Suspected?" the male guffaws. Collins, I remember. Collins is his namesake. "You didn't tell me?"

"I wanted to know for certain. And I didn't want to give that scumbag any fucking hope."

Collins sighs long and hard. "So you let the diggers go, breaking the ground, knowing full well there might be something beneath it, disturbing god knows what." His voice rises. "And almost killing yourself in the process. Fuck, Shelby, you could've at least told me! We could have scanned for infrastructure faults, scouted for a subverted entrance! We could've pierced the top layer of terra with the ship's asteroid needle!"

I peel back my lips and bare my fangs. The male glares at Shelby, ignoring my warning to move away. She begins to pace, saving his life, again, and drawing my gaze.

"I didn't know there was going to be a sublevel. I followed protocol and kept my cards close. I couldn't trust you giving the information to Peter. What if we did what you said and pierced the outer core, only to destroy our one lead in finding the tech? It was too risky. Too much is riding on this mission, and it's already dangerous enough with Peter going off the rails."

"That wasn't your choice to make!"

Shelby flinches, and I slip my tailtip around her boot when she comes to a stop, claiming her without either of them noticing. I want to pet her, reassure her that she does not need to suffer this treatment.

But I am also deeply curious about her. Watching her interact without preamble with another is... interesting.

"Of course I would have told Peter," Collins waves his free arm. "He may have put less fucking pressure on you and let you back onto the ship where you're safe! Whoever is hounding him from Central Command may have gotten off his balls!" Collins shoots me an angry look, and I bare my fangs. He scowls and diverts his eyes.

Good. Underestimate me. Look away.

He is letting down his guard. I lick the roof of my mouth.

He doesn't know how fast I regenerate when I rest. Neither of them do.

This play... I've been in it many times before. It is best to wait and listen. I am a creature of the water, not of the land. When it came to dealing with those of my kind who dwelled upon ground, patience was key.

Everyone underestimates the water serpent until it's too late. Zaku was smart to throw me off the mountain when he did at the beginning of the hunt. I would have killed many.

"So I could spend all my time rotting in a five-by-five cell? Yeah, I made the right choice," Shelby argues. "Even though I hate that man with every fiber of my being, and I don't care if someone's riding his balls, I'd rather do what I can for our people than sit idly by while they die. While innocent children die."

"Sooo self-sacrificing. Always self-sacrificing. If you sat idly, maybe Peter wouldn't suspect you're not pregnant!" Collins roars. "You kept this info to yourself, where it was no use to anyone. Own up to that. We could have died because of your choices. The rest of the team might already be dead!"

Shelby's face falls, her lips parting. Fury flashes across her glowing eyes. My chest constricts, captivated by them.

'*...suspect you're not pregnant?*'

My female's not gestating. She did lie.

I knew it. I'd been studying her for weeks. Glancing down at my tail, I recall the way I reacted to her...

"Fuck you, Collins. Don't put this all on me. I kept this secret to save face for all of you. If there wasn't something down here, then what would happen? Central Command wants facts, not *hope*. If you told them we discovered a sublevel and there wasn't one... can you imagine?"

My ear twitches. There are more humans than those here on Earth. Something called a Central Command whom they both seem to respect and fear. They're here on a mission, and she does not trust Collins. At least not enough to share her secrets with him.

Is this why they wanted old tech? Offering their females for it? I could not understand these humans when they first arrived.

I'm beginning to understand them now.

"Well, there was a secret sublevel, and now we're beating around the block about what ifs. You should have told me," Collins repeats.

"You're not going to change my mind," Shelby says while stepping out of the protective circle of my tail, stumbling over the rocks and onto the floor where the path is mostly clear. "We can argue about it all day or we can move. I say we move." Her voice lowers. "The ceiling doesn't look—" Suddenly her hands shoot out, her knees wobble, and she braces her body against the wall, sliding toward the floor.

The space dims from the sudden loss of the light from her eyes.

I hiss, jerking upward to catch her.

Collins yanks out his gun and aims it at me before I can, letting her fall. "Don't you fucking move." He steps toward Shelby, grabbing her arm, keeping his eyes on me the whole time. "Are you okay? Is it your head?" he asks her, his voice softening.

I growl, wrenching my hands shut, letting my scales drop.

He will die.

Swallowing down the venom pooling into my mouth, I let him pretend he's in charge for a little longer.

Shelby stabilizes and slowly straightens, rubbing the back of her head, then quickly pulling her hand away. "Yeah," she says. "I'm just a little dizzy. Got a little headache." She rolls around until her back is upon the wall and her hands are on her knees. Deep wrinkles are etched over her brow from eyes closed tightly.

Collins sheaths his weapon. "Can you move?" he asks.

"Yeah, just give me a minute." Shelby opens her eyes, and they're no longer glowing blue. They fall on me. "Can you?" she asks.

I cock my head. *Why are your eyes not glowing anymore, little female?* "You do not need to worry about me," I say, giving her my tail to use as a crutch to keep her from falling again. "You are what is important."

"He's not coming with us," Collins snaps. "It's nice that this place still has some working lights."

Ignoring him, I rise to join them. "Yesss," I hiss, answering Shelby's question. "I can move."

The only question worth answering. Collins is no more than the dust on my tail.

"Fuck this. We saved him, and that's it." Collins scowls. "He's not coming with us. No fucking way."

"We may need his help," Shelby whispers. "He's strong, stronger than us both. We need him."

Need.

She *needs* me.

Excitement wells inside me from her words. And with it, determination. Some of my internal agony fades away. Any pain I endure, it is for her. I can endure it, if it's for her.

Collins gawks. "No—"

I hear something give way and then a thunderous crash. Shelby jumps from the wall. Collins twists to face the hole. I brace, readying to grab Shelby and flee.

"Go," I rumble to her, ignoring the male. "Before we're back where we ssstarted."

A knowing expression falls across her face when she looks at me. A glimpse of panic forms.

You are mine.

Mine.

I make sure she sees it in my expression. It's better than seeing her panic.

And then the three of us are off as rocks shift precariously overhead.

SIX

DEEPER AND DEEPER

Shelby

WE MAKE it out of the area, and just in time.

Something behind us booms and reverberates the cement floor. The sounds of collapsing walls and the whoosh of dirt falling reach my ears soon after. A wave of dust hits my back, and I fall to my knees, catching my body on Vagan's tail.

Sleek yet velvety scales slip under the pads of my fingers, and he coils his tailtip up my arm in response. He's cold now, outside of where we were pinned tightly. With that thought, I yank my hands off of him, and look up, meeting his eyes. Collins grabs my other arm as Vagan gently tugs me up with his tail.

"Sorry," I say, my head spinning. Removing my limbs from both of them, I rub my brow.

"Are you sure you're okay?" Collins asks. "How's the wound?"

Dropping my hand, Vagan is still watching me. His tailtip brushes over my boots.

Inside them, my toes curl as if he touched them directly. I'm glad no one sees me do it.

"Yes, yes," I say a little quickly, stepping away from both of them. "Let's just keep moving. I can rest once we know what we're up against." Collins tries to take my arm again, but I shake my head. He sighs and drops back a step, returning to the rear.

Vagan's on point, and I'm between them. Collins isn't thrilled with the positioning, wanting to keep me as far from Vagan as possible. Except in doing so would have made me point. He'd rather have me in the middle and near Vagan than exposed in any way

Which leaves me sandwiched between them.

Right now, there's only one direction for us to go, and the passageway we've found ourselves in isn't nearly big enough for Collins's liking

"As soon as we're back above ground," Collins growled, "we fucking split up. He's not one of us and can't be trusted."

That was a little while ago, and my headache has only gotten worse.

Flicking my eyes to Vagan, I frown. *He's hurt.* He's trying to hide it, but it's easy to see. Pain creeps into his expression when he doesn't think anyone is looking at him.

No one could hold up hundreds—possibly thousands—of pounds of rubble without suffering wounds.

Wiping my face with the back of my hand, I still feel his sweat dripping onto me. Even if he's strong, he's not invincible. No one is.

We were both certain we were going to die. We were dying, staring at each other...

I shudder.

I need to talk to him. I want to talk to him. I want to ask him about Daisy, and if he knows anything about Gemma. I'm curious about how his kind came to be here on Earth. My gaze moves from the floor to the back of Vagan's arms.

He keeps a hand pressed to his stomach.

I haven't been able to get a good look at what he's covering but I'm guessing it's a wound. I want to ask him. I want to check him over, help him. Only Collins is hurt too. He doesn't trust Vagan and for good reason.

Showing either of them any extra attention will infuriate the other. We've only been together for an hour, maybe, and I already know they hate each other deeply. The tension between them is heavier than the rocks above us.

Tearing my eyes off Vagan, I peer around. The hallway—if that's what we're in—is large and we haven't passed any doors or forks in our path. The pathway seems more like a road of some sort. And the more we walk, the more I think that's exactly where we are: an underground tunnel for vehicles. It's curving, keeping us from seeing too far ahead. The lights aren't flickering as much this far from the cave in. They're embedded in cement walls in long tubular strips, receiving power from a hidden source.

For as much as I crave the safety of being above ground, I want to explore these tunnels just as much. I spent weeks investigating a power source under the facility, and now I've found it. Kind of.

What was Earth's old military doing down here? And why so far underground? The military facility spans a mile, though much of it had been lost over the years, taken over by the forest. All that is left are remnants of buildings, old machines, and broken roads.

None of which would help us in searching for the lost tech—or *any* tech for that matter.

It was only in this spot that the sentinels and scanner bots had found unusual readings.

Vagan comes to a stop.

"What's going on?" Collins barks when I stop too.

"Ssshhh," Vagan says, lifting his hand, peering into the dimly lit gloom ahead of us. He's staring at something.

Stilling, I glance ahead and then back at him, seeing nothing except more of the same tunnel, curving out of sight. Pausing to listen, there's only silence. Collins moves to stand next to me, his gun in hand.

"What is it?" I whisper when Vagan continues to stare ahead.

"We are going down," he hisses.

My brow furrows.

Collins takes a step forward. "What do you mean?"

Vagan cocks his head without turning. "The tunnel is sloping downward. It's getting colder. We're going deeper."

Looking ahead again, the ground appears flat. "Are you sure?"

"Yesss."

Collins sheaths his gun. "Great. So we should head back and take our chances climbing."

"The ground is unstable. If we go back, we could be crushed. And it's too high to climb." I look up. Even here, the ceiling has to be fifteen feet. "This has to lead somewhere if we keep going, right?"

Vagan looks my way, his dark eyes rooting me to the spot. His gaze makes me shiver, the way they trace my face. Like there's nothing else in the universe but... *me.*

Collins turns full circle and lets out another sigh. He's upset with me and I understand why.

This is my fault. At least he's made that apparent.

"Look," I say, "We only have two directions. One is clearly unsafe, and the other—"

"Is going down?" Collins interjects.

"Yes," I respond dryly. "We can keep going forward and hope it changes or risk going back. I say we go forward. This tunnel has to lead somewhere, right?"

"And if it doesn't?"

"Then we turn back and try climbing out. If that's what happens, then it'll at least give the ground time to settle."

Collins looks at Vagan. "What are your thoughts, snake boy?"

Vagan doesn't respond, keeping his eyes on me.

Uncomfortable with the fierceness in them, I turn away. "We're wasting time. Let's go." I start walking again, letting them decide to follow me or not.

I don't have it in me to argue. My head is killing me. I hear Collins's footsteps soon after as Vagan slips ahead of me, his tail brushing the side of my leg.

The sounds of falling debris continue for some time behind us, displacing the random bouts of eerie silence. The noises echo through the tunnels, and for a time, no one says a word, listening to the death trap we barely escaped. Hours go by, maybe minutes, and I find my eyes closing more and more. I stop watching where I'm walking and stumble again.

Vagan twists and catches me before I fall.

"Are you okay?" he asks, his eyes clouded with concern.

"We need to stop and rest and check your wound," Collins orders, taking my arm and helping me right myself.

"No." I wave them both away and keep walking. "A little farther." I go back to massaging my brow, feeling both of them watching me, analyzing my every move. My head is getting worse, fast, and I gently touch my wound, feeling fresh blood. "I can go a little farther. Tunnels end. They always do."

"I don't like this, Shelby. I'm worried about you."

"I know you are, but this is what I've trained for, Collins. The end can't be much farther. There will be machines, perhaps even a radio, a first aid kit. I'll be fine," I assure him.

"You can't be sure."

"We're in a military facility," I grumble. "I've never been more sure."

Collins stays at my side, and in doing so, Vagan slows down to join me at the other side, sandwiching me between them. Again. My world spins a little more as I walk a little faster, trying to escape the masculine tension radiating from both of them. It's making everything worse.

I need space. Gasping quietly, they're almost worse than a ton of rocks crushing down upon me...

Seeing something ahead, I can suddenly breathe again. "Look!" I quicken my pace.

And come to a stop, discovering bones. Lots and lots of human bones.

Vertigo hits me hard and I collapse, staring at the indent in the tunnel and the corpses piled before it.

"Shelby, get back," Collins snaps.

"A door," I mumble, pointing, staring in shock, refusing to accept the bones' existence. "See..."

My world blackens as a steel band coils around me, pulling me away.

SEVEN

THE FIRST CIRCLE OF HELL

Vagan

Grabbing Shelby, I yank her into my arms before she drops on her side, cold as death in my embrace. Collins shouts something, but I tune him out, instead putting my ear to Shelby's lips. Her shallow breaths fan my skin, and I clutch her tighter.

"What are you doing?" Collins growls, grabbing my shoulder. "What's wrong?"

"Get the door," I snap at him, and he takes his hand off of me. Lifting Shelby in my arms, heading for the entryway she pointed at, I scatter the bones of old humans in my wake.

The tunnel continues to curve, but there is so much more than the door Shelby collapsed in front of. The tunnel opens up to a much larger room with vehicles, ramps, and large crates. There are machines between them and walls with large grates with the bodies of long-dead humans between them. I see no other doors except the double ones Shelby indicated. Hearing Collins chase after me, I pick up speed.

"Put her down or I will shoot you," he threatens, pressing something into my back when he catches up. "I swear to the swift winds of Colony 8 I will."

"She is unconsciousss," I hiss, stopping at the doors. They're made of thick, banded metal. "She smells of blood. We do not have time for your silly threats, human. We need to get her somewhere safe. She needs water." We both do.

"Fuck you and… fuck," he curses, scowling at me, glancing at Shelby. I hate seeing worry flash across his face. "I knew it was worse than she was telling me." Collins shoots me a warning look, kicks the bodies in front of one of the doors out of his way, and then yanks on it. The door doesn't open. "Ancient security systems," he mutters. There's a flashing panel on the wall next to the doors that he slams his fist into.

I feel Shelby shivering, and I curl around her as much as I can, giving her what warmth my body has to offer, which is very little.

"Back up," Collins warns, tugging something out of the belt latched around his waist. He sticks that *something* to the door. "I'm gonna blow it."

Blow it?

Grunting with frustration, I slide back, but only when he does, following him to where he crouches behind one of the larger vehicles. "Shield her," he warns, giving me and Shelby a once-over. "She's pregnant and doesn't need to be hurt any worse than she is. She's been through enough. This could get messy." He presses a button on the thing in his hand and covers his head.

Pregnant? My chest tightens with anger at this male's blatant lies.

She's not pregnant.

The tunnel erupts, and debris flies everywhere, raining down. The blast makes me flinch and startles Shelby awake. I duck and curl my tail around her. A siren goes off, and red lights pulsate from where the lights used to be. Shelby fights my hold on her, pushing at my chest, my wounds. Gritting my teeth, I curl further around her as the tunnel rings and the reek of corrosive salts fills my nostrils.

She settles after a moment, and we stay like this until the dust clears and all that's left is sirens and red lights.

"What's happening?" she gasps, looking around wildly, trying to see over my arm.

I lift off of her. "The male is '*blowing it*,'" I say.

She frowns and then flinches again with a nod.

"Come on!" Collins yells, standing and heading for the place the door used to be. Rising with Shelby, my curiosity on this '*blowing it*' disintegrates as Collins pulls back out his puny weapon and approaches the hole. His back hits the wall next to it, and he glances inside it. "Clear," he barks as I join him. He sheaths his weapon.

Strange.

This male is strange.

He made more rocks fall when we just escaped falling rocks. He is loud. He would not survive in my forest. Not for long, at least. Loud things attract animals, my kind, and evil robots. Loud things do not last long being loud.

He's also a liar.

Shelby is not pregnant with his litter. But she will be with mine, soon enough. It is inevitable between mates.

I follow him into the space beyond anyway. It's another hallway, smaller than the one before, and at the end is another pair of double doors with another panel. Collins tries the doors, and they don't budge. He curses some more.

He curses a lot, making more noise. I debate leaving him to it and taking Shelby somewhere else for her to rest.

But then he looks at me and her, palming his face. "I only had one grenade. You have an idea on how to get through these? If not, we're going to need to come up with a new plan quick," he says.

Shelby moans. "Let me down. I might—"

I tighten my arms. "I will break it."

He bursts into laughter. "Break it?" Collins swings his arm behind him, indicating the doors. "These are solid steel security doors built by the military. They're not made to be broken. Blown maybe but not broken."

His laughter draws my ire. There is nothing funny about our situation.

"You look like you've been digging your way out of the seven circles of hell, snake boy. You're not breaking anything," he continues, turning back to the doors.

I gently place Shelby on the ground where she can lean against the wall. I'd rather her be on the ground than in this male's arms, even if he's willing to protect her. Facing Collins and the doors, I slide toward them. He steps back when I place my palms on the metal and goes to Shelby, crouching by her side.

Anger rises in me.

He is getting on my nerves. If he were a naga, we would have battled by now and settled who was alpha. Clearly, I am, but he acts as if I am not. I will have to watch him carefully so he does not put Shelby in any additional danger.

Pressing my palms into the metal, I push, testing what I am up against.

"I told you. Solid metal. Nothing's getting through," he taunts.

Bristling, I coil my tail under me, biting through the pain. Picturing Collins instead of the door in my way, I tense my limbs and brace. Striking out with all my strength, the doors cave inward, bowing out from the momentum. I strike again several more times, and they fly off the wall. Swiping them out of our path, I brace against the wall before I collapse, biting back an agonized groan as the bones in my tail shred up my insides.

Collins is silent as he helps Shelby stand. He wraps his arm around her and leads her through the broken entryway, shooting me a wary look. There's no laughter from him now.

I take a minute before I follow them, letting my anger simmer. Seeing his arm around her, seeing her accept his touch so easily bothers me. Jealousy bubbles its way back into my head, imagining them together in... *his* nest.

Pushing off the wall, I go after them.

On the other side is yet another hallway, with more doors on either side and many more corpses. To my right is a small alcove with old human furniture. I find Shelby sitting on a dusty couch, facing away, and Collins is shifting through her dark braids behind her. Her hair hangs over her shoulders to the middle of her back. She trembles with her face in her hands.

"Please make the sirens stop," she whimpers into her palms. "My head is going to pop."

Her words make me pause. "I will stop them."

Turning to find their source, Collins calls after me. "Wait, snake boy. If you find some water, bandages, a first aid kit, anything that could help her, snag it and bring it back with you. She's got a gash that needs cleaning. If it gets infected, she's fucked."

Do not tell me how to care for a female! My female!

My claws dig into my palms.

It takes a lot more than that to not strangle him and fling him away. Picking the doors to my right, I break them open. At first, I find nothing, just rooms with furniture, desks, and chairs. Some have bodies in them.

Leaving these rooms behind, I discover others with machines.

Midway down the hall, I come upon the source of the sirens and smash the speaker. The noise comes to a stop, and I move to the next speaker, destroying that one as well.

I destroy all of them.

Afterward, I come across a room with counters and large containers of liquid. What looks like water sloshes within one of them, and my nerves scream. Breaking one open, I drench the stale liquid over my limbs. *Water.* My whole body gasps, sucking it up.

Dripping wet and snagging some discarded human clothes on a rack, I haul one of the containers back with me to where Shelby and Collins await.

His hands are no longer on her when I return.

Together we work to clean Shelby's wound, dabbing her blood and making bandages out of the clothes. Both humans watch me gulp some of the water down before they take sips themselves.

"Better than nothing," Collins mumbles. "We'll rest up here for the night and continue on afterward." He settles onto the dusty couch and closes his eyes as Shelby curls her legs up and lies down beside him, placing her head on the armrest. She meets my eyes.

"Thank you," she says, pushing a braid behind her. "For the water and stopping the sirens. Thank you." She yawns. "For everything."

I nod. "Rest now. The scent of your blood is thick in the air. I do not enjoy the smell."

She stares at me for another moment before closing her eyes and slumping into the cushions. After a few minutes, the strain on her face eases.

It is a beautiful sight to behold.

I settle against the opposite wall to watch her and find Collins studying me. He picks up Shelby's feet, pulls off her boots, and places them in his lap.

Laying claim.

I hold his gaze as he takes his weapon back out and lays it on his thigh.

"You might have saved her life, but so did I. And I'm the one she has history with," he warns. "Try all you want, but at the end of all of this, she's leaving this planet with me. Earth isn't her home. It never will be. I am her home."

I keep my features expressionless, giving him nothing, though rage simmers hot in my veins. Eventually, he realizes that I will not attack nor speak to him, and he drops his head back and closes his eyes.

For a time, I study him, letting my mind wander to dark places, to ways I can dispose of him without her knowing.

He can have his history. I'll take the rest. Shelby has a new home waiting for her.

EIGHT
BONES, BLOOD, AND WATER

Vagan

Hours slip by, and eventually the sirens deeper in this place stop. Silence returns and the only noises left are the quiet breaths of the two humans sleeping in front of me. They are small compared to me, with no natural armor. They can be easily hurt. Tensing my tail, a raspy breath wheezes through my teeth.

I pull my limb close and feel where my bones are broken. Once found, I claw through my scales and slice open my hide to dig them out.

"What are you doing?"

My eyes snap to Shelby, who's leaning on her elbow, watching me with bleary eyes.

"Removing bone," I say, keeping my voice low. "Go back to sleep."

Blood wells up between my fingers as I dig.

She doesn't listen. Instead, pulling her feet out of Collins's lap, she tugs her boots back on. "Here, let me help." She comes to me before I can stop her. I don't want to stop her. Her scent invades my nose as she nears and she takes my hand.

I go rigid at her touch. It is warm. So, very warm.

"I'm sorry. Can I take a look?" she asks, hesitating. "Would that be all right?" She tries letting go of me, but I grip her back, caging her hand in my bloody one. Sliding my thumb to her wrist, her pulse thrums under it. I caress it in circles with my thumb.

"Vagan?" she whispers. "What are you doing?"

I hum, pleased. "Again," I order.

She tries to pull her hand out of my grasp. "What?"

"Say my name again."

Catching her eyes, she leans back from where she's crouched beside me, a small wrinkle deepening over her brow. "I don't—"

"Say my name again." This time I demand it.

"Vagan...?"

Closing my eyes at the sound, I exhale. "Shelby," I respond. She pulls at her hand again, and I let it go. "You can look," I say.

Confusion washes over her features, but it quickly vanishes. She wipes her hand on her pants and peers down at where I was clawing my tail open, gasping quietly. "You weren't kidding."

"Kidding?"

She shakes her head, gently touching my scales around the cut. "That you were... removing bone. We need more light for this."

Suddenly, light cascades from her eyes, flashing across my tail as she blinks. Her light falls upon my wound.

"How do you do that?" I ask, awed by her human magic.

She pulls at my scales gently. "With my eyes? Everyone asks that when they meet me. I'm surprised it took you so long."

My brow furrows.

"I guess with our current circumstances, that makes sense. It's not like we've had time to talk." She probes my tender flesh. "I got them installed after I finished my training in xenoarchaeology. And no, it wasn't because I was going blind. I had my original eyes removed." She looks up at me, and my pupils dilate from her brightness. "Sorry," she says, and her eyes turn off. "We need more water, maybe a scalpel, and supplies to see what's going on with your tail." She touches the back of her head. "We both do."

"Why?"

She glances at me. "Why?"

I scan her face, her soft features, her full lips. Have her lips always been so full? "Why did you have your eyes removed?"

Her eyes go distant. "Because I'm the best, and the best uses the finest equipment. Some people didn't believe I should have these eyes when there were others..." She shakes her head. "It doesn't matter. I proved to them that I was serious, and that's all that matters. It's all in the past now."

Her words leave me with more questions, but she stands and looks around before I can stop her.

"I'm going to scrounge through some of these rooms and see what I can find that can help us and that tail of yours while Collins sleeps. Maybe find a map of this place or an old radio. Something besides all this dust and decay."

She starts to move away, and I spring upright, grabbing her arm, spinning her to me. "Not alone you are. Never alone."

Wide, unbright eyes meet mine. They're dark again, brown under direct light from outside her body. I've come to realize the blue glow comes from inside her, not outside. Feeling her pulse under my fingers, I search them, waiting for her inner light to return. Her lips part in surprise, and I let her go.

Why? Why are her eyes so different from all the other humans? Brown of blue, they are mesmerizing.

"Did I hurt you?" I ask, glancing at where I grabbed her.

"N-No."

She pulls her arm close, curling over her chest. "Then come with me? I'm not going far. Maybe you can answer some of my questions while we search?" She indicates my tail. "But it might be better if you stay here, especially if your tail is broken."

I hiss, slipping past her. "Do not worry about me. I am fine, female."

"Right." I hear her sigh. "In my culture, I'm called a woman, by the way."

I am glad she agrees.

For the first couple of rooms, she looks in and moves to the next, just like I had earlier, finding nothing of use. She riffles through cabinets and drawers, huffing when everything inside them crumbles or turns to dust. "Wow, is this... a stapler?" she mutters, lifting a small object to her face only to discard it.

When we get to the room with the plastic water capsules, her face lights up. "Supplies."

I break another one open, and she pours some of the water over her hands, cleaning my blood off of them. We both drink until we're full and then she moves to the counter. She digs through the stuff atop it, then the stuff within it, the glow having returned to her eyes.

Fascinating. I have never thought it was possible to replace one's appendages.

"Yes!" she exclaims and pulls out a case. She sets it on the floor and opens it up. "An aid kit. Not a very good one, it looks like. There's no boosters or even a scalpel, but there are tweezers and..." She lifts something. "Scissors and string. Let me see your tail."

I slide my open wound next to her, lowering my upper half to the floor. She pulls the large water capsule to her side and upends it over my tail.

"This is going to hurt," she warns.

She digs into my tail, and my hands curl. *It's her touch*, I remind myself. I will endure her touch even if it hurts. *She's touching me...* Willingly. My hands unclench, feeling her fingers inside me.

"I'm sorry," she mumbles, plucking out a shard. "The quicker I do this, the easier it will be for you. You helped me with my head, let me help you with your tail."

Dropping my chin to my chest, I do not argue her logic.

It takes time for her to pull out the bigger pieces, having to fight them from my ropey muscles. But she makes do, and after a time, with her constant mantra of 'sorry' singing in my ears, I relax. When the stabbing lessens, I push her hands away and finish up, digging out smaller pieces still hidden within that she keeps missing.

She hauls over another water capsule, screws open the top, and pours it over the wound. By the time we're done, we're both drenched and in a pool of bloody water. The wetness feels good on my hide. Enjoying this moment, I have forgotten what it's like to be cared for.

What it's like to be touched by another willingly, without the intention to cause pain, but to prevent it.

I want to savor every second as Shelby sews my wound closed.

When she's done, she's panting, and her sweat scents the air.

I inhale. *Deliciousss.*

"Now, what's wrong with your stomach?" she asks, her gaze dropping to my middle.

Tensing, I remove my arm that's over it. "Nothing."

"You've been cradling it since the rocks," she accuses. "You wouldn't be doing that if nothing's wrong with it. There's scarring? Were you... hurt before the fall?" She starts to reach for me.

"It was a mistake," I hiss.

She jerks her hand back. "Your wounds?"

"Letting another get the better of me," I correct. "I was not in my right mind when these wounds were inflicted."

Her head slants and her eyes narrow. "Was it Daisy?"

Stilling, I look away.

"You might as well tell me. I've already heard her side of the story."

"It is not a story, and you lie, little female. Zaku would never let Daisy leave his den."

"Zaku..." Shelby says the other naga's name and glances at something behind me, her eyes going distant. "She said his place is safe."

My mood darkens. "Until someone like me proves otherwise."

Shelby's eyes snap back to mine. "You hurt her."

"I was not right in my head."

"That is no excuse. What happened between you two? She was terrified of you, terrified for me, for..." she trails off.

"For your litter?" I spit.

"What? Litter? What are you talking about?"

I scowl. "Your *young*. The young you are *not* carrying."

She straightens, rising to her feet. "How do you know?"

"You said so yourself, arguing with that ridiculous human male. He is loud. He does not listen to you like I do."

"I didn't—"

"Are you with him?"

"I—"

Anger and jealousy streak through me, tightening my limbs for combat. "Are you with him?" I ask again, rising over her. I need to know. I have to know.

How she answers...

"I was, once."

I bare my fangs.

"I-I'm not with him anymore," she stammers, taking a step back.

She was with him? Once? Once is too much. Red crosses my vision. The male does not deserve her, he is loud and reckless. He does not listen!

He is not strong, not like me!

"Please don't hurt him, Vagan," she begs suddenly, saying my name again, the fear I want to vanquish having returned. "We're not together anymore, and that shouldn't matter, but Collins is my friend. He's a good guy despite what you may have seen. He's just..." she trails off, taking a short step back. "He's been through a lot. More than most people I know, and he's still trying to make the universe a better place. He's..." she trails off, taking another step back. "You promised."

I am scaring her.

Do not scare the female you wish to nest with.

"I promisssed," I say, scowling. I do not care about this male's past, only Shelby's. Reaching out, I slide forward and pick up one of her long braids, bringing it to my nose, inhaling her scent. "You are mine now, little human. Mine. Not his. You belong in my nest, no one else's. I am only tolerating him for you."

Her mouth parts and all I want to do is slip my tongue between her lips and sink inside her.

"I'm no one's," she whispers, watching me sniff her hair, eyes wide with shock. "No one tells me what to do or makes my choices for me. You have no way of knowing whether or not I'm pregnant." Her lips flatten. "Just because we're not contracted—"

"I know you're not gestating, female. I have always known."

"That's not possible." She swipes her hand out, forcing me to release her. "We've only just met! Stop interrupting me!"

"Met? I've been studying you for weeks. You do not view that male as your mate, nor did you try and nest to protect your litter. I would catch your scent on a breeze now and then as you walked back and forth from the ruins to your spaceship. It was not long ago that I smelled ovulation, ovulation *and* blood. One moon cycle apart. Eestys was the same."

"Eestys? That's ridiculous."

"Ridiculous? I have no meaning for that word, female. Though your tone suggests you do not believe me. I am forever changed because of you. Let that be the answer to any question you feel you need to ask me. That, and who you've been claimed by because that male *friend* of yours thinks you are hisss." I growl out the last part.

Every minute, I feel my strength returning, and with it, clarity. My member swells with new seed, hardening for the first time since Zaku's. The pain of needing to breed returns with it, pain I had thought behind me. With hydration, my emotions rise faster. And so does my need to rut.

To mate.

I am a patient naga until I am not.

Anger crosses Shelby's features. "I am not some piece of meat that can be claimed by any alien male at his whim! There are laws, and codes, and so much more than that. You know nothing about me."

She is mesmerizing when she is mad.

"If you must know the answer to your question," I ground out, lowering my voice. "You are right. The other female—your Daisy— stabbed me repeatedly while I lay unconscious and paralyzed. She was right to do so. I had sought to use her as a way to control Zaku, and I attacked them."

My female's shoulders sag. "Why would you do that?"

"Because you were not brought to the plateau. Because my need for you is difficult to control."

Her pretty brown eyes come back to mine, and I am enraptured all over again. It was the glow from them that originally drew me to her, that and my curiosity for what she was up to, yet seeing them now, again, makes my mouth water.

"Vagan..." She breathes my name and shivers, saying it so sweetly I might fall, enslaved to her every whim. "You can't just claim me," she mutters, rubbing her face. "I don't even know you. You don't just claim people, Vagan. It doesn't work like that."

I catch a braid with my finger and twirl it. "You are welcome to think as you must."

She groans and drops her lovely eyes.

Something touches my stomach, and my eyes drop with hers. Her fingertips slip gently over the wounds healing there. "It's not that easy."

I capture her hand. "Don't." I don't want her touching those wounds. They don't deserve it.

"What the hell is going on here?"

Shelby startles and jerks her hand from my grasp, stepping away. Growling, I find Collins standing in the doorway. Dirty and ruffled, there's fire in his eyes. He's braced to fight.

"I was helping him stitch up his tail," Shelby says, taking another step away with a huff.

Sliding my tail after her, I circle it around her feet. *You are still mine, little female.*

"Right," Collins snaps. He reaches his hand out. "Come here, Shelby."

A hiss tears from my throat. I wind my tail tighter around her.

Shelby throws her hands up in the air. She steps out of my coil, storming to Collins and pushing past him out of the room. "For fuck's sake, I've had it about here with the two of you. I'm going to find a way out of here myself," she grates, her voice trailing down the hallway. "Alone!"

Collins and I glare at each other.

Only one of us can have her.

And it's going to be me.

NINE
THE WAY IS UNCLEAR

Shelby

Infuriated, I storm through the hallway, peeking into room after room, finding only offices and storage closets. I'm relieved when I hear neither Vagan nor Collins chasing after me.

I touched his abs. Why did I touch his abs?

Am I now married to him? He thinks I am.

Talking about claiming and nests, and... litters.

Have I broken a cultural norm? My fingers twitch, remembering the reprimanding my professors would give me for doing such a thing to a sentient alien.

They'd say it's my mistake, a woman's mistake.

Then again Vagan's not as alien as he seems. He seems almost human. Sometimes. There are glimpses of humanity that give me pause, only for those glimpses to quickly revert to the strange being that he is.

All aliens are strange, Shelby.

All of them.

Grumbling under my breath, I wipe my hands on my pants. It's not like me to touch another, especially not without purpose, alien or not. Helping Vagan with his tail was a necessity. That was enough to break cultural norms. Norms that have already been broken dozens of times since arriving here.

I knew he was hurting, but having bone shards broken up inside you? And hiding that from everyone? I shake my head. I'll never understand the male mind. Of any species, apparently.

Right now, they're all exasperating.

And my dead friend had stabbed him repeatedly, probably hoping to kill him.

Daisy wouldn't do that...

Who am I kidding? I'd only known Daisy for a couple of months, less than that in the few times we encountered each other during the mission. I didn't know Daisy that well. Stabbing an unconscious alien to death might be commonplace for her. She was a soldier—a pilot—fighting the war against the Ketts before she ended up being Peter's pilot.

She had attacked Peter.

Ducking into an empty room, I catch my breath. It's not like any of it matters anymore anyway. Vagan is clearly not a rabid, savage rapist, and Daisy is *still* dead.

All that matters is getting out of this place alive. Preferably before Central Command declares Collins and I dead and leaves us here on Earth. Leaving my hiding spot, I go back into the hallway.

And stop dead in my tracks, seeing the remnants of several humans up against the wall ahead of me

These humans died a long, long time ago, I remind myself.

Approaching them slowly, Daisy, Vagan, and Collins drop from my thoughts.

The bodies are sitting next to each other, like they were once friends. One is leaning against the wall while the other has fallen on its side. Had they been friends? Or just coworkers? Did they know what was happening above and were stuck down here, hoping they would be safe? Or were they waiting for their inevitable end?

I curl my arms over my chest.

Everyone died after the Lurkers left. Even those who were deep underground.

Like me. Right now. I hug my body tighter.

I've gone through thousands of records, listened to thousands of wayward signals that had been sent from Earth during those final hours. Hundreds of people before me had, hundreds will after me, all trying to glean information about what actually happened back then and why the Lurkers ultimately chose to do what they did to us. Not only that, but where they had gone afterward as well.

There are so many theories, yet none can be proven.

The Lurkers vanished as surely as everything on Earth died. Fifteen hundred years later, we're still looking for them.

I crouch in front of the corpses.

The one still sitting is wearing a lanyard with cards dangling at the end of it.

A keycard.

Gingerly taking the lanyard off, the skull falls to the ground.

"Sorry," I say. "I need this now."

I dust off the card. The plastic has faded, but the words on it are still clear. There's a barcode and swiper on the back, while the front has an employee identification number and name.

"Thank you, Omar Hal," I say softly, wiping the keycard on my shirt and putting the strap over my head. I head to one of the locked doors nearby and try it. The door clicks, and I'm able to push it open. Finding another empty office, I go back to searching for a way out.

The hallways change as I continue. Broken furniture litters them now, torn off doors, and half the lights are flickering, cracking. I come across more bodies, but these new bodies are scattered or are in corners, as if a fight had broken out, or a mob had rushed through. Entire security panels are shattered, the grates in the ceiling have been torn off, and doors are hanging off their hinges. Heading to the wall to my right, my brows furrow as I lift my finger to the holes in it. I hit something with my boot, and it rolls away.

Bullet shells?

I swallow thickly, feeling my heart ramp up. Ahead of me are a lot more corpses. A lot more bones. They're piled in front of a set of double doors, just like the door leading into this place.

Taking a step back, two hands grasp my arms as my back hits something hard.

I twist around, and Vagan's scaled blue form fills my vision. "You scared me," I gasp.

"You should not wander off alone. Never. No female should."

"Well, this female can handle herself." I swallow, very aware of his hands still on my arms and how warm they are, how large they are.

"There's nothing alive here anymore. It's just an old building," I add. "I think I'm fine."

"Are you sssure about that?"

His gaze falls upon the corpses, and I pull from his grasp. "Yes. I'm sure."

"There you are," I hear Collins say as he appears, stepping over debris, giving Vagan a dirty look as he comes to my side. "You shouldn't wander off alone, Shelby."

I sigh. *Males.* "While you two were off comparing dicks," I snap, "I found a key. And I think we need to go that way." I point to the double doors. "It's..." I glance around with a shudder, "where everyone else was trying to get through, apparently. Maybe we'll find our exit, at least maybe a radio of some sort?"

"Don't think a key is going to work. If it had, there wouldn't be bodies here," Collins mutters, scattering bullet shells as he makes his way toward the doors, clearing a path. "But we can try. This might be another task for *snake boy.*"

Vagan hisses and my flesh prickles. Wishing I still had my uniform jacket, I rub my arms. Aware of how close I'm standing to Vagan, I follow Collins, picking my way through the bones. "Vagan's wounded. He shouldn't be breaking through anymore steel doors."

Collins grabs the back of a chair and shovels the rest of the bodies away from the door. I swipe the card at the lock—where there are deep grooves as if someone tried clawing it—and nothing happens. Trying once more, I shake my head. "Doesn't work."

"Thought so. Okay, alien, you're up. Let's see if you can crash through metal twice," Collins goads.

"He's hurt—"

"He doesn't look that hurt to me," Collins says, eyeing him behind me.

"Ssshelby, stand back," Vagan whispers into my ear, making me jump.

His breath sends my nerves zinging. I lick my lips and back away, getting a whiff of the delicious spicy scent again. Before I can react, Collins grabs my hand and leads me over the bones, pushing me behind him.

"All clear." He shoots Vagan another pointed look. "Unless you're in too much pain?"

The next instant, a loud noise is ringing in my ears and then the doors are gone. Vagan's drawing his tail back behind him as I hear the doors thud and bang down the hall on the other side.

My lips part, wanting to say something, awed by his strength.

Collins grumbles, gripping me harder, pulling me after him. With Vagan now at my back, we enter another shorter hallway. One body faces where the doors had been, holding a gun poised at them. Behind the corpse is a large square elevator with glass doors and walls.

"What the fuck do you think happened here?" Collins crouches in front of the body with the gun.

"I don't know." Feeling increasingly uneasy, I go to the elevator and press the button to call it. The doors immediately open, and I step inside and check out the buttons, seeing I need keycard access to use it.

"This guy was a soldier," Collins says, tugging at a badge on the body's chest. "He's got a keycard too."

Half-listening, my heart drops, eyeing the buttons. The number on the wall across from me makes my heart fall even further. "We're on the first floor," I breathe. "There's nowhere left to go but down. It only goes down."

Collins stands. "You can't be serious. We're already underground."

My uneasiness grows, and I peer back at the pile of corpses. "These people weren't trying to get out. They were trying to get *in*."

It makes sense now. There were bodies outside the other door too...

The Lurkers were leaving, killing everything behind them. Of course they were trying to get in.

Feeling Vagan's tail bump my leg, his dark eyes pin me with an unreadable expression and another shiver goes through me.

I want to leave this place. I want him to break through the walls and dirt and get me out.

I don't want to be here anymore.

Collins stands and wipes his hand over his mouth, eyeing the elevator and the corpses behind us.

"Maybe we should go back," I say. "Check the other doors that are locked?"

"They're dead ends."

"How do you know?"

"There's a layout of this floor on one of the walls where we came in. We entered through an underground shipping deck. If we go back, we'll find the bays, but it doesn't look like there's another access tunnel except for the one we fell into. This is the only elevator on this level."

I start to pace. "So we either try climbing through the rubble or we go down. We go down and hope there's another way out of this place, or we take our chances of being crushed by falling rocks?"

"That's what it looks like."

"What could be down there?"

Neither Vagan nor Collins respond.

I turn to Collins. "What are the odds of Peter and the others searching for us?"

"If they survived, the odds are pretty good. They will at least have the sentinels scout for bodies, but if you're looking for an immediate rescue, it's not coming."

"What do you mean?"

"Think about it, Shelby, the facility was collapsing all around us. There's a lot of rubble to go through. Even if they can pinpoint our last location, it will take time just going through the wreckage, let alone what might be in the dirt. You didn't tell anyone there might be something beneath the facility. They might not know to look deeper."

Collins's face softens when mine falls. He walks over just as tears spring in my eyes and grabs my shoulders.

"Look, you made a call, the wrong call, but that happens to the best of us. I've made plenty of shitty calls too. So many I've lost count. I shouldn't have yelled at you earlier because I understand why you did what you did. I probably would have done the same if I were in your position."

"I didn't mean for any of this to happen," I whisper.

"None of us does when shit goes down." Collins's reassurance settles me a little. He's always there when I need reassurance. "Luckily, I'm trained to fix things when shit hits the fans," he laughs and winks, trying to make me smile. "I'm pretty good at it too."

He leans down and softly kisses my brow as my lips twitch. His soft lips barely touch my skin, gentle in their affection.

Suddenly, he's gone, torn away in a wind of limbs. I stumble backward as his hands disappear from my shoulders. Collins hits the wall opposite me with Vagan's tail coiled tightly around his chest and neck.

Vagan rises on his tail over him.

"You dare put your mouth on her?" he hisses, his muscles bunching, his face contorting with fury. "You dare to put your mouth on my female?" Vagan's voice is dark and low, terrifying in its intensity.

"Savage fucking alien," Collins chokes. "I knew it—knew... you couldn't be trusted."

Vagan slides him up the wall by his neck

Rushing forward, I grab his arm. "Vagan, stop!" I cry. Muscles of steel meet my fingers. "You're killing him! Stop!"

"He put his mouth on you."

"You promised! Remember?" I beg. "You promised!"

"He put his mouth on *you*."

"That's not a reason to kill someone! In any culture," I continue to beg, growing more frantic at Vagan's lack of response.

Collins kicks his legs. "Do it, snake," he rasps, straining. "Kill me. She'll still never be yours."

Vagan's face darkens.

"Stop!" I scream. "Please, please don't kill him!"

Collins's cheeks go red, water leaks from his eyes. "Do it," he wheezes, his voice cracking. "Make her hate you. You've already killed her friend."

I wrap my arms around Vagan and yank, putting all my strength into trying to stop him. "Please, Vagan, don't!" I shout at the top of my lungs. "Stop!"

Something presses into my middle, and I stumble away, pushed back into the elevator. Flinging my arms outward, I swipe the elevator buttons. A light from above scans me, recognizing the keycards on my chest. The elevator shudders. I hit the wall and twist around just as the doors begin to close. I rush forward, slamming my fists against the glass right as they shut.

"No!" I scream, seeing Collins reach for the gun in his belt. I press all the buttons, praying the doors will open back up. I swipe the cards on the reader. "Open, open, open."

The elevator drops.

"No!" I wail, falling to my knees as they vanish out of sight, hearing a gun go off mere moments after.

TEN
STRANGER IN A STRANGE LAND

Shelby

Shocked, I brace against the wall, staring at the cement wall on the other side of the glass—gunshots ringing in my ears.

Daisy was right.

Shaking, I push back until I'm in the corner of the space, wrapping my arms around my middle. Too stunned to move any further, I watch the cement wall slide by through the glass, taking me deeper. When I remember to breathe, it's only short gasps that come out.

They're both still alive. They have to be.

Or they're now both dead.

More tears form in my eyes. I press my fingers to my brow where Collins's lips brushed me. The spot tickles. His lips had barely touched my skin. He'd kiss me this way once before, when he promised he would keep me safe from the nagas, from Peter...

My heart constricts.

Fucking men. Fucking stupid men.

I never gave them the time of day, not until Collins wanted to contract with me. That had been well over a year and a half ago. I felt I had to say yes, I had so many feelings when it came to him.

Collins just wanted to protect me. *And Vagan...* I shudder. *I should've listened to Daisy. But he saved me! We spoke.* He called me his, but I hadn't put much thought into it. I'd been convinced he was more human than he really was, too focused on the situation and how I felt a connection to him. He had called me *his*, twice, and I... I brushed it off.

Feeling my headache returning with a vengeance, I force my feet under me and go to the elevator buttons, wiping my stupid tears away.

I need to get back to them. Right now. I don't want anyone to be hurt on my behalf, nor anyone dying. Yet no matter how hard I try to do the right thing, people get hurt anyway. *Others* get hurt.

This is all my fault. I focus on the buttons, barely seeing them.

Focus, Shelby. They're fine. They have to be. I almost convince myself.

Despite there being many buttons, there are only three levels, including the one I just left. Three isn't that many. My fingers shake. I turn from the panel and pace. *No more than a couple of minutes and I'll be back with them.* Only a couple of minutes...

As more and more cement slides by, my teeth grit.

The elevator isn't going fast, and it's very large, like it was meant to be used for machinery, except that doesn't explain the glass walls. I turn to the doors and wipe my arm across it, removing a layer of dust.

I should have reached another level by now, right? I go back to pacing, wanting to scream the further the elevator drops.

Vagan kissed me too. Pressing my fingers to my lips, I caress them, remembering it. Heat rises to my cheeks, hating myself for not stopping Vagan, for kissing him in the first place. I'd thought we were about to die. It felt right at that moment, a *thank you.* I wanted to kiss him. Who am I kidding? I was trapped beneath him, and he was the only thing stopping me from losing my mind. I loved him right then, knowing absolutely nothing about him. How could I not feel something, thinking we were about to die together?

That he had tried to save me, ending his life as well in the process.

Except he did save me, and we both survived.

That warm, chaotic, panic-inducing frenzy—I feel it even now, constricting my throat and burning up my insides. Cursing, I hit the glass, frustrated that all my choices, as small as I think they are, all end up being horrible mistakes.

This isn't my fault. This is their fault. If they could have just put their toxic masculinity behind them for five minutes and worked together—I wipe my eyes again.

Something appears, catching my attention. The cement slides out of view, and below a whole new world appears.

"What the..."

Twisting around, there's still cement behind me, but the room has opened up in every other direction.

"What the ever-living hell..." I breathe.

Before me is a giant circular dome that I'm descending into. And below is a wild forest. It's so thick, vines are growing up the sides. Though large, I can see the other side of the dome easily—the cement wall across—and know that there are no other elevators in or out of this place.

Moving my gaze from the forest—that is getting closer and closer every second—my eyes shift to the middle of the dome where a large, mechanical structure is rising over the trees.

The structure is streaked on every side with dazzling red and blue lights, giving off enough light to brighten the entire dome. The lights surge up and down like electrical waves, though I know that doesn't make any sense. Bursts of white light brighten the strips when the colors touch, making me flinch. I've never seen anything like it, in person or my studies of aliens and old human technology. Something about it makes me think it's not humanmade, not completely.

Lurkawathian tech? I can scarcely form the thought.

I blink hard and turn on my eyes.

Even from where I'm standing, a field away, the machine's power envelopes me. The trees closest to it are larger, bigger, more voluptuous than those farther out.

Nearing the tops of the tallest trees, I quickly scan the rest of the dome, taking in as much as I can. Large shafts and pipes are all over the walls, with faded labels I can't read from a distance. Glancing up at the ceiling, it's solid with what appears to be a large screen, now turned off, or no longer working, I can't tell. There are several large cracks in it.

Dropping beneath the tree line, the elevator snags and jerks. Catching the wall with my hand, it gets rougher the lower I go. I hear a cracking, snapping sound beneath me. Glimpsing outside, thick branches and plants are pushed up against the glass.

The elevator halts. But then it breaks through whatever it is beneath us and stutters to a final stop. The elevator trembles again, and I wait for the doors to open. They try to, stopping at the midway point. Peering out, I'm still well above the ground.

Glancing at the buttons, it still says I'm on the first floor. I press them all again, but nothing happens.

Panic comes rushing back.

Refusing to wait for a miracle, I pry my fingers between the glass doors and help them along. Spreading them as wide as I can, I crouch to see more of what I'm facing.

At first, there's only overgrown foliage, though, through it, I see the floor. It's broken where roots have torn through. Swiping the branches away with my left arm, I duck my head out to see what's stopping the elevator.

The elevator shunts, and I tear away from the opening. I hear more rustling and cracking and I peer back at the buttons.

It's signaling as if it wants to go back to the first floor.

They're alive! Painful hope clutches my throat. Then it vanishes, knowing it might not be both of them. The elevator tries to lower again, and I hear more tree limbs breaking.

I'm going to have to clear them out to go back up.

Crawling back to the opening, it's big enough for me to slip through. I get into position with my legs first and slide out. Sticks and leaves abrade me as I get my bearings, meeting the floor with my feet.

I immediately see what's stopping the elevator from landing—part of a tree. A partially crushed one, splintering with each tremble of the elevator trying to lower upon it. Grabbing a broken branch, I tug it out of the shaft, shifting backward to let it drop on the dirty laminate and realizing that it's going to take me hours to clear the way.

I get to work.

Breaking, tugging, cursing under my breath, I slowly empty the shaft of everything I can.

With only one large branch left, the elevator shunts atop it, unable to break through it. I pivot to look for something to remove or weaken the wood.

The elevator is in an octagonal glass room that's mostly clear further away from the elevator. There are three sets of double doors, two closed firmly shut with key panels next to them, and rounded glass tunnels leading out from them through the trees.

Hearing a crack echo behind me, I spin to the elevator just as it breaks through the branch.

"Yes," I gasp, swiping the sweat from my brow. The elevator drops with a ding as I rush back to it. The doors I pried open begin to close. Thrusting my arm through, they continue closing, biting into my skin. "No!" I grate, fighting them. Jerking my arm out with another gasp, I watch as the glass shuts on me, and the elevator lowers deeper into the shaft.

To the next floor.

"Fuck!" I shout as it vanishes out of sight. "Don't do this to me. Please, don't do this to me! Fuck," I scream, slamming my fist against the wall that closed off the shaft behind it.

Turning off my eyes, I don't want to record what happens next.

I spin around and scream at the top of my lungs.

I expel everything from me. The stress, the exhaustion, Peter, the nagas. Bending forward, I scream until my throat feels like it's full of needles and I can't any longer. My screams echo back at me, encouraging me on.

I don't know when I stop, only that I'm holding my head and kneeling on the ground when the branches beside me shift and an acrid, sour smell invades my nose.

Lifting my head to see if the elevator has miraculously made its way back to me, my eyes fall upon something in the shadows, through a broken portion of the glass that shows the forest beyond.

What could cause that? My heart stutters to a stop, realizing too late that there might be something alive down here with me.

Slowly switching my eyes back on, I pierce the shadows with soft blue light.

The glint of vertical, dark red pupils meet mine, set high and deep within a smoothly rendered face. Black spikes of thick hair—or cartilage—pop out right above the creature's eyes to the back of its angular head. Its skin is brownish-green and roughly textured, peeking through the foliage, half camouflaged.

I can't see anything else.

Fingers shaking, I slowly reach for a gun that I know hasn't been on my hip in over a month.

I hear the ding of the elevator and startle, my eyes slicing to the doors.

Escape... The word whispers through my head.

With fear strangling my throat, the creature growls as I shimmy into the elevator beside me. Snapping my gaze back to it, I hitch.

Its head has shunted forward, and as I stare, its mouth opens—from the side of one eye and to the other, razor-sharp teeth appear in a grin.

And I know exactly what I'm looking at.

I scurry to the back of the elevator.

"Close, close, close, close," I beg the doors. "Close, close—please fucking close."

Hearing the branches shift and leaves rustle, I jump up, rush to the buttons, and slam my hands across them. "Close!"

The creature appears in the doorway, and I drop back again until my back is flushed to the wall. A lumbering, lithe, leathery body appears behind a nightmarish reptilian head poised outward and forward, a thick tail swaying back and forth behind it.

A Lurker.

The first one seen since the day they left Earth and murdered billions.

"Human," it rumbles, the word menacing and full of hate.

Clawed hands grab the frame of the elevator's opening as it comes toward me.

"No," I whimper, wetting myself.

It grabs my leg and drags me into the dome.

ELEVEN
THE LURKAWATHIAN

Vagan

"You kissssssed her," I hiss, needing Collins's blood all over my hands. "She is mine." The words claw from my throat, furious and strained.

Hearing a ding, a gasp, and a banging beside me, I don't look, unable to take my eyes off the human male suffocating under my grip.

It is all I care about. Piercing madness rushes through me in waves, igniting nerves that have been dormant for weeks as I healed. With my shaft engorged, my patience is gone.

This male put his lips on my female. Lips I will rip off his face. Lips I will desecrate.

Seething, the male's mouth opens wider to try and suck in the air I refuse to let him have, and a primal sense of rightness rushes through my veins at his wasted efforts. Fighting for a female is instinctual.

I am stronger, bigger, deadlier than this creature.

There is no contest. Yet he thinks there is. I will make sure he thinks about it no more.

Eyes leaking with wetness, his face reddens, and I slide him higher on the wall, watching the last of his life leave him, seeing the realization cross his face that he *lost*.

"Fucker," he spits, and saliva sprays my face.

A loud noise splits the air, startling me. Pain erupts throughout my body. I fall back when the stabbing pain clusters at my abdomen. Collins drops to the ground with a wheezing grunt as I slowly look down at my middle.

I see blood. A lot of blood. Reaching down, my clawtips slip through it, meeting fresh, open wounds. Hissing, I bring my fingers to my eyes.

How?

Falling further backward, the agony builds. Blood oozes from the open wounds, and I search wildly for what hurt me. To make sure it doesn't hurt me again. My gaze falls upon the male slumped on the ground. I see the puny weapon in his hand, falling out of his fingers.

I stare at it in shock.

Shelby... It dawns on me that she is not here. She would be screaming, fighting, throwing her body between us. My gaze snaps to the elevator.

It's gone.

I grow lightheaded trying to understand how that's possible, clutching my stomach. Weakening, I crash to the floor. I try to rise, finding I can't, only weakening further. My vision wavers and everything goes black.

I wake to a ding, to two glass doors opening, and the elevator room returned to its place. But there's no Shelby waiting for me beyond them. There's nothing. Groaning, I pull my tail under me and lift onto my hands.

"Shelby," I rasp.

Where is she? How long have I been out?

Glancing back, Collins is still on the ground. His chest moves, and I know he's not dead. Fresh blood trickles from my new wounds as I snag his weapon with my tailtip and bring it to me.

I crush the weapon and fling it away, making sure it'll never hurt me again.

Looking back at Collins's form, I debate whether to finish the kill and take out my competition once and for all.

He is not as weak as I thought he was. I will not make that mistake again.

You promised. Shelby's voice flutters through my head.

I turn away, my rage having diminished somewhat.

Dragging my body to this *elevator*, I remember Shelby and Collins talking about the buttons and floors to this place—that it goes deeper. Inhaling, her scent hits me, and it's no longer fresh. And with it the reek of fear, sharp salt, and her tears. There's a sour, stale aroma as well that sends my nerves zinging. I release a pained, frustrated hiss. I am not a dirt naga, a forest naga, a land naga. I am a sea serpent, and these wretched human ruins are not for one such as me.

Raising my hand from my wounds, blood gushes down my fingers.

I will find you.

The strong smell of her fear sends a chill up my spine. I still don't understand why she's not here. I told her not to go anywhere alone. Females should always listen to their males.

Swiping all the buttons, pulling the rest of my tail in when the doors close, the corpse falls into the room with me, breaking apart across the floor. A light comes from above and scans something attached to the body.

The room drops, and I lose sight of Collins's form.

Feeling alien things inside of my body, I peer at my gored stomach. Alien things that are *not* bones. I stuff my fingers into my wounds and search, finding hard rocks. Huffing in pain, I dig three of them out and collapse against the wall, closing my eyes.

I hear another ding, and my eyes snap open.

I'm facing a forest, piles of broken branches and leaves, but it's the putrid reek in the air that gives me pause. It wafts into the elevator and cloisters, stealing all that is Shelby away.

I shoot upright and out of the room before the doors close, coming face-to-face with broken glass and tree litter. Shelby's scent is stronger here. Plants press against glass walls that partially divide me from the forest outside, and with those plants are trees with strange leaves and vines. They creep up the walls inside and out of the space I'm in.

There are forests under the dirt?

I hear the elevator doors shut, and then nothing at all.

Everything is still. There's no breeze to rustle the branches, no chirping of insects or even bird calls.

Grabbing the leaves off a branch I plaster them to my wounds, threading them through my scales so they stick, and slither through the pile of branches. The pungent odor thickens.

It smells like a rotting naga corpse.

Slipping into clear space, I realize that I'm not in a forest, not completely. I'm in a glass room with tunnels leading out. Some of the glass is broken where trees have broken through. There's light, but it's dim and blinking, coming through the thick canopy above. My brows furrow.

"Get off of me!"

Twisting around, I hear Shelby's shriek coming from outside the room. I surge toward the broken opening and into the forest.

"Shelby!" I shout, hoping she'll call out again.

She screams again, and my mind shuts out all else.

Hearing a ruckus ahead of me, I tear off branches, swiping the overgrowth clear, needing to get to her like it's my last breath. Thorns graze my scales, and sappy flowers stick to my hide. A rough, hitching clicking sound fills my ears, followed by gaspy cries and grunts.

I hit the back of a beast, knocking it into the nearest tree, coiling my tail quickly around it. Tough flesh meets mine, and large, bulky limbs. Seeing Shelby's fighting form still grasped by the creature, I sink my fangs deep into sinewy muscle.

The monster lets go of Shelby's leg, and she scurries out from under it. It rears back with a roar and grabs hold of me. I constrict around it harder as it yanks at my tail.

"Vagan!" Shelby cries out at my side.

Spikes shoot out of the creature's back, stabbing into my scales, forcing my fangs to loosen and let go of its shoulder. It spins around and slams me into the trunk of the nearest tree. I strike out. Rounding my arm around its neck, I squeeze, trying to suffocate the creature like I did Collins. Guttural noises fill my ears, coming from the both of us.

The spikes from its back rip through my scales and into my wounds.

My hold falters.

Out of the corner of my eye, I see Shelby come closer.

Terror fills me.

She raises and swings a large branch, hitting the creature's back. It halts its beating upon me, and I shunt out from between it and the tree trunk, uncoiling my limbs from its bulky form. She raises the branch again and hits it in the face.

It reels back and then snaps its head forward in her direction, revealing a large mouth with rows of sharp teeth.

"Run!" she screams, falling on her butt. She pivots down the path back to the first room. Slamming my tail once more into the monster's face, I take off after her. She's climbing through the broken opening when I catch up. Helping her through, I hear branches shake and snap behind us.

"Where's the elevator?" she yells, hitting a panel on a vine-covered wall when we're on the other side.

The elevator room is gone.

I grab her and spin her around. "We have to hide," I rasp. Her face falls when she sees my blood, my stomach. "Now," I urge.

I don't know what the creature is—I don't know what we're up against.

Fear flashes across her face, and she turns and rushes to one of the sets of double doors. Grabbing the handle, she tugs. It doesn't open. "Fuck, fuck, fuck. Where's the keycard?" Her fingers grasp the thin rope on her neck, spinning it around.

"You are not a human," a thick voice snarls behind me. I twist to find the monstrous being climbing through the opening.

I strike it with my tail, pushing it back into the forest. Red eyes meet mine as it immediately straightens.

"Vagan! It's open. Go!" Shelby shouts.

Launching through the doors, she closes them behind me with a bang. Shelby stumbles back several steps, and I catch her against me. Coiling my tail around her, I draw her behind me. The doors shudder, and the creature screams.

I brace for the doors to fling open, cradling my stomach with an arm.

The banging grows frantic. My muscles bunch. The roar morphs into a rapid clicking sound.

The doors hold.

Pushing Shelby further back, we slip deeper into the glass tunnel.

"There's another door," she wheezes.

I keep my gaze on the rattling doors as she steps out from my coil.

"Vagan, come on," she calls. I back up toward her voice, crossing this second threshold.

Click click click click click.

The new doors shut, breaking my view, and the clicking vanishes. Shelby's arms thread around me, and I finally tear my gaze away. She presses her face to my side and sobs.

Curling my arm around her protectively, I tug her small form against me. "It isss okay," I say weakly.

It's the last thing I do before I collapse.

TWELVE
DRIPPING WET

Shelby

Vagan lowers to the ground, and I press my face harder into him.

When the Lurker dragged me out of the elevator, I thought I was as good as dead. The alien hauled my thrashing body deep into the dome's forest and to a circular copse of trees where it clearly lived. The reek of excrement is still in my nostrils, making me nauseous amongst everything else I'm feeling.

I'd only gotten away because the Lurker had let me down to find something to tie me up with. I ran, praying I'd make my way back to the elevator, only for it to reach me first, pinning my body to the ground.

If Vagan hadn't arrived when he did...

His hand slips down my body as I shudder deeply, imagining what would have happened if he hadn't found me. How is it that I've come to rely on him so much so soon? How all I want to do is sob because he's here?

Vagan's hands fall off me, and I lift my head to find his mouth slack and his eyes hooded. "Vagan?" I move off of him. He drops and sprawls across the floor. There's a lot of blood covering him—and me. "Vagan?" I say louder, dropping to my knees beside him.

He doesn't respond.

Leaning over him, I cup his cheeks. "Vagan, wake up! Wake the fuck up right now!" My voice comes out shrill. I release his face and his head rolls to the side. "Shit!"

Stumbling to my feet, I look around frantically.

The room we're in is right outside an atrium to another that is filled with white counters, glass cabinets, sleek machinery that I don't recognize, and bed slats. I realize we're in some sort of research lab, and Vagan and I are in the clean room leading into it.

The lab is large and round, with another closed-off room opposite us, and only portions of the outer walls are glass. The forestry overgrowth presses against them from the other side. The ceiling is covered in pipes and ducts that vanish into the walls.

The space is faintly lit up as if everyone had just left for the night and would return tomorrow. Some machines hum while others are off. Besides some broken glassware on the floor, the lab appears mostly untouched.

Shooting to my feet, I swipe my keycard through to the bigger space. A gust of air pummels me, and I start opening cabinets, searching for supplies, snatching the first aid kit that's hanging on one of the walls. There's a smaller room to my right with seating and an oval table, an old large television screen on one wall. Two bodies are hunched over at the table, each with a gun in their hand. The backs of their skulls are shattered.

I rip the guns from their hands and turn their safety switches on, seating them in the waistband of my pants.

Returning to the lab, I rush to the sink. Water comes out in brown spurts and spits. Leaving it running, I run back to Vagan and the 'clean room' where lab coats and hazmat suits are hanging on the walls, placing the first aid kit beside him. Grabbing some of the coats off the walls next, I head to the sink and soak them.

Two minutes later, I'm wiping off the blood from his wounds and praying the medical tape in the first aid kit will still have enough functioning glue to seal them.

"You are not going to die on me," I mutter under my breath—except my hands are shaking. When I finally get the medical tape in position, I place the first strips haphazardly. "You've survived this far. You'll get through this damnit."

Talking keeps me grounded. He still doesn't respond.

"Don't you dare leave me alone down here," I growl, closing up the bullet holes. Collins got him. Blood gushes over my fingers, making them slip.

"Water," he rasps.

My eyes dart to his face and his parted, dry lips.

"Water," I whisper, half-dazed. "You want water."

Sprinting back to the faucet and grabbing the nearest, cleanest beaker, I fill it. Water sloshes as I return to Vagan and gently pour it between his lips.

"More," he says, swallowing weakly. I tip the beaker. His throat bobs and I give him the rest. "More," he demands, louder this time. I leave and come back with a full glass. "More."

"But your wounds—"

"Leave... them."

Shaking my head, excited enough that he's even able to talk, I rush back to the lab and find a bucket, filling it to the top. I lug it back and fill the beaker when Vagan shunts over the bucket and dunks his face in.

Confused and maybe a little bit in shock, I stare as he gulps it down, as he lifts the bucket and drenches his body, as his wounds visibly stop bleeding soon afterward, his scales puckering around them.

"You're... a water-based lifeform?" I stutter.

"Yesss," he sputters. "A water naga."

I go back to the lab and start filling every container I can find, only returning to drench him. After my fifth trip, his bleary eyes start gaining focus again.

I drop down at his side in exhaustion and place the rest of the medical tape on him, closing up the rest of his wounds while he watches me. When I'm done, I lean back onto the wall next to him, panting.

I have yet to catch my breath. My head hurts like a cragnoid, slamming its claws into my skull. Sliding the first aid kit toward me, I dig around for a painkiller, finding several sealed pills. I swallow them back, knowing they probably won't work.

We sit there in silence for a time, listening to each other breathe. Vagan rolls onto his side and drapes his arm over my legs as if he needs reassurance I won't leave his side.

He's physically very strong, but seeing him do such a thing, such a vulnerable gesture, tightens my chest.

Reaching down, I grip him back. "I'm not going anywhere," I whisper. "I promise."

Wet, in pain, and alone—with a Lurker hunting us—I drift off without meaning to. My heartbeat slows down, and the constricting in my throat loosens. Shivering, exhaustion invades my limbs, and a quiet, deep, dread settles in my mind. I'm wounded, have eaten next to nothing in days... My thoughts muddy just from the effort of having them.

We're alive now, but for how much longer?

Statistics and analytics aren't my forte, though our chances of survival are easy to see. They're getting worse by the hour.

We're no longer pinned by rocks, but this despair reminds me of that all the same. At least I'm not alone. My hold on Vagan tightens.

"You vanished," he rasps. "I never want to hear you scream again."

An absurd laugh escapes me at his words. "Same."

I don't mention Collins.

We fall silent again, and more time slips by. Vagan's eyes close, and I lean my head back against the wall. He's hurt badly, and I'm afraid if I move, it'll just make it worse. And I don't want to move. Every limb and joint in my body aches.

Scanning his form, he's partially coiled around me, his tail in a wide arch below my feet. Most of his sapphire scales glisten with water, drawing my gaze up and down the length of his long, thick limb. His orange tailtip, his orange face, offset the blue of his body in such a way that it's impossible to look away once your eyes are trapped upon him.

Without his wounds and the blood still trickling from his smaller gashes, I'd say I've never seen anything in the universe remotely like him. Vagan's one of a kind. And even while resting next to me, he's all male. Very, very male.

He has rippling muscles and a long, lithe frame, delicately cushioned with strong yet sleek and pointed scales. I touch the nearest one—a scale on the side of his neck—and trace it with my fingertip. It's smooth, soft, except when I press it lightly there's a firmness within that offers natural armor.

As I inspect his scale, his tailtip winds gently around my ankle, sliding up my leg. I draw my finger back when it reaches my thigh.

He stops his ascent, and I stare at the orange tip pointed toward the crux of my thighs, unconsciously clenching my sex. Pressing my legs together as much as I can, a blush rises to my cheeks.

The blush reminds me I'm also growing colder by the minute, that if I don't get warm soon, I'm going to get sick. I lean over Vagan's back for warmth, and he groans.

I move off of him. "Sorry," I say, teeth clattering. "Didn't mean to hurt you."

He pushes up on his hands and meets my eyes. Stoic pain molds his features and with it a wildness that should send me running all over again. His pupils are so dark, they're unnerving. Instead, all I want is to press against him and seek comfort, warmth.

"You are cold," he says.

Another desperate laugh escapes. "My adrenaline is wearing off. I'm not sure that's a good thing..."

Vagan continues to search my face, making me increasingly uneasy, especially since his tailtip still rests on my thigh. I do not touch others, human or otherwise. This amount of touch unsettles me. "Do you like being cold?" he rasps.

My brow furrows. "No."

He straightens with a wince, and I scramble up after him. "What are you doing? You'll open your wounds. You shouldn't be moving."

Vagan tugs me into his arms anyway.

I whimper for his wellbeing when he hauls me into them. "Vagan, please be careful." I don't have much fight left in me. I press my face into his chest. If we get attacked again right now, I'm dead weight.

He carries me out of the wet clean room and into the lab, snagging some of the lab coats when he does, peering around the laboratory. We enter the darker conference room where the bodies are. Going to the back corner, he sets me down and drapes the lab coats over me.

"What are you doing?" I ask when he starts dragging the empty chairs from around the table toward us.

"A nessst," he wheezes out a weak hiss. "Building... a nest. For us."

For us...

Pulling the coats up to my chin, I watch as he positions the chairs in an arc around me, closing me to the wall. When he's done with that, he flips the table on its side, scattering the bones, and creating a barrier between us and the door. I reach into the lip of my soggy pants and remove the guns, placing them at my side.

Vagan returns and coils his tail between me and the chairs, erecting the final barrier.

All of his wounds, his scars, his beautiful vibrant scales are now displayed out for me to study again at my leisure, his lithe male form spread out in an arch around me.

A surge of warmth blooms in my chest. Even in the pain he's in—which I can't even imagine—he's thinking of me.

No one in their right mind would be thinking about another in the state he's in.

Or be able to do the things he does with wounds such as his.

He can endure a lot, more than any human, and it makes me even more curious about him and his kind.

Collins's face slips into my mind, recalling the last time I saw him, and my sudden warmth runs cold. I don't dare bring him up; I can't deal with the news that he might be dead. Especially killed by the being who is giving me the comfort I sorely need without even asking for it.

Vagan promised.

I'm going to place trust in that promise right now. Wrenching my eyes shut, prayers wet my lips for Collins to stay put wherever he is.

Vagan leans back on the wall next to me and presses his long tail against my other side.

I open my eyes. "Do you think we're safe here?"

"For now."

"That creature..."

"It's not a creature, it's a monster."

"A monster?" I ask hesitantly. "It's a Lurker. One of the aliens that—that committed genocide against my people."

"We call them monsters, beasts like that."

"You've seen them before," I say rather than ask.

"Yesss."

Not able to take that information any better than the possible news that Collins might be dead, I press into Vagan's shoulder. How could there be Lurkers here, after all this time?

What does that mean for us?

Shuddering, I push the lab coats off of me and begin removing my wet clothes. Tugging off my boots is the best decision I've made in a long time, but removing my dirty, drenched socks is even better. I wiggle my toes and sigh. The small act of self-pleasure only makes me more tired.

When I start sliding my pants off, Vagan stiffens beside me.

"What are you doing?"

"Taking off my wet clothes so they can dry, so I won't be as cold. If I get sick, I won't be much help," I say, tossing my pants to one of the chairs and then removing my shirt. I throw it on the chair with my pants.

I'm taking a big risk. We could be attacked again, and I'd be mostly naked if that happened. I wouldn't have time to dress.

I'm also on an alien planet, and my immune system can't handle me getting ill without the resources on the transport ship. I've heard of these 'colds' from Earth and decide I'm willing to take the gamble.

When I'm just in my undergarments and the lanyard with the keycards, I place the lab coats back around me, draping one over Vagan. He's watching me, his dark gaze sliding across my bare shoulders and legs, petting my bare ankle with his tailtip. Strangely, I trust him not to do anything. At least not in the state he's in. He snags my hand before I can settle into place.

He brings my hand to his lips and kisses my fingers. "Are you warm now, little mate?" His tailtip coils around my lower leg.

"I will be soon," I say, unsure of what is happening and too tired to really care. "I'm not your mate," I whisper. "Call me something else." Even if I wanted to be his 'little mate' I couldn't. Trying not to dwell on it, I adjust the bandages that have miraculously remained over my head wound, pulling them off.

I suppose this is a sort of test. If he tries something, I'll know his true nature and if he doesn't, then I know I can trust him completely.

He reaches out with his other hand and gently tangles his fingers into my hair. "Your braids are unraveling. There is water in them that will keep you cold."

Glancing down, the ends of more than half of them are broken open. I finger one. The staying serum is wearing off. I haven't had the luxury of wearing a scarf since Peter's betrayal, and the serum was all that was keeping them out of my way.

The lab coat falls open, and I quickly pull it closed over my chest. My tattered bra is still on but my breasts push heavily against it, and Vagan doesn't need to see that.

Tugging my braids out of Vagan's grasp, I push my hair behind me. "They'll be fine. The coats will keep me warm enough."

"Let me," he says, shifting upward.

Before I can say no, he's collecting my hair and nudging me to face away. "What are you doing? You need to rest," I argue. I try to turn, settling for looking over my shoulder. "We need to rest while we..." I trail off as he gently pulls my hair away and squeezes droplets of water out of my braids.

It doesn't puddle in the small space between us... Vagan puts the ends of my hair into his mouth and sucks on the drips he releases.

Dazed, all I do is stare.

Braid after braid, he works the water out and into his mouth. Warmth floods my chest when his eyes catch mine.

His voice is low and reverent when he lifts a new strand to his lips. "Like my tail, you wear your hair as such. Long and slender, we are alike. *We are alike*," he hums.

What is happening? My lips part.

Vagan wrings and gathers portions of my strands, sucking on their tips, making sure there isn't a single drip from them that won't end up on his tongue. His fangs catch in my tight curls now and then, prickling my scalp from the tugs. Several more of my braids come undone, and my loose ends start to cinch.

"Until my braids are freed completely," I murmur because I don't know what else to say, "and then any semblance of a tail is gone." I smile slightly despite watching my riotous hair breaking free. "It's okay if they fall out. My hair needs a break."

"I would like to see your hair free. Why do you wear your hair like tails?"

Only Collins has ever seen me without my hair braided... I wince and push the thought away. Soothed by Vagan's grooming, my gaze hoods upon him.

People usually only ever ask me about my eyes, or question my academic position.

"Braiding my hair makes it easier to manage," I say. "I also like how it looks."

Too soon, he's done playing—the excess water gone—and I'm shifting down to the floor to rest against his arm. He moves a portion of his tail under my head, pillowing it, draping his arm around me, above my head. I find I miss the tugs, the petting, and the attention.

"One of us should keep watch," I yawn.

"One of usss will."

"It should be me."

He doesn't answer me, instead removing the lab coat that I placed upon him and putting it over me. I snuggle into it and pass out.

THIRTEEN

MONSTER

Vagan

SHELBY SLEEPS FITFULLY BESIDE ME, all while I try to keep her as warm as I am able. It should have occurred to me that humans are warm-blooded creatures because I am not. I have cold blood running through my veins. I seek warmth often, being as such, but a creature like a human also seeking warmth?

I should have realized even warm-blooded creatures can get cold.

She continues to shiver, and I curse, feeling like I am unable to provide basic care for her. Glancing around the mostly bare room, there's nothing within reach that I can use to make her more comfortable. She already has all the remaining dry coats from the other room wrapped around her.

Doubts emerge when she curls her legs into her chest and brings her hands to her trembling lips.

Will she still let me take her to my nest? My nest is above ground, near the water, and I can provide many hides to keep her comfortable. But the cave is cold, and so is the water.

Making my nest warmer and more comfortable will be the first thing I do when we are free of this place, and if I am lucky, she will enjoy helping me so I do not make a mistake.

Lifting one of her curls to my nose, my thoughts drift with her scent so fresh inside me. I have saved her again. But it is not enough. She is still hurt, tired, and wary of me. I know she is. Glints of mistrust sheen her eyes when I capture them with mine. My fingers pinch her braid. I have not done a good enough job in keeping her safe.

If she had been on the plateau like she was supposed to be...

I look around the room again, upon the shoddy barrier I erected, and bristle. *She would be safe in my den, in my nest, and not here in this humanmade pit. She would be in my arms where no one could take her away from me, fully healed with no aches to bear.*

We wouldn't be hiding from a monster.

She is in my arms now, though we are far from what I could call safe.

I press my hand to the closed wounds on my stomach and groan, sitting straighter. I can just see the window in the other room over the barrier. Strange foliage is pressed up against it, so tightly I see nothing else. The monster is out there. He's prowling, searching for us, and planning his next move.

It's a hunter.

I've never seen a monster quite like him though it has similarities to many of the beasts I have encountered in the past. Each aggressive, rabid, angry. Wrong.

Except this one talks.

This one speaks words that I understand.

I do not like that I understand it, especially after killing so many in the past. It's been many years since I last saw one. Could they have evolved? Could they have retreated below the ground and gotten stronger?

If there are forests under the ground, it is possible.

I shake my head, keeping my eyes on the window. The other nagas who hunted them would have known. They would've shared such information to their clans, and the few nagas they trusted. Information on monsters would have eventually spread because the monsters needed to die. It was something we all agreed on, like the killings of the evil nagas who drove our females off, monsters had to die.

Besides their viciousness, I never knew why that was the way, and I never questioned it. But that was before one of them spoke to me... *They have never spoken before.*

Not only that, none of the other monsters looked quite like the creature outside. This one is more humanoid, and less... broken. The others rarely had any symmetry to their bodies, with legs, arms, and heads of unusual shapes and sizes. Only, they each were scaled and sometimes could look like *me*.

My tail goes rigid at the thought.

Leaves upon the glass shift, and my eyes narrow. *He is out there. He knows we will leave at some point.*

I have no intention of staying here with my mate for long. Once we have recovered and I am certain I can withstand a fight, we are leaving.

Hours pass, and Shelby continues to sleep. Her fits from the beginning having settled. Gently, I pull away from her form and enter the larger room to check it over for anything that might be useful, or anything that might hurt her.

She has found two puny weapons like that one Collins had—and I destroyed—but I allow her to keep them, knowing they might save her life.

Going to the sink Shelby had gathered water from, I turn the handles and drink until my body is flush with hydration and my wounds soothe from moisture. I pour some water in a clear container to bring back to my female.

Afterward, I find cloths and human clothing materials, gathering them in my arms. Returning to Shelby with my findings, I settle back at her side. Hours have gone by, hours in silence, and now that I know what it's like again to have company, someone to care for, someone to protect and converse with, loneliness creeps in.

Pressing the extra coats and cloths around her, I make our temporary nest more comfortable. It is the best I can do with what is available. There is not much else here I can offer.

She wakes briefly, moaning, and then settles back down into the cushioning to fall asleep again.

I absently pet my female's remaining braids—her snake tails—for a time. The monster can't get to us. If it could, I would have already faced it. For now, Shelby is as safe as I can make her. Now, I just need my full strength to return and my wounds to close.

Closing my eyes, my mind settles.

Wayward curls tangle in my claws and I brush them out. I like her hair. I like her snake-like braids. Now that I have them under my fingertips, I never want to stop touching them. She is alive, and my tail is coiled around her. She is in a nest I made for her, erecting as much security as I can provide in our current predicament. This all comforts me.

For a time, I run my claws through her strands and drift.

Her scent blooms in the air, and I inhale greedily, tightening my tail around her small form.

I must earn her.

My nostrils flare. *Yesss.*

This hellish, ancient place is my test. If I am to mate a rare, human female, I must prove worthy first. *Yesss.* It makes sense now.

This is a test.

I hiss.

With this revelation, I'm invigorated. It's not my desperation that's fueling me any longer; it's blood, water, and my own persistent need. It's building with each breath of Shelby's scent I suck in. Fresh fluids course through my limbs, and my mouth waters. My hissing deepens. My loins swell, and my member engorges.

And fill, and engorge further. Baring my teeth, a groan wheezes out of me. The scales locking my slit draw back, and my shaft emerges, hard and thick.

She cared for me, my wounds. She rests next to me, seeking my protection...

I cup my shaft with my free hand and groan again, petting her hair some more.

Weeks, I have not felt like this, not once in weeks. I spilled all my spill and had no sustenance to take in to create more after the fight at Zaku's. I drained my body dry, overcome with the changes forced upon me when Shelby entered my life.

I had wanted her more than anything, turning into a rabid monster like all those hunted down long ago, having been denied her.

I squeeze my member.

She moans softly, and I still. Gripping my shaft harder, I take in a steadying breath, hoping not to wake her. My claws rake her curls with a shudder.

Do not lose control. Not again. My chest tightens, and try as I might, I can't remove my hand from my shaft, or her hair. Wrenching my eyes close, I recall all the bad occurrences in my life in hopes that my member will ease and drop back down in my tail. I can't protect Shelby if I am focused on rutting, on claiming...

If I spill...

Curses whip out from between my lips as I start yanking on my member hard and fast. My tailtip curls up Shelby's leg, seeking her feminine heat and the need to conquer her most hidden spot. The place I long to be buried deep inside of. I don't need to touch it—I just need to be close. My mind will do the rest.

I need to be the male, the only male, allowed so close.

So close that if a claiming happened to occur, I would be one move from dropping atop her and taking her completely. In all the ways I desire to most.

My mouth waters at the notion. Wet, and fresh, and right. I could take her now that there is no one to stop me... There is no other male here, naga or otherwise.

We are alone, and in a nest. Not a very good one, but a nest of *my* creation. Nest sharing only happens between mated pairs and their offspring. It is a sacred place for any naga, especially a male who seeks to woo a mate.

The scales on my tail rise as I inch my tailtip closer to the crux between her legs, slithering under the lapels of the coats draped over her. My hand quickens, and I drop my head back against the wall. I swipe my tongue across my fangs.

She hitches and I go still, knowing full well what I am doing is wrong.

My hand halts on my shaft as my eyes open and drop to where she lies beside me. Her dark skin brings out the sapphire of my scales and as my heart jolts, wondering if she is awakening—if it is my fault—my hand slides over my swollen knot and seed spurts everywhere before I can stop it.

Some of it lands on her cheek.

Her eyes blink open, and she brings a hand to her face to wipe it off. She yawns and smears her fingers on the lab coat, covered in seed, and as I stare, horrified, she realizes that it's not water that has landed on her skin.

The rest of my spill trickles down my shaft and over my hand.

Eestys would gut me alive for being so perverse.

Shelby turns her head to look up at me. Her brow furrows, and I jerk away, untangling my fingers from her hair.

"Vagan? What? What's wrong?" she asks quickly as I try pushing my member back into my tail, hiding it under my tailtip. "What's on my face?" She reaches up and wipes the rest of my seed off of her, bringing her fingers to her eyes.

"I do not want to ssscare you," I hiss. Leaning away, my shaft pops right back out of my slit before my scales can lock it shut.

"Scare me?" her voice heightens as she sits up. "Are we in trouble? Did you hear something? What is this?" She looks around wildly, glancing again at the watery cream between her fingers.

Clothes shift, and I pivot to stop her as she pulls her legs under her, catching her just before she pulls her pants off of the chair. Ripping the pants from her grip, I put them back.

My eyes go straight to her glistening cheek.

"I did not mean to wake you. Go back to sleep," I insist, cupping her shoulders, staring into her wide eyes. "Nothing is wrong."

She reaches up to wipe her cheek again. "I don't understand?" she says, rubbing the pads of her fingers together. "What's on me?"

I back away and uncoil my tail from around her. I don't wait for her to realize with what's upon her, what I've wasted. "I'm going to take a look around. Sleep, female."

"Woman," she breathes, still studying my seed curiously. "Shelby. My name is Shelby, not female. I'm a *woman*."

I cock my head. Yes, I know this.

Her eyes lift to mine.

Then they fall to my chest, over my wounds, and to my large leaking member protruding out from me. Her breath hitches, and my jaw clamps. I grab my shaft and push it back into my tail.

"I did not mean to wake you—"

My member falls right back out.

Her lips open and close. "You..."

I straighten and try pushing my member back into my tail again.

"Your..." She lifts onto her knees. "You do have a cock."

Again, my member falls out.

I stop trying to hide it and frown at her words. Cock? Member, she means?

She wipes the end of the lab coat over her cheek as she studies me. Her eyes trailing over my aching shaft. There's no horror or fear in her eyes like I had expected. Like how the other females on the plateau looked when they saw cocks hanging out. I also don't hear Eestys's voice shame me for having mine on display.

I can't help it sometimes.

And now, since my body has changed, has grown tenser, I can help it even less.

But to not have one at all?

"I do… have… a cock," I say, figuring the word cock refers to my shaft since she's staring at it with fascination.

Shelby shuffles toward me on her knees, and I straighten even further. "Daisy said she was nearly raped but from those of you I've seen, there were no genitals. I assumed she meant in another way, like how the Gentri manipulates minds." She takes yet another knee forward, and her lab coat opens up, revealing much of her body.

I clench my fists, digging my claws into my palms.

We are different, yet I find her attributes more enticing than any female naga's. I've seen more human women—in pictures and old screens—than I ever had of females of my own species. It's hard not to have a preference.

And with her curious eyes, intelligent eyes, her tail-like hair, her darker hide, dark in a shade like my own, I had never seen a more alluring female.

She continues to come closer not knowing the dangerous game she is playing, speaking her words. "And that smell you're giving off right now," she says breathily, her eyes hooding. "I smelled this under the rocks. Spicy and rich, like food from my home, food my mother used to cook. Different, yet somehow so similar." She inhales hard, nostrils flaring, staring at my member. "I can't seem to get enough of it," her words fade. "It… makes me hungry."

Standing within arm's length of me, I slip my tail to curve around her as she continues to focus on my member, trying not to hurt her with my building need. I sink my fangs deep into my tongue.

Her gaze slowly comes up to catch my equally hungry one.

"Vagan, your scent…" She blinks, her eyes turning on and off rapidly. "It's—it's making my chest—" she drops her face as she places her hand between her breasts "—warm. What's happening to me?" she whispers.

Her words make me pause as her head lifts and she goes back to staring at my member.

And then I smell it too.

Sweet, luxurious, a scent that is so sweet it shouldn't exist. My tongue twists as I try to taste it, knowing full well what it is, and where it comes from. From her. It's her arousal.

My loins strain. *She is aroused!*

Shelby's pupils grow bigger. Her lips part. She leans forward, her head at the level of my member and takes a deep breath. I lean forward as well. She brings her hands up as if she's going to touch me, and my insides twist. Her fingers tremble as she reaches for me.

It's too much.

I need her to touch me. Her fingers draw nearer.

The whisper of air between our bodies is more sensation than I can handle.

"Do it," I urge through a hiss, nearly begging. Not once have I ever begged before, not until her. "I am yours. It is yours however you like."

Spill leaks from my tip.

Her fingers halt right before they touch me. "Vagan," she says with a gasp. "What's happening? I can't—I can't—"

There's fear in her voice. "You can," I tell her.

Her fingers continue to shake just above my taut, sensitive rod. "M-My body... it's acting strange... your smell..."

"You are changing," I say, understanding dawning on me.

Her eyes flip back up to mine. "Changing?"

Unable to take us not touching any longer, I clasp the back of her neck and hold her there, leaning forward. "I changed for you, the first time I caught your scent in a breeze. Now, it seemsss, you are changing for me, little one."

I knew we were fated. This proves it.

Her brow furrows, her eyes search mine, and I increase the pressure of my hand on her neck. Her arousal perfumes the air between us, rushing more spill to my knot.

Suddenly, she scurries back, pulling out of my grip. She turns around and scrubs her hands over her face. "This isn't happening. This can't be happening. There's never been an alien species compatible with humans. We almost fucking died, twice in the last day—or days?" She looks up but not at me. "Has it been days down here? I don't know... I don't even know!" Her words come quicker, ripe with worry. "We're stuck, lost, and no one knows we're even alive! How is this happening? Why? And now of all times?" She grabs her hair and tugs on it.

Her denial hurts. Yet, I understand. I lift my bloody palm where my claws dug deeply to my lips and lick my wound. "I did not have a choice either."

She twists to face me. "Choice! Yes," she says. "I still have a choice, right?"

My hand drops.

"Your pheromones—that's what it is, that's what I'm smelling—are strong, but I can..." She nods, her eyes slipping to my member again. "I can fight this. I... just..." She rubs her hands over her face again. "Why are they affecting me? I'm not a naga."

Fight this? "You are mine," I warn. "I told you this. I do not want you to fight me."

Shelby's face falls. She brings her hands to her nose, cups it, fear flashing across her face again.

Anger bursts through me, and I grab her wrists, snatching her up to me.

"Breathe me in, female," I growl. "I did not have a choice. There are no choices, just me. I am the only male here. The wind of this land pushed your scent right into me, despite the barrier you hid behind. I will never let you go. Never. I am your choice, the only choice."

She whimpers, and something in me snaps. I release her. She sinks to the floor before me, shaking, wrapping her arms around her middle. "Vagan, please," she breathes then moans.

Cursing, I move away. Every inch of space between us brands me like fire. "But you are right," I growl again, barely able to contain my mood, wishing she had not fought and was exploring me as badly as I want to explore her. "We need to get out of here and to my nest. I will not risk your life." I push through the chairs, the table, and toward the door. "Finish resting," I head for the exit. "I will remove my scent if that is what is causing your fear."

My scent affects her as much as hers affects me.

"Vagan."

I stop but don't look back at her. I can't risk it.

"Did you kill Collins?" she whispers.

Fury explodes through me at the mention of the other male.

"I promisssed," I hiss furiously.

A relieved moan answers me. My fury grows.

"A promise I wish I had not made," I add.

Stalking out of the nest before she can say anything more, I strike my tail out and break everything in my path.

FOURTEEN
THE LABORATORY

Shelby

I STARE AFTER VAGAN, listening to him thrash and destroy. The destruction comes to a stop quickly, and then I hear the flow of water from the faucet. Debating going after him and begging him to make this heat inside me go away, I hold still, tensing and relaxing all my muscles again and again.

I don't know what's happening to me, and despite the slick clenching between my legs, my frown deepens.

I fell asleep anxious and almost comfortable beside him and now, I'm completely aware of how little clothing I have on, how my lab coat must have shifted while I tossed and turned, and what that must've done to a male like Vagan.

You are mine.

I've been taking those words far too lightly so far, shucking them off for being nonsense. I didn't even think he had compatible genitalia until now. Now, the memory of his bulging, blue cock is branded in my head like a curse.

Or worse: my body's own, personal salvation. Which doesn't make any sense. But pressing my hand to my forehead, my flesh is hot and feverish. My nipples are peaked. Seeing him by the sink, the sound of the water between us, my body wants nothing more than to go to him and...

Cool down.

He could cool me down...

Fuck.

My eyes trail up his spine, to the beautiful scales there and downward to his hips. More than anything, I want them pounding away at me firmly between my legs. Twenty minutes ago, my body was too exhausted to feel anything except hard sleep and tension.

Sex is on my mind. Sex shouldn't be on my mind. It rarely ever is. There's too much sensation pulsating through me to do anything but feel whatever his scent is doing to me.

It has to be his scent. There's nothing more alluring, nothing except... Trailing my gaze back over Vagan's lithe, muscled form, I blanch, forcibly keeping my hand from going between my legs and rubbing my clit.

Each flex of my inner muscles, the power of his potent pheromones weakens, and after a time, I can take a normal breath without being infused with more of it. Luckily, with this place still having a source of power, the ventilation systems are still in effect. My eyes sluggishly drift to the ceiling and the ducts humming there.

Collins is alive.

Then he drops from my head like a weighted brick because it's still too damn hard to focus on anything but how close Vagan is and how profoundly empty I feel suddenly.

I bring my hands to my chest, feeling like I'd just experienced going into heat, or what going into heat feels like. Humans don't go into heat, or ruts, or anything of the sort. We women ovulate when we're most fertile, but we don't melt into a puddle of desire when we smell a human male's pheromones...

Or any species' pheromones for that matter.

And I can't ovulate... not really, not anymore. It happens, though nothing can ever come from it. I gave up the ability to have children to prove to dozens of *men* in my field that I wasn't going to run off with expensive and rare technology just to go into contract to have children. Men who wanted to keep me oppressed just because of my biology.

Putting them in their place had been rewarding and vindicating. Sometimes I wonder if it was worth it.

Not liking where my thoughts are going, I push them out. Hard.

So, what the hell just happened to me? I switch on my eyes to scan my body. Checking my flesh for hidden bites, needle pricks, or anything else that would give me red flags, I find nothing amiss. Only the dull ache where I hit my head and the scratches and some bruises from fighting off the Lurker. Either the painkillers from the kit are working or the sleep helped.

Vagan didn't inject me with anything or bite me. Which further proves it's the smell he's giving off. I'm certain I would've felt it if he had dosed me with something. Sighing, I shift my lab coat back into place, covering my body.

With my thoughts growing less muddied by the minute, I look around for my clothes, finding a full beaker of water near me, and more coats and cloths cushioning Vagan's 'nest.' Tossing back the water, some of the heat in my chest cools.

Even while I was sleeping, he cared for me, for my comfort. Even while he's hurting. I stare at the empty beaker in my hand a little dumbfounded.

Snatching my clothes, they're still damp, though on their way to being dry. *I must've been asleep for hours.* Wringing them between my hands, I help them along since I have nothing else to do.

And I'm not ready to face Vagan just yet. I don't dare.

What just happened between us now scours my thoughts, and I wince. I sniff my fingers, getting another hint of his scent, and wince harder when my sex quivers.

Well, this is going to be a problem.

With the rest of the water that's left in the beaker, I wet a cloth and clean my cheek and fingers.

Afterward, I eye the laboratory beyond, still seeing Vagan at the sink, peering down the front of his body.

Washing his cock?

I swallow, unsure why my mind is still so fiercely focused on him right now, even though I no longer smell him.

His back muscles are just as enticing as the front of him, symmetrical and tight, gracefully covered in his scales.

Biting my tongue, I realize I'm stuck, and I'm still flushed. I can't risk going near him right now, especially if he's scenting up the place.

Feeling my sex clamp with just the thought of his scent, of the cock I spent way too much time memorizing because I was desperate to smell it, lick it, nuzzle it, I groan and drop to the floor, resting my back to the wall.

What am I going to do now?

Thoughts of the cave-in, of him keeping the rocks from crushing me, come to my mind. The indomitable strength he's shown... Heat returns to my cheeks as his kiss takes over my thoughts. Hard, desperate, demanding, it was a branding. I let my mind wander, imagining what it would be like to be with him at a sexual level. I saw his soul in those terrible moments, and it wasn't dark. Not like how Daisy made me believe.

I lift up to get a glimpse of him and find him still by the sink, splashing water over his scales, clearly tense, clearly refusing to look back at me.

It makes me wonder if he's suffering as much as I am right now.

He said his body changed when he smelled *me*. Maybe there's something in his pheromones that triggers arousal in human women?

He would have to be compatible with them if that's the case. I furrow my brows and swallow.

His scent reminds me of innocence and the grain fields of Luntra. Of golden forests and Luntra's large sun. Of happy days playing with the other kids at the women's birthing center. Some were my siblings; most weren't. Mom and the other women treated us all as their children, so it never mattered who belonged to whom. It had been peaceful at the center, and when I reached five sun rotations and was forced to leave to begin my testing and eventual training, I'd been heartbroken.

I've seen my real mom only a couple times since. She's no longer a contractual breeder, but a midwife at the center now, and she only leaves every couple of years to visit her older children. I'd go back and visit her, except the place has a purpose, and someone like me isn't welcome there anymore.

It's not like I'd be able to join the program—or even qualify for it anymore. I never wanted to be a contractual breeder. It's near impossible to 'become' a breeder at the center anyway. The highest-caste women took jobs there. Women who didn't want a man around but who also wanted children, and a peaceful place to live, went there.

How can I live happily, birthing innocent children into a universe that would only just chew them up and spit them out?

We're at war.

It's that thought that finally sobers me.

Spreading out my clothes, I tug on my pants, my boots, and drop the lab coat to put my undershirt back on, replacing it afterward. Vagan's scent is a problem, but it's manageable. Rising, I shove the guns in the coat's pocket, tie one of the longer cloths over my face to mask my nose and mouth, and leave the room. I pause on the threshold.

Vagan stops splashing his tail and turns. Slitted, black eyes scan me from head to toe.

Stiffening, I suck in my stomach without meaning to and a rush of what I felt before crashes through me. "I'm going to look around," I say, though it comes out raspy and dull through the cloth, "and see if I can't figure out what this place is and how we get out of it." I don't mention what just occurred between us, though a blush rises to my cheeks anyway.

I also need to find a place to clean my body and find some sort of sustenance, but I don't tell him any of this.

He responds by keeping me pinned with his intimidating gaze, by not saying a word to ease this horrible tension now between us.

The fury in Vagan's expression is gone, but his demeanor makes me think he's on the verge of attacking something—maybe me. My heartbeat thumps, and I hold my breath.

Is he going to let me explore?

I don't dare drop my eyes to see if his cock is still jutting out from his tail. I think I see its shape in the periphery of my view.

"Your eyes are bright again," he says, startling me.

"I-I was searching my body for wounds," I whisper. I'm nervous. Why am I nervous? Men, human or otherwise, have never made me nervous. Why does Vagan make my nerves want to jump right out of my skin?

Curling my arms across my middle, I shield whatever I can from his gaze.

What would have happened if I took hold of his cock when I had the chance?

My body flushes all over again.

"Are you in pain?" he asks, turning fully toward me.

"No. Only minor aches..." I glance around uneasily. "I'm fine otherwise. I think."

I hear him hiss, and my skin prickles.

"You ssshould rest while you can. It will help with the gash on your head."

"I can say the same to you," I snap. "I don't think I've even seen you sleep yet. I don't know how you're able to talk, let alone move after being shot several times in the stomach."

"I do not need sleep, not like you."

"Is that so? Because it looks like your wounds could really use some R and R." His brow furrows, and I shake my head. "Never mind. I've already figured out that you can withstand a lot. A lot of pain, a lot of…" I trail off, not wanting to jinx us. "I'm not going far. I want to take a look around the room for something that might help us."

I peer past him and at the large circular space that's closed off. "Maybe see if I can get to that reactor outside and figure out how it's still working," I murmur. "If it's what's making this place have power. I can't sleep any more right now anyway."

It's a shit idea, but it's better than doing nothing. If I do nothing, my mind will wander to dangerous places. Heady places. Places my mind does not often wander because there's always something pressing to take care of.

I look back to Vagan, who's still staring at me. My toes curl.

"I won't leave this room," I add when he doesn't respond.

"Do not go near the windows."

I nod. "And I'll make as little noise as possible. I do have common sense, Vagan. I am only reassuring you because I'm beginning to understand that you feel like you need to protect me. I can protect myself too."

"Do not leave this room, or go where I can't sssee you." His tail strikes out and swipes the floor. Glass and debris from all the things he broke go flying to the walls. "I will be watching you."

Bristling now, I start walking toward the clean room and the puddle of bloody water that's still there. "Great, make me feel like I'm a captive again. First Peter, now you? Are you my warden now? I'm just grabbing the first aid kit," I add. A deep hiss follows me as I key into the smaller room. "You should know I'm carrying guns now too. I have pretty decent aim and can hold my own," I keep talking just to fight against the tension between us that wants to take over. Stepping into the space, I snatch up the wet first aid kit. Closing the top, I bring it back into the laboratory space. "See—"

A wall of chest and scales eclipse my view. My eyes slowly climb up the mountain of scarred blue muscle before me.

"Ssshelby," Vagan growls my name. "I will do whatever it takes." He grabs both my arms, lifts me from the floor, and plants me behind him. I see him wince from the act, almost imperceptibly. *He's still hurt, still suffering...*

My heart constricts, and I hear the doors to the clean room click closed.

Vagan's eyes find mine as he moves back to the faucet, hooded and predatory. His tailtip stays back to coil around my boots and cinch my ankles. "Poke around if you must, but if I am ready for you to be done, you are done," he warns. "The monster is prowling." His gaze shifts to one of the windows.

This time, my skin prickles for a completely different reason.

"I'll be careful," I say with all seriousness. "I promise."

We're lucky. Very lucky. And I forgot... Our luck could run out at any time.

"But you have to do something for me," I add, furrowing my brow. "You have to try and get some rest now. I'm awake and aware, I can keep watch while you do."

He hisses, and I stop him with a hand.

"We need to get out of here, and to do that, we may have to face that Lurker again. I'm not going to be able to do it alone." I swallow. "I need you. I need you to take care of yourself too."

For a moment I think he's going to argue with me, but then he tilts his head and nods, his gaze softening. "I will rest," he rumbles. "But I will stay here with you while I do."

I lick my lips. "Thank you. I'm... worried about you." I am. How can I not be? I eye his stomach and chest, fingers twitching to reach out and touch him, to feel his scales.

Vagan leans into me, bringing his face close to mine, and I stop breathing, thinking he may pull down my mask and kiss me. He trails the back of his fingers down the side of my face. "I will not have you worry on my account, female."

"Shelby," I whisper, correcting him, unconsciously leaning into his hand.

"I know."

He pulls away.

"Vagan," I say, making him pause in his retreat. "I need you to-to stop producing that scent, if you can. It'll be safer, much safer, for us if..." I swallow thickly, feeling my cheeks heat. "If you *contain* it. I don't think we should leave until you do."

His cock is still jutting out of his tail, drawing my gaze, making me increasingly nervous.

I lick my lips nervously. "Just… do what you have to." I can barely form the words, wanting to impale my soul onto a pike for how embarrassed I am suddenly. Because there's a large knot in his cock, and the tip of his shaft keeps leaking seed like he needs to release the build up.

He doesn't respond, only moving back to the sink. I stare after him until I hear the water running again. But when I hear a raspy groan and a quick slapping sound, I inhale sharply and decide death would be more endurable.

Forcing my gaze away from the lean curves of his backside, and what I *know* he's doing, I begin my search around the lab, suddenly hopeful, although partially frightened.

Because part of me wants to turn around, go to him despite that fact he's jacking off and I just ordered him to do so, and demand more answers about what's going on between us—except I'm afraid that if I do, I won't be prepared for the answers or what might happen afterward.

The Ketts are killing us, ravaging entire human colonies, and are chasing after us. It's a problem I am desperately trying to help solve. I'm not equipped to fight, to join the military, but I have a good mind. I risked my life coming to Earth, knowing its past, and I'll keep taking risks because at the end of the day my homeworld, Luntra, will never be safe until humanity pushes back the Ketts, and until then, there'll be no peace for me, or anyone.

My eyes shift to Vagan, and my throat constricts. We shared something under those rocks. He saw my soul laid bare. Something I've never let anyone else see.

If only it was so easy.

I shift my eyes away. I'm not his destiny, nor he mine. It's not possible for me.

There's no *mine* in my future.

<h1 style="text-align:center">FIFTEEN
A BRIEF HISTORY</h1>

Shelby

A SHORT TIME LATER, Vagan settles in a spot by one of the outer walls and drops down onto his tail, dripping with a fresh coat of water. He leans his back against the wall, closing his eyes. His wet orange hair is plastered to his face. His cock still out, and from what I can tell, the knot in it is smaller, but I don't sneakily eye it for long, still beyond embarrassed by the whole situation.

He cups his bulge as I eye him again in my periphery anyway, and I dart my gaze away when he moves his hand up and down.

For how well he communicates, I keep forgetting how primitive he still is. How alien he is.

How bizarre that our horrible circumstances have taken on an even dangerous change.

I know he's not going to allow himself to sleep, and I know he's watching me despite his eyes being closed. I can feel it. I can even feel him pleasuring himself in a way, because whatever remains of this heat inside me wants to cry because he's not pleasuring me as well.

But I let it go because we need each other and having his protection, despite how alarming and domineering it can be, is...

It takes away some of the fear.

One of the machines beeps, and my eyes drift to the window.

There is a Lurker outside these rooms.

I clench my hands. Having a real Lurkawathian to study and question would be momentous for Central Command—it could save us—or end us. Except the one outside is aggressive and nothing like the Lurkers I read about in my studies. The species, although reptilian, are extremely intelligent and incredibly old. They've been around far longer than humans.

They've also conquered space, intergalactic travel, modern medicine, and so much more.

Just because they look like terrifying monsters with razor-sharp teeth and wide mouths doesn't mean their evolutionary path is any different than a human's. When they first contacted Earth, they wanted peace. They deployed diplomacy. Humans, on the other hand, were suspicious.

The peace treaty Earth solidified with them had taken years to create. Stipulations being, no testing upon either species without delegates of both being present.

I rub the back of my head while I find a private corner to relieve myself, and head to the sink afterward to wash what I can of my body like Vagan did.

Without taking off my clothes, I clean everywhere I can, reaching under them to wipe away any sweat or grime still on me. Grabbing some of the cloths from our 'nest,' I also clean around my head wound and change the bandages.

I'd hoped that all my reactions to Vagan had been a delusion, that the bump on my head was a lot worse than it really is, but I'm disappointed. The wound is healing, smaller than before. After I'm done, I head to the nearest lab bench and shuffle through the first aid kit and grab the remaining painkillers, gauze, and glue before stuffing them into my pocket, heading to the computers by the entry to the inner relay.

Sitting in one of the swivel chairs, I touch the screen and turn on my eyes. Swiping my finger across the screen, it hums to life. It flickers, crackles, as if it's trying to remember how to work. On the table next to me, an old tablet and several white orbs are sitting on charging platforms. I've seen the orbs before, having dug up several broken ones around the pit.

Picking one up, it turns on. "How can I help you?" it asks in a clear, feminine voice. The orb jumps out of my hand, making me flinch, and hovers beside me.

Glancing at Vagan, he's still lying prone against the wall. But his cock is gone—thankfully, finally back within his tail—and his eyes are closed.

"What is this place?" I ask the orb a little hesitantly.

"This place is Eagle's Rest Military Base."

I knew that. It was in the mission documents I helped create for onboarding the rest of Peter's team. "Where am I inside the base?" I ask instead, comfortable now that I know I'm using an old communication system and excited that it works.

The orb spins once before answering me. "You are currently inside Eagle's Rest Military Base's research hive."

Research hive?

"What kind of research?" I ask, seeing if Central Command had been correct about this place having the answers we need.

"Extraterrestrial lifeforms and bioware research."

"Wait, not technology and weapons research?"

"I do not understand your question," the orb responds.

My brow furrows. Those who arranged this mission had told us this base was used for Lurkawathian technology research, as per the treaty, but also more. Glancing outside, a shiver streaks up my spine. A biodome, deep underground, in a military base where weapons development and testing were supposedly done, could easily be corrupted from fear of a bigger, stronger species magically appearing.

That humans are not the alphas of the universe has only been one of the problems we've had to overcome in the last fifteen hundred years. Our mortality is another.

Sometimes these weaknesses make us afraid.

I've had a theory for a long time. A theory a lot of my colleagues refuse to acknowledge...

What if it's something we did that made the Lurkers commit genocide against us? What if it was *our* fault?

"Orb," I force out, "what do you know about... Lurkawathians?"

"Lurkawathians, the first sentient alien lifeform to contact humanity, arrived outside Earth's exosphere in 2132. Seeking peace, the first great extraplanetary, extraterrestrial treaty was signed between two species in 2138, and Lurkawathians first set foot on Earth. From then on, Lurkawathians, also known as Lurkers, have been an integral part of

Earth's economical, agricultural, ecological, astronomical, and techno-logical systems. As a species who has conquered space travel and has knowledge of other alien lifeforms and extraterrestrial space law, they became our mentors, providing us access to other worlds and galaxies, and furthering our knowledge of the vast universe we live in."

The breath I wasn't realizing I was holding *wooshes* out of me. I spent my whole life being told Lurkers were evil and murderous, only coming to Earth to destroy us. Hearing old human technology recite their history on this planet with nothing but diplomatic respect is strange to me.

It had been a long shot, but it was worth trying all the same. Ques-tioning the orb will only get me so far. It's only going to have basic information.

"Orb, what is your function here?"

"I relay information between classified sections here at Eagle's Rest."

"Like a communication device?"

"A communication device powered specifically by Eagle's Rest's relays."

"I don't understand?"

"I am a singular cell belonging to a much larger one. More than a communication device, I am threaded with artificial intelligence technology."

Licking my lips, I give the orb my whole attention. "Can you link to other devices? Devices not belonging to these relays?" Could the orb contact the team, the transport ship? *The Dreadnaut?*

"I can only link to other devices connected directly to the relays."

"And these relays? What are they?"

"The three Eagle's Rest base relays are nuclear-powered hubs controlled by Stigma, an artificial intelligence built by the government to protect and monitor the highest level of classification. They feed power to everything near it, spanning miles in each direction, whether the technology is directly linked or not. Using microscopic dark matter, the relays at once react as a security system, as well as a failsafe to all digital data in its vicinity."

I stare at the orb, trying to process what it's telling me.

"Can you connect to other... orbs linked to Stigma?" If it can do that, I could still contact someone on the surface. I could call for help.

I glimpse Vagan who's still resting by the wall. Though his eyes are closed, I know he's listening.

"If the orb is powered and I have a direct contact code, I can connect to it."

"Can I send a message? Speak to someone?" My excitement builds.

"Yes."

"But I need a code?"

"Yes."

Heart thumping, I cup the orb in my palms, covering it with the blue glow of my eyes.

They flash, scanning the orb, immediately sending signals to connect with it. Databytes scroll across my gaze as my eyes flood me with analytics. My eyes also have threads of artificial intelligence embedded in them. Besides recording everything I see when on, they're experts in ancient human and alien technology.

Numbers appear. Codes. Connecting with the orb directly, I see tendrils of electrical connections streaking out of it, to other devices in and outside this room.

Highlighting all of them, not knowing which goes where and hoping for the best, I send out a distress signal.

Nothing happens at first.

"Anybody out there?" I ask the orb, keeping my voice low. Nothing. I try again. "Is anybody out there?"

Nerves zinging, I pray for a connection, an answer, anything, glancing at the window where I know the Lurker awaits. Feeling my palms grow clammy, I beg for a miracle.

Minutes go by and there's still no response. I'm about to give up and try something else when I decide to give it one more go.

"Please, answer. This is Shelby from *The Dreadnaut*, and we're in trouble."

I wait another minute but still get no response. Losing hope, I drop my hands from the orb.

"Shelby?" A familiar voice suddenly comes from it. "It's Gemma. What's wrong? I'm here. Are you okay?"

Gemma?

Gemma!

I jump out of my seat, scarcely believing the voice who answered is actually her. Scarcely comprehending what's happening. "Gemma! Oh, hell. You're alive! Thank god you're alive. It's good to hear your voice, any voice."

"What's the matter? What's happening? Are you okay? Where are you?"

"I'm trapped," I say, grabbing the orb to me roughly. "Under the facility. I'm trapped with *him*."

"Who—"

"There's something you need to know," I tell her, eyes darting to the window. "I've found something—" A crackle fills my ears, and the orb powers off.

"No!" I shake it, hearing a rattle inside it. Trying to turn it back on, it stays dead.

I reach for another one when a hand covers mine. "You are making too much noise," Vagan hisses.

I nearly jump out of my seat. "I reached Gemma. She's alive!" I gasp, turning to him. "She's one of the women who was at the plateau," I add. "I need to connect with her again." I try pulling my hand from Vagan's grip, but he doesn't let me go. "Why are you stopping me?"

"If you bring her here, will she save usss?" he asks harshly. "Is she capable? More capable than me? Then that other male? Or will she come here to die?"

"I..." Any argument I had dies. Gemma would have already returned to the facility if she were able.

Guilt grips me, realizing I should have demanded where she *was* and how I could save *her*.

"You will risk her life," Vagan continues.

"I can try contacting someone else," I say.

"Only nagas use the orbs." His hand tightens on mine in warning. "I will not have you lead all the males across the forest here to fight each other in hopes of claiming you. We will return to the elevator when the last of my wounds close and find our own way out, a safer way," he growls.

Vagan releases my hand to curl his finger around one of my braids. "There could be others listening."

Others.

Monsters, aliens, Lurkers. He doesn't have to say any more to make me understand.

I close my eyes. "You're right. I won't reach out again." Not yet at least. We're managing right now, and soon Vagan will be well enough to safely get us back to the elevator. From there... I don't know, but all hope isn't lost.

He grabs one of the other orbs off of the table.

"How do we get out of here?" Vagan asks once he's turned it on.

His tailtip curls around my ankle and up my leg as if he's laying claim to me, even warning off these orbs...

Breathing only through my mouth now, I press my thighs together, tensing my muscles, finding his overly protective nature as unsettling as it is comforting.

"Eagle's Rest Military Base is connected to two—"

"How do we get above ground," Vagan barks, interrupting it, "if the main way is blocked?"

The orb stutters, pauses, and then answers.

"There are two access points to this floor," the orb says, stealing my attention. "One being the main entry point elevator that leads to the surface and the other through the maintenance elevator outside the relay in the biodome."

"And that will take us above ground?" Vagan questions.

"There is an elevator outside the relay that will take you to the biodome's main research space, equipment and storage below us. From there, you can access the main entry point elevator and head up to the surface."

Vagan and I share a look. It's not quite the answer we were looking for, but it's a useful answer all the same.

We can either go back the way we came, possibly encountering an ambush, or we can go deeper and reach the elevator through the floor below us. Either way, we'll have to risk encountering the Lurker again.

Vagan releases the orb and sets it down on the charging base. My eyes lower further. Glimpsing the hefty cock fully erect, again, standing at attention outside his tail. I gasp and startle away and out of his coil when a drip of seed falls from it.

"Vagan," I say his name in warning, holding my breath, getting a whiff of his scent anyway. "I thought you fixed it! I thought—"

My mouth waters.

My cheeks heat.

He hisses and jerks away and back to his corner. I stare after him, wanting to follow him and press against his side. Rooting my feet to the floor, I fist my hands. When he settles back into his spot, his eyes remain open.

His hand goes back to gripping his length, and this time, while he touches himself, he's looking at me while he's doing it.

I wait for the rush of heat to pass, snared with sudden fever and embarrassment, staring as he squeezes his knot.

Minutes or hours go by, I have no idea, watching each other the whole time, listening to the soft hum of the vents above us and the deepening, groaning hissing tearing from his throat.

SIXTEEN
WORTHY OF A MATE

Vagan

SHELBY DOES NOT MOVE from where I left her.

I am trying to give her the space she needs. The *air* she needs.

It is hard.

My gaze trails her form and my mouth parts to bare my fangs. The scales of my tail slide back, and my member pulsates, hardening further, expanding in the middle. I try to hide it with my hand because it refuses to stay within my tail. I have tried to put it away, I am trying not to frighten her, but she is right.

If we leave these rooms, and she reacts to me like how she did when I woke her, I will mount her like the wretch I am, knowing I will not be able to resist. Even if we're being hunted, even if other males will see.

I am not an evil naga.

I am not.

No matter how badly I want her to come to me, to touch me, to initiate a claiming, I know she's nervous and fearful. Instead, she watches me with wide eyes like I am wrong, wrong in every way that matters.

Eestys would be ashamed, having fended off other naga males who'd tried to hurt her. She would see me with my swollen shaft, desperate to rut, and turn away with disgust. I squeeze my knot in frustration, wishing it would go back to being small so I can tuck it away.

Spill leaks from my tip and over my hand, and Shelby's eyes go straight to it. I have spilled and I have washed, spilled again only for it to swell immediately after. The waste of my seed washed away.

Despite wanting her to come to me and accept that I am her mate, to end my misery, I also don't want Shelby to view me how I always feared Eestys would.

Clamping my hand harder around my shaft, I milk the ache away, trying to force Shelby to turn away from me and my shame.

Because if she doesn't, my control might break. If she continues to stand there, watching me, I may become everything I have always tried not to be...

Evil and rabid.

Like the Death Adders or Black Mambas.

Coiling my tail around her middle and dragging Shelby's body across the floor and under mine is all I want to do. Was this how it was between naga males and females? Was this why the females left, because resisting this, this... this tension was too much? Annoyed, I stiffen. My ears prick.

Shelby takes a step toward me.

I hiss with frustration, releasing my swollen length. It was easier when I was in pain, thirsty, and near death.

Hissing again, she takes a step back.

"You do not have to fear me," I grate. "I am not a rapist. Stab me if you must, bleed me out and weaken me again if you are afraid, but it will not change anything." I begin peeling off one of the strips she put over my wounds to reopen it with my claw.

"Vagan," she breathes my name, the blue light from her eyes piercing the space between us. Her brow wrinkles, and some of her fear wanes.

"I will not have you be afraid of me," I grunt, widening the gash. If this is what works, then I will spill blood instead of seed. I can handle thirst and blood loss and still be strong. If she won't mate with me, then we only have one other safe choice before we make our escape...

I can be bait.

Blood smells, especially fresh blood.

"Vagan! Stop!" she orders, suddenly running to me and pulling my hand away. "What the hell are you doing? Have you gone mad!"

She goes quiet, and I look down at her, finding her staring at my chest.

"Ssshelby," I rasp, clasping her chin. "You will smell me if you do not move away." I clasp her chin harder, making her aware that I do not want her to leave despite this.

Her mouth parts, and her tongue swiftly wets her lips. She sucks in a long, shaky breath and places her hands on my chest. Her fingers curl, her hands fist, and she trembles, leaning into me. The scent of her arousal floods my nose.

Thick and delicious.

My muscles strain, and my tail coils outward, circling her, eliminating her ability to escape.

Her breath fans my scales. She inhales again, and her eyes flutter closed. "You smell... you smell like home. Like everything I've always wanted. Everything I won't allow myself to want," she whispers.

"Why?" I lift her chin because her words confuse me. "Why deny this?"

"I'm... I'm not. I'm... so confused."

Confused?

I search her face, her glistening eyes. "Why are you confused?"

Her hands flatten on my chest. "I need to prove..."

My eyes narrow. "What?"

Her gaze hoods as she considers my question, and as she does, she lowers onto her knees and presses her body to mine. Tensing, I grasp her shoulders, pushing her away, before she traps my aching member between us. Every fiber in my body goes still, because if I move, I'll spill. I'll be pressed against her body, and I will spill.

She presses upon me anyway, and a groan slips from my throat.

She has nothing to prove to me.

"I'm trying," she starts slowly, shuddering. "To show those who think I'm incapable of doing this job, that I am. That I'm worthy of the investment they've put into me." Her eyes drop, and I release her chin. "That... the choices I've made weren't a mistake."

Even more confused by her words, I cup Shelby's cheeks. Her eyes sparkle with unshed tears. Tears that make me thirsty. "You are here, aren't you?" I ask softly. "Haven't you proved what you needed to?"

I don't know what she's talking about, only that she has nothing she needs to prove to *me*. Clearly, being on this planet brings power to those who've been chosen to leave the skies. Some human gave her this opportunity. Someone she must consider to be important.

Bristling, I can't help but think another male is seeking to win her. A male who is on her mind, even now, while she is with me. Because she has nothing to prove to me... *If what is stopping her is another potential mate...*

I grit my teeth, jealousy arising.

Of course there will be other human males who want Shelby as a mate! Not just the lonely nagas outside. Collins can't be the only one. She is too beautiful to be alone. Too brave. Too interesting. Scanning her face, a tear forms, trickles from her lashes, and catches on the tip of my thumb. I rub it away because it's not meant for me.

"I haven't proven anything. It's only getting harder," she says as another tear falls for me to catch. "You make it harder. It's not fair you're here, that you smell like home, that I trust you, because I can't... I can't!" More tears brim and trickle down to cover my hands. "I've made a mistake!" She sobs, pulling away from me and covering her face. "Your smell is messing with my head."

Shelby stumbles away. Stunned, I watch as she rubs her face furiously into the sleeves of her coat. "Coming here was a mistake," she continues through hitches. "Maybe my mentors were right. Maybe they should've given these eyes to a man."

This is about her eyes?

"Fuck," she says, wiping her nose. "I shouldn't be crying at a time like this. And not to you." She gulps down a breath, straightens, and heads to where she left her weapons. "It's not like you'll understand." She hitches again. "I should be thinking about Gemma, about Collins, about finding the technology that will save us all. Not *this*."

I rise swiftly and pull her into my arms. She gasps but doesn't fight me when I spin her to face me. "Why do you have to prove something for your eyes? Make me understand."

They widen, bright and blue upon me. "Vagan—"

"No male is waiting for you in the skies? No other I need to fight?"

Her brow wrinkles.

"Tell me," I growl. "Tell me no male is waiting for you."

If there is, he'll be waiting a long, long time. Only a crazed male would let his female leave his side to be claimed by another.

"T-There's no male waiting for me."

My hold on her eases.

"I don't have anyone waiting for me," she whispers.

Relief floods through me. "Then I am the only one." I won my battle against Collins; I've captured Shelby away from all the other nagas. There is only me. Trapping her to me, I wrap my arms around her, coiling my limbs. "Mate," I murmur, resting my cheek upon the top of her head.

She's stiff at first, and I understand why. I can easily hurt her. But if she's beginning to trust me then she knows that I would never. Shelby settles in my arms and leans into me. Even with my member hard between us, she rests.

For a time, neither one of us dares to move.

But as the moments continue, the tension in me grows, so much worse than before. Her breathing grows heavier, and the ache in my loins builds. I want her so badly, it hurts. She rubs her cheek in soft circles over my scales, her fingers playing with their outlines. Aware of every little move she makes, my thoughts blur.

Clenching my hands, I go rigid.

The only way to make her think of me, and only me, is to claim her.

Claim. Her.

Yesss.

And as if she knows my thoughts, she presses her mouth to my chest. The warm, wet lash of her tongue slips across the sensitive skin between my scales, and I lose it.

I rip off her mask, capturing her face once again, and take her mouth with mine. Swallowing her breath, my tongue thrusts between her lips before she can close them.

She strains against me, her nails digging into my shoulders, and I sink as deeply inside her mouth as I can. Her arousal blooms heavier in the air, invading my senses. She pushes at me once then stops, losing the fight, then grasps me back.

She doesn't try to move away from me again. *Yesss.*

Her lips dance with mine. Kissing her, tasting her delicious, human flavor, sends my tail coiling up our bodies. I seek her heat, pushing my tailtip between her legs, searching for the warmth between them. She is warm where I am cold, and I want to burrow into her and burst into flames. I am hungry for her wetness.

My body is ready to be on fire.

There is nothing I want to do more than to feast upon her essence and bathe in her arousal, wetting my scales, my tongue, my member.

But she wears ridiculous human clothes.

Tearing my mouth away, I haul her into my arms and carry her to one of the tables, sweeping everything off of it. Hooded eyes find mine as I lean forward, placing her a top it and spreading her legs, trapping her with my larger body.

Claim her.

Now!

"Vagan," she whimpers, arching her chest. "Help... me." She rubs at her nose, panting wildly.

Claim me, is what I hear.

Yes. Finally. *Yesss.*

Shuddering, my bulge expands, surging with so much seed, spill juts out and over her pants. Pushing against her, more of it spurts out, and my mouth dries up. Needing her wetness now, I clutch her head and press my mouth back to hers, licking her teeth and lapping at her tongue.

She arches against me.

"Vagan... stop!" she gasps, turning her head away. Clawing my back, touching me everywhere, I lift up to peer at her. When I do, she puts her heels on the table's edge and pushes her sex against my member. "We shouldn't do this. You need to get away from me! Oh my fucking god."

"Am I hurting you?" I rasp, confused.

She's shaking, and there's fear etched across her expression. Fear? Again?

"I... need..."

"Need? Need what?"

Do not tell me to back off. With the way she is spread out and open for me, her sex splayed at the perfect height for my shaft and its knot, I do not think I can. Not without a taste.

Not without a sip.

Whimpering, Shelby drops her head back onto the table.

Am I being too rough? Too fast? I thought humans kissed during mating, but perhaps I'm wrong.

"Tell me," I growl, raking my claws across the table on either side of her body. "Tell me what to do!"

A cry of frustration leaves her, and she sits upright, forcing me back. She kicks off her boots, grabs the lip of her pants, and yanks them down her legs. Shyly, she looks at me as she shimmies out of the scrap of cloth covering her sex.

Her sweet scent fills the air as she slowly parts her legs again.

Rearing back, my eyes drop to take in the gift she's giving me. Dewy, wet lips eclipse my vision, her dark flesh haloing a strip of glistening pink. She is as hairless here and my fingers strain to feel her, to slip them over her, to open her up and see where my shaft will go, where my knot will be seated.

Before me is my female's most sacred, secretive spot, and she is baring it for my eyes to feast upon. Hunger rams my gut; thirst tightens my throat. My tail slides up the table to circle around her.

My claws scrape the table on either side of her, digging into metal and leaving their mark.

She wants me as badly as I want her.

But when I glimpse her face, she's not looking at me. Her eyes are closed tight, and her body is flushed and shaking as if she is ill. The coat has fallen open, and her shirt is still on. She shows me her sex before she allows me to see all of her? She hides her face but not her sex?

She has seen all of me. I want all of her.

"Look at me," I demand.

"Please." Her voice is barely a strained gasp. "It's too much. I can't bear it."

Gently cupping her thighs, I lean over her. "Bear what? Your body changing for me?"

"Your scent," she gasps. "I can't!" she abruptly cries out, dropping her head back. "I can't!" She shunts her hips up into me, and her hot sex slips across my scales. "You need to do this, and fast. We need to get out of here. Please, make it fast! I can't get pregnant."

"Not take you, mate you," I correct, rising up. "Why are you afraid?"

"Vagan!"

I grip her legs harder. "Why?" I demand.

Why am I so confused? Don't humans mate like my kind?

She is acting like she does not have a choice...

"Because I don't know what the fuck is wrong with me right now and if you don't—" she sits up, pushes at my chest, and grabs my member with both hands "—fuck me, I'm going to scream at the top of my damn lungs and bring that alien down upon us. We don't have time for this!" she shrieks. She squeezes my knot, and I spill all over her chest. She cries out. "Not my shirt. It's on my shirt. Now, we're going to die," she sobs.

I tear her hands off me before I spill even more on her body and clothes, suddenly, deeply unsettled by what is happening. "That doesn't answer my quessstion, little mate."

Do humans not change for their mates?

Is what she is experiencing as new for her as it was for me?

Does she not know what is happening? "Fate wants our bodies to join," I say when she doesn't answer.

She kicks and squirms, pushing against me, at the same time clutching me closer. "Fate? Humans don't react like this. Like heat—going into heat. We don't go into heat, Vagan! Something alien is happening to me and I'm," she sobs again, "scared."

Catching her shoulders, I pin her to the table. "I will not have you fear me," I snap.

I think of what is happening, what she's going through. She wants to rut, needs to rut, like she might die if she doesn't. She needs to spill. She needs to spill like how I needed to spill weeks ago, beyond desperate, confused and lost.

Because it's her body forcing her this way, and not her mind.

I must show her, teach her, soothe her.

"I did not want my body to react like this either," I say, softening my voice. "I will not mate you while you are afraid. You can fight through this."

She stops thrashing and her glazed eyes find mine. "You won't have sex with me?"

"No." The word claws from my throat, more painful than any wound.

"But I need—"

"To spill?"

"S-Spill?" she stutters.

Until now, she has been headstrong, and forward, speaking her mind. Right now, she is none of those things and despite my need for her, my unease deepens.

"Ease the ache," I say, petting her thighs. "Make it bearable." Grabbing my member, I lift it to show her, tugging on it once to release a trickle of seed. "It helps. Not as much as being sick and weak has done for me, but it helps. Bleeding out helps."

Her eyes land on my shaft.

Groaning, I ask, "Do you want me to leave?"

"No!" She scrambles up onto her elbows. "Tell me what works."

Warmth fills me at her adamance, and then my own terror rises. I can barely hold back from her, breathing her in, and seeing her in such a state. And now she wants to *talk?*

"How?" I grate thickly, remembering I am being tested. "But only pain and exhaustion helps, or spilling. Tell me how I can help you spill because I will not hurt you. Either that, or let me leave."

She is much smaller than me, much weaker overall. My fantasies of rutting her are brutal and vicious, but I can't be that way with her. She would not survive. I may not survive. *Please, let me leave.*

She licks her lips, and I nearly come undone. "Touch me," she breathes. "Between my legs. I-I can't ease myself without help." She winces at her words.

Nostrils flaring, we stare at each other. She knows what she's asking of me. She can see my body shaking with restraint. She trusts me enough to keep my word anyway. She lowers back onto the table, holding my gaze, and positions her legs so they're spread wide.

Yesss, she trusts me. We are good together.

My eyes drop to her sex at the same time, and I dive forward, slicing my tongue along her slit. She cries out my name and grabs my head.

I lash her harder, overcome with her taste. Her essence quickly coats my tongue, making my shaft jerk in response. Her fingers tangle into my hair. My scalp prickles, shooting the scales along my tail upright.

She moans my name.

A strange emotion hits me.

Joy? I slide my tongue up and down her slit. I lick her faster. Growing hungrier, more anxious, I want more. If she needs to spill, she'll need to spill a lot more than what her glistening sex offers up.

When my body reacted to her scent, I spilled for hours, and still had more to give. There was little relief even after I was drained, only madness and thirst. It felt like I was on fire.

And that madness that nearly got me killed. I can't have my female go through the same torment, not when I'm here to help her through it. Not with other males and monsters lurking nearby. Moving my hands between her thighs, I spread her nether lips and her little human opening appears. It quivers as I set it to memory. It's small like she is, and I will need to stretch it for her to take me.

Reaching down, I palm the head of my shaft.

Shelby's hand slides down her body to rub a small nub above her opening. Curious, I push her hand away.

"What is that?" I rasp.

"My clit," she gasps, putting her fingers back upon the nub. "It feels good when rubbed."

I push her fingers away again and pinch it gently.

Her hips jerk. "Oh, god, yes."

Pleased with her reaction, I lean down and swirl my tongue over it. When her hips come off the table, I catch them, force them down. "Do not move," I growl. "Let me help you spill."

She buckles once then holds still beneath me.

I swipe her sensitive nub harder, caressing her slit with the fingers of my free hand.

Leaning back in, I lick her faster, harder.

Shelby's nails dig into my scalp.

Still... There is no spill...

Why isn't she spilling?

Rolling my thumbs, I massage around her sex, urging her to release. Desperate, my throat constricts, ready to drink her down, ready to fill my belly and to know her in such a way as I have not imagined. My tail coils, wrapping around her left leg, gently squeezing it. I slide my tailtip toward my cock to rut it.

"More!" she cries when I falter.

I growl.

I tear my mouth off of her nub and thrust my tongue inside her.

She screams my name, and my thoughts scramble.

Diving, licking, probing, and tasting, I learn every inch of her tight sheath, finding the rough spot inside her to be my favorite. Her flavor floods me when I tease it.

"I need... I need..." I slam my tongue hard into her rough spot, and her body stiffens. She tries to push my head away. "I'm coming!" she gasps.

Coming? Coming where?

Shelby's body seizes, and she goes silent, straining every limb against me. Her sheath clamps down on my tongue, and wetness trickles down my chin and over my cheeks. I widen my mouth around her little hole and brace to swallow every drop that she will soon give me.

Panting excitedly, my mouth waters in anticipation. I've never been so desperate for a sip. I might go mad if there's not enough.

Still, there is no spill.

Her sheath flutters, constricting around me, and I imagine what it would be like to have my member cradled so perfectly.

I spill all over the floor before I finish the fantasy, shoving my member hard against the side of the table. Her limbs give way, and she collapses beneath me. Chest heaving, her arms drop to her sides as if she's just been felled by the enemy.

"Thank you," she sighs. "Thank you," she whispers again right after.

Swirling my tongue through her clenching sheath, I search for her spill.

"V-Vagan," she stutters after a moment, and she rises on her elbows, "I..." Keeping my mouth firmly on her, I peer up when she looks down at me.

Hooded and glistening, dark and wild, they widen, no longer blue.

Slowly, her limbs strain and lock again around my frame. Her eyes drop to the seed I've spilled, and her nostrils flare.

I'm not going to stop until she's spilled too, and she's coming to realize this. Her breathing grows heavier, and the slight redness on her dusky cheeks heightens.

I lift off of her, replacing my tongue with a curious finger. "You did not ssspill," I hiss, swirling it, exploring her tight channel, wishing it was my shaft it milked.

"I did," she whimpers. "I came..."

That word again.

I slide part of my tail under her head for her to rest against. Liking the way her tight hole feels, I push in a second finger to search and tease, to stretch her.

"There is no ssspill."

She shakes her head.

"When I spill, it is everywhere. It drenches," I tell her.

Her head falls back when I lower and tease her nub with my tongue. "Vagan! That's not—"

"I will not stop until you do. The madness of it is dangerous." I should know. "The pressure, unbearable."

"Vagan, I can't spill like you! Women—human women—don't release like that. Not usually. Not like you do." Her hips jump as I probe her rough spot with both fingers. "We really shouldn't be doing this knowing so little about each other," she adds with a quick hitch.

"Human females don't spill?"

"No!"

I pause my attentions, still trying to understand. Females don't spill? How do they find relief?

She writhes and curses at my inaction, her legs hooking around my middle, clamping back around me. Then she looks around the room, her hooded gaze going to the seed smeared across her thigh, ending on me.

I wait for her direction, muscles taut, hips rocking. Petting her wrinkled spot with vigor, I practically beg her to give into my dominion, to finish the claiming.

There's a heat in her eyes that primes my body. The madness has taken over her. I rock my hips harder in excitement.

A hiss wheezes out between my fangs. I can't help the savage glee that fills me—and the guilt that comes with it.

SEVENTEEN
DANGEROUS GAMES

Shelby

I want to cry.

Thrash.

Scream.

I want to pummel him with my fists for bringing me so low.

But most of all, I need him to be inside me, pressing his hips between my thighs.

For a brief moment, there was bliss. Real bliss, climaxing at his curious fingers and mouth. I've never known such a feeling, not even the couple times I'd been with Collins. Excitement, embarrassment, exhilaration for something other than my work… I've never known anything else could make me feel that way. There was sun on my skin, wind in my hair, and golden fields of grain. And a moment of peace. The kind people chase their entire lives to experience, only for it to end too soon and Vagan's pheromones to go to work on me again.

Pleasure, especially self-pleasure, is not something I've ever focused on, living in the world I have lived in. Duty comes first.

I shouldn't be focusing on it right now.

Touching my thighs, my skin is heated and flushed, my sex clamping around horrible emptiness. I'd been filled for that blissful moment only for it to be ripped away, leaving me emptier still.

Vagan's blatant confusion about how his scent affects me is the only thing that's keeping me grounded right now. He doesn't know about his kind. It's obvious from our interactions. He's alone. He hasn't mentioned any kin. He hasn't mentioned his culture at all.

Because he doesn't have one. Not really. I'm beginning to realize this. The nagas are very primitive despite their knowledge of the common tongue and the ruins of Earth.

In the back of my mind, reality is trying its hardest to claw its way back to the forefront.

Pushing Vagan back some more, I slide off the table and brace against him, my knees giving out. His cock rubs up against my stomach, and my mouth floods with saliva. Furiously hot, my skin burns, even pressed against his colder body.

Sliding my hands down his chest, whispering my fingers over his wounds, I grasp his cock with both hands. My sex clenches, happy with my reckless decision.

He's a different species.

It's thick with an ever-expanding bulge widening its middle. Wet with seed, my hands slide down to his root, cupping his knot as they slip back up to his tip. He's big, larger than any human man could ever be. But it's also long and tapered, making the massive knot in the middle a little less frightening.

The trapped thoughts in the back of my mind scream out. But a deep hissing sound fills my ears, shooting delightful shivers up my back. Vagan shunts his hips, accidentally throwing me backward against the table.

If this happens, I could be mating him, binding him to me for life.

"Not take you, mate you."

His words come back to me.

It happens in other alien species, and sometimes in animals. My eyes widen. Lifemates? For humans? Is that even possible? Vagan leans his face into the crook of my neck and slides his tongue from my collarbone to my ear.

If I let this happen, there will be consequences. Still, my body shudders with pleasure despite my anxiety ratcheting.

Grasping his cock harder, I drift my gaze from his member, up to his vibrant body, to meet his eyes. Dark, animalistic hunger stares back at me. My lips part.

He's already inside me.

He has been since the beginning.

He's... *my hero.*

"Vagan," I say, beyond fear and straight terrified now.

Saying what I wish I could, my lips seal shut instead. The hunger in his expression grows fiercer as I hesitantly pump his cock. It frightens me even more because the savagery in his expression makes me breathless and needy.

Releasing him, I sit back on the table. His gaze drops to my sex, and embarrassment snags my courage. I start to close my legs, but his hips lodge between them.

"Don't make me beg." Beg for him? Beg to stop? Beg for more? If I beg, I don't know what I'd be begging for.

Vagan clasps my waist with his hands as he nudges his tip to my opening. His seed immediately splashes my insides. Shuddering, it drenches me, making me hotter, as he jerks away. I press my knees into his sides, stopping him.

He hisses, slides back and then forward.

Vagan lines his large tip to me again and pushes in. Flinching from the sharp sting of penetration, I clench around his tapered head. "You're big," I barely muster the words. *And strange,* I think, staring at the sapphire and indigo blues of his very alien prick.

"Mate," he hums that word again, holding his body prone.

I start to shake.

He presses further into me.

My head drops back as a cry tears from my throat.

"My little female is... sssmaller than me," he says. "Yet her body givesss."

My legs strain against him. The sting intensifies, and Vagan leans over and licks my neck, my ear. The swipe of his tongue relaxes me, and the sting cools. Pleasure swirls and builds.

"Ssssweet mate, I will open you and take your madnessss away. *Yesss.* I will open you up like the rare gift you are," he rumbles, nuzzling my throat. "I *am* worthy."

His words flit and float in my head without solidifying. Nothing about what's happening between us is solidifying.

Falling back, I land on the slightly cushioned hardness of his tail.

His tailtip coils over my shoulder and slides down the front of my body. He sinks deeper into me, stretching me even further.

I gasp. "Slower."

Rough fingers fall on my clit, and they begin to play with it, pressing it hard like a button. My hips jump into the air, and Vagan's cock slips out.

He lets out a growl and grabs my hips, pinning them roughly to the table. And then he presses into me again, this time thrusting all the way to his knot. Crying out, I constrict around him, trying to push him out. "Ssstop moving," he orders. "Or I will spill all over your outer flesh again. I do not want any more of my seed to go to waste."

Waste...

Waste?

Vagan rolls his hips, and the word floats away with the others. He pushes, pressing his bulge to my opening. My hips shudder against the hard wall of a male trying to conquer me. Sweat beads on my brow, and his tongue strikes out to lick it away. He pushes a little more, his movements roughening.

I try to relax. There's no pain anymore, only pressure. Pressure that clears my mind, but only a little, because it means I'm not empty anymore. Encouraged, my body settles against the table as I close my eyes and let the sensations take over.

If this is going to happen, it'll be easier if I'm a willing participant.

"Yesss," he encourages, sliding partially out of me.

He thrusts forward and forces his large knot in.

A shocked scream tears from my throat. Kicking my legs out, Vagan traps me to the table. My inner muscles go to work, trying to force him out. He stops, fully seated, holding me down. Squirming, my limbs seize up, bracing for the pain, for the strangeness of his alien cock invading me. I push and thrash and writhe, clenching and loosening, trying to adjust to his size. Stars fill my vision as the pressure builds.

And builds.

I stutter his name.

Vagan hisses in my ear as my mind reels. "Sssssshhhhh." His hands run up my body, over my shirt, and then back down. His hissing turns into an even deeper hum. The vibrations make my nerves dance.

My muscles unlock. Now he hums against my ear.

The coolness of his scales seeps the heat from my skin. The pain I feared never comes. The power of his body cages me in on all sides, and all I see is him wherever I look. Blue scales and glimpses of bright orange shields me away from the world.

It makes it easy to forget everything else.

Sucking in another breath as I accommodate his cock, my gaze lands on him hovering above me. His dark eyes pin me, and I gasp as my mind unwillingly shifts to a bad place. A trapped place.

My eyes dart left and right to Vagan's straining arms on either side of me, and it's like we're back beneath the rocks. A trickle of his sweat slides from his brow to the tip of his orange nose.

If it lands on me like it had then...

"Shelby," he grunts, forcing my eyes back on him. The darkness in them is gone, and all that's left is a softness that unnerves me even further. His fingers tangle into my braids as he lowers and brushes his lips to my parted ones. "You are safe with me," he growls.

Like he senses my panic.

I *am* safe. Tears threaten to well in my eyes. *I'm safe with him.*

Right?

We're not about to face our doom.

We're not slowly being crushed. I tighten my legs around him. They're free, and so are we. I press my chest up into his, inhaling his sweet scent before the vents steal it all away, and I bask.

It's like we never left the cave-in.

This is better.

"You are mine," he rasps, saying what he did before, and heat erupts deep inside. "Mine. Mine. *Mine*," he growls thickly. His cock jerks hard, and he shoots off me, arching his back, rising up on his arms. His tongue swipes the air as his hips shudder and twitch. The pressure builds.

His knot grows bigger, spreading me even further, forcing my inner muscles to give way to him.

I buckle.

Bliss returns hot and fast, streaking out to every nerve ending. Trembling, I reach up and pull him down to me, and our limbs lock together. His seed floods me, returning the uncomfortable heat to my body, but his tail undulates, shifting my hips, rubbing his knot directly against my inner spot. Mouth parting in a hurried moan, I press my lips to his chin.

Silently screaming in pleasure, he spills, and my sheath milks his seed.

His tail shunts forward, and my legs strain against his brutal hips.

Vagan hisses my name again and again as he thrusts, and each time he does, there's more pressure, more seed.

Too much seed.

He pulls out hard, and I gasp, clenching wildly. His cum splashes my sex. Pressing my feet back to the table, I lift my hips, begging for him to return. Already my body wants bliss again, wants the pressure of his cock forcing me to accommodate it.

"Again," I cry.

He pushes back inside me.

Lifting on my elbows, I watch him enter me, watch my body accept such a virile male. Sinking his knot inside, I fling my head back with a cry of pleasure.

He pulls out and thrusts back in.

This time, I drop as he grabs my waist and fucks me savagely.

My body shifts up the table, dragged back down, impaled again and again in quick succession. Pressure and relief, he drags his tail off the table and behind him, thumping it roughly. Feeling my sex scorched with pleasure, my moans trill to heightened cries. His nails bite into my skin as he continues to growl my name with each rough slam. Consumed by his scent, I meet him mid-thrust and impale my hips onto him, coming undone.

Vagan catches my legs and hauls me into his embrace, pounding into me as my mind scrambles. Seeing dots across my vision, I clutch him as he ruts a violent orgasm from my body.

It's still not enough. I rock my hips through the bliss.

When he seeds me again, I beg for it, rocking faster.

Slick and wet, he lowers us to the floor, and I straddle his hips, jerking them like an animal gone rabid. I can't get enough. He clutches my hair and tugs it behind my shoulders as I undulate frantically. There's a sharp ache from where I'm wounded, but then it fades.

"Claim me, mate," he orders, and I manage to peer at him through hooded eyes, seeing his tongue slice across his fangs. The wicked sight rattles me. Grabbing his head, I slam my mouth to his. His tongue invades and lashes every corner of my mouth.

When his knot thickens again and I can no longer take its stretch, I drop onto his chest with a scream feeling an even heavier surge of pleasure burst from my body. Nearly clawing at him, suddenly violent from too much sensation, he coils his tail around my back as he presses my face to his throat. I bite down on his neck

And when I think I'm about to lose my mind, satiated exhaustion hits.

I shudder and twitch, shaking on his cock, I close my eyes. Holding me to his chest, he pets my back over my clothes as his tailtip caresses my left foot. He spills once more, trapping his seed inside me.

Time passes as his scent fades and gets sucked up into the vents. Warm and happy, I cuddle his chest, not wanting to move. The heat tormenting me from the inside out begins to cool, and troubling thoughts start to worm their way back into my mind.

I try to push them out... but they stick. Inhaling deeply, they remain even though I can still smell Vagan's pheromones. And with them, embarrassment rushes through me red and hot.

I just...

I just had sex with him.

He's a different species.

I realize that I've just broken so many laws, standards, and morals that my body goes rigid. I did it even knowing there would be consequences. Even after he attacked Daisy. Even knowing we could be attacked at any moment.

Blinking my eyes open, I stiffen further against his chest.

He seems to know something's changed because he stiffens too.

"What's wrong?" he asks.

Flinching, it's the last thing I want to hear him say. I push off his chest and divert my eyes. "Nothing," I say, realizing I'm still wearing my lab coat, shirt, and bra. I never even took off all my clothes...

"Shelby?" Vagan tries to get me to look at him, but all I want to do is stare at the place where I'm naked and straddling his body and all his cum everywhere. *Maybe if I stare hard enough, long enough, I'll vanish.*

"We have to clean up," I mutter quickly, jerking off of him. "We have too—" I gasp when he doesn't slip right out. Pushing at his chest, I try to rise off his cock again. The swollen pressure of it stops me. "Vagan, why aren't you slipping out?" I lean back and look down at where we're joined.

"My knot is filled with seed."

"Still?" I squeak. "Are you serious?"

He growls. "Why wouldn't I be?"

Lifting up harder, I wince when I find I'm trapped. It's like his bulge is enlarging further with each try. "Help me!" I say, grabbing his root, already feeling his pheromones go back to work on me. Not again.

Please not again. Looking around for something to help, I just see an ancient human laboratory, and my heart sinks further remembering where we are.

Vagan groans when I squeeze his base.

"Come again," I say quickly, already clenching.

"Come?" he asks, running his palms up my thighs.

"Spill!"

He hisses and rolls me over. Pinned beneath him, I bite down on my lower lip hard as he pushes back into me. Beyond embarrassment, shame hits me hard despite the eruption of pleasure. His tail pushes under me, over me, coiling me up tight.

Hitching, he slams into me hard. "Vagan!"

Curling my fingers against my mouth, he pounds in shallow, pressurized bursts, spreading me wider than before. Unable to brace from his weight, I push my butt back into him and try to keep my wits.

Despite my best efforts, I can't help but moan each time his knot rubs my inner spot.

Vagan floods my sheath with seed, pushing my hips to the floor from the effort.

Scurrying out from under him, he slips out, and a sigh of relief leaves me. He's still spilling when I tug out of his limbs and move away. He reaches for me, and I grab his hand before he pulls me back beneath him. "Why?" he groans.

Clenching, needy for another round, I press my thighs together. "I'm sorry," I whisper as he continues to spill all over the floor, just as his spill leaks from me. I feel terrible for what I'm doing but also way out of my depth.

I'm not experienced, not really. I've been with men but never like this. Never in a way where all the horror and pain drifts away and I can just be happy.

I can't.

Unconsciously, I raise my fingers to my eyes. My throat tightens as Vagan stares at me like he's trying to understand.

I can't...

Never have two words hurt me so much, and I don't even say them aloud. I part my lips to tell him when something moves in the corner of my eye and I glance away, seeing several leaves shift over the glass outside the window. Glancing back at Vagan, I realize there's no breeze down here.

I look back at the window.

Gooseflesh rises on my arms and legs. "Vagan..." I begin to say and trail off.

The leaves have stopped moving, and I second guess myself. Regardless, the hair on the back of my neck rises.

"What's wrong?" Vagan asks. His tail shifts and coils.

"The leaves..." I murmur, staring at them, too afraid to look away.

They shift again, so slightly it's barely noticeable, and a form appears. The outline of a large, hunkering beast camouflaged within the foliage. My heart stutters to a stop.

"Vagan!" I shriek as the Lurker's red eyes flick and its camouflage falls away. I scramble backward and slip in Vagan's seed. "Behind you!"

EIGHTEEN

THE ELEVATOR

Shelby

My back hits the wall on the far side of the room. Digging into my pocket for the guns, I remember they're still sitting on the desk.

Vagan snaps upright and strikes his tail at the window. The Lurker doesn't even flinch.

Clenching, wet, and covered in seed, I tear my eyes off Vagan to my pants and boots on the ground beside him. Hearing a wild pounding noise coming from the window, my whole body flinches. Running a hand roughly down my face, I rush across the floor to grab my clothes, dodging behind the table to pull them on.

The pounding on the window worsens.

"Can it get in?" I call out, heart racing with fear.

Peeking around the corner, Vagan's still at the window, his back turned to me. The pounding stops, and then there's a long, loud screech. I cover my ears and close my eyes as the Lurker rakes his claws down the glass.

"Get away from there!" I yell when Vagan doesn't move away.

Through it all, his scent continues to invade me, making my nerves zing uncomfortably.

This is what I didn't want to happen.

The pounding starts back up. Rising on my feet, I dash to the desk and grab one of the guns. Straightening, I face Vagan to scream at him again, catching a glimpse at the Lurker on the other side. With a mouth parted open to reveal its sharp teeth, it looks like it's grinning. Deeply set slitted eyes and its reptilian features give way to predatory interest as they shift to me.

My fear skyrockets back.

"Vagan," I say, nervously, taking a step toward him. "Look at me." *Why isn't he responding?*

"He speaks," Vagan mutters. "They've never spoken before."

"They?" I ask, hearing the Lurker scratch the window again.

"The other monsters. They were beasts. Even the ones that look like me..."

"Face me." I reach out and touch his back. "The Lurkers are a completely different species than you. You're not the same."

His body jerks as if coming out of a trance, and he hisses, shooting out his arm to keep me from coming any closer. He turns to face me.

"Ssshelby," he hisses my name, and the confusion in his eyes nearly breaks my heart. "Are you sure about that?"

"You're not a monster—"

The Lurker slams his fists onto the glass, and we both startle back. Vagan's tail coils around me.

"The glass will hold, r-right?" I stutter quickly. "Right?"

"He will break it. He can break it, if he wants to."

"What?" That's not what I wanted to hear.

The banging on the window gets louder.

"If he is that desperate to get through," Vagan mumbles distantly, turning to look at the Lurker again. "I got through."

I shake my head, having no idea what he's talking about. "Through where?"

He doesn't turn to look at me again. I back up a couple of steps and out of his tail. "Vagan," I say, worry filling me, "we need to go then before that happens."

We need to go right now.

The Lurker's grin is back. The glass trembles and the hollow noise reverberating from it reminds me of the blasters of a spaceship just before exhaust shoots out. I wince.

"Zaku's barrier," Vagan finally says.

"This isn't Zaku's barrier! Vagan, snap out of it!" I shriek. "We have to go!"

He turns back to me just as an ear-splitting crack cascades across the room. Focus returns to his gaze, and he flings toward me and away from the window.

Behind him the glass fractures.

The Lurker draws back and slams his shoulder into it. More fractures form.

"Watch out!" I scream, switching the safety off on my gun.

Hands trembling, I aim as the alien pummels the glass again. He throws his body against it, sending web-like fractures through the window. He draws back as I try to hold the gun steady. He crashes through on the next hit and I shoot, praying a bullet lands. Vagan grabs me and rushes to the central doors as I continue to press down on the trigger. The Lurker jerks, and I cry out as it crashes to the ground with an agonized grunt.

It doesn't stay there long.

"The key," Vagan growls, grabbing the lanyard around my throat. It yanks against my skin as the alien rises and stalks toward us. I hear a beep and then Vagan's tail curls around me, shunting me through the opening doors.

The Lurker sprints forward as Vagan slams the doors shut behind us with his tail.

They jerk open before they have a chance to lock. Vagan releases me to brace his body against them. The Lurker roars as it rams into them.

"Run!" Vagan yells as I find my footing.

Throwing the empty gun away, I search for the elevator. "Fuck, fuck, fuck, fuck," I curse, gazing at the thick vines and trees all around us. We're back in the forest, not another laboratory or hallway. The glass tunnel here is completely broken apart. Overgrowth crushes against us from all sides. Seeing red and blue lights through some of the branches, I push through toward them.

The reactor rises up before me, electrical static energy blasting out of it.

Vagan grunts loudly as the Lurker's pounding grows frenetic and vicious.

I hear another crack, and my eyes tear from the reactor. "I don't see the elevators! It's just trees!"

"Hide!" he bellows.

The Lurker breaks through, crashing right through the overgrowth to my left. It spins and sees me as it catches itself. Vagan's tail shoots out and wraps around the Lurker's torso, knocking it down to the forest floor before it can attack. Vagan drags the alien toward him as it tears at the ground, reaching for me.

The Lurker flips over and swipes his long claws at Vagan's tail. Seeing Vagan try and jump atop its back, he bares his fangs and aims for the meaty flesh of the Lurker's shoulder.

It rears up and knocks Vagan off of him.

Vagan's not going to win, not with his wounds. I need to create a distraction.

Gunfire goes off to my right. Covering my ears, Collins strides out of the trees with a rifle in his hands. "This way!" he shouts at me as he aims at Vagan and the Lurker.

My throat tightens seeing him, but as he heads straight for me, my gaze shifts to his gun.

"Don't shoot Vagan," I cry.

"There's an elevator behind the vines to my right," he yells, grabbing my arm and hauling me to my feet. "Go," he orders, indicating the area. He pushes me toward it.

Stumbling forward, I come to a wall. Grasping the vines on it, I shove them aside, searching for the mechanism that the last elevator had. Ripping a clump off, I find a partially destroyed panel with some torn and rusted wires. The walls on either side are streaked with claw marks.

The mechanism is gone.

More gunfire goes off, and I flinch, dropping the vines in my hands.

I wrench my eyes shut, saying a small prayer, and reopen them, turning them on. The blue light flashes out as I scan the panel. And in a few short seconds, my eyes begin feeding me directions to repair the mechanism.

Attach the wires. Grasping the ends of several, I brace to be shocked and begin twisting the ends. Collins shouts and fires another shot. Fingers shaking, I scrape off rust with my nails and hope for a good connection, twisting the final ends together.

"Shelby, fucking hurry!"

The panel sparks, and I hear a humming noise. Seeing the call button flicker, I slam my hand to it.

The elevator doors slide open.

"Now!" I scream.

Collins backs up toward me. He pushes me into the elevator before I can stop him. "We can't leave without Vagan!"

Collins lowers his rifle and grabs my arm. "We have to. That creature won't stop."

Tugging my arm, Collins's hold on it tightens. "Vagan!" I scream, calling for him to come before the elevator closes, as a red light reads my keycard.

The trees shift outside, and Collins hits buttons with his elbow.

"No!"

The doors begin to close.

Collins hauls me against his chest as I try to stop them from shutting.

Vagan appears through the vines, slicing through the closing doors and catching his tail on them. He falls against the wall and the doors start to open. The Lurker sprints forward. Vagan knocks him back before coiling his limbs in the small space. Collins releases me and shoots at the Lurker until the doors shut.

The pounding on the metal booms as the elevator jerks once and lowers. Sliding down the wall, I press my face into my hands.

NINETEEN

THE BREAKUP

Shelby

I LOOK up to find both Vagan and Collins staring at me.

Rough, dirty, and wounded, they look like they've been through hell, and so do I. I'm certain. Vagan has fresh wounds on his upper chest and arm—claw marks from the Lurkers' nails—and Collins's uniform is ripped open, with dirt covering much of his exposed skin and chest. He's no longer wearing a jacket.

Exhausted, my gaze glides over the both of them, taking them in as they do the same to me, and each other. For a long time, we all just stare at each other.

Vagan's tailtip coils behind my back, around my hair, tugging it behind my shoulders.

"Are you hurt?" he asks, breaking the silence first.

"No, but it looks like you are again," I say sadly.

He touches his arm. "Yesss."

I turn to look at Collins, and he's studying Vagan. "You're alive," I whisper, pulling up to my feet.

The elevator comes to a stop, and we all face the doors as they open. Collins raises his gun. I shift my feet, ready to run.

But nothing is waiting to kill us and we collectively sag with relief.

Collins's gaze shoots to mine, and he steps between the elevator doors before they close. Behind him is a long, dimly lit hallway with white walls. It's empty except for some piping along the ceiling and some floating dust motes.

"No thanks to him," Collins snaps, cocking his head at Vagan, finally responding to me. "If I hadn't shot him, I would be dead."

Glancing at Vagan, I see the truth of Collins's words in Vagan's furious expression. My heart twists.

"Looks like you lived having three bullets lodged in your gut," Collins continues, scowling at him. "What a fucking waste of ammo."

Vagan's lips twist, revealing dripping fangs.

My whole body jerks in reaction. "Stop!" I yell. "For all our sakes, both of you just stop! That Lurker is still alive, and we barely got away from it. We need to work together or we're never getting out of here alive, understand? Just stop."

Glaring at Collins, I tell him straight. "I know you don't trust Vagan, but I do. I know he attacked you, and if he does it again, I'll kill him myself," I threaten both of them, pinning Collins with my gaze. "You are not my father, my brother, or even a contracted partner anymore, I don't need you to protect me from him. I can do that myself because there are bigger things to worry about. And Vagan," I say, facing him, "Collins is my closest friend. He's not out to steal me away so you need to calm down, because—" I run my fingers through my hair "—I can't have you hurting each other because of me." There. I said it. "I can't. We just barely survived..."

Tears want to well and fall, but I don't let them.

I have never had boy trouble before. Never. And thank god for that because it's exhausting and it has nothing to do with the alien hunting us.

"So that's how it is," Collins growls.

"Yes," I grate, "that's how it is."

Collins takes a step toward me, and Vagan strikes his tail between us. Collins and I both jump in reaction.

"Stop!" I scream, pushing Vagan's tail aside. "Both of you. I am not a thing to be owned by either of you!"

"That's not how I see it, Shelby. His kind wants to *own* you. I saw how they wanted Gemma and Daisy, how they looked at them. I put three fucking bullet holes in his stomach, and you're still with him?

How does that make me feel?" Collins scowls. "Why do you both smell like sex?"

I flinch. "He saved my life." He's saved my life more times than I can count.

"Fucking hell! Did you have sex with him?" Collins yells.

"It's not what you think—"

"Holy hell, you did! And right after he tried to murder me, am I correct? Forgive and forget? Or is it fuck and forget?"

My guilt returns hot and fast. The proof is there for all to see soaking my upper pants. I never had a chance to clean up. I never had a chance to process. My thoughts are still addled. I glance at Vagan, feeling sick. "He told me you were alive," I say softly, answering Collins. "I—"

Collins balks and throws his hands up into the air. "Barely. I almost wasn't. Was it fucking good at least? Did he blow your mind?"

My face wrenches, and I turn away.

"You're upsetting her," Vagan rumbles, his tone full of warning. "Back away, human."

"Good! She should be upset—I'm fucking upset! I wake up alone, thinking my windpipe might be crushed, to an open and empty elevator covered in blood. Shelby's blood! I don't just stumble upon an underground fucking jungle but a goddamned Lurkawathian wanting to tear me limb from limb! Thank fuck the guard left me a rifle because you'd both be dead without me. That fucking thing hunted me relentlessly, and he almost had me until he went quiet. Then I heard you two... And I had thought you both fucking dead!" Collins runs his fingers through his hair. "The forest is not that fucking big!"

"I'm so sorry," I whisper. "I didn't know. We escaped into the hallways."

Collins's eyes fall on me, and his voice lowers. "I thought you were dead. I thought that blood was yours and *he'd* hurt you—" he says, indicating Vagan "—and that I had been right. I was going to kill him for taking you from me, for almost killing me, and for being a fucking snake, but I see now that's not what happened at all." Collins reaches for me but drops his hand. "Because then the doors opened and a fucking Lurkawathian attacked. Fuck!" he bellows, turning and storming out of the elevator. "And you had sex. Sex!"

"Collins—" I call after him.

He spins and comes back. "What? You want to tell me to *stop* again? You're alive, and I can't deal with this right now." He points at Vagan and me. "If it's because of him, fine, that's great. Kudos to you, alien fucker. But you mean more to me than you want to accept, Shelby. You may have written me off, but I haven't written you off. You're my fucking girl, and I'm not going to quit until you realize that." Collins storms away. "And now I'm going to take a fucking walk before I kill this motherfucker."

I stare after him until he turns a corner. He's furious. I've never seen him lose his head like this. I should've known he wouldn't stay put, should've known he'd come after me.

His girl?

My heart sinks into my stomach.

He wants to be with me. I suspected as much when he took our lie about being pregnant seriously. I just hoped it was a crush, nothing more. Guilt slams into me anyway. *I knew it was more... I just didn't want to acknowledge it.*

I never set him straight when he was protecting me from Peter, from the nagas.

My chest constricts.

"I was going to kill him."

Closing my eyes for a moment, I inhale, and look at Vagan. "Because I'm yours?" I ask softly. Heat swirls inside me when I say the words and so does another wave of tremendous guilt. Only the guilt fades some.

I'll have to figure out how to set Collins straight, without anyone getting killed.

Vagan cups my cheek. "He kissed you."

"You were willing to break our promise because... he kissed me?"

His eyes darken. "Yesss."

I pull away. What am I supposed to say to that?

"It's not good to kill people over a kiss," I say. "Promise me you won't try and kill him again? I need you to *promise* me."

"I will not make another promise I might not be able to keep."

Sighing deeply, a bone-tiredness floods me, and I face him head-on. "Thank you for your honesty, but I can't accept that. I've known Collins since I was a child, he's my friend, the closest person I have to family. You don't know him like I do. He's suffered so much. I can't let you hurt him, Vagan. Because when you do, you're hurting me."

I search his eyes, praying he understands. Trying to swallow, my throat tightens instead. How do I get through to something that isn't human?

"I will never hurt you."

"Then you have to keep your promise, otherwise..." What am I supposed to say? Otherwise we can't see each other again? We can't be friends? We can't associate? We can't work together to survive? I break eye contact with him. Otherwise, *what?* We can't be together?

Is that even possible? The heat that wants to make an annoying return between my legs builds.

We might both be dead this time tomorrow.

Vagan grabs my arms and forces me to face him. I don't have the strength to stop him.

"I promise I will never hurt you," he says.

"Then don't hurt Collins. Why is that so hard to understand?"

He releases my arms with a growl, striking his tail against the opposite wall. I flinch.

"He just saved our lives," I say.

"He is a male who seeks to mate you!" His hands clench, and fresh blood trickles out from his wounds. "He wants you. How can you ask me to go against my instincts? I am the only one worthy of you. Not some small human who can't even keep you safe. If you had been on the plateau, you would be mine right now, unharmed and sssafe within my nest. He kept you from me and seeksss to keep you from me. I will not remake such a promise!"

"You're forgetting something," I snap at him. "I haven't chosen to be with you one way or another. I am not your mate. Why not seek out a female of your kind?" I bite out because, in the back of my head, I need to know why *me*. Why not go after someone available? One of his kind? "Why me, Vagan? Why not go after someone you don't have to make a promise to if it's so much trouble?"

His hissing deepens. "I can't."

"Can't?"

"They left many years ago."

Great. That's a lot to unpack. I have too many bags as-is.

"So I'm a consolation prize? Just a woman who happens to be in the right place at the right time? Or is it the wrong place at the wrong time? Is that it?" Feeling hurt and lied to, my chest swells with emotion. "You want me because there's no other option? Great. Good to know." His wet seed on my skin and pants is beginning to make me feel like a grade-A slut. A slut who's been manipulated and taken advantage of.

"You are the only one left," he says.

The building heat inside me, the way I reacted to Vagan, thinking there was something special between us, our stolen moments, kisses, all we've been through together in the last few days, and how we... I shake my head, rubbing the chill from my arms. Nausea churns my belly and with it, shame. *How I reacted to his smell...*

Vagan doesn't want *me*. He wants a female, any female.

Because there are no other options, the only two were Daisy and Gemma, and one of them is lost, the other dead.

I'm all that's left, apparently.

Finding it hard to be in Vagan's presence, I move away and into the hallway. Because it hurts. It hurts a lot more than it should, and I don't want him to see it. I don't want to be vulnerable in front of him. Not like this.

I don't let my hormones or emotions get the better of me. And no amount of magic alien pheromones should have changed that. *I'm stronger than that.* At least... I thought I was.

"Ssshelby," Vagan hisses my name, sliding his tail after me.

"Don't." I keep walking. Collins has the right idea. "I need to be alone for a bit. Don't follow me. *I* may kill you if you do."

Vagan grabs my arm before I make it another step. He twists me to face him.

"You are the only one I want," he says, leveling his dark eyes with mine.

His words make me flinch.

Swallowing thickly, flutters dance in my stomach despite finally knowing the truth.

I'm a consolation prize.

"But am I? Really?" I say, hating the vulnerability I'm showing.

His eyes bore into me anyway, and I can't look away, caught up in their intensity. He could trap me here forever with his abysmal gaze. There's loneliness and something else in them...honesty maybe? Perhaps it's all just wishful thinking on my part.

Breathing in, I risk inhaling more of his scent but do it anyway. His aroma floods me, and I feel my eyes dilate, my sex clench unwillingly, already begging to be filled. His hand on my arm burns as my awareness of him grows. Of the sex we had, of his seed drying on my legs, and how badly I want to do it all over again despite the Lurker, Collins, and the lies.

Male. Strong. Dependable…

Hard to kill.

Attractive.

My body sends these signals straight to my core. I take another deep breath. This time through my mouth and not my nose.

And I take another.

I start to lean into him and stop before I do, needing to prove that I can withstand his allure. I also need to prove that not everything we've been through was simply chemical manipulation. It doesn't take a mastermind to understand my reaction to him, pheromones at work or not. I've felt connected to Vagan since I woke up underneath him, and his scent wasn't nearly as strong then. It was there, I realize, but I wasn't affected.

I wasn't affected until we were in the lab… when we were alone and relatively safe.

Taking another deep breath through my mouth, the heat erupting inside me eases.

Everything that happened between us before this was real. I sag when my shame and the heat dissipate. *He didn't need to dive into the pit and save me. He did it anyway.*

Exhaustion hits, and I pull away from Vagan. I don't know what to think or do anymore.

"I'm going to find somewhere I can clean up," I say, dodging, pulling my arm out of his grip. "And maybe look for something to eat." *And process. And get my head on straight. And try not to cry.* "You should get some rest too. Your wounds will heal faster if you sleep," I tell him numbly, turning around and walking away.

I stop and glance over my shoulder at him. "I'll be careful. If I think something's wrong, I'll yell, and I won't go far, and Vagan," I add, "I mean it. Don't follow me. Your scent is too powerful. I need to think clearly. If you… if you mean what you say, you'll give me space."

This time, he doesn't stop me when I walk away.

And I've proven that I can withstand his biology.

TWENTY

VILLAINOUS

Vagan

I WATCH SHELBY LEAVE, the plea in her voice hurting my heart.

Now that I know what it's like to be inside her, what it's like to taste her, explore her, and be the one she grabs onto when she loses her mind, when she's at her most vulnerable, letting her walk away takes a terrible toll.

I wanted to bleed the Lurker dry for scaring her and taking her away from my arms, but then I remember she was already trying to get away from me before the creature attacked.

Was it something I had done? Had I hurt her? She is upset that I lied to her, though I didn't, not really. I did not kill Collins in the end. I could have, but I didn't.

I am trying to keep my word and prove to her that I am not an evil naga like so many others... My hands clench and my claws dig into my palms.

She turns a corner and heads in the opposite direction of Collins. My tail loosens, and I coil it under me, having been ready to stop her if she'd gone the other way. Despite what she's said, I do not want her with him, and especially not alone. She may not want to be his mate, but he is of a different mind. He doesn't care about her wishes.

Doesn't she see that?

Collins isn't stronger than me, though he is stronger than her. He could steal her away as I had planned to do from the very beginning. If he found a way to get out of this hole and he takes Shelby with him, he could bury me here and win. I can't let that happen. She does not want him. She said as much.

She does not want him. A growl tears from my throat.

Because stealing her away is what I hoped to do.

Perhaps I am...*evil.*

If not kill Collins, trap him in a place where he can't follow. If I can get away with it, the option to do as much still holds merit. Collins is thinking the same in regards to me. I do not like human males, and him least of all. We both saved Shelby from being crushed, except it was me who was willing to give up my life for her.

She will forgive me if she doesn't think I trapped Collins on purpose... She never has to know.

Shelby will forgive him for the same. Another growl releases from me, realizing the truth of that thought. She is bonded to the human male in a way I do not understand, especially for not wanting to mate with him.

Like how Eestys and I bonded.

Stilling, I don't know why she comes to mind.

Eestys came to me first as a mother, then as a friend, and almost a mate if I had it my way. Except I did not want Eestys, not like how I want Shelby. I thought I did, but I would have gone after Eestys if I had. I would have tracked her to the ends of this land if I wanted her nearly as much as Shelby.

Why?

Shelby asked me why...

My eyes drop to my straining slit—barely holding my member—at the groin of my tail. I have spilled and spilled again inside her, and all I want to do is continue spilling.

Why?

With Eestys, it seemed like the natural next step for us. She had long since stopped taking care of me, and the maternal aspect of our relationship had been so far in the past, it never occurred to me that there was something wrong with the way I felt toward her. She was a female, and I, a male. She was alone, unmated, unnested, and unprotected.

But Eestys never really needed protection. She was from the Boom-slang clan and could vanish within the forest as easily as if she were part of it. As a sea snake, there was no way I could catch her.

She was my secret, one of the last females in the land. By the time I was a proud, fully grown male, one who had snuck up and listened to the other nagas as they sought water to drink, I knew I was her only branch to the others. She would visit me, share her treasures, her food, her information, and I, in return, did the same.

Except I never reacted to her as I have with Shelby. My body never turned against me. I looked forward to Eestys's visits even though she never joined me in the water, and I rarely ventured into the forest back then.

She did teach me that knowledge was power and the technology on land held the most knowledge. That I needed the technology to survive. She taught me how to be a good, clever male, and for that, I was loyal to her and no one else.

Still, my body never reacted to her.

The other nagas who sought mates, despite knowing that mating them would kill them, would come to my nest because there was a rumor of a female living near me.

I killed many, many males back then. Eestys's existence was my secret. Mine.

I stole knowledge from these young seekers. I stole their weapons, their tech, and whatever they had on them, what others had to scavenge for. I grew excited when another male would seek me out and spill their secrets in hopes I would spill mine, knowing that at the end, if they truly sought Eestys, we would fight each other until one of us were dead.

A Blue Coral male does not share.

And Eestys? She hated that males would come to me as much as she needed them to. Even if she hated that I killed them even more. I was her first defense, and she used me as much as I used her.

She begged me to be merciful.

But I never wanted her. Not really. I never even knew where her nest was. She had never taken me to it, nor offered to show me where I could find her.

Brows furrowing, I realize now...

She didn't trust me.

When I tried to lure her to be mine, it wasn't out of lust or friend-ship, it was for power. There was no tension, no rabid need to spill, no scent coming off my body. It was only about keeping the upper hand in our relationship. If she was in my nest, she wasn't in another's. She would be safe with me, and we would be mates in every way except the way that would kill her.

Mating Eestys, putting my litter in her womb, was never what I wanted. The thought alone always brought up memories of my mother's corpse and the wails of my litter mates.

Shelby doesn't bring up those horrible memories. When I see her, think of her, there's hope in my chest that my future will be more than just surviving.

That there's a future at all.

Shelby trusts me. Cursing under my breath, I know I'll lose her trust if I hurt Collins. She'll never willingly join me in my den—my nest—if I do. She may not want to mate him, but she could always choose another naga to mate with, one she *could* trust.

I will have to take her against her will or let her go.

Tracing my fingers around the Lurker's claw marks, I realize I haven't heard Shelby's footsteps for a time.

Hissing, I go after her. Damn her wants.

Something is wrong, really wrong, I scowl, hating the pressure in my groin as much as I need to find her, mount her, and rut her all over again. In the vicious way my body needs. Claiming her was not what I was expecting, and it's shaken me. She is too; I can sense it. It has nothing to do with Collins.

She did not want to mate, and then she begged for it. She says it's my scent.

Is she still afraid of me? Even when I tried to soothe her, help her?

There is something about this place that I do not like. The monster is still alive. A monster who has shown intelligence and has spoken.

A creature with a forked tongue, sharp claws, and a tail like me. When I looked at the beast on the other side of the window, it was me I was looking at. I saw myself outside Zaku's, banging on his glass, out of my mind with desperation and lust.

We were the same. The monster and I.

Scowling harder, I turn the corner and glimpse Shelby staring at something. She glances up at me, her chest rising and falling rapidly, and then she looks away, slides the card against something on the wall and yanks open a door.

"Ssshelby," I hiss in warning.

She steps through, shutting the door in my face just as I get to her. Slamming my fist against it, a loud thump echoes down the hallway. Maybe I am nothing more than a beast as well. My scales rise. I try the door handle, but it's locked.

What if she isn't safe?

Beside me is a series of windows looking into rooms. Hissing, I shift to the one beside the door and search for her within. The room appears a lot like the one we just escaped from, with machines and tables throughout. But there's also giant glass tubes, and a haziness that makes me think the inside is cold. There are things in several of the tubes that I can't make out. They're suspended in murky water.

My throat constricts and I swallow, envious of their water.

I see Shelby staring at me through the other side and I raise my fist to hit the window when I stop midway. Dropping my fist, we stare at each other. She curls her arms over her middle and then looks away.

Don't.

She glances at me and then walks deeper into the room. I pound my fists on the glass, and she jumps. Watching her scurry further into the space, I draw back, furious that I may have frightened her.

How else am I supposed to act right after claiming my female? She should be resting in my nest... I twist away with a frustrated grunt because I'm losing my head again.

She's right. I need to rest. Water. Sleep.

I also need to rut and claim and conquer. And make these thoughts and furious instincts go away.

But not until I make certain she is safe.

I go back the way I came. The hallways are not much different from those we've been in prior. Besides the windows allowing me to view into many of the rooms, they're the same except that each door requires a key to enter.

It's quiet except for a faint hum.

Rounding another corner, I find another long hallway with viewing windows. Flickering half-dead lights glint the glass. Seeing several doors open ahead, I move to them, and the humming grows louder.

Expecting another room like the others, I come to a large room with rows upon rows of aisles facing a central hub of machines and old human items. There's a large empty cage in the middle with metal bars, a long slat table, and orbs scattered and broken on the floor. In the middle kneels Collins, hovering over a flashing orb.

I bare my fangs, drawing forth my venom, and stalk forward.

Collins doesn't look up. He's not even aware that I'm behind him.

The orb says something I can't hear, and I quiet my movements even more, stalking forward. Readying to strike Collins and be done with him, I start to make out the orb's words.

'*Specimen A106 of section 4, reptilian class testing 36 has been sedated. She will be given Genesis 8.*'

There's a pause.

'*Specimen A106 is now being given Genesis 8. If she responds favorably, she will expand in form and begin developing sexual organs compatible with a Lurkawathian. If she does not, she will die.*'

There's another pause. Something shimmers on the floor in front of Collins, and I see a small screen. It's showing an image of the center of this room. A man in a white coat, like the one Shelby is wearing, is sticking a long, thin needle into a small creature.

A snake-like creature. Long and thin, it has no distinct pattern or coloring. Its only feature is that it's brown.

'*Specimen A106 has now been given Genesis 8. She is already reacting favorably.*'

The man draws the needle away.

Nothing happens at first, and I lose my interest, but then the creature twitches, drawing my attention back to it. Starting with its tailtip, the shiver goes from one end and toward the other. The whole body convulses when parts of its flesh branch out. Its hide stretches, causing it to shudder. There's a crack, and its tail shoots outward.

It wakes up with a shrieking hiss, and the voice in the background curses. The last thing I see is a rock smashing the creature's head. I flick out my tongue in disgust. The screen flickers and there's another different creature in the same place the other was.

A new specimen.

A naga. A female naga.

THE TRUTH

Vagan

SHE'S TINY, *barely larger than the male's arm. Female nagas aren't small...*

And it's not a youngling. It looks like an adult female with appropriately proportionate appendages.

Confused and unnerved by what's playing out on the screen, my lips lower over my fangs. Not once, in all the years, have I seen another one of my kind as they were in the past. The forest is filled with human relics, not naga's.

I don't even know why we're called nagas. It was a term Eestys taught me.

Collins shifts on his knees and I hear the breath woosh out of him.

'Specimen A208 of section 6, reptilian class testing 81 is now being given Genesis 8. This specimen has been shown to respond to Lurkawathians and to humans. If she reacts favorably, she will grow larger, more intelligent, and her genome will potentially branch both species. She will be able to copulate with both. Being as she still is partially a reptile, some intellect is needed to communicate with her. Unfortunately, this will be our final test, as she is the last of her litter.'

The male sticks her with a needle. She twitches slightly, and then her skin lifts and bubbles like the prior creature's. Cracking fills my ears as her bones push out, stretching her flesh, and she begins to grow. When she's about double her original size, she wakes up screeching, her head enlarging far quicker than her body. The screen blinks off right as her eyes bulge.

I jerk to save the female but then remember she's not here. I look around the stage, feeling my heart pound wildly, she was *here* at one point. A long, long time ago.

Collins curses, wiping his mouth, and I nearly draw away from him when a new image appears from the orb.

This time, it's a partially naked human male.

There are machines and screens all around him. He's strapped down to the table, and his head is in some type of vice.

'As you have all been made aware, we have moved on from female specimens due to their inability to survive gestation after copulating with a Lurkawathian. On the other hand, the males we have created from our combined genomes can breed with both species without dying because they do not carry young. Through many trials, we have eliminated the failures. We have discovered we share strands of DNA with the Lurkawathians, but we have remained incompatible. Today, we will conduct our first test on a fully-grown, healthy human male given Genesis 8. Officer Patrick has been kind enough to take the first dose.'

The male on the tables eyes are closed. He's either sleeping or unconscious. The other 'speaking human' walks around him, indicating that the male is this Patrick human.

'And what about the hybrid females you've created?' someone offscreen asks. *'From the cross litters of human, reptile, and Lurkawathian DNA?'*

The male in charge smiles. *'We are still working with them to bridge the gap in interspecies sexual relations. They take Genesis 8 better than the males, are more submissive, and less likely to strike out. These are qualities we want for our hybrids as they make them easier to control.'*

'Does that mean the males you've bred are not like this?'

The human in the coat hesitates. *'Not... exactly. The hybrid males tend to show other... qualities. They are strong, efficient, and predatory, with a keen intellect melded to a ruthless animal cunning. After receiving Genesis 8, they grow rapidly in size but tend to veer toward their more—how should I say it?—animalistic and alien attributes. They are possessive of the females in their litters, produce venom based on the* species of snake used, and are hard to control. Their bodies react to Lurkawathian technology, but they are not stable enough to use it.'

'So what you're saying is that your research has been a failure thus far?'

'A failure? Not quite. Yes, our hybrids are small, and Genesis 8 isn't working how we hoped it would with regards to size while still keeping their bodies and minds intact. But that is with created litters from our lab. These smaller hybrids are still able to use Lurkawathian tech. We have successfully spliced our DNA with a Lurkawathian using reptiles, but we are still not yet able to crossbreed with them. We are unable to usurp their traits, and in turn their technology, and make them our own.'

The male's eyes flare.

'What we do today will change this. For the last two decades, we have been infiltrated, taken over, and been made painfully aware of our short-comings when it comes to strength, intelligence, and endurance as a species. After today, that will be no more. Now that we are ready for our first human trial, I am certain all of you will agree with me. After today, Officer Patrick will be the first human to be able to use Lurkawathian technology, and he will pass on these traits naturally.'

'And the creation of a subspecies from our two species will accomplish this?' someone says dryly. Others snicker. My tail coils under me. 'Seems morally suspect just for being able to use their technology.'

'Not a subspecies, an intermediary. A chimera,' the male on the screen snaps. 'A temporary one—humanity's bridge to the stars. True moral failure is letting an alien lifeform take over our planet, our technology, our way of life, without giving more than the meanest glimpse of the secrets they hold. They keep their knowledge from us, dangling it over our head like scraps of meat before a slavering hound, supreme in their arrogance as our perceived masters. We are physically unable to use their weapons or machines. What's to stop them from conquering us tomorrow? Next month? Next year? What if we go to war? Genesis 8 will eliminate this obstacle.'

'You're expecting there will be a war?'

'Only a fool plans for everlasting peace.'

The room goes quiet as the dominant male moves to the unconscious one's side and prepares a syringe. 'As you are all aware, we can't breed with them, despite what we've accomplished, but with Genesis 8, given to an adult human, and not a spliced hybrid, we can impregnate a female of our own kind using a male who has been... amplified with *aggressive alien DNA. The resulting children will be human in aspect, but in reality a perfect hybrid born from the womb. They will have the qualities of both species, will be able to breed with both—'*

'Don't get ahead of yourself, Moseley.'

Moseley's hand clenches at his side but he continues. *'We shall not only create a generation of hybrid humans with enhanced physical and mental attributes, but these humans will be able to naturally synthesize Genesis 8 themselves and pass it on. But most importantly—and why we're all here today—we will be able to interact with and use alien Lurkawathian technology. Do not lose sight of what we stand to gain.'*

'What if today's trial is a failure and Officer Patrick doesn't survive the transformation? Do you have a woman on staff, or a womb to inject his semen into? It would be a shame to waste the dose.'

Moseley's smile returns. *'He won't, and we do.'*

'And who, may I ask, volunteered to be the candidate? Officer Patrick's wife?'

'Her name is classified. Any other questions before we start?'

A pregnant silence falls, Moseley and several other humans surround the male on the table and double-check his straps. Lights flash from the machines, and the unconscious male is tilted upward. Someone places a strap between his slack lips. When they're done, the people move away until it's only the original male, Moseley, and the unconscious one left.

'If Officer Patrick reacts favorably, he will grow slightly in size, develop temporary flu-like symptoms during the transition period, and has the potential to develop some attributes of a Lurkawathian. Namely, rapid regeneration, higher intellect, and strength. Administering Genesis 8 now.'

Riveted, I watch the screen as a large needle is stuck into the man's arm and its venom is injected straight into him without a fight.

Nothing happens at first, and my gaze trails to Collins, who's still crouched in front of me. He's just as curious as I am about what's happening.

Because it couldn't be real, right?

The strain in my limbs says otherwise. Fingers trembling, my hands shake at my sides. Most of what is said I do not understand, but I understand one thing...

That was a female naga on the screen. And a human male bashed her head in.

'*What's happening?*' a voice breaks the silence.

My eyes fall back onto the screen.

The reclined male's body jerks upright, straining against his bands. His skin turns a pasty white as all the color bleeds from his flesh. His body jerks once again, settling back onto the table, only to jump and strain against the bands once more. The dark trails of his veins show in stark relief against his pallid skin.

'*It's okay, everyone.*' I hear Moseley's voice. '*The serum is spreading through his system.*'

But the body continues to jerk, spasming more and more fiercely. The orb is quiet except for the unconscious groans coming from the male. He's under a spotlight, making every detail of his reaction easy to see. He goes still again, falling upon the table as if to signify the end.

A strange tension rips through me, relieved for the male.

And then his eyes snap open, black and beady and far too familiar.

'*Shit! Chrisy, pull the kill switch. Now! Get the tranquilizers.*'

The male screams, breaking free of his bonds, tearing at his chest. He claws the skin right off, digging at it like he's trying to free something. His skin quivers throughout like lapping waves over his joints, only to stop and stretch over them as they pop out. I hear cracking, and something snaps, making the male groan louder.

He fights at his bonds as people surround him.

Suddenly, they are all thrown back as an agonizing scream tears through the orb. Legs bent at an odd angle, arms twisted at his sides, his skin shreds.

There's yelling, pandemonium in the background as the more courageous of the humans grab and hold the male down. Their hands come away with bloody strips of skin.

Beneath are wet, newly formed leathery scales pushing out, stabbing through whatever hasn't fallen off. Rippling muscles can be seen forming.

'*Shoot him! Shoot him now!*'

Moseley rushes forward. '*No! It's working. Don't kill him!*'

The male breaks free of his bonds and attacks the closest human, throwing them across the room. Blood and bits of bone rain from the male's face, and it takes me a moment to recognize the flecks as human teeth.

Sharp incisors emerge in their place.

The male turns on Moseley just as his fingers expand and rigidify to form claws.

'Calm down, Officer Patrick, this will pass—'

The screen flickers and the image vanishes. Staring down at a dusty floor, I wait for the screen to come back on.

It doesn't.

"What the fuck?" Collins says, also still staring where the holographic screen was. He lifts his hand and palms his mouth.

Still unsure what I just witnessed, alarmed by the image of a helpless female being murdered, I grip the back of his neck and squeeze. Collins tenses and drops his hand from his mouth.

"So, we're back to this?" he murmurs, holding still. "Are you going to break my neck, or are we going to face each other, man to man?"

"I am not a man."

"No. You're just some test tube baby that crawled back out of the haz waste bin. A failed experiment."

"I am a naga, not an experiment," I growl. I was born here next to the water. How can I forget?

"That's not what it fucking looked like to me."

I throw him to the side, bringing forth my venom. He catches his body and rolls onto his feet. Facing me, spreading his feet, he braces for me to tackle him.

"Man to man it is!"

Striking my tail at his legs, he dodges, jumping over it. When I swing my tail back, I knock him off his feet. Collins lands on his back with a grunt. Moving to his side, I lean over him, letting the venom leaking from my fangs drip onto his face.

"You can't win againssst me," I taunt. "Why even try?"

He wipes my venom off. "A soldier doesn't give up, ever. Especially if what he's fighting for is important."

"She will never be yours. I will not relinquish her."

"You keep telling yourself that," he sneers. "She's only interested in you because you're a means to an end."

Fury fills me at his words, but they give me pause. "Means to an end?"

Collins laughs, and my scales rise. "Once we're out of here, she's going right back to *The Dreadnaut* with *me,* with the rest of the team she came here with, with *her* people. People she knows and cares for. She'll get a promotion, a hell of a lot of money, and fame. She'll be a universal expert, consulting with every branch of the military and sought after by every corporation from here to Colony 42. People will write books about her. She'll go down in history as the woman who fought a Lurker and lived. She won't have time for you.

"She'll be too busy traveling the universe, meeting with important people, and trying her damnedest to help humanity have a brighter future. Do you think she'll really stay here? On this dead planet? Giving up her work? For you? No room to spare on a spaceship for a pet snake. Shelby is mine. She has been the moment I laid eyes on her. I've protected her since then. Some alien isn't going to come between us."

I frown.

Collins lifts on his elbows and laughs again. "You did. You really think that! Do you even know why she's here?"

He doesn't give me time to respond.

But then again, I have no response, feeling something malicious creep into my mind.

Paranoia.

"She's here to help locate and study Lurkawathian technology. Advanced technology beyond our imagining, technology that could change the tide of the war. Well, we fucking found it, or the next best thing to it, *alien.* You. You and all of this and Genesis 8."

Collins cocks his head at the room and the dusty machines around him. "This place is the find of a century. Even if she did feel something for you, she'll never be able to stay. She needs to prove her worth, having a mother as a breeder, needs to make a difference. She's not doing that fucking a snake. She's already sacrificed too much. Are you going to follow her into space, across the universe? If you hate me, you have no idea what you're in for. Humans are not kind. We're at war. Are you willing to go to war for her?"

As he speaks, Collins stands, holding still as I coil my tail around his neck, completely unafraid.

When he is done, he huffs and grabs my limb, yanking it off. He wipes his uniform afterward like he's trying to get me off of him. The churning in my soul expands, taking over every corner of my mind.

I can see it; I even hear the truth in Collins's voice.

The image of the tiny female naga brings dread to join in with my paranoia. Trying to push it away, it comes flooding right back.

Inhaling, Shelby's scent fills my nostrils, little tendrils of it that still cling to me from when we mated. The paranoia fades away.

I am worthy of her.

I can be.

I am. A puny human male I do not trust will change this. He is jealous.

"The best thing you can do for her now is to let her go. You can't survive in our world, snake. You wouldn't last a day. Ask her yourself if you don't want to believe me—she'll tell you the fucking truth."

"And you can't sssurvive in mine," I hiss, pinning him with my eyes. I coil my tail back, preparing to strike him down one final time. "I would rather go to war."

TWENTY-TWO

COMING TOGETHER, COMING UNDONE

Shelby

I WAIT for Vagan to leave, busying my hands at the computer within the cold space. Doing anything to stop from looking up and at him.

I barely even acknowledge the screen when it lights up my face. But seeing movement at the corner of my vision, I rush to the window when he slips away. I count to one hundred and open the door to peer out.

And sag—inhaling a deep breath of pheromone-clear air—when I find the hallway empty.

"Running diagnostics," a robotic voice sounds, startling me.

Peering back, machines hum to life around the room. There are large tubes along the walls with creatures inside them. I take a step toward one, studying it.

And quickly realize what it is I'm looking at. Waterlogged, partially decayed reptilian creatures that I can barely make out through the sickening murk of the liquid they're floating in.

Snakes, bent claws, webbed feet, and flimsy scales. Animals from the old Earth who met sad ends, forgotten in their tubes to perish.

Creatures that remind me of the Lurker we just escaped.

Heading to the computer, I turn on my eyes, praying for an answer to all of this. I might die down here, and if I do, I want to at least have some answers. I've been searching for answers my whole life.

A file catches my eye, making me stop. Leaning forward, I read it a dozen times over to make sure what I'm seeing is real.

Naga.

The simple word, right there. The name of Vagan's people—species. In front of me, for no reason at all. It's not a file about the Lurkers, or their technology, it's about Vagan. Vagan and his kind.

Brow furrowing, I'm missing something. Something important.

Naga.

I click on the file and it remains locked. Encrypted.

Damn it.

I trigger my eyes to take the file from its original source and add it to the cloud of data in my head, putting the AI within them to work on encrypting it. A matrix of numbers and screens appear in front of me— everything my eyes have recorded all there for me at any time.

Something in one of the vials moves, and I scurry for the door, slipping out. I can't leave it fast enough, unnerved by the things within.

I lick my lips, shifting my eyes in each direction of the hallway as a sickening feeling twists my stomach.

On top of it all, I can't help how frustratingly horny I am.

I need to get Vagan's scent off of me. Now.

Two hours ago!

I scrub both hands down my face. If I make it out of this alive, I'm going to have to destroy at least half the data my eyes have recorded. In terms of research, understanding, and science, it makes me sick. For me and Vagan, it's what's best to keep him safe.

I don't care what happens to me, but the file could destroy his kind— whatever his kind is... I don't know what part his species has to play in all of this, but it can't be good. Whatever it is, he and others of his species have survived the death of this planet. That alone, now that I'm certain they originated here, is going to make Central Command interested.

Spying a women's bathroom symbol on the wall to my right, I head straight for it, hoping it means what I think it means. Discovering a lavatory with stalls inside, I nearly cry for joy, shutting the door behind me. A flickering light turns on when I enter.

Without waiting another moment, I strip my clothes off until I'm completely naked—keeping the keycard around my neck—and turn the knobs on all the sinks. There's a groaning in the walls, and brown water jets out of them. After a couple minutes, the water clears.

I need to make sure Vagan rehydrates.

I scrub my clothes, my skin, and even dunk my head and wet my hair, determined to clean everything as best as I can. The bandages for my gash are long gone at this point. Soon, I'm smelling nothing and my flesh cools to the point that I'm shivering violently. Shaking out my limbs, I press the hand dryer button, and hot air hums out.

I nearly burst into tears again as I shuffle my body and my clothes under it to dry, and reach up and press the button repeatedly. With heat blasting my scalp, I bring my knees into my chest and enjoy this precious moment. All that matters right now is removing Vagan's scent from me and keeping my thoughts straight.

Except my time is short, and the longer I meander, the more likely Vagan and Collins will run into each other. Or they'll come searching for me. I turn on my mechanical eyes and draw forward the naga file, and begin skimming it. I might not have another chance.

I need to know what's happening to me, him, the Lurker—all of us.

Files within files emerge, each one headed by a series of letters and numbers. There are old presentations, data prints, testing schedules, and more information than I'll be able to go through in a month's time.

A tingling, frightening niggle of doubt worms its way into my head as I scroll through the enormous amount of data.

If the Nagas have any relation to Lurkers... I almost don't want to finish the thought. *They'll all be captured, studied, tested upon, interrogated, or worse.* I say a little prayer that they're just another alien species that have no relation whatsoever to what Central Command wants. That perhaps they're alike, or aligned with the Lurkers and nothing else. Maybe the Lurkers brought them to Earth.

Pressing the button on the hand dryer to start it back up, I choose a random tab and get an academic article.

I start at the beginning.

And blanch coming upon the word *hybrid* immediately. My breath catches in my throat. Damn it all to the void.

Nagas are human and Lurkawathian hybrids.

That's impossible.

Isn't it?

Someone would've known humans and Lurkers could breed—someone! We've been researching them for the past fifteen hundred years.

Something as important and extraordinary as a human-alien hybrid would be everywhere. It's hard to believe.

We've never come close to breeding with any alien, nor have we wanted to.

Naga sapiens, a genetic pairing of Lurkawathians and Homo sapiens, are the result of using reptilian DNA from certain species on Earth to bridge the gap in each species' genome. Through years of pairing and breeding reptilians with the corresponding DNA from both, the Naga sapiens are the least volatile of the hybrids created.

Most are failures.

Though having characteristics of both Lurkawathians, and serpentine reptiles, Naga sapiens still retain many human features. They have heightened strength, intelligence, and can carry Genesis 8 naturally.

What's Genesis 8?

Though hard to control, the males can pass on Genesis 8 to their offspring, allowing future generations of hybrids to use Lurkawathian technology. The females, though easier to control, also carry Genesis 8, but are unable to survive gestation. It's a messy affair.

Hearing a noise, I glance at the bathroom door. When I'm certain it was nothing, I go back to the file and skim further down.

Genesis 8 is hard to produce naturally, and when given to an adult human, it can kill them as easily as transform them while increasing their aggression. Only one human male has been given Genesis 8, Officer Patrick Holds. During his transformation, he murdered eight men and women, escaping from his bonds. Though he can transfer Genesis 8 naturally and handle Lurkawathian technology, albeit not well, he is ultimately unable to procreate with a human female without killing her.

My throat tightens. But what about the pheromones? I keep reading.

The above leaves us with one current solution: using his semen to artificially inseminate human women. Thus, creating the first true Naga sapiens on record. The first gestation resulted in a full litter of hybrids that all respond to Lurker technology, allowing us to finally use and test their technology first hand. Unfortunately, gestation is rough on the female, and the human females in question are unlikely to volunteer to host future litters.

Unable to attract viable sexual partners, we have solved this problem by splicing naturally created pheromones into the male's sexual glands. Like a virus, the pheromones attack the female's immune system, much like the aggressive nature of Genesis 8, reforming their makeups to that of a scent that would appeal to both human females and even human males. Once the male Naga sapiens goes into a rut, he releases the newly formed pheromones to entice his chosen mate, getting her sick. If the virus has adapted correctly, the human female will enter into a heat cycle beyond anything that could happen naturally.

She will carry the virus for life.

And any future pheromones from other Naga sapiens males will be seen as a threat and attacked and destroyed upon entering her system, causing further flu-like symptoms for the duration. Unfortunately, women with strong immune systems can fight off the virus and only experience a mild form of heat. If the chosen woman's immune system weakens at a later time, the male Naga sapien can initiate a mating with her then.

Swallowing thickly, I slam my fist against the button again, annoyed, almost fucking furious.

Once the pheromones leave her system, and the male is no longer in a rut to procreate a litter with her, the heat cycle will end. The virus goes dormant when the female is either gestating or no longer able to procreate. This has greatly increased our chances of creating a new generation of humans that have naturally occurring Genesis 8.

Pulling out of the files, I rise and go to the nearest sink, lowering my face to gulp down water and wash the acrid taste from my mouth. Leave it to men to fuck women over. Leave it to us to take the brunt of the work. God, why am I not surprised? I have a virus running through my system, one given to me by some ancient human assholes, a virus that I'm going to have for the rest of my life.

Fuck.

At least men can be affected too.

And Genesis 8...

This Genesis 8 is needed to use Lurker technology. Vagan and his kind carry it naturally?

The little Lurker tech that I've studied firsthand had all been deemed broken and unusable. Maybe that's not true. Maybe I was just unable to properly use it.

Peering down at my body, and the faded scar on my abdomen, my brow furrows.

What am I going to do?

Does Vagan know any of this?

Based on our conversations, I'm scared he's in the dark as much as I am and I'm a little relieved by that. If he got me sick on purpose, if everything that happened between us was a manipulation on his part, I would never forgive him. I'd hate him for the rest of my life. But I don't, and I'm certain what has transpired was at least genuine.

What really scares me is what the information I now have stored in my head will mean for us.

Because if I get out of this, I only have two choices.

Return to *The Dreadnaut* and have the data synced to the systems for Central Command to download and read, or stay here on Earth and hide.

I could delete it all, but that still leaves *me*. All Central Command has to do is dose me with a psychoactive serum the moment they suspect I'm keeping something from them. I'll spill everything. And if that happens, they'll still come down to Earth and capture every naga they can to study.

Uncomfortable where my thoughts are going, I fling out my damp clothes and tug them on. Taking some of the gauze out from my lab coat pocket, I tie my wild hair away from my face and suck in a deep breath as half-undone braids and crimped ringlets fall out to frame my face.

Jittering, my stomach growls loudly. I haven't eaten in days. At least I think it's been days.

I leave the bathroom and head back toward the elevator and keep walking when I find it empty. Stumbling upon another lounge area and finding some old granola bars wrapped in plastic, I stuff them in my pockets while ripping one open and tasting it. Hard as a rock and salty, I wince as I chew it down.

The next few hallways are empty and quiet, and I peer into the windows into other rooms as I go. As the moments lengthen and I don't come across either Vagan or Collins, I pick up the pace.

Where are they?

The hairs on the back of my neck rise, and I glance behind me but find the hallway empty.

My shoulders sag when I hear their voices a few moments later. Then I rush forward to find them, entering a large auditorium.

Please don't be killing each other! I can't trust anyone right now, not them, and especially not me.

Below me, on a stage covered in laboratory equipment and

machines, Vagan and Collins are facing each other, their stances aggressive. Vagan has his tail poised and raised behind him.

"What's going on?" I call down quickly, hoping I've made it in time to diffuse the situation.

Neither of them turns my way.

The only indication they heard me, is both of them going quiet.

Hurrying down the steps, I maneuver my body between them. "What's going on?" I ask again, slower this time. "What's wrong? Why aren't you answering me?"

Collins shifts his gaze my way first. "Nothing that's not new. Just giving your snake here a sorely needed reality check." He looks me up and down, probably noticing that I'm wet. "The floor is clear so unless the Lurker can suddenly start working the elevators without a key, we should be safe. For now."

Remaining tense, I look again between Vagan and Collins. Vagan's fury is palpable. His tail remains above and behind his head, ready to strike.

"That's good..." I say, reaching slowly into my pocket and handing Collins a couple of bars, staring at Vagan. "I found sustenance, and there's a working bathroom with water back near the elevator. Vagan, are you okay?"

He doesn't take his eyes off Collins.

"He's just dandy," Collins snaps, tearing into a bar. "We had a good talk, him and I. Pretty much resolved our issues to beat."

I turn to Collins. "What does that mean?"

"Exactly what I said it means. He and I resolved our issues. We need to make camp and come up with a plan to get out of this hellhole and back to the surface. How's your head?" Collins lowers his voice when he indicates my bump. "Does it still hurt?"

Suspicious and nervous, I continue looking between them, bracing for the worst. "I found some painkillers in a medkit and have more in my pocket, if you'd like one. For now, I'm okay."

His eyes soften, and my back straightens as he steps between me and Vagan. "You keep them. I'm sorry about yelling earlier," Collins says, his voice turning serious. "I really thought you were dead. That fucker upstairs hunted me for hours, and I spent every second thinking that at any moment I was going to stumble across your body. I can't do it again, Shelby. I can't see someone I love dead in front of me."

His eyes are tired, so very tired.

I've never seen Collins tired before.

Biting down on my tongue, I don't know how to take his words. He's talking about his mother, which can't be good. "Collins... I'm sorry," I tell him, searching his eyes, trying to get him to see what I'm trying to say without breaking him further. "I mean it." I've never been sorrier. I'm not just sorry about what he went through in the dome, and what I was doing during that time, but for not loving him the way he wants me to love him. For knowing, no matter how badly he wants it, I'll never be his.

"I'm going to get you out of here," he warns, ignoring what I'm trying to convey. "Your sacrifice won't be for nothing." He glances at my stomach, and my spine goes rigid. "On my life, I'll make certain of that."

"Collins..."

"You still trust me?"

My brow furrows. "I do. Of course I do."

"Good. I'm going to check out this bathroom and clean up." He steps away and toward the stairs, refusing to look at me. "I don't want these scrapes on my arms to get some sort of alien infection."

"You're going?" I ask, following him with my eyes. "What about coming up with a plan?"

"I'm covered in sweat, blood, and alien fluid," he grumbles over his shoulder. "And I may already have a plan. But we'll need to rest up first." He stops at the threshold and peers down at me. "This time tomorrow, you'll see the Earth's sun, Shelby." Then he turns from me and walks away.

Staring after him, confused, I don't hear Vagan close in until he's pressing against my back and wrapping his arms around me. I sink into his embrace before remembering that being near him is dangerous. I pull away, but his grip on me tightens. Turning in them, I push against his chest.

"Vagan," I say, my voice trembling, refusing to breathe through my nose. "We need to talk."

TWENTY-THREE
THE SACRIFICE

Shelby

"Yesss," he says, agreeing with me. "We do."

But the look on his face makes me swallow, makes my heart pound even faster. Feeling his hands slide up my back to cup my neck, shivers streak down my back. His scent isn't as strong with the shallow breaths I'm taking. Resisting is harder than I'd expected.

I want to smell him, inhale him. I like the way he and his pheromones make me feel.

His scent makes me believe he's a part of my past. That he's a piece of my homeworld, Luntra.

My throat tightens as I study him, studying me. How much longer do we have? Because if Collins is right and this plan of his works, we'll be above ground soon and I'll have to make a decision.

For how badly I want to survive this, I'm not ready to say goodbye. I've said so many goodbyes in my life that the thought of doing it again makes me want to rear my head back and scream. I fear them.

Goodbyes terrify me now.

"What were you and Collins talking about?" I ask.

His eyes harden and the tension from a few minutes ago comes flooding back to his limbs. "You," he hisses.

I pull from his grasp and take a step back. "Me? What about me?"

Pinning me with his gaze, his tongue flicks the air. "He told me you have sacrificed a lot coming here and that you are fighting a war."

I wince. "Yes."

There is that...

"A war is when two different sides fight until one wins, like a battle, except bigger. Right?"

"Yes." I place my hand on my chest. "Humans are fighting to keep their homes and all we have built and accomplished since losing Earth from an alien race known as the Ketts. At least that's the name we've given them."

"Are they coming here?"

"I don't know. There are many colonies between here and where they last attacked, but if we don't push them back, if we don't do something soon, they might come here eventually."

His eyes narrow. "I don't understand."

I swallow thickly. "We're losing, Vagan. *Humans* are losing. If any other species are fighting the Ketts, we have yet to encounter them. The Ketts... they're not like us, you or me, they're... evil. Evil and hungry. They can't be reasoned with, can't be fought one on one. They're large and bulbous and envelop everything around them in their desire to eat and dominate. They consume advanced sentient organic matter to survive, and humans procreate quickly, making us desirable. The more they eat, the stronger they become. We can take down their ships, if we're lucky, but that's it. Their bodies are like sponges, and our weapons do not affect them once they invade a planet. They swarm, devour, and move on. They steal our knowledge and use it against us. We believe they have a... *being* who controls them, but we're not sure. And if they do, we have no idea where they are."

"Do you think something here will help you win against them? Something you are willing to make sacrifices for to find?" Vagan looks at me but does not see me, studying my eyes like an object. What did Collins tell him?

But it's more than that.

"Yes," I say, feeling my throat constrict around the words. *You.*

My face falls. Vagan's expression softens, and he reaches up to spin one of my curls. "We will find it, female, but no more sacrifices. I do not like thinking of you making sacrifices. We will discover what your people need to win and we will win."

His words erupt like wildfire inside me, and an overwhelming sadness takes me over. *If only it were so easy.*

It isn't winning versus losing. Yes, humans *want* to win, but we also need the Ketts to fear us, to avoid us, and to develop a defense system against future attack and invasion. War in outer space isn't easy because there are no lines drawn in the sand, because there's no sand at all.

We know little about the Ketts, where they originated from or how far-reaching their dominion is. They will always exist because of it, and so will always be a threat.

My brow furrows. We'd destroy them at the source if it were possible... wouldn't we?

Is that what the Lurkers did to us? Seeing what we were becoming?

And we survived anyway, we hardened, we built new cities, new ships. There is no *winning* involved in war anymore...

Not liking where my thoughts lead, I press into Vagan and bury my face against his scales, wishing we had never left the cave in. That it was just he and I still buried under rocks, with no one else but each other until the end. His arms wrap around me, trapping me to him, his tail sliding up my legs.

I should tell him. I should tell him everything I've learned about him...

But as soon as the words form in my mouth, I swallow them away. His fingers thread into my hair, loosening the gauze. More of my hair slips out.

"I will go with you when you leave," he says, pressing his cheek to my head. "I will follow you wherever you go. That is what I told the human male."

Wrenching my eyes closed, there's only more sadness at Vagan's declaration. Pushing away, I cup his cheeks and kiss him.

He goes still.

At first, his lips are soft, pliant under mine, and slightly chapped. I rub mine over his, caressing back and forth, unable to go further, needing him to respond, just needing comfort. This connection. This strange bond we have, wanting it to be more. His scent remains faint, and the longer I rub my lips to his, the more emboldened I become.

I've proven that I can resist his pheromones. I relax in his embrace. The emotion that floods and swirls in my chest isn't a manmade manipulation; it's real.

I trust myself enough to know this.

Slowly, Vagan's fingers curl in my hair, his claws grazing my scalp. He tips my head back and coaxes my lips to open for him, giving me what I need.

Silence, gentle touches, and all the softness in the world.

Slipping my tongue out to lick his lip, he meets me halfway, sliding the forked end of his tongue up mine and into my mouth. Opening for him, Vagan tugs me harder against his chest with a groan.

I feel his cock emerge from its hiding place to press against me.

Inhaling sharply, I draw back. "We can't."

He stiffens and draws his fingers out from my hair. "You are leaving me when we are free of this place," he says so matter-of-factly that I don't have the wherewithal to keep my face blank. "Even if I follow you, you will leave without me."

"Vagan…"

His gaze hardens. "You are going to make more sacrifices even if I don't want you to."

I avert my eyes, trying to keep my tears inside. "It's not like that. You're oversimplifying."

"Am I? Stop looking at me with sadness in your eyes then."

Wrenching them shut, I reopen them to meet his gaze head-on, knowing he'll still see my grief. "I'm not going to lie to you."

"Then why?" he asks with almost a growl.

Pulling further away, I step out from the coil of his tail. "I haven't made any choice yet. I can't. I won't." I look around the room, and at all the empty chairs. "I'm afraid."

His fingers clasp my chin, forcing me to face him. "Because of how I will be treated?"

"What *did* you and Collins talk about?" I bite out.

"What your world is like, what is in store for you, and for me. They will not treat me kindly, being what I am."

"Humans don't allow other sentient species on their ships unless they are a sanctioned diplomat for their peoples, and are accompanied by a diplomat of our own. An expert. It's not because you're an alien and look different—"

"An experiment, you mean."

My spine straightens. "What? What did you say?"

Vagan coils his tail under him, bringing an orb between us with his tailtip. "I am an experiment."

I look between him and the orb. "What do you know?"

He hisses, dropping the orb into the palm of his hand. "Humans created us because they were unable to use certain technology. They killed a female, a small one, because she did not meet their requirements."

"On that orb?" I ask carefully.

"Yesss, Shelby, on the orb. You came here for this alien technology, technology you will not be able to use. I might be able to."

"You don't know that, not for certain. We don't know that."

"Why else am I here? It makes sense. I have lived amongst the ruins of an old world all my life, a world that was ruled by you. It is not my species depicted in books and videos. It is always yours, never mine."

"Vagan—"

"Do not tell me otherwise! I never thought much about it, but it makes sense. I am part-human, part-snake, and part-Lurkawathian. Tell me I am not."

I snatch the orb from his hand and throw it against the ground, shattering it. Lifting my foot, I stomp the pieces that remain until they're unrecognizable. Even then, I crush what's left with my heel.

"Shelby." Vagan's hand clamps down on my shoulder. "Stop."

Huffing, I glare at the pieces strewn across the floor. "We don't know for sure."

When I finally lift my eyes to meet his gaze, he's watching me curiously. "Destroying the orb does not change anything."

"No. It doesn't. But it makes me feel better."

"You are here for something to save you, you have made sacrifices for this, and yet you have not found what you are searching for, except me."

"Don't, Vagan, please."

"I know where it isss."

Startling, my eyes snap back to him. "You know where there's Lurkawathian tech? Like, real tech? Weapons, ships, servers?"

He nods.

"And when were you going to tell me?"

"Does it matter?"

"Yes!"

"I will show you then, when we are free. When you accept that I am coming with you."

Spinning away, I growl. "You are not coming with me. You can't. Collins may have told you what it would be like, but did he tell you there's almost no water? There's no forests, or rivers, or lakes. There's just endless cold steel walls and constant buzzing. You won't even fit in half the spaces, and any space you're allowed to have is small or shared. You'll be surrounded by humans, all the time, if they even let you stay with me—"

"You are mine."

"Central Command won't give a damn what you want, think, or say. The moment they know what you are, you'll be taken from me, dissected, stitched back together, and used until there's nothing left. If what you say is true and humans really can't use Lurker tech, you'll..."

I look around the room again, a shiver streaking up my back. "You'll..."

"What?"

I wave my hand at the space around us. "This will all happen again. Do you understand? Even if you join me, you'll never be able to stay with me. I won't be able to protect you. The moment someone sees that we care for each other is the moment they use us against each other. They'll kill you inside and out."

"You do not underssstand," he hisses.

I turn on him, frustrated, terrified. "Understand what? I think you're the one not understanding, Vagan. What you're asking of me, what it means if you offer yourself up..."

Just imagining what would happen if someone above learned about the pheromones Vagan and his kind can naturally create... Just that thought alone terrifies me.

"You do not understand, Shelby, because the moment you leave, I will be as good as dead already."

Vagan curls his tail around me and hauls me back against his chest. Stiff and shaking, he runs his hands up and down my back, trying to comfort me.

But there's no comfort anymore, only fear.

I can't let him join me. I can't let him follow me up into the stars and back onto *The Dreadnaut*. I can't. He's asking too much. I hadn't even considered it, and refused to any further. It hurts too much.

He already knows he's a hybrid, carrying the genes of humanity's greatest enemy of old in his body. Central Command will destroy him. They'll destroy all the nagas.

And if it really is true, and this Genesis 8 is what is needed to use the technology I seek, it wouldn't matter if we ended the war against the Ketts. A new one, a worse one, will take its place.

This time when I push away from him, there's only conviction in my eyes. "You won't die, Vagan. We fucked. That was it. And even that was forced upon us by chemicals your body naturally creates. There's nothing between us. Whatever Collins told you, he was right. Once we're out of here, this" —I move my finger back and forth— "ends. I'd never be respected by my peers if they knew I slept with an alien."

"Ssshelby," he hisses my name in warning.

I head for the stairs. "It's ridiculous that you think you could own me." I chuckle. "It's laughable. You really need to get some sleep. I'm going to find Collins and tell him about what we learned above—"

Suddenly, I'm torn off my feet and held in a cage of muscled arms. Spun around, Vagan shoves me back against the metal wall of one of the larger machines. Pressed against it, my feet dangle as he rams his pelvis into mine. With metal behind me and Vagan everywhere else, there's no escape. I go still.

The rage on Vagan's bright face could only be described as a roaring fire, the orange of his face inflaming his eyes with cast-off sparks.

"You forget, female," he rasps, lowering his face to mine, using the word I told him not to. "I don't care what happens to me."

He slams his mouth to mine, capturing me completely. Unable to breathe, I gasp, sucking in sharply as he forces my lips open.

His scent floods me and I forget.

Everything.

Everything except him.

TWENTY-FOUR
RESISTANCE IS FUTILE

Vagan

Thrusting my tongue into her mouth, I battle hers. At first, she tries to close her lips, biting down, but I push through her defenses, coaxing her open. Her lower teeth graze my lip, and the frantic desperation in my limbs build.

She fights like a rabid creature, her teeth biting, nipping at me, catching my tongue. She purses her lips and pushes at my chest. I groan, allowing her to attack me, tasting her sweet flavor all the while.

When she begins to taste me back, allowing me free range of her sweet mouth, I pull back, knowing I've won.

"You will not leave me like Eestys. I will not allow it. You are mine," I growl, forcing my mouth off hers. "Mine!" I roar, making her flinch, and shunting my hips between her legs, forcing her to feel the swollen girth of my knot, my length in its entirety. "I can survive what is put in my path, female, but I will not endure you walking away from me!"

I don't know why I bring Eestys up, but the female naga popped into my head the moment Shelby tried leaving me. Murderous thoughts, resentment, and loss invaded like a rare storm, and next I knew, I had Shelby against the metal wall of one of the machines.

"Do you think I will let you so easily walk away now that I have you?" I snarl, licking the air between us. "I have claimed you and as long as you are alive, I will never stop coming after you, wherever you try to go." My tongue swipes her cheek and the fresh taste of her flesh fills my mouth.

I am not afraid of war.

Feeling my member lengthen and grow ever more, I ram it into her, making it very clear that she'll not only have to escape this place, but me as well if she ever wants to go back to the sky. "You have come here for answers, and I will help you find them but I will have you in exchange! That is the truce we have made with your human leader!"

Zaku and the others had the way of it. They knew how to approach this situation best. I realize that now. The females will walk away otherwise!

"Vagan," Shelby gasps, her hands gripping my shoulders, nails biting into my scales. "What are you doing?"

I clasp her chin, sliding my free hand over her front and cupping one of her breasts. "I am reminding you who is the alpha here. And that I have caught you. That you are mine."

Her eyes glisten and then hood, and I know she's becoming the lusty female I had in my arms earlier. The one who wasn't the Shelby I know.

But it is her, and this is *me*.

Grabbing my member, I squeeze my knot and spill against her legs, dirtying the clothes she just washed. She can argue all she wants, but she will always wear my mark.

"Vagan, look at me," she pants, already pushing her hips out to accept a mounting. I suck in a breath, scenting fresh arousal beginning to bloom in the air between us.

Sweat dews her brow, her lips raw and puffy from our kiss, and her eyes swirl with emotion. Her reactions, even the simplest ones, excite me.

"I'm trying to save your life," she whimpers, grief and desire molding her features. "Like you've saved mine." Her words are so low I barely hear them.

And just like that, my rage slips away.

"Ssstop," I hiss, "Just stop." I capture her mouth again in a desperate kiss.

She doesn't fight me this time, kissing me back. Her hands clutch my neck, and she pushes into me as I press her body against the wall. Her fingers catch the wild ends of my hair, and she pulls on it.

Thrusting my tongue back into hers, she meets me and thrusts back. They tangle.

She clutches me to her and I soften, moved by her caring.

I never expected my female to care for me, or my wellbeing. Now that I know Shelby does, my need for her, to keep her, turns monstrous.

I will not give this up.

Jerking my hands down her body, I grab the lip of her pants and yank them down, but they don't go far. She groans, knocking her head back on the wall, and helps me unlatch the front of them, shimmying them down her legs. Catching on her boots, I lift her foot with one hand and tear a boot off with my tailtip, the other foot right after.

She grabs me to her when she's bare below the waist, and I let her, rocking my throbbing length to her skin, dirtying her with more wasted spill. *Mark. Mark. Mark.*

Then I tear her off me, press her to the wall.

"Vagan," she gasps, reaching for me. Her gaze falls from my face to stare at my member. Upright and ready to be mounted, the seed painfully forcing my knot to expand begins to weigh it down.

"I want to see you," I rumble, tugging her white coat down her arms. Nagas don't wear clothes, so why does she?

She doesn't say anything as I spin her around, pulling the rest of them off of her, and drink in the vision of her body.

Soft flesh, dark skin, and curves that make me pause because it looks like her body was meant to have a tail like mine... Venom leaks from my fangs as I take her in, imagining her wearing my scales. Spreading my hands on her upper back, she pushes her butt out with a begging whimper, displaying her sex to me. The pink slit beckons my attention, the scent of her arousal rushing through me. I groan thickly, pressing my shaft's head to it.

Slick, I spill on her there too, unable to control my urges.

She hitches and pushes her butt out even more. Plagued with instinct, running my hands down the curve of her back, I grab her hips and yank her against me.

"Vagan, please," she cries out as I run the length of my knot up and down her slit. Her body trembles under my hands, and I push my tail in front of her to hold her up.

"I cannot make you spill, but you will make me spill, mate," I warn, rubbing her. "You want what's inside me. You want to take it."

Isn't that why she's here?

"I have been bred for thisss," I growl, maneuvering her to her hands and knees, lining my tip to the puckering opening above her slit.

"Vagan," she squeaks, stiffening under me. "Wrong hole!"

Peering at the bud displayed, I lean back as she looks at me over her shoulder, through her wild, curling hair.

Slipping my fingers through her slit, I quickly find the right one and thrust them in to make sure. My mouth waters when my fingers come away wet. Catching her gaze, I lick them clean. Then I thrust them inside her tight channel once more and do it again for another taste.

She shudders and turns away, pressing her brow to my tail.

Coiling my tail under her middle, I yank her backside into the air, and press my tip to the right one. Grabbing her hip again with my free hand, I force her quivering sex to still. This time when I push into her, she gasps my name.

Like before, her tight flesh fights my penetration and tries to push me out. I have to force my way in, battling clenching muscles. In small thrusts, I coerce them into submission, spreading her a little more with each small shunt. Moving my tailtip to caress her spine, she reaches between us to rub her clit.

Excited, I stare, thrusting in small bursts, watching her lips part in pleasure, watching her help me seat my prick inside her. Such a sweet mate...

And when a gasping moan fills my ears, her backside completely open and on display for my attention, I work my swollen knot inside her.

Her hand drops, and she goes back to hugging my tail, straining against me.

"I want you to feel it," I snarl, slowly pushing my knot further in, stretching her tight opening to accommodate. "Feel who's claimed you."

It's time for me to take over from here on out.

"*Vagan*," she hitches my name.

She releases another whimpering moan. Pressing a little more into her, she jerks forward and cries out. "Too much, too good." She tosses her head, and kicks her legs.

"Stay still!" I warn.

I do not want to hurt her.

"Vagan, I can't," she breathes against my scales. "I can't."

Smearing my fingers through the seed I spilled on her flesh, I bring them to her nose. "You can. Breathe me in, little mate."

She inhales sharply and then grabs my wrist, sucking my fingers into her mouth.

Going tense, her tongue slips through them and my mind falters. Halfway conquered, I thrust the bulk of my remaining bulge deep inside her. My hand catches her scream as she bites down on my fingers. Seated fully, crazed, needy, possession takes over my head and I roar. I roar hoping Collins hears.

Yanking out, thrusting back in, I begin rutting her in the way I've always wanted.

Shelby's whimpers quickly turn to moans. I retrieve my fingers and slam my hands on the metal wall on either side of her, leaning in, keeping her prone with my tail. Slapping flesh fills my ears, her nails tearing into my hide, and overwhelming pleasure bursts through me. Tight, constricting flesh heats my shaft to a furnace, and I hiss gutturally, frantic in my need to release.

I know when she comes because her body tenses beneath mine, her legs buckle, straightening, her feet pushing against the floor as her backside lifts simultaneously. Her channel strangles my painful knot and milks the seed right out of it.

She comes again as soon as she's done. She is right; she does not spill.

I thrust wildly as my excess spill slips out between us, my palms flush to the wall. I look down at her small, soft body and delight in the wicked excitement it brings me.

I will have her like this nightly. Naked and precious and all mine because I have earned her. It doesn't matter where we are, she will accept me. I know this. I watch her spine arch and sway, her messy dark hair slipping everywhere, and my tail strains out with tension.

Seed pumps through my loins and into her, little bursts to fill her womb.

Sweet relief.

Feeling pressure building in my tail, my muscles go rigid, her channel clenches and flutters continuously now, and my tailtip coils around her tighter, lifting her slightly. She wraps her arms around the part holding her up and screams out as her body spasms again.

Seeing something move at the corner of my eye, I glimpse Collins standing in the doorway, watching us.

I yank Shelby against my chest and unravel, laying my claim, warning him against interrupting and marking the satisfaction across my features.

It is not him she is mating, opening her smooth, human legs to receive a swollen knot. It's me. And she is the most beautiful female in the universe because of that.

Straining against her pliant body, I spit venom in Collins's direction and spill every last drop of my seed inside Shelby. She cries out my name, making Collins's face redden. If she is going to carry anyone's litter, it will be mine.

"Vagan," she moans, her cries of pleasure diminishing with exhaustion. Still, she's undulating her body tiredly back upon me. I glance down at her and brush her hair from her face, petting her cheek gently. So beautiful...

When I look back up, Collins is gone.

Lifting Shelby into the cradle of my arms, I nuzzle her, soothing her quivering frame, and search for a place to take her to rest. Picking up her clothes and boots with my tail, I leave the wretched space behind and find a quiet alcove where there's a sink, and cabinets.

Coiling around her, dropping my tail in front of the door so no one will get the jump on us, I fall asleep as she settles in a nest of my arms.

TWENTY-FIVE
THE BOTTOM OF THE PIT

Shelby

I WAKE WITH A START, sitting upright, startled that I'd fallen asleep at all. Inhaling sharply, I peer around the room I'm in, immediately seeing Vagan's tail coiled around me and across the floor. My shoulders sag, finding we're alone, and it's quiet. Only the dim glow from one working strip of light brightens the space.

The room is small compared to the others I've been in, but I recognize it, recalling Vagan taking me here after...

After sex.

I reach down between my legs, brushing my fingers across my slit, and swallow thickly. Wet and sticky from Vagan's spill, it aches from his rough thrusting. A blush rises to my cheeks because I wanted it. I liked it—a lot.

Rubbing my brow, I look at him.

He's sleeping, his back leaned up against the wall, his chin against his chest. His breathing is deep and even, and I quiet my own so I don't disturb him.

I'm not going to be able to walk away from him. Not so easily. I rub my face again.

The old scent of pheromones and sex fills my nostrils and I tense, waiting for my body to react. When there's only a slight stirring, I relax and rise to my feet, moving out from Vagan's limbs as gently as possible.

I head for the sink where I see my clothes and boots piled next to it, wondering how much time we've been like this and how much sleep we've gotten.

Can't be long if Collins isn't here...

But then I glance down at my naked body, Vagan's dried seed across my legs and thighs, and hitch, refusing to acknowledge the horrible thought that Collins knows exactly where we are and what we've done. Turning the faucet on, the walls groan, and I glance back at Vagan.

He stirs just as water spurts out and his tired, hooded eyes find mine.

"I didn't mean to wake you," I whisper, waiting for the water to clear. He lifts a hand and threads his fingers through his tousled hair, smoothing it back. "How are your wounds?" I ask, glimpsing his stomach.

He reaches down and touches one of the bandages sealing a bullet hole. "Better."

I turn back to the sink just as the water clears. "Good. We need to find Collins and get out of here," I say quickly before he brings up sex, splashing water over my body.

A hiss fills the small space, and I hear Vagan close in behind me. Tensing, I wait for him to press against my back or to haul me against him. Instead, he reaches around me and wets his hand. My throat tightens as his large presence threatens to swallow me whole. I wait for him to tell me I'm his again. I wait for him to touch me, to nuzzle my neck, to play with my hair, to addle my thoughts and fill the room with his pheromones.

He moves his wet palm away.

I don't know if it's relief or disappointment that I feel watching his hand disappear behind me.

I startle again when he presses it between my legs.

"V-Vagan," I stutter, twisting to face him. "We can't."

"Sssssh," he shushes and hisses softly, placing his wet hand back upon me. "I am helping clean you."

My skin prickles at his words.

Going rigid, I don't move as he cages me to the counter and wets my body with his palms. The next few minutes float between us like a dream.

He washes me everywhere. His large hands and long fingers wiping, cupping, probing, swiping every curve and divot of my body. Methodical and careful, as if washing me is a sacred ritual to be done at one's leisure, he removes all the dirt, seed, and grime upon me, stoking me with worrisome heat.

When he presses a finger inside me, I widen my legs and lean back, unable to resist. Spinning it in gentle circles, his black eyes pin me to the spot. His forked tongue slips out to lick my cheek.

"Your eyes have not turned blue in some time," he says low and thundering, coiling his finger inside me to massage my roughened sweet spot.

Clenching hard, I gasp, "There is nothing I-I want to record."

His thumb presses my clit. "Record?"

"They record when they're on."

"Why do you not want to record?" he asks, tilting his head.

His strikingly sharp and handsome features are suddenly boyish and curious.

I shake my head, rolling my hips. "I-I don't want anyone to see you like I see you."

He leans in and presses his face to the crook of my neck and shoulder. "Why?"

Because you're mine. The words sprint to the tip of my tongue, and I almost say them. Curling my toes, I stop them before they're given a voice.

I shake my head again, whimpering when his fingers tease me harder. "I don't know."

"Do you like this, Ssshelby?" he asks.

Hips rocking, I lick my lips. "Yes."

His hand stops abruptly. "Are you clean enough?"

I'm horrified at the sudden loss of pleasure and pressure. "No!" I gasp quickly, pushing into his hand.

"Will this make you... come?"

He didn't say spill.

"Yes."

He presses his body to mine.

His fingers quicken, returning to their playful yet deliberate exploration. His scent sharpens but doesn't flood me, much weaker than before. His cock doesn't emerge from his tail, and I wonder why.

But then he thrusts a second finger into me and grazes his fangs across my shoulder.

Yelping, my body goes taut as an orgasm rips suddenly, brutally through my body. Riding his hand like a madwoman, I knot and constrict around his fingers, seeking the pleasure radiating from their tips, wanting them to roughen and pump. Grabbing his shoulders, I rock into his hand as waves of bliss eradicate the tension still held from the last few days.

When it becomes too much, I push his hand away.

He brings it to his mouth and licks it clean, watching me slyly all the while.

Panting, all I do is stare.

I'm fucked.

He doesn't even give me a knowing, wicked smile, like I would expect him to. Like any man who knows he's won would. He just eyes me darkly, possessively, licking my essence off of his fingers.

Before I lose my mind any further, I twist around and splash my face and grab my clothes. I move away and start dressing. Tugging my pants up my legs, Vagan grabs my hand.

"What is that?" he asks, dropping to peer at my lower stomach.

Covering my scar, I try to twist away again. He doesn't let me.

"Just an old wound."

"Who did this to you?" he hisses.

I tug at my arm. "No one did. It was a machine."

He looks up at me. "A machine cut you?"

"Yes." I try to free my arm again but his hold on me only tightens. "Vagan, it's nothing. An old wound."

He continues to stare at me.

"It's nothing..."

He hisses. "It is precise, like it was done by a claw."

"A scalpel," I correct.

"Why?"

"It doesn't matter. Can you let me go so we can find Collins and get out of here?"

"Why?" he demands.

I flatten my lips.

Vagan slides up to tower over me, pulling his tail under him, challenging me to not tell him. My heart pounds harder in my chest as the seconds tick away and he doesn't release me.

"I have bruises all over my body, as well as scratches. Why do you care about an old scar?"

"Because it is deliberate."

"I had a hysterectomy, okay? You can release me now."

And he does. His grip on my arm softens. "Hissterectomy?"

"It was the cost for my eyes." The words scrape out of my mouth like sandpaper. I straighten the shirt bunched in my hand and tug it over my head, hiding the old wound from sight.

"You were clawed open for... your eyes?"

"Yes," I say.

"Ssshelby," he rumbles my name in warning when I throw on the lab coat after yanking out some painkillers from my pocket.

"I can't have children, okay?" I snap. "They weren't going to put these eyes inside me if I was going to be a liability, if I couldn't be trusted to dedicate my life to the job. There are many scholars who wanted them, many *male* scholars who used my sex as a reason why I shouldn't *qualify* for them. Why give them to a woman when she's just going to get pregnant and not put them to good use? It didn't matter if I was better than them at the work or if I was smarter, not with a Central Command predominantly run by men. So I had them remove my uterus to prove that I'm dedicated, that my work comes first and that the future of the human race is my first priority!" I yell, unable to keep my voice from rising and yanking on my boots.

"Resources are limited, you see? Up there." I point at the ceiling. "Water, food, clothes, even *space*. How else was I going to show them that I'm the best person for the surgery?"

I storm away, furious for even having to bring it up, and hurt, because now Vagan knows. I'm still a red-blooded woman; I'm just a woman who can't have children.

Children that his anatomy is obviously urging him to create, if the strength of his pheromones have anything to do with it.

"Are you happy now?" I grate, double-checking that my keycard is still around my neck.

I tug open the unlocked door and walk back into the medical auditorium.

He doesn't say anything as I climb the stairs, more than ready to be out of this awful place. The only indication that he's behind me at all is the quiet shifting of his tail.

You picked the wrong female to hunt.

I frown as the thought rises in my mind.

The wrong one to infect with a virus. I briefly squeeze my eyes shut, entering the hallway. *The wrong one to save.*

Window after window goes by, door after door, as I search for Collins. Still, Vagan is silent behind me.

I guess it's for the best, I laugh inwardly. *Now he'll let me leave Earth without a fight.*

Seeing a bright light piercing out from a room ahead, I step over the bones of a long-dead human. They scatter shortly afterward from the sweep of Vagan's tail.

I pick up my pace.

Feeling tears brim my eyes, I blink them away before they're able to fall. Inhaling sharply, I stop at the open doorway of the lit room, finding Collins deep within and standing before a large, partially frozen cabinet.

"Collins?" I say his name and step into the room. "Let's hear this plan of yours."

He looks up at me, his face blanched, eyes bloodshot and sunken from lack of sleep, lips dry and twisted into a reserved, questionable frown.

I stop in my tracks.

In his hand is the largest hypodermic needle I have ever seen.

"For you," he says numbly, stabbing it into his chest. "For us."

TWENTY-SIX

SACRIFICIAL LAMB

Shelby

I RUSH FORWARD. "No!" Grabbing the needle, I yank it out of his chest, throwing it across the room. Facing the sweat-soaked flimsy white undershirt he's wearing, I push at him. "What have you done?" I cry. "What have you done?"

Vagan's tail coils around me and yanks me back.

Collins doubles over, bracing his hand on the counter, his hair falling into his face.

"Collins!" I thrash against Vagan's coil, horrified and confused. "What the hell did you do?"

"For you," he rasps, dropping to his knees. "For you. Now I will be the one who saves you, gives you everything you want." He coughs, spitting out blood. "I will have everything you need, *we* need, to... to..."

My brow furrows, and I stop fighting Vagan as he drags me back toward the door. Mouth opening and closing, I shake my head.

"We have to leave. Now," Vagan growls in my ear when I dig my heels into the floor.

Collins's head snaps up. "You will take her nowhere, snake!" he snaps, eyes reddening further, sweat trickling down his face.

Vagan thrusts me behind him as my confusion builds. I don't know what Collins injected into his chest. I don't know what he's saying. I glance at the needle in the corner and the blood dripping from its sharp end.

"You have made your grave, human," Vagan warns. "You know what will happen next."

"I am stronger than him! Stronger than you!" Collins bellows.

Trembling, I look around Vagan's frame as Collins pulls himself back to his feet, his whole body shuddering from the effort. "Collins, what did you do..."

His wild eyes snap to mine. "I saw you."

I shake my head again. Trying to go to him, Vagan tightens his hold on me.

"I saw you with him!" he roars, stepping toward me just to drop to his knees again. I jerk in response. "I did this for you, Shelby. For us. Now there's no one who... will," his voice cracks, "take you... from me. I can save you."

"What have you done?" I whimper. Try as I might to get to him, Vagan keeps me restrained with his limbs. "Vagan, we need to help him!" I shout. "Find a medkit, fast!" Yanking violently out of his hold, reason returns hot and fast, but he grabs me again as I start frantically searching for a medkit. "Stop," I cry. "We need to help him!"

"Release her," Collins orders, dragging his body toward us.

Vagan ignores him and me. Instead picks me up and carries me out of the room.

"He is beyond our help."

"Leave her!" Collins shouts, his voice guttural and wet, arm outstretched towards me. "Shelby!"

"No!" I yell, fighting Vagan as he takes me away. "We can't leave him. We have to go back. Please!"

"He's already gone."

"He's not gone!" I climb up Vagan's chest, clawing to look over his shoulder as he moves away from the room. "He hasn't slept," I beg. "He's sick, maybe even hurt. We have to go back! Why did he do that? Why?"

I see Collins crawl out of the room just as Vagan turns a corner.

"Collins!" I scream when I lose sight of him again.

Turning my attention to Vagan, I pound at his chest. "Let me go. Let me go!" I kick at him, overcome with fear for my friend. For the thoughts I know are breaking him down. When Vagan doesn't release me, doesn't even loosen his grip. The fight quickly leaves me, and I pant from lack of food and adequate rest. "Please," I beg, my voice falling. "Please... It's not about me," I cry. "He needs help."

Somewhere behind us, I hear a terrible scream. I hear my name roared. I hear threats.

"I will kill you, snake!" Collins voice cracks, making me go still with fear in Vagan's hold. "I will rip off your tail and feed it to you! I will dismember your bowels and let the flies feast!"

Vagan comes to a stop and lowers me to the ground. "Where's your key?"

I stare down the hallway, listening to Collins's threats and screams, hands trembling.

"Ssshelby, the key!" Vagan prompts.

"I-I..."

He grabs the cord around my neck and tugs the key out from under my shirt. Something beeps behind me.

"Shelby, look at me," Vagan orders.

I barely hear him, listening to Collins, staring down the hallway. There's bones and old corpses up and down it, some having broken and scattered from Vagan's passing.

"I will tear out your spine and carry your head on a pike!"

Vagan's hands clamp down on my arms and spins me to face him. "Look at me," he orders again.

My gaze shoots to his, and his black eyes fill my vision. He cups my face, keeping me from looking over my shoulder.

"We have to help him," I mutter, hearing more horrifying threats roar and echo in my ears. Threats that Collins would never say. I blink the dewy tears out from my lashes.

"He is turning."

I blink again, this time actually seeing Vagan. "What?"

"Like on the screen, he is turning."

"I don't understand. What screen? Turning how?"

"He injected Genesisss into his body," Vagan says, his tongue flicking.

I startle at the word. "Genesis 8," I correct him, immediately switching on my eyes and drawing forth the file.

'Genesis 8 is hard to produce naturally, and when given to an adult human, it can kill them as easily as transform them while increasing their aggression. Only one human male has been given Genesis 8, Officer

Patrick Holds. During his transformation, he murdered eight men and women, escaping from his bonds.'

Vagan's eyes narrow slightly, and he nods.

Collins bellows grow louder.

"Why?" I ask. "Why would he do that?"

"It turns him into one of those monsters—the Lurker—above us. It makes him more... *like me.*"

The mention of the Lurker startles me further, yet still Vagan keeps his hold on me, refusing to let me glance away. "Not like you," I whisper.

"He is a weak human male, that is why."

"He's not weak," I snap and wince from the scream Collins releases right then.

"He is right now," Vagan grits out. "He will not be soon. I need you to ssstay here," he says when I stop trying to pull away from him. "Can you do that? Can you?" he asks again when I don't respond, unable to stop listening to Collins's screams.

He's not making threats anymore. All I hear are screams. Agonizing, horrific, animalistic screams.

Vagan shakes me, forcing me to focus.

"We have to help him."

"I will, but I need you to stay here and wait for the elevator to come. Promise me, Ssshelby."

Startling again, I swallow. "You'll help him?"

He nods. "But you will have to wait here for the elevator. It is a long descent. It will take time."

I jerk out of his hold, and he lets me go so I can look at the elevator beside us, realizing where we are. Vagan's taken me to the main elevator, the one we rode down into the dome. The one that will take us all the way back up to the top floor.

It has to be. According to the orb, there's only two.

"What about the Lurker?" I mutter.

"If we encounter him again, I will deal with him."

"I thought—"

"*Shelby!*" Collins roars my name abruptly, making me flinch and twist around. Coming from around the corner, he appears, clawing and dragging a bent body I don't recognize toward us.

Vagan's hissing deepens as he thrusts me behind him.

"What's happening to him?" I gasp, half-crying.

"He's becoming the creature in the dome."

"He's not a Lurker, Vagan. He's human. The file says it'll only make him aggressive."

"So was the other one on the screen. It changed him anyway."

This screen he keeps mentioning, I recall how I smashed the orb on the ground.

How I wish I had watched what was on it.

Collins's back arches, drawing me out of my horrific thoughts, bending him in two. Hearing snaps and cracks as his mouth opens wide in a chilling shriek, his eyes clench then bulge. His bare arms are rimmed with bulging veins, like webbing, emerging from his flesh. Half his teeth are missing, and blood pools out of his mouth and down to drench the clothes that still remain on him.

His fingers crack—making me want to vomit from the sound—shooting outward from his hands, curling into claws.

"Shelby," Collins groans as more terrible snapping fills my ears.

Sobbing out in response, I watch as he twists and turns, heading straight for me, knowing if I rushed to try and help him that I'd most likely die.

Only one human male has been given Genesis 8, Officer Patrick Holds. During his transformation, he murdered eight men and women, escaping from his bonds.

Vagan moves away from me and heads toward Collins.

He's going to kill him. My vision blurs with tears. There's no other way to save him.

He's going to break our promise.

A large leathery tongue emerges from Collins's mouth, stretching out his lips.

"Vagan," I warn as he moves slowly toward Collins.

He pauses but doesn't look back at me.

Collins crashes to the floor with an agonized wail.

"Please..." It's all that comes out.

Please make it quick.

Please don't hurt him any further than he's already suffering.

Please...

Be merciful.

Vagan strikes forward and smashes his tail down on Collins's head, and I scream from the brutality.

TWENTY-SEVEN

THE ASCENT

Vagan

I HEAR the elevator doors opening just as my tail connects with Collins's broken form. Shelby screams, and the sound is filled with anguish.

Collins grunts once, then drops flat to the floor. His muscles strain under my tail but don't rise.

Pulling back my long limb, I pose to strike again, pausing briefly to take in his twitching body. My lips twist. *Where's your weapon now?*

I was always going to win. I always win. Promises mean nothing when one is patient enough to wait...

Except staring down at him, there's only pity. The anger, the possessiveness, the jealousy, even the hate I had for him is gone. All that is left is this pity, and... relief. He's not a male anymore, just a poor creature desperately trying to take hold of something that was never his to possess. It's not even a battle.

It *never* was.

Slamming my tail back down to finish him, his arm shoots out and catches it with his hand. Sharp claws digging into my scales, I yank it back, hissing with annoyance.

He lifts his head and looks at me.

His eyes are no longer human but slitted and yellow. What is left of his skin is taut and moist over the hide with scales emerging underneath. "Snake," he wheezes between broken, human teeth.

I snatch my tail from his grasp.

He rises to his feet, dragging his claws along the wall as he does.

"Collins?" Shelby gasps behind me.

I twist to stop her from moving any closer but she's still standing by the elevator. My eyes snap to the doors which are scratched and bent, and not flush with the floor. I hear a groaning, crunching sound as if the small moving room is pushing against something below.

"Sssnake!" Collins barks, his voice a wet croak, dragging his broken body closer.

"Shelby, the elevator," I hiss at her when she just stares at him with a horrified expression. "Shelby!" I snap.

She jumps and turns to look at it.

"Face me!" Collins yells, hearing him move closer.

Shelby peers between the slats of the elevator's doors then jerks back. "Tree branches," she says breathlessly. "Branches I had to break, some fell—"

Something stabs my tail, and I pivot around, losing her words. Collins's claws are digging into my tail. Growling, I slam it against his chest, barreling him to the ground and pummel my fist into his stretched face. He laughs. Breaking his teeth, newer, sharper ones pop out to take the old ones' places.

He snaps at me, unconcerned by the damage I'm doing to him.

I snap back, pressing my lower arm hard to his throat.

Something wet and hard curls around my neck when I grab his head and pummel it into the floor. He stays down, and I grasp the band strangling me. Hands slipping, I try to pull it off.

"Vagan, watch out!" Shelby shouts.

Suddenly flung to my back, Collins claws atop of me. A large, long limb shoots out of his bent spine. I tug harder at the coil around my throat. A thick tail of roped muscle rips Collins's clothes, tearing from the bottom of his spine.

He rakes his nails down my chest, reaching for my bandages, and I spit venom into his eyes. Rearing back, he wipes at his face with a shriek. Skin sloshes off of him.

Striking his side, I throw him down the hall and rise as he lands hard against a wall, only to recover almost instantly. Naked except for his pants, even his boots are torn open by the new limbs forming within, barely resembling the male I hated.

Now he's just putrid waste.

I brace, wiping my mouth clean of the blood that had splattered there.

Shelby grunts, and Collins's gaze flicks over my shoulder to her.

"You have to get through me to get to her," I growl, bringing forth more venom.

He sprints forward, connecting with me, throwing me straight down the hallway. I crash through a door.

Shocked, I rush my coil under me to grab his leg.

But he's not next to me. He's where I was a second ago, stalking toward Shelby.

I hiss, punting forward.

She flings around to flee just as Collins grabs her. There's a broken branch in her hand, half-pulled out from under the elevator. "No!" she screams when he hauls her against his chest.

I hit his backside and his tail knocks me away. He rears his head and bites Shelby's arm, tearing a chunk of her flesh straight off. He draws back his claws and streaks them down her front, shredding her clothes, her flesh.

Her screams make my ears bleed.

Dashing up, I strike at Collins's legs, pinning my arms. He releases Shelby, and she drops to the ground with a wail.

I sink my fangs into Collins's neck. He reaches for me, tries to tear me off of him, railing his new tail hard against any limb it can hit. I tighten my hold, injecting him with as much venom as I can muster.

Must paralyze him.

His body locks up, his limbs swelling against mine. He slams backward into the wall, trying to dislodge me. Stabbing my claws into him, I hold on.

Eventually, he drops to his knees, succumbing, and I coil my tail around him in a pin.

It is the same every time. Always.

Now to finish the kill.

Still, he tries to fight off the effects, fingers twitching, tail taut along my side.

I lift off of him when he goes completely still.

Pounding my tail down once more, his body finally slackens.

Crying fills my ears, and my gaze tears to Shelby. She's sitting with her back against the wall beside the elevator, her hand clutching her arm, tears streaming down her face. Her body is shaking, her hair plastered to her stunned, agony-etched expression.

My heart drops.

I rush to her side. "It'sss over," I tell her. Her eyes are wide with shock, staring mutely ahead of her. "Let me see," I demand, trying to get her to look at me.

When she doesn't respond, I grow more frantic and pull her hand away from her arm. Finding only torn cloth and blood, I grab the lab coat and rip it with my claws, tugging it off of her to see the damage. Seeing a definitive bite wound on her upper arm, I grasp her shoulder and lower arm, pressing my mouth to it.

She screams as I suck, pulling her skin into my mouth. Swallowing her blood, her taste, her fear, I search for poison.

"Vagan," she cries, thrashing between me and the wall. "It hurts. It hurts!" she screams.

Her words alone send more pain through my body. I unlatch from her and grab what's left of the lab coat. She tries to hide her arm from me, but I take hold of it anyway and wrap it up tightly in the cloth.

"Hold this in place if you can," I order her.

There's a groan behind me.

Glancing back, I haul Shelby into my arms. Collins's fingers scratch at the floor, trying to rise. Slamming my tail hard to his head once more, he goes still.

"We have to go," I say, turning for the elevator. Seeing the branches keeping it from landing through the door slats, I release Shelby and yank them out.

The elevator drops with a resounding crack, and the doors open.

She doesn't fight when I pick her back up and carry her through. She doesn't do anything but shake and whimper. There's dried blood, dirt, broken glass, leaves and twigs strewn about, and I sweep them all to the side as I take the keycard from around her neck and unlock the elevator. Swiping the buttons, the doors begin to shut.

I hear Collins groan again. "No."

A bloody, scaled hand shoots between the doors just before they close. Furious, I strike it down. His other hand grabs at the side. The glass is murky and smudged.

"No," he gurgles again. "I'm ssssoorrry," he yowls. His face appears, his expression somewhere between murderous and bereft, and I strike him again.

The doors close again just as he begins to rise on the other side.

"No!" he bellows. "No! I'm sorr—"

The elevator shakes and lifts as Collins thumps the other side wildly. There's a loud groaning, thumping, and I grasp Shelby closer to me when her shaking worsens. I feel her weaken as blood drenches the bunched cloth haphazardly rounding her arm.

She's bleeding too much. I need to get her somewhere safe and soon. I don't know how much blood a human can lose before they die, and I do not want to find out.

Not with her. Never with her.

Something bangs the floor beneath us, and I coil my tail under me to raise Shelby off of the ground. The thumping stops then starts up again.

The elevator beeps, and I glance at the doors as they begin to open. The banging beneath me loudens.

I straighten, clutching Shelby's body.

On the other side is the Lurker.

TWENTY-EIGHT
REUNION

Vagan

We stare at each other.

Neither he nor I move.

Arms outstretched at its sides, the thumping beneath me becomes more chaotic, more frantic. Collins is climbing up the elevator room's tunnel; it is the only thing that could be making the noise. The Lurker's eyes drop to the ground, and I slip out of my coil, warning him away.

When the doors begin to close, the Lurker grabs the edge of one and stops it. His large mouth opens to reveal sharp teeth. I shift Shelby in my arms, knowing I will have to let her go if he attacks.

"Human," the Lurker crows, his gaze going to her. He says the word with disgust.

Shelby turns her face further into my chest. Her breaths are shallowing upon my scales. She doesn't have much time. The coppery reek of her blood, of Collins's blood is all I smell now.

"She is mine," I announce, threatening the Lurker off.

The Lurker tilts its head.

"I will fight for her," I growl.

His gaze comes back to mine, and his mouth widens into a grotesque grin. "You are like me," he says, scanning my body.

"Not like you," I hiss back.

His smile grows as his large tail swings back and forth. He points one long outstretched finger at me. "The key," he rumbles. "Give it to meeeee."

I tighten my grip on the cord in my hand.

He clicks his tongue when I do, rising up on hind legs, expanding bulky muscles. I slap my tail on the floor, doing the same.

"Humans are to die," he snarls. "There is no other way."

"Not this one."

He flares his nostrils and tilts his head again. "We have our orders."

The noise under the elevator goes from thumping to breaking and scrapping.

"We must follow our orders," the Lurker continues. "The key, scaled one," he prompts. "And you will live. You will live."

All I hear are lies.

Cradled by my tail, I slowly let Shelby slip to the floor, and the Lurker's face brightens in triumph. Then I slide her as gently as possible to the back corner and behind me.

"I cannot live without her," I say. "I need her. I will die for her," I warn. "I will fight for her."

"Then you have been compromised. You can not be trusted."

"Compromised?"

"They have poisoned your mind." The Lurker pounces, pummeling into me as I meet him half-way. Swiping fingers, he lacerates my hide, aiming for the slit that hides my genitalia. "Your scent reeks of mating!" he shrieks. "Compromised! Filthy!"

I drive him back, shielding Shelby from him.

We tear into each other, simultaneously defending our limbs while doing as much damage as possible. I strap my tail around him and squeeze. He tears a chunk out of my chest. I grit through the sharp agony, feeling my thoughts muddle.

All I know is that Shelby's not making any noise anymore. Not even a whimper.

Desperation unfurls my limbs, and I wring my hands around the Lurker's meaty neck, squeezing with all my might. He sinks his teeth into my arm, biting his way up it at rapid speed. More agony slices through me, and my tail drops from shock.

Bellowing out from the pain, any remaining strength I have seeps from my limbs. The Lurker rolls me over and climbs onto my chest. My hands slip from around his neck, thumping at my sides. He straddles me, slicing his claws through the air, shredding the flesh on my chest to ribbons.

Shelby...

"No!" Shelby cries out suddenly and flings her body atop the Lurker.

Horror rises in me as he swipes her off him like she's nothing but a mild nuisance. She hits the wall and drops, unmoving.

A deep, terrifying rumble releases from my throat.

Snapping my arm out to stop the Lurker, I snatch his throat and slice my claws through it.

He roars and yanks my hand off him, spurting blood.

The floor beneath me tears open just as he recovers. We roll to the side as Collins bursts through. "I'm sorry!" he sobs, long and winded.

Vision hazing, it's not really Collins that comes through but something else entirely, breaking apart cement and metal. He sees the Lurker on me, and Shelby's unmoving from crumpled against the wall next to us. He shrieks, and the noise makes my head erupt with overwhelming pressure. Shelby falls to her side with a cry, covering her ears.

Collins slams down onto the Lurker's back and tears him off of me, throwing him back through the open elevator doors. Trembling, I pull my tail under me, rising on my arms.

Collins jumps and lands directly on the Lurker's chest as it swipes its claws at him. Collins opens his mouth and tears out the Lurker's throat, spraying gore across the room, killing it instantly.

He goes in for another bite, and I strike once more, twisting until I hear his neck snap. He falls atop the Lurker.

They don't stir. A pool of blood forms around them.

Unable to move, clutching my middle, I stare, waiting for one of them to move again.

It's not until I hear the rattle of the elevator doors beginning to close that I pivot and fall to Shelby's side, pulling my tail back within the confines of the small space. I cradle her shaking form in my arms and watch the doors close tightly, firmly on Collins and the Lurker.

The elevator jerks and starts to complete its ascent.

"Sssshhhh," I coo soothingly, hissing and purring against Shelby's ear. "Ssstay with me, female," I beg, shaking with her. "Stay with me. Do not leave me."

When the elevator doors open again a few minutes later, I gather

Shelby into my arms, careful not to disturb her arm or the wounds along her front, and carry her back the way we came. With the last of my strength, I slip through the empty halls, the bones of long-dead humans, and out into the tunnel. The scent of dirt and murk fills my nose, clearing some of the putrid coppery blood.

"Ssshelby," I say her name softly. "Stay," I continue to beg. "Stay with me."

But she still doesn't answer, and the cloth around her arm sags from moisture. It drops from her body.

I push onward, eyes blurring from my own wounds, new and old. Feeling my body surrender, a different type of chill cools my scales. Far, far past the point of exhaustion, the constant regenerating my flesh and frame usually undergoes isn't happening. I slip and dive forward, nearly losing my hold on Shelby before catching my weight.

Exhaling, I keep going.

There are no plumes of dust or sounds of tumbling rocks anymore. The tunnel is silent and still, as if the cave-in had never happened. Everything that has fallen has fallen, and the way is clear until it's not.

Coming to the place I saved Shelby from being crushed, the first time I had her in my arms, there are far more rocks and boulders, pipes, and detritus than there was before, having fallen after we fled.

Blinking through the dusty murk, almost in complete darkness, there's one small strip of sunlight streaking down from far above.

The rest of the tunnel forward is completely blocked off. Looking up, the way is steep and jagged and would not be an easy climb for a forest naga, let alone a dying water serpent carrying his wounded mate.

Blinking at the sunlight, I collapse, pressing Shelby's cold form against me.

Using the last of my strength, I coil the larger part of my tail around her body and band my tailtip tightly around the wound on her arm. Shifting a wet curl off her cheek, I press my face into her hair and close my eyes.

My body twitches as something tickles it.

Groaning, I open my eyes to find dust and pebbles scattering down upon me from above. The light has dimmed, and I reach up to swipe at my face. Glancing up, I shield my eyes with my other hand.

"Keep digging!" someone says. A distinctly feminine voice. "There's something down there!"

"Gemma, ssstay back. The ground is shifting."

More dust and pebbles tumble, and I move to the center of the hole to escape the worst of it.

"She's down there. She has to be! She said she fell. Where else would she have gone?"

"Female, it has been a week since we heard her on the orb. If she has fallen, she is dead."

"Stop, Vruksha, we can't know that for sure," the female breathlessly snaps. "Shelby was alive then, and she could be alive now. I'm not leaving again until I know for sure."

Vruksha... I know Vruksha...

"Then stay back and let us dig," he grumbles. "So we don't have two females that need saving. It is getting dark."

Uncertain of what I'm hearing, I stare blankly at the light piercing down from above. Sand, dirt, and rocks continue to fall as the hole slowly widens. I look down at Shelby in my arms and recall all that we've been through and wonder if any of it was real or not.

But then I shift my tailtip off of her arm to check if there's a wound. I hiss through my teeth, quickly covering it again when I discover the bite mark and large chunk of flesh still missing.

"There's something moving."

My gaze snaps up again. There's a dark form leaning over the opening, and behind the form is the sky. Bright white, I blink, trying to make out who it is.

And if they are another enemy.

Another dark form appears and then a third.

"Hello?" the female calls down. Shelby twitches in my arms at the female's voice.

"Hello?" she says again, "Is someone down there?"

"Gemma?" Shelby mumbles. It's the first response she's made since the elevator, and I squeeze her to me.

"There's someone down there. I see movement," the female gasps.

One hard look at Shelby and her frailty has me calling out. "She's hurt."

There's a scattering of commotion and more dust falls upon me. Voices filter down to me, to Shelby, and the weakness pulsing through my limbs grows. The light fades, and I can't be sure if it's because it's evening or it's just me.

"We'll get you out of there—hold on!" the female shouts, cutting through everything.

Hold on. I nuzzle Shelby and slip back to the ground.

Hold on.

TWENTY-NINE

OLD FRIENDS AND NEW FEARS

Shelby

LIGHT FLASHES BEHIND MY EYELIDS, startling me out of the dark. There are noises all around me, and hushed voices. Going rigid, fear grips my throat. Every time I've woken up in the last however many days, I wake up like this, the events of the recent past rushing through me in a burst.

But there's no fear in the voices I hear. There's no real sense of urgency. Slowly, my mind and my overly tense limbs relax.

Sighing when I fully settle, relief hits me like a soft breeze. Vagan is alive. Collins must be alive.

I'm alive.

And then the pain hits. Agony floods my body, making me cry out. Reaching for my arm and my chest simultaneously, hands grab my limbs and pin me to the ground.

"Stop her from moving!" someone orders.

I open my eyes, wildly looking around me. A silent scream tears from my throat, and I hitch, arching upward, fighting through torment all while trying to understand what's going on.

There's a fire beside me, bright and flickering, blurring my vision.

There's smoke in my nose, quickly gusted away by a short blast of frigid air, and then there's Vagan, looking at me from above.

His face is recognizable anywhere.

Some of my fear ebbs. But the pain... the pain remains.

He cups my cheeks with a harried look on his face, saying over and over that I'm safe, that I'm above ground and he's with me. I stare into his eyes, wheezing through clenched teeth until the radiating sting only takes up half of my thoughts.

Vagan's face is covered in grime. There's dirt and dried blood over the majority of his neck, arms, and chest, his vibrant coloring diminished in the firelight despite the glow upon his orange face.

"Vagan," I whimper. "My arm."

It feels like someone is sawing it off.

"Tip her head up! We need to give her water. Try and hold still, Shelby," I hear a familiar voice as someone moves me. Crying out, my gaze darts to the side because it's not Collins.

"Gemma," I rasp, seeing her appear in the golden hue of the firelight. I stare until I'm convinced it is really her next to me. My lips tremble.

She looks exhausted but nowhere near as bad as Vagan. Her riotous red hair is pulled back from her face. She's staring at my arm, where the worst of the pain is coming from, and not at me, her lips pinched into a line.

"Gemma," I rasp again, barely believing she's here.

"Just hang on, Shelby. You've lost a lot of blood. We cauterized the wound while you were unconscious, but you need to drink. Can you do that? I'm almost done."

"Done?"

"Stitching you closed," she says, not even taking a moment to meet my eyes. "Some of your wounds are too deep."

Something pushes my head up—Vagan's tail—as he takes something from another figure beside him. I barely manage to part my lips when he places a cup at my mouth. I take a sip and sputter, and then take another. Swallowing is hard, but I force back everything poured into my mouth.

When the water is gone, Vagan settles me to the ground. I try not to cry out as Gemma moves my arm, then leans over to do something to the gashes on my chest.

"What's happening?" I gasp.

"You fell, were underground, and were... attacked," Gemma says, glancing at Vagan before meeting my eyes. "We got you out, and now we're taking you someplace safe, someplace where you can heal and rest."

"The ship?"

"Not the ship. The ship is gone."

I lick my lower lip. That's all I can do.

Gone?

"Try and get some rest now if you can. Tomorrow will be hard," she says instead of saying more, a look of worry across her face.

It's good to see her. Seeing her gives me hope. She's clearly alive, healthy, and safe.

It makes me feel less... alone.

My gaze slips to Vagan, who's watching Gemma work on me intensely, then to the forms behind him. Two other nagas. A red one, I think, and a brownish one. Focusing on them helps distract me from the pain. Firelight licks their features and hurts my head. I look back at Vagan.

The concern on his face has only grown. I want to reach up, grab him to me, press against him and breathe him in, but I can't. Everything leading up to my wounded arm comes rushing back, and a terrible ache hollows out my chest.

Vagan leans down and presses his brow to mine, in *our* way.

"Sssleep," he hisses.

"Where are we?" I rasp, seeing dark shapes and shadows on every side.

"In the forest, near the river and at the edge of the mountains," he says.

"How did... how did we get out?"

"The same way we fell in."

Up through the pit, through the rocks, pipes, and boulders. Somehow his answer only floods my head with more questions.

But my eyes begin to droop, and I wonder if Gemma put something in my water. There are medicinal plants on this planet...

"Will you be here when I wake?" I ask instead.

"Yesss, female. I will. I will always be here."

I curl my fingers into the grass beneath me. "Get some water," I tell him, searching his exhausted expression. "You need it."

He hisses softly in reply.

My eyes close and I fall under, Vagan's face the last thing I see before comforting darkness pulls me away.

I wake again to sunlight, cradled in Vagan's arms. We're moving upward, and there's cliffs to one side of me. I cock my head to see a vast landscape and a lake on the other.

Vagan hums down at me when he sees me awake. Glancing up at him, his neck and shoulders, the dirt and blood upon his scales are gone. I'm clean as well, and I wonder if he or Gemma washed me while I was asleep. *They would need to, to fight off infection.*

"I disturbed you," he says softly.

"You didn't." Hooding my eyes upon him, the concern on his face fades, and I settle into the crook of his arms.

His hair is clean, soft and tousled away from his face. His black eyes glint with sunlight, and the coloring of his unique form is almost enough to steal my breath. He was beautiful in the shadows and under the flickering lights beneath the ground, but he's absolutely stunning in broad daylight. The orange of his face brightens the blue of his shoulders and chest, and vice versa.

There are scars upon him that I now see, though not many. The wounds on his chest are healing.

He's hydrated.

I suddenly want to see him swimming in the lake far below. Would he slice through it like a knife? A ribbon in the water? Would it be frightening and mesmerizing all at once?

I'm jostled as we ascend a ledge and I wince.

I test my arm. It's positioned atop my chest and covered in bandages. So is my chest, and I realize I'd be naked from my pants up if my breasts weren't wrapped with them.

Hearing the crunch of footsteps, I look around.

Ahead of us is Gemma and a red naga. He's taken the lead but keeps his tailtip behind him next to her. She grasps it as she climbs.

Are they...?

It doesn't matter. She's clearly safe and well, and that's enough for me right now.

Hearing something behind Vagan, I cock my head to see who it is. Collins? Someone from the team? How many survived the cave-in?

I find another naga. The brownish one from the night before. He's got strange, flowy stripes in shades of beige and cream upon his body. But it's his face that gives me pause. He's stunning. Human stunning, not alien stunning, despite how alien he is. With flowing golden-brown hair, he looks like he belongs in the sun.

His eyes find mine, and I hold his gaze. My heart thunders in my chest the longer we stare at each other. His eyes are a soft brown, the same color as the lighter beige of his scales. There's a distinct pattern to him that's different from both Vagan and the red naga with Gemma. When his tail swishes to the side, it's shorter than both, but thicker, his patterning of darker brown stripes interspersed all the way to his tailtip.

Ripped with muscles, he reminds me of one of the juggernauts, the ground troops in our military. A familiar forked tongue comes out to taste the air as we take each other in, the red appendage accompanied with a single hiss.

I'm the first to look away, searching for others.

"Where..." I start, finding my throat a little raw. "Where's Collins, everyone else?"

Vagan tightens his hold on me at the mention of Collins. But it's Gemma who stops and lets us catch up to her. My eyes go to her as she walks beside Vagan. I notice the red naga slowing down too so his tail remains by her side.

The red one has ridges, unlike Vagan and the brown one. And he has wicked features.

"You're awake," she says. "How are you feeling?"

Sweat beads her brow. It's then I notice she's no longer pale, but tawny with sun damage, her skin a darker shade than before. She's glowing.

"Tired," I respond honestly. "Confused. I don't like not knowing what's happening, what's going on," I say a little too quickly. "Or where I'm headed." Any other person, I'd keep my worries to myself, but with Gemma...

We're far beyond that now. There's no regime watching our every move.

She gives me a tight smile and then opens her mouth to speak.

"Collins is gone," Vagan rumbles, and my gaze shoots back to him. "He came after us—you—in the elevator room. He attacked the Lurker and..."

He trails off.

Feeling a terrible pressure fill my head and chest, I prompt him, "And?"

"And saved our lives." Vagan gives me an indifferent look then tears his eyes away. "He killed the Lurker, and I snapped his neck before he came after you again. I took my chance to end him quickly."

His words are like thunder in my ears.

"I'm sorry, Shelby," Gemma whispers. "I'm really sorry."

Silence descends upon us after that. I can barely open my mouth to speak, swallowing down the tightness in my throat. Memories invade my head, good and bad, all of Collins, and our time together. And how it all ended horribly.

I'm angry at Vagan. And then I'm not. Something confusing and sad settles in my heart because I know I'll never know for sure. My eyes have been 'off' for a long time. I think of those last few minutes of Collins in the lab, right before he stuck himself with a needle full of Genesis 8, and—I shudder—how he tore a chunk out of my arm.

How he was there when I cried as a child, and how we kept each other's secrets. I wrap my hand over the wound and blink away the tears. I wish I could have seen him glow like Gemma does now.

After a while, Gemma moves back ahead to the red naga's side, and we dip down into the forest briefly and stop at the edge of the lake. The Earth's sun is falling and the shadows deepen when Vagan finally sets me on the ground.

The brown and red naga leaves to scout our surroundings as Gemma pulls out something she calls a flint torch from the pack on her back and lights some wood on fire in a pile between us.

"We'll make camp here tonight," she tells me. "We'll head up that mountain tomorrow." She points to the largest one in the range around us. I can just barely see its peak through the trees.

Vagan pulls off my boots and helps me shift to lie on a patch of grass. The deep cuts on my chest sting terribly from being cradled all day. Gemma moves to my side, bringing her pack with her.

"It's really good to see you," I say as she tugs at my bandages.

"I'm glad to see you too. I was so worried when I heard your voice. I didn't think I'd be able to get to you in time."

"I'm sorry."

"Don't be. Here, bite down. This may hurt." She hands me a bunched cloth and helps stuff it in my mouth. "Vagan, hold her down."

Quietly, he grabs my limbs, coils his tail over my middle, and I wrench my eyes shut.

Gemma peels off my bandages, partially crusted to my skin, and I grit into the cloth from the sharp pain. My flesh burns from the cauterizing, and I want to beg for someone to hit me over the head so I'm unconscious for whatever is about to happen.

And then Gemma starts to clean my wounds with water from the lake.

By the time she's done, night has fallen and the other nagas are back. Blustering from snot and tears from the pain, she offers me water and some painkillers from her bag, and I take them greedily. I accept all her administrations with ease, finding that I trust her more now—this woman she's become—than I ever did while we were on *The Dreadnaut*.

Vagan, having been nearly completely silent this whole time, leaves briefly to the shore and vanishes within. He's back at my side less than a minute later.

Gemma and the other nagas talk in hushed voices about the trip tomorrow. She offers me a bar, packaged in plastic, and I shake my head.

"You have to eat."

"In the morning," I beg. "I don't have the stomach for anything except water right now."

She gives me a hard look and I expect her to pull rank, but she doesn't, putting the bar back into her pack. "In the morning then," she concedes.

The red naga coils his tail around her as she settles on the opposite side of me and Vagan. Staring into the fire, she leans upon the red naga when he comes to her side. I study them for a time, praying I don't see any warning signs.

"Are you together?" I ask softly.

"Yes." They both answer at once.

It brings a smile to my lips. "He... caught you?"

Gemma smiles. "You can say that."

I exhale a tired breath, reaching for Vagan with my good arm. I eye the third naga, the one who's alone, and find him tensely staring into the shadows of the forest.

Keeping watch.

"That's Krellix," Gemma says, answering the question I didn't have to ask. Krellix keeps his eyes on the shadows. "His nest was destroyed when we took over the facility months ago."

"We have a lot to talk about," I whisper to Gemma.

She shifts and our eyes meet, and I see my exhaustion reflected back at me. "Yes, a lot to talk about."

"Thank you," I say, listening to the crackle of the fire.

"Don't thank me, thank him." She cocks her head at Vagan. "He got you out of that pit. We only had to drop him a canister of water." She shakes her head.

"Enough now," the red one orders, his face fearsome when he scans Gemma over. "You need sleep, female, or I will be carrying you tomorrow as well."

Gemma harrumphs but nods, moving to settle into the coil of his long red tail. "Fine." But then she lifts her head. "Is Krellix taking the watch again tonight?"

"Yesss," the red one answers. "He does not have a female to sleep upon him."

"Stop being an asshole, Vruksha, or he's just going to steal me out from your arms."

Vruksha, so that's the red one's name.

"If he tries, there will be nothing left of his corpse to feed the pigs."

Vruksha and Vagan hiss deeply in agreeance, and my gaze goes to Krellix, who appears completely unconcerned about the threat or by having others talk about him.

Turning my attention back to Vagan, I press my face into the side of his wet tail, breathing him in. A faint trace of his scent fills my nostrils, mixed with the smoke from the fire.

We have a lot to talk about as well, he and I.

A lot.

And it makes me afraid.

By the evening of the next day, we come to the stop at a bluff at the top of the mountain. A hidden mountain trail that only Vruksha and Gemma seemed to know about cuts the ascent time in half, and I'm grateful.

The pain has receded into a place into the back of my mind. Between food this morning, several nights of rest, and water, some of my strength has returned.

Vagan remains uncharacteristically silent, and I can't be sure if it's because of the others or me, or something else entirely. We've had no time to be alone.

He's acting differently than he had when we were below ground. He's just as watchful, perhaps more so, but he's not nearly as aggressive as he was with Collins toward the other nagas. I worried there would be a fight breaking out between the males at any moment. Besides some warning hisses and one tail strike in Krellix's direction, there has been no violence, no overt masculine tension. And Vagan and Vruksha have generally agreed about every decision made.

Is it because of Gemma? Vruksha is clearly protective of Gemma, almost to a frightening degree, though allows her to be by my side, and in turn, Vagan's side. It's like they have a silent pact, or an understanding.

I'm terribly curious about their relationship.

But between the pain and simple exhaustion, I don't have the energy to do anything except take in my surroundings and try not to be a bigger burden than I already am.

All I know is that we're traveling further and further away from the facility. Further from Collins. The Lurker, and everything I know.

"Zaku's den," Gemma says with almost an excited sigh. "I can't wait to take a bath." Vagan turns and then I see it, a pile of bones stacked high, a lawn scattered with skulls of many shapes and forms, and the towering glass window shining the sunlight right back into my eyes. Gemma stomps to the doorway with Vruksha directly behind her.

Krellix has mysteriously vanished, and Vagan, Vagan doesn't move.

"Vagan?" I say his name when he just stares at the glass. "What's wrong?"

"I am not welcome here."

Zaku's den.

Daisy.

Gemma and Vruksha brought us here?

I wiggle in his embrace, and he begrudgingly lets me down. Swallowing thickly, I clutch my bad arm. There's noise where Gemma and Vruksha have gone, and I search for them.

In their place is the largest naga I have ever seen, and the flaring cowl upon his head brings me right back to that day I first saw him forcing his way through the barrier around towards the facility. He hisses, rising up on a long tail, just as Gemma yells.

The male barrels straight past me and toward Vagan. Pushed aside by Vagan's tail, Zaku tackles him to the ground.

I scream.

Suddenly there's shouting all around, and I try to intervene only to be pulled back by Gemma. Crying out from pain from being thrust away, Vagan finally responds to Zaku's attack and sinks his fangs into Zaku's cowl.

"Stop! Zaku, stop!"

Vruksha yanks Gemma away, in turn yanking me away as well, bringing me to my knees when the wounds on my arms and chest go taut. The two nagas coil around each other, viciously tearing at each other's hides.

It's not until I hear another voice that Zaku pauses in his attack.

My head whips around to see Daisy, round in the middle, standing at the doorway sobbing.

"Zaku, stop," Gemma shouts again. "Daisy needs you."

Stunned, Zaku and Vagan tear away from each other and Zaku rushes to Daisy's side. She curls her arms around him as he sags slightly from Vagan's venom.

It's not until Vagan vanishes into the trees without looking at me that I realize I'm being led toward the house. That everyone else has already gone inside, and it's just me and Gemma now.

"What about Vagan?" I ask.

"He'll be fine," Gemma says, pushing me through the open glass doors of Zaku's home.

Still searching for Vagan amongst the trees, I tremble, brows furrowing deeply. I want to go after him, refuse whatever safety is being presented unless he's with me, but as I call out, deciding as much, the doors shut, locking me inside with a resounding thud. He's been the only constant in all of this. He's the only thing keeping me grounded and going. I don't want to be alone. I'm alone without him.

I can't lose him, not after losing Collins. I don't want to be trapped inside a stranger's house. Not without Vagan.

I shake my head as grief hits me again at the thought of Collins and my confusion grows. As the rocks and dirt closes in around me. Then worry fills me as I scan the bones again outside and the old pyre near them.

Gemma puts her arm around me and forces me away from the glass. "I should have warned you."

I'm trying not to panic. "Warn me?"

"That Vagan attacked Daisy and Zaku."

"I already knew... I thought..."

Gemma studies me, confusion flitting across her face.

My eyes land on Daisy across the space. She's sitting on a couch, wiping her eyes. "Daisy," I say mutely, still unable to believe that she's alive.

That she survived the crash. Except she didn't survive without a lot of pain… Tears flood my eyes as I take in her scars.

"Please forgive me," I beg.

THIRTY
ZAKU'S CASTLE

Vagan

Days have passed since arriving at Zaku's, and not once has anyone left. Not even Vruksha. I see them all sitting together on the seats behind the glass barrier, talking, but I can't hear them. I do not know what they are discussing. Nor what they are deciding.

I stay in the shadows of the sparse trees nearby, keeping watch, keeping Shelby in my sight as much as possible. I always know when they talk about me. Zaku now and then hisses at me from within, and I take it, knowing he has a right to do so.

When Vruksha and his female, Gemma, suggested coming here, every muscle in my limbs strained. Zaku's den was once considered an impenetrable place, where none have been able to trespass, that was, until my need for Shelby had grown so crazed, I broke down his walls and attacked his female.

I sought to steal her, to use her as leverage.

But Vruksha's female insisted that it was the safest place for Shelby. Not only to heal, rest, and recuperate, but also be protected from other, nasty nagas, animals, and monsters while she recovered. That Shelby would do best being with other females of her kind and that Zaku had a human medical device that could ensure that Shelby's wounds would not get infected, even healing them.

I almost didn't believe it until Vruksha agreed with her. Vruksha is not the agreeable sort.

If I'm willing to follow Shelby into the skies, I can face Zaku and do what I can to help her heal. Even if I die in the end.

Seeing Zaku's female alive and well, and clearly gestating, hasn't taken away any of the guilt festering in my chest. Palming it now, knowing if I had not been beaten down by them and that she could have died because of me, my heart stings. I would not forgive me if I were in Zaku's place.

Zaku owes me nothing, despite my part in bargaining for the females. And because of that, Zaku is allowed to distrust me for what I have done, but Shelby? I worry for her.

She watches for me at the glass barrier now and then, concern etched across her face. Sometimes I let her find me when her eyes turn distant and lost.

Other times I will stare at her for hours even after she's pulled away.

Is she considering going back to her ship and her people? Is she going to leave me? The last place I want my female to be is near this war, where great battles happen. I could lose her. I've almost lost her already, multiple times.

Clenching my fists, *I can keep her safe.*

I have killed many, many monsters. I can kill many more. Sudden bloodlust streaks through my veins and I unclench my hands.

Shelby's at the glass again, watching me. She's dressed in new clothes now, though her boots are the same. She's braided her hair and has it pulled tightly away from her face. Her dusky skin has taken on a radiance. She's clean, clearly fed, and is getting the rest she needs.

She is getting better.

It makes me agitated that I am not the one providing all of this for her, that I never even had a chance to. That it's Zaku and his generosity and the other human females who are giving Shelby the things she needs to mend. It agitates me as much as it excites me that she is recovering from Collins's and the Lurker's attacks.

Swiping my claws across the healing wounds on my stomach, it is my punishment.

Being left in the dark, atop a cold mountaintop, with little access to water while I watch my female from outside a barrier, is my punishment. It is hellish. Back to the shadows, the waters, and away from the others, is where I always end up.

Outside looking in...

Shelby coming to visit me keeps me grounded. Late at night, when everyone is asleep, she comes to see me, pressing up to the glass, gazing into the darkness, like she is right now. She has not forgotten about me.

Her face lights up slightly when I stalk from the shadows and go to her.

We'll sit together in silence, sometimes until dawn, when she scurries away before the others rise.

I can't smell her. I can't taste her. I can't talk to her. Though I can see her.

And she can see me.

It is enough. It has to be.

She can't have young...

It is the last real conversation we had and it replays in my head when she walks away. I have never heard of a female who can't have young.

I will never have to worry about her safety during gestation—I will never have to experience what my father had with my mother—and that relieves my soul. I eye the other female, Daisy, and her growing belly, and shudder with fear for her, for Zaku, and then I'm grateful it's not Shelby. More grateful than I ever thought possible.

More grateful than when I was told she was gestating Collins' young...

I realize Shelby would not be here at all if she had not had this *hisssterectomy*. She would be far from me, somewhere in the sky.

But as one day turns into another and she is not returned to me, my frustration at our separation grows.

My wounds are healing, the stinging and deep aches becoming easier to bear. I no longer have to grit my teeth and force the pain away.

I am ready to have her back in my arms, ready to take her to my nest.

And I know Zaku won't let her remain in his den long-term, not unless he takes her to *his* nest to mate, and if that happens...

My tail coils, and a blistering growl roils my throat.

I will accept this punishment from Zaku, but I will not accept that.

So on the fifth day, when there's a scattering of movement inside, I unclench my straining limbs when Vruksha and Gemma head for the doors, followed by Shelby and Daisy. The females gather and embrace each other, tears slipping down their cheeks, and more than that as well...

Shelby is holding several 'orbs,' and her eyes are glowing blue. They gather around her as she does something with each orb and hands them to the other two females afterward. They take them and clutch them to their chests. They embrace again, and then Vruksha and Gemma move to the door.

Stiffening, my excitement palpable, the thick glass barrier opens up, and they step through.

Shelby remains on the other side. She does not follow.

Hissing, I head for Vruksha and cut him off. Our eyes meet, and the muscles of his arms go taut, his scales rising in warning. He pulls his spear forward.

"How is she?" I ask.

It's Gemma who responds, coming to a stop next to Vruksha. "Hi, Vagan. Shelby is doing good. She had a fever the first couple of days but has since fought it off." She eyes me up and down. "You... look better."

"Move out of our way, Vagan. I am taking Gemma home."

Home.

Gemma sighs and flicks her eyes to the sky. "He's concerned, Vruksha. We can take a couple more minutes before we head back," she tells him. "It's the least we can do for him saving my friend's life."

"Though he attacked another?" Vruksha growls.

Gemma's cheeks redden. "Yes."

Vruksha neither lowers his spear nor settles at Gemma's words. I can't blame him. He may not know how deeply I've claimed Shelby, or if my attention will roam. My attention will never roam.

I swallow, my dry throat constricting. "She is safe? With Zaku?"

Gemma's lips twitch upward. "Zaku's got running water, electricity, and just about everything a girl could want. She's safe. She's with Daisy."

"And... Zaku?" I ask again.

"He does not want you on his land," Vruksha rumbles.

"I will not leave without her," I snap.

"That's Shelby's choice," Gemma interjects sternly. "Not yours." She sighs again and steps forward. Vruksha's tail immediately shoots out to wrap around her loosely in warning. "Give her time, Vagan," she lowers her voice. "She's been through a lot. We all have. She has a lot to think about."

My eyes shift to Zaku's den.

"She'll come out when she's ready," she whispers.

Meeting Gemma's eyes, I nod once and slip back into the trees. I hear her and Vruksha descend down the mountain path, and then I don't hear them at all.

Finding my shadowy alcove, where there's moisture in the soil my body can absorb, I let her words swirl in my head as my gaze lands on Shelby, who's at the glass, watching me.

Tensing all over again, I clench my hands as she studies me, her expression blank. Beautiful in the light and in the darkness, I can't tear my eyes off of her. I forget how to breathe.

Minutes pass, maybe hours, before I realize she's wearing boots.

And that she's alone.

Not alone. There are those thin, stick-like house robots around her, around the room, cleaning and lasering it. When she slowly heads for the exit, I still haven't taken a breath, nervous if I do, she'll feel it and flee from my sight.

Her lips move and one of the robots comes to her. It opens the door, and she steps out.

I rush forward before I think better of it, stopping directly in front of her, rising up on my tail until she has to crook her neck to keep my gaze. Her smell rushes me. Sweet and satisfying, and... clean. Too clean for me. Floral and rich, flowers fill my nose, and none of her pure, feminine scent. Her sweat, her blood, her salty tears that I can always taste on the tip of my tongue. It's all gone.

I inhale anyway, deeply, fully, until I smell her real self beneath the soap. The smell that's *Shelby*.

My Shelby.

Her brow furrows slightly as we stare at each other and her throat bobs. Her mouth parts and closes then parts again as if she wants to say something but can't find the words.

"Ssshelby," I say at last, clenching my hands so I don't snatch her to me and steal her back to my nest.

I would do just that if I knew how her wounds were doing...

"Vagan," she whispers.

I nearly groan at the sound of my name on her lips.

"I wanted to thank you," she continues.

"Thank me?"

She curls her arms around her middle, averting her eyes. "For saving me... back there. For getting me out of that place alive."

Reaching forward, I hook one of her braids with my finger and tug it. She tenses, her gaze darting to my hand.

"Do not thank me for that," I say, leaning down to smell her braid.

There she is.

"I-I've decided not to go back."

Our eyes meet briefly. "Back? Back where?"

She shifts on her feet, clearly uncomfortable, not immediately answering me. My eyes narrow. Behind her, deep within the home, I notice Zaku and Daisy watching us.

"To... *The Dreadnaut.*"

My gaze snaps back to Shelby. She averts her eyes again. "Why?" I ask.

"Well, that the transport ship is gone changes things." She swallows, still avoiding my gaze. "And Gemma and Daisy are staying here, with their..." She clears her throat. "Daisy is pregnant, with perhaps the first true human-alien hybrids of our time. And knowing what I know now..." She shudders. "I can't leave her—won't leave her—not after everything..."

She trails off.

"Shelby—"

"You're a hybrid, Vagan," she says quickly. "You and Vruksha and Zaku, and the rest of the nagas. You're all hybrids. You have the blood of our enemy running through you, Lurker DNA, as well as human. You carry Genesis 8, and now so does Daisy, in a way. Your scent, when aroused, creates a virus that infects the female you crave, altering its makeup to entice her to mate with you. Zaku and Daisy are guarding a... reactor—relay—something that's manipulating life here on this planet and... it's the same thing we saw down in the dome, the same thing powering it. Gemma and Vruksha are aware of an army of some sort, of weapons, of unidentifiable monstrosities, deep within the mountains. I'm afraid, Vagan, really afraid," the words spill from her like a flood.

She shifts on her feet and inhales, closing and opening her eyes. "The knowledge in my head... it will destroy you, us," she ends in a whisper. "But it can also make a difference, here on Earth, before it's too late."

"Too late?" I say slowly, taking in what she's telling me.

"Someone will discover all of this, someone who will not care how many people—or nagas—they will hurt in taking it for their own. It's why we're here, Vagan, Gemma, Daisy, and I, all for different reasons, but it's why we're here. The Lurkers are—were—so far advanced in regards to humans, they could not only probably fight back the Ketts but destroy them entirely, like they tried to do to us. That power..." She shakes her head. "We need Genesis 8 to use it. It's all here." She taps her temple. "I know everything about you, where you came from, why you're here at all. I mean, not right this very moment, but why *you* exist."

"Ssshelby," I hiss when the worry on her face grows. I let go of her braid and caress her cheek. I want to tell her I do not care about any of this, but she keeps going.

"We talked, the three of us, a lot these last few days. If I go back, what's in my head will transfer to the systems on *The Dreadnaut*, accessible to my superiors. Everything my eyes recorded, the file, some of what happened down there, everything that happened with Peter and Collins. You and the nagas. You'll be hunted, all of you. Every last square foot of this forest and these mountains will be taken over, and that... I can't let that happen. Not to you, not to Daisy, nor anyone else. There's nothing I would be able to do to convince them that this—" she waves her hand in a sweeping arch "—is not the answer we're looking for. This is dangerous."

"And your war?"

She finally meets my gaze. "We're never going to win the war, Vagan. If it's not the Ketts, it'll be something else. It'll be... *us*."

She inhales and rubs the back of her hand across her nose, going silent. Circling my tail around her feet, I cup her face when she tries to look away again.

"Us?"

Her eyes glisten, tears budding on her lashes. "I don't want it to be me," she says so softly I barely hear her.

I press my brow to hers.

Some of her tears fall. "But I don't know where to go from here."

"Home," I say. "We go home."

She lets out a quiet sob, and I press her to my chest, coiling around her.

Reminding her that she's safe and if anyone comes for us, they'll have to get through me first.

THIRTY-ONE
THE CHOICE

Shelby

Vagan holds me until my tears dry, and I push out of his arms. I try to look at him but find it too hard to do so. He's being kind, he's here, and he's watching me, stealing time with me, except I don't know if it's because he really wants me, not anymore.

It's stupid. I know he wants me. I know he cares. There's something disquiet, fiery, and powerful between us, what we've shared, what we've been through together. We've risked our lives for each other.

But is it enough to contract with me for more than a couple of months? What about for the rest of our lives? Marriage contracts are permanent. They can't be undone. And he's an alien, a primitive alien, and half Lurker.

Besides all of that, rarely do couples go into marriage contracts without children. He knows I can't have them now. The only one who does, at least here on Earth.

For the job, it was everything. For me and him? I have no idea.

I'm able to tell him all the reasons I've decided to stay, despite how much I've been through in my search for peace for humankind, but I haven't told him the main reason.

Him.

I want to stay *for* him, to be with him. To never have to face another choice or decision alone, but to always do it with *him*. He says he'll take me home. His home, I assume, except for how long? Is he willing to share it with me forever?

Will he take on that burden?

He's my peace.

He's just not anyone or anything else's.

He wasn't Collins', and that's okay. Once things have settled down, Gemma promised to come with me to help retrieve Collins's corpse and to give him a proper burial. But that's if no more ships come down in the meantime. And we'd have to return, traveling deep underground and into a catacomb of bodies. The likelihood of it happening is so slim, I have no hope in it.

Collins saved my life, and I... miss him. There's no one here who'd understand that and it makes the loneliness swirling in my chest all that much worse. Rubbing my arm absently, I swallow, staring down at Vagan's tail curled around me on the ground. It shifts under my perusal, and I can't help but glance at Vagan's groin. Shut tight, I swallow down another lump in my throat.

I don't scent him, not his pheromones at least.

God, how I miss his scent.

"Ssshelby," he hisses my name with a question. "What's wrong?"

"You haven't been drinking enough water, have you?" I try to divert from the question.

"The soil is wet enough."

"That's not nearly enough—"

"What is wrong, female?" he demands this time, clearly not letting me change the subject.

"Forever," I rasp out. "Your home will be my home, forever?" I eye him, suddenly intimidated to peer too closely into his dark eyes.

His brow wrinkles, and he reaches for me again. I slip away before he takes me in his arms.

"Yesss."

"Despite..." I press my hands to my stomach. "This?"

His gaze drops and a flash of fury crosses his face. I draw in a breath and take a step back.

"I will follow you into the stars," he growls. "To your war. Why is there so much worry and fear in your voice?"

"You don't want what Daisy and Zaku have?" I whisper.

"What they have?" He thumps his tail. "Living behind walls, scared of the land? I want you. I never want what they have."

The vehemence in his voice makes my eyes widen.

"Children," I correct. "Why?" I frown.

His eyes snap to something over my shoulder, and I turn to find Daisy and Zaku watching us from inside.

"Children..." Vagan pauses in thought then shakes his head. "I watched my mother die having me," he says, lowering his voice, "and my litter mates perished soon afterward. I never want to experience that again. The fear I might lose you like how my father lost my mother... it would make me crazed."

I'm taken aback by his words. "I'm so sorry."

"It was long ago."

"I'm still sorry," I whisper. "No one should have to go through that."

He tilts his head in Daisy's direction. "Will she be fine?"

Glancing her way, I'm thankful for the change of subject. "She's doing well. The medical device Zaku has says she's healthy, and the fetuses are developing well. It's only naga females who can't... survive..." I swallow the rest.

He looks back at me. "Good. I want to take you home now," he states firmly.

I glance at his groin again and blush, my doubts slipping away. "I'd like that. I'd really like that."

He shifts his tail out from around me, prompting me to do more than just stare and get lost in my worries. But I've been lost in them for so long, I don't know how not to be. Forcing them away, at least for now, I head inside to grab the few things I've been given.

Zaku moves to bar my way.

But he's not looking at me, he's glaring at Vagan outside.

"You are not welcome here," he rumbles. "We are enemies."

Vagan hisses in response.

"I'm leaving with him," I tell Zaku, shuffling past him to grab my bag. The one I hoped I'd need. Daisy comes rushing to me, wrapping me in her arms.

She's forgiven my lies.

She and Gemma both.

"Do you have to go?" she asks against my ear. "Please stay. I want you to stay."

"I can't. You know I can't. It's best, safest, for all of us if we're separated," I remind her. "We don't know who or what's still out there, nor where the transport ship is. Where Peter is, or the others. We don't know what they know…"

If we're lucky, they know very little.

"But with him? Why does it have to be him?"

Daisy's afraid of Vagan. She risked her life to save mine, fearing Vagan would hurt me and the 'child' I was pretending to carry. She almost died because of us, several times.

Seeing her covered in scars makes my stomach churn, and yet she's forgiven me. If only I could forgive myself.

The least I can do is protect her, and her babies, with everything I have left. I'll start making amends.

"Yes. With him," I say softly, releasing her and then stepping out from her arms. I indicate the orb she's still clutching in one hand. I'd reconfigured several of them so we could communicate long-distance. Hopefully, it'll be the last time I will ever have to use my eyes. "Comm me every day," I say. "Keep me informed about your progress, and," I glance behind me at Vagan, "when you think it's time, I'll be here."

"Promise?"

The word gives me pause.

The word hurts.

"I promise on my life."

Hauling my pack over my shoulder, Zaku moves out of my way to let me by. I know he's glad to be rid of me. He and Vruksha know everything I've learned. About their kind and why they exist.

And Zaku…

He hadn't been entirely surprised. Which makes me believe some nagas know a lot more than others.

I step between him and Vagan, and Vagan takes my bag. I hear the glass door shut behind me and take a step toward Vagan. He tears his eyes off Zaku on the other side and coils me back within his tail.

Sapphire blue and indigo scales surround me, and his stunningly orange tailtip slides up my spine. Shivering from the feel of it, he reaches out and takes my hand, tugging me to him.

A strange sensation rushes through me. One I haven't felt in so long, that I nearly forget the word for it. It tightens my chest and trembles my fingers. It parts my lips and flushes my face. It fills me with excitement and exhilaration.

Vagan leads me away from everything I know.
And I'm free.

THIRTY-TWO

A WATERY ABODE

Shelby

THE TREK TAKES us two days, going down the mountain the opposite way we came up. Afterward, we head south and through a dense gorge, where we come across bears, wolves, and numerous Earth animals.

Vagan scares them all away, striking his tail in warning, while relaying to me how dangerous they can be. He captures a small animal, something he calls a rabbit, and cleans it for me to eat. It's up to me to make a fire, and I'm really thankful for the supplies Zaku let me have, otherwise I don't think I could stomach the strange, raw meat uncooked.

Our first night alone in the wilds brings something out in me, something I thought I'd lost long ago.

My imagination.

There's no walls or weapons, robots or others to offer protection, it's just Vagan and me, the small fire I built and am trying to keep going, the glowing orb of Earth's moon, and the sounds of the night. Vagan spent the trek answering all my questions about this land and his world, feeding my desire for knowledge, except now that the sun is down, my curiosity has diminished with it and my mind wanders to those things that live in the dark.

Feeling terribly exposed, I go to a nearby tree and have Vagan help me break off a branch from it. With the pocket knife in my supplies, I begin to whittle it down to keep my mind busy, designing it after Vruksha's spear.

He let me examine his at length, and as much as I would have loved to have scanned it with my eyes, I didn't. I already knew what I was looking at.

Lurker technology of a very primitive variety. A basic weapon that was clearly designed by humans, using resources here on Earth, copying that of the Lurkers. A Lurker wouldn't need a spear as lightweight as Vruksha's, not with their claws and teeth and speed. Not with their regenerative skills and intelligence. They had far more advanced ways to destroy their enemies.

But it was fascinating to see the spear, to hold it, even if it didn't work for me. It also brought a theory to mind about the reason there was a living Lurkawathian deep below the ground as well...

Had some of them defected from their species and helped humans beyond their mandates? Or was it more nefarious? Had the Lurker been a captive and used for testing? The Lurkers helped humanity before they ended the world, but with weapon creation as well? There's nothing in my file about him, or these weapons like the one Vruksha has. In fact, there was almost nothing about the Lurkers at all.

There's still so much I don't know.

And if I manage to find my way back there to retrieve Collins's body —I shake my head. There's too many ifs. Dwelling on what happened down there—what is down there—makes my heart thump uncomfortably.

So, I whittle my wooden spear until my eyes hood and Vagan pulls it from my hands.

Tense in his hold, I realize I'm still nervous around him. But he coils his tail around me and gently pulls me against his chest and near a dense copse of bushes away from the firelight. He doesn't do anything more than that, and I quickly fall asleep in his embrace.

By the end of the second day, we come to a lake hidden deep within the thickest part of the gorge. It's smaller than the previous one that can be seen from some of Zaku's windows. Vagan clears the overgrowth leading to the shore and drops my pack. I watch as he slips into the water and quickly disappears beneath.

Finding a boulder to sit upon and rest, I take off my boots and slip my feet into the water. Vagan emerges some distance from me, wet and stunning, his hair plastering the sharp features of his face. He glides my way, his tail swaying from side to side in the water behind him.

He stops at my feet, gathering them in his hands, looking up at me from below.

He grazes my arch with his claw, and I inhale sharply, curling my toes.

"We are near our home," he says, doing it again, but with my other foot. I hitch as sensation streaks my nerves and goosebumps rise on my arms.

I look past his glinting eyes and to the rippling water behind him. "You do live on land, right?"

I had never thought to ask.

He kneads my soles with his thumbs. "I live in and on both."

"Both?"

"You will see." He tugs on my feet. "Sssoon."

"I'm not good with water. I can't swim," I say. "I probably should have mentioned that, you being a water creature and all, but I forgot."

He cocks his head to the side, giving me a curiously sly expression. "I will teach you."

"To swim?"

"Yesss."

"I would like that." I smile, gathering my braids and retying them in a knot above my head. He straightens as I shift off the boulder and into the water with him.

"Your wounds," he says, stopping me from going further.

"They'll be fine. They're healing well. What's not fine is how sweaty I am from two days of hard travel." I glance at the deepening shadows of the forest and the golden cast of the setting sun upon the water. "I want to be in the water with you." If he's in the water, then I know it's safe.

That's how much trust I've put in him. I've never trusted anyone as much as I trust Vagan.

He watches me for a moment before moving aside, letting me walk deeper into the lake.

His tail slides against my calf as I move past him. "It's safe, right?" I have to ask anyway, almost teasingly. "There's nothing that will come from the depths to eat me?"

"Only me."

With a shiver from me and a heating expression from him, I swallow thickly and slip into the deeper waters. Yes, there's him.

Him...

I suck my lower lip into my mouth.

I forget sometimes that we're different. That he's not entirely human. I just see Vagan when I look at him now, and not the parts of him that are completely different from me. I see blue and orange, I see scales and a tail, I see a forked tongue, pointed ears, and glinting eyes, but then they fade into completion, they fade and it's just... him.

Right before my feet lose the bottom, he's next to me, keeping my afloat. He takes my good arm and pulls me away from the shore.

"My boots," I gasp, trying to keep my head above the water. "The pack."

"I'll return tomorrow and retrieve them."

"Tomorrow?"

Slashing through the quiet waters, he moves me farther and farther away, following the shoreline. "Tonight, you will sleep in my nessst," he hisses, diving his head beneath the water and bringing it back up.

His nest.

Golden trickles of water slip down his face, over his lips. I lick my own in response.

His eyes drop to them. For a tense moment, he stares.

Curling my toes all over again, I clench between my legs, heating there despite the chill of the water. Grasping Vagan harder now, he tears his eyes from me and swims us past the forest and into another gorge where the lake turns into a river. Against the current, he never loses any speed as tall, jagged rocks rise high on either side of us. A ledge that's far too steep to climb.

Then the sounds of rushing thunder, booming and vacuous, fill my ears, and I mistake it for the rapids. Tightening my grip on him, we turn a slight corner and a waterfall comes into view.

"Vagan," I say in warning as he aims directly for it, caught up in its beauty. "*Vagan!*" I shriek just before he grabs my waist and dives us under the water. Sputtering when we emerge, trembling with cold, I hiss at him in anger. "You could have warned me!" I wipe the water from my eyes as he continues pulling me along and into a hidden cave.

But there's no darkness like I expected. Instead, there's a stream of water, and on the walls on either side and on the ceiling are bioluminescent creatures. They give off a faint white glow.

Vagan glides up to a ledge and helps me out of the water.

"What is this place?" I ask, turning as he hauls his long body up afterward.

"Home," he says.

Nearly lost in the way the water slips over his lithe body and taut muscles, I avert my eyes to take in our surroundings, stepping deeper into the space.

The cave is narrow where we are but just ahead is a large, open cavern and a pool of water where the stream ends. And around the pool are ledges, some high, some low, circling it. Across from me, on the other side of the water is what seems to be an old walkway with metal bars as a railing. The walkway goes deeper into the cavern but also out toward the waterfall, leading to a carved-out stairwell.

A way in and out, built by humans long ago.

Vagan curls his tailtip around my waist and takes my hand, leading me toward the cavern. The way is dry, though in some parts there's water trickling down the walls, and with my bare feet, I'm happy for the help.

I've never seen anything like it. A grotto. A fantastical place to someone who's spent the majority of their life on a spaceship.

In the cavern, there's hides covering the walls of all shapes and sizes, and items, furniture and otherwise, neatly placed throughout. There are piles of pieces and things that I can't identify, though the layout itself is orderly. The ceiling is high, and I start scouting for a place where I can make a proper fire pit.

"I do not have food for you so I will need to catch fish for us," Vagan starts telling me as he leads me towards one of the higher ledges. "I have not been back here since your ship came down from the skies."

"That was months ago," I say, eyeing him.

All he does is sway his tail in response.

"Have you been... Were you watching me?" I ask instead. "All that time?"

I think back on the months I've been here, what I've done, and wonder how long and how much he's seen. How long has he wanted me?

"Only after I saw you the first time," he answers casually. "Before that, it was out of curiosity."

"And when was that?"

He twists and meets my eyes. "The first time you walked off the ship, I believe."

Months. He's been watching me for months. I shiver, and I'm not sure if it's from being wet and cold or how determined he was to have me. I hug my middle. Right now, I'm very thankful he was. If he hadn't been, I'd be rotting and crushed under a ton of rock.

I tear my eyes off him first. "I like it. Your home," I add.

"Our home."

A smile pulls at my lips. "I've... never had a home before, not really. Not since I was really young. Since then, it's only been one small room after another."

He moves to stand in front of me, slipping a finger under my chin. "This is your home now, Shelby."

"It's beautiful," I whisper, pulled back into his gaze. "Is it safe?"

"Yesss. No one knows of its existence but me, and you now. Those who did are long gone."

I swallow. "And your nest?"

He drops his finger from under my chin and pulls back. The scales at the groin region of his tail pull apart and his cock falls out, tapered, knotted, and hard. Seed beads his tip, and I inhale deeply, getting my first whiff of his scent in days.

"You are cold," he rumbles.

Trembling harder than before, I nod stiffly.

"Let me warm you, female," he rasps low.

Breathing in, his scent suddenly floods me, and my lips part in a gasp. My cheeks heat furiously.

"Shelby," I say softly, reminding him.

He moves back in front of me, forcing me to look away from his cock, and cups my cheeks. "Ssshelby," he repeats.

Unable to move, unable to do anything but breathe him in, he tugs me toward the back of the cavern.

Piles of rocks, placed in patterns in a rounded formation at the edge, come to view. Trickling water from one of the walls in the back glides through the pile, keeping it cold and wet, before it drips into the pool below.

His nest.

Vagan releases me as I walk around it, seeing deep grooves where I am sure are his favorite places to sleep.

But the whole rock formation isn't wet, only the middle is, and on the sides are draping, thick hides. Feeling one, it's plush and dry, though worn down with use.

"You will have to help me make a new one," he says. "One we can share. One that will keep you warm and comfortable"

"Would you be okay with that?"

"Yesss," he says, brushing against me. "Yes. Let me be worthy of you."

I tilt my head to look at him, but he yanks me to his chest before I'm able to respond.

"Let me warm you. The only way I know how."

Wet heat splashes my leg, and I know he's spilled. Gasping in a fresh wave of his pheromones, I let him pull off my drenched clothes and fling them aside. His scent engulfs me and I suck it in, knowing what it will do to me. Now I know Vagan, I'm not afraid, and I do not resist. I welcome this.

Flames burst in my chest, harder, heavier, hungrier than before. The chill of the water vanishes, and I grasp Vagan's cock with both hands, tugging it.

More of his spill releases, getting all over me, and I bask. In his scent, in the rising heat, in everything.

My stress disappears, and finally, *finally* it's just Vagan and I again, just us, us and soft darkness, hidden from the universe in our own little paradise away from everything that wants to tear it apart. Surrounded by rock, on the brink of something more, alone, but together. Always together.

I squeeze his shaft hard, wanting more.

Is it selfish to want everything?

Suddenly my pants are being torn off, my shirt goes next, and he's pushing me into the rock formation and toward a cushion of hides near the side.

"I'll get them wet," I mutter, my hair dripping water down my bare curves.

He hisses and then dives down behind me, streaking his tongue up my spine. "I like you wet, mate." He laps at my hairline at the base of my head, lifting my sagging braids and squeezing them with his hands so water pools everywhere. "I am always thirsty. Always. If I could, I would drink my fill from your body, or off of it."

He says this as he lowers to drip the water from my braids into his open mouth.

I watch him, transfixed, as he sucks the ends into his mouth, making sure he gets every last drop of water from them.

Shivering from the piercing look in his eyes, he nudges me down between the grooves of several smooth boulders and gently rolls me onto my back. Keeping our eyes locked, he lowers and slides his tongue through my folds, over my clit, up my belly, to end at my mouth where he dives his tongue into me.

Splaying my legs as wide as possible, he covers me completely, pushing against my opening. Slick and ready for him from the moment his pheromones entered me, I cup his neck with my hands and press my face to his chest.

His gentleness only lasts until his tip is buried, stretching me. He keeps his body above me so he doesn't disturb my wounds, holding himself over me with two hands grasping the rocks on either side. Clenching around his girth, Vagan groans and shunts his massive knot into me, forcing me to take all of him in one, brutal push.

I strain, arch, grit my teeth. My feet slip on the rocks and fall into a pile of soft hide. He spills inside me all while I try to adjust to his size all over again. Tight pressure gives way to pleasure soon after. Sweet, primitive pleasure.

I followed him to his den, even to his nest for this very reason. For him to claim me in every way possible.

I gasp his name when he shifts his hips, rubbing his swollen knot deliciously against the spot that gives me the most pleasure. I've hurt so much lately, I need pleasure, all the pleasure he could force me to endure.

Vagan keeps his dark, alien eyes on me as I milk him, making him tremble with each jet of seed that splashes hot and deep. He pins me with his eyes, studying me in a way that makes the butterflies in my stomach fly away in fear. Heated from the inside out, any remaining chill of the water vanishes. Holding onto him tightly, I push my pelvis to his, needing more.

"You won't hurt me," I breathe through moans. "You won't," I whisper against his ear, sliding my hands from his neck to tangle into his wet hair.

He pulls out and slams back into me in response.

An airy shriek tears from my throat. He does it again, harder. Much harder.

"More," I urge him, already slipping up the rock behind me from force.

I want his savagery. I want the male who stalked me for months, who threatened others for me, who risked his life again and again, for *me*. I want all his fascinating strangeness and broody quiet to conquer me as I graze his scaled back with my nails, taking it all. I don't want him to be gentle.

I need him to remind me that we survived.

And we're going to survive, always, because we're together.

"I—" he grunts, grinding his hips hard "—I want to be worthy of you."

Again he says that, spinning my mind with those words. "You are," I cry out when he thrusts like he's trying to put all of his body inside me. "You are!"

Pulling his head down to mine, I kiss him, shoving my tongue into his mouth, swiping his fangs. Saliva, blood, and stinging thrusts erupt between us and he shoves me back, trapping me on all sides, cushioning me down.

I take his weight. His brutal, heavy weight.

Our mouths tangle, and he loses control, snapping his hips in quick succession, pounding his knot against my sweet spot. Hooking my legs around his tail, he ravages, filling my body entirely with him, amplifying the torturous pressure, forcing me to forget.

His rutting grows faster, more desperate, hurried like we're running for our lives, and not even after I've cried out, begged, and climaxed more times than my mind can number, slipping from one sensation to the next, does he let up. He mates me like he'll only ever get one chance to do so.

Embracing him, I remind him I'm not going anywhere.

I'm not returning to *The Dreadnaut*.

That I choose him, and this life here on Earth. Finding the decision to be the easiest of my life.

When the blistering heat nearly suffocates me, he lifts up and watches me come undone, slamming, grinding his hips as I suck in cold air into my lungs. He drops his tail at one point, and water sprays down from us from above. It's the only glimmer of awareness I have, the speckles of that brief chill across my skin.

Still, I know he's holding back.

Knowing what runs through his veins...

I stare into his dark eyes as his hips shunt hard and devastatingly into mine, stoking the pressure inside me again. My naga is a horny male. Reeling, it's his gaze I need, his alien savagery, that makes me peak again with gut-wrenching screams.

They echo through the cave.

When I thrash this time, it's a fight. He dives, covering my mouth, pinning me down as I struggle and claw and lose my mind. Pleasure rips through every nerve-ending, shunted continuously with his stabbing, needy cock.

He told me about his spill. He's always producing more... I gasp, thinking about my poor body and the continuous workout it's going to get until this tension between us ends.

He holds me down until it's over, until we're both depleted. And with him still buried deep, he shifts me to rest in the crook of his arm, and we sleep.

I wake to him spilling again inside me. I wake to more rough thrusting, his tail holding my legs open, and another orgasm.

I fall asleep again afterward, and wake once more to him sliding out, to him lifting me into his arms, gathering my hair and carrying me to the pool. He bathes me, impales me on his tailtip from behind while I hold onto the ledge, and drinks the water that gathers on my skin and in my hair.

He dominates my mind with pleasure and sensation. Two things that were nearly taboo in my old life.

And I love him for it.

THIRTY-THREE
A NEW BEGINNING

Shelby

We eat, we rest, we mate.

We swim.

We barely speak, only conversing about our current needs and wants, avoiding all other topics completely. One day turns into another, and when we do converse, it's about his world and mine, and our many differences.

Everything he tells me fascinates me.

True to Vagan's word, we are safe, and nobody calls out my name to save me, and though that pains my heart terribly in its own way, I feel better when I curl around Vagan's tail and he circles his limbs over me, protecting me in every way I need. I'd rather be with him and free than beholden to men who are evil.

The next time I fall asleep, I wake to find my boots and my pack amongst the supplies. Rising, I drape a hide around my shoulders and go to it. Every muscle in my body aches, but it is a sweet ache.

Vagan has adequately proved to me we're compatible—well mostly—the tight stretch of his large cock likes to remind me that I'm much smaller than him.

Inside is my orb and I pull it out, checking to see if either Gemma or

Daisy have reached out to me. Neither have, and I breathe a sigh of relief.

Hearing Vagan slide up behind me, I lean back into him when he takes hold of my hair and pushes it forward over my shoulder, rebraiding one of my strands in the process. He licks up the column of my neck.

Shivering from the touch and twisting in his arms, I notice a pile of wood in the corner. I glance from the pile to him, a smile twitching my lips. "You've been busy. Are you sure you still want me here?" I tease. "Now that you know what you're in for? Can you even handle a fire pit in your space?"

His expression remains stoic. "You are hiding," he accuses abruptly. "It is time for you to stop."

My face falls. "I'm n—"

"You are."

My lips part, then close, then part again, trying to find an excuse, anything to stay in our bubble of bliss longer. Nothing comes to mind. I reach for his cock to tug it out of his tail but he grabs my hand and stops me.

"I know," I finally whisper. "I am hiding. It's... easy. Hiding, that is."

He searches my face. "Do you want me to leave?" he asks after a moment, his voice softening.

Do I want him to leave? To stay? Would he even want to? I press my face to his chest. "I want you to stay. If that's all right? Please."

"I will stay."

He releases me, and I look around, letting sadness enter my heart. It's been easy keeping it out, keeping it from bothering me having Vagan around to distract me, but he's right, it's still there. It's there and festering, poking at me at the darkest hours of the night and during the first rays of sunlight in the morning, brightening the falls at the grotto's opening.

Collins told me I'd see the sun again. That he had a plan.

If I had known at the time he wouldn't be seeing the sun with me...

I inhale a shaky breath.

Fisting my hands, I move around the pool, to the other side of the stream where there are old metal railings from long ago, and take the path toward the falls. Vagan follows behind me, letting me move at my own pace.

Coming upon a rounded, smooth rock, I pick it up and wipe it clean with my hands, letting some of the spray from the falls wet it. Shuffling through the rest of the tunnel, I emerge on the other side of the waterfall to a broken pathway leading up the steep rocky ledge to my left. So ruined, it doesn't even look like a carved-out stairway from a distance.

Pulling the edges of my blanket tightly over my shoulders and tying it upon my body, I climb the stairs.

Lush forest greets me, and a wide view of the watery gorge we swam down days before stifles my panting. Beyond is the lake. The early morning sun glistens the smooth surface of it.

I walk along the edge, searching for the perfect spot.

Closer to the lake, there's an outcropping where the sun hits the stones directly, and I choose the place upon first glance.

It's near me, though far enough away that I have to travel specifically to it to pay a visit. Gathering all the loose rocks and stones nearby, I bring them to the spot.

Vagan hands me one as I begin building.

It takes me all day to get it right.

And as the sun sets in the distance, and the lake takes on a golden hue, I scratch Collins's name onto the first stone.

When it's done, I place it on top of the death marker.

"Thank you," I say, rubbing my arm. "Thank you," I breathe out, knowing the words are shallow in these circumstances. Saying nothing seems worse though...

Who knows if I'll ever have the chance to return and retrieve his body, if it'll even be possible? I loved him. He's the closest thing I had to family. And despite what happened between us, I trusted him too. I've always trusted him.

But I also failed him, and I'll have to live with that for the rest of my life.

He deserves to see the sunlight every day.

No tears fall from my eyes, though a burden lifts from my chest as Vagan leads me back home in the dark.

Once we're within the grotto, I go to the pile of wood and grab some to create a temporary fire, not wanting to say goodbye to the light quite yet. The fire pit will have to wait another day.

Vagan leaves and returns with several fish just as I manage to get the flames roaring.

Watching him gut the fish with his claws, trying to memorize how to do it in the future, I realize we haven't spoken since this morning.

"You keep saying you want to be worthy of me," I say, breaking the silence, listening to the wood crackle and snap. I get up and move to Vagan, dropping to my knees before him. "But am I worthy of you?"

He stops what he's doing and meets my eyes.

I hold my breath as he scans my face, his expression unreadable.

He releases the fish.

"Are you?" he asks, throwing the question back at me.

I look around our home, the pool, our nest, and finally back to him. "I want to be," I tell him. "Please help me be so. Teach me?"

His gaze softens, and his lips twitch into a smile.

The first smile I've ever seen from him. I smile back. I can't help it. Vagan is...enchanting when he smiles.

He cups my cheeks and presses his brow to mine. "You already are," he hums. "My brave one. I could not do what you did today, and I have lost someone too, long ago."

"You have? Your parents?"

"Not my parents. I never knew them but yesss, I have lost someone. She went west to join the other females. She was... my mother. My friend. She saved my life. She was the only family I have ever known. She found me there, on the shore bank, near death. She saved my life."

The other females, the ones Gemma and Daisy told me about. The naga women.

"She sounds wonderful," I say softly. "I wish I could have met her. What was her name?"

"Eestys. She would have liked you."

Eestys. I remember that name.

"I hope so." Vagan starts to pull away, and I cover his hands, keeping them on me, not wanting his touch to go away. "I love you, Vagan. I need you to know that. I love you, and I think I've loved you since... since..." I trail off, not wanting to bring up that first moment again.

He cocks his head as if he's never heard the phrase before. Then his eyes lighten, rather than darken.

"I love you too, Ssshelby." He coils his tail around me and then taps his chest with his tailtip. "Here."

I press my palm to my chest as well, smiling. "Same." But then I sniff fish guts and my nose wrinkles, and I wipe my cheeks. "You got fish all over me," I gasp, smearing slime down my face. "Oh, god, it's so gross!" I cry out, rushing to the pool.

And he laughs.

He laughs, and it's the best sound I have ever heard in my life, and for the first time in more months—years—than I can count, there's hope in my heart.

Real, true, hope. The kind you spend your entire life chasing, searching, bleeding for.

Sacrificing for...

Hope.

It's the last thing I hear as he dives into the pool and pulls me in after him.

Hope.

EPILOGUE CHAPTER ONE: WHAT IS PEACE?

Shelby

ONE MONTH LATER...

"Push!" I urge. "Breathe and push!"

Daisy screams, legs spread wide, and I'm between them, waiting for her to crown. She grunts and wails, threatening Zaku all the while, but it's just me and her and the medical device she's lying upon. Lying upon and strapped down to.

I had to kick Zaku out to the hallway because he was stressing Daisy and me out more than he was helping. He clearly can't handle seeing Daisy in pain, and his tense, terrified manner was more burdensome than funny.

And it was funny. Really funny seeing the giant would-be king of this land, unable to do anything but stare with horror as Daisy screamed at him, ordering him to add his skull to the ones on the lawn outside.

"Shelby, I can't," Daisy cries.

"You can and you will. Now, push!"

Blood is all over my hands, and my eyes are on, spotlighting between her legs. Try as I have to not use them, to not record anything more that could put us all at risk, there have been times it's been necessary.

Like this. I couldn't keep Collins alive, but I'll die trying to keep Daisy and her babies happy and healthy. I will fucking learn.

I'm a doctor, just not the type of doctor Daisy needs, and the data in my eyes, thankfully, has information on childbirth, at least alien childbirth. Gestri childbirth, even Kett copulation and gestation.

It's enough. It has to be.

But Daisy's scars keep her from spreading her legs too wide, pulling her skin taut, and her pushing is causing her more pain and discomfort than I can imagine. Face flushed red, sweat beading both our brows, her eyes are wrenched shut so tightly that tears couldn't fall even if she was crying.

"You can do this, Daisy," I encourage. "If anyone can do this, you can."

She has to do this.

"You escaped, you traveled across this forest, took on Peter and bloodied his face. You survived the crash," I tell her. "You can do this. You can survive this!"

She has to survive. I'm going to do everything in my power to make sure that happens. Hybrids have been born before from human women in the past, at least from what I'd discovered, so I know she can survive...

The crowd gathered outside Zaku's home apparently wants proof. They want to see Daisy live. They want to see her babies.

"Where is Gemma?" she cries.

"Coming, sweetheart. She's on her way. She'll be here soon."

Getting Gemma through the nagas outside is another thing entirely though. Vagan is out there, ready to intercept her and Vruksha and help them get to Zaku's house without bloodshed, but I'm worried. I can't help it.

Somehow news of Daisy's pregnancy and labor has traveled.

Boy, has it traveled.

One glance at the windows outside the room is enough to keep my head down and be everything Daisy needs me to be because otherwise it'll be me staring at a lot of fearsome faces.

There's a lot of scary alien males out there, and I'm suddenly very thankful I didn't have to face what Gemma and Daisy faced on the plateau. Although the researcher in me wants to speak to and analyze every single one of them that's gathered, to interrogate them until it's *me* chasing *them* through the forest.

Because they clearly didn't escape from the facility.

So how have they survived Earth's collapse, and where did they come from? Where did any of the nagas, animals, and plants come from?

Seeing a head emerge between Daisy's legs, I shift her legs, helping the baby move through the pelvis.

"Push!" I scream, when she abruptly sags in exhaustion. "They're coming!"

Daisy shrieks and bears down.

The first baby rips through her and into my arms. The whimper the little one gives floods my chest with love, and I quickly wrap it up, handing it to Daisy. She cries and clutches her child to her chest just as another one appears.

"Again," I order her. "Push!"

The second one slips right out, having none of the stress upon them as the first one. I bundle them up and call Zaku back into the room.

He's at my side the next instant. "Help Daisy with the babies," I tell him. "I need to cut the umbilical cords and deliver the placenta now. Daisy, you still need to keep pushing or you'll hemorrhage."

I see Zaku gather the babies in his arms, remaining next to Daisy.

The next few minutes are some of the most stressful of my life. If it weren't for the medical device keeping Daisy hydrated and reporting her vitals to me, I don't know what I'd do. There's a lot of blood.

Vagan and I raced here like we were being hunted all over again. I haven't slept since.

But when it's done, and Zaku's house robots come and start cleaning everything up, I sit back on my stool and say a quiet prayer.

Hearing soft laughter, winded gasps, and screams giving way to coos, is everything. Wiping my hands clean on a towel after rinsing them, I take a moment to watch Daisy, Zaku, and their two babies curled up together at the head of the medical table.

Both babies are male, scaleless—for now, I imagine—and oddly enough, one has a tail while the other one has legs. They both have filmy cowls coming from their heads and attached to their backs, like their father. Gently, I squeeze between the machine on Daisy's left and join them at her other side.

"Can I?" I ask, indicating the babies.

Daisy smiles and nods. With Zaku's watchful eyes on me the whole time, I pull back each of the little ones' lips to check for fangs.

"Oh, thank god," I mutter. "You'll be able to breastfeed them."

It takes Daisy a moment to understand what I mean. "Thank god."

"Is she going to be fine?" Zaku interjects.

I nod. "Yes. The placenta came out intact, and I've stitched her up. She's going to continue bleeding for several more weeks as she sheds her lochia. No sex, for a long time," I order, giving him a stern look. "If your thing is anywhere as big as you are, Zaku, you'll want to wait a year."

"A year?" they both sputter.

"Three months at least, and take it easy the first time." I wave my hand, not even wanting to imagine how their bed play works. "Take it easy every time, in fact. Make sure she gets a lot of bed rest. I don't know what..." I trail off and lick my lips, not wanting to say the wrong thing. "I don't know exactly how the next several months will go for her, having hybrids. Every woman is different, but take it easy, keep Daisy close to the device, and keep her fed and hydrated. Also, keep me updated. Full human pregnancies take at least nine months for gestation, and, well, it's been what, six weeks, eight weeks maybe? The next couple might be just as interesting..."

Daisy looks at me, her brow wrinkling. "What do you mean?"

"According to what I've read, nagas—hybrids—grow fast, much faster than human children. And according to Vagan, who has clear memories of the first day he came into this world." I caress the top of one of the baby's smooth heads. "They might be listening to us now. Do you remember, Zaku?"

His gaze slits, and then he shakes his head. "I only remember my father."

"Don't say anything that'll... disturb them," I say anyway, smiling. "You're already going to have enough on your hands."

"Thank you, Shelby," Daisy says, turning back to her babies.

I head for the door. "It's the least I can do," I say softly. "I'll give you guys some time to bond, but I'll be back shortly to check you and the babies over. I think—"

There's a loud noise and then footsteps speeding our way. Before I can react, I hear Gemma's voice calling out just as she crashes into me.

"Where is she!?"

Steadying myself, I move out of Gemma's way as she shoves Zaku aside. "I'm so, so sorry I'm late," she whines. "We came as fast as we could. Vruksha had to carry me up the mountain." She's completely disheveled, dirty, and sweaty.

"Wash your hands before you touch them!" I yell just before Gemma encloses Daisy in a hug.

She jumps back, eyes wild with adrenaline. "Shit, yeah. Fuck. I'll be right back."

Daisy, Zaku, and I share a winded look.

"I'm going to give... your guests... the news they're here for and tell them to get the hell away and leave you guys alone," I finish. I almost make it out the door when Daisy stops me.

"Shelby, will you stay? For a few days at least?"

I stop and face her, leaning on the doorframe. "Hell yeah I'm staying. I've been eating nothing but fish for the past month and am dying for a hot soak in one of your tubs."

"Good," she says.

I escape into the hallway and take a long, steadying breath, finally able to relax a little. The last few days have been hellish, and I wouldn't wish them on my worst enemy. Worrying about Daisy, and getting to her in time, was worse than the entire ordeal beneath the facility... almost.

Straightening, my eyes land on Vagan immediately out on the bluff. Next to him is Vruksha.

He carried me here too; it was faster that way. I head to the kitchen and find a large bowl, filling it with water. With access to Zaku's home, given only to Gemma and me, I head for the door with the eyes of at least a dozen males following my every move. I recognize one of them... Krellix, I believe, waiting in the background. Beside him is a light green male with large black eyes.

Vagan and Vruksha meet me at the door, and Vruksha heads into the house.

"She's fine, the babies are well, and she's resting with Zaku and them now," I say loud enough for everyone to hear. There's commotion among the males, hissing of every variety, and looks of relief flashing across the faces of several.

Out of the corner of my eye, I see a streak of black and purple just as it vanishes into the shadows of the forest beyond the lawn.

Turning to Vagan, I hand him the bowl of water, which he gulps down. I leave and return with another, stopping at the threshold. Half of the males are gone when I come back.

"They won't be an issue?" I ask, glancing at the several who remain.

"No." Vagan caresses my cheek with the back of his claw. "They are curious. Nothing more."

"Good."

"Are you okay?"

Leaning my face into his hand, I nod. "Just tired. I'm going to stay for a few days and make sure everything is good."

"I will misssss you."

I can't help but smile. "Miss me? There's no need to miss me."

He hums. "I miss you always."

I meet his eyes. "Same."

When one of the babies starts crying, I jump, looking behind me. "I should..."

This time, he nods. "Go."

"You'll be here?"

"Watching. Waiting. Always."

"You're good at that," I tease.

Vagan backs away, keeping my eyes. "I know."

He slips into the shadows of the trees, and part of me wants to follow him, to grasp him close and tell him, I've always felt his eyes on me.

There will be plenty of time for that later. Vagan and I have only begun our journey. Turning, I make my way back to the room where my new family is waiting for me. It'll take some work, it'll take time, and a lot of forgiveness and trust, but someday I know Vagan will redeem himself and be welcomed.

But that's another fight, for another time.

Seeing Gemma curled up on the medical bed next to Daisy, she's clean, her hair damp. I go to the other side and force my way onto the bed with them. "Shuffle over."

"There's not enough room!"

"Well, make room," I huff. "I want in."

Squeezing onto it, Zaku's left cradling one of his sons while Daisy works on helping the other latch.

"It's like he gets a harem without even asking for one," Gemma teases Zaku.

"I do not want a harem," he mutters dryly.

"I wouldn't mind having you two around all the time." Daisy laughs. "Why won't he latch, Shelby?"

I reach between them and curl my fingers around Daisy's nipple. "He could be having a problem with the scars. Start with his bottom lip. We'll work on it," I yawn, absently helping her squeeze colostrum into the baby's mouth. The baby's tongue is forked and tickles my finger as it slips out to explore.

"How do you know so much?" Gemma asks, stifling her own yawn.

"I don't. Not really. I asked the orb a lot of questions, and the rest... I guess I just remember from being around so many babies when I was a kid. My mom was a breeder."

Daisy settles back. "On a colony? Those types of breeders?"

"Yeah."

"Lucky."

"Yeah."

Hearing a soft snore, I lift to see Gemma passed out on the other side of her. Daisy gives me a tired smile of her own. "I think she's tired."

I lie back down, cuddling into Daisy's side. "Me too. Aren't you?"

She nods.

I won't be able to lie for long; I have too much to do, but for a few minutes, I rest with my sisters. Like with Vagan, I'd die for them, I'd fight for them, and I'll protect them with everything I have. We may have not chosen our fates, but we made them our own regardless.

We found love in the process.

And that...

That is everything.

EPILOGUE CHAPTER TWO: MONSTROUS

Collins

I WAKE UP, finding my head killing me. The room already spinning, I still my limbs and quiet my breathing, immediately aware of who I am and what I've done. My training instincts kick in, and I settle back into the prone position I'm in.

Then I wait and listen, feeling out my body without making a noise, learning what I can from my surroundings.

Silence.

There's only silence.

I sense no one around me, watching me, waiting to see if I'll wake up. After a while, the fact that I'm completely alone dawns on me.

And that means I'm safe—for now—and Shelby is gone. Dead or gone, I don't know yet, but I can move without alerting anything that I'm alive.

Testing my limbs, every joint hurts only there's no crippling pain. There should be pain. The last thing I remember is hands around my neck, snapping it, breaking my spine. I also recall an overwhelming urge to fight, to destroy everything in my path, and to eat.

I was ravenous. I still am.

It's this hunger that has me throwing caution to the wind and rising on my elbows to peer around.

And immediately regret doing so, seeing the corpse I'm lying atop of.

Stiff from rigor mortis, the Lurker is just as fucking ugly as the first time we met. Except now its throat has been ripped out, and—I spit—some of it's still in my mouth.

I push off the dead alien and roll onto the ground next to it, staring up at the ceiling, chewing absently on the remaining gristle between my teeth. My hunger grows, and I try to fight it, this yawning, hollow ache in my stomach, knowing it's a losing battle. With rot in my nostrils, I flip back over and take a bite out of the alien's side.

Each swallow, each tear of flesh, I wince, spit, and groan at the disgusting thing I'm doing. At the horrible act I'm committing. Chewy, tough flesh gums between my teeth, shredding on my sharp incisors. The Lurker's been dead for a while.

The corpse has lost all its warmth.

Growing stronger with each gagging swallow, becoming less hungry, my mind sharpens. The events leading me to this moment strike my skull like bullets.

I gave myself a healthy dose of 'grade A' Genesis 8, not even caring about the half-life of it, nor its immediate effects upon me. I knew what I was in for. I just wasn't aware of... the hunger... All I cared about was being strong, strong for Shelby, desperate to be her hero, to have her look at me the way I always dreamed she would.

I hadn't spent years orchestrating my life to follow hers just to lose her so easily to another.

But she's gone now, she's made her choice, and I've made mine.

I can taste her blood in my mouth, even now, even amongst the rot. I'll never forget her taste. I'll never forget that split-second where I couldn't hold back from her. I was so mad, so tired, so... in love.

She was right to run.

I tried to eat her, knowing all the while how much she means to me.

Apparently, transforming is hungry work. The fucking snake was right to end me. I don't know what I would have done otherwise...

A wail of remorse escapes me.

Finishing up with the Lurker's corpse, feeling the pain in my head, the aches in my joints fade away, I rise and finally get a good look around.

I'm in the foyer outside the first elevator, at the entrance to the dome. *A goddamned underground forest.* A forest I know far too well after being hunted through it for hours by the fucker at my feet.

I glance at them and spread out my toes.

My feet... they're not human feet anymore. Reaching down, I tear off the remainder of my military boots, revealing hooked, clawed toes and tough scales. From there, I realize my whole body is covered in tough scales. I rip off what's left of my pants, sliding my fingers up my leg.

They're longer, taut with muscle, and no longer resemble anything human. Standing takes some work, but when I find and adjust to my new balance, there's power coursing through my limbs. I'm naturally armored. Inhaling sharply, my shoulders roll, and my back cracks.

Moving to one of the dome windows, I study my form in the faint, pulsing reflection cast from the distant lights pulsating out from the dome's central relay.

Awash in red and blue hues, I see my face for the first time and lick my lips.

It's me.

I'm still here.

My face might be broader, sharper, perhaps a little longer, but I recognize it amongst my new features. My hair is gone and so are my eyebrows. My eyes are darker, almost swollen with black ink, and the tears I hadn't realized were falling are creating dark tracks down my leathery cheeks.

I taste one of them, finding it salty, like a human tear.

Hmm.

My fingers are longer, my chest broader, my muscles bulging. What-ever is left of my uniform hangs off my frame in tatters.

And my cock...

I grip it, annoyed seeing it out of my clothes—clothes that couldn't hide it even if I wanted it to at this point—and test it with a squeeze.

My cock is hard as steel in my grip, and it's one change I can get behind. It's grown as well, the girth aligning with the larger frame of my new body and no longer as sensitive. My testicles are gone, and I grunt, pushing this concerning change in anatomy out of my mind for now.

I need to get out of this place and get back above ground.

Now that my hunger is gone, I know I can't stay here. I'm not going to die, not easily, and becoming like the dead alien, stuck in a dome, is not a fate I'm willing to suffer.

Turning toward the elevator doors, a new emotion floods me.

Fury.

Plain, unhindered rage.

Shelby's gone.

My life is gone.

Everything I have ever wanted, worked endlessly for, is gone. The training, the ranks, the blood, sweat, and tears to someday prove myself enough to Central Command and be promoted to captain, gone. Signing a marriage contract with Shelby, having children with her, gone.

And for what?

I look down at my hands, clenching them.

Someone is going to pay, and I know exactly what I need to do.

Going to the elevator, I tear open the metal doors and climb the shaft to the top, climbing through the hole I punched when I was after Shelby. The scent of her blood swarms my nostrils, and I hiss, a long, thick tongue shooting out of my mouth, tasting the scent in the air.

Old. It tastes old. Days? Weeks? I can't tell. Stumbling to the wall, I look around, afraid I'm going to stumble upon her corpse.

There's just blood, a lot of blood, dried brown and crusted. I claw open the doors and push my way out of the small, gore-covered space, and find the hallway with the old bones of the security guard. Heading back towards the tunnels, I follow Shelby's scent all the way back to where we fell.

Eyeing a single shaft of light, I peer upward, seeing a long, jagged tunnel, slightly obscured by boulders and pipes above me.

My nostrils clear, and I close my eyes.

She made it out.

The fucking snake got her out.

I wish I could say I hated him for doing what I would have never been able to do, even if I had gotten her this far, but I don't. She needed the both of us to survive. He got her out when I had failed her terribly.

And I was there when she needed me the most...

She'll be safe with him. Safer with him than with me.

I sniff the ground where I know they lay, practically seeing them curled together on the rocks, and grit my teeth.

I begin to climb.

My fury returns as I haul my body up and through the passageway, knowing I'm getting closer and closer to my target.

Knowing I'll have him screaming for mercy soon.

For what he's done, for what he's caused, he'll suffer. If not on my behalf, or Shelby's, then for the other teammates who have died or been hurt because of him. He will suffer.

Peter will pay.

If I have to hunt him across the universe, he will *pay*.

AUTHOR'S NOTE

Thank you for reading *the Naga Brides Box Set*.

If you adore cyborgs, aliens, anti-heroes, and adventure, follow me on Facebook or through my blog online for information on new releases and updates.

Join my newsletter for the same information.

Naomi Lucas

Turn the page for Death Adder Naga Brides Book Four!

DEATH ADDER'S BLURB

Females have returned to Earth, brought here by technology I do not trust. They've been claimed and nested, kept far from me.

The broken one. The dark one.

I will always be alone.

When a ship lands in my territory and a black-suited human female appears, I am in awe. I am in NEED.

Only she is surrounded by men.

So, I will sneak up on her.

I will stalk her, learn everything about her, and wait for the right moment.

And when the time comes, I'll set my trap.

She will be caught.

Then she will be claimed.

By no one else but ME.

Click here for Zhallaix's story... And turn the page to read the first chapter!

DEATH ADDER
CHAPTER ONE: LANDFALL

Celeste

"In and out, guys. That's the goal. We get the target and we get out. This isn't field practice. This planet is dangerous, and previous reports indicate that the locals are prone to aggression."

"Oh, come on, Captain. It's not like we're dropping into Hellion. This is Earth. We all know what's down there. Nothing but dust and bones."

I don't give Roger my attention. He feeds on jokes and easy sentiments, feeling the need to always lighten the mood of my squad. He does it when he's nervous.

"Kyle, tighten your straps. Until we lose the pod, the descent will be much rougher than you're used to," I say.

Roger smiles from where he sits across from me. "Nobody wants to smell like vomit on their first mission."

Once our ship is close enough to the planet, we're dead falling in a battle box. The ship's pilot will drop the container we're in, aiming it at our target location. Until we make contact, we'll be in freefall. The descent will be rough. They always are in battle boxes. Soldiers have died because their straps weren't tight enough.

Sometimes they died anyway.

Those in command aren't giving us a ship. There's already one waiting for us on Earth—the same transit that brought Peter's team here. We just have to find it, figure out what happened to Captain Peter and his team, and bring both home.

As my men settle back in their seats, I check the satellite map of Eagle's Point. The ship is currently several miles north of the original mission site and sits at the base of a mountain. Peter's ship hasn't moved for several months, not since its emergency takeoff.

And its subsequent crash.

Peter's ship never made it off of Earth, and shortly afterwards, all contact was lost. Since then, Central Command has been in the dark.

Central Command does not like being in the dark.

"Countdown commences in one minute."

I lower the map and pull down my goggles.

Peter's mission was supposed to be an easy one: find the whereabouts of the enemy's technology and bring it back to *The Dreadnaut* in hopes that we can discover a way to fight the Ketts. We need anything that would give us an advantage. Because we're running out of options.

"Steady now," I remind my team. "Deep, even breaths. This'll be over before it's begun."

Stoney silence answers me as I scan my squad one last time. They're focused and aware.

Good.

The box trembles, and it's lifted from its track—disconnected from the transport ship. Reaching up, I clutch the straps over my chest and join my men in bracing.

We're close to Earth now.

Our homeworld.

How did I ever end up here?

The pilot's voice over the intercom begins counting down from thirty. My fingers strain, and the cushions on either side of my head tighten, locking my head in place. The light above us flickers when the box lurches. Then the light goes out entirely.

My men are silent through all of it, probably holding in their stomachs and swallowing the ball of anxiety lodged in their throats.

Nobody likes being dropped, especially in the dark. I inhale and hope to god that we land on level ground.

"Five. Four. Three—" my eyes wrench shut *"—Two. One."*

We rattle as a hollow, static sound envelops everything. That hollowness stabs into my gut and my head, making me lightheaded, even shaky. I grit my teeth against it.

The *woosh* of air—of cutting pressure—encompasses the space inside the box, and my boots lift off the floor. I press them down as the sensation of weightlessness grows, as one second becomes a hundred more.

My body lurches upward, thrusting my soul out of my body, and we stop as I jerk just as violently down. The pressure clears. The lights flicker on, and then there's a moment of strained tension as everyone peels their eyes open.

I pry my fingers out from around my straps. "It's done."

Roger curses. "I think I pissed my pants."

Officer Ashton rises from his seat first. He has been with me the longest and is my team's analyst as well as my co-pilot. "When don't you piss yourself?"

They continue to bicker while I straighten my uniform and push up my goggles. I unlatch my supplies from under my seat and tug on my weapons' straps and walk to the back of the box to grab my rifle from the cabinet. When I'm certain it's not jammed, I throw on my beltpack.

My hand pauses over the lump in my right pocket, checking the small recorder Dr. Laura gave me an hour before takeoff. It's undamaged. Sighing, I walk to the front where Ashton is kneeling at the hatch and peering down at his tablet.

I peer over his shoulder at the screen. "What do you see?"

"The temperature is 76F, the air is clear of radiation particles, oxygen and hydrogen levels are good, and we're on level ground. Captain Briars knows his math."

"And the ship?"

He flicks his screen and brings up another. "Peter's ship is southeast of us by about five kilometers."

"Good. That's not too far."

"As I said, Briars knows his math."

"Captain, there's something wrong with Liam!"

Josef stands next to Petty Officer Liam, who is bowed over, and coughing up spittle. He loads his medical scanner and begins checking him over.

I open my water canister and head to them. "Drink," I order.

Liam wipes his mouth and takes my water. "Thanks Captain."

"His vitals are normal but elevated. He's fine," Josef mumbles and puts his tool away. "He's just green."

Liam wipes his mouth again and hands the canister back to me. "Of course I'm fine."

"This is your first drop. It happens."

"Someone always vomits," Roger quips.

I return to the front and secure the rest of my gear. Liam and Josef follow me and do the same.

Pulling my rifle forward, I face my men.

"We're not supposed to interfere with the local alien life unless absolutely necessary. We're not supposed to make our presence known at all," I remind them. "These *nagas* are sentient and are highly intelligent beings, according to Captain Peter's reports. If you see one, you'll know it. They look like us, but are not bipedal. Let's make this quick, short and sweet. We head straight for the ship."

"What happens if we get there and everyone is dead?"

I meet Liam's eyes at the back. His face is white as a ghost, and it's clear he's not feeling well. Maybe the water wasn't enough. "Let's hope that's not the case. We cover each other's backs, understand?" I look at each one of them as I say it. "This is Earth, remember that, this isn't a war zone. What's our motto?"

"Life's too short for shit."

"Exactly."

My men know what they're doing and I'm confident in their abilities. Although Liam and Kyle are new to me and are mainly serving as extra manpower in this mission, Josef, my team's medic, and Roger, my second in command, are both full-fledged officers and have been with me since I was transferred from the front lines to serve on *The Dreadnaut*. Both men are excellent officers, but Ashton and I go back even further.

I had been the only surviving soldier after the Ketts' takeover of Colony 4's airspace. My ship crashed outside Huryanta City just as the aliens turned their attention to the planet and the people still trapped upon it. I managed to get into the city, make it to the local base and help the citizens hold the Ketts off long enough to repair one of their few remaining ships.

Now that the people had a pilot in their midst, they had hope.

Getting that ship off the planet should've been impossible, but the stars aligned for me, saving not only my life, but also Ashton, the brother of a Colonel of *The Dreadnaut's* military. He followed me when I was then transferred to *The Dreadnaut*, where I was awarded medals, bumped up in caste, and given my own squad.

The Colonel said a woman with a strong survival sense shouldn't be wasted on the Ketts. I was a hero now. I could be utilized better, and I agreed because if I ever faced a Kett again, I knew it would be the last thing I saw.

I was lucky and afraid. I agreed and became a Captain.

But nobody gets that lucky twice.

Meeting each of their gazes one last time, Roger gives me a twitchy smile back.

I punch the release code into the battle box's panel. Pressure floods my ears as the door gives way and disappears into the confines of the box's inner walls.

Shrouded in darkness, an alien wilderness greets me.

Breathe, says Laura's voice in the back of my mind.

Inhaling sharply, I turn my night vision on and step out onto sacred ground.

Click here for Death Adder!

ALSO BY NAOMI LUCAS

<u>Naga Brides</u>

<u>Viper</u>

<u>King Cobra</u>

<u>Blue Coral</u>

<u>Death Adder</u>

Boomslang (Coming Soon!)

<u>Cyborg Shifters</u>

<u>Wild Blood</u>

<u>Storm Surge</u>

<u>Shark Bite</u>

<u>Mutt</u>

<u>Ashes and Metal</u>

<u>Chaos Croc</u>

<u>Ursa Major</u>

<u>Dark Hysteria</u>

<u>Wings and Teeth</u>

<u>The Bestial Tribe</u>

<u>Minotaur: Blooded</u>

<u>Minotaur: Prayer</u>

<u>Stranded in the Stars</u>

<u>Last Call</u>

<u>Collector of Souls</u>

<u>Star Navigator</u>

<u>Venys Needs Men</u>

To Touch a Dragon

To Mate a Dragon

To Wake a Dragon

Naga (Haime and Iskursu)

Valos of Sonhadra

Radiant

Standalones

Six Months with Cerberus

Cyber Pool Boy

9 798987 221341